Mary White

Heiress

Heiress

A NOVEL BY
Janet Dailey

LITTLE, BROWN AND COMPANY
BOSTON   TORONTO

Second Printing

Library of Congress Cataloging-in-Publication Data

Dailey, Janet.
  Heiress.

  I. Title.
PS3554.A29H45 1987   813'.54   86-27538
ISBN 0-316-17092-5

The characters and events portrayed in this book
are fictitious. Any similarities to real persons,
living or dead, are purely coincidental
and not intended by the author.

MV

*Published simultaneously in Canada
by Little, Brown & Company (Canada) Limited*

PRINTED IN THE UNITED STATES OF AMERICA

Part One

1

Sunlight pierced the thick canopy formed by the branching limbs of the oak trees and dappled the century-old marble monument that laid claim to this section of the Houston cemetery as the Lawson family plot. Cut in the shape of an ancient obelisk, the monument had been erected more than one hundred years ago to watch over the graves of the first Lawsons to be buried in Texas — and to commemorate the Lawsons who had died far from their East Texas home while proudly serving the Confederacy. Again mourners had gathered, and the hallowed ground was opened to receive the body of yet another member of the family, Robert Dean Lawson, Jr., known to all as Dean.

The suddenness of her father's death — for Abbie, that had been the hardest. An accident, the police had said. He'd been driving too fast and missed a curve. Ironically, he'd been on his way home from the airport, returning from a business trip to Los Angeles. Killed on impact, Abbie had been told, as if that made his death easier to accept.

It hadn't. The pain, the regret came from not having the chance to talk to him one last time, to tell him how very much she loved him, and maybe . . . just maybe . . . hearing him say that he loved her. It sounded so silly, so childish to admit that, yet it was true. She was twenty-seven years old, but she still hadn't outgrown the need for her father's love. No matter how she had tried to get close to him, something had always stood between them, and years of battering hadn't broken down the wall.

Numb with grief, Abbie lifted her glance from her father's closed casket, draped in a blanket of Texas yellow roses, and scanned the crowd massed around the grave for the services. Admittedly the turnout wasn't as large as the one at her grandfather's funeral nineteen years ago. Even the governor had come to it. But that was to be expected. Her grandfather R. D. Lawson had been one of the pioneers in the petroleum industry. He was the one who had refilled the family coffers after they had been virtually emptied during those terrible years of Reconstruction that had followed the Civil War. Bold, shrewd, and very sure of himself — that's the way Abbie remembered him, even though she'd been a child, barely eight years old, when he died. Judging from the stories she had heard, he had been a colorful and charming character, and occasionally ruthless about getting what he wanted. In those early days in the oil business, sometimes a man had to be.

But the Lawsons weren't oil millionaires. Whenever people insinuated as much to Abbie — christened Abigail Louise Lawson after her grandfather's mother — she loved to steal her grandfather's famous line: "Not oil, honey. We made our money in mud." The startled expressions on their faces always made her laugh. Then she would explain that *mud* was the term given to drilling fluids that were pumped into a well to soften up the ground for the drill bit, carry off the tailings, and maintain pressure to prevent a blowout. In the early days of rotary drilling in the oil fields, a mixture of clay and water — literally mud — was pumped into the hole. Later, additives such as barite and bentonite were included in the mixture to increase its weight. In the late 1920s, after working in the booming Texas oil fields, R. D. Lawson came up with his own formula for "mud" and marketed it himself, starting a company that he eventually built into a multimillion-dollar corporation.

Following her grandfather's death and the subsequent sale of the company by her father, the Lawson family's role in Houston had changed considerably. No longer were they members of the vast petroleum industry. Without the company's power base, their influence on the oil community was minimal, reduced to long-standing friendships with former associates of R.D. However, with the family's wealth and heritage, they had remained a major part of the

Houston social scene, as evidenced by the number of prominent Texans among the crowd of mourners.

Looking at all the well-known faces, Abbie thought it was odd the way one took note of such things at a time like this, as if the living needed an affirmation of the importance of the loved one who had died — an affirmation that could only be measured by the number of influential people who came to the funeral.

Catching a movement out of the corner of her eye as her mother slipped a silver lace handkerchief underneath the black veil of her hat and dabbed at the tears in her eyes, Abbie started to turn to her. At almost the same instant, she noticed the young woman standing near the memorial obelisk, a woman so eerily familiar that Abbie had to take a second look. She stared at her in shock, the blood draining from her face. The resemblance was uncanny.

"Now let us pray," the minister intoned, bowing his head as he stood before the closed casket. "O Lord, we have gathered here to-day to lay to rest the body of your servant, Dean Lawson, beloved husband and father . . ."

Abbie heard the minister's call to prayer, but the words didn't register. She was too stunned by the sight of the woman in the crowd. It isn't possible. It can't be, she thought wildly, suppressing the shudder caused by the chills running up her spine.

As the woman stood with her head slightly bowed, a breeze stirred the mass of lustrous nut-brown hair about her face — the same rich shade of hair as Abbie's. But it was the color of the woman's eyes that had Abbie completely unnerved. They were a brilliant royal blue, fathomless as the ocean depths — the same vivid color as her own. "Lawson blue," her grandfather had called it, boasting that it meant their eyes were "bluer than a Texas bluebonnet."

Abbie had the distinct feeling that she was looking into an imperfect mirror and seeing a faintly distorted image of herself. It was a strange sensation. Unconsciously she raised a hand to her own hair, verifying that it was still sleeked back into its French twist and not falling loose about her shoulders like the woman's across the way. *Who was she?*

With the question echoing over and over again in her mind, Abbie leaned closer to Benedykt Jablonski, the manager of the Arabian stud farm at River Bend, the Lawson family home southwest of Houston. Before she could ask him about the woman who was virtually her double, a murmured chorus of "Amens" signaled the conclusion of the graveside services, and the previously motionless throng of mourners began to stir. Abbie lost sight of the woman. One second she was there, and in the next she was gone. Where? How could she disappear so quickly? *Who was she?*

As the minister approached their chairs, her mother stood up, the black veil screening her wet eyes. Abbie rose to stand beside her, as always feeling protective toward this slender reed of a woman, her mother, Babs Lawson. Like her father, Abbie had made it a practice, from the time she was a child, to shield her mother from anything unpleasant. Babs just couldn't cope with problems. She preferred to look the other way and pretend they didn't exist, as if that would make them miraculously vanish.

Not Abbie. She preferred to confront situations head-on and usually led with her chin, mostly due to that Lawson pride and stubbornness that she had inherited in abundance. Just as now, unable to shake the image of that woman from her mind, she scanned the faces of the people milling about the grave, vaguely aware of the words of condolence offered by the minister to her mother, but intent on locating the woman who looked so much like her. She had to be here somewhere.

Instinctively she turned to Benedykt Jablonski, seeking his help as she had done nearly her entire life. Dressed in a tweed suit that was nearly as old as he was, he held his small-billed cap in front of him. His thick, usually unruly iron-gray hair was slickly combed into a semblance of order.

Age had drawn craggy lines in his face and faded his dark hair, but it hadn't diminished the impression that he was a bulwark of strength. Nothing ever seemed to faze him. Considering all he'd been through during World War II, with the Nazi invasion and occupation of Poland and the immediate postwar years under Soviet control, perhaps that wasn't so surprising.

Now, standing next to his solidness, Abbie recalled the way she used to say that everything about this man was square: his jaw, chin, shoulders — and his attitude. Yet Ben had been the steadying influence in her life. It was to him she'd gone as a child with all her questions and problems.

A solemn man who seldom smiled, he studied her briefly, reading her body language the way she'd seen him do so many times with a young Arabian colt in training. "What is wrong?" His voice carried the guttural accent and the lyrical rhythm of his native Poland.

"A moment ago, there was a woman standing near the family marker. Did you see her?"

"No," he replied, automatically glancing in the direction of the monument. "Who was she?"

"I don't know," Abbie replied, frowning as she again skimmed the faces of the people milling about. She knew she hadn't imagined the woman. Absently she ran a hand across her waist, discreetly smoothing the black Chanel dress, the crepe de Chine soft and silky to the touch. Determined to find the woman, she turned back to Ben and said, "Stay close to Momma for me, Ben."

"I will."

But Abbie didn't wait to hear his reply as she moved out among the graveside gathering, pausing to speak with this person, accepting the press of hands in sympathy from another, nodding, smiling faintly, murmuring appropriate responses — all the while looking for the woman she'd seen so briefly.

Just as she was about to decide the woman had left the cemetery, Abbie saw her standing on the fringe of the crowd. Again she felt unnerved by the striking resemblance between them. Next to her stood the gray-haired Mary Jo Anderson, her father's longtime legal secretary, who had more or less run his limited law practice single-handedly over the years. Shocked and confused, Abbie stared at the two of them. What was Mary Jo doing with her? Did she know her?

Fingers closed around her arm as a man's deep voice came from somewhere close by. "Miss Lawson? Are you all right?"

"What?" Turning, she looked blankly at the tall, dark-haired man now beside her gripping her arm.

"I said, are you all right?" His mouth quirked slightly, lifting one corner of his dark mustache in a faint smile that was both patient and gentle, but his narrowed eyes were sharp in their study of her.

"I'm . . . fine," she said, mentally trying to shake off her abstraction as she stared at his rough-hewn features, conscious that there was something vaguely familiar about him.

Remembering the woman, she glanced back over her shoulder to locate her. The man curved a supporting arm around the back of her waist. "You'd better sit down." He started guiding her in the opposite direction.

Abbie stiffened in resistance. "I told you I'm fine." But she was propelled along by his momentum to a nearby folding chair. There she took a determined stand and blocked his attempt to seat her. "I feel fine," she insisted again.

Eyeing her skeptically, he cocked his head to one side and let his hands fall away from her. "You don't look fine. As a matter of fact, Miss Lawson, a minute ago, you looked like hell."

It was his bluntness more than the sight of Mary Jo Anderson walking away from the gravesite alone that caused Abbie to center her whole attention on him. She thought she had learned to hide her feelings over the years. Perhaps she hadn't — or maybe he was just more observant than most.

Either way, Abbie tried to cover her previous reaction. "It was probably the heat."

"It is hot," he acknowledged with a faint nod of his head, but Abbie suspected that he didn't think the stifling afternoon heat was to blame. As his gaze moved lazily over her face, its look still sharp and inspecting, the action reinforced the feeling that she'd met him somewhere before — and he'd been just as thorough in his study of her that time, too.

"I am all right, though. Thanks anyway for your concern . . ." She paused, unable to supply his name.

"Wilder. MacCrea Wilder." The name didn't ring any familiar note with her and he seemed to sense that. "We met briefly this past spring, in your father's office."

Her memory jogged, Abbie suddenly could see him taking up most of the big leather armchair in her father's private office, the look of irritation that had crossed his face when she had barged in unannounced, interrupting their meeting, and the way he'd leaned back in the chair and watched her while absently rubbing a forefinger back and forth across his mustache and upper lip. That afternoon he'd been dressed in a khaki shirt with the cuffs turned back and the collar unbuttoned at the throat, revealing a faint smattering of chest hairs. She remembered the ropes of muscles in his forearms, the slick look of bronzed skin, and the breadth of his shoulders. But there had been something else, too. She frowned, trying to recall the thing that eluded her. She breathed in and accidentally inhaled the musky fragrance of his masculine cologne.

"Oil." Mixed in with the aroma of her father's pipe tobacco had been the smell of the oil fields. "Wasn't that what you were talking to my father about?"

"Indirectly. I'm flattered you remember."

"Are you?" Somehow he didn't seem to be the type to be influenced by compliments one way or the other.

"Who wouldn't be flattered to have a beautiful woman remember him from a chance meeting?"

"I could name a few." Abbie wasn't fooled by his smooth charm, any more than she was fooled by hard muscles. She was usually good at sizing up people.

"Your ex-husband, for instance?"

Automatically Abbie covered the bare ring finger on her left hand. The platinum wedding rings, dominated by a brilliant three-carat sapphire encircled with diamonds — the very set she had chosen at Tiffany's after she and Christopher John Atwell had romantically breakfasted outside the Fifth Avenue store in New York — no longer adorned her third finger. Ten months ago, she had thrown them at him and watched the intertwined pair tumble to the floor and break apart — like their disastrous six-year marriage. She had walked out of their home on Lazy Lane in Houston's River Oaks section that very afternoon, moving home to River Bend and taking back her maiden name. Certain things in her life she regretted, but the end of her marriage wasn't one of them.

Still, she resented his trespass into her personal life. "You seem to know a great deal about me, Mr. Wilder," she replied, challenging him ever so faintly.

"As I recall, you had received your final divorce decree that day and wanted to celebrate. A man doesn't exactly forget when a young — and strikingly attractive — woman announces her availability."

Until now she had forgotten the reason she had barged into her father's office that day. "You remember?" she said, her tone softening. "I'm flattered."

"Are you?"

She looked at him with new interest, surprised at the quick way he had picked up the cue and turned her own words back to her. A part of her felt alive for the first time since she had received the news of her father's death, but only briefly. She couldn't escape the soberness of this occasion, not with her father's closed casket still visible and the oppressively hot air heavy with the sweet scent of roses.

MacCrea glanced at the brass-encrusted coffin. "I want you to know how sorry I am about your father's death."

Abbie regretted the return to trite phrases — and equally trite responses. "Thank you. And thank you for caring."

The instant he walked away she felt his absence, but she didn't have an opportunity to dwell on it. Someone else was waiting to offer her more words of sympathy, and Abbie began making the rounds once more, but her gaze was always moving, searching for that woman, still wondering who she was.

Rachel Farr watched her from a distance, observing the grace and assurance with which she moved through the crowd. It was that expensive little black dress that did it, Rachel decided — so simple yet so elegant, with its black satin accents at the cuffs, placket, and mandarin collar. Or maybe it was the way she wore her hair — all swept up in that sophisticated French twist that made her look so stylish and poised. She certainly didn't appear to be suffering from the heat and humidity the way Rachel was. Her dress wasn't sticking to her skin and her hair wasn't damp with perspiration like Rachel's. Rachel had expected the heat, but not the humidity. Texas was supposed to be dry, brown, and flat. Houston was flat, but lushly green and obviously wet.

Rachel glanced down at the single red rose she held clutched in her hand. Its velvety petals were already drooping from the heat. She'd bought it at the flower cart in the terminal of Houston Intercontinental Airport shortly after she'd arrived from California yesterday afternoon. She wanted to place it on Dean's coffin as a symbol of her love for him, yet she was afraid to make this one simple gesture.

Last night she'd gone to the funeral home, but she hadn't found the courage to go inside, fearing the family's reaction and reluctant to cause a scene. And today, she'd sat outside the church while they held services for Dean inside, wanting to be there, yet oddly feeling too unclean to attend. Finally, she had followed the procession of Lincolns, Mercedes, Rollses, and Cadillacs to the cemetery on the edge of town.

Over and over she kept thinking that if his secretary hadn't telephoned her, no one would have notified her of Dean's death. It might have been days, weeks, perhaps months before she'd found out otherwise. She had tried to express her gratitude to Mrs. Anderson, but she had sensed how awkward and uncomfortable the woman felt with her at the funeral.

It wasn't fair. She had loved Dean, too. Surely his family could

"Who are you?" she demanded again.

"I'm his daughter."

Abbie recoiled in shock and anger. "That's impossible. *I'm* his daughter, his only child."

"No, you're —"

But Abbie didn't want to hear any more of her preposterous lie. "I don't know who you are or what you're doing here," she declared, struggling to keep her voice down, "but if you don't leave now — this very minute — I'll have you thrown out of this cemetery."

understand that she wanted to grieve with them and share the pain of their mutual loss. She'd had so little of him and they'd had so much. She would place the rose on his coffin. She didn't care what they thought.

Not giving herself a chance to have second thoughts, she set out quickly, walking blindly along the narrow strip of ground that separated the rows of graves. Her low heels sank into the thick carpet of grass that covered the ground as she moved in and out of the dappling shade cast by the towering oak trees that stood guard over the dead. It seemed as though she was traveling in a vacuum, encapsulated by a grief that dulled her senses, the sights and sounds of her surroundings making little impression on her.

Yet, despite all the hurt and suffering she felt, Rachel was conscious of the irony of the moment. Since she'd been able to have only small pieces of his life, it was fitting somehow that she was only allowed a small piece of his death. But just as she had railed at the inequity of the former, she cried over it now. There was nothing she could do that would change it. Dean was the only one who had possessed the power to do that, and he was dead.

Suddenly the casket was before her, draped in a blanket of sun-yellow roses. Rachel stopped beside it and hesitantly laid the wilted red rose on top of it. The bloom looked so forlorn and out of place she wanted to cry. She blinked at the tears that stung her eyes and trailed her fingers over the edge of the casket in a last good-bye as she turned away. When she looked up, she saw Abbie standing a scant fifteen feet away, staring at her with a confused and wary frown. For a split second, Rachel was tempted to hurry away, as if she were guilty of something. She wasn't. So why should she run? Gathering her fragile pride, Rachel lifted her chin a little higher and started forward at the same instant that Abbie did.

They met midway. Abbie spoke first. "Who are you? Should I know you?" Her voice was lightly laced with a soft Texas drawl, like Dean's. Rachel noticed that she was taller than Abbie by a good four inches, but it didn't make her feel superior in any way, only awkward and gauche.

"I'm Rachel. Rachel Farr from Los Angeles."

"From Los Angeles?" Abbie's frown deepened. "Daddy had just returned from there."

"I know." Realizing that Abbie had absolutely no idea who she was, Rachel suddenly felt very bitter and hurt. "Dean used to say we looked a lot alike. I suppose we do, in a way."

❖ 2 ❖

Barely able to see through her tears, Rachel bolted from the grave, making her long legs carry her quickly away. She wished she had never come to the funeral. It had been a mistake — an awful mistake.

How had she expected Abbie to react when she met her? Had she thought Abbie would throw her arms around her and greet her like the long-lost sister she was? Half-sister, at any rate. Had she hoped that Abbie would invite her home? No, that would have been awful.

She could imagine nothing worse than seeing all the trophies Abbie had won competing in horse shows on Dean's horses. Rachel had long ago begun haunting the Los Angeles Public Library, going through its magazines and out-of-town newspapers to satisfy her hunger to find out more about the father she saw so seldom. What did he do when he wasn't with her? Where did he live? How did he live? Over the years River Bend had been featured in several magazines, mainly those dealing with Arabian horses, but a few society-type publications as well. Dean had rarely mentioned any of them to her, but in them she'd seen too many photographs showing Abbie astride some gorgeous Arabian with Dean standing proudly at its head.

She'd seen pictures of the family's Victorian mansion, and of the expensive fashions worn by his wife and other daughter when they attended their lavish parties and balls. She'd read all about Abbie's formal coming-out in the society columns of the Houston newspapers: she didn't want to look at pictures of her, stunning in an elaborate white gown, dancing with Dean at a debutante ball. Abbie, so beautiful and daring — and looking so much like her it hurt.

She couldn't bear the thought of hearing about Abbie's travels with Dean to England, Europe, and the Middle East; she had never gone anywhere with Dean except to Disneyland and Catalina Island.

All her life she'd been filled with envy, knowing that Abbie had Dean with her all the time. He was there to tuck her into bed at night. He was there for every holiday, every Christmas morning when she got up. He was there for every important occasion, from piano recitals to graduation. But Rachel had been lucky, especially since her mother died, to see him four times a year.

It was obvious whom he had wanted to be with, whom he had loved. She doubted that she had ever been more than an embarrassing burden to him, an unwanted complication. She thought she'd put all that pain and bitterness behind her. After graduation from UCLA, she had tried to make a life for herself without him. She had a good job and a promising career as a commercial artist with a large advertising firm in L.A. But today, all the old wounds had been opened again. And the hurt went deep — deeper than ever before.

She paused, trying to get her bearings and locate her rental car. Just as she spotted the tan Firebird, a long black limousine pulled onto the shoulder of the cemetery lane and parked in the space behind her car. A uniformed driver hopped out and opened the rear passenger door. Absentmindedly Rachel stared at the silver-haired man who stepped out.

The man said something to the chauffeur, then walked away from the limousine, striding briskly toward Rachel and the gravesite behind her. Something about his strong facial features reminded Rachel of Dean. He was in his middle fifties — about the same age as Dean. She wondered whether his eyes would crinkle at the corners when he smiled the way Dean's had.

A moment later she saw that they did as he noticed her and smiled quickly. "How are you?" The warmth, the sincerity in his voice gave meaning to the question, changing it from an offhand phrase of greeting. Rachel was startled to find herself shaking hands with him in the very next second.

"Fine, thank you." Hurriedly she wiped away a tear that had slipped onto her cheek, certain she probably looked awful, her eyes all bloodshot and puffy. But the kindness in his look told her he was too much of a gentleman to notice.

"The services are over, aren't they?" he asked instead. "I'm sorry I was late, but I . . ." He paused, a frown flickering across his expression. "Excuse me, but you aren't Abbie, are you?"

"No. I'm not." She wanted to die when she noticed the way he unconsciously drew back from her. All her life she'd fought against this sense of shame. She'd done nothing wrong, yet she had never been able to escape this feeling of guilt. Trembling with agony of a different kind, Rachel turned to leave.

"Wait. You must be . . . Caroline's daughter."

She paused, tears of gratitude welling in her eyes. At last she'd been recognized by someone, someone who could truly understand the deep loss she felt. "You . . . knew my mother?" Hesitantly she faced him.

"Yes." A smile of understanding crinkled the corners of his eyes. "Your name is Rachel, isn't it?"

"Yes." She smiled for the first time in days. "I'm sorry," she said, shaking her head a little vaguely, too choked with emotion to say much more. "Your name?"

"Forgive me. I took it for granted that you would know me. My name is Lane Canfield."

"Mr. Canfield. Yes, Dean spoke of you often. He . . . thought a great deal of you."

There were some who claimed Lane Canfield owned half of Texas — and the other half wasn't worth buying. According to newspaper accounts Rachel had read, his holdings were vast and widely diversified, ranging from real estate developments to luxury hotels and giant petrochemical plants. Photographs had rarely accompanied the articles. Rachel seemed to remember hearing that Lane Canfield shunned personal publicity.

"To be truthful, the feeling was mutual. Dean was a remarkable man, and a loyal friend. He will be missed by many people."

"Yes." She bowed her head with the grief his words elicited.

"Do you still live in Los Angeles?" Gently he directed their conversation to a less emotional subject.

"Yes. He'd just been out to visit me. His flight back was delayed. He was late. He was hurrying to get home when . . . the accident happened." Hurrying back home, to Abbie, the daughter he loved.

"Will you be staying in Houston long? Maybe we could have lunch, or dinner, together. I think Dean would like that, don't you?"

"You don't have to do that." She didn't want to be a duty, an obligation, to anyone.

"I don't *have* to do anything. I *want* to do it. What hotel are you at?"

"The Holiday Inn, the one near the Astro," Rachel heard herself answer.

"I'll call you tomorrow after I've had a chance to check my schedule."

"All right."

After their good-byes were said, Lane lingered to watch the young woman as she walked away. The resemblance between father and daughter was strong. She was tall and slender like her father, with his thick brown hair and incredibly blue eyes. Sensitive and vulnerable — yes, she was very much like Dean.

Abbie didn't waste any time locating her mother, convincing her that it was time to leave, and hurrying her off to the waiting limousine. She didn't want to take the chance that her mother might run into this woman who claimed . . . It didn't matter what she claimed. The very idea was ludicrous, absurd. The woman was obviously crazy.

The snarl of departing cars on the narrow cemetery lane slowed all movement to a crawl. Her nerves tense and brittle, Abbie leaned back in her seat, wondering how many of their friends that woman had talked to, told her lies to. Texans dearly loved a scandal.

Covertly she glanced at her mother. "Babs — that's short for babbling brook"; supposedly that was the way R. D. Lawson had frequently referred to her, partly in jest and partly seriously. Abbie had to admit that it was a singularly apt description of her mother. Her mother was bubbly and bright, flitting from this thing to that. She could chatter for hours and not say anything. Her life seemed to be nothing more than one long stream of parties. She loved giving them as much as going to them.

Abbie felt that two people could not have seemed less suited for each other than her parents. Yet Babs had absolutely adored Dean. She didn't make a single decision, no matter how trivial, without consulting him. She believed in him totally. Any and everything he did, she thought was perfect.

Not quite everything, Abbie thought, frowning slightly as she recalled arguments that had taken place behind closed doors: her mother's shrill voice and the sound of crying, her father's angry and de-

termined, yet pained, look when he stalked out. Her mother always
remained in the room, sometimes for hours, emerging pale and drawn,
unusually silent, her eyes puffy and red. Some of the early memories
were dim, yet Abbie had the impression that their arguments were
always over the same thing — and that *thing* was somehow con-
nected to the frequent business trips her father made to California to
see one of his clients.

Once, shortly after she had gone off to college at the University
of Texas, Abbie had suggested to her mother that she accompany
him to Los Angeles. "After all," she had reasoned over the telephone, "now that I'm not at home anymore, why should you stay in
that big house all by yourself? This is the perfect opportunity for
you to start going places and doing things with Daddy."

She could still remember the strangled yet adamant *no* that had
come over the line.

"Momma —"

"I hate California," had come the retort, with uncharacteristic bitterness.

"Momma, you have never even been there."

"And I don't care to ever go, either." Abruptly Babs had changed
the subject.

With anyone else, Abbie would have demanded to know why.
She could become incredibly stubborn when confronted with a wall
of any kind. If necessary, she'd take it apart brick by brick just to
find out what was on the other side. But it had been obvious this
was something Babs didn't want to face. Now Abbie wondered why.

That Rachel woman had said she was from Los Angeles, Abbie
recalled unwillingly. Of course, that was just a coincidence — like
the distinctive blue of her eyes. Lawson blue. Made uneasy by the
thought, Abbie frowned, haunted by the memory of the way her
father used to stare at her when he thought she wasn't watching, his
expression vaguely wistful and pained, a look of sadness and regret
in his eyes, eyes the same shade of deep blue as her own — and that
Rachel Farr woman's.

She had always thought he looked at her like that because he wished
she had been a boy. What man didn't want a son to carry on the
family name and tradition? None, she was sure. He had tried to love
her. And she had tried desperately to gain his love without ever fully
succeeding.

Maybe that was her fault. Maybe if she hadn't argued with him
so much . . . Half the time she had picked a fight with him just to

make him look *at* her instead of *through* her. They had fought over everything from horses and homework to pot and politics. Their last major confrontation had been over her divorce.

"Abbie, I think you're being too hasty, as usual," he'd said when she told him she had left Christopher. "Every married couple has problems. If you would try to be a little more understanding —"

"Understanding!" she had exploded. "Tell me just how understanding a wife is supposed to be when she discovers that her husband is having affairs — even with women she knows!"

"Now that doesn't mean —"

"What do you expect me to do? Condone it? Are you suggesting that I should look the other way while he makes a fool of me in front of all our friends? I won't be humiliated like that — not again."

"I can understand how you would be hurt by his . . . indiscretions." He had chosen his words with care and slowly paced in front of his desk as if presenting his case to a panel of jurors. "I doubt that he meant for it to happen. Things like that can begin so innocently. Before he knows it, a man can find himself more deeply involved than he ever intended to be. It wasn't planned. It just happened."

"Is that the voice of experience talking, Daddy?" she had caustically shot back at him, only to notice the way he blanched and turned quickly to avoid her gaze. He had looked guilty. Never one to miss an opening that could give her the advantage, Abbie had charged in. "Have you been unfaithful to Momma? Is that why you are siding with Christopher against me, your own daughter? Don't you care that I'm unhappy?"

"Of course, I do," he had insisted forcefully.

"Do you? Sometimes I wonder." She had turned away from him, struggling to control the bitterness she felt. "Daddy, I know you think I should forgive and forget what has happened. But I can't — and won't. I can't trust him. Without trust, there's no love. Maybe there never was any. I don't know anymore, and frankly, I don't care. I just want out of this marriage and Christopher out of my life."

"Dammit, Abbie, no Lawson has ever gotten a divorce."

"In that case, I'll just have to be the first, won't I? It's time somebody set a precedent." On her way out of his study, she had paused at the door. "But don't worry, Daddy. I won't ask you to represent me. I'll get some other lawyer — one without your high scruples."

The subject was rarely broached again after that. Yet Abbie knew he had never truly reconciled himself to the divorce. She had returned home, conscious of the new tension between them and determined to outlast it. Only she hadn't. He had died first. She felt a choking tightness in her throat and tears struggling to surface.

Beyond the tinted glass of the limousine's rear windows, Abbie saw Rachel Farr standing among the gravestones. Had her father had an affair with another woman in the past? Was Rachel Farr the result of it? Was the possibility really as preposterous as she'd first thought?

Too many half-forgotten memories were making it seem more than just a string of coincidences. Snatches of arguments she'd overheard between her parents, the constant trips to Los Angeles, four and five times a year, the way he used to look at her as if seeing someone else — things she had never regarded as pieces to a puzzle were all fitting together now. Devoted husband and father. Had it all been an act? All these years, had he kept another child hidden away in Los Angeles?

Struggling against a sense of betrayal, Abbie stared at Rachel, again considering the startling similarities: the hair color, the shape of the face, and the blue eyes. The prepotency of the sire — that's what Ben would have called it, in horsemen's terms. The ability of a stallion to stamp his offspring with his looks.

It felt as if her whole world had suddenly been turned upside down and shaken hard. Everything she had ever believed to be true, she now questioned. All these years, Abbie thought she knew her father. Now he almost seemed like a stranger. Had he ever really loved her mother — or her? She hated the questions, the doubts . . . and the memories now tainted with overtones of deception.

"Abbie, look!" her mother exclaimed. Abbie instantly stiffened, certain her mother had noticed Rachel Farr. "Isn't that Lane Canfield?"

So consumed with Rachel, Abbie hadn't paid any attention to the man she was talking to. It was Lane Canfield, her father's closest friend. She hadn't seen him since her wedding six years ago, but he had changed very little. He was still trim, still a figure of authority, and still managed to look cool and calm in the afternoon heat despite the suit and tie he wore. If anything, his hair — always prematurely gray — now had more white in it, giving it the look of tarnished silver.

But what was he doing talking to Rachel Farr? Did he know her? He acted as if he did. If all this was true, wasn't it logical that her father would have confided in Lane? That logic became even more damning when Abbie remembered that her father had named Lane Canfield the executor of his will.

"It is Lane." Her mother pushed at the switch on the armrest, trying to open the limousine's automatic windows. Finally the window whirred down, and the humid heat of the June afternoon came rolling into the car. "Lane. Lane Canfield!"

Hearing his name, Lane turned then walked over to greet them. "Babs. I'm so sorry I wasn't able to get here sooner. I was at a meeting in Saudi Arabia. I didn't receive the news of . . . the accident . . . until late yesterday. I came as quickly as I could," he said, warmly clasping her hand.

"It's enough that you're here. Dean valued your friendship so much, but I'm sure you know that." Babs clung to his hand. "You will ride back to the house with us, won't you?"

"Of course. Just give me a minute."

As he walked away, Abbie wondered if he was going after Rachel. But no, he walked to a black limousine parked several cars ahead and spoke to the driver, then started back. She felt numb, not wanting to believe any of this.

When Lane Canfield climbed into the back of the limousine and sat in the rear-facing seat opposite her mother, Abbie saw the way he looked at her, taking note of her every feature and obviously making the comparison with Rachel. He didn't seem surprised by the resemblance between them — which meant he must have expected to see it, Abbie realized.

"You will stay for dinner tonight, won't you, Lane? The Ramseys and the Coles will be there, and several others said they'd be stopping by. We'd love to have you join us," Babs insisted.

"I'd love to." With difficulty, Lane brought his attention back to Dean's widow, still an attractive woman at forty-eight. "Unfortunately I'll have to leave early. I have to get back to town tonight and attend to some business."

"I understand." Babs nodded, her voice quivering. For an instant, she appeared to be on the verge of breaking into tears, but she made a valiant effort to get hold of her emotions as she turned to Abbie. "Lane was best man at our wedding. But I guess you know that, don't you, Abbie?"

"Yes, Momma."

"I don't think I will ever forget that day." Babs sighed, her face taking on a nostalgic glow. "Do you remember, Lane, how our car wouldn't start? Dean must have worked on the motor for nearly an hour. He had grease all over his tuxedo, and I just knew we were going to have to leave on our honeymoon in that carriage. He tried everything, but he just couldn't get that car to run."

"I believe there were a few parts missing." Lane smiled, recalling how he and his cohorts had sabotaged the vehicle.

"No wonder." Babs laughed, a merry sound still infectious after all these years. "You loaned us your car, I think."

"Yes." He reminisced with her aloud as his mind wandered back to the start of that long-ago day.

3

Guests had begun arriving at River Bend long before the wedding ceremony in the garden was scheduled to begin. Everything was pristine white for the occasion. The stately mansion, the ornately carved picket fence, the elaborately scrolled gazebo — all sported a fresh coat of whitewash, as did every building, barn, and fence on the place.

No expense had been spared: even the Spanish moss that naturally adorned the towering oak and pecan trees on the grounds had been sprayed with silver dust, leaving the guests in no doubt that R. D. Lawson whole-heartedly approved of his son's marriage to Barbara Ellen Torrence, the daughter of an old Texas family reputed to have the bluest blood despite the fact that financially they were in the red, victims of the stock market crash of '29; and leaving the guests in no doubt that the Torrences were not too proud to let the nouveau riche R. D. Lawson pay for this lavish and elaborate wedding. As far as R.D. was concerned, no other setting would do but River Bend, restored, virtually rebuilt, to its former glory.

Located on the Brazos River less than twenty miles southwest of the very center of Houston, River Bend was surrounded on three sides by croplands and rice fields, the flatness of the coastal prairie unbroken except by the occasional farmhouse or tree. But the one hundred acres that remained of River Bend conjured up images of the Old South. Here, the strongest and tallest of the oaks, pecans, and cottonwoods that grew in the thick woods next to the river were left standing, towering giants bearded by the lacy moss and strung with wild grape vines.

Set back from the main road, nearly hidden by the trees, the main house was a magnificent fourteen-room Victorian mansion. A wide veranda wrapped itself around three sides of the house, outlined by a handsome balustrade repeated as a parapet around a narrow second-floor balcony. A cupola crowned the third story, which contained R.D.'s billiard room, and provided a center balance point for the corner turrets.

Once this mansion had been the heart of a thousand-acre plantation founded back in the late 1820s by a Southern cotton planter, Bartholomew Lawson, who was drawn to the area, like so many others of his kind, by the rich alluvial soil along the Brazos River bottom. As R.D. liked to remind everyone, there was a River Bend long before there was a Houston. Lawson slaves were in the fields back in 1832 when a pair of land speculators from New York were peddling lots in the tract of land they had bought on Buffalo Bayou.

River Bend flourished for nearly half a century, but the Civil War and the abolition of slavery changed all that. During the years of Reconstruction, large parcels of the plantation were sold to satisfy old debts and claims for back taxes. When R.D. was born at the turn of the century, only three hundred acres of the original plantation were still in the family; not a trace remained of the slave quarters near the river that had once been home to nearly a hundred blacks; and the mansion was a hayshed, its vast lawn and surrounding pecan grove a pasture land for the cattle and hogs. R.D. — his momma called him Bobby Dean — lived with his parents in the cottage that had been built to house the overseer and his family.

At the age of fifteen, R.D. went to work in the Texas oil fields. That's where the big money was. It made sense to him that if he was going to dig in the dirt, he might as well get paid for it. He got hired on by a man with the wishful name of "Gusher" Bill Atkins, who owned a rotary drilling rig. His first job was working in the mud pits. Eventually he graduated to a "roughneck," working on the floor of the drilling rig, handling the pipe. Within a few years, he'd tried his hand at nearly every job on the rig.

Those were the wild, freewheeling years of the oil business. The whole nation was certain the country was on the verge of running out of oil. Dire warnings were regularly issued by the government in the late 1910s and early 1920s, accompanied by statistics that showed production and consumption of oil were increasing at a considerably faster rate than new reserves were being found. The rush to find new fields was on, led by the "wildcatters," the independent oil men. For the most part, the major oil companies, who had the pipelines, the refineries, and the distribution market, sat back and watched, letting the wildcatters take the risks in a new area. Once oil was found, it was a simple matter for them to step in and buy up leases on adjoining land, or buy a piece of some wildcatter's action, or simply purchase the crude oil he produced.

It didn't take much money to drill a well back then, and little scientific knowledge was required. New drilling sites were selected on a basis that was pretty much "by guess and by golly." The only way to know for sure whether there was oil beneath a particular formation was to drill.

More than once, R.D. had been tempted to raise some money and drill his own well. But he'd heard too many stories and seen too many wildcatters who were rich as Croesus one year lose it all in a string of dry holes the next. The only ones consistently making money, other than the majors, were the men supplying materials and equipment.

Maybe because it was his first job, or maybe because he'd been raised a dirt farmer, R.D. was fascinated by the drilling mud used in the hole. All he had to do was scoop up some in his hand and he could tell by the feel and the texture of it — sometimes by the taste or smell of it — whether it was the right consistency for the job, or if it needed to be thinned or thickened.

After six years of working in oil fields, R.D. recognized the many functions mud performed. It did more than soften the formation the drilling bit was cutting through, more than bring the bit's cuttings to the surface for disposal, and more than sheathe the wall of the hole to stabilize it so it wouldn't cave in. If the mud was the right weight, it exerted more pressure than any gas, oil, or water formation the bit encountered, thus preventing the blowout of a well. Over the years, he'd seen his share of blowouts — lengths of pipe, the drill, and other equipment thrown high in the air and turning into lethal missiles. Whenever a blowout was caused by natural gas, invariably there was fire. A gusher was nothing more than a blowout caused by oil. As spectacular as they were, they were still dangerous and a colossal waste of oil.

As his fascination with mud grew, R.D. began experimenting with different mixtures and ingredients, picking the brains of geologists and chemists in the oil fields, and learning terms like *viscosity*. In 1922, he came up with a formula that seemed to be consistently successful. That same year his father died, killed when his horse bolted and overturned the wagon he was riding in.

R.D. found himself back at River Bend, faced with a difficult decision. His mother, Abigail Louise Lawson, better known as Abbie Lou, couldn't work the farm by herself, and they couldn't afford a hired hand. But how could he stay and run it when his heart was in the mud pits of the oil fields? To make matters worse, that skinny little neighbor girl, Helen Rae Simpson, had grown into a doe-eyed young woman while he was gone, and R.D. found himself in love.

Determined to do the right thing, he stayed to farm River Bend and follow in the tradition of his ancestors. He married Helen, and a year after their wedding, Robert Dean Lawson, Jr., was born. He should have been happy: he had a son, a lovely wife, a home, and a farm that was producing enough for them to get by. For three years R.D. tried to convince himself that a man couldn't ask for more, but he just couldn't stop talking about mud.

Abbie Lou Lawson recognized her son's discontent. One December night at the supper table, she — who had given him her dark hair and blue, blue eyes — offered him a solution that would provide him with the means to achieve his dream. They would sell the roughly two hundred acres of River Bend's cropland and keep the rest. The old mansion was a white elephant nobody would buy, and the one hundred acres of pasture wouldn't bring much either. The money from the sale would start him in the mud business and she would keep the books, the same as she had for the farm.

Within three months, the plan became a reality. R.D. applied for his patent and began peddling his products, making the rounds of the various oil fields and calling on drillers. But it was hard to make sales. Few were interested in such revolutionary ideas. Only the drillers in trouble with stuck drill pipes or cave-ins were willing to listen. Most of them were skeptical, but desperate enough to try anything. However, his successes usually only guaranteed him that the next time the driller was in trouble, he would call R.D.

Those first years were discouraging. And that discouragement was compounded by the stock market crash and then the death of his wife. A few times he would have given up, but his mother wouldn't let him. She encouraged him to expand, to set up a laboratory to test new products and equipment, and to hire field representatives to sell the company's products and educate the drillers on their use.

The world might be suffering a depression, but the oil industry wasn't. Within ten years, he went from being a one-man operation to having seventy people on the payroll. He started buying up smaller companies, taking over their patents, quadrupling the size of his business. Suddenly he was a millionaire several times over.

Thanks to the woman who believed in him: Abigail Louise Lawson. R.D. gazed fondly at the gilt-framed photograph of her taken a year before her death. Blue eyes smiled back at him from a face crowned with snow-white hair swept atop her head in a mass of curls, a pair of chandelier drop earrings dangling from the delicate lobes of her ears.

"Real diamonds, they are, too." R.D. winked at her, as he had the day he'd given them to her. "You and me, we made 'em sit up and look, didn't we? Hell, we never did do what they expected. They all figured we would buy us one of those big fancy homes in River Oaks, but we fixed up River Bend instead — and reminded them all that Lawsons had been here long before most of them were. This time Dean's the Lawson who's foolin' 'em, marryin' that Torrence girl. And a damned fine wedding it's going to be, too."

The gold mantel clock chimed the quarter-hour from its perch on the carved walnut shelf above the fireplace. As if he could hear her reprimand, R.D. grimaced faintly and faced the mirror above his dressing table once more.

"I know I left this getting-ready business a bit late." He made his third attempt at tying the black bow tie. "But I had to go down to the barns and make sure they had the mares all harnessed up right and the carriage ready. Remember that fancy horse carriage I bought you so you could ride in that parade we sponsored to get people to buy war bonds? That's what the bride's gonna arrive at the wedding in. She's over at the cottage with her family, gettin' ready."

He paused for a minute to stare at his reflection. He just didn't feel like a man about to turn fifty, despite the gray spreading through his thick hair. His face had the look of smooth leather with permanent creases worn across his forehead and around his mouth and eyes. There was no sagging skin along his strong jawline, although maybe just a little under his jutting chin, emphasized now by one end of the tipsy-tilted bow tie.

Exasperated, R.D. yanked it loose and started over again, absently resuming his conversation with his mother's photograph. "You should see that carriage. Garcia has it covered with white flowers. Lilies of the valley, gardenias, and apple blossoms. It reminds me of those buggies they use in the Rose Parade. I'm having it pulled by those two matched gray Arabians. White as milk, those two mares are now. I've got 'em in the black harness with white plumes. That young Pole polished the leather on that harness until it shines like a pair of patent-leather shoes on a fancy nigger. I like that Jablonski boy." He nodded decisively. "He definitely has a way with horses. And he knows a helluva lot about the breed. Although, half the time I can't understand him, his accent is so damned thick." Again the bow tie sat askew. "Hell, I never could tie these damned things," R.D. muttered and ripped it apart. "Dean!"

His booming voice sent the silver-lead crystals on the master suite's chandelier jingling as he stalked out of the room, dressed in the required tuxedo with the tie dangling around his neck, but minus his shoes. He padded down the hall toward his son's turret bedroom, his feet making little sound on the hardwood floor of heart pine.

The bedroom door was ajar. R.D. started to push it open, but he paused when he caught sight of his son in the room. Dean was every bit the gentleman R.D. had hoped he'd become. Well aware of his own rough edges and lack of formal education, R.D. had been determined his son would have it better. The rough-and-tumble days were gone.— the days when a handshake was all it took to make a deal. That's why he sent Dean to Harvard Law School after he'd graduated from the University of Texas. Ever since the boy was ten years old, R.D. had worked him every summer in the company, making him learn the business from the ground up. He sent him to the best schools and made him learn about the arts and manners. That's what it took in today's world. And, from the beginning, R.D. had been grooming Dean with one thought in mind: that someday he'd take over the reins of the company.

And there was the result, lounging on the arm of an overstuffed chair, totally relaxed and comfortable in his formal attire and smiling affably at his former college chum at Texas, his best man for the wedding, Lane Canfield. Dean was tall — although not as tall as R.D.'s six feet — and good-looking, with the Lawson eyes and thick, brown hair. His face still had the smooth, fresh look of a boy without a care in the world. But when had he ever had to worry about anything? Sometimes R.D. wondered if he hadn't given the boy too much, made life too easy for him. But then he remembered how he had worked him every summer while most of his friends played.

If R.D. could change one thing about him, he wished Dean had some of Lane Canfield's gumption. From what he'd been able to learn, Lane had taken over much of the operation of his family's petrochemical plant in Texas City and almost single-handedly put it in the black. Rumor claimed that he planned to enlarge the facility.

So far, Dean simply hadn't shown R.D. he could be that aggressive. But he hadn't had a chance to, either. All that was going to change now that Dean was coming on board full-time — as soon as his honeymoon was over, that is.

A door slammed somewhere in the house. As Dean glanced over to the door, R.D. hesitated a split second, then pushed it open the rest of the way and walked into the room.

"I think you forgot your shoes, R.D." Dean grinned.

"I've been fighting with this damned tie for twenty minutes."

"Let me tie it for you, Mr. Lawson." Lane walked over to him and took the mangled ends of the tie and adjusted the two to the proper length.

R.D. tilted his head back to give him room and eyed his son, still calmly perched on the chair arm. "I expected to find you pacing up and down, pawing the ground like an eager stallion at the trying bar."

"That's what Lane keeps telling me, but there'll be time enough for that when the ceremony's over," Dean replied with a negligent shrug of one shoulder, then rolled gracefully off the arm of the chair and stood up. "Lane and I were just going to have some of that champagne Jackson brought up. Care to join us and toast the end of my bachelor days?"

"Sure, but don't pour me any of that champagne. I'd just as soon have some bourbon and branch water, if you got any handy."

"Coming right up."

When Lane finished tying the bow tie, R.D. inspected the result in the dresser mirror. The knot was squarely in the center and the bow was perfectly straight. "I'll be damned if I can ever get it to look like that."

"Practice. That's all it takes," Lane assured him.

"I suppose. It's for sure I never had much cause to get duded up like this when I was a young man. Formal attire wasn't the required dress in the oil fields." Smiling, R.D. turned from the mirror. "Some of those old boys would get a real belly laugh if they could see me now."

"To hear him talk, you'd think he didn't like getting all dressed up. But believe me, Lane, he loves it," Dean said, coming over to hand them their drinks and remaining to lift his glass in a toast. "To my last hour as a free man."

After a clink of glasses, they all took a sip, then R.D. raised his. "I think we should drink to havin' a woman in the house again to make this place come alive."

"Hear, hear," Lane agreed, not quite certain whether Dean's hesitancy had been imaginary or not.

Ever since R.D. had entered the room, Dean's behavior had changed. True, they had been laughing and cracking jokes before, but it had been a way of easing the wedding jitters. Dean had been nervous — plucking at upholstery threads on the chair and smoking cigarette after cigarette. But all that had vanished the minute his father walked in. Dean had thrown his guard up, become subtly reserved and aloof, and disguised it with his teasing banter. Although Lane would never say as much to him, it was obvious Dean was intimidated by his father.

"I stopped by the cottage a little while ago to make sure there weren't any last-minute hitches," R.D. said.

"Did you see Babs?" Dean inquired, ever so casually.

"No, but I heard her, tittering and tee-heeing away in the back bedroom."

"That sounds like Babs." His mouth quirked in a half-smile as Dean reached for the champagne bottle to refill his glass.

R.D. watched him closely, his forehead puckering in a frown. "This is probably going to sound like a dumb question, but . . . you do love the girl, don't you?"

"If I didn't, I wouldn't be marrying her." But one look at his father warned Dean that such an offhand reply wouldn't suffice. He wanted to know more. R.D. wanted him to open up and tell him how he really felt. That had always been difficult, if not impossible, but Dean tried. "I'm not sure I can explain it, but . . . when I'm with her, it's like the sun's always shining. She . . . makes me feel important — like I was someone special."

"Well, you damned well are. You're a Lawson."

Realizing that his father didn't really want to hear the truth, Dean recovered and managed to force out a laugh. "I meant in the way a woman can make a man feel important and special." Which was to say that, around his father, he sometimes felt like something less than a man. Lord knew he tried to be the son his father expected him to be, but too often he fell short.

A few minutes later, R.D. finished his drink and left the room. "Your father's quite a guy," Lane remarked.

"Yes. He is," Dean agreed. He loved him. That's what made it so hard, knowing he failed to measure up to R.D.'s standards. Lane was the kind of son R.D. should have had. "Yesterday he took me over to the company and showed me my new office. It's right next to his. He's really been looking foward to the day when I join the company full-time."

There wasn't any way Dean could disappoint him. But he knew in his heart he was no more cut out to be the head of a mud company than he was to be a lawyer. More than once he had wished that if R.D. wanted him to manage something, why it couldn't be the Arabian breeding operation here at River Bend. The horses were Dean's real love, and the one common bond he had with his father.

It all began when R.D. bought him a pony-sized horse, reputed to be Arabian, for his seventh birthday. The mere thought that he had a horse just like the one Valentino had ridden in *The Son of the Sheik* had been enough to capture Dean's imagination totally. He promptly dubbed his new horse Araby. As he galloped Araby beneath the pasture's moss-draped pecan trees, he used to pretend they were in the desert, racing across the sands. He even used to steal sheets from the clothesline to wrap around himself in an attempt to mimic the flowing robes Valentino had worn in the movie. No more did he have to ride that broken-down old mare and wear his legs out trying to kick her into a trot. He had a horse that could run like the wind — and followed him around like a puppy dog.

But R.D. had been impressed by that combination of spirit and docility — and remarkable stamina. While he was on the road, he started tracking down previous owners of the gelding and discovered that the horse was sure enough a purebred Arabian, sired by a stallion named Hamrah, imported from the desert by a man named Homer Davenport — a fact that absolutely thrilled Dean.

R.D. had bought the gelding on impulse, drawn by the claim it was Arabian. Years ago, when he was learning to read, his mother used to sit him down at the kitchen table and have him read aloud to her while she fixed the evening meal. They didn't have many books. As a change from the Bible, she used to let him read from the yellowed pages of an old journal kept by an ancestor, dated in the late 1850s. In one part, this Lawson ancestor had extolled the virtues of a young racehorse recently purchased from a man named Richards in Kentucky, marveling at its ability to gallop for miles and miles without showing any sign of tiring, boasting of its blazing speed, and admiring the beauty of its head, the largeness of its dark eyes, the proud arch of its neck, and the high carriage of its tail. The horse was an Arabian.

R.D. never knew what happened to that horse, but he suspected that like so many other things, it had been a casualty in the ensuing Civil War. So he'd bought Dean the small Arabian gelding and told him the story about the previous Lawson who had owned an Arabian, too.

But buying the horse had revived his own childhood interest in Arabians. During a business trip to the California oil fields, R.D. heard about the Kellogg Ranch and decided to attend one of their regular Sunday shows for the sole purpose — he thought — of obtaining a photograph of Jadaan, the gray stallion ridden by Rudolph Valentino in *The Son of the Sheik,* for his son. But R.D. was totally captivated by the horses he saw, especially the stallions Raseyn and Raswan. He had to have them — or if not them, then their offspring. At the time it meant nothing to him that both were imported from the Crabbet Park Stud in England, both sired by the Polish-bred stallion Skowronek. He just knew he liked what he saw.

Less than six months after Dean's seventh birthday, four more horses arrived at River Bend: three fillies and a stud colt. R.D. hadn't planned to get into the horse-breeding business, especially with his company currently suffering from growing pains, but he was. He reasoned that this way he was putting that one hundred acres of pasture land to productive use. Besides, it was just four horses, not counting his son's gelding. Little did he realize that in the early 1930s there were less than a thousand purebred Arabian horses in the whole United States, making his five rare indeed.

But the first time his friends saw R.D.'s dainty-boned, delicate-faced Arabian horses, they broke out in laughter. Texas was Quarter horse country. Next to those compactly built, powerfully muscled animals, his horses looked like pissants. By then R.D. had done some reading up on Arabians, but his friends weren't interested in his explanations that Arabian horses weren't a breed but a subspecies of horse with distinct anatomical differences, whereas the Quarter horse was a man-made breed, formed by the mixture of different blood types, including Arabian. Nearly all light horse breeds traced back to the Arabian: Thoroughbreds, Morgans, Saddlebreds, Tennessee Walkers, Standardbreds, and Quarter horses.

But the ribbing didn't stop. In defense of his Arabians, R.D.

began riding them as soon as they were old enough and competing in open horse shows against their Quarter horses, usually entering nearly all the classes to prove the Arabians' versatility and stamina, frequently placing and occasionally winning. He let Dean ride them in the junior classes as well, to show that despite their spirited looks, they were gentle enough for a child.

Dean loved the show ring. And he loved the horses. They were his best friends, his playmates and confidantes. Riding them was the one thing he was good at; the proliferation of ribbons from those first shows and from subsequent all-Arabian horse shows proved it. Arabian horses were one thing he didn't have to take a backseat to his father on. In fact, he thought he knew more about them than R.D. did.

Over the years, the Arabian horse population at River Bend had grown from five to thirty-five, the bloodlines heavily weighted in favor of Crabbet imports of Skowronek and Mesaoud lineage. In Arabian horse circles, River Bend Arabians had earned the reputation of being among the best in the country. If R.D. would just give him the chance, Dean knew he could turn River Bend into the top Arabian horse farm in the country — maybe even the world.

True, he had received his law degree and passed the bar exam, and as of yesterday, he had been made a vice-president in the company. But those were meaningless titles. He wasn't a lawyer or an executive; he was a horseman. He wondered if he'd ever be able to get R.D. to understand that.

Lane lifted aside the French cuff of his shirt sleeve and checked his watch. "It's time we were going down. One of the duties of the best man is to make sure the groom doesn't keep the bride waiting."

"Knowing Babs, she'll keep *us* waiting." But Dean started for the door anyway, the thought of his bride-to-be bringing a smile to his face. In the back of his mind, though, he was wondering how he was going to convince Babs that they should cut their honeymoon in New York by a couple of days so he could stop in Illinois on their way back and look at some of the Egyptian-bred Arabians at Babson Farm.

A picket fence surrounded the small yard of the overseer's cottage, which was built in the same architectural style as the mansion but on a smaller and less elaborate scale. A pecan tree, gnarled and twisted with age, spread its broad limbs above the small house, its canopy of leaves providing shade from the unrelenting Texas sun.

A pair of white horses hitched to a carriage decorated with white flowers came to a prancing halt on the narrow dirt lane in front of the cottage. Their coats gleamed like ivory satin, a contrast to the ebony sheen of their hooves.

Benedykt Jablonski cast one last inspecting glance at them as he hopped down from his seat beside the driver, a stable groom decked out in a top hat and tails for this auspicious occasion. Ben struggled not to smile when he glanced back at him, certain he looked equally strange in the footman's uniform his employer, Mr. R. D. Lawson, had insisted he wear.

Ever since the actual preparations for the wedding had begun the day before, Ben had watched it all with growing awe. It had always been his understanding that only royalty went to such extravagant lengths, but here it was in America, on a grander scale than he'd ever seen. But how much had he seen in his twenty-five years of life? How much besides war, with its devastation and hunger, and the oppression of foreign occupation?

That was Poland; that was the past. This was America; this was his present. He was free, and his life here was good. Again he was being allowed to work with his beloved Arabians. And he was part of the young master's wedding, however small his role.

With shoulders squared, he strode through the gate to the front door of the cottage and rapped loudly twice. A heavyset man in formal clothes opened the door, glowering at him like an intruder.

Nervously, Ben cleared his throat. "For the bride, we wait."

The man stared at him blankly, the frown on his forehead deepening as if he didn't understand what Ben had said. Then he noticed the carriage waiting by the front gate and turned, calling to someone in the cottage — in a heavy Texan accent that Ben found equally difficult to understand — "Betty Jeanne, the carriage is here. Are you about ready in there?"

In the back bedroom, Babs Torrence anxiously turned to view her reflection in the mirror. "Momma, is it that time already? Am I ready? Have I forgotten anything?"

No. It was all there: the veil of Brussels lace, "something old" from her grandmother; the wedding gown of white satin, "something new"; the pair of pearl and diamond earrings, "something borrowed" from her mother; and the cerulean ribbon around her bridal bouquet, "something blue."

"You look lovely, darling. Absolutely lovely." Betty Jeanne Torrence discreetly shooed the maid out of the bedroom, then finally called an answer to her husband. "Tell them we'll be right there, Arthur, dear. And don't get yourself all in a dither. You know how it makes your face red."

But Babs didn't hear a word her mother said as she looked worriedly into the mirror. The satin gown, a Dior original, was the essence of femininity, with its high lace collar and heart-shaped neckline, the satin material curving snugly in to hug her waist, making it look no bigger than a minute, then flaring out into a floor-length skirt.

"Momma, this Merry Widow is hooked too tight. I just know it is," Babs complained for the fifth time about the strapless undergarment that was a combination of brassiere, corset, and garter belt.

"Nonsense," her mother retorted as she busily poked another pin through the veil to hold it more firmly in place, smoothing a stray strand of Babs's ash-blonde hair as she did so.

"It is," Babs insisted. "I just don't dare take a deep breath or I'll pop right out of it."

"Honey, if you have room to take a deep breath, then it's not tight enough."

"If this is a dream, I wish someone would pinch me," Babs declared and turned from the mirror, the gown and the petticoats beneath it making a soft rustling sound. "I can't believe Dean Lawson is really marrying *me*. Do you think he truly loves me?"

"He's marrying you. That's what matters," her mother insisted brusquely, then tempered her callousness with a smile. "You're going to take his breath away when he sees you coming down the aisle on your father's arm. Now, you remember what I told you about tonight?" Babs nodded, desperately wishing her mother wouldn't go on about her approaching wedding night. "It will all seem strange and awkward at first, but . . . you'll get used to it. And don't worry. I'm sure Dean will expect a few tears."

Her father appeared in the doorway. "Betty Jeanne. They're waiting for us." Smiling quickly, Babs turned, welcoming the interruption.

"And it will be worth it," she declared, gazing with pride at her daughter.

"I'm ready." Babs picked up the front of her skirts and hurried from the room at a running walk, brushing a kiss across her father's florid cheek as she went by. "Hurry, Daddy. We don't want to be late." As she emerged from the cottage, she stopped to stare at the carriage lavishly adorned with bridal-white flowers. She was reminded instantly of the Confederate Ball that marked the opening of Houston's debutante season. That night she had made her debut. That night she had met Dean. He had been the handsomest man there. She couldn't believe her luck when he asked her to dance, not once but twice. It wasn't until after the second dance that she found he was *the* Dean Lawson. By then, it didn't matter that her parents had been anxious for her to marry well; she was already in love.

She felt exactly like Cinderella about to climb into her coach drawn by white horses and ride off to marry her Prince Charming. All that was missing was the glass slipper. But she didn't care. She was about to become Mrs. Robert Dean Lawson, Jr.

There was a smattering of applause from the guests seated in the rows of chairs spread across the lawn when the carriage pulled up to let its precious passengers out. The lawn had been transformed into an English garden, with huge pots of white azaleas competing for attention with equally large tubs of yellow roses. Dividing the rows of chairs into two sections was a carpeted runner of pure white that led to the altar in the gazebo, its white trellises laced with more flowers. A stringed orchestra played the "Wedding March" as Babs started down the aisle on her father's arm with yellow rose petals strewn in her path. She could just as easily have been walking on air.

The wedding ceremony was merely a prelude to the lavish buffet reception on the lawn that followed. The four-tiered wedding cake was an architectural wonder, each layer separated by frosted columns of white, stairstepping to the top tier where the figures of a bride and groom stood inside an exact replica of the gazebo. After the ritual cutting of the cake, the new Mr. and Mrs. Dean Lawson toasted each other. Glasses were raised by the guests, filled with either champagne from the silver fountains or, for those who preferred, hard liquor from the bars set up on the lawn.

The newlyweds posed endlessly for the official photographer, then mingled with their guests, always together, Babs clinging proudly to Dean's arm, reveling in her new status, the princess to her prince. As she deferred nearly every inquiry about their future to him, Dean seemed to grow taller by inches. "Whatever Dean wants," "I'll let Dean decide," "You'll have to ask Dean about that," were beautiful words to him.

Twilight was settling over River Bend as Dean and Babs, she in her pale pink traveling suit, made their dash amidst a pelting shower of rice to his car — a car that wouldn't start, creating hoots of laughter among the onlooking guests. All sorts of advice was shouted to Dean, which he largely and wisely ignored as he raised the hood and checked the wires. When Dean attempted to enlist Babs's aid in starting the car, the typical husband-wife interchange created more peals of laughter.

"Dean, you know I can't drive," Babs protested.

"You don't have to drive. Just start the car. Now, when I tell you, turn the ignition and pump the gas pedal."

"Which one's the gas pedal?"

"The one on your right."

"This one?"

"Yes, honey, but . . . not now. I'll tell you when." After several attempts failed, Dean suggested, "Use the choke."

"What's that?"

Dean told her, and Babs promptly turned on the radio. In the end, Lane took pity on them and gave Dean the keys to his car so they could leave to spend their wedding night in the Houston hotel suite before boarding the train for New York the next day.

4

s the white board fences that outlined the boundaries of River Bend came into view, Lane was momentarily disconcerted by the feeling he had been literally transported back in time. It was as if the same horses were grazing beneath the sprawling limbs of the oak and pecan trees, their satiny coats shimmering in metallic shades of bronze, copper, silver, and gold. Beyond them, he expected to see the grounds clogged with cars, the wedding guests still lingering.

After watching Dean and Babs drive away, he remembered turning and finding the usually brash and robust R. D. Lawson standing silently beside him, his look distant and thoughtful. Then R.D. had glanced sharply at him, as if suddenly realizing he was there.

Lane remembered that he'd said, "Well, they're off. They looked happy together, didn't they?"

R.D. had stared after the car. "I wonder about her," he had said, then added hastily and forcefully, "I like the girl. But if she keeps acting helpless and dumb, pretty soon she's going to believe it. It's a damned shame she never knew my mother. Now, there was a woman," he had declared and slapped Lane heartily on the back, clamping his hand on Lane's shoulder. "Come on. There's still some partyin' left to be done."

At the time, Lane had regarded R.D.'s description of Babs as unfairly demeaning. But after more than thirty years, Babs still possessed that endearing childish quality. She still reminded him of a little girl who needed someone to look after her. Babs, who loved parties and beautiful clothes. Lane wondered if R.D. had been right. Had she been playing a role? Had that role become reality?

Covertly, Lane studied the Babs before him, the face behind the veil still relatively unlined, her hair still femininely styled in soft curls, its color still the same shade of dark blonde — whether naturally or artifically retained, he didn't know. The sad, lost look in her hazel eyes, however, was poignant and real.

"Dean never tired of their antics," Babs remarked when a half-dozen yearlings bolted away from the fence in mock fright as the limousine passed by. They streaked across the pasture with their tails flung high, and fanned out among the ancient oaks to watch the vehicle traveling up the driveway. "Beauty in motion, he called them. Living art."

"Indeed." But he couldn't help thinking that even in death, she was clinging to him.

The limousine rolled to a stop in front of the house. Lane waited until the driver assisted Babs out of the car, then he stepped out to join her. From the stable area, the shrill, challenging whistle of a stallion shattered the late-afternoon quiet. Drawn by the sound, Lane absently noticed all the improvements Dean had made since he'd taken over at River Bend following his father's death some nineteen years before.

The old barn had been torn down to make room for the large stable complex with its attendant paddocks and support facilities, a complex that covered more than twice the area of the original. All the new structures mimicked the gabled roof and cupola of the mansion. In the distance, a bay stallion strutted along a high fence, its neck arched and ebony tail flagged, its small, fine head lifted high to drink in the wind's scents. Lane guessed that he was also the source of the shrill call that had rent the air a moment ago.

"That's Nahr El Kedar." The statement came from Abbie Lawson, the first words he'd heard her speak since they'd left the cemetery. "You helped Daddy import him from Egypt."

"I'd forgotten all about it. That was a long time ago." Somewhere around twenty years, if he remembered correctly. His participation in the project had been relatively minor, mainly consisting of putting Dean in touch with some of his contacts in the Middle East to facilitate the handling of all the red tape of importation.

"Would you like to see him?" There was something challenging in the look she gave him. Lane suspected that Dean would have described it as one of his grandmother's "You-come-with-me, and-you-come-with-me-*now*" looks.

"Abbie," Babs began hesitantly.

"Don't worry, Momma. I won't keep him long." Without waiting for his assent, she set off confidently toward the stud pen. Lane found himself walking along with her.

After matching her for several strides, he realized that she wasn't as tall as he'd thought. The high heels she wore gave the illusion of height, plus she carried herself as if she were tall, but she was actually several inches shorter than he was. That seemed odd. He remembered . . . Lane caught his mistake. It was Rachel who had been his height.

"I saw you talking with her at the cemetery."

Lane was momentarily taken aback by Abbie's remark, coming as it did directly on the heels of his own thoughts. "You saw me . . . talking with whom?" he said, aware that he was treading on delicate ground.

"I believe her name is Rachel Farr." She turned the full blaze of her blue eyes on him. "She claims that Daddy was her father. Is that true?"

Lane didn't relish being the one who removed that last element of doubt. But it was equally pointless to lie. "Yes." Immediately she began staring at some point directly ahead of them and kept walking, but with a new stiffness of carriage that revealed the inner agitation she was trying desperately to control.

"But why would he —" The instant Abbie heard the naïveté of her question, she cut it off. She had already experienced firsthand the infidelity of a husband, with no real cause, no adequate justification . . . and no flaw in their sex life. Yet the idea that her father had been unfaithful to her mother — it shook Abbie. "I always thought my parents were happy together."

Only now when she tried to remember how they had acted together did she realize how very little they had in common. Her father had been all wrapped up in the horses, but her mother took little interest in them, except to attend the social events at major shows. And their conversations: her mother never talked about anything but parties, clothes, new room decor, gossip, and, of course, the weather. Abbie hated to think how many times she'd heard her mother brightly declare, "I never discuss politics, business, or economics. That way I never show my ignorance." And she didn't. If any conversation took a serious turn, she either changed it or moved on. But that was just Babs. She was funny and cute, and engagingly frivolous. Everyone loved her.

Heavens, there were times when Abbie had wanted to shake her. She had never been able to run to her mother with any of her childhood problems, no matter how trivial. She wanted more than her mother's pat answer, "I wouldn't worry about it. Everything always works out for the best." Too frequently, her father hadn't been available either. Abbie had invariably poured out all her troubles to Ben.

Was that what her father had sought in a mistress? Someone to talk to? Someone who would listen and understand? Someone who was more than a decoration on his arm? Someone to stimulate him intellectually as well as sexually? Almost immediately, Abbie shied away from such thoughts that smacked of disloyalty to her mother. Even if her mother was a disappointment to him in some ways, her father had no right to take another woman. He had betrayed her. He had betrayed them all.

As Lane and Abbie reached the stud pen, she walked up to the stout white boards. The dark bay stallion, his satin coat the color of burnished mahogany, strutted over to her, snorting and tossing his head, then arched his neck over the top board and thrust his finely chiseled head toward her.

A picture of alertness, the stallion stood still for an instant, his graying muzzle nuzzling her palm, his large dark eyes bright with interest, his pricked ears curving inward, nearly touching at the tips, his nostrils distended, revealing the pink inner flesh of their passages. For all the refinement of his triangularly shaped head tapering quickly to a small muzzle, the width between his eyes, and the exaggerated dish of his face, there was a definite masculine quality about the horse.

Abruptly the stallion lifted his head and gazed in the direction of the broodmares in the distant pasture, ignoring Abbie as she raised her hand and smoothed the long black forelock down the center of his forehead, the thick forelock concealing the narrow, jagged streak of white. With a snaking twist of his head, the stallion moved away from her and wheeled from the fence to pace its length.

"Kedar's in remarkable shape for a stallion twenty-two years old," Abbie said, just for a minute wanting the distraction he provided.

"He's a fine-looking animal," Lane agreed.

"His legs aren't all that good. He's calf-kneed and a little down in the hocks. But he has an absolutely incredible head, and Daddy always was a headhunter. As long as an Arabian had a beautiful head, he assumed it had four legs. Arabians of straight Egyptian bloodlines are noted for having classic heads. That's why all the Arabians on the place trace directly back to Ali Pasha Sherif stock — all, that is, except for that two-year-old filly over there." Abbie gestured to the silvery-white horse standing at the fence in the near pasture. "Her dam was the last of the Arabian horses my grandfather bred. I wouldn't let Daddy sell her when he sold off all the others after Granddaddy died. Daddy gave me her filly last year."

"You've obviously inherited your father's love for horses."

"I suppose." When the stallion came back to the section of the fence where they were standing, Abbie idly rubbed his cheek. "If I wanted to spend any time with him, I didn't have much choice."

Immediately she regretted the bitterness in her statement, especially since it was only part of the story. Horses had been her companions and playmates all her life. She loved working with Arabians and being around them — not just because of her father, but because of the feeling of satisfaction it gave her.

Blowing softly, the stallion nuzzled the hollow of her hand. Abbie returned to the subject that was really on her mind. "My mother must have known about this all along. Why did she put up with it?" Abbie didn't really expect an answer, but Lane gave her one.

"I think . . . . they reached an understanding."

"Momma does have a knack for ignoring anything remotely unpleasant," Abbie admitted, wryly cynical. But his answer explained why she had childhood images of her mother shutting herself in her room for hours and coming out with red and swollen eyes whenever her father left on a "business" trip to California; yet in recent years, Abbie could only recall her mother being unusually silent right after he'd gone. "How many other people knew about Daddy's . . . . affair?"

"Initially there was some gossip, but it pretty well died out a long time ago."

"And this woman, the one he had an affair with — what happened to her?"

"She died several years ago. Rachel's been pretty much on her own since she was seventeen."

"You expect her to be named as one of the beneficiaries in Daddy's will, don't you?"

"I think it's logical to assume he would have included her."

"And if he didn't, she could contest the will and demand her share of his estate, couldn't she?" Abbie challenged, voicing the fear that had been twisting her insides all during the long ride from the cemetery — a fear that filled her with anger and deep resentment. River Bend was her home. It had been in the Lawson family for generations. This Rachel person had no right to any part of it.

"That will depend on how the will is written. Dean may have directed the bulk of his estate to go to his widow, Babs, or he may have set up a trust, giving her a life estate on the property and providing for it to pass on to his heirs upon her death."

" 'Heirs'? If you're going to use the plural, shouldn't it be 'heiresses'?" she suggested stiffly.

"Until the will is read, Abbie, I don't think we should be anticipating problems."

"I'm not like my mother, Lane. I prefer to face every possible contingency. And you can't deny that this might end up in a long and messy court battle."

"It's possible."

Looking away from him, Abbie gazed out over the shaded pastures all the way to the distant line of trees that hugged the banks of the Brazos. She knew every foot of River Bend, every bush and every tree. The horses out there — she could call them all by name and list their pedigree. This was her heritage. How could Lane stand there and tell her not to feel that it was threatened?

"Who was his mistress? What was she like?" She sensed his hesitation and swung back to face him. "I want to know. And don't worry about sparing my feelings. It's better if I know the truth after all these years. Momma probably doesn't know what it is anymore. You're the only one who can give me that."

After studying her thoughtfully for several seconds, Lane began telling her all he knew. "Her name was Caroline Farr. She was from somewhere in the East, I believe. Dean met her at a private showing of an art exhibition at the Museum of Fine Arts here in Houston."

5

Hot and tired, Dean tugged at the knot of his tie as he climbed the grand staircase to the second-floor suite he shared with his wife. He wished to hell he could shed all the pressure and frustration of the office as easily as he could shed the business suit and tie he wore to it. For three damned long years he had tried, but he just didn't fit the mold. Whereas making business decisions was so easy for R.D., Dean would agonize for days before recommending a course of action, and even then, most of the time he hadn't considered half the options R.D. raised. He had never felt so inadequate.

A long gallop before dinner, that's what he needed, Dean decided as he pushed open the door to their bedroom and walked in. He paused when he saw Babs, clad in a dressing gown and seated at the vanity table, primping in the beveled mirror.

"There you are, darling." Her reflection smiled at him from the mirror. "How was your day?"

"Rotten." Dean pulled the loosened tie from around his neck and closed the door behind him.

"That's too bad. But tonight you can relax and forget all about it and just enjoy yourself," she declared airily and waved a hand in the direction of the four-poster bed with its delicately carved maple posts ending in ornate finials and its Marlborough feet. "I had Jackson lay out your clothes, and your bathwater is already drawn."

Dean stared at the evening suit so precisely laid out on the peach and green floral-striped spread and began to tremble with anger. "What's going on? Don't tell me. Let me guess. It's another one of your damned parties." He couldn't hide the disgust he felt. Night after night, there was always something: a formal dinner invitation, a charity benefit — or if they stayed at home, they invariably had company over to dine, when they weren't the ones giving the party.

"Darling." Babs partially turned around to look at him, her hazel eyes widened by the look of hurt surprise he had come to know so well after nearly three years of marriage. "Tonight they're holding that private showing at the museum. When I asked, you said you wanted to go."

Maybe he had. He didn't remember. Too many other things were on his mind. "I've changed my mind, and we're not going."

"But everyone's expecting us to be there."

"Just once, can't we have a quiet evening at home?" "And talk," he wanted to add, but he had already learned that Babs didn't want to listen. Every time he tried to express the doubts he had about his role in the company and the dissatisfaction he felt, she brushed them aside with some variation of "It's hard now, but I know you'll work it out. You always do." He tried to tell himself that it was wonderful to have a wife who believed in him, who believed he could handle it. But he couldn't handle it. What would she think of him when she found that out?

"We'll stay home if that's what you want. I honestly didn't know that you didn't want to go tonight. I'm sorry. Truly I am." She rose from the peach velvet cushion covering the seat of the carved maple bench and crossed the room to cup his face in her hands. "I want to do whatever you want. So if you don't want to go, neither do I."

She smiled brightly, but he knew it was a lie. She loved all these social functions. It gave her the chance to be a little girl again and play dress-up. He felt guilty for depriving her of that. Just because he was miserable, that was no reason to make her evening miserable, too.

"We'll go." He caught one of her hands and pressed her fingertips to his lips. "You're probably right. I need to go out and take my mind off the office."

"I know I am." Raising on her tiptoes, Babs kissed him warmly. "Now, hurry and take your bath before the water gets as cool as rain."

Minutes later, Dean was stretched out in the long, claw-footed bathtub, letting the tension float away and sipping on a bourbon and water Babs had thoughtfully fixed for him. He listened with only half an ear to Babs as she chatted away to him from the other side of the door to their private bath.

"You're just going to love the new gown I'm wearing tonight, Dean." There was a slight pause before she continued. "Remind me to wear these stiletto heels the next time we're going to a party where there will be dancing. They are positively deadly. Once and for all I'm going to cure that left-footed Kyle MacDonnell of stepping on my feet. Oh, talking about cures, that reminds me . . . I was talking to Josie Phillips the other day, and she told me that if I wanted to guarantee myself of getting pregnant that we needed to make love on a night when there is a full moon."

"What?" The water sloshed around him as Dean sat bolt upright in the tub, hoping his hearing had deceived him.

"A full moon. Isn't that the wildest thing you've ever heard? But Josie swears that all four of her children were conceived when she and Homer did it on nights when there was a full moon outside. I checked the calendar, and there won't be a full moon again until the middle of this month."

In a flash, Dean was out of the tub. He was still dripping water as he opened the connecting door and walked into the bedroom, absently tying the sash of his terry-cloth robe around his waist.

"Babs, just how many people have you told that you haven't been able to get pregnant?"

She gave him a blank look, then shrugged. "I don't know. It's hardly a secret. People aren't blind. They can see for themselves that I'm not going to have a baby," Babs declared, smoothing a hand over the close-fitting waistline of her off-the-shoulder evening dress in a black-on-white floral silk. "What am I supposed to say when people ask when we're going to have a baby? That we don't want one yet? You know we do. And you know how anxious poor R.D. is for us to have one."

"I don't think it's something you should be going around telling every Helen, Mary, and Jane about." He had enough trouble without having to face friends who knew he couldn't even manage to get his wife pregnant. "If you want to talk to someone about it, talk to a doctor."

"I have." She slipped on a long white-kid evening glove, carefully fitting the snug material between each finger. "He said I was just being too anxious and that what we needed to do was stop trying. Have you ever heard anything so preposterous? How in the world does he expect me to get pregnant if we don't do anything?" She reached for her other glove. "You really need to hurry and get dressed, honey. R.D. is already waiting for us downstairs."

At the private showing of the art museum's latest acquisitions, Dean viewed the new paintings with indifference. A low hum of voices surrounded him, the volume mostly subdued, although occasionally a cultured laugh rose above it. Despite the setting, there was a sameness to the gathering — the same people, the same conversation, and the same high-fashion look that made up nearly every affair Babs insisted they attend.

He wished now he hadn't given in and agreed to come. He could have been home at River Bend with the horses. There was a show in two weeks and he wanted the half-dozen Arabians they were taking to be in top condition. Not that he really needed to worry about that — not with Ben on the job. He envied Ben being able to work with the horses every day, all day. All he could manage was an early-morning ride.

When Babs wandered on to another painting, Dean drifted along with her, managing to appear interested even though he wasn't. The work was some surrealist thing, an incongruous mixture of colors and images. R.D. joined them, with the MacDonnells in tow.

"Amazing work, isn't it?" Beth Ann remarked, studying the painting as if mesmerized. "So full of power and energy, don't you think?"

Dean nodded and wished he had a drink.

"I think" — Babs paused as she contemplated the painting a little longer — "he must have really liked red."

For an instant, there was absolute silence. Then R.D. burst out laughing. "Babs, you're just too precious for words," he declared, wiping the tears from his eyes. "I swear, those are the first honest words I've heard tonight. Come on." He hooked a big arm around her small shoulders and herded her toward another painting on the other side of the room. "You've got to see this one over here."

A slightly embarrassed Beth Ann trailed after them dragging Kyle along with her, but Dean stayed behind and pretended to study the painting on the wall. Right now he wasn't in the mood for his father's company.

"Do you like it?"

Dean glanced sideways at the woman who had come up on his right. He was faintly surprised to discover he didn't know her. That in itself was a novelty, but so was the woman. She wasn't dressed like Babs or any of her friends. Instead she wore a plain black sheath and absolutely no jewelry. Her dark hair was lifted back from her face, then allowed to fall in a thick cascade onto her back — a style that didn't remotely resemble the curls of Babs's Italian cut.

As unusual as the woman's appearance was, Dean wasn't interested in making idle conversation with a stranger. "I find the painting very interesting," he said and started to move on.

"Then you don't like it," she stated flatly.

"I didn't say that." Dean frowned.

"No," she agreed. "You said it was 'very interesting.' That's what everybody says when they don't really like something."

"In this case, it isn't true. I happen to like surrealism," he replied, mildly irritated by the hint of censure in her voice, and tired of others believing that they knew what he liked or wanted.

"This isn't true surrealism, not like Dali." She continued to study the painting, her unusually thick eyebrows drawn together in a slight frown. "It's too coherent for that. This is more like a picture puzzle."

She spoke with such certainty and authority that Dean found himself drawn in by it. "What makes you say that?"

"Because . . ." And she went on to explain the symbolic use of numerals to represent mankind and the human intellect set against the blazing red of the sun, the vivid green of the land, and the swirling blue of water, creating an allegory of man and his relationship with nature.

Dean followed only part of it. Somewhere along the way, he became fascinated by her intensity — an intensity that was both serious and passionate. It was there in her gray eyes, the dark gray of the clouds on the leading edge of a thunderstorm, clouds shot with lightning and jet black in the center. It seemed perfectly natural to shift his attention from her eyes to her mouth. She had soft, full lips, the lower one pouting in its roundness — blatantly sensuous, not at all dainty like the sweetheart shape of Babs's. Dean started wondering what they would look like if she smiled.

"Do you work here at the museum?"

"No, I don't."

"You spoke so knowledgeably that I thought. . ." He shrugged off the rest of it.

"I've studied art extensively and spent two years in Europe going from museum to museum, poring over the works of the old masters."

"Are you a collector then?" Although he had never been good at judging a woman's age, she seemed young — young for an art collector, anyway. Dean doubted that she was any older than he was.

"No." She looked at him with a kind of amused tolerance. "I'm an artist."

"You are. Don't tell me this is one of your paintings." Dean stared at the oil she had lectured about so intelligently only minutes ago.

"No." She smiled for the first time — just a curving of the mouth, her lips together. "My style is much more turbulent, more emotional, not landscapes of the mind like his." As she gestured at the painting, Dean noticed her hands, the long fingers and the short nails. The hands of an artist, graceful and blunt.

"What's your name? I have the uncomfortable feeling that I'm going to be embarrassed when I find out who you are."

"I doubt it." Again there was that little smile. "I'm what is known as a struggling artist. I don't think the name Caroline Farr is going to mean anything to you. Maybe someday, but not now."

"I'm Dean Lawson." As he formally shook hands with her, Dean noticed the strength of her fingers and the firmness of her grip. He also noticed that his name didn't mean a thing to her. More than that, she didn't seem all that impressed by him. It pricked his ego just a little bit. Between his looks and his name, Dean had never had any problems attracting women, but Caroline Farr was obviously different. "I'd like to see some of your paintings sometime."

"I should warn you they're not surrealistic."

"My wife will be glad to hear that. She doesn't care for it at all."

At that point their conversation returned to a discussion of art, and the inability of many to appreciate its different forms and styles. More precisely, Caroline talked and Dean agreed.

"Your accent . . ." Dean tried to place it and failed. "You're from somewhere in the East, aren't you?"

"Connecticut."

"Are you just visiting here in Houston?"

"Not really. Right now I'm staying at a friend's summer house in Galveston." When she said that, Dean automatically began to scan the milling guests, trying to remember which one had a beach house on Galveston Island. "It doesn't belong to anyone here."

"Was I that transparent?" Dean smiled.

"Yes."

"Sorry. But, since you're not from here, you're obviously someone's guest."

"Why?"

"Because this affair tonight is by invitation. The collection doesn't go on public display until tomorrow."

"Tomorrow I'll be in Galveston. I wanted to see it tonight."

"My God." Unconsciously Dean lowered his voice. "You mean you crashed this? You just walked in?" He hovered between incredulity and stunned admiration of her audacity.

"Of course." She was very matter of fact about it and indifferent almost to the point of arrogance. "This isn't someone's home. It's a public museum. Why should it be open to one — privileged — class of people and not to all?"

"That's a good point." He tried not to smile. "However, most if not all of these guests are patrons of the museum."

"Because they have donated works of art or money, does that entitle them to special treatment?" she countered in a challenging tone.

"They think so."

"I don't."

"Obviously." Dean had never met anyone like her before. He'd heard that artists were a proud, temperamental breed. Wealth and status supposedly meant nothing to them. Dean found that hard to believe, even though this Caroline Farr seemed to feel that way. "You know, I really would like to see some of your paintings."

She gave him a long, thoughtful look. "Most afternoons you can find me on the west end of the beach."

Someone came up to speak to him. When Dean turned back, she was gone. He was surprised to find that he wanted her still to be there — that he wanted to talk to her and learn more about her. He was intrigued by her seriousness and her passion, the intensity that emanated from inside her and charged the air around her. He caught sight of her across the room, tall, statuesque, dramatic in black. He wanted to go over there to her, but he didn't. He'd already been seen talking at length with her. It wouldn't look right if he sought her out again. Dean smiled faintly as the thought occurred to him that Caroline Farr would probably mock such a conventional attitude. She wasn't bound by the rules that restrained him. He wondered what it would be like to feel free to say and do what he wanted, without worrying about whether he was living up to someone else's expectations: his father's, his wife's, or his friends'.

A seagull swooped low in front of his car as Dean drove along the deserted beach, the window rolled down to admit the stiff breeze blowing in from the Gulf. His jacket and tie lay over the back of the passenger seat. The sleeves of his shirt were rolled up and the collar unbuttoned. He felt like a kid playing hooky for the first time — a little guilty because he hadn't returned to the office or gone home after the meeting, and a little excited because he was doing something he shouldn't.

But the farther he drove on the tideline's hard-packed sand, the more his excitement faded. For the last half-mile, he hadn't seen a single soul, not even a surf fisherman. She had told him he could find her here "most afternoons," but obviously not this one. Admittedly it was late, Dean thought as he squinted into the glare of the sun hovering low in the western sky. He wondered if maybe it was just as well that Caroline wasn't here. He'd be better off if he forgot all about her. Of course, he'd tried that, but he just hadn't been able to get her off his mind these last four days.

More than once, Dean had questioned why, out of all the women he knew, he was constantly thinking about Caroline. Her looks were striking, but he could name any number of women who were more beautiful. And his marriage was basically a happy one. Sure, there were times when he wished he could talk to Babs about some of the things that troubled him, but that didn't change the way he felt toward his wife. That was just silly, lovable Babs, and he really didn't want her any other way.

As he thought about Babs, Dean realized that he had no business being out here. He was about to turn the car around, when he saw Caroline about fifty yards ahead on the edge of the sand dunes. In that second he forgot everything: vows, loyalty, and convention. It was all gone, lost in the excitement of seeing her again.

Intent on the canvas propped on her easel, Caroline didn't even look up when he stopped the car a few yards away and climbed out. Dean walked over to her slowly, taking advantage of the chance to gaze at her unobserved.

Her hair was caught up in a ponytail secured with a string of red yarn, but the strong sea breeze had tugged several long, dark strands loose and now lashed them across her face — a face that was a study of concentration, her gray eyes narrowed, flicking their glance sharply from the canvas to the scene she was trying to capture, then back again, her dark eyebrows drawn together, and the line of her mouth pulled taut in determination, her full lips pressed firmly together. There was a paint smudge on her cheek, and another on the point of her chin.

More paint was splattered on the man's plaid shirt she wore with the tails tied in a knot at her waist. The looseness of the shirt failed to hide the outline of her breasts, thanks to the breeze that shaped the cotton material to her body. A pair of snug capri pants was stretched over her full hips and emphasized her long, slender legs. She was barefoot, her toes half buried in the sand. Somehow Dean had guessed she would have beautiful feet.

"The artist at work," he said.

"I'll be finished here in just a . . . few . . . short . . . minutes." Each pause was filled with decisive strokes of the brush.

"Do you mind if I look?"

"Not at all," she replied, shrugging her indifference but not taking her concentration off the painting except to dab her brush in more paint from the palette she held in her left hand.

Dean circled around to stand behind her left shoulder. Flames radiated from the canvas, a core of red-orange spreading to yellow-orange, then gold, and yellow-white to tan. Swirled in amidst them from both sides came shades of light blue and dark green. The fiery turbulence of the painting made such a visual impact that Dean didn't immediately see the image of a late-afternoon seascape with the waves reflecting the long trail of light cast by the setting sun.

"It's very powerful," he said quietly.

The Sun and the Sea, she called it as she paused to study it critically. "I like to take subjects that have been painted endlessly by artists and see if they still can move us."

"I think you've succeeded." Dean didn't pretend to be an expert, but he was impressed with the sensation of intense heat and light that the painting evoked.

"Maybe. Either way, I'm losing the sunlight effect on the water that I want." Smoothly, efficiently, she began cleaning up and stowing her paints and brushes away. "Care to join me for a drink?"

"Sure."

The summer house sat off by itself in a sandy meadow of sea oats. Supported by a network of pilings that protected it from high water, it resembled a large square box with legs. Once the house had sported a coat of sunshine yellow, but long ago the sun had bleached it to a shade of cream.

During the short drive to the house, Caroline had explained that it belonged to the parents of a friend, a fellow teacher. Caroline, it seemed, was a struggling artist rather than a starving one, who supported herself by teaching art classes in elementary school. She devoted all of her summer vacation to her own artwork.

"What made you pick Galveston?" Dean took the easel out of the backseat and followed Caroline up the driveway of crushed seashells.

"It was a place to live rent-free. Truthfully, it was more than that. I'd never stayed on this side of the Gulf Coast before. Just around Sanibel Island on the Florida side." She climbed the flight of wooden stairs to the wide porch that ringed the beach house. From the porch, the shimmer of sunlight reflected on the rolling water of the Gulf could be seen. "I've always been drawn by the sea. As a child I lived in a house only three blocks from the Sound. Maybe that's why I always want to be close to it. It's so . . . primordial. We all come from it. Even the fluids in our bodies have a high saline content. Without salt, we'd all die. So maybe my need is much more primitive than just being used to living near it." As Caroline pulled the screen door open, Dean caught it and held it open for her, then followed her inside.

The kitchen, dining, and living area was all one big room, starkly furnished with the bare essentials of table, chairs, and sofa. The rest of the space had been turned into a temporary art studio. Caroline walked directly to it and propped the partially finished painting on an empty stand.

"You can set the easel by the door," she said. "There's cold beer and part of a bottle of wine in the refrigerator. Help yourself."

"What would you like?" Dean hesitated for an instant, then set the easel against the wall by the door and went into the kitchen.

"I prefer wine. A holdover from my sojourn in France, I suppose."

After she finished putting her paints and equipment away, she washed the paint from her hands and face in the kitchen sink. But she didn't attempt to freshen up any more than that, neither brushing her windblown hair nor applying new makeup to her clean face. Not that Dean thought either was needed to improve her appearance, but he was slightly taken aback by her lack of vanity. As she sat on the couch next to him, curling one long leg beneath her, Dean silently admired her strong self-confidence.

They talked, covering a variety of subjects. One drink led to two, and two led to three. In many ways they were so different, coming from totally diverse backgrounds and lifestyles, yet Dean couldn't remember a time when he'd enjoyed a woman's company so much.

Caroline drank the last of her wine and reached down, setting the glass on the floor. There was no end table. She turned back to face him, sitting sideways on the couch with an elbow propped on the backrest near his head.

"I wasn't sure I wanted you to come here," she admitted, letting her gaze wander over his face.

"Why?" He suddenly didn't feel too sure of his ground, not with her.

"Because I was afraid you were going to be one of those insufferable bores who brags all the time about how much he's worth and what he owns." She smoothed the lock of hair at his temple, then let her fingers trail into his hair. "I'm glad you're not."

"So am I." Reaching up, Dean cupped his hand over the nape of her neck and slowly drew her face closer.

The moment was inevitable. It had been since he met her on the beach. This was what he'd come for, what he wanted. Caroline did as well. He could see it when he looked into the velvety depths of her gray eyes.

As he kissed her, her lips opened and Dean groaned at the silken feel of her mouth, taking him in, wanting all of him. He felt as if he'd been swept into one of her paintings, fiery-hot and turbulent, his need for her consuming him, primordial as the sea.

In one sinuous movement, she uncurled her body and turned to lie sideways across his lap, never losing contact with his mouth. Her body was there for him to touch and explore. As his hands roamed over her, cupping a breast, stroking a thigh, curling over a hip, she was all motion beneath them, her soft buttocks rubbing across his stiffening joint in exquisite torture.

She nuzzled his ear, the darting of her tongue creating more excitement. "I want to undress you, Dean," she whispered. For one split second he was too stunned to react. Jesus God, he thought. He'd heard artists were uninhibited. He tried to imagine Babs saying something like that to him, but even drunk, she would be incapable of it. "I want to see your body."

Everything from that point on had the quality of a dream: Dean standing motionless while she removed his clothes, piece by piece, the touch of her hands on his naked skin setting off a wildness he had never known, the bright glow that had leaped into her eyes when she saw his erection, and the sound of her low voice telling him there was nothing more beautiful than a man's body. Her own clothes seemed to disappear in the blink of an eye. In that instant, Dean knew there was nothing more beautiful than this woman's body, with its firmly shaped breasts, slender waist, and wide hips made to cradle a man.

Then he was holding her, loving her, rolling his tongue around her taut nipples while she writhed against him, her hands urging, her body exhorting, her legs twining around to draw him inside. There was no sanity, only hot sensations rocking through him, carrying him to a depth of passion, a stormy rapture.

Afterward Dean surfaced slowly, knowing he had never been loved nor given of himself so completely. This incredible woman in his arms had reached into his soul and brought out emotions he hadn't known he could feel.

By the time he could make himself leave Caroline, it was late. That night when he got home, he made tender love to Babs, letting his body beg forgiveness for his adultery, knowing he would do it again and again.

From that night on, Dean saw Caroline whenever he could, stealing an hour here, two hours there, sometimes an entire evening. It meant he had to lie, to make up fictitious appointments and invent excuses for coming home later than usual. He shied away from pretending he had to work late, fearing that his father might begin to question that. Most of the time he used Lane Canfield, claiming he had a meeting with him or he'd run into him somewhere, knowing that because of his long friendship with Lane, such an excuse wasn't likely to arouse suspicion. Other times it was an Arabian horse somebody had that he'd gone to see.

Dean tried not to think about the double life he was leading: on one hand, the devoted, loving husband, maintaining the routine of married life as if everything were normal, and on the other, the eager lover, cherishing every second spent with his mistress. Not once did he let himself wonder how long it could go on. There was only now. Nothing else mattered.

With Caroline, Dean felt free to be himself for the first time in his life — sexually free, confident that nothing would shock or offend her; and emotionally free, certain that he could talk openly about his feelings and know that she would understand.

At the same time that he told her about his dream to someday turn River Bend into the top Arabian stud farm in the world, a contemporary rival to the legendary Crabbet Park Stud in England or Janow Podlaski in Poland, he admitted the mixed feelings he had about working in his father's company, wanting to please him while knowing he lacked the ability ever to run the multimillion-dollar corporation.

"He's wrong to expect you to follow in his footsteps, Dean," Caroline stated in the black-and-white way she had in her opinions. "No one can do that — and shouldn't. You are an individual. His way will never be yours. You need to tell him that. Make him understand what you want. Just because the company is his life's work, that doesn't mean it has to be yours. He probably won't like it when you tell him that, but what can he do? He has to respect you for taking a stand. And he has to know that you didn't reach this decision without ever trying to see if it was something you could do."

Although Dean was willing to concede that she was right, he was hesitant to take such a giant step. Caroline had never met R.D. She had never seen him tear someone's logic to shreds, then piece it back together, creating a totally different conclusion. But he did sit down with R.D. and discuss his desire to take a more active role in the breeding operation and relieve R.D. of some of that responsibility. R.D. agreed to it almost immediately. Dean felt that if he could prove himself with the Arabians, his father would be more receptive to the idea of Dean dropping out of the company.

Life suddenly seemed very good to him — complicated, perhaps, but good just the same. Everything seemed to be within his reach: Caroline, the horses — everything.

Whistling a catchy tune he'd heard on the car radio driving home, R.D. crossed the living room's parquet floor of light chestnut and dark walnut boards and paused in the archway leading to the hall to do a mock little sashay, then proceeded to the staircase. He paused at the bottom and hollered up, "Babs, girl! I'm ready to go do a little dancin' if you are!" He started whistling again as he waited for her to come down. When he failed to hear the sound of her footsteps in the upstairs hall, he stopped and cocked his head to listen. Nothing.

"Babs?" he called again, then started up the stairs. It wasn't like her to be late for a party, and certainly not when it was gonna be a good ol' Texas barbecue.

When he reached the second-floor landing, he turned and walked over to the door to the bedroom suite that belonged to Babs and Dean. R.D. paused outside to listen and heard a faint noise that sounded like Babs was sniffling. He knocked once and reached for the doorknob. She was standing at the window with her back to the door when he opened it. A lace shawl was draped around her shoulders, covering the Mexican-style peasant blouse that went with the bright full skirt.

"Babs, are you ready to go?" R.D. frowned at the startled way she jumped when she heard his voice then hastily wiped her nose with a wadded handkerchief. He wasn't sure, but he thought she dabbed quickly at her eyes before she turned away from the window.

"I'm sorry, R.D. I guess I didn't hear you." Her voice was tremulous as she went through the motions of looking around her. "I know I laid my clutch purse somewhere."

"Here it is." R.D. picked it up from its resting place on the marble-topped side table by the door. "What's the matter? Are you coming down with a summer cold?"

"Maybe a little one." But she avoided looking at him as she walked over to get her purse from him.

She looked unnaturally pale. When she got closer, R.D. could see the telltale redness of her eyes. "I don't think you've got a cold. Those look like tears to me."

"Nonsense." She airily tried to brush aside his comment, but R.D. had never been one to be brushed aside easily.

"I know tears when I see them. Now either you've been peeling onions or something's the matter. Why don't you tell me what's bothering you, girl?"

"I — Oh, R.D., I don't know what to do." After a faltering attempt to deny anything was wrong, she started to cry again.

"There, there." He put an arm around her shoulders and guided her over to the apricot-colored chaise longue. There he sat her down and gave her his clean handkerchief. "It can't be as bad as all that."

"That's what I keep telling myself." Babs sniffled. "But what if it is?"

"Why don't you stop this boo-hooing for a minute and tell me what this 'it' is?"

"I — it's Dean." She lifted her tearful glance to his face. "I . . . think he's seeing . . . another woman."

He felt first disbelief, then a kind of dazed shock as he looked back over the last two months and saw a pattern to Dean's absences. Still, to Babs, he denied it. "Whatever gave you that silly notion?"

"He's been late so much and . . . and . . . Tomi Fredericks told me this afternoon that he's been seeing a woman in Galveston." She rushed the awful words in her haste to get them said. "Some . . . bohemian artist," Babs added, as if that made it worse.

"Now how in the name of Sam Houston would she know?" R.D. wondered aloud.

"She said that . . . Billie Joe Townsend saw them together on the beach last Friday night when Dean said he'd gone to look at a horse. According to him, Dean kissed her right there in public and then . . . they went walking off down the beach together, so close that you couldn't have got a slip of paper between them. And Tomi claimed that . . . others have seen them, too."

"And you call that proof?" R.D. chided. "Somebody saw somebody who looked like Dean. Did any of them talk to him?"

"I don't think so," she admitted.

"Well, then it seems to me your so-called friend Tomi is just trying to stir up trouble."

"But what if she isn't? What if it's true? He's been so different lately — so preoccupied. Tonight he said he was going to have a drink with Lane and meet us at the barbecue. But what if he isn't? What if he's really with her?"

"And what if cows fly? There's about as much chance of that as there is of Dean leaving you for some other woman. And that's the truth." He'd see to it. "Now, when I take a girl to a party, I expect her to be smiling and happy. So you go wash away those tears on your face and meet me downstairs in" — R.D. made a show of looking at his watch — "five minutes."

"Five minutes." She gazed at him with a glimmer of a grateful smile on her face. "I just love you to pieces, R.D." She pressed a wet kiss firmly on his cheek.

"You'd better behave yourself, girl, or folks'll start talking." He winked at her and smiled.

But the smile faded from his face as he went downstairs and closed the pocket doors in the library before he reached for the telephone.

The next morning, Dean stifled a yawn as he entered the office of his secretary, Mary Jo Anderson. "Late night?" She smiled and peered knowingly at him over the tops of her horn-rimmed glasses. Trained as a legal secretary, she had joined the company six years ago and knew more about the mechanics of the company than he did. Bright and efficient, she had covered his mistakes many times.

"That's putting it mildly." He stopped at her desk to pick up his telephone messages. "If it had been left up to my wife, we still would be dancing. Luckily the band packed up their instruments and went home at two in the morning."

"There's a message there from Lane Canfield. He wanted you to call him back as soon as you came in. He said it was important."

"Will do." He separated it from the others and put it on top, then continued on to the connecting door to his private office, smothering another yawn. "Better bring me a cup of coffee, Mary Jo," Dean said over his shoulder as he pushed open his door.

"Black with lots of sugar?"

"You've got it." Leaving the door open, he walked straight to his desk and picked up the phone. After dialing Lane's number, he settled himself in the swivel chair behind his desk. Directly in front of him on the opposite wall hung the painting Caroline called *The Sun and the Sea*. Every time he looked at it, it was like having her there with him. "Lane," Dean said when his voice came on the line. "How the hell are you?"

"Busy as usual. And you?"

"The same. Mary Jo said you wanted to talk to me right away. What's up?" Just at that moment, she walked in bringing his coffee.

"I had a strange phone call from your father last night," Lane said. Dean froze. For a split second he couldn't think. He couldn't even breathe. "Dean? Are you there?"

"Yes." He felt the first rush of panic as Mary Jo set his coffee cup on the desk. "Yes, just a minute." Covering the receiver's mouthpiece with his hand, he held it away from him and struggled to keep his voice pitched normally. "Would you mind closing the door on your way out, Mary Jo?"

"Of course."

Dean waited until he heard the click of the latch before he uncovered the mouthpiece. "Sorry, I'm back now. You said R.D. called? What did he want?"

"He was looking for you. He had the impression we were supposed to be together."

"What did you tell him?" Dean felt himself breaking into a sweat. He should have guessed that sooner or later something like this would happen, and been prepared for it. But he hadn't.

"I wasn't sure what to say. So I . . . gave him a story that I had gotten tied up with some last-minute paperwork and we were supposed to meet later."

"Thanks," Dean said, exhaling the breath he'd unconsciously been holding.

"He didn't leave any message. Just said he'd talk to you later."

Lane paused expectantly, but Dean couldn't fill the gap. "Would you mind telling me what's going on?"

After carrying on a silent debate with himself, Dean realized he had to tell somebody. He couldn't keep it to himself any longer. And he knew he could trust Lane. Dean started talking and didn't stop until he had told Lane practically everything about Caroline and his relationship with her. "I know this probably sounds trite, but Caroline is the most incredible woman I've ever met. I love everything about her." Dean paused, and smiled self-consciously. "I guess I kinda got carried away with my answer, didn't I?"

"A little."

"I want you to meet her, Lane." It suddenly seemed very important to have his best friend meet the woman he loved. "I've got an appointment in Texas City late this morning. Caroline is going to drive up to meet me for lunch. Are you free? Could you join us?"

"I had planned to drop by the plant this afternoon. I probably could get away from here a little earlier than that."

"Try," Dean urged.

Lane promised that he would.

Initially, Lane had been prepared to dismiss Dean's voluble praise as the rantings of a married man enjoying his first taste of forbidden fruit. But after seeing Caroline and him together at the small café, communicating with a look or a touch, and completing each other's sentences, he knew he was wrong. This wasn't some infatuation that would eventually burn itself out. It was much more serious than that.

Lane could even understand what had attracted Dean to Caroline in the first place. She was intelligent and articulate, serious and dedicated. Nothing was ever halfway with her — not even love. She either loved something or someone totally and completely, or not at all. She was the antithesis of Babs.

As he watched them, he had the feeling he was looking at a pair of star-crossed lovers. No matter how much in love they were, Lane could see that they had nothing in common. Their clothes typified it, Dean in his Brooks Brothers suit and Caroline in her black pants and shirt. Their attitudes and their outlooks were nowhere near the same. Saddest of all, Lane recognized that, individually, they couldn't — and wouldn't — change.

As the three of them left the café, Lane started to say his good-byes and leave, but Dean stopped him. "You can't go yet. Caroline has something for you."

Curious, Lane followed them over to her vintage Chevrolet. A framed and mounted canvas sat in the backseat, carefully separated from a clutter of rags, easels, and boxes. With Dean's help, Caroline lifted it out and presented it to Lane.

Shades of gray, white, and black swirled out at him, shot with splinters of silver-gold. Within the enveloping mists of the painting, Lane had the impression of spires, tall cylinders, and a long vertical shaft.

"Do you recognize it?" Dean asked, his eyes alight as he watched Lane's face.

"There is something familiar about it," Lane admitted, but the images were too faint, hidden too well by the swirl of white and gray.

"It's the San Jacinto Monument with the tank farms and chemical plants in the ship channel in the background, shrouded in the early-morning fog and the smoke and fumes from the chemical plants."

As soon as Dean explained it, Lane was suddenly able to discern the faint outline of the lone star, the symbol of Texas, atop the monument's limestone shaft. "Yes, of course."

"I call it *Progress*," Caroline said.

A somewhat cynical observation, Lane thought, then decided that he was becoming too sensitive over anything that even implied criticism of the pollution around the ship channel. He also recognized that she could have depicted a scene much worse than the reality of the acidic haze and smoke that blanketed the area. She could have painted the waterway itself on fire.

"I like it, Caroline," Lane stated, after studying it a little longer, then he smiled. "And if I was supposed to get a message, I did. I'll hang it in my office just to remind me."

"Dean said you wouldn't be offended." As she looked at him with approval, Lane couldn't help wondering if he had just passed some test. "I have to be going," she said and turned to Dean.

Lane quickly interjected his good-bye and carried the painting to his car so the two lovers could have a degree of privacy. As Caroline drove out of the lot, Dean rejoined him.

"Didn't I tell you she was talented and wonderful?"

"You certainly did," Lane agreed.

"I'm glad you like the painting. You know, she won't let me buy her any presents. I should say, expensive presents. Canvas, paints, brushes — those she'll accept. But she just isn't interested in material things like clothes, jewelry, or perfume. Can you imagine meeting a woman like that?"

"No — at least, not until today."

As Dean gazed in the direction she'd gone, his faint, musing smile changed into a vaguely troubled frown. "I keep wondering why R.D. never mentioned anything about calling you when I talked to him at the barbecue last night."

"Maybe it just slipped his mind."

"R.D.?" Dean retorted skeptically. "He has an elephant's memory."

To play it safe, Dean had stayed close to the office and home for the next three days, but his need for Caroline outweighed caution and he'd finally had to see her, just for a little while. Even so, the fear that his father might suspect something forced Dean to look at his present situation and try to decide what he wanted to do about it. He loved Caroline and he wanted to spend every minute of his time with her, yet he still cared for Babs — not as deeply as he did for Caroline, but just the same, he didn't want to hurt her. She was completely innocent. She was a good wife, a loving wife. None of this was fair to her. But he also knew that he'd never be able to give Caroline up. Selfishly, what he wanted was for things to go on the way they were.

As he looked over the new crop of foals grazing in the near pasture with the mares, Dean felt an empathy with the foals. Right now, their world was perfect — their mothers right there by their sides offering comfort, protection, and a ready supply of milk — but soon they would have to be weaned. The separation of mare and foal would cause suffering. If Man didn't do it, Mother Nature would. It was unavoidable. Dean knew he was personally faced with a similar situation. It was unrealistic to pretend things didn't have to change. The trauma of a separation was inevitable, but a separation from whom? That's what he'd kept asking himself when he'd gone to see Caroline after work that afternoon.

Sighing, he pushed away from the fence and walked toward the house. Not a breath of air stirred the leaves of the ancient oaks and pecans that shaded the lawn. The hot, sultry weather of an East Texas early August had settled over River Bend with a vengeance. By the time Dean climbed the veranda steps, his cotton shirt and jeans were sticking to him, the denim material drawing tightly against his legs with each stride.

Some claimed that air-conditioning was man's greatest gift to Texas. Dean wholeheartedly agreed with that as he stepped inside and paused a minute to let the coolness wash over him. Intent on a shower and a change of clothes, he headed for the stairs, the heavy thud of his cowboy boots on the foyer's heart-pine floor echoing through the house with its fourteen-foot-high ceilings. But before Dean reached the massive staircase, R.D. walked into view and paused beneath the curved archway to the library.

"Would you mind stepping in here, Dean? I need to talk to you." R.D. turned and walked back into the library. Dean hesitated a minute, then followed him inside the room lined on two walls with glass-enclosed bookcases of heavy walnut. As R.D. rounded the curved hunt desk that faced the fireplace, he glanced back at Dean. "Close the doors."

Suddenly uneasy, Dean backtracked and pulled the pocket doors shut, then turned around and moved hesitantly forward. "Is something wrong?"

"That's what I'd like to know." R.D. sat down on the walnut-framed swivel chair padded with navy-blue leather and tilted it back to fix his gaze on Dean.

"I don't follow you." Frowning, Dean shook his head slightly, all the while feeling more uncomfortable.

"I think you do," R.D. stated and rocked his chair forward to rest his arms on the desk in front of him. "Where did you go after you left the office tonight?"

"Why?" Dean struggled not to look guilty, well aware that inside he was squirming just like he had when he was a kid, caught doing something he shouldn't. "Did something happen?"

"Just answer the question."

Lying had become second nature to him. "Babs has a birthday coming up. I . . . was out looking for a present for her."

"Like you met Lane the other night?"

Dean tried to laugh. "I don't know what you're talking about."

"Dammit, boy! Don't lie to me!" R.D. brought a hand crashing down on the desktop. Then he stood up and breathed in deeply, making a visible effort to control his temper. "You know damned well what I'm talking about. You've been seeing some woman in Galveston, so don't bother to deny it. She's an artist, I understand — no doubt the one who did that yellow painting you've got hanging in your office."

"Her name is Caroline Farr."

R.D. snorted. "I wish she was Farr — far away."

"I'm in love with her." It was almost a relief finally to admit that to his father.

For a moment there was only silence in the room as R.D. looked away, his face expressionless, as if he hadn't heard what Dean had just said. "It's one thing for a man to get a little somethin' strange on the side now and then, but it's another to let himself get involved." He swung back to glare at Dean. "Have you forgotten you're married? That you've got a wife upstairs?"

"I haven't forgotten." Dean couldn't meet the accusing look in his father's blue eyes.

"She knows. You do realize that?"

"How?" Dean frowned.

"You've been seen and the talk's gettin' around."

"I didn't know." He hung his head, realizing just how complicated the situation had become — and how much worse it could get.

"Tell me one thing, Dean. Just what do you plan to do about it?"

"I'm not sure. I —"

"Well, you can be sure of one thing. There has never been a divorce in the whole history of the Lawson family. And there isn't going to be one now. That little gal upstairs is your wife and you married her 'for better or worse.' "

"I know that."

"Well, if you know it, then you bring this little affair of yours to an end — and damned quick."

"You don't understand, R.D." Dean raised his hands in a helpless and angry gesture of frustration. "I'm in love with Caroline."

"I'm truly sorry about that," R.D. stated. "But I don't see where that changes anything."

A fan whirred in the corner of the beach house, slowly wagging its head from side to side, the blades spinning to circulate the air. But Dean hardly noticed its refreshing draft as he sat slumped on the living-room couch with his head resting on the seat back, his legs stretched out in front of him, and Caroline's dark head pillowed on his stomach. He was glad of the silence. A half a dozen times in the last hour, he had tried to get the words out that would tell her it was better if they didn't see each other again, but every time they'd become lodged in his throat. Regardless of what R.D. said, no matter how he tried, he just couldn't imagine life without her.

"I like your nose. It has a very noble line."

Dean glanced down to find Caroline watching him with her dissecting artist's eye. "It does, eh?"

"Yes." She shifted her position slightly, changing the angle of her head on his stomach to give herself a better view of his face. "Have you ever wondered what a child of ours would look like?"

"No, I haven't." Such talk was painful to him. It spoke of the future, and Dean wasn't sure they had one. "I think I'll get another beer." He slid a hand under her shoulders and gave her a little push off of him. Obligingly she swung her feet off the couch and sat up. "Want anything?" Dean asked as he walked over to the refrigerator.

"No."

He took a long-neck out of the refrigerator and pried the top off with the opener that was lying on the counter beside the cap of his last bottle. Turning, he took a swig of beer and saw Caroline standing by the counter island, her hands stuffed in the side pockets of her shorts.

"I'm going to have a baby, Dean."

"You're . . . you're what?" After the first shock of disbelief passed, Dean started to laugh — happily, uproariously. This changed everything. Even R.D. would have to agree to that. There was no other choice now except for him to divorce Babs and marry Caroline. He couldn't allow a child of his to be born illegitimately. The bottle of beer sat forgotten on the countertop as Dean lifted her off the floor, holding her high in the air, and spun around the room.

"Dean, stop. This is crazy," Caroline protested, but she was smiling, too.

"Crazy. Wonderful. It's all that and more." He kissed her shoulder, her neck, and her lips before he let her feet touch the floor again.

"I'm glad you're happy about it."

"Happy? I'm delirious!" He gazed at her, certain she had taken on a new radiance. "How long have you known?"

"A couple of weeks."

"A couple of weeks? Why didn't you tell me before?"

"I wanted to be sure this was what I wanted. I've always liked children, but I've never seriously thought about having one of my own before. My paintings were always my children. But I had to face the fact that I'm twenty-nine years old. In a few more years, I'll be too old. It's a case of now or maybe never." When she paused to look at him, she lost her serious expression and smiled. Dean was relieved. She had sounded so coldly logical that it had scared him a little. "And besides, I happen to love the father of this baby very much."

"And I love you, Caroline." He drew her into the circle of his arms and held her close, shutting his eyes tightly as he rubbed his cheek against her hair. "We'll get married as soon as I can arrange the divorce, but I promise you, it will be before the baby is born."

She seemed very still in his arms. "And then what, Dean?"

"What do you mean?" He nuzzled her hair, wondering whether it would be a boy or a girl. He still felt a little dazed at the prospect of becoming a father. A father.

"I mean" — gently but firmly she pushed away from him, creating some space between them — "what will we do? Where will we live?"

"At River Bend, where else? I'll breed my Arabians and you'll raise our baby — and maybe one or two more — and paint. Maybe we can talk R.D. into turning his billiard room on the third floor into a studio for you."

"I don't think so." She turned out of his arms and walked a few feet away.

"It's worth a try. Give him a grandson and R.D. will probably give you the moon." Dean laughed.

"I meant that I don't think that would work." Caroline twined her long fingers together, revealing an agitation that was totally foreign to her. "I love you, Dean. I'll always love you. But I would *hate* living there."

"You don't know that," Dean protested, stunned by her statement and its implications. "Wait until you see it. It's a beautiful old home with turrets and bay windows . . . the design of the parquet floor, you'd fall in love with it. The craftsmanship of the woodwork —"

"The beautiful furniture, the crystal, the china, the elaborate clothes and the entertaining that goes with them — I don't like that kind of life, Dean. Please try to understand that's not the way I want to live," she said insistently.

"You're being emotional right now. It's the baby." Dean grabbed at any excuse rather than accept what she was saying.

She sighed heavily with a mixture of exasperation and despair. "Could you live anywhere else than River Bend? Would you be happy for the rest of your life living in a house like this one, without all the fine and beautiful things you're used to?"

"I . . . could try." But he just couldn't imagine it.

"I won't ask you to, Dean. I don't expect you to give up your life for me and I can't give up mine for you. Just the same, I'm glad that you wanted to marry me."

"What are you saying?" He stared at her, icy fear clutching at his throat.

"I love you, but I won't marry you." She turned her back on him and faced the table strewn with brushes, paints, cleaning fluids, and rags. "I was offered a teaching post at a private school in California. I've decided to accept it." Her shoulders lifted in a little shrug. "After all, I've never seen the Pacific Coast. I'll be leaving in ten days."

"You can't! You're going to have my baby."

"I can have it in California as easily as I can have it here." She sounded so callous.

"If you love me, how can you leave me?" As he caught hold of her arm and turned her around, he saw the tears in her eyes. "Dear God, Caroline, I don't think I can live without you."

"Don't —" Her voice broke. "Don't make this any harder for me than it already is."

"Then stay."

"I can't."

No amount of cajoling, demanding, begging, or arguing on Dean's part could persuade her to change her mind. In the following ten days, he tried time after time with no success. She was going to California. "If you want to see me, you can come there," she said and gave him the address and phone number of the school in Los Angeles. When he tried to give her some money, she shoved it back in his hands and informed him that she would not accept any financial support from him. If he wanted to pay part of the medical expenses he could, but she insisted that she was more than capable of raising the baby without his help.

That first week Caroline was gone, Dean went through hell. Twice he called the number she'd given him; both times he was told she hadn't reported in yet. When he was almost driven crazy with the thought that she'd disappeared from his life for good, she called. She'd had car trouble in Arizona. No, she was fine. She'd found an apartment in Malibu, near the beach. The Pacific was so different from either the Gulf or the Atlantic, she could hardly wait to start painting it. And she missed him.

Life suddenly seemed worth living again. Dean started making plans to fly to California and see her as soon as Babs was feeling better. Two days ago she had collapsed at a charity luncheon. The doctor was certain it was merely a case of exhaustion brought on by the heat and a slight case of anemia. With a couple of weeks of rest and a well-balanced diet, she would be on her feet again.

As soon as he arrived home that night, Dean went upstairs to see her. She was reclining in the chaise longue, wrapped in a ruffled silk robe of mint green. A bed tray was across her lap, but Dean noticed the food on it had barely been touched.

"You're supposed to be eating," he admonished as he bent down to drop a kiss on her forehead. "Doctor's orders."

"I don't want it."

Dean glanced at the food on the plate. "You've always liked spinach omelettes. Surely you can get down a few more bites."

"That tastes like . . . squashed meat."

"How about if I have Justine fix you something else?"

Babs turned away to look out the window, but she couldn't turn far enough to hide the quivering of her lower lip. "I don't care."

"Babs, what's wrong? This isn't like you." He sat down on the edge of the chaise and took her hand in his.

"You don't really care," she retorted, sniffling and lifting her chin a fraction higher.

"I certainly do." Dean frowned.

"I know you don't love me anymore."

"Babs —"

"It's true. You think I haven't noticed the way you've been acting this last week. Well, I have. You've been mooning around here like —"

Never once had Babs accused him of being unfaithful, even though, as R.D. had told him, she knew. Grateful for that, Dean tried now to ease her mind a little. "She's gone, Babs." He heard her quick little intake of breath. "She left last week. I never meant for you to be hurt. I'm sorry."

"Then" — she gazed at him hopefully — "you're going to stay?"

She was so vulnerable, so childlike, constantly needing assurance. How had he forgotten that? "Yes."

"I need you so much now." She clutched at his hand, a wondrous smile breaking through the tears. "Darling . . . we're going to have a baby."

Babs's pregnancy was a complicated one, and toxemia had kept her bedridden for the last few months of her term. Dean managed to squeeze in two short trips to Los Angeles in the next few months to see Caroline and assure himself that all was healthy and normal for her. He didn't like the garage apartment she had rented, but Caroline insisted it was adequate for her needs and flatly refused to move into a five-room house he found. But as Babs grew closer to term, Dean was too concerned about her health to leave her, trusting that healthy and self-sufficient Caroline would somehow manage, as she claimed.

Two weeks before Babs's due date, her doctor decided to take the baby by caesarian section. Dean sat out the operation in a private waiting room with R.D.

The doctor walked into the waiting room, still clad in his surgical gown and cap. "It's a girl, Mr. Lawson. Five pounds ten ounces and bawling her head off."

Dean came to his feet as R.D. stopped pacing. "Babs — how is she?"

"She's going to be fine," the doctor assured him. "They have taken her to Recovery. She should be coming out of the anesthesia fairly soon."

"I'd like to see her."

"Of course. Come with me," the doctor said.

"Here." R.D. reached inside his jacket. "Have a cigar."

Dean was there when Babs came to. She was groggy and a little silly, but for Babs, that was normal. Relieved, Dean joined his father at the nursery window.

"There she is." R.D. pointed to a red-faced, squalling infant wildly waving her little fists. A downy mass of black hair covered her head. "Strong little tyke, isn't she? And a Lawson through and through. Look at her yellin' her head off, lettin' the world know she's here. And those eyes, too, they're Lawson blue."

"All babies have blue eyes when they're born, R.D." But Dean smiled at the obvious pride his father took in the child. He felt it, too.

"Not blue like that. Are you still going to name her after your grandma?"

It had been Babs's suggestion to name the baby after the woman who had raised both himself and R.D. if it was a girl. Dean had agreed, knowing how much it would please R.D. "You're looking at Abigail Louise Lawson."

"I like that." R.D. nodded approvingly, a softness entering his expression before it slowly turned thoughtful. "When's the other one due?"

Dean was surprised by the reference to Caroline. R.D. had rarely mentioned her since that day last August when Dean had informed him Caroline was going to have his baby. R.D. hadn't said much except to remind him that a father had as much responsibility as a mother to see that a child was properly brought up, provided for, and educated. But the lecture had been unnecessary. Dean knew he could never abandon Caroline or the child born of their love.

"Soon," was all he said in reply.

At the Lawson Company headquarters the next morning, Dean waded through a gauntlet of backslapping congratulations on the birth of his daughter before he reached the haven of Mary Jo Anderson's outer office. "Sorry." He held his suit jacket open to show the emptiness of his inner pockets. "I'm fresh out of cigars. Those guys out there got them all. At this rate, I'm going to have to buy them by the case."

"I don't mind. R.D. would probably have a heart attack if he walked in here and saw me smoking a cigar anyway. Congratulations, just the same." But she didn't seem as enthusiastic as everyone else. Dean wondered if it was because she knew about Caroline. He'd had to confide in her. As his private secretary, Mary Jo screened all his mail and phone calls, and handled a lot of his personal bills. In an emergency, Caroline had to be able to reach him. Where else was safer than here at the office? And someone had to know where to reach him when he went to California, especially when Babs had been so ill during her pregnancy.

"She's a beautiful baby, Mary Jo. We decided to name her Abigail Louise after my grandmother, but we're going to call her Abbie." Feeling self-conscious about the way he was carrying on, Dean walked over to her desk and picked up the previous day's messages. "Have a dozen yellow roses sent to Babs at the hospital, will you?"

"Of course." She paused a moment then said, "You had a phone call yesterday that's not with your messages."

Tense with anticipation, Dean looked up from the now unimportant pieces of paper. "Caroline?"

"Yes. She had a baby girl yesterday morning. Rachel Ann."

Yesterday. The same day that Abbie was born. Stunned by the coincidence, the terrible irony, Dean was speechless.

6

The bay stallion snorted restlessly and tried to elude her hand, but Abbie continued to hold him there and rub his cheek. She needed this excuse to avoid looking at Lane. She didn't want him to see the tears that smarted in her eyes.

"I remember stopping by his office one day," Lane said, continuing with his story. "You would have been . . . probably four or five years old at the time. Dean was sitting behind his desk, reading a letter. There was a color snapshot on his desk of a little girl with big blue eyes and long dark hair . . . pulled in a ponytail, I think. She had on a swimsuit, and there was sand in the background. The little girl stood there smiling shyly at the camera. I thought it was you and said something to that effect to Dean. He corrected me.

" 'That isn't a picture of Abbie,' he said. 'It's Rachel. It's amazing, isn't it, how much they look alike?' I must have picked up the photograph, because I remember Dean took it from me and stared at it. 'And both born on the same day, too,' he said. 'Every time I look at Abbie, I see Rachel. It's almost like having both of them with me all the time. When I go places and do things with Abbie, I can almost believe that Rachel is there, too.' "

When Lane paused, Abbie sensed he was looking at her, probably seeing the striking resemblance again. She hoped he didn't expect her to say anything, because she couldn't. The muscles in her throat were so achingly tight, she couldn't even swallow.

As the silence threatened to lengthen, Abbie realized Lane was leaving it up to her to break it. "And Momma — when did she find out? About his other child, I mean."

"I'm not sure, probably a couple of years after you were born. With all the trips Dean was making to Los Angeles, she became suspicious that he was seeing Caroline again. When she confronted him, he told her about Rachel. How much, I don't know. I do know he promised Babs he would never leave her, even though he was deeply in love with Caroline and intended to visit her and Rachel whenever he could. I'm sure your mother didn't like it, but she accepted the situation. After all, she was desperately in love with him, too." Lane paused, a frown gathering on his forehead. "By that, I don't mean to imply that Dean didn't have any feelings for her. He did care about Babs very much."

"If that's true, then he wouldn't want her hurt any more than she's already been. I hope you'll agree that there isn't any reason for Momma to see the entire contents of the will if it can be avoided. She has suffered enough, I think. Surely as the executor of Daddy's will you can arrange that."

"To a degree. However, the will has to be filed with the probate court. It will be a matter of public record."

"I see," she said tightly.

"I'm sorry, Abbie."

"I know. Everybody always is." She couldn't help sounding cynical and a little bitter. That was the way she felt.

"Abbie," Lane began, "I hope you can appreciate how difficult, mentally and emotionally, it must have been for your father. He was in an extremely awkward situation and he handled it the best way he could. It's the most natural thing in the world for a father to want to love and protect his children, and to spare them from unnecessary hurt. And it's just as natural that he would want to provide for them in the event anything should happen to him."

"What about . . . Caroline?" Abbie questioned, only now struck by the possibility that she, too, might be one of his beneficiaries.

"She died several years ago — from an aneurysm, I believe."

Several years ago. "I see," was all that was left for her to say. A misting of tears blurred her vision as she lightly stroked the stallion's soft nose. "I appreciate your frankness, Lane. You'd probably better go to the house now before Momma starts wondering what's keeping you."

"Aren't you coming?"

"I'll be there soon."

The stallion attempted to pull away from her again, but Abbie kept him there until Lane had walked away. Then she let him go and watched him, her father's favorite, as he galloped around the small pen and stopped at the far end to call to the mares in the pasture, his sleek body quivering in anticipation. But his love call went unanswered.

Abbie turned and walked blindly away from the stallion run that butted up to the stud barn. The gray filly nickered plaintively to her, but Abbie's misery was so great she was unaware of the horse. She felt the tears coming and had to find a place where she could be alone and cry.

She sought refuge in the building that housed a reception area for visitors as well as the manager's office, the tack room, and her father's private office. Attached to the main stable by a breezeway that her grandfather had always called a dogtrot, it commanded a view of the stables, the stud barn, and the pastures. A black wreath hung on the door. Another time Abbie would have been moved by the gesture of the stable help to show their grief over her father's passing, but she didn't even look twice at it as she pushed through the door and headed directly to her father's private office, pulled by memories of the times she'd spent with him there . . . memories that now seemed so false.

Once inside, she closed the door and leaned against it to look around the room, her throat tight, her chin trembling. Sunlight, filtered by the pecan trees outside, streamed through the window onto the richly paneled walls covered with trophies, framed photographs, and show ribbons. A heavy oak desk sat in front of the window, strewn with papers, notes, and breeding charts. To the right of it stood antique file cabinets that contained the papers, pedigrees, and breeding files for every horse at River Bend. Behind the glass doors of the corniced and columned oak bookcase, shelves held books on equine ailments, horse husbandry, and genetics. Along the near wall stretched a chesterfield sofa upholstered in Madeira-brown leather and trimmed with brass nailheads. Partners to it were the wing chair and ottoman.

Abbie walked around to the big leather armchair behind the desk and ran her hand over the hollow curved into the headrest. She remembered how hard she had tried to please her father — to make him proud of her. Abruptly she turned away from his chair, fighting the writhing anger and hurt inside.

She almost regretted asking Lane to tell her about her father and

Caroline. Before, she'd at least had her illusions. Now she didn't even have those. But she had asked for the truth and she got it. It wasn't Lane's fault that it wasn't what she'd expected.

She thought he'd tell her that it had been some cheap, meaningless affair; that her father had made a regrettable mistake he'd had to pay for for the rest of his life; that some tramp had tricked him into getting her pregnant then blackmailed him with the child; that . . . somehow, he'd been trying to protect the family honor and spare them his shame.

Instead, she'd heard a story of tragic love — of two people from different worlds, deeply and passionately in love with each other, but destined to remain apart — and the child born from that love.

No wonder she'd never been the daughter he wanted. She was the wrong one. All she'd ever been was a look-alike stand-in, a double, right down to having the same birthday.

Abbie longed to scream and release all the pain she felt inside, but what would that change? Nothing — nothing at all.

With hands and teeth clenched, she moved away from the desk and fought to convince herself that she didn't care that he hadn't loved her. She wasn't a child anymore. She didn't need his love. But Abbie didn't think she could ever forget — or forgive him for — the years of deception. As a hot tear rolled down her cheek, she blinked to clear her burning eyes, and wondered how she could have been so naïve all this time.

On the wall in front of her was an old photograph of her grandfather, R.D. Lawson, taken at the Scottsdale Arabian Horse Show the year he died. He stood there beside the two-year-old gray filly, River Wind, named Champion Filly of the Scottsdale Show — the dam of Abbie's filly, River Breeze. A Stetson hat concealed the iron gray of his hair, but it didn't hide the proud smile that wreathed his face and softened its hard angles. The picture showed a robust man who carried his years well.

As Abbie stared at the photograph, memories came flooding back. She was finally forced to admit that she hadn't been blind to what had gone on all these years: she had simply refused to see it. Innumerable incidents had contained clues, but she had ignored them all.

She remembered the last time she'd seen her grandfather alive. He'd gone to the airport to see them off on what Abbie regarded as a family vacation. In actuality, it had been combined with a business trip her father was taking to check on the company's overseas offices and to look over Arabian breeding stock in other countries for possible purchase and importation. She had been all of eight years old at the time, so the reasons for the trip hadn't mattered to her. They were going: Abbie, her parents, and their black maid, Justine, brought along to look after Abbie.

*L*ondon was the first stop on their overseas tour. Abbie, with her boundless energy, fueled by excitement, didn't suffer from jet lag and didn't understand why the first full day of their vacation in a new city had to be spent so quietly. She wanted to go out and explore this town where people drove on the wrong side of the road and talked so funny she could hardly understand them. She wanted to ride on one of those red double-decker buses and see the palace where the queen lived.

"Babs, why do I have the feeling she is going to hound us until we agree to do something?" Dean caught hold of Abbie's hands and forced her to stand still in front of his chair.

One look at her father's tolerantly amused smile and Abbie knew she had him. "Ben says it's because I'm just like my grandpa. I won't quit no matter what."

"Ben just may be right," Dean conceded, aware that at times, his daughter's persistence bordered on sheer bullheadedness — a trait tempered by a naturally warm and outgoing nature. Not at all like the shy and sensitive Rachel, Dean thought, recalling the way she watched him with those haunting blue eyes of hers. Rarely did they sparkle and dance the way Abbie's did now.

"Ben's always right," she announced pertly.

"Most of the time, anyway." Affectionately he tweaked her nose, then glanced over at Babs, still clad in her Italian palazzo pajamas, and propped up with a cushion of pillows on the sitting-room sofa. "Let's take the child for a walk, Babs. The fresh air and sunshine will do us good."

"I doubt it, honey." She groped for the cup of coffee sitting on the end table, the last that remained from the late morning breakfast they'd had served in their hotel suite. "This is worse than the mornings after one of the MacDonnells' barbecues. My eyes feel like a pair of peeled grapes full of pits. And I know I must weigh two hundred pounds, as heavy as I feel."

"If she's gained that much weight, then she really does need to exercise, doesn't she, Daddy?" Abbie grinned slyly.

"She certainly does."

"I have a better idea," Babs said, pausing to take a slow sip of her coffee. "You and Abbie go for a walk and let me stay here and rest."

"No." Abbie pulled free from Dean's hands and walked over to the sofa to take the coffee cup out of her mother's hands. "You have to come with us. This is our vacation and we're supposed to have fun."

After a considerable amount of joint prodding and coaxing, an hour later the three of them were strolling down the London streets. At least, Dean and Babs were strolling. Abbie was skipping ahead, eager to experience the sights and sounds of this city that was so new to her.

Abruptly she turned and started walking backward, a perplexed look on her face. "Why isn't there any fog today? Isn't there supposed to be fog in London?"

"Not every day," Babs said. "It's like at home in Texas. Sometimes it will roll in at night, or early mornings. And sometimes it will just hover on the river, like it does on the Brazos, sneaking around the trees on the banks and spooking into the pastures."

"It gets scary then." But Abbie's eyes were bright with excitement at the thought.

"Turn around and watch where you're going before you run into somebody," Babs admonished.

"And don't get too far ahead of us," Dean added when Abbie started to take off at a run. "You'll get lost."

"Yes, Daddy." Unwillingly she slowed down.

If that was Rachel, Dean knew she'd be right at his side holding on to his hand, especially when they were at some public place with a lot of people around. She said it was because she didn't want to get separated from him, but Dean suspected that Rachel was a little too timid and insecure to venture off by herself. Abbie, on the other hand, didn't even know what a stranger was. Night and day, his daughters were, regardless of how much they looked alike.

"I forgot to tell you, Babs, before you were up this morning, I made arrangements with the concierge for a guide to take you and Abbie around London tomorrow and show you the sights. I'll probably be tied up the rest of the week handling things with the company office here."

"Abbie isn't going to be too happy about that." Neither was Babs, but she wasn't about to admit it.

"She'll have too much to see and do to notice I'm not around. Look at her." Dean smiled. "Her head's swinging from side to side like one of those dogs on the dashboard of a car."

During the next three days, Babs and Abbie took in all the must-see sights, accompanied by the unobtrusive Justine and their guide, Arthur Bigsby. They watched the ceremonial Changing of the Guard in the forecourt of Buckingham Palace, but Abbie was disappointed that she didn't get to see the queen — and she didn't think the palace was as nice as their home at River Bend, although she did concede it was bigger. She was impressed by the glittering array of Crown Jewels and royal regalia at the Tower of London. She argued with Arthur when he tried to tell her Big Ben was the large bell in the Clock Tower of the Houses of Parliament in Westminster. Everyone in Texas knew Big Ben was the clock.

Westminster Abbey was all right. She couldn't imagine why anybody would want to be buried in a church, especially kings. That's what cemeteries were for. She fed the pigeons in Trafalgar Square and laughed when one sat on her head.

When they met Dean for lunch, her array of observations and the questions they raised was endless. Why wasn't there a circus at Piccadilly Circus? Why did they call cookies biscuits? Why did they call supper high tea? If there was high tea, what was low tea?

Dean finally pointed at her plate and said, "Eat."

"Poor Arthur should have tried that," Babs said. "She absolutely wore the man out. And me, too."

"Well, tomorrow will be different. I thought we might drive down to Crabbet Park and look at their Arabians."

"Really, Daddy? Are we honest and truly gonna go there tomorrow?" Abbie asked excitedly.

"Yes. I thought we'd leave bright and early in the morning so we can spend as much time there as we want."

"You and Abbie go. When it comes to horses, I can't tell a gelding from a stallion."

"Momma, that's easy. Ben says all you have to do is —"

"Abbie, it's not polite to interrupt." Dean tried to look stern and not laugh.

"I'm telling you, Dean, some of the things she knows would make Justine blush," Babs declared, then went on with what she had been about to say before Abbie interrupted her. "Anyway, I want to go to this boutique in Chelsea called Bazaar. Some new designer named Mary Quant has it. Her clothes are supposed to be all the rage now. I haven't had a chance to do any shopping yet."

"I'd like to go shopping," Abbie said wistfully, then quickly added, "But I'd rather go to Crabbet Park with you, Daddy."

"Is there any reason why we can't go shopping after we finish our lunch? I haven't had a chance to do any shopping either." And he wanted to send something to Rachel from England — something nice.

"I have an appointment to have my hair done," Babs said. "I can't very well cancel it if you expect me to look presentable tonight when we have dinner with your London manager and his wife."

"In that case Abbie and I will go, and meet you back at the hotel later."

A taxi dropped them off at the main entrance to Selfridge's Department Store. Usually Dean had trouble choosing something for Rachel, especially when it came to clothes; he was never sure she'd like it or whether it would fit. With Abbie along, he hoped to solve at least part of the problem.

As they entered the children's wear department, Dean spied a girl's dress in lavender-checked gingham trimmed with white lace. "Abbie, do you like that one?"

"It's okay." She wrinkled up her nose. "But I don't like lavender. Look at this blue dress, Daddy. Isn't it pretty? I'll bet it just matches my eyes."

"It sure does. Why don't you try it on? And the lavender one, too."

"Daddy," she protested at his first choice.

"For me. I want to see what you look like in it."

"Okay," she declared with an exaggerated sigh of agreement.

A few minutes later Abbie emerged from the fitting room, wearing the gingham dress. "See, Daddy." She did a slow pirouette in front of the mirror. "It doesn't do a thing for me."

Dean was forced to agree that it didn't suit her at all, yet looking at her, he could see the quiet and reserved Rachel wearing it, her dark hair tied up in a ponytail with a matching lavender ribbon. "Take that one off and try the blue one on." As Abbie disappeared into the fitting room again, he turned to the sales clerk. "I want that lavender dress, but I'd like to have it shipped, please."

"But your daughter —"

"I'm not buying it for Abbie."

"Very good, sir. We'll be happy to ship it wherever you like."

After the blue dress, Abbie tried on a half-dozen other outfits ranging from sport clothes to party dresses. Finally she chose three that she just couldn't live without. As Dean was paying for the purchases, Abbie noticed another sales clerk wrapping the lavender gingham dress in tissue. She pulled Dean aside.

"Daddy, I told you I didn't like that dress."

"You mean the lavender one?" He pretended not to know. "I think some other little girl is getting it."

"Oh, good." She rolled her eyes ceilingward in a dramatic expression of relief. "I was afraid you were buying it for me." As the clerk handed Dean the packages and receipt, Abbie hovered at his side. "Where to next?"

"Wherever you want. Although it is getting late. Maybe we should head back to the hotel."

"But I thought you wanted to do some shopping." Her eyebrows arched together in a bewildered frown.

"I already have." He held up the packages as evidence.

"Oh, Daddy." She broke into a wide smile. "I love you."

Back at their hotel suite, Justine took charge of the packages and Abbie, and informed Dean that Mrs. Lawson hadn't returned from her beauty appointment yet. Checking his watch and mentally calculating the time difference, he walked into the master bedroom and closed the door. The telephone sat on the nightstand between the twin beds. Dean picked up the receiver and dialed the operator.

A very British voice came on the line. "May I help you?"

"Yes, ma'am. I'd like to place an overseas call to California." After supplying the needed information, Dean waited through the innumerable clicks and cracklings before finally hearing the dull ring on the other end of the line. Then, above the faint hum of static, he heard Caroline's voice. As always, it brought that same soaring lift of his spirits.

"Hello, darling." He tightened his grip on the receiver as if that could somehow bring her closer.

"Dean." Her voice was filled with surprise and delight — with just a trace of confusion. "But . . . I thought you were —"

"I'm calling from London. I'm missing you so much I just had to hear your voice. How are you? You sound wonderful." Swinging his legs onto the bed, he reclined against the pillowed headboard and gazed at the room's high ceiling, but saw her face in front of him.

"I'm fine. So is Rachel. As a matter of fact, she's standing right here, tugging at my arm. I think she wants to say hello."

"Put her on."

There was a moment of muted voices in the background, then Rachel came on the line. "Dean, is it really you? You are calling from England?" Amid the excited rush of her questions, there was a touchingly tentative quality to her young voice.

But that didn't cause the quick twinge of pain Dean felt. It was the use of his given name. Rachel never called him Father or Papa or Daddy — always Dean. Caroline had insisted on that from the start, just as she had insisted on Rachel knowing about her illegitimacy from an early age. Caroline didn't believe in hiding from Rachel the truth that her parents were neither married nor divorced like those of other children. Her classmates and friends were bound to ask questions and make remarks that would ultimately hurt, but not as much if they prepared her for them. In Caroline's opinion, the use of his given name gave Rachel a degree of protection from unwanted questions about her father and allowed her to decide what she wanted to tell about him. Although Dean was forced to agree with Caroline, he didn't like it. He hated the fact that Rachel knew about his other family, his other daughter. He hated the questions she asked about them — and the guilt he felt.

"Yes, it's me, calling from England." But it was a struggle for him to keep the light, happy tone in his voice. "I bought you something today. It's being sent, so you probably won't get it for a few weeks."

"What is it?"

"I can't tell you. It's a surprise. But I think it's something you'll like very much. By the way, guess where I'm going tomorrow?"

"Where?"

"To Crabbet Park. Remember the book I sent you for Christmas about Lady Anne Blunt? We sat and read parts of it when I was there in January."

"Oh, yes!" she cried excitedly, animation taking over her voice. "About how she traveled with her husband, riding on horseback to Persia and India, and all through Arabia and Mesopotamia and Egypt, and crossing flooded rivers and deserts way back in the eighteen hundreds. She lived with the Bedouins and learned to read and speak their language. And she learned all about the Arabian horse and bought the best she could find so they wouldn't become extinct. The Bedouins called her 'the noble lady of the horses.' And even though she had a home in England, she loved the desert and horses so much that she went back to Egypt to live. And that's where she died. But her daughter in England loved Arabians, too, and she kept them all and bred them and raised the finest horses in the world." Rachel finally paused and released a dreamily heavy sigh. "It was a wonderful story. I've read it over and over."

"I can tell." Dean smiled, feeling a sense of pride that she was developing a love for Arabians, too.

"Mommy has to help me with the words sometimes."

"I'm sure she does." There were some Arabic ones even he couldn't pronounce. "Anyway, tomorrow I'm going to the stud farm that was owned by her daughter, Lady Wentworth."

"Are you? Oh, I wish I was going, too."

"So do I, honey," he said tightly. "So do I. But maybe someday." Yet try as he might, he couldn't imagine the day ever coming when he could openly take Rachel with him on trips like this.

"Yes." She didn't sound too hopeful either, but she quickly tried to hide it. "I forgot to tell you, Dean: I convinced Mom to let me take riding lessons this summer. I had my first one yesterday. My riding instructor says I have a natural seat and good hands. Of course, I told him that you've taken me riding before and shown me some things."

"It sounds like I'd better start looking for a good horse suitable for a new, young rider."

"I'd like that, Dean, more than anything," she declared, the fervor in her voice eliminating any doubt that she meant it.

"I'll see what I can find when I get back." He talked with Rachel for a few more minutes, then spoke again to Caroline. Much too quickly Dean heard the door to the suite open, signaling Babs's return. Hastily he said his good-byes to Caroline and hung up.

Don't let her know, don't let her see, don't let her hear; just let her pretend none of it existed. That was his agreement with Babs. He did his best to keep it and not cause her any more anguish.

After a short drive south of London through the Sussex countryside on the way to Brighton, they arrived at the famed Arabian stud farm founded in 1878 by Lord and Lady Blunt on his ancestral estate. Even though the land wasn't Texas-flat, the lush green pastures, the big old trees, and the beautiful Arabian horses in the paddocks reminded Abbie of her home at River Bend. She hadn't realized how much she missed it until she saw Crabbet Park.

"Grandpa says the horses here are relatives of ours." Abbie scanned the sleek horses, searching for one that might remind her of River Rose, River Sun, or River Magic.

"Some of them, maybe," her father agreed as they followed one of the stable hands across the thick grass of the manicured grounds that had been the site of the famous annual Sunday parades during Lady Wentworth's days.

"I wonder if they'll show us Skowronek's stall. That's the way you pronounce it: Skov-ro-neck. Ben says that in Poland all the *w*'s are pronounced like *v*'s. That's vhy he talks the vay he does." She longed to hear his voice and listen to his endless stories and the fascinating things he knew about horses, especially Arabians.

"I know."

"Did you know that when Skowronek first came to England from Poland, he was used as a hack? Can you imagine a famous stallion like that being used as an ordinary riding horse and rented to people? Ben says that's what a hack is."

"But he wasn't famous at the time. And remember, there was a war going on. World War I. So people had other things on their minds beside Arabians."

"Ben says it was lucky that Skowronek was here because Communist soldiers stole the horses from the farm where he was born. And when the stallion that was his father — Ben says he'd always been a very gentle, well-mannered stallion — started to fight the soldiers that were trying to take him out of his stall, they shot him. Isn't that terrible?"

"It certainly is."

"Anyway, like Ben says, it's a good thing Lady Wentworth saw him and recognized what a great stallion he was. He was pure white, you know. They call him a gray 'cause he had black skin underneath like all Arabians, except where they have white markings, then the skin is pink. But Skowronek looked snow-white. Both Ben and Grandpa said that's very rare."

"That's true."

"Look, Daddy." Abbie spied the clock below the roof peak of the arched entrance to the Coronation Stables, built of brick, the muted color of terra-cotta. "Ben says the main stables at the stud farm in Poland where he worked had a clock tower. We should put a clock in ours at River Bend so we can be famous, too."

"It takes more than a clock, Abbie." Dean smiled down at her. "You need a stable full of outstanding broodmares and two or three really great stallions."

"But we have that, don't we?"

"Not yet, but we will."

"Are you going to buy some of these Arabians?"

"Maybe. First we have to look at what they have and see if it's what we want."

They spent the better part of the day looking over the Crabbet Arabians available for sale, walking around each horse to study its conformation from all angles, observing its action at a walk, a trot, and an airy canter, and studying it close up. Everything from yearling colts and fillies to Arabians under training to aged broodmares was paraded out for their inspection. Iridescent chestnuts, flashy bays, dappled grays, all slickly groomed, their coats glistening in the sunlight — Abbie wanted to buy nearly every one of them.

Although Dean found it difficult to fault the majority of them, none had aroused more than a passing interest. He couldn't define exactly what it was he was seeking — a look, an aura that made one horse stand out from all the others, something that would spark the gut feeling, "this is the horse."

As they drove away from the stables, Abbie felt the sting of tears in her eyes. One part of her hated to leave the familiar surroundings and the other part of her just wanted to go home to the real thing: River Bend.

"I think Grandpa would have liked that gray filly. She looked a lot like River Wind, and he loves her." Just talking about her grandfather made her feel worse, but she couldn't admit to feeling homesick for fear her father would not take her with him on another trip. "How come you didn't buy any horses? Didn't you like them?"

"I liked them, but they weren't quite what I wanted. Maybe we'll be luckier next week in Egypt," he replied, his mouth twisting in a crooked smile of wry hope.

"It's gonna be a while before we go home, isn't it?" Abbie asked. "I'll bet Grandpa and Ben are really missing us."

Teeming Cairo: a city of cacophonies, with its honking of horns, babbling of Arabic tongues, braying of donkeys, chanting of the muezzin, and bellowing of camels; a city of contrasts, with its modern buildings sharing the skyline with minaret-topped mosques, its cars and trucks traveling the narrow streets with donkey carts, caleches, or camel herds on their way to the slaughterhouse, and its people in Western attire walking along the crowded sidewalks with those in the more traditional robe and headdress; a city of extremes, with its abject poverty and limitless wealth, and harsh desert edges and verdant river bottoms.

Cairo was chaos after the quiet order of England. Babs hated it and refused to set foot outside their Western hotel. Justine was terrified of the strangeness of this city inhabited by heathens. Stuck in the hotel with nothing to do, Abbie grew all the more homesick.

After much persuasion, her father convinced her mother that she at least had to make one excursion out of the hotel to see the Pyramids of Giza on the outskirts of Cairo. Elaborate arrangements were made through their guide, Ahmed. When they arrived at Giza, a pair of horses was waiting for Abbie and her father, all saddled and bridled, ready to take them closer to the Great Pyramids.

Despite Ahmed's insistence that the horses were true steeds of the desert, Abbie was quite certain these skinny, narrow horses were not Arabians. She climbed on just the same and cantered her placid mount alongside her father's. Together they rode beneath the blazing sun toward the Pyramids that stood out starkly against a sky of pure blue. Abbie was just a little bit disappointed to discover that the ancient Pyramids looked just like the pictures she'd seen of them, only older maybe and more crumbled.

Near the base of the Pyramids, they rendezvoused with the car bearing Ahmed and her mother. The horses were taken away and replaced by a camel that its driver called Susie. All of them had to take a ride on this groaning, moaning "ship of the desert." Both Abbie and her father broke into laughter as her mother shrieked and grabbed at the protruding horn of the strange saddle when the camel rolled to its feet in a slow lurch. However, Abbie didn't think it was at all funny a few minutes later when she tried to pet the camel and it spit at her, literally ending their excursion on a sour note.

At dinner that night, her father suggested that Abbie accompany him the next day to visit the El Zahraa Arabian stud farm. She leaped at the chance, her head filled with visions of another Crabbet Park — another River Bend.

Located outside the city limits of Cairo in Ein Shams, the stud farm occupied sixty acres of desert. Before the overthrow of King Farouk, it had been known as Kafr Farouk and run by the Royal Agricultural Society. But with the recent ascension of Nasser to power, its name had been changed to El Zahraa and its governing board now went by the more democratic name of the Egyptian Agricultural Organization. Prophetically, perhaps, the neighboring land to El Zahraa stud farm had once been the site of the Sheykh Obeyd, the Arabian stud farm established by Lady Anne Blunt in Egypt.

A dust as fine as powder enveloped the car as they traveled down the long driveway lined with palms leading to the main stables of El Zahraa. Beyond lay sandy, grassless paddocks. Abbie saw immediately that this was not Crabbet Park or River Bend. There wasn't an oasis of green here, just more dry sand and hot sun.

At a distance, the horses in the paddocks looked positively skinny to her. Up close, she found out they didn't look any better. They had the delicate heads, arched necks, and high tail carriage typical of Arabians, but where were their satiny coats, and why did they look so lean?

When she put the question to her father, he replied, "The Egyptians like their horses slender. They think ours have too much flesh on them. Their favorite saying is 'We ride our horses, we don't eat them.' "

In Abbie's opinion, this was a wasted trip. She was certain there couldn't possibly be anything here that her father would be interested in buying to ship back to River Bend.

But Abbie was wrong. After more than three hours of walking, looking, and reviewing, Dean saw *the* horse he'd been looking for all this time. As they approached a group of yearlings, munching on a pile of berseem hay in a paddock, a bay colt lifted his head to gaze at them. The colt had the most incredibly classic head Dean had ever seen, his profile showing almost an exaggerated dish and his eyes large and dark. Dean stopped and just stared.

Here was the horse of his dreams — here in the desert sand

beneath a blazing blue sky, surrounded by shimmering waves of heat. For a moment, Dean was afraid he was looking at a mirage. If he blinked, the colt might disappear. His eyes began to water. Unwillingly he did blink, but the colt was still there.

"I'm telling you, Babs, that colt had the most gorgeous head I've ever seen on an Arabian." Dean stood in front of the dresser mirror, tying his tie while Babs continued to add the finishing touches to her makeup in front of the mirror in the bathroom.

"I didn't think he was all that great," Abbie inserted, not caring that she hadn't been asked. Already dressed for dinner with Justine's help, she wandered about her parents' bedroom in the hotel suite, pausing now and then to twirl about and watch the full circle the skirt of her new blue dress made.

"I don't have any idea how much they want for him, but with a colt like that, price doesn't mean anything. You talk about charisma. This colt has it and then some. El Kedar Ibn Sudan, that's what they call him." Dean pulled the knot tight and adjusted it to sit squarely in the center of his shirt collar. "The head man wasn't there today. I'm going to have to call tomorrow and arrange to see him. They wrote his name down for me. I've got it here somewhere." As he reached for his tie tack, he scanned the items lying on top of the dresser. "It must still be in my jacket pocket. Abbie, my jacket's on that chair by you. Will you bring it here?" She scooped the wheat-tan jacket off the arm of the chair, letting it dangle upside down, and whirled around so her skirt would flare out.

"Careful," Dean warned. "You're going to dump everything out of the pockets."

Abbie stopped just as a postcard slithered out of a pocket to the floor, landing facedown. "Did you send Grandpa a postcard?" Bending down, she picked it up and started to read the writing on the back of it. "Dear Rachel —"

"It's not polite to read other people's mail, Abbie." Dean took it from her before she could read more.

As he walked over to slip the postcard into the pocket of his dinner jacket, Abbie tagged after him, frowning curiously. "Who's Rachel?"

He darted a quick glance at the open bathroom door, then smoothed a hand over the top of her head and smiled, "Just somebody I know, okay?"

"Okay." Shrugging, she moved off to inspect her reflection in the mirror vacated by her father. She stared at the dark-haired, blue-eyed girl, wearing a new blue dress, white patent-leather shoes, and lace-edged anklets, then wiggled her hips to watch the skirt swing out.

Busily clipping on a diamond earring, Babs emerged from the bathroom, the pink silk chiffon of her Empire-style evening dress whispering about her. "Do you think I should wear the necklace, too, Dean, or would it be too much?"

"I'd wear it."

"Would you? You'd look positively silly in it," Babs replied, her hazel eyes twinkling outrageously, but her expression otherwise perfectly serious. Dean laughed.

Catching their playful mood, Abbie wanted to join in. "Momma, guess what?" She danced over to her and glanced slyly over her shoulder at Dean. "Daddy's sending a postcard to a girl named Rachel."

Silence. Absolute silence came crashing down as the smile faded from her father's face. Sensing that something was dreadfully wrong, Abbie turned to look at her mother. She was white with shock, her expression almost pained as she stared at him.

"Babs . . ." He took a step toward her, his hand reaching out.

"Abbie, leave the room." The words came from her mother with a rush, yet there was something desperate in the tone of her voice, as if something terrible was about to happen.

"But . . ." A little frightened, Abbie stared at her mother, so motionless, never taking her eyes off her father.

"Leave the room now!"

Abbie recoiled instinctively at the sudden movement her mother made when she swung around, turning her back on Abbie to face the highboy against the wall, her body so rigid it was trembling. Abbie felt the touch of her father's hand on her shoulder.

"Go find Justine, and have her brush your hair." Firmly but gently, he steered her toward the door to the suite's sitting room.

Once there, she turned back to him. "Daddy, I —"

"I know, honey, It's all right." He smiled at her.

But Abbie knew it wasn't. She didn't understand what she'd done wrong. She'd only been teasing when she mentioned that postcard. Didn't they know it was a joke? She was just trying to have fun like they were, teasing each other.

As the door started to swing closed, shutting her out, Abbie heard the taut accusation that burst from her mother, her voice low and barely controlled. "How could you, Dean? How could you let her find out?"

"She doesn't know anything. I swear it."

"How can you be sure? What did you tell her?"

"Nothing."

The door latched tightly shut, muffling the rest of their argument. Abbie slowly turned away from the door and moped over to one of the chairs. Fighting tears, she slumped onto the cushions and stared at the blue skirt of her dress. She didn't like it anymore.

The telephone in the sitting room rang once, then twice. On the third ring, the tall, slender Justine came out of the adjoining bedroom to answer it. Abbie didn't even look up. More than ever she wanted to go home to River Bend.

"Lawson suite, Justine speaking. . . . A call from America? Yes, I'll stay on the line."

Abbie looked up. "If that's Grandpa, I want to talk to him."

But Justine waved a shushing hand at her, then pressed her fingers over her other ear, shutting out any sound but that from the telephone. "Hello? This is Justine. . . . Yes, Miz Anderson, he's here. He and Miz Lawson are getting dressed for dinner." Discovering that it was only her father's secretary, Abbie slumped back in the chair. "Why, yes, Miz Anderson, I'll get him right away." Justine hurriedly laid the receiver down next to the phone and almost ran to the master bedroom door, her dark eyes wide with a look of concern. "Mr. Lawson?" she called his name as she knocked loudly.

"What is it, Justine?" Despite the muffling door, the impatient snap in his voice came through. Abbie sank a little lower in the chair.

"It's your secretary on the phone. She has to talk to you right away. There's . . . been an accident."

"I'll take it in here."

"What kind of an accident?" Abbie wanted to know.

But Justine just looked at her without answering and walked back to the telephone. After making sure the bedroom phone had been picked up, she placed the black receiver back on its cradle, then stood with her head bowed in an attitude of prayer.

Abbie frowned. "What happened, Justine?"

At that instant, she heard a wailing cry come from the bedroom, dissolving into terrible sobs. She scrambled out of the chair and dashed to the connecting door, hesitating only a second before pushing it open and running into the room. Abbie paused when she saw her father holding her crying mother tightly in his arms. He looked stunned, and close to tears himself.

Haltingly, she moved toward them. "Daddy . . . what's wrong?"

"Abbie." His look of pain intensified as he loosened his hold on her mother. Together they turned toward her, Babs making a valiant effort to check her crying.

Their hands reached out to her, but Abbie was almost afraid to go to them. She wanted to turn and run before this terrible thing claimed her, but her legs carried her forward within reach of her mother's clutching hand.

"Darlin', it's . . . your grandpa," her mother said, then quickly covered her mouth, as more tears rolled down her cheeks, smearing the makeup she'd so carefully applied.

Abbie didn't want to ask, but she couldn't stop herself. "What about Grandpa?"

"There's been an accident, honey," her father said, briefly closing his eyes before looking at her again. "He was crossing the street and . . . stepped in front of a car."

Frightened, she looked from one to the other. "He's going to be all right, isn't he?"

Her father simply shook his head. "I'm sorry, honey. I'm truly sorry." He tightened his grip on her hand, making her fingers hurt. "I know how much you loved him."

"No." Abbie shook her head, not wanting to believe they were trying to tell her he had died. "He'll be all right. You'll see. When we get home, you'll see."

Her mother turned and hid her face against her father's shoulder, crying softly, brokenly, as he pulled Abbie closer and put his arm around her, too. But Abbie wouldn't cry, afraid if she did, it might really be true.

"I wanta go home, Daddy."

"We are, honey. We are."

The funeral was big, even by Texas standards. Everybody came, including the governor. But Abbie didn't cry, not at the funeral. The tears didn't come until later, after they had returned to River Bend and she'd run off by herself. Ben had found her in River Wind's stall, crying herself sick. It had taken a long time for him to convince her that she wasn't somehow to blame for her grandfather's death.

His death changed many things. Within a year, Dean had sold the drilling fluids company R.D. had founded and made a return trip to

Egypt to purchase the Arabian colt of his dreams. In addition, he bought three fillies. With all the paperwork involved, the lengthy sea voyage, and the sixty days of quarantine in the U.S., it took nearly a year before the new horses finally arrived at River Bend.

In the meantime, the old barn was torn down and a new stable under construction — the first step in an expansion program that created many more new facilities at River Bend during the next ten years. The practice established by R. D. Lawson of using "River" as a prefix in the names of all the Arabians foaled at River Bend was altered somewhat by Dean. He registered his newly imported Egyptian-bred Arabians with the prefix "Nahr" attached to their names — the Arabic word for "river." El Kedar Ibn Sudan thus became Nahr El Kedar.

Buying trips to Egypt became annual events. Abbie didn't go with him again until she was in her teens, but she was never able to share his enthusiasm for the lean, narrow Arabians bred in Egypt, nor his fascination with the barren desert. Nor did she agree with his decision, when the stallion Nahr El Kedar turned five, to sell all the Arabians at River Bend bred by her grandfather, regardless of their worth or championship potential, and breed solely Arabians with newer Egyptian bloodlines. It was as if he were rejecting everything her grandfather had built — first the company and now the horses. Loving him as she did, Abbie tried to understand and not regard his actions as being even remotely disloyal.

Truthfully, she didn't have a lot of time to dwell on his possible reasons. Too many things were happening in her own young life to claim her attention. In addition to the Arabian horse shows that she continued to participate in, and the preparations for them, there were school, friends, and dates. Without any false sense of modesty, Abbie recognized that she was becoming a strikingly beautiful girl, extremely popular with her male classmates. Of course, she also recognized that having wealthy and prominent parents didn't hurt her popularity either.

With the advent of her senior year in high school, Abbie's life truly became hectic. Following in her mother's tradition, this was the year she would be one of the debutantes presented during the Houston season, which meant she would require a lavish haute couture wardrobe in addition to the formal presentation gown in the requisite debutante-white. Babs insisted that nothing less would do.

The selecting of some fifteen ballgowns, the fittings, the shopping for accessories, the planning for parties — it all seemed so endless to

Abbie. She'd lost five pounds and the season hadn't even started yet. It had sounded like a lot of fun, but it had turned out to be a lot more work than she thought.

"That was good." Babs nodded approvingly as Abbie gracefully straightened from the full court bow, her taffeta underskirts rustling beneath her ankle-length skirt. "Now do it again. A little lower this time."

Abbie groaned. "Lower? Now I know why they call this the Dallas Dive."

The traditional forehead-to-the-floor curtsy performed by all Texas debutantes went by many names: the Dallas Dive, the Texas Dip, and naturally the Yellow Rose curtsy. When done correctly, with grace and dignity, the deep court bow was a thing of regal beauty. But a misstep, a slight imbalance, and it could be the ultimate in ignominious disasters.

"If you practice it enough now, it will become second nature to you. It will be all one fluid motion, sweeping and grand — and easy."

"It will never be that," Abbie muttered into her skirt as she dipped her upper body as low as it would go, practically sitting on the floor in the process, the muscles in her legs and ankles screaming with the repeated strain on them.

"Now, turn around and practice it in front of the full-length mirror. And remember, one long, flowing motion." Babs proceeded to demonstrate what she meant.

"You're cheating, Momma. You have on pants," Abbie retaliated, a little envious of the smooth, effortless bow executed by her mother.

"Most girls make the mistake of practicing in pants or shorts or regular skirts. Then they're thrown by all the yards of long material in the skirts of their ballgowns." A laugh broke from her. "I remember at one ball, Cissy Conklin caught her heel in the hem of her gown and went sprawling headfirst on the floor. It was so hilarious seeing her spraddled there on the floor like a dressed-up duck on a platter, I laughed 'til I cried. She was such a know-it-all little snob that I was glad it happened to her. Of course, when she saw me laughing, she had a hissy-fit right there on the spot."

"Momma, I'm surprised at you," Abbie teased. "That wasn't nice."

"Neither was she. Not that it mattered." Babs shrugged. "Her daddy gave a new meaning to the word *well-oiled*. He had more pumpjacks on his land than ticks on a cow's back."

"I'll have to remember to tell Christopher that one. He thinks you come up with some of the funniest phrases." Abbie stepped in front of the full-length mirror and smiled a shade triumphantly. "All the girls turned positively emerald green when I told them that Christopher is going to be my escort at the Confederate Ball."

"Which is just three days away," Babs reminded her. "So practice."

"Oui, Mama." Mockingly obedient, Abbie swooped low to the floor and held the pose to glance at her reflection.

Behind her stood the scrolled iron bed, enameled in shiny white with brass and alabaster finials topping the end posts, and covered by a floral bedspread of blue cornflowers, a match to the blue walls in her turret bedroom. To the right of the bed was a doorway to the second-floor hall. A gray-haired Jackson, the black houseman hired years ago by R.D., appeared in the opening, as always very reserved and proper. Delicately he cleared his throat, letting his presence be known.

"Yes, Jackson." Abbie straightened, turning with a little flourish.

"Miss Lawson, Mrs. Lawson," he said, acknowledging both of them with a nod. "Mr. Lawson asked me to let you know he was home. He's in the library."

"Thank you, Jackson," Babs replied.

He retreated, as soft-footedly as he'd appeared. Abbie stared after him for a minute. "Do you know . . . in all these years, he's never slipped — not once — and called me Abbie."

"And he never will either. Jackson takes a lot of pride in what he considers to be his role in this household. Part of that is keeping his distance. I admit, I've always felt he's the authority here. He runs the house, and us, very well."

"That's true." But Abbie's interest in Jackson faded, replaced by the information he'd relayed to them. "I'm going downstairs and show Daddy my progress in the Texas Dip. Maybe I can talk him into brushing up on his waltz steps."

Quickly she was out the door before her mother could insist that she practice more. At the stairs, she gathered up her long skirt and the voluminous taffeta slip and ran lightly down the steps. Halfway down she heard the phone ring, but it was quickly silenced. Since there was no summoning call to the telephone for her, Abbie swung around the carved newel post at the base of the staircase and headed for the library.

The pocket doors stood closed. Gripping the fingerholds, she slid them open wide and stepped into the room. Her father was behind the desk, the telephone in his hand. She had that one glimpse of him as she went into her full court bow, briefly feeling like a princess paying homage to her king and wanting to laugh.

But as she straightened to walk to his desk, he held up his hand as if to stave off her advance, turning his face away and hunching over the telephone. She sensed something was wrong — very wrong.

"Daddy, what is it?" She watched as he hung up the phone, gripping the receiver tightly — so tightly Abbie expected it to snap in two. "Daddy?"

When he stood up, he seemed to be in a state of shock. He walked blindly toward the door without even looking at her. His face, his eyes, everything about him looked haunted. Worried, Abbie went after him.

"Daddy, are you all right?" She caught his arm as he entered the foyer.

He looked at her, but she didn't think he could really see her. "I . . ." His mouth moved wordlessly for several seconds. "I have to . . . go. I . . . I'm sorry."

As he pulled away from her and headed toward the front door, Abbie saw her mother coming down the stairs. "Momma, something's wrong with Daddy. He got a phone call and . . ."

Babs ran the rest of the way down the steps and hurried to his side. "Dean." She had never seen him look so lost and broken before — not even when R.D. had died so suddenly. "What's happened? Tell me."

He gripped her arms, his fingers digging into her flesh, but she was afraid to tell him he was hurting her, afraid he'd let go. "Oh, God, Babs." The words came from some deep, dark well, wrenched from his soul. "I can't believe it. I can't. Please, God, she just can't be dead."

Babs stiffened, something inside her hardening in the face of his shock and grief.

"Momma, what is it?" Abbie questioned, not standing close enough to have heard.

"There's been a death. An old . . . friend of your father's in California." She looked at Dean, tears stinging her own eyes. "I'm afraid he'll have to go out there. Would you . . . leave us alone, Abbie? Please."

Vaguely Babs was aware of Abbie slowly climbing the stairs, but all her attention was on Dean. It tortured her to see him this way.

"You do understand, Babs. I have to go," he said brokenly. "I have to be there."

"Yes. I know you do," she stated flatly.

When he released her arms, her flesh tingled painfully. She walked with him to the front door and watched as he hurried down the steps to the car parked by the front gate. Slowly she closed the door and leaned against it, sobbing softly. Caroline's name hadn't passed between them, but she knew he'd lost the woman he so deeply loved.

"I'm glad," she whispered, and buried a fist against her mouth. "God forgive me, but I'm glad she's dead."

8

*A*bbie remembered how hurt and upset she'd been when she learned her father wouldn't be returning in time to present her at the Confederate Ball. She hadn't understood why he couldn't come back for it. Why he had to remain in California just because someone he'd known for a long time had died.

The Confederate Ball was the most important event in her life. It was her launch as a debutante. He was supposed to present her and dance the first waltz with her. She couldn't walk out there alone: it wasn't done. Of all the hundreds of parties and balls that would follow, why did he have to miss this one?

Her mother had tried to console her by assuring Abbie that any number of their friends would be happy to stand in for her father. Lane Canfield was out of the country, but Kyle MacDonnell or Homer — But Abbie had stormed out of the house, insisting that if her father wouldn't be there, neither would she.

She had saddled up one of the Arabians and gone tearing down the lane, galloping across the hay fields and drained rice fields of the neighboring Hix farm, making a long, wide circle that brought her to the banks of the Brazos, and following it back to River Bend. Ben was waiting for her when she returned to the barns. She remembered the silent disapproval in his expression as he inspected the sweat-lathered mare.

"I'm sorry. I'll cool her out."

"Yes, you will," Ben had replied. "We both will, and you will tell me what this is all about."

Most of her anger had been spent in the ride, but not her hurt and bitter disappointment. As always, it had been so easy to pour out all of her troubles to Ben.

"I told Momma I wasn't going to the Confederate Ball and she could just cancel everything. It's all a lot of nonsense anyway. This is nineteen seventy-one, for heaven's sake. Who cares about being a debutante in this day and age?"

"You do, I think."

She had desperately wanted to tell Ben that that wasn't true, to insist that she was a liberated young woman and all this parading before Houston society like a slave on an auction block was sexist. Maybe all the pomp and pageantry was silly, but it was her moment in the spotlight, when all the eyes of Houston would be on her.

"I'm not going to be presented by some friend of Momma and Daddy's," she had stated forcefully, again close to tears. "If Grandpa were alive . . . but he isn't. Can you understand, Ben? I don't want just anybody presenting me. It's got to be somebody —" She had started to say "like my father" just as she had turned to look at Ben. "— somebody like you." Someone who knew and loved her; some-one who had always been there when she needed him; someone she cared about. "Ben, do you know how to waltz?"

"Me?" He had been so startled Abbie had laughed.

"Yes, you. Would you present me?"

"Me? But I am only . . ." He had started to gesture at the stables, but she had caught his hand.

"You're the only man I'd walk out there with other than my fa-ther." She had caught a brief glimpse of tears in his eyes as he bowed his head and stared at the hand clutching his.

"You honor me." His voice had been husky with emotion, one of the rare times she ever remembered Ben showing any. Then he had shook his head, as if to refuse.

"There's nothing to it, Ben. All you have to do is walk out with me when I'm introduced and the announcer talks about my Confed-erate ancestors. Then we'll dance the first waltz until my escort cuts in. We'll have to rent you a black tux and white tie . . . and gloves. You'll look so handsome. And I'll tell everyone you're our dearest, dearest friend from Europe. With your accent, they'll go crazy over you." When he wavered, Abbie had pressed her advantage. "Please,

Ben. At least come to the rehearsal with me. They'll walk you through everything."

"I have not waltzed since I was a young boy."

"Let's see how rusty you are." Still holding the mare's reins, Abbie had placed his hand on her waist and raised the other one. "Ready? One, two, three. One, two, three." While she hummed a waltz tune, they had started to dance, haltingly at first, then with increasing ease. "You see, Ben, it's just like riding a horse. You never really forget how." They had waltzed across the stable yard, leading a tired and bewildered mare.

The night of the Confederate Ball, Abbie, arrayed in an off-the-shoulder antebellum gown of white satin designed by St. Laurent, her hair piled atop her head in dark ringlets, arrived at the country club in a horse-drawn carriage that was met by a member of the Albert Sidney Johnston Camp of the Sons of Confederate Veterans, the sponsor of the Confederate Ball, dressed in full Confederate regalia. To strains of "Lorena," an erect, square-shouldered Ben, completely transformed by the white gloves, white tie, and black tuxedo he wore, walked proudly at her side as she was presented and made her full court bow to an applauding, cheering throng of guests. After all the debutantes were presented, Abbie danced the "Tennessee Waltz" with him until her escort for the evening, Christopher Atwell, cut in and fastened a corsage on her wrist, an act that traditionally symbolized her assumption of responsibility for her social destiny.

Even though it wasn't the same as if her father had been there, Abbie had fond memories of that evening — because of Ben, ill at ease, yet going through it for her.

By the time her father had returned after a week's absence, Abbie had been too caught up in the whirl of parties, teas, and balls to take more than passing notice of his apathy. Now, hindsight enabled her to see that he had been a man bereaved by the death of the woman he loved.

Abbie remembered it all so clearly, the brooding silences, the far-away stares, the pained look in his eyes. Her lips felt wet and she pressed them together to lick them dry, tasting the salty moisture of tears . . . her tears. She could feel them running down her cheeks, one after the other.

No wonder she'd never been able to be the daughter her father wanted.

No parent ever loves his children equally, no matter how he might try or pretend. There is always one that is the favorite, one that is special. But it hadn't been her. Never her. Obviously it had always been Rachel, the daughter of the woman he had loved for so long. Yet all this time he'd let her believe she was the only one; all this time she'd wondered what was wrong with her, certain that something had to be — otherwise he'd love her. Hurt and angered by the deception, Abbie dug her fingernails into the palms of her hands, needing the physical pain to ease the emotional one.

Behind her the office door opened. Instantly she stiffened, opening her eyes wide to try to clear them of the stinging tears.

"Your mother asked me to find you."

Abbie slumped at the quiet sound of Ben Jablonski's voice. She didn't have to hide her feelings from him. "Ben, did you know about the woman and child Daddy kept in California?"

There was a long pause before he answered. "I heard some talk . . . among the help."

"It was more than talk. It was true." She poured out the whole agonizing story to him, and its obvious conclusions. "Why, Ben?" She choked on a sob, as always demanding from him the answers she couldn't find. "Why?" She felt the light pressure of his big hand on her shoulder and swung around to face him. "Why couldn't he love me, too?"

"Ssssh, baby." Gently he gathered her into his arms and crooned to her in Polish.

She leaned against his shoulder and doubled her hands into tight fists. "I hate him for what he did, Ben. I hate him!"

"No. You don't hate him." He smoothed her hair with a gentle touch. "It hurts so much because you loved him."

Abbie cried, this time for herself.

9

$\mathcal{T}$he distinctive skyline of downtown Houston soared above the flatness of the sprawling Texas city. Coming from Los Angeles, Rachel hadn't expected to be impressed. In her opinion, city downtowns were all alike — a collection of skyscrapers crowded together to form concrete canyons jammed with traffic — a place you only went if you absolutely, positively had to.

But as she turned down Louisiana Street, she was radically revising her opinion. Initially she was struck by the high-rise buildings themselves, each one unique, like an architectural signature written against the sky. Contemporary in design, their individual use of shapes, angles, and glass was unusual, if not controversial. She couldn't help marveling at the progressive mixture that combined to make a single statement of dynamic growth.

She felt the energy and vitality that surrounded her. In almost any direction she looked, construction was under way on a new tower. She couldn't shake the feeling that she was driving through an outdoor gallery devoted to architecture. Yet the wide streets, the short blocks, and the building setbacks gave the downtown a sense of space. In fact, when she stopped looking up at the bronze and silver reflecting towers and noticed the small plazas, the spraying fountains, and the sculptures scattered about, Rachel caught the mood of the city center: vital yet leisurely, with a kind of laid-back energy, Texas-style.

Nowhere was the impression stronger than when she turned off Louisiana Street onto Dallas and approached the landscaped entrance to the Hotel Meridien, where she was to meet Lane Canfield for lunch. Designed in the form of an elongated trapezoid tapering to a sharp point at its western end, the building was faced entirely with bronze glass, echoing the color theme of the off-white concrete and bronze used so effectively in adjacent structures. But the severity of its form was broken by the zigzag construction of its front that faced the plaza entrance and added dimension to the hotel.

Although Rachel hadn't inherited her mother's creative talents with a brush, only a technical skill, she had acquired an appreciation for art from those early years of constant exposure to it. To her mother, art had been everything. It was her great love. After that came Dean. Rachel had never been sure where she ranked with her mother, but it had been somewhere down the line. Caroline had loved her, but when a choice had to be made, art had always come first. She had lived her life the way she wanted, compromising for nothing and no one.

It was a selfish attitude that Rachel had frequently resented when she was growing up, especially when she learned that Dean had wanted to marry her mother. She was certain her life would have been very different if they had married. She wouldn't have grown up so lonely, feeling unwanted and unloved — and ashamed of who she was. During those first years in elementary school, she had learned very quickly that being a love child wasn't the wonderful thing her mother had claimed, and that *love child* wasn't the term ignorant people usually used to describe her. The feeling had never really left her, even now, in this supposedly enlightened age.

Maybe that's why she'd always had this vague fear of drawing attention to herself. She wanted to blend in, be like everyone else. It was almost better to be a wallflower; then people wouldn't be whispering behind her back.

But when she parked her rental car and entered the hotel, Rachel felt uncomfortably conspicuous. The California layered look of her dirndl skirt, knit top, and belted overblouse didn't fit the understated elegance of the hotel's French-flavored decor. Too self-conscious to approach the clerk behind the genteel reception desk, Rachel approached a bellman and asked him for directions to the hotel's Le Restaurant de France.

Inside the restaurant's entrance, she hovered uncertainly. This formal atmosphere was the last thing she'd expected to find in Texas.

Texas was supposed to be barbecue and boots, cowboy hats and chili peppers. Despite the restaurant's name, she hadn't dreamed Lane Canfield had invited her to a place like this for lunch. All her life, she'd wanted to have a meal in surroundings like these, but she'd never gone to a fancy restaurant, certain that she'd end up feeling out of place.

And she did — from the top of her long, straight hair to the bottom of her sandaled feet. As the maître d' approached her, wearing a uniform that had the unmistakable stamp of custom tailoring, Rachel realized that even he was better dressed than she was — a fact he noted in one sweeping glance at her.

"May I help you?"

She felt intimidated and struggled to suppress it. "I'm supposed to meet Mr. Lane Canfield here for lunch."

"Mr. Canfield." An eyebrow shot up, then quickly leveled as he smiled respectfully. "This way, ma'am."

Seated at a secluded table for two, Lane Canfield sipped at his bourbon and water and stared absently at the empty chair opposite him. Idleness was unnatural to him. Usually every minute of his day was crammed with business: meetings, phone calls, conferences, or reports of one kind or another.

Lane frowned absently, trying to recall how long it had been since anything had taken precedence over his business. There'd never been time in his life for anything — or anyone — else. Sex wasn't even a diversion to him. He hated to think how many times he had arranged for one of the prostitutes from his carefully screened list to come to his penthouse apartment, then screwed her while he mentally plotted out some new corporate strategy. Why? What did he want? What was he killing himself for? More money? More power? Why? He was millionaire a hundred times over.

Dean's death had affected him in ways he hadn't expected. He wondered how he could fairly say he'd been Dean Lawson's friend. Yes, he had interrupted his busy schedule to attend his funeral, but in the last ten years, how many times had he seen or talked to Dean? Eight, maybe nine times. No more than that. Yet Dean had made him the executor of his will.

And what had he done? Turned the paperwork over to one of his staff to handle — too busy, his time too valuable for him to get involved with any of the details beyond the contents of the will.

Reaching up, he felt the front of his suit jacket, making sure the letter was still in his inside pocket — the letter that had been addressed to him marked PERSONAL: ONLY TO BE OPENED IN THE EVENT OF MY DEATH, with Dean's name signed below.

It had been buried among the papers, bills, and documents collected from Dean's law office by his secretary, Mary Jo Anderson. He had assigned the task of sorting through them to his own personal secretary, Frank Marsden. Frank had found the sealed envelope and delivered it into Lane's hands late yesterday afternoon. This morning, its contents had been verified.

Lane knew it was the letter in his suit pocket that was partly responsible for all his soul-searching. The opening lines of the letter haunted him:

> Dear Lane,
>
> I hope you never have to read this. I promised myself long ago that I would never tread on our friendship. But now I find myself in a situation where I must ask a favor of you. There's no one else I can trust. It's about my daughter, Rachel, Caroline's child. . . .

Trust. The word nagged at Lane. He had done so little to deserve it. What troubled him more was the doubt that there was anyone among his own circle of friends whom he could trust with something so very personal in nature. Not a single name came to mind. The people he dealt with and called friends were not that at all. It was a sobering discovery at the age of fifty-six to realize you had no one you could turn to.

But whom did Rachel have? Motherless. Now fatherless. No blood relative who wanted her. Abbie had made that clear. Since meeting her at the cemetery, Lane had thought about Rachel often: the sadness, the hurt in her blue eyes, haunting him at odd moments. He wondered if she had suffered much from the stigma of illegitimacy while growing up. He doubted that she could have escaped it entirely, considering how thoughtless and cruel other children could be at times.

Roused from his reverie by the sound of approaching footsteps, Lane glanced up and saw Rachel following the maître d' to his table. As he rose to greet her, he noticed how stiff and tense she appeared.

"Hello, Rachel."

"Hello. I'm sorry I'm late." Immediately she sat down in the chair the maître d' pulled out for her, then awkwardly helped him move it closer to the table.

"You're not late." Lane resumed his own seat. "I was able to leave the office sooner than I planned. It gave me a chance to relax and have a drink."

She seemed self-conscious and ill at ease, her glance skittering away without even meeting his as she opened the menu in front of her. "I know how busy you are and I'm grateful that you could spare the time to have lunch with me."

Her cheeks looked flushed to him, and he doubted it was rouge. She wore very little makeup, but with her skin and eyes, he didn't think she needed any. "It's my pleasure. It isn't often that I have lunch with an attractive woman."

She glanced briefly around at the other customers in the restaurant, her glance lingering on one or two of the more fashionably dressed women in the room. "You're very kind, but I doubt that, Mr. Canfield."

"You shouldn't. It's the truth." Belatedly he realized she was embarrassed about the way she was dressed. He blamed himself for not saying something when he had suggested meeting here, but it hadn't occurred to him. "Would you like something to drink before we order lunch?" he asked as the waiter came up to their table.

She hesitated briefly. "Perhaps a glass of white wine."

"A chardonnay or Riesling? We have a very nice —"

"The chardonnay will be fine," she interrupted.

"We'll trust your judgment on the vineyard and the vintage," Lane inserted to stave off the anticipated inquiry from the waiter, guessing — he was sure correctly — that Rachel wasn't knowledgeable about wines. "And I'll have another bourbon and water."

"Very good, sir."

"This is a beautiful restaurant," she remarked as the waiter left.

Personally, Lane regretted his choice, observing how uncomfortable she was there. He'd assumed that Dean had taken her to places like this in Los Angeles. Maybe not, though. Caroline certainly wouldn't have been impressed by it.

"It's a little stuffy, but the food is excellent."

"I'm sure it is."

Dammit, he felt sorry for her, although he suspected his pity was the last thing she wanted. He had intended this lunch to be something personal. He felt he owed that to Dean. More than that, he felt Rachel deserved it. He didn't want this to become a business discussion about the contents of Dean's will and the letter in his pocket. That had to be dealt with, but not now. After their drinks arrived and they ordered their meals, Lane started asking her questions, trying to get her to talk about herself and her work as a commercial artist, and relax a little. He discovered it wasn't easy to draw her out of her shell, but he persisted, responding to the challenge.

"Are you still living in Malibu?" he asked after his questions about her work gained him only meager responses.

"No. I have an apartment in the hills near the riding stable where I keep my horses."

"You have horses?" He remembered how involved Abbie was with the Arabian horses at River Bend. He should have guessed that Rachel would pick up Dean's obsession for them as well.

"Well, only two, actually. Ahmar is the gelding Dean bought me when I was twelve. He's the first horse I ever owned. Before that I had a pony — a Welsh-Arabian cross. Ahmar is nineteen years old now, but you'd never guess it. He still loves his morning gallops and gets jealous if I take my filly Simoon out instead."

"Ahmar. He's an Arabian, of course," Lane guessed.

"Of course," she laughed for the first time. He liked the warm spontaneity of the sound. "A fiery red chestnut. In Arabic, *Ahmar* means 'red.' He's my very best friend."

A horse for a best friend, Lane thought, noticing that she appeared embarrassed by her admission. If that was true, then her life must be lonelier than he'd thought.

The waiter returned with their food order: a lobster salad for Rachel and duck terrine for himself. He let it absorb her attention for a few minutes.

"You said you have another horse," he prompted.

"Yes, Simoon, a three-year-old filly. Dean gave her to me as a yearling. She's out of one of the mares he imported from Egypt a few years ago, and sired by his stallion Nahr El Kedar." Rachel described her at length, for a little while completely forgetting herself. It was a different Rachel that Lane saw then, warm and glowing, that wall of reserve lowered, but only briefly.

"What about boyfriends? I'm sure there's someone back there in L.A. waiting for you."

"No." She picked at the remains of her lobster salad. "Between my job and my horses, I don't have a lot of free time for dating. I go out once in a while, but not often."

Lane could tell by her expression that the experiences left a lot to be desired. As sensitive as she was, there was no doubt in his mind that she'd probably been hurt at one time or another. And the old saying "once burned, twice shy" was probably more than apt for her.

After Rachel had refused both dessert and coffee, Lane asked for the check. "I enjoyed the lunch very much. You were right. The food was excellent." She laid her napkin on the table and picked up her purse. "Thank you for asking me."

"Don't leave yet," Lane said, checking the movement she started to make. "I thought we might take a walk in the park across the street. There are a few things I want to talk to you about."

With a hand at her elbow, Lane guided her across the street to Sam Houston Park. They strolled together across the rolling green, past historical St. John's Church and the gazebo to the rushes growing along the bank of Buffalo Bayou. There Rachel turned and looked back at the modern skyscrapers of downtown towering over the small park.

"The architecture here fascinates me." A gusting wind blew her long hair into her face. She combed it out of the way with her fingers and held it, the pose pulling the loose blouse tautly across her breasts. Lane was not so jaded that the sight failed to arouse him. Rather, he felt a healthy stirring of desire in his loins, and had to remind himself that she was the daughter of a friend — not that he was entirely sure what difference that made. "I guess I get that from my mother. I don't know." She shrugged absently. "When I think of all that Los Angeles is doing to try to revitalize its downtown area and then . . . see this. I mean, there's construction going on everywhere."

"Counting cranes is Houston's favorite pastime," Lane said, referring to the giant construction cranes that poked their long necks from nearly every building site. "Some people want to declare them the state bird."

"I can believe it."

"If you want a better vantage point of the downtown buildings, we can walk over to Tranquility Park. It's just a block or so from here."

"I know you're busy. And I can't keep taking up your time. . . ."

"It's my time." With a wave of his hand, he pointed out the direction they would take. "Before you leave for California, you should take a drive around Houston. There are high-rise buildings clustered miles apart on the outer loops with architectural styles that rival what you see here."

As they walked across the park with the sun beating down on them and the wind tugging at their clothes, Lane did something he hadn't done in years — decades, maybe. Impulsively he took off his tie, unbuttoned his shirt collar, and removed his jacket, hooking it over his shoulder on his finger. It was as if a weight had been lifted from him. He felt lighter, freer — even a little younger as he directed Rachel across the street again to the futuristic Tranquility Park.

Named after the Sea of Tranquility on the lunar surface, the park was built as a Bicentennial tribute to the Apollo flights to the moon, and constructed atop the concrete deck of a multilevel underground garage. As they wandered past the reflecting pools, Lane explained some of the symbolism in the park's design, with its grassy knolls representing lunar mounds, and the fountains, ascending rockets.

"I'm told it's beautiful in the late afternoon when the angle of the sunlight hits the fountains just right and turns the water golden," he said, then admitted, "Actually, this is the first time I've ever been here."

"It's peaceful here."

"It certainly is."

She walked over to a bench and sat down, gripping the edge of the bench with her hands. "You said you wanted to talk to me about something."

"Yes." Lane joined her. "I'm sure you must have guessed that Dean's will has been read. He named me as the executor of his estate."

"I see."

"Rachel." The rest was hard for him to say, even now. "There was no mention of you in the will. Legally, you could contest it . . . and probably be awarded a third of his estate. At this time, I can't tell you what that amount might be, but —"

"No." She shook her head, her expression sadly fatalistic. "I won't do that. River Bend, the house, the horses — all that is theirs. It never belonged to me. I won't claim part of it now."

"Rachel, I'm sorry." He could tell she was hurt.

"Don't be," she insisted with a tight little smile, trying to pretend she didn't care. "I think I always knew I'd be left out. I mean, why should anything change just because he's dead?" She bowed her head. "That sounded bitter. I didn't mean for it to."

In her place, Lane thought he would have been more than bitter. Even in death, Dean hadn't publicly acknowledged her existence. "I don't want you to misunderstand me, Rachel. Your father didn't forget you. It seems that shortly after you were born, he set up an irrevocable trust fund in your name. Today, between the contributions he made into it and the accumulated interest, the fund totals over two million dollars."

"What?" She stared at him incredulously.

Lane smiled. "The exact figure is something like two million, one hundred and eighty-seven thousand dollars, plus change. The way the fund was set up, the money was to come to you when you reached the age of thirty — or in the event of his death . . . unless of course you were under twenty-one at the time."

"I can't believe it." Tears swam in her eyes, but her expression was joyful. "Daddy — Dean did that for me?"

"Yes." Moved by her poignant display, he smiled even wider, more gently. As her hands came up to cup her nose and mouth and catch the tears that spilled from the inside corners of her eyes, Lane swung away the suit jacket he'd carried and reached out to draw her into his arms. "Child," he murmured, but she felt like a woman against him.

At first, she simply let him hold her and comfortingly pat her shoulder while she cried softly. But the tears seemed to wash away some invisible wall she'd built around herself. Soon she was leaning against him, letting him support her, her face buried in the crook of his neck, her fingers clutching the front of his shirt. Lane rubbed his cheek and jaw against the silken top of her head, wondering when he'd last felt as deeply as she did. His own emotions had been buried too long in his work.

"I don't believe it." She sniffed at the tears that wouldn't stop and wiped at her nose and eyes, trying to regain her control. "He must have really loved me. Sometimes, I —" She pulled back, gazing at Lane with haunted eyes. "Is this another of his presents to buy off his guilty conscience?"

"I think he loved you very much. And, like any father, he wanted to provide you with some financial security for the day when he couldn't look after you." That much Lane believed was true, but he wouldn't speculate on whether Dean's concern had been motivated by a guilty conscience.

Maybe Dean had lavished presents on her in the past to make up for the time he couldn't spend with her. Thousands of people did that. Was that a guilty conscience or an attempt to buy a child's love? Was either one really wrong? Lane had never been a parent. He couldn't say.

"I will tell you this, Rachel. He wouldn't have been much of a father if he hadn't taken steps to provide for your future."

"He *was* good to me — always." She moved away from him a little as she finished wiping the last of the tears from her face. Then she smiled wryly at him. "I can imagine what you think of me, falling apart like that."

"I think . . . you're beautiful." And he'd never meant a statement more. Impulsively he leaned forward and lightly kissed her lips, briefly feeling their softness and tasting the salt of her tears. Then it was his turn to wonder what she thought of him. But the look in her eyes seemed to be one of trust. He was stung by the possibility that she had regarded his kiss only as a fatherly peck.

"I'm not really sure any of this is happening to me." She shook her head vaguely. "Yesterday, I was wondering how I was going to keep both my horses. Dean always paid the boarding fees on them. I was going to look for a cheaper apartment when I got back. Now, with that much money, I can live anywhere I want, do anything I want."

"Indeed you can."

"It's staggering. I always knew Dean was wealthy, but I never dreamed I would ever have that much money. I'm not even sure what to do with it."

"What have you always wanted to do? No, seriously," Lane encouraged, observing her show of reluctance. "What's something you've always dreamed about having or doing if you had the money?"

Glancing down, she fingered her blouse. "I've always wanted to have a closet full of beautiful clothes — and a real home. But my dream . . ." She hesitated, glancing sideways at him, her self-consciousness returning. "This is going to sound silly and childish to you, Mr. Canfield."

"I'll only answer that if you call me Lane."

"Lane. Practically all my life, I've dreamed of owning an Arabian horse farm. Simoon — the filly Dean gave me — she was going to be my start. I've been saving money for the stud fee so I could breed her next year. Then I could sell the foal and use that money to buy me another broodmare, and slowly build a herd that way. I've been trying to find some land I could buy or lease, but it's all so expensive in California I can't afford it on my salary. And I never could bring myself to ask Dean to help me. He already had a farm, and, even though he never said so, I know he would have been uncomfortable if I got into the Arabian horse business, too. He knows all the top breeders everywhere in the world. How would he have explained me? And, of course, there was his family."

"You don't have to worry about any of that now. Money can't alter the past or make you happy, but it can help you to realize your wildest dreams. So go ahead and dream, Rachel. That's what it's for."

"It is, isn't it?" she mused. "Back in my apartment in L.A., I have the barn all designed for my dream farm. I mean, it's complete right down to the dimensions of the foaling stalls, the veterinary lab, the video equipment, everything — even the materials to be used in the construction."

Lane listened to her dream and remembered the way he had talked, back in the beginning when he was getting started. Those were the good days, when he'd had time to rejoice in his successes and savor the sweetness of them. Now, he was too busy. Watching her, he realized how much he missed the excitement of dreaming. He envied her the feeling.

"Have you given any thought to where you would like to build this?"

"I always assumed it would have to be California. Which is fine. Most of the major breeders are located in either California or Arizona. But where would I *like* to build it?" She paused, a slight ruefulness twisting her mouth. "Dean always talked so much about Texas."

"You will have to spend quite a bit of time here — at least initially. There's going to be a considerable amount of paperwork involved in transferring the funds into your name. Naturally you're going to need someone you can trust to advise you on the best way to invest a sum that size. I'm sure there are qualified people in California who can help you, but I think your father would have wanted me to assist you in making such decisions. You don't put over two million dollars in a savings account to draw interest. You can, but it isn't wise."

"I can't even comprehend that amount," Rachel admitted. "And I would like you to advise me. I know how much Dean trusted you. And how could I be sure I'd find someone else like you? But I hate the thought of bothering you —"

"Rachel, I would be happy to do it. I would never have volunteered myself otherwise. Have we got that settled?"

"Yes." She smiled and Lane felt warmed by it.

"Now, back to your dream farm. Tell me how you would go about accomplishing it." He encouraged Rachel to expound on her plans, enjoying the animation in her face, the free play of expression, and the total absence of the air of reserve behind which she'd hidden her feelings earlier.

"To start with, I'd like to find three or four really good mares," she began. "Ideally, I'd buy older broodmares — twelve or thirteen years old probably — proven producers. That way I could have better quality mares for a lower price. Even though their most productive years would be over, I could still hope to get three, maybe more good foals from them. If I could be lucky enough to buy broodmares already in foal, I'd have the choice the following year of selling the foals as weanlings to start generating an income or keeping the really good ones to build my own herd."

She continued to talk, telling him all her plans, her breeding theories, and her ambitions. Occasionally Lane would insert a comment or question, but mostly he just listened. For one so young, in his eyes, she had impressive knowledge of horses and various bloodlines. Then he remembered the way Abbie had talked, and decided that maybe it wasn't so surprising after all. Like father, like daughter.

"Look at the fountains." Rachel halted in surprise to stare at the molten-gold cascading water. "Have we talked that long?"

"We must have." Lane was surprised that he'd so completely lost track of time, as well. Appointments usually made him a prisoner of the clock. Yet he hadn't glanced at his watch once since he'd been with Rachel. He realized it was a good thing he'd told Frank to clear his calendar of all appointments this afternoon.

Rachel hastily stood up, smoothing the front of her skirt and withdrawing behind her wall of reserve again. "I'm sorry for boring you like that."

"My dear, you could never bore me." Lane straightened, reluctant to part from her. Rachel had awakened desires in him that he'd forgotten he'd ever felt. They were more than mere sexual urges, easily gratified. Their makeup was more complex, evoking a longing to arouse and please, to cherish and protect, to give and delight in the giving. Sobering feelings — all of them.

"It's kind of you to say that, Lane, but I know I did." Her lips curved faintly in a smile of regret, then she glanced down the street. "I left my car parked at the hotel."

"I'll walk you there." He swung his suit jacket over his shoulder again and curved his arm around the back of her waist, trying to keep the contact casual, as they set out of the park. "What are your immediate plans?"

"I've . . . made reservations to fly back to Los Angeles tomorrow morning." But she seemed to question whether she should cancel her plans.

"I'm sure there are plenty of things you need to take care of there as well as here. All the document signing and paperwork for the trust account can wait until next week. It isn't going to vanish between now and then."

"That's true. I could fly back here the first of the week."

"If you're short of funds, I'll be happy to advance you some money."

"No, I . . . I can use my savings. There's no reason not to now, is there?" She still seemed a little dazed by the news. "It's hard to think of myself as being rich, an heiress to a fortune."

"That's exactly what you are. Let me know what day you'll be coming back. We'll have dinner. I still haven't shown you that painting of your mother's I mentioned at lunch."

"I'd forgotten all about that."

"I hadn't." Any more than he'd forgotten what it had been like to hold her in his arms and kiss her as he'd done a little while ago. "Would you have dinner with me next week?"

"I'd like to, yes, but —"

Lane didn't want to hear another self-effacing comment about taking up his busy time. He cut in to stop her: "Then let's consider it a date," realizing that he meant it in the strictest old-fashioned sense.

"All right." She nodded in agreement, smiling faintly as if pleased, yet afraid something would happen to change it. Lane wondered how many times Dean had made a promise to her that he hadn't been able to keep. He didn't like the impression he had that Rachel was preparing herself to be disappointed. No one should be that insecure. He vowed to change that.

10

*T*he sound of Abbie's footsteps on the stairs disturbed the stillness that enveloped the house. There'd always been an empty feeling to it whenever her father was gone. Now that feeling would be permanent. Abbie paused near the bottom of the staircase and glanced at the closed doors to the library. They had always been kept shut when he was away.

Not needing such a reminder, Abbie ran down the last three steps and crossed the foyer to slide the doors open, then paused to stare at the neat, tidy top of his desk, not at all the way he'd left it.

This past week she'd gone through the room, cleaned out his desks — both here and at his office in the stables — and sent what few pertinent documents she'd found to Lane Canfield. But there hadn't been any letters, photographs, or mementos that pertained to his mistress and child in California. If there were any, Abbie suspected that he'd probably kept them at his law office. That was Mary Jo Anderson's province.

There had been many things to do this past week, things her mother hadn't been up to doing: notifying the accountant to send her father's records to Lane, forwarding the bills to him, cleaning out her father's drawers and closet, throwing out his old clothes and packing the rest into boxes for distribution to local charitable and religious organizations, sorting through personal articles such as jewelry and toiletries and deciding which ones to save and which ones to discard.

It hadn't been easy to remove the physical traces of him from the house.

Even though they were gone now, he still haunted it. Somewhere a clock ticked, marking time against the low hum of the central air-conditioning and echoing the feeling of expectancy that permeated the house, as if any second he was going to walk through the front door. But he wasn't . . . not now, not ever!

Abbie pivoted sharply and strode across the foyer to the living room arch, letting the heels of her riding boots strike the polished boards of the heart-pine floor as hard as they wished in an attempt to chase away the ghosts — and the nagging fears.

From her chair near the bay window, her mother looked up from the stack of sympathy cards that surrounded her. "Is something wrong, Abbie?" Babs frowned quizzically.

She resisted the impulse to say yes. How could she tell her mother that, despite the fact that Rachel hadn't been mentioned in the will, and despite the fact that Lane had informed her that Dean had made separate provisions for Rachel and it was extremely unlikely she would contest the will, she still felt uneasy about it? Until the estate was actually settled, the possibility remained. And she couldn't ignore it.

"Nothing at all," she lied. "I just wanted to let you know I'm headed for the stables. I thought I might work River Breeze a little."

"The way you came marching in here, it sounded like we were being invaded by the whole Russian army or something."

"Sorry. I'll be outside if you need me."

"Don't forget: the Richardsons are coming for dinner tonight at seven."

"I won't."

Abbie turned and left the room, more quietly than she'd entered it. Outside, the summer sun had begun its downward slide and the oak trees in the front yard cast long shadows across the lawn. Abbie paused in the shade of the wide veranda and turned her face toward the cool breeze that came whispering through the trees, letting its freshness calm her nerves.

A battered old pickup truck was parked in front of the stables. Abbie recognized it instantly. No other truck was in such sorry shape in the entire county. Her father used to joke that rust was the only thing holding it together. It belonged to Dobie Hix, who owned the neighboring farm to the west of them. Abbie smiled wryly, guessing that his brand-new pickup was probably parked in his garage. He rarely drove it, except to town. He didn't want to get it all beaten up bouncing over the rutted lanes to his fields, so he drove the old one most of the time.

Ever since Abbie could remember, he'd always been like that: buying something new, then never using it until it was old. It didn't matter that he could probably afford ten new trucks. Between the land he owned and the acreage he leased, he farmed close to fifteen hundred acres. More than once Abbie had heard her mother insist that Dobie was tighter than the bark on a tree with his money. His tightfisted hold on a dollar had become almost a standing joke in the area. Abbie had laughed about it once or twice herself, but never in front of him.

She wondered what he was doing here at River Bend. He sold them the hay they used to feed the horses, but the hay shed was practically full. Her curiosity aroused, Abbie headed over to the stables.

As she neared the breezeway, she saw Ben standing in its shade, talking with Dobie. "I am certain you have nothing to worry about, Mr. Hix."

"I figured that." Dobie nodded his head in agreement, the rolled brim of his straw cowboy hat bobbing up and down with the motion. As usual, he was dressed in an old pair of faded Levi's, a plaid shirt, and a leather belt with his name stamped in fancy letters across the back of it. "I've always known Lawson was good for it. It's just —" He spied Abbie and halted in midsentence. "Hello, Abbie." Quickly he swept off his hat and self-consciously ran his fingers through his fine strawberry-blond hair, trying to comb it into some kind of order.

"Hello, Dobie." She glanced at the sprinkling of freckles that gave him such a boyish look despite the fact that he had to be, at least, thirty-five. "What's the problem?"

"No problem," he insisted, smiling. "Leastwise, nothing that you need to worry your pretty head about." Then he ducked his head as if regretting the compliment he'd paid her.

More than once since her divorce, Abbie had gotten the impression that, with the least little encouragement from her, Dobie would renew the suit he'd pressed throughout almost her entire senior year of high school, particularly at the Gay Nineties debut party held here at River Bend, the Victorian mansion providing the theme and backdrop. It had been an elaborate bash thrown by her parents. All the invitations, bearing a tintype photograph of Abbie dressed as a Gibson Girl, had been hand-delivered by uniformed messengers wearing flannel trousers, bow ties, and straw skimmers, and riding a bicycle built for two. A carnival had been set up on the grounds, transforming it into Coney Island, complete with a midway — and a kissing booth. Dobie Hix had been very free with his money that day, Abbie recalled, buying up all the tickets when she was selling kisses. Her mother had insisted that they couldn't leave him off the invitation list, when he was their closest neighbor. Truthfully, Abbie hadn't objected — until she had to endure the embarrassment of his monopoly on her kisses, and later his broad hints about their lands adjoining and the advantages of combining them.

Nearly every time she'd gone riding after that, she'd run into him somewhere: down by the river, along the fence line, by the road. She'd had the feeling he hung around and watched for her. He hadn't really given up until she announced her engagement to Christopher Atwell. But she'd never been frightened of him, only irritated by his persistence.

His hands dug into his hat, crumpling the brim. "I saw you at the funeral. I would have come over, but . . . I want you to know how sorry I am about your daddy. He was a fine man."

"Thank you, Dobie."

"If you ever need anything — anything at all — remember, I'm just up the road. You let me know if I can help in any way."

"I appreciate that, but I can't think of anything right now. Ben and I have things fairly well under control, I think."

"I'm sure you do." He glanced at Ben, then hesitantly back at her. "Maybe the next time you're out riding, you can stop by the farm and visit." But he didn't wait for a response to his invitation. "Well, I'd best be gettin' along." With a bob of his head, he moved by her toward the rusty pickup, shoving his hat onto his head as he went.

As the truck rattled out of the yard, Abbie turned to Ben. "What did he want?"

"He came about the hay bill. When he delivered the last load, we had not yet paid him for the winter hay."

"Daddy must have overlooked it. Make a note of the amount and send it to Lane so he can make sure it's paid with the rest of the bills." But Abbie frowned, aware this wasn't the first inquiry they had received regarding past-due bills.

"I will see that he receives it."

With that settled, Abbie glanced toward the paddock where her silver-gray filly was kept. "I thought I'd lunge Breeze. She's had it easy this last week."

"It would be good . . . for both of you. You go," Ben prompted gently. "I will bring the halter and line."

She smiled at him, briefly acknowledging his gesture, then headed for the paddock gate. The filly trotted forward to meet her with an effortlessly floating stride — gliding over the ground, all delicacy and grace, head up, neck arched, her silvery tail erect and streaming behind her like a banner in the wind. As Abbie came through the gate, the filly nickered a welcome and impatiently nuzzled her arm.

Laughing softly, Abbie turned and caressed the filly, rubbing her favorite place just above the right eye. The texture of the filly's coat was slick as satin beneath her hand. Here and there, a smoky dark hair was hidden among the dominant white coloring, but beneath, the filly's skin was as black as the haircloth tents of the Bedouins in which her desert-bred ancestors had lived. The mares were prized above all others by the nomad raiders of the sand.

"Lonely, were you?" Abbie crooned, watching the filly's small ears move to catch every inflection of her voice. "And I suppose there was no one around to give you any attention. Well, you don't have to fret anymore. I'm back now."

She embraced the filly, hugging her neck, feeling the affection returned, the warmth of another body. The sense of being wanted — needed — was strong. Abbie responded to it, talking, sharing, and never minding how silly it might sound, not until the filly alerted Abbie to Ben's presence at the fence.

"I think she's happy to see me." She took the halter from him and slipped it on the young horse.

"She missed you."

"I missed her." She buckled the throatlatch and snapped on the lead rope as Ben opened the gate.

The silver-gray horse came prancing through the opening behind Abbie, animation and eagerness in every line, yet, for all the show of spirit, there was still slack in the lead rope Abbie held. Ben studied the filly with a critical eye, looking for any faults or imperfections.

"She reminds me of Wielki Szlem. What a magnificent stride he had."

"That's when you were at Janow?" Janow Podlaski was the famed state-run Arabian stud farm in Poland where so many of the great Arabian stallions had stood: Skowronek Witraz, Comet, Negatiw, and Bask.

Ben nodded affirmatively as a faraway look came into his eyes. "I was fifteen when they hired me to work at Janow." He'd been talking about the past more and more of late, Abbie noticed. "That was before the war with Germany, when many of Janow's grooms were drafted into the army."

Many times Abbie had heard the story of his experiences in Poland during World War II: the dramatic flight to evacuate the valuable stallions and broodmares in advance of the invading German army, only to be turned back by Russian forces; the horses that were left at farms along the way; the ones confiscated by the Russians, including the great Ofir, sire of Wielki Szlem; the years of occupation by the Germans; the horrors of the Dresden bombings that claimed the lives of twenty-one prized horses; the valuable bloodlines that died out; the maneuvering that had enabled the Janow stud to come under British jurisdiction immediately after the war; and Ben's eventual immigration to the United States entrusted with the care of a stallion that subsequently died of colic on the long sea voyage. As a child, Abbie had thrilled to his tales. Even now, when she thought of him leading a horse through Dresden in the midst of an air raid, with bombs exploding all around, it raised chillbumps.

From the stud pen an elegent bay stallion, an inbred son of Nahr El Kedar, nickered shrilly at the gray filly Abbie led. Ben cast a contemptuous glance in the stallion's direction. "Racing, that is the test of a stallion. It is not how pretty he looks. Look at that one. Does he have heart? Does he have courage? Does he possess the stamina and disposition to endure the rigors of training and competing on the racetrack? Will he pass it on to his get? Who knows?" He shrugged his shoulders. "Many times I argued with your father on this, but never would he listen to me. The horse has a pretty head. That was all he cared about."

"I know." Just as she knew that Benedykt Jablonski based his opinions on the breeding practices in Poland, where racing played a vital role in the selection process of breeding stock. And Abbie had agreed with him even though it put her at odds with her father.

Ben had always disapproved of her father's practice of close inbreeding. "Incest breeding," he called it when Dean bred father to daughter or brother to half-sister. It set the good traits — the big eye, the dished profile or long neck — but it often exaggerated the faults — slightly sickle-hocked hind legs became severe, or a hint of calf knees became decidedly such. Abbie didn't like it either, especially when she saw that the overall quality of the River Bend Arabians had declined because of it.

She led the young filly into the work arena. Inside the solidly fenced area, she switched the lead rope for a lunge line and took the whip Ben handed her, then walked the horse to the center.

Having been raised on the farm, surrounded by horses, with no neighbor children her age living nearby, Abbie had naturally turned to horses as friends. They had become her companions, her playmates, and her confidants. But more than loneliness had drawn her. Any affection or loyalty shown by them was genuine. Unlike humans, they weren't capable of pretense, and they'd never betray her trust.

Most of the other girls Abbie knew had gone through a horse phase sometime in their early years, but hers had carried over into adulthood. When she was with horses, she felt good about herself. That had never changed.

After Abbie had succeeded in getting the filly to relax and trot smoothly in a counterclockwise circle around her, she saw Ben Jablonski leave the arena fence and head in the direction of the barns. She smiled faintly while keeping her attention focused on the filly. Once Ben would never have allowed her to work a young horse unsupervised. Compliments from him were rare, and when they came, they were invariably stated by his actions, as now.

Rachel slowed her car as she approached the entrance to River Bend, marked by a white signboard, the name written in black scrolled letters with the black silhouette of an Arabian horse below them. She stared at the horses grazing beneath the huge, moss-draped trees in the pasture, none of them close enough for her to see clearly.

She had driven here straight from the airport, returning to Houston a day earlier than she had planned. During the short time she'd spent in Los Angeles, she'd managed to quit her job, pack and store everything she didn't bring with her, and sublet her apartment to one of her co-workers. Everything had gone so smoothly that Rachel was even more convinced that her decision to move to Texas was the right one. As soon as she found a place to live, she would have her horses shipped from California. Except for them, that life was behind her, a part of the past.

Flexing her grip on the steering wheel, Rachel hesitated, then turned the car onto the narrow lane and followed its winding path through the trees. Ever since Dean had given her Simoon, she had wanted to see the filly's sire and dam in person, not just pictures of them. And she wanted to look over the facilities at River Bend that she had read so much about.

As the car neared the heart of River Bend, the trees parted — like an honor guard before their ruler — and revealed the towering mansion with its gables and turrets, its skirting veranda and parapet. It was a stately, elegant home. Yes, *home* was the word, Rachel realized. There was nothing cold or austere about it for all its grandness. It looked like a place filled with hidden delights and wrapped in a warm invitation to come and explore.

Staring at it, Rachel remembered the spare apartments of her childhood, cluttered with her mother's paintings and permeated with the smell of paints and thinners. This home could have been hers. The thought swelled inside her — a bitter, choking thing.

Almost unwillingly, Rachel recalled when her mother had died, so suddenly, so unexpectedly. She'd come home from school and gone upstairs to the studio loft — and found her mother lying on the floor in front of an unfinished painting. When she had failed to get her mother to respond, Rachel ran to a neighbor's for help. After that, everything was a blur. She remembered being at the hospital and some man in green telling her that her mother was dead. She no longer knew whether Dean had arrived that night or the next day. But he had come. And she had cried and cried and cried in his arms.

At some point, either before the funeral or after, Rachel wasn't sure now, she had asked, "What's going to happen to me?" She'd been seventeen at the time, but she'd felt like seven — left alone and frightened.

"I've made arrangements for you to stay with Myria Holmes," he'd said, mentioning one of her mother's artist friends. "She offered and —"

"I don't want to live with her!" She had almost cried, "I want to live with you," but she'd stopped herself before the words came out. It had been so painful to realize she had secretly hoped all along that Dean would take her back to Texas with him; that he wouldn't be able to bear the thought of leaving her here alone, with no one; that he loved her too much to go away without her. She had been crushed to learn that she wasn't going to be leaving with him.

"It won't be for long," he'd hurried to assure her. "Next year you'll be going to college and living on campus with your friends."

But he'd never understood that she didn't have any friends, not really. They'd come in and out of her life, some staying longer than others, letting her believe that maybe this time she had a best friend she could trust, but each time she'd been disillusioned. Now that her mother was gone, no one loved her or wanted her around all the time — not even her own father.

God, how she longed to be wanted and loved — and feared it would never be. Her horses, that was all she had. And she told herself they were all she needed. Their affection, their companionship was enough.

Just ahead, a lofty oak tree split the lane into two branches, one leading to the white mansion and the other veering off to the huge stable complex. Rachel swung the car to the right — to the horses.

After a twenty-minute workout, Abbie led the silver-gray filly out of the work arena, the perimeter of which was solidly boarded to eliminate outside distractions. Snorting and blowing, the filly paced alertly beside her. As they approached the stables, Abbie felt a tug on the lead rope. Mistaking the pull for a show of eagerness to reach her stall and receive her evening measure of grain, Abbie glanced sideways at the filly, chiding, "Worked up an appetite, did you?"

But the dainty ears and huge dark eyes were trained on the car parked near the stables' office annex. Abbie didn't recognize the late-model car. One of the grooms approached from the direction of the annex.

"Who does the car belong to, Miguel?" she asked curiously, not immediately seeing any stranger in the vicinity. "Is it just someone wanting to look at the horses?" Visitors — some prospective buyers, some not — frequently stopped at River Bend to look at their Arabians.

"Si. She wanted to see El Kedar. I pointed out his pen to her. I was just going to get Señor Jablonski."

By then Abbie had already seen the tall, dark-haired woman crossing to the reinforced stallion run. She was nondescriptly dressed in a natural gauze blouse and tight-legged jeans minus any distinctive label, her long hair worn straight, sweeping past her shoulders. Rachel. Abbie recognized her immediately, and every muscle in her body suddenly grew taut.

"Never mind getting Ben," she told the groom. "I'll handle this one." She pushed the lunge line, lead rope, and whip into his hands. "Take Breeze to her stall and see that she gets a good rubdown before she's fed."

Without waiting for an acknowledgment, Abbie set off for the stud barn and its adjacent runs. Somehow she wasn't surprised that Rachel was here, but she seriously doubted that Rachel had come to look at the inheritance she was giving up. It was probably just the opposite.

Rachel stood pressed against the heavy rails, gazing admiringly at the aging bay stallion on the far side of the paddock, who was suspiciously testing the air to catch the scent of this stranger. At first she wasn't even aware that Abbie had joined her. Then she darted a quick glance at her and self-consciously drew back from the fence.

"He's magnificent," she said, a slightly nervous edge to her voice as she turned her attention back to El Kedar.

"My father thought so." Abbie wasn't sure why she'd said that, except in some way, she knew she wanted to challenge Rachel and assert her claim to him — to River Bend, to everything that she had once thought of as solely hers.

"At his age, I expected him to be heavier . . . thicker-necked, maybe, and stoutly muscled. But he looks lean and fit."

"We've always had trouble putting weight on him, especially during the breeding season. He was born and raised in Egypt. They don't believe in putting flesh on them. He was a three-year-old when he finally arrived here at River Bend — practically skin and bones after the long sea voyage and the quarantine. He'd never seen a blade of grass, let alone walked on it or ate it. And he'd never had room to run free." In a paddock separated from El Kedar's, a bay stallion similarly marked trotted boldly up to the fence and whistled a challenge to his older rival. "That's Nahr Ibn Kedar, his son."

"He doesn't have El Kedar's presence, does he?"

Abbie was briefly surprised by Rachel's observation. She hadn't suspected that she was so knowledgeable about Arabians. "No. El Kedar has never reproduced himself." Abbie paused, fighting a tension and an anger she couldn't quite understand. "Exactly why have you come here?"

Again she noticed Rachel's hesitation, that trace of uncertainty and nervousness in her expression. "I've only seen pictures of El Kedar. I've wanted to see him in person ever since Dean gave me his daughter, Nahr Simoon, out of Nahr Riih."

Abbie stiffened, remembering the filly, one of the best of El Kedar's daughters — the filly her father had supposedly sold. But that was yet another lie he'd told. She couldn't admit that, certainly not to Rachel.

"You called him by his first name?" she said instead.

"Yes. It was my mother's idea. She thought it would create fewer questions than if I called him Father or Daddy." Just for an instant, a wryness, faintly sardonic, crept into her voice and expression. But it was gone when Rachel turned from the fence and swept the stable area with a glance. "I was hoping I might tour the facilities here."

"Why?" Abbie wondered. To appraise its worth?

"I . . . I just wanted to see it. I've heard so much about it."

"I'm sure you'll understand that a tour isn't possible." Pushed by some territorial compulsion, Abbie wanted only to get her away from there, off of River Bend, *now*. Rachel had no right here, none at all. "River Bend isn't open to the public. And it won't be again until the estate is settled."

"Surely it wouldn't hurt anything if I just . . . looked around," Rachel suggested tentatively.

Over my dead body, Abbie thought, trembling with the rage she felt inside, not really knowing where it came from — and not really caring. "I can't allow that." She managed to keep the pitch of her voice calmly even and firm, but it wasn't easy.

"I see." Rachel held herself stiffly, looking a little hurt. "In that case, I guess there isn't much point in my staying here any longer."

"I guess not."

"Thank you for at least letting me see El Kedar."

"You're welcome."

As Rachel walked back to her car, Abbie felt the tears burning in her eyes. She was afraid, and it was the first time in her life she could remember feeling fear. So much had happened. She'd lost her father. She'd lost her illusions of the past. She couldn't stand the thought of losing even one small part of River Bend.

Surely Rachel hadn't really believed she would blithely show her around. Did Rachel really think she was so stupid that she hadn't guessed she intended to claim part — maybe even all — of it? Abbie wondered as she watched Rachel slide behind the wheel of her car and close the door. Well, she was wrong if she did.

Abbie started to turn and walk back to the stables. Out of the corner of her eye, she caught a movement along the fence and glanced over, expecting to see Ben. But the tall, dark-haired man in a wheat-tan sports jacket and crisp new jeans bore no resemblance to the elderly Pole.

She breathed in sharply, fighting to bring her emotions under control, as she stared at MacCrea Wilder. She wondered how long he'd been standing there. How much had he heard? She saw his glance follow Rachel's car as it pulled out of the yard. When they'd met at the cemetery, Rachel had been involved that time, too, Abbie remembered.

"Mr. Wilder. I didn't hear you walk up." She studied his angular face, noting the aggressive jut of his chin and jaw. Despite the smooth darkness of his eyes, his was a hard face, she realized.

"I guessed that." Unhurriedly, he moved toward her. When he reached the approximate place where Rachel had stood, he stopped. "Did I understand right? She's your half-sister?"

Abbie didn't have to wonder anymore about how much he'd overheard. "Do you know anything about horses, Mr. Wilder?"

His mouth quirked in a little smile, lifting one corner of his mustache. "I know which is the back end."

"In the Arabian horse business, the term half-sister is restricted to fillies foaled by the same mare. Rachel Farr and I share the same sire."

Idly MacCrea studied her, catching the glitter of moisture in her blue eyes. He frowned briefly, realizing that he'd unwittingly touched a sore spot. She had looked so calm and poised to him before, completely in control, that he hadn't noticed the fine tension emanating from her. He could see it now in the firm set of her lips and the almost rigid lines of her jaw.

"Sorry. I guess I put my foot in it, didn't I?"

"All the way up to your boot tops," she retorted curtly.

"But I couldn't know that, could I?" he reminded her, squarely meeting her gaze and holding it until hers fell away.

"I don't suppose you could," she admitted grudgingly, leaving him with the impression that she would have preferred to battle it out with him and let him be the scapegoat for her anger. But a fight with Dean Lawson's daughter was the last thing he wanted. "Is there something I can do for you, Mr. Wilder? I presume you didn't come out here just to eavesdrop on a private conversation."

"I stopped by to see your mother."

"You'll find her at the house."

"I figured that. But I wasn't sure she was receiving visitors yet, so I stopped by the stables to check. That's when I saw you."

Abbie believed him. She didn't want to, but she did. "I was just on my way to the house to change for dinner. If you'd like, you can walk along with me."

"Thank you, I will."

11

"Momma." Abbie entered the foyer, conscious of MacCrea Wilder following her — just as she had been conscious of him during the walk to the house. She'd forgotten what it was like to be physically aware of a man, to be alive to the close swing of his arm next to hers, the inches it would take before they accidentally brushed. When had the sensitivity been buried? During her years of marriage to Christopher? Had she taken a man's nearness so for granted that she'd become indifferent to it? Maybe familiarity did dull the senses, she decided. Practically every man she'd dated, both before her marriage and the few afterward, she'd known for years. Maybe that's why it was different with MacCrea. She didn't know anything about him, not his background, or his tastes — or even the way he kissed. Abbie smiled at herself, amused that she even had such thoughts, considering all the things she had on her mind. Yet she almost welcomed the diversion he offered.

"Someone's here to see you, Momma." She led the way into the living room.

As she turned, she caught the sweeping glance he gave the room before he focused his attention on her mother. Despite his seeming casualness, Abbie suspected that he had noted every detail. She doubted that those ever-watchful dark eyes missed much.

But she wondered how he'd seen it, as she looked around the room, taking in the wainscot's striped pattern of alternating chestnut and

walnut boards that matched the parquet floor, the walls painted a
cool shade of blue above the wainscot, the elaborately carved walnut
molding around the fireplace, the neo-Victorian tufted velvet sofa
and swan chairs, and the lace curtains at the tall windows. She wondered whether he liked it, then almost laughed. What did it matter
whether he liked it? This was her home, not his.

"I haven't had the pleasure of meeting you before, Mrs. Lawson.
I'm MacCrea Wilder," he said, shaking hands with her mother.

"Mr. Wilder. I'm happy to meet you." But she threw a questioning look at Abbie.

"After meeting you in person, I can honestly say that the photograph your husband kept on his office desk doesn't do you justice."

"You're obviously a Texan," Babs laughed, beaming at the compliment. "Only a Texan can tell tall tales like that and get away
with it."

"It's no tale. I promise you," MacCrea chuckled, the sound coming from low in his throat. Abbie was warmed by it.

"Now I know it is," Babs declared, and waved a hand at the sofa
and chairs. "Make yourself comfortable, Mr. Wilder. Jackson?" As
she turned to summon their houseman, the ubiquitous Jackson appeared in the archway, carrying a tray of iced drinks. "Oh, there
you are. And you brought extra glasses of iced tea."

"Yes, ma'am. I heard the gentleman and Miss Lawson come in,"
he replied, walking in and pausing to offer each of them a glass from
the tray. "Will there be anything else, ma'am?"

"I don't think so, Jackson. Thank you." As the black houseman
withdrew, they each found a place to sit, Abbie on the blue-flowered
velvet sofa with her mother and MacCrea in a pale-blue swan chair,
but she noticed he waited until they were seated before he sat down
himself.

Abbie also noticed that the swan chair didn't suit him at all, with
its gleaming walnut arms carved in the shape of swans with necks
bowed and wings curved back to form the chair's sides. With his
broad shoulders and lean hips, he was much too masculine to look
natural in such an ornate chair. Abbie remembered that her robust
grandfather had referred to the twin chairs as the "bird seats" and
claimed he always felt ridiculous sitting in them, but he sat in them
anyway. Like MacCrea, he didn't let them bother him or make him
uncomfortable.

"You knew Dean?" Babs prompted.

"Not well. My relationship with him was mainly business." Crossing his legs, MacCrea hooked his hat on the bend of his knee. "He was helping me with a project of mine."

"Are you involved with Arabian horses, too?" Babs guessed, influenced by the boots, the hat, and the jeans, even though they were fairly standard dress in Texas.

"Mr. Wilder's in the oil business," Abbie inserted. "He's one of those wildcatters." In her opinion, he fit the mold of the independent oil men — a bit of a gambler with shrewd instincts.

"Not exactly," MacCrea denied smoothly, meeting her glance. "I'm a drilling contractor by trade, although on occasion I have taken a small piece of action in a well."

"Then what was your business with my father?" Abbie had assumed her father had been putting together a limited partnership to raise the capital for some new well, a fairly common practice of his.

"Truthfully, I was hoping he had talked to you about it, Mrs. Lawson," he said, shifting his gaze to her and watching her expression closely.

"Dean knew better than to discuss business with me," Babs declared. "What I know about it wouldn't fill a beanpot."

Abbie caught the look of disappointment that flickered briefly in his eyes, then it was deftly smoothed away, leaving only the grim set of his jaw to indicate that her reply wasn't the one he had wanted to hear.

"What kind of project was Daddy helping you with?" Abbie leaned forward, her curiosity thoroughly aroused.

He hesitated, as if trying to decide how much to tell her . . . or how much she'd understand. "With the help of a computer friend of mine, I've come up with a system that can test the downhole performance of drilling fluids. Without getting too technical, it will allow an operator to better determine what kind of drilling fluids he might need."

"You mean mud." Abbie smiled.

His mouth crooked in response. "Yes. The Lawson name is somewhat legendary in the mud industry. I grew up hearing the old-timers telling stories about your grandfather."

"R.D. was a character," Babs recalled fondly, her expression taking on a reminiscent glow. "He never did anything small. With him everything had to be big — and I mean Texas-big. This house was so alive when he was here. He just filled it up. Not that he was noisy, although his voice could boom when he wanted it to. He said it came from all those years he spent in the oil fields, trying to talk above the racket going on. But when he was home, you just felt like you could relax 'cause everything was going to be all right. He'd see to that." She paused to sigh. "I always thought it was a shame Dean sold the company R.D. worked so hard to build and took such pride in. Was your family in the oil business, too, Mr. Wilder?"

"My daddy was a drilling contractor. He was born in the Permian Basin area west of Abilene on the family ranch. That's where he caught the oil fever." MacCrea didn't bother to add that the ranch had been lost in a foreclosure sale during the depression, making his father's venture into the oil fields to find work a necessity.

Nor did he consider it advisable to talk about his own childhood. By Lawson standards, it would probably be regarded as rough. His mother had died when he was barely three years old. He had traveled with his father after that, living in whatever drilling site the rig was sitting on, playing in the mud pits, and eating with the crews. Texas, Arkansas, Oklahoma, Kansas, Wyoming, Louisiana — he'd gone to school all over the country and started working in the fields when he was twelve. When he'd turned eighteen, his father had made him a full partner and changed the signs on the trucks to WILDER & SON DRILLING CONTRACTORS. They were going to make it big together. John Thomas Wilder had been more than his father; he'd been his partner and buddy, too.

"Your father: is he . . ." Abbie hesitated over the question.

"He's dead. Killed in a freak drilling accident several years ago." Thirteen years ago, to be exact, he remembered, conscious of the hard flatness in his voice and the effort it took to suppress that memory and keep it locked in the past with his feelings. He took a sip of the cold tea, then lifted the glass in the widow's direction. "This is good tea, Mrs. Lawson. Some people make it too sweet for my taste."

As MacCrea Wilder raised the iced-tea glass, Abbie noticed the effeminate crooking of his little finger. The mannerism struck her as being totally out of character with his otherwise ruggedly masculine presence.

"The secret is not the amount of sugar you add, but the amount of lemon. Even with something sweet, you like that hint of tartness," Babs replied.

"That's the way Grandpa always said he liked his women," Abbie recalled, guessing it was MacCrea's reference to him that made her remember that.

"Your grandpa knew what he was talking about." He looked at her when he said it.

Abbie wondered whether he intended it merely as a response or as a personal reference to her. More than once, she'd been accused of having a sharp tongue. She had to admit that, earlier at the stables, she'd hardly been cordial to him. He drank down the rest of his tea, curling that little finger again.

"It was kind of you to let me take up your time this way, Mrs. Lawson. But I don't want to keep you any longer." He set his empty glass down on the tea table beside his chair, picked up his hat, and rolled to his feet, all in one slow, fluid motion. "Thank you. For the tea as well."

"It was our pleasure, Mr. Wilder." Babs stood up to shake hands with him.

He held on to it. "I meant to tell you how sorry I am about your husband."

"Thank you." There was the faintest break in her composure.

Abbie covered for her. "I'll walk out with him, Momma."

"There's no need for you to do that," MacCrea inserted.

"I don't mind." She shrugged. "You left your pickup parked by the stables, and I have to go there anyway."

With the good-byes over, Abbie left the house with him. She couldn't help noticing how preoccupied he seemed to be as they went down the porch steps to the sidewalk.

"You never did say exactly how my father was helping you."

He glanced at her absently, still giving her the impression that his thoughts were elsewhere. "He had talked about possibly becoming involved financially, but mainly he was going to put me in touch with the right people. Even though he wasn't in the business anymore, he still had contacts. That's why I went to him."

"Why?" Abbie frowned, not following him. "I mean, what was the purpose in introducing you to these contacts?"

"Right now, all I have is a prototype of the testing equipment, so I could get a patent on it. But that's all it is — a prototype. Working models have to be built and extensive field testing done. I'm not in any position — financially or otherwise — to develop and market it by myself."

"So what are you trying to do? Sell the patent?"

"Only as a last resort. It's my baby. I've worked on it a long time. I don't want to let it go completely if I don't have to. But maybe I won't have a choice." He shrugged to conceal the anger he felt at finding himself back at square one. All the groundwork he'd laid with Lawson was wasted time and effort. He had to go out and do it all over again. He was beginning to wonder if it was worth it.

"Grandpa always said, 'Houston attracts people who make things happen. You can't keep 'em down, no matter what.' " She smiled carelessly at him. "So, at least you came to the right place."

"Maybe so." He couldn't help noticing the wide curve of her lips, their expression of warmth, and their soft fullness.

The first time he'd seen her at Lawson's office, he'd been aware of her striking looks, that unusual combination of rich, dark hair and incredibly blue eyes. He was a man capable of being aroused as readily as any other by a beautiful, well-built woman, but that day he'd been turned off by her brittleness and demanding ways — phony and spoiled, with nothing behind that beautiful window dressing. At the funeral, he'd seen she could be vulnerable. And now . . . now, he wondered if he'd been mistaken about her. Maybe she wasn't the spoiled, shallow woman he'd thought she was.

"What will you do now?" she asked.

"Start over."

"I might know some people you can talk to." Lane Canfield was the first name that came to her mind. "I'll make some calls and see what I can find out. Is there someplace I can reach you?"

He took a business card out of his pocket and scratched a telephone number on the back of it with a ballpoint pen. "You can get ahold of me at this number," he said, handing it to her. "Don't pay any attention to the one on the front of the card. It's an answering service."

"What's this, then?"

"The phone at the drilling site south of here in Brazoria County. You can reach me there day or night."

"Don't you ever go home?"

"That is home. Once we start making hole — drilling, in layman's terms — I'm there around the clock," he explained, glancing at her sideways, a lazy gleam in his eyes challenging her. "Have you ever seen a rig in operation, Miss Lawson?"

"Lots of times. This is Texas," Abbie asserted, then smiled in mock chagrin. "Of course, I've seen them all from the road."

"For a Texan — and R. D. Lawson's granddaughter — your education has been sadly neglected."

"I suppose it has," she conceded lightly, feeling oddly invigorated by his company — really alive for the first time in a long while. She wondered if he felt the same. But he had a face like her grandpa's. It only revealed what he wanted it to.

"Want to correct that with a tour?"

"With you as the guide?"

"You guessed it. If you're not busy after lunch tomorrow, come out to the site. I'll show you around." He supplied her with concise directions as they reached the cab of his truck. "You can see the mast from the road, so you can't miss it."

"It doesn't sound like it. I'll see you tomorrow, then."

He nodded and climbed into the dusty black truck and pulled the door shut. As he started the engine, Abbie stepped farther back and lifted her head in acknowledgment of the casual, one-fingered salute he flicked in her direction. Then he reversed the truck away from the stables and swung it toward the lane.

"Another visitor?" Ben Jablonski spoke beside her.

Abbie turned with a start. The noise of the truck's engine had drowned out the sound of his footsteps. She hadn't heard him walk up behind her. "Yes," she replied absently and glanced back at the dust being churned up by the departing truck, then realized what Ben was implying by his phrase "another visitor." "You saw her," she stated.

"Yes."

"Why do you think she came here?"

"Perhaps she was curious."

"Maybe." But Abbie doubted it, the feeling again returning that her world was being threatened. As the grimness and tension came back, she turned toward the stables. "I think I'll go check on Breeze."

The oil industry had changed considerably since its early boom days when the famed Spindletop gusher turned Houston into a city and a center of the oil industry with its inland port, oil refineries, and petrochemical plants. Technological and scientific advancements had brought more sophisticated equipment and techniques into use. Environmental and federal controls had reduced pollution and waste, and increased costs. Demand and deregulation of oil and natural gas prices had sent the world price of crude oil soaring in 1980 to more than thirty dollars a barrel, with predictions of future prices reaching fifty, sixty, maybe even seventy dollars a barrel.

One factor remained constant: the key role played by the independent oil men, the wildcatters. They still drilled the vast majority of test wells in the exploration for new fields, as high as nine times the number drilled by the giant oil companies. The wildcatters were responsible for some 80 percent of the gas and oil discoveries in the United States.

Few, if any, wildcatters absorbed the full cost of drilling. They spread their risk, selling off percentages of ownership to the majors or other independents, giving up percentages to the landowner or the drilling contractor or both, and selling limited partnerships to private investors. The successful ones were cautious and conservative gamblers.

MacCrea Wilder might call himself a drilling contractor, but Abbie knew better. She'd listened to too many discussions between her ex-husband and his banker father not to know that most financial institutions were reluctant to speculate on newcomers. They wanted to look at a wildcatter's track record and examine his staying power. With his small deals here and ownership percentages there, MacCrea was establishing a performance record in wildcatting and generating royalties that were both an asset and an ongoing cash flow. His drilling company gave him an independent income and a business history, as well as knowledge and experience in the field.

When everyone from mail-order promoters to lease brokers called themselves wildcatters, Abbie wondered why MacCrea played it so low-key. She smiled at herself, amused by her own curiosity about him. There was no doubt that the man had thoroughly aroused her interest.

In every direction she looked, the scenery was all sky, a blue dome towering over the flat coastal prairie of cropland, broken now and then only by a ground-hugging farmhouse occasionally shaded by a lonely tree. A crop-dusting plane swooped low over a rice field, releasing its white misty trail of pesticide or herbicide, then buzzing her red Mercedes convertible before climbing higher, giving the pilot an eyeful of the dark-haired beauty behind the wheel, dressed in a simple backless sundress in royal purple, belted at the waist with a chain of silver conchos, lizard-skin sandals on her feet.

Still smiling thoughtfully, Abbie returned the pilot's wave and continued down the road, speeding by a pasture scattered with slow-bobbing pumpjacks rhythmically drawing crude oil from completed wells. She watched the horizon to her right, looking for the distinctive iron skeleton of an oil derrick. According to MacCrea's directions, she should see it any minute now.

Suddenly there it was, poking its head up about a mile off the main road. She slowed the car, anticipating the turnoff that would take her to the drill site. Less than a quarter-mile ahead, a gray-white strip converged on the highway at a right angle. Abbie turned onto the road spread with oyster shells and followed its straight line to the iron-ribbed tower in the distance.

The tall derrick dominated the drill site from its perch atop the substructure platform. Sprawled at its feet were the support components: the diesel engines that powered the rig, the racks of pipe stacked in layers, the mud pumps and pits along with their auxiliary equipment, the fuel tanks, and the on-site office trailers. All were interconnected by a system of walkways and stairs.

More than a half-dozen vehicles were parked in the clearing that surrounded the drilling rig. Abbie parked her Mercedes in the space next to MacCrea's black pickup. The steady roar of the diesel engines covered the slam of her car door as she paused to look around. Several workers were in sight, but none of them seemed to notice her arrival. Without the cooling draft of the moving car, the heat became oppressive. She tucked her hair behind her ears, grateful for the turquoise sweatband across her forehead.

As she started toward the nearest office trailer, MacCrea stepped out, dressed in a pair of blue-green coveralls and a hard hat. Right behind him came a second man, dressed in street clothes — a print shirt and tan trousers — but wearing the requisite hard hat.

"Hello." She walked over to MacCrea, glancing questioningly in his companion's direction. "Have I come at a bad time?"

"Not at all," he replied and introduced her to the on-site representative of the major oil company that had contracted the drilling of the well. "Like me, Chuck lives on the site," MacCrea explained, gesturing over his shoulder at the trailer behind them. "I promised Miss Lawson I'd give her a tour of the operation."

"Be my guest. Anyone who's been in the business any length of time at all has heard about your grandfather. Here." He removed his safety helmet and offered it to Abbie. "You'll need this."

"Thanks." Like them, she had to speak louder to make herself heard clearly above the steady din from the power plant and the equipment in operation.

After MacCrea had adjusted the inner band of the hat to fit her and set it on her head, they started out along the walkway. He took her by the mud pits first, showing her the heavy gray-brown fluid that had been the basis of her family's fortune. He explained how the mud was pumped from the pits through a discharge line to the vertically mounted standpipe on the near leg of the derrick (properly called a mast, since it needed no assembly), and from there it entered the kelly hose down the kelly, the drill pipe and collar exiting at the bit at the bottom of the hole. Abbie discovered that, with all the noise in the background, it was easier to understand everything he said if she read his lips, too.

From the mud pits, they traveled down the elevated walkways to the steel pipe that carried the mud and bit cuttings circulating out of the hole and dumped them onto a vibrating screen called a shale shaker. He pointed out the raised earthen pits behind it where the cuttings were dumped after being extracted from the mud. The mud was recycled back to the pits after passing through some other processes that Abbie didn't follow completely — although that was only indirectly MacCrea's fault. He introduced her to the mud engineer on the site, and when he learned that he was talking to R. D. Lawson's granddaughter, his explanations became very technical.

"You made a big impression on him," MacCrea observed dryly as they headed for the stairs leading to the rig's raised platform. "He'll be bragging to everybody how he explained modern drilling-fluid methods to R. D. Lawson's granddaughter."

"Too bad I didn't understand any of it."

At the bottom of the narrow set of stairs, MacCrea paused and let her go in front of him. As Abbie mounted the steps, she was conscious of the beads of sweat forming above her upper lip — and of the curious glances from the crew when she reached the top. She paused to let MacCrea take the lead again.

"The floor of a rig isn't the cleanest place in the world. There should be an extra pair of coveralls in the doghouse." He directed her to the small storage shed atop the platform a short distance from the stairs. Inside the storehouse, he took a pair of blue-green coveralls, like his, off a hook and handed them to her. "They aren't the latest fashion, but at least they'll keep your clothes from getting dirty."

Abbie could tell just by looking at them that they were too big and too long, but she put them on anyway and rolled up the pant legs. She felt like one of those clowns in baggy pants, and judging by the gleam in MacCrea's eyes, she looked like one, too.

But he was right: the floor of the rig around the hole was slopped with the grayish mud. There was relatively little activity at the moment. MacCrea introduced her to the driller, who operated the drilling machinery from his control console and supervised the work of the other floormen. She met a couple of the rotary helpers, too, known as roughnecks in the old days.

MacCrea attempted to explain some of the equipment and its uses, but by the time he got done talking about monkeyboards, catheads, ratholes, catwalks, and mouseholes, Abbie wasn't sure whether she was on a drilling rig or at a zoo.

Her head was pounding from the noise, heat, and mental confusion when they finally descended the steps back to the ground. She felt the guiding pressure of his hand between her shoulders and glanced up, wondering what he could possibly want to show her now. He pointed at the near trailer. She walked to it gladly.

As he opened the door for her, she felt the blessed coolness of air-conditioning and practically ran inside. There she paused and gratefully swept off the hot helmet and her sweatband, shaking her damp hair loose with a toss of her head. As the door closed behind her, muffling most of the rig's noise, the telephone on the desk started ringing. Abbie stepped out of the way as MacCrea walked over to answer it.

"Wilder Drilling."

Abbie unzipped the protective coveralls as she glanced around the Spartan office. A pair of filing cabinets stood against the wall behind his desk. A Naugahyde sofa that showed the abuse of the drill site faced it from the opposite wall. Two straight-backed chairs completed the furnishings. The paneled walls were blank except for a framed photograph propped against the paneling on top of a filing cabinet.

"Yeah, Red. Just a minute." MacCrea covered the phone's mouthpiece with his hand. "There's not a lot I can offer you in the way of refreshments, but there's a little kitchen through that door. The coffee in the pot is probably black syrup by now. If you want to make fresh, go ahead. There's beer in the refrigerator and a jar of instant tea in the cupboard. Help yourself."

"Thanks." Abbie stepped out of the coveralls and laid them across one of the straight chairs, her own clothes sticking to her skin.

The trailer rocked slightly as she crossed to the door, already partway ajar, and pushed it the rest of the way open. The cupboards, range top, and sink took up one short wall in the compact kitchen, with the refrigerator against the opposite wall. A table and two chairs took up the rest of the floor space. Beyond the kitchen a door leading to the rear of the trailer stood open. Unable to resist the opportunity to explore, Abbie peeked to see what was back there.

A bed, its covers all rumpled, hugged one wall. Opposite it was a built-in dresser next to a closet. Beyond it the door to a small bathroom stood open. She realized MacCrea had been serious when he said he lived here.

In the kitchen she fixed herself a glass of iced tea, then, on impulse, made one for MacCrea, adding sugar to both, and carried them into the office. He smiled his thanks when she handed it to him and took a long drink before continuing his conversation on the telephone.

Sipping at her own, Abbie wandered over to take a closer look at the photograph on the filing cabinet. A much younger MacCrea smiled back at her, minus the mustache he now wore. She was struck by the differences between the MacCrea she knew and the one in this picture. An occasional lazy gleam had replaced the laughter shining out of the dark eyes in the photograph. The same lean, strong features were in the picture, but they hadn't been honed to a hardness yet; the lines and creases were missing. She had no impression of determination or inner toughness when she looked at this younger version of MacCrea. This one had the world by the tail, and was ready to whip it into shape.

Curious, she shifted her attention to the older man who MacCrea had his arm around. He, too, grinned proudly at her, almost hiding the tiredness in his weathered face. Abbie saw the resemblance between them, and realized the older man had to be MacCrea's father. The love between them was obvious to anyone looking at the photograph. Abbie felt a sudden stab of envy, followed by a twisting pain from her own loss — a loss rooted in more than just the death of her father, but in the bitter discovery and disillusionment that came after as well.

"Yeah, I'll talk to you later, Red." MacCrea hung up the phone, the chair squeaking as he pushed out of it. Abbie continued to stare at the photograph, giving herself time to control that sudden surge of resentment.

"That's your father, isn't it?" The ice cubes clinked in her glass as she used the hand holding it to indicate the picture.

"Yes. It was taken a month before he died." Taking a drink from his tea, MacCrea turned away from the filing cabinet and the photograph. Again, Abbie noticed the total lack of emotion in his voice when he referred to his father or, more specifically, his death. She sensed it was something he didn't like to discuss. "Sorry about the interruption. That was my toolpusher on another site, filling me in on their progress."

"A toolpusher." She felt inundated by the flood of new terms she'd heard in the last two hours. She was amazed by how much she'd thought she knew about the oil business, when she actually knew practically nothing.

"A toolpusher is in charge of the entire drilling operation and co-ordinates everything with the company man. That's temporarily my job here," he explained. "My regular man is in the hospital with a broken leg. Normally I'm not tied to one site like this."

Abbie caught herself watching his lips when he talked. Slightly disconcerted that she had allowed the practice to carry over from the tour of the drilling operation, she quickly averted her glance, focusing it instead on the iced-tea glass in his hand. Immediately she noticed the peculiar crooking of his little finger, its suggestion of daintiness completely at odds with the smooth toughness conveyed by the rest of him.

"Why does your little finger bend like that?" She thought it might have been broken at some time.

"This?" He glanced down at it, his mouth quirking, tilting one side of his mustache as he lifted a shoulder in a shrug of indifference. "I was born with a shortened tendon in the first joint. It's a family trait."

"I wondered," she admitted, smiling.

The trailer door opened behind them, letting in the noise from outside. As Abbie turned toward it, one of the roughnecks poked his head inside. "We got a kick, boss."

In the next second, MacCrea was brushing past her, shoving his tea glass on the desktop and grabbing up his hard hat as he went by. "Does the company know?"

"Not yet," the roughneck replied, pulling back as MacCrea charged out the door.

"Tell him," MacCrea ordered, his tone sharp and abrupt.

She didn't understand what was going on. Why had he sent for the company man? Had they hit oil? Intrigued by the possibility, she hurried to the door before it swung shut, reaching it in time to see MacCrea bounding up the steps to the rig floor, covering them two at a time. Abbie started to run after him, then remembered she didn't have her safety helmet on. When she went back for it, she saw the coveralls on the chair. She hesitated briefly, then pulled them on over her clothes and hurried out the door, still struggling with the stubborn zipper.

By the time she reached the raised metal platform, MacCrea was standing off to one side, holding a conference with the company man, Kruse, and the mud engineer. Everyone else seemed to be just standing around, waiting. Then Abbie noticed that the level of noise had fallen off and saw that the rotary table wasn't turning. She realized they'd stopped drilling. But she still didn't know what that meant.

She walked over to MacCrea to ask him. None of the three men paid any attention to her at first, too intent on their discussion, which was totally beyond her limited knowledge. MacCrea glanced briefly in her direction, his brow furrowed in concentration as he kept his attention focused on the mud man.

Suddenly he shot another look at her, and recognition turned into anger. "What the hell are you doing here?" In two strides, he had her by the arm.

"I was just —" Abbie tried to explain as he roughly spun her around and propelled her toward the stairs.

"You get back to that trailer and you stay there! Do you read me, lady?"

"Yes, I —" She was stunned by the anger that seethed from him, as palpable as the sun's burning heat.

"Then get going," he snapped, shoving her down the steps.

Abbie grabbed at the rail to stop herself from falling, wrenching the muscles in her left shoulder and arm in the process. When she regained her footing, MacCrea was gone. Embarrassed that others had witnessed her rude eviction from the premises, Abbie ran the rest of the way down the steps and walked back to the trailer, holding herself stiffly erect.

The minute she set foot inside the trailer, she rubbed her aching arm and nursed her wounded ego, her embarrassment turning to indignant anger. She stripped off the coveralls and the hard hat, dumping them both on top of his desk. She started pacing about the room, letting her anger build.

Abbie had no idea how long she waited in the trailer before he returned, but she knew it was a long time — more than enough time for her to have cooled off, but she hadn't. She was boiling mad when he opened the door and walked in.

She didn't even give him time to shut it before she launched into him. "Just who the hell do you think you are, pushing me around like that?" He looked tired and hot, sweat making dark spots on the front of his coveralls and under his arms, but she didn't care.

"You had no business being there," he muttered, shouldering his way by her, barely even glancing at her.

"And just how was I supposed to know that?" She followed him, addressing her demanding question to his back as he swept off his hard hat and combed his fingers through the curly thickness of his dark hair. "You never said anything to me. You just barged out of here without so much as a word to me."

MacCrea swung around, glowering at her. "Dammit, you heard Pete say we had a kick!"

"You had a kick." She longed to give him one. "Hasn't it occurred to you that I don't know what that is? And I still don't. But did you bother to explain? No. You —"

"So it's another damned lesson you want, is it? Well, honey, you damned near got more than that. A well 'kicks' just before it blows out. Have you ever seen a well blow?"

Taken aback by his explanation, and the danger it implied, Abbie lost some of her anger. "No. But I've heard —" she began, considerably subdued.

"You've heard," he mocked sarcastically. "Well, honey, I've *seen*. And let me tell you, it isn't a pretty sight. You don't know what's down in that hole — gas, saltwater, or oil — or maybe all three. And you don't know how much pressure it's packing. Whether it's got enough to blow you and your rig sky-high. Or if it's gonna be a ball of fire. You could have been standing on a damned powder keg out there."

"Well, I obviously wasn't," Abbie retorted. "I'm still standing here. Nothing happened."

"Nothing happened." He repeated her words through clenched teeth as he seized the undersides of her jaws, the heel of his hand pressing itself against her throat. For an instant, Abbie was too startled to resist. "I ought to —"

"Wring your neck" was what she expected him to say, but it never came out as he suddenly crushed his mouth onto her lips, brutally grinding them against her teeth, shocking her into immobility. After interminable seconds, the pressure eased. Short of breath and with racing heartbeat, Abbie waited for his mouth to lift from hers. But it lingered there, motionless, maintaining a light contact but nothing more. Cautiously, she looked at him through her lashes. He was watching her, the fiery blackness in his eyes reduced to a smoldering light that strangely bothered her more than his anger.

Then he broke all contact and turned, stepping away from her. He stopped with his back to her and sighed heavily, his hands resting on his hips. "Would it make any difference if I apologized?" he asked, almost grudgingly.

"Only if you choked on it." She was trembling, but she was faking her anger now.

"Good." He swung around to face her, his features set in grim lines. "I won't have to say something I don't mean. The method I used to get you off the drilling floor might not have been polite, but you have to admit it was effective. And I didn't have to waste a lot of time on explanations — time I couldn't afford. As for kissing you —"

"That wasn't a kiss."

"Maybe it wasn't," he conceded. "But you wouldn't have liked the alternative any better. I have enough problems right now out there without getting the riot act read to me by you all because of your damned ignorance and hurt pride. So if you'll excuse me, I have a lot of work to do."

As he turned and opened one of the file-cabinet drawers, Abbie walked blindly out the door, stung by the things he'd said and hating him for making her feel so wretched, when he'd been the one at fault.

12

*A*wed by the expensive decor in the penthouse, Rachel wandered into the spacious living room, artfully done in a subtle blending of gray, peach, and cream. It was like something out of the decorating magazines, everything precisely arranged with an eye for symmetry and balance. Nothing gaudy or overdone, just an understated elegance.

Her glance was drawn to the large windows that overlooked the city. Rachel walked over to them, anticipating the panoramic view of Houston at sunset, the glass-walled towers reflecting the sky's fuchsia hues, and the first dull glow of the streetlights far below.

"What do you think?" Lane came to stand beside her.

"Breathtaking," she said, then looked at him and smiled. "And fitting, too, to have Houston at your feet."

"I don't know about that last part," he replied.

His modesty was sincere. During the few times she'd seen him, Rachel had discovered that was one of his traits. Sometimes it was difficult to remember that this was only the third time she'd seen him, counting the funeral. The feeling was so strong that she'd always known him. She admired that confidence he exuded, never overtly, always calmly. She liked him. Sometimes she worried that she liked him too much.

"You've been so kind to me, Lane." She didn't want to misinterpret that kindness, to build her hopes too high.

"It is extremely easy to be kind to a beautiful woman, Rachel. Don't misunderstand me. I didn't invite you to dine with me this evening out of any sense of obligation to your father. I wanted your company."

Rachel believed that. The first time he'd asked her to have lunch with him, she had thought he'd invited her to fulfill some duty he felt he owed her father. The first may have been an obligatory gesture, but not the second. She could tell he wasn't patronizing her. His interest seemed genuine. Truthfully she was flattered . . . and a little thrilled that a man of Lane Canfield's standing would want to spend his time with her. It made her feel important.

That's why her minor shopping expedition into Houston today had turned into a major one. None of the clothes in her closet had looked suitable; all of them were too casual, appropriate for California maybe, but not for dinner with Lane Canfield. She'd spent the better part of the morning and early afternoon combing the shops in the Galleria, looking for something sophisticated yet simple, this time not letting price sway her.

Finally she'd found this white linen suit with a matching camisole top on a sale rack. Its lines were simple and timeless, yet the epaulets of pearls on the padded shoulders gave it that touch of elegance Rachel had wanted.

After buying the evening suit and the accessories to go with it, she'd gotten up enough nerve to take the final plunge and stopped at the Neiman-Marcus salon to have a complete makeover done by one of their beauty consultants. A woman named Karen had shown her how to use makeup to soften her features, add fullness to her lips, and bring out the blue of her eyes. She had her hair cut to shoulder length and styled to curl softly about her face. For the first time in her life, she felt sophisticated and confident enough about her appearance to accompany Lane to the most exclusive restaurant in Houston. But what could be more exclusive than his penthouse apartment in Houston's Magic Circle?

"I have to confess, Lane, that I didn't accept because you were a friend of Dean's. I came because . . . I like being with you." Rachel felt bold saying that, but she wanted him to know her true feelings.

"It's mutual, Rachel. I can't begin to tell you how much I enjoy being with you. If I did, you'd start thinking I was a lecherous old man."

"No. Never that." She didn't like it when he talked about himself that way. She had never felt so comfortable with any man before.

The men she'd dated seemed like immature boys in comparison — not that she had ever dated all that much.

"It's a curious thing, the way the aging process works. Chronologically the body gets older, but the mind — well, I think and feel about twenty years younger." He smiled, his eyes crinkling at the corners the way she liked. "To put it in your vernacular, when I'm with you, I feel like a young stallion."

She laughed softly. "I hope not. Young stallions can behave so foolishly at times."

"Maybe that's what worries me, Rachel. That I am being foolish where you're concerned."

Behind the quiet statement, there was a question. Rachel heard it and felt the sudden skittering of her pulse in reaction. She wasn't any good at being coy and flirtatious. Abbie probably was, but Rachel couldn't think of anything flattering or witty to say. She had to resort to the truth.

"I don't think you are." She practically whispered her reply, conscious of how much she was admitting about her own feelings toward him. She gazed at his face, liking the lines that gave it so much character. They told so much about the man he was: his strength, his confidence, and his sense of humor — although there was little evidence of the latter in his expression at the moment as he studied her intently.

"I hope you mean that," he said.

She felt the light grip of his hands on her arms, bunching the thick shoulder pads of her boxy jacket. He drew her gently toward him. The warm touch of his lips was firm and persuasive, not demanding a response, yet seeking one.

Hesitantly she returned his kiss, letting her lips move against his while controlling her ardor, not wanting to appear gauchely eager to a man as experienced and worldly as Lane Canfield. Tentatively she let her hands touch the sides of his waist, the rich fabric of his jacket feeling like silk beneath her fingers.

His hands glided onto her back, his arms folding around her to draw her closer still, and his kiss now spoke to Rachel of need and want, two emotions she felt in abundance. She answered him, warmth spreading through and filling her body. As her breathing deepened, she inhaled the masculine fragrance of his cologne. It was neither musk nor spice nor citrus, but some exotic blend that made her feel almost giddy.

Someone in the room coughed delicately, but the sound hit Rachel with all the shattering force of a lightning bolt as she realized they weren't alone. She jerked from the kiss and averted her face, hot with embarrassment. Lane loosened the circle of his arms while retaining a light hold on her.

"Yes, Henley. What is it?" Lane sounded tolerant, not the least upset by the intrusion of his butler. Then Rachel recalled that he'd introduced Henley as his houseman, although the man's aloof bearing, his cordial impassivity, had reminded her of a butler.

"A telephone call, sir. I believe it's somewhat urgent."

"I'll be there directly." Lane dismissed him and returned his attention to Rachel.

She didn't know what she was supposed to say or do in a situation like this. Then she was doubly mortified by the discovery that her fingers were clutching his jacket. She would have looked ridiculous if he'd tried to leave just then. Hastily she let go as her face felt as if it had caught fire. Lane tucked a finger under her chin and gently turned her face toward him. Rachel tried to look at him, but her glance skipped away from the amusement that glinted in his eyes.

"You blush beautifully," he murmured.

"I'm sorry." She felt dreadfully inadequate. She had tried so hard to appear sophisticated so he would like her and respect her, but she had failed miserably. She always did.

"Why?"

"You must think I'm naïve."

"Because you were embarrassed when Henley walked in right in the middle of our kiss?"

She nodded.

"My dear, I would have been disappointed if you weren't. I considered that kiss to be special and private — not something to be shared with others. You obviously did, too, and I'm glad."

He started to kiss her lightly, but their lips clung moistly together, unwilling to part. Rachel wanted it to go on, to recapture that warm feeling that had just started to grow inside her when the last kiss was so abruptly halted, but she couldn't block out the image of formal and proper Henley hovering somewhere out of sight, waiting, knowing what he'd seen and what their silence meant. Reluctantly she drew back.

"Your telephone call," she said.

"Ah, yes." With a rueful smile, he let her go. "I won't be long."

*   *   *

"Is he there?" Babs Lawson anxiously hovered close to Abbie's shoulder.

"Yes. He's being called to the phone right now." Absently she twisted the receiver cord around her fingers, her impatience growing with the lengthening delay. "Before I forget, tell Jackson we'll need another place setting for dinner tonight, Momma. Dobie Hix will be joining us."

"He will? Why?"

"Because I invited him," Abbie snapped, then sighed, realizing that she'd been snapping at everyone since she'd come back from the drilling site. "He came by the stables this afternoon and I decided to ask him to stay for dinner." She didn't mention the broad hints Dobie had made . . . or the unpaid hay bill.

"If we're having company, maybe I should have Jackson get out the good china. What do you think?" She made it sound as if it were a major decision that required discussion.

"I doubt that Dobie would know the difference. Do whatever you want, Momma." She had too much on her mind to be bothered with such trivial things. Distracted by her mother, Abbie almost missed hearing the voice on the other end of the line. "Hello. Lane?" She tightened her grip on the receiver.

"Yes."

"This is Abbie Lawson." She didn't waste time apologizing for bothering him at his home but went straight to the point. "We've been receiving quite a number of phone calls from creditors wanting to know when they'll get their money."

"Give them my office number and tell them to call me. I'll handle it." His response was too pat. It irritated her; nearly everything did.

"That's what we've been doing. But . . . how long will it be before they're paid?"

There was a lengthy pause at the other end of the line. Abbie sensed that, at last, she had his full attention. "Why don't I come out to River Bend on Thursday," he finally said. "That way I can sit down with both you and your mother and explain the situation to you."

"The sooner the better."

"Yes. I'll see you then. And give Babs my regards."

"I will." But the line had already clicked dead. Abbie frowned and replaced the receiver on its cradle, wondering why she didn't feel relieved. That long pause, the strange tone of his voice before he'd hung up — they troubled her.

"What did Lane say?"

Abbie shot a brief glance at her mother. "He sent you his regards and . . . said he'd be down on Thursday to talk to both of us."

"I'm glad. This is all so embarrassing — the phone calls and the questions."

"I know, Momma." Abbie nodded.

As good as his word, Lane was back within minutes of leaving her alone in the living room. But Rachel noticed immediately how preoccupied he looked, not anything like the smiling, jaunty man who'd left the room.

"Is something wrong?" Her question seemed to startle him out of his reverie.

Quickly he fixed a smile on his face, but she noticed that it didn't extend to his eyes. "No. Nothing at all. Just a business matter." He reached to take her hand. "Henley informed me that dinner can be served whenever we're ready. Are you hungry?"

"Yes." She let him lead her into the dining room.

The table was set for two, replete with white candles burning in silver holders and champagne chilling in a silver ice bucket. On one of the china plates lay a long-stemmed red rose. Henley pulled the chair away from the table directly in front of it and held it for her.

"See how optimistic I was tonight?" Lane said as Rachel scooted her chair closer to the table with Henley's assistance. "Candles, champagne, roses, and privacy." Henley popped the champagne cork from the bottle with a practiced *whoosh*. Lane glanced at him, then back to Rachel, and smiled faintly. "Well, almost privacy."

Rachel tried to hide her smile, even though Henley gave no indication that he'd heard a single word Lane had said. He filled their glasses with champagne, then retreated from the room via a side door.

"To a beautiful evening, and a beautiful lady." Lane lifted his wineglass and Rachel touched hers to it, the melodic tinkle of crystal ringing softly in the air. She sipped the champagne, noticing over the rim of her glass how thoughtful Lane had become again. This time he caught himself. "I was just thinking — wondering is probably a better word — whether you'd like to have dinner with me again this Friday night. I'll be tied up probably all of Thursday at River Bend. Otherwise —"

"I'd like to, yes." Rachel rushed her acceptance, still debating whether she should mention her own visit to River Bend. She decided against it, unwilling to recall how unwanted — and uncomfortable — she'd been made to feel.

13

After Ben had broken the news to the half-dozen stable hands, Abbie stepped forward to explain the situation to them. She knew she was in an awkward position, and their stunned, quizzical looks didn't make her task any easier. She slipped her fingers into the side pockets of her jodhpurs, trying to appear relaxed and in control despite the tension she felt.

"We want you to know that your layoffs are temporary. It's obvious that we need help to take care of all these horses. Unfortunately, until my father's estate is settled, we don't have the cash available to pay you. It's legally tied up by the court." Abbie doubted that they understood the judicial system or the inheritance laws any better than she did. "We can't ask you to continue to work at the farm and wait until later to receive your wages. We know you all have families." Still, she had her fingers crossed that some of them would volunteer to stay on.

"How long do you think this will be before we can get our jobs back?" Manny Ortega inquired in his heavy Spanish accent, his brow furrowed in a troubled frown.

"I don't know." Lane Canfield had been reluctant to speculate on that when he'd spoken with Abbie and her mother that morning. She saw the discontented shakes of their heads. "Maybe six weeks," she held out hopefully.

But their expressions didn't change as they nervously fingered the pay envelopes Ben had passed out to them. Three of the stable hands glanced at Manny, looking to him to be their spokesman. "You will let us know when to come back, no? Señor Jablonski will call us?"

"Yes, he'll call." Nettled by their reaction, Abbie watched them as they shuffled off to their vehicles, where they congregated briefly to talk among themselves, then went their separate ways.

"How bad is the problem?" Ben stood beside her.

"It's just a temporary situation," she insisted. "Nearly all Dad's personal and business accounts are frozen." Lane had explained it in more detail, but that was the gist of it. "We knew we were short on funds, but we expected to get a check from the insurance company. Now, we've learned that Dad cashed his life insurance policy last year and neglected to tell anyone."

"Why was this done?"

"I don't know. It's spilt milk now." Abbie shrugged. "We don't have it and we're not going to get it. And what with Dad's law practice, the farm, and his personal finances, things are in a tangle. Lane says it's going to take longer to sort them all out than he first thought. The loss of the insurance money is just frustrating, that's all. We'll make it . . . in spite of them." With a jerk of her head, she indicated the vehicles driving out of the yard.

"What did you expect them to do?"

"I thought Manny would stay. He's worked here for six years steady."

"He has a family to feed," Ben reminded her with his usual tolerance, but he recognized the signs that indicated her mood was turning argumentative. From the time she was a child, she reacted this way when things went wrong. It was as if she had to pick a fight with someone to release her pent-up anger and frustration.

"Maybe. But it just proves to me that a man's loyalty is bought." At the moment, Abbie didn't care how angry or cynical she sounded.

A pickup drove into the yard, dust swirling around it like an enveloping fog. At first glance, she thought it was Manny's truck, that he'd changed his mind and come back. But that hope came crashing down when she recognized MacCrea Wilder's black pickup even before he stepped out of it.

All too clearly, she remembered the way he'd treated her the last time she'd seen him. She felt her temper rising and didn't even try to control it as she strode across the stable yard to confront him. He paused beside the truck's tailgate to wait for her, letting her come to him — which irritated Abbie even more.

"Afternoon, Miss Lawson." His words were polite, but his look was icy-cool.

"Don't tell me you've reconsidered and decided to apologize for your rudeness — or should I say 'crudeness' — the other day," she chided, sarcasm in her voice as she relished the opportunity to make him squirm.

"You mentioned the other day you might know some people I could talk to about the computerized test system I've developed. I came by to get their names from you, if you have them."

The man's gall amazed her. "A couple of them did call me back this last week," she informed him, although she had deliberately not mentioned his project to Lane Canfield. "But I'm not about to give their names to someone like you. I don't help someone who has manhandled me. I thought you would have guessed that."

MacCrea breathed in deeply, then released it slowly, eyeing her coolly all the while. "So you still think I owe you an apology? All right. I'm sorry I was even remotely concerned for your safety. As you pointed out, nothing happened. Of course, if the well had blown, you'd be thanking me for saving your life even though you were 'manhandled' in the process."

Abruptly he pivoted and walked back to the cab of his truck, leaving her standing there, struggling to come up with some cutting retort, but she couldn't summon any of her previous venom as he climbed in the cab and slammed the door. As much as she hated to admit it, MacCrea was right. If the outcome had been different, she would have been grateful.

He didn't even glance in her direction as he drove away. Abbie lingered, watching until his truck disappeared down the winding lane. Then, slowly, she walked to the house.

With twilight only a couple of hours away, the shadow racing beside Abbie's Mercedes was long. A sheet of paper with the names and phone numbers of two men who had expressed an interest in MacCrea's invention lay on the passenger seat next to her.

The turnoff to the drill site came quicker than she expected. Abbie braked sharply to make it, the front tires grabbing at the oyster shells as the rear end started to fishtail on the loose surface, but she made the turn.

When she reached the drill site, the activity there appeared normal. She knew, even before MacCrea had told her, that once drilling was started, three separate crews worked round-the-clock shifts until the contracted depth was reached. She parked her car beside MacCrea's pickup in front of his office trailer, picked up the paper from the passenger seat, and stepped out.

Still dressed in her jodhpurs and riding boots, she paused in front of the trailer door and took a deep, steadying breath. She had never found it easy to swallow her pride. Most times she preferred to choke on it. She knocked twice on the metal door, then opened it, doubting that her knock could be heard above the noise from the drilling operation.

As she walked in, she saw MacCrea sitting behind the desk, a bottle of beer in front of him. She hesitated, then pulled the door shut behind her. He rocked back in his chair, staring at her with his dark, impenetrable eyes, his features showing no discernible expression. Then his attention shifted to the bottle of beer as he picked it up.

"What do you want here?"

What had she expected? Abbie wondered. A red carpet rolled out for her? She gripped the paper a little tighter and crossed to his desk.

"I brought you those names you wanted." She managed to inject an air of bravado into her answer as she held out the paper to him.

"Just lay it on the desk." He took a swig of beer and turned the chair sideways, then rolled out of it to walk to the file cabinet, as if dismissing her.

She felt a surge of anger and clamped down on it tightly, reminding herself that she had come to apologize, not to clash with him again. She glanced down at the scatter of papers and reports on his desk.

"Just anywhere?" Abbie challenged.

"Yup. I'll find it." He opened a metal file drawer and started riffling through its folders.

As she started to lay the paper on his desk, she noticed the rough draft of a lease agreement for the mineral rights to a piece of property. She'd seen too many of those forms at her father's law office not to recognize it. She laid her sheet down and picked the document up.

"What's this? Are you planning to drill your own well?" She skimmed the first page, noting that the legal description referred to a piece of property in Ascension Parish in Louisiana.

The trailer shook slightly under the force of the single, long stride MacCrea took to carry him to her side. "My plans are my business," he said curtly, taking the document from her and laying it back down on the desk. "Now, if you're through snooping, the door is behind you."

"I didn't come here just to bring you those names." She touched the edge of his desk, hating the awkwardness she felt. "I could have easily mailed them to you."

"Why didn't you?"

Stiffening at the challenging tone of his voice, Abbie tipped her head back to look at him. No matter how she might try, her pride wouldn't let her appear humbly contrite.

"I came to apologize," she retorted. "I know that this afternoon, and the other day, too, I behaved —"

"— like a horse's ass," MacCrea broke in, his mouth crooking in a humorless smile. "Remember, I told you I knew that end of a horse when I saw it."

Abbie forgot her carefully rehearsed speech as anger rushed in. "Dammit, MacCrea, I'm trying to apologize to you. You're not exactly making it easy."

"No easier than you made things for me."

It didn't help to know that he was right. Somehow she managed to get her temper under control, however grudgingly. "All right, I was an ass today —"

"I'm glad you agree."

Swallowing the angry response that rose in her throat, Abbie glared at him. "For your information, just before you arrived today, I had to lay off all our stable help and most of our servants at the house because we don't have the cash to meet their payroll until my father's estate is settled. Now, maybe that doesn't excuse the way I behaved to you, but I wasn't in the best of moods when you showed up. I know it was probably wrong to take my frustrations out on you, but . . . that's what I did. And I'm sorry," she finished on a slightly more subdued note, not really understanding why she had told him about their financial problems except that he'd provoked her.

"I didn't know."

Uneasy under his contemplative gaze, Abbie stared at the desktop. "How could you? Any more than I could know there was any real danger the other day. You could have explained it a little better. You know, you're not exactly a saint either, MacCrea."

"I never claimed to be," he reminded her.

"Look, I came here to apologize, not to get into another argument with you. I hoped —" What had she hoped? That he'd understand the vagaries of her temper when no one else did, not even herself? That maybe he'd feel sorry for her because financially they were having problems? That maybe they could start fresh without this hostility? "I hoped you'd accept that."

For an unbearably long second, there was only silence. Then MacCrea offered his hand to her. "Apology accepted, Abbie."

She hesitated a fraction of a second, then fit her hand into the grasp of his and watched as it became lost when his fingers closed around it, leaving only her thumb in view. His skin was brown as leather, a contrast to the tanned, golden color of her own. The calloused roughness of his fingers reminded her of the pleasant rasp of a cat's tongue against her skin. She looked up to discover his eyes watching her closely. Something in their depths made her pulse quicken.

"How about a beer to wash the bad taste from your mouth?" A smile tugged at the corners of his mouth.

Abbie smiled back, discovering that even though the apology had been difficult to get out, it hadn't left any sour aftertaste on her tongue. "I'd like one."

"Make yourself comfortable while I get your beer." He gestured at the tan Naugahyde sofa.

As MacCrea disappeared into the trailer's compact kitchen, Abbie settled onto the sofa, turning to sit sideways on the cushion and hooking a booted toe behind her right knee. When he returned, he held an empty glass and the long necks of two bottles of beer. Unconsciously she studied him as he approached her, taking in the width of his shoulders and the narrowness of his hips. His dark, almost black hair was thick and wavy, a little on the shaggy side, but that seemed to suit him. Yet it was his face, with its hard strength stamped in the sculpted bones of his cheek and the carved slant of his jaw, that she found so compelling. She kept wanting to describe the bluntly chiseled angles and planes of his features as aggressive, arrogant, and impassive, but she was never able to define that quality about them that attracted her.

As he set the glass down on the end table closest to her and poured beer into it, she let her curiosity again direct her gaze to the narrow line of his hips, then glanced up quickly when he straightened and moved to sit on the other side of her.

"There you go," he said, folding his long frame onto the sofa cushion.

"Thanks." Abbie lifted the glass, briefly saluting him with it, then took a sip of the cold beer, conscious of his arm extended along the sofa back, his hand resting inches from her shoulder.

"What will you do now that you don't have any help to take care of the horses?" MacCrea's question touched a wound that was still sore.

"Naturally Ben is still there. He's practically family. Between the two of us, we'll manage." But Abbie didn't know how they would. Ben might look like an ox, but he was an old ox. Even though there was still a lot he could do, much of the heavier work would fall to her, she knew. "I'd rather not discuss it."

"Why?"

"Because . . ." She caught the sharpness in her voice and paused to sigh heavily. "I guess it bothers me that none of the stable help volunteered to stay on. Most of them have worked for us for several years and never once missed a paycheck. You'd think they would trust us to pay them as soon as we got the money from Daddy's estate."

"Maybe they knew their landlords and bill collectors wouldn't trust them. A lot of people around here live from paycheck to paycheck. If you've never lived like that and tried to raise a family, then you can't appreciate what it's like."

"I know," Abbie admitted, recognizing that she'd never had to worry about money her whole life. There had always been plenty of food on the table and clothes in her closet. The material necessities of life she'd known in abundance; it was the emotional needs that she hadn't always had met. But she didn't want to talk about that either.

"Financially, it can be rough after someone dies. Wilder Drilling Company owned five rigs the day my father was killed when a well blew out. The insurance check was sitting on his desk, waiting for his signature. Two other workers were injured in the same accident. I wound up losing everything but one rig. It wasn't easy, but I managed to build the business back up." MacCrea studied the long-necked bottle of beer in his hand, staring at the brown color of its glass as he remembered that he'd only been two short years away from getting his degree in geology when he'd had to quit college, and how he'd struggled through those early years on his own when few companies wanted to hire a young, untried contractor to drill their wells.

"Your father was killed when a well blew?" she repeated, stunned by the news. "No wonder you reacted the way you did with me. If I had known . . . Why didn't you tell me?" she demanded.

"You didn't give me much of a chance," he reminded her dryly.

"I guess I didn't." She paused briefly. "What happened? Do you know?"

"Yeah, I was there. He'd made me a toolpusher that summer — his man in charge on the site. Of course, he covered himself by putting his top men in my crews. It was my second well. He'd stopped by to see how I was doing. I went to get the company man. He was up there, joking with the driller while the guys were tripping in a length of pipe. I heard somebody yell and turned around just as a ball of flame engulfed the mast." He shook his head, seeing it all again — the human torches leaping off the raised platform of the rig's floor, trying to escape the inferno. One of them had been his father. "He was killed."

He took a swig of beer, then set the bottle down on the side table and rubbed his hand down the top of his thigh to wipe off the bottle's moisture. Abbie observed the action. She wanted to tell him she understood his pain. She'd lost her father, too. Then she noticed his hand as it lay flat on his leg. His little finger rose prominently above the others, bent while the others lay straight. A family trait, he'd said.

"Your finger really is crooked, isn't it?" She leaned forward to examine it more closely. "Won't it lie flat at all?"

"If you hold it down it will. Go ahead. Try it."

Abbie hesitated. "Does it hurt?"

"No."

She reached out and tentatively pushed the first joint down with her forefinger. There was no sense of resistance as she held it down, but the instant she lifted her finger, it popped back up again. "I've never seen anything like that."

"It runs in the family."

The little finger appeared perfectly normal except for its jutting angle. As Abbie started to study it again, a lock of hair swung forward into her eye. Before she could reach up to push it back, she felt the brush of his fingers across her brow and temple as he lifted her hair back. She looked up, feeling the warm tingle as his fingers lingered to caress her cheekbone lightly. The intensity of his gaze, heavy-lidded, revealed a man's interest. Abbie recognized it instantly, and it ignited a breathless excitement in her.

"You have the bluest damned eyes," he murmured.

"I know."

His hand slid to the cord in her neck where blood throbbed in her vein. The pressure was light yet insistent, guiding her to him. But Abbie didn't need its direction as she moved to meet him, closing her eyes when his mouth was finally too close to see. The soft hairs of his mustache tickled the sensitive edges of her lip an instant before his mouth covered hers.

She explored the gentle contours of his mouth in the most tactilely stimulating way, satisfying the curiosity that had merely been whetted by the brief meeting of their lips several days earlier. His kiss was more than she'd expected, warm and firm, persuasively arousing in its devouring investigation of her own lips. Desire was building inside her, her breathing deepening, and her body straining to move closer still. Abbie realized how easily this could get out of hand, and she wasn't entirely sure that's what she wanted yet.

With an effort, she broke away from his spellbinding kiss and pushed herself back a few inches to bring his face into focus, discovering that at some point she had braced her hands against his chest for balance. She was beset by a whole new awareness of him — the natural heat of his body burning through the cotton of his shirt, the faint ripple of powerful muscles drawing breath into his lungs, and the heavy thud of his heart beating beneath her hands. Then she felt the weight of his hands on her, one resting idly on her lower ribs and the other absently massaging her upper shoulder.

It was crazy. All this time she thought she'd been in control of everything that was happening. Only now did she realize how totally absorbed she had been by the kiss. She studied the strong lines of his face in wonder, stunned by her response to him. His gaze traveled over her face.

"Now that was a kiss." Her voice sounded just a little throaty to her ears, as she subtly reminded him of the violence of their previous encounter.

"I wondered if you would notice the difference." His husky voice was like a caress.

As his dark eyes focused their attention on her lips, a faint tremor of want quivered through Abbie. "This is much better, MacCrea," she murmured as his hands exerted pressure to draw her back to him — not that she needed their coercion.

Her lips parted when they met his mouth, inviting the full intimacy of his kiss. When it came, she drank him in, letting his tongue mate with her own and probe the recesses of her mouth, a rawness sweeping hotly through her that made her ache for more. A storm of sensations buffeted her — the taste, the smell, the feel of him — and she let them engulf her.

His hands shifted their hold on her, now gripping and pulling. Abbie felt oddly weightless, boneless, as he effortlessly lifted her onto his lap. She slid her hands around his neck and into his thick hair, unable to remember the last time she'd felt so alive. Ever since her father had died, she'd been filled with so much pain and bitterness. Now that was gone, and it was as if she was being reborn in MacCrea's arms, her senses awakened again to all the exquisite pleasure of life and living — of love and giving.

How long had she ached to love and be loved? It was happening to her now. Each caress, each response, each demand she made was diminished by the magnitude of his. And Abbie didn't care why. If it was merely lust, it didn't matter. Selfishly, she wanted to feel more of these sensations — of being needed and wanted.

His arms bound her tightly to him, fitting her snugly into the cradle of his body, while his hands stroked her body, exploring the curves and hollows of her, the roundness of her hips, and the firmness of her thighs — always stimulating, always arousing, always urging closer contact. And all the while, the kiss went on and on, their breath rushing hotly together, their throats swallowing the intoxicating taste of each other.

When at last he moved his mouth from her lips and brushed it along her jaw to the sensitive hollow behind her ear, Abbie exulted in the low groan that came from his throat and turned her head slightly to allow him to kiss her neck. Quivers of sheer pleasure danced along her nerve ends as he nibbled at her skin, taking exciting little love bites. She felt his fingers at the buttons of her blouse and breathed in sharply when the pleasing roughness of his hand met her bare skin and cupped her breast. Desire seemed to throb through every inch of her body. It was like being consumed by a fever that heated every inch of her flesh, and MacCrea offered the only relief.

"You know where this is leading, don't you?" His thickly spoken question was slow to penetrate her sensation-riddled consciousness. MacCrea lifted his head to look at her face, resisting the pressure of her hands to pull him back to her.

She wasn't sorry he'd partially broken the spell of passion to question her intentions. It would have happened at some point, mentally if not verbally. Very early in her sexual experiences with men, Abbie had recognized that it was invariably the woman who controlled the situation and determined the degree of intimacy. Most men went no farther than the woman let them, stopping, however reluctantly or angrily, wherever she drew the line. Abbie had never made love to any man unless it was what she specifically wanted.

His question hovered in the air. Abbie bridged the space between them and nuzzled his ear, lightly rubbing her lips over its inner shell. When she answered him, her voice was barely a whisper. "I hope it's leading to the bedroom." She darted her tongue into the dark opening and smiled at the raw shudder that quaked his body, enjoying her ability to arouse him sexually.

A second later, his fingers dug into her arm as he forced her away from his ear. Desire had darkened his eyes to black, yet amusement lurked in them, too. "You do, do you?"

"Yes. Don't you?" she murmured.

"It would be a helluva lot more comfortable than this."

"I agree." She touched his face, exploring the high ridge of his cheekbone and tracing the slanted line of his jaw, then directing her fingertips to his mouth, which fascinated her so.

He caught hold of them and pressed them to his lips, then gently scooted her off his lap onto the sofa. As he stood up, he kept hold of her hand, as if unwilling to break contact. Abbie wondered if he thought she was going to back down. She wasn't. Once she made up her mind about something, she never changed it. But she let her actions tell him that as he pulled her up to stand in front of him, actions that she regarded as neither wanton nor brazen, but merely a reflection of her feelings.

His arm circled the back of her waist, drawing her against the length of his body and lifting her onto the toes of her boots as he bent his head to reach her mouth. She leaned into him, arching her back and pressing her hips against his thighs, conscious again of the difference in their heights, but more conscious of the differences in their bodies.

After kissing her thoroughly, MacCrea straightened and let her rock back onto her heels. Turning, he kept an arm around her waist to draw her along with him, and guided her toward the bedroom.

Abbie paused, aware of MacCrea behind her, and started to undo the rest of her buttons, the ones he hadn't bothered to unfasten. This was always the awkward time, the moments spent apart undressing. It always took the bloom from her passion and turned it into something calculated.

"No, you don't." MacCrea caught her by the arm and turned her around to face him. Startled, she looked at him in confusion, then he pushed her other hand out of the way and unbuttoned the last two buttons of her blouse. "I'll have this pleasure, thank you."

Abbie doubted that he intended to undress her fully. Maybe the blouse and her brassiere, but after that, he'd become too impatient. Strip and hop into bed, that had been her experience — and that of her friends as well. It didn't matter. This was more than she usually got.

He pushed the blouse off her shoulders, taking the bra straps with it, and bent to nuzzle her neck and the ridge of her shoulder. Abbie shivered at the delicious shudders that raced through her body, ignited by his nibbling kisses. Slowly, he pulled the blouse down her arms, caressing her skin as he went. Then it was free. She caught a flash of white out of the corner of her eye as he tossed her blouse onto a chair.

Then he turned her away from him, but the exciting nuzzling didn't stop. She felt his fingers at the hook of her brassiere and unconsciously held her breath, waiting for its release. It came a second later and her breasts hung free. As the brassiere went the way of the blouse, one of his large hands glided around her ribs and cupped the weight of one breast in its palm. The second one was quickly claimed by his other hand. Abbie couldn't stop the sighing moan of pleasure that rose from her throat.

Fighting the weakness that attacked her limbs, Abbie leaned against him and turned her face toward his chest as his thumbs drew lazy circles around her nipples, stimulating them into erectness. Her stomach muscles tightened, and a hollow ache started low and spread quickly.

All of a sudden she was lifted into the air and turned. Abbie wanted to scream in frustration, knowing this was when it would stop, that his own desire demanded consummation at this critical point when her arousal had just begun. So certain was she about his intentions that she wasn't surprised to find herself seated on the edge of the bed.

When he picked up her leg and started to tug off her riding boot, she stared at him, not knowing what to think. The second boot hit the floor soon after the first one. Her heavy socks followed them, each slowly peeled away, allowing him to caress her feet in the process. Until that moment, Abbie had never considered her feet to be a part of her body that she wanted caressed, never regarding them as particularly sensual. MacCrea showed her otherwise.

After that, she didn't know what to expect from him. He pulled her upright, then spanned her waist with his hands and lifted her up to stand on the bed. As his hands slid to her breasts, she breathed in sharply and deeply, then couldn't quite release it as he nuzzled one of her breasts, rubbing his lips over its roundness and across the nipple, his tongue darting out to lick it and making it harden even more. Moaning at the exquisite torment, Abbie dug her fingers into his thick hair and urged him closer.

As his mouth opened to take in the point of her breast, a searing pleasure rocketed through her. She forgot all about his hands until her lower stomach muscles contracted sharply with their contact with his flesh. He'd unzipped her jodhpurs. Shot with frissons of raw passion, Abbie knew she'd never felt so weak with desire in her entire life. He pushed the pants off her hips and the weight of the material slid them partway down her thighs. A boneless feeling nearly overwhelmed her as his hands glided over her bare bottom and paused to knead the soft cheeks, then moved on, down the backs of her legs, dragging the jodhpurs with them. She felt her knees start to buckle under the warmth of his hands. When he swung her off her feet, Abbie instinctively wrapped her arms around his neck and curled her body against him. One final tug stripped the jodhpurs from her.

Totally enraptured, she studied his profile, his face so close to hers she could see every pore in his leather-tan skin, his hair all rumpled and furrowed by her fingers, and his mustached mouth still moist from sucking her breasts. The slanted angle of his forehead continued along the straight ridge of his nose and ended with the natural thrust of his chin. Despite all the aggressive lines, MacCrea suddenly seemed incredibly handsome to her.

She watched his gaze wander over her nakedness. When he turned his head to look into her face, she saw the desire that darkened his eyes and weighted their lids. She wanted him. She wanted all of him. Slowly he set her onto the floor, his hands trailing over her skin as if reluctant to release her.

"Now, it's your turn." His voice was low and deep, its huskiness belying an otherwise even pitch. "This is the part I enjoy."

For a split second Abbie didn't catch his meaning, then realized she was supposed to undress him. Her own desire was so strong at that moment that she wanted to protest the delay in consummation. But she knew she wasn't being fair.

Trying to speed up the process, she practically ripped the buttons from his shirt, but when she bared his chest, she was overwhelmed by the need to touch him, to press her own body against his muscled torso and feel the wall of his chest flatten her breasts. She discovered how exciting, how stimulating it could be to run her hands over him, to let her lips explore his hard flesh, and to taste the faint saltiness of his skin.

As she slid his shirt down his arms, she began to appreciate the sensual joy to be found in unveiling him a little at a time, feeling for herself the bulge of his biceps and the sinewy cords in his forearms. She could tell that he was enjoying it, too, by the faint tremor that shook him when she unfastened his jeans and unzipped his fly.

At last the moment came when his Jockey shorts were the only article of clothing that remained. She was conscious of the trembling of her hands as she slid her fingers under the elastic waistband and pushed them slowly down — conscious, too, of his erection straining against the confining cloth. Her throat was tight as she watched it spring free when she slid his shorts down.

Bending, she continued to pull the shorts down his legs, not stopping until he stepped free of them. She straightened and lightly, very lightly ran her fingers down the underside of his shaft, smiling at the convulsive leap it made into her hand, and the hiss of his indrawn breath that muffled his half-curse.

He grabbed at her hand and yanked her against his body, naked and hard, the heat of his flesh firing her skin. "Who taught you that?" he growled.

"You did," she whispered. "Just now."

Abbie wondered if he realized just how much he had taught her. Before this moment, she'd never known so much pleasure could be derived from exploring a man's body, that it was something to be enjoyed as much as the kisses and caresses.

With a twisting motion, MacCrea lowered her onto the narrow bed and followed her down to lie along her side. She turned to him eagerly. "Make love to me, MacCrea," she urged, more than ready for him, she thought, only to have him show her how wrong she was as he kissed, fondled, and caressed her body, building the aching tension inside her until she was raw with need, while he resisted the stimulation of her hands and the urging of her lips.

At last, when the throbbing ache was almost unbearable, he shifted his weight onto her and entered her as smoothly as a blade into its sheath. A storm of sensations drew her into its vortex, everything centering lower and lower, the fusion culminating in a glorious explosion that sent her soaring, for a few shattering seconds transported to a purely physical plateau where all was sensation.

Then it was over and she lay nestled in his arms, her head on his chest. After all that she'd learned about MacCrea in the last hour, she wasn't surprised that he continued to hold her instead of rolling over to light a cigarette or climbing out of bed to get dressed. This intimacy after the act was part of making love, too. She was so content she wasn't sure she ever wanted to move.

But she rubbed her cheek against his chest and sighed. His chin moved against the top of her head. "You know you are damned near perfect, Abbie?"

"And I thought I was perfect," she mocked, smiling.

"Maybe if you were a little taller."

Like Rachel, she thought and immediately wished that name had never come to her mind. All her contentment seemed to flee, as if a moment ago it hadn't even existed. Abbie stirred restively, her peaceful mood gone.

"What's the matter?"

Abbie pretended to glance at the curtained window and the blackness of nightfall beyond it. "It's later than I thought. I'd better be going." She left the warmth of his arms and swung out of bed, reaching for her clothes scattered around the room.

"There's no hurry, is there?"

"Momma doesn't know where I am. I don't want her to worry." She finished tugging on her jodhpurs and sat down on the edge of the bed to pull on her boots. The mattress shifted as MacCrea sat up.

"She'd probably be more worried if she knew."

"Probably." Abbie smiled at him.

He combed the hair back from the side of her face. "I still say you have the bluest damned eyes."

So does Rachel. Dammit, Abbie railed silently. Why was she thinking about her? Trying to block out the unwanted thoughts, she leaned over and kissed him. She waited for him to say something, to indicate that he wanted to see her again. But he made no response.

She left the trailer a few minutes later without knowing whether she'd ever see him again.

14

One more bale of hay would do it. Pausing to gather the needed strength and breath, Abbie wiped the sweat around her mouth onto the sleeve of her blouse, every limb trembling from her overworked muscles. But no matter how sore and weary she was, the horses had to be fed.

Bending her aching back, Abbie slipped her gloved fingers under the baling twine and attempted to heft the heavy bale onto the flatbed with one mighty swing. But she rammed it against the edge of it instead, unable to lift it high enough, and quickly used her body to pin the bale against the flatbed. Then grunting and straining, she struggled and shoved to push it over the edge. Almost immediately, she collapsed against the flatbed trailer, letting it support her, too exhausted to stand on her own and too tired to cry. She didn't even feel human anymore, just an itchy mass of hay chafe glued together with sweat.

"Why do you not wait for me to help with those bales?" At the sound of Ben's scolding voice, Abbie hastily straightened to stand erect. "What you think? That you are Superwoman?"

In no mood to be lectured about her strength or lack of it by an irritable old man, Abbie swung around to snap at him. But one look at his tired and wan features reminded her that these last six back-breaking days had taken their toll on him as well. They were both cranky and out of sorts from the mental and physical strain of trying to take care of all these horses, working practically from dawn 'til dusk. Even then there'd been tasks they'd had to neglect, like the training of the yearlings and two-year-olds, and the cleaning of the empty stalls in the barns.

"I was trying to save time." Abbie lied rather than hurt his pride by telling the truth, that he was too old to stand up under this kind of heavy labor. "How is Amira's foal?"

Problems just kept coming their way. One of the new foals had come down with a severe case of scours, a relatively common occurrence when the dam came back into season. They had isolated the pair immediately to avoid the risk of spreading the diarrhetic condition to other sucklings in the pasture.

"She is not good."

He needed to say no more. Abbie knew how critical it was. Foals had little reserve. If the lost fluids weren't replaced, the resulting dehydration could kill them or weaken them so badly they'd contract other diseases.

Abbie glanced toward the house. "Maybe we should call Doc Campbell."

"We will see."

She opened her mouth to argue with him, then closed it, deferring to his judgment. If Ben didn't believe the foal's condition was critical enough to warrant calling in the vet, there was no point in questioning his decision. He had years more experience than she did. And, Lord knows, they probably already had a huge outstanding veterinary bill that had accumulated over the spring foaling and breeding season.

Judging by the barrage of phone calls they'd received in the last few days, they owed practically everyone in the whole county. Abbie sighed dispiritedly. Nothing could be done about any of that until the estate was settled, so there was no use thinking about it, not when they had so many horses to feed before dark.

In an attempt to cut down on the amount of time spent distributing hay and grain to all the horses, they had turned most of them into the pastures for mass-feeding from wooden troughs. This meant that some of the horses would be bullied out of their portions by the more dominant members of the herd, but it couldn't be helped.

"We might as well get on with this." Abbie turned and faced the flatbed trailer and laid her hands on its wooden floor, preparing to jump onto it, but her weary muscles simply refused to make the effort. "Will you give me a leg up, Ben? I can't make it." She didn't even try, and instead stepped onto the cupped hands he offered and let him boost her onto the trailer. As he walked toward the tractor hitched to the flatbed, Abbie stopped him. "I meant to ask you if they're going to deliver that grain tomorrow. We don't have much left."

"They wanted to speak about the bill to your mother first."

"That's right. You told me that." Abbie frowned, irritated with herself for forgetting. "I meant to call them this afternoon. As soon as we get done here, I'll phone Mr. Hardman at home tonight."

And this time she vowed she wouldn't forget. She let her legs dangle over the side of the hayrack and leaned against the bale behind her, too grateful for its support to mind the bristly stalks that poked her back. The tractor roared to life and jerked the flatbed after it, briefly jarring Abbie, but she didn't move, conserving her energy for the moment when she'd have to hop off the back and scurry around to open the pasture gate.

She couldn't remember ever being so tired and sore. Every bone, muscle, and fiber in her body ached. The only thing that kept her going was the certain knowledge that this situation couldn't last much longer. The estate would be settled. There was a light at the end of the tunnel. But why did she have the feeling it was a train?

Above the noisy engine of the tractor, she heard the rumble of a pickup truck. She felt a little leap of anticipation in her heart, hoping it was MacCrea's. She hadn't seen or heard from him since that night. Maybe . . . She sat up and tried to swallow the bitter disappointment when she recognized the rusty old pickup that belonged to Dobie Hix. He pulled in front of the pasture gate and stopped, blocking the entrance. She had a pretty good idea of why he'd come.

As the tractor lumbered to a halt, Abbie jumped off the back of the flatbed and charged around to the front to confront Dobie as he climbed out of the truck. "If you've come about the money we owe you, we still can't pay it. Nothing's been settled yet. There's your precious damned hay." She gestured wildly at the hayrack behind her. "Go ahead and take it!"

A look of shock crossed his face as he swept off his battered straw cowboy hat and held it in front of him. "That's not why I came, Abbie. I don't want that hay. You all need it for your horses. It's yours. I just came to give you a hand. I know you don't have any right now and —"

"Dobie, I . . . I'm sorry." She was miserably ashamed of the way she'd unjustly lashed out at him. Feeling incredibly tired and defeated, she ran a gloved hand over her face, wondering why she'd said those terrible things. "There was no excuse for what I said."

"You're tired. This isn't work for you to be doing. Those bales are heavy even for a man to lift." He waved his hat in the direction of the flatbed. "Let alone a gal as little as you."

"I'm stronger than I look," she flared.

"I know you are, but it still isn't work you should be doing."

What other choice did she have? How else were all these horses to be fed? Was she supposed to let Ben do it all? What if he suffered a heart attack? What was she supposed to do then? Somehow Abbie managed to keep all those angry questions to herself. No matter how illogical and chauvinistic Dobie's statements were, she recognized that he was merely trying to be thoughtful.

"We appreciate your offer, Dobie. Thanks."

"That's what neighbors are for." He shrugged. "I only wish you had let me know that you were shorthanded. I would have been over to help sooner."

"You will stay for dinner."

"There's no need in that."

"I insist." She didn't want him or anyone else to think they didn't have enough food in the house to eat. Their present straitened circumstances were temporary, and she didn't want anyone imagining otherwise. "I'll tell Momma to put another plate on the table." And she'd make that phone call she'd forgotten earlier.

As she started for the house, Dobie climbed back into his pickup and moved it out of the way. Abbie listened to the sound of its engine, wondering how she could have mistaken its clattering roar for MacCrea's. She guessed she'd simply wanted it to be his, even though she'd known when she'd left his trailer that night that he probably wouldn't come around again. Why should he? After all, she hadn't made that a condition for going to bed with him.

MacCrea was a wildcatter, a gambler, hardly the type she could expect to have an ongoing relationship with. He was the kind who was here one day and gone the next. It wasn't as if she'd lost anything that she hadn't expected to lose, so why was she still thinking about him? But the answer to that was easy. With him she had felt alive and whole, possibly for the first time in her life. It wasn't a feeling she could easily forget.

She entered the house through the back door and stepped into the kitchen. Her mother turned toward the door, a slightly panicked expression on her face, and quickly placed her hand over the mouthpiece of the telephone receiver she held.

"Abbie. I'm so glad you're here," she rushed. "It's a Mr. Fisher on the phone. Long distance from Ohio or Iowa — I can't remember which. He's calling about some horses he sold to your father last year, but he says he never got paid for them. Abbie, I don't know what to say to him. You talk to him." She pushed the receiver at her.

"Just give him Lane Canfield's number and have him call there. Lane knows more than we do," she insisted wearily.

"I can't. You tell him, Abbie."

Stifling her irritation at her mother's inability to cope with something so simple, Abbie took the telephone and barely listened to the story the man recited. Her response was the same as the one she gave to all the recent callers: a referral to the man handling the settlement of the estate. Afterward, she hung up the phone and stood facing the wall, feeling mentally, physically, and emotionally drained.

"It's all so upsetting when they call like that, Abbie," her mother declared. "I never know what to say to them."

"I told you to leave the telephone off the hook," Abbie said tiredly, wondering why she had to deal with everything.

"But what if our friends tried to call and couldn't get through?"

What friends? Abbie thought, wondering if her mother had noticed how few had called since word had gotten out about their present financial straits. Maybe she should have expected it, but it still rankled. After all, they weren't broke. This was just a temporary situation.

She picked up the telephone and dialed the home number of the owner of the local feed-and-grain company. As soon as she identified herself as a Lawson, she had no difficulty convincing him to send out another load of grain, despite their outstanding account. She sighed as she hung up, relieved that the Lawson name still carried some weight.

"Before I forget, Momma . . . ." Abbie turned and saw her mother standing at the sink, peeling potatoes — a sight that still seemed foreign. In the past when her mother had puttered in the kitchen, it had usually been to supervise the meal preparation, adding a touch here and changing something there, but never to cook herself. Now, she had no kitchen help to supervise. No one except Jackson, and cooking and cleaning were two things he assisted with only grudgingly, considering both to be beneath him. The brunt of the housework and meal preparation had fallen on her mother. ". . . we're having company for dinner tonight. Dobie Hix came by to help with the horses, so I invited him to eat with us."

"In that case I'd better peel more potatoes, and maybe fix another vegetable. Perhaps some broccoli . . . with cheese sauce."

Abbie left her still mulling over ways to stretch the evening meal to feed four and returned to the stables. With Dobie lending Ben a hand to feed the horses, Abbie set out to clean some of the stalls.

All the doors and windows in the stable stood open to allow cross-ventilation, but little of the evening breeze reached the interior. Abbie paused to wipe the sweat from her face, then laid the pitchfork across the wheelbarrow and gripped the handles to roll it to the next stall.

"Let me do that for you, Abbie." Dobie came up behind her just as she lifted up on the handles.

"I can manage." Once she got it balanced and rolling, it practically pushed itself. It was just a matter of getting it started. She strained forward, pushing with all her weight. It moved an inch, then Dobie's hands were gripping the wheelbarrow as he shouldered her out of the way.

"It's too heavy for you to be pushing." He rolled it effortlessly to the next stall.

"How do you think it got this far, Dobie?" Abbie muttered, but she really didn't object to letting him push it. It was heavy and she was tired.

She swatted absently at a fly that buzzed around her face, then reached for the pitchfork. She didn't dare stop to rest. She was afraid if she did, she wouldn't be able to get herself moving again, like the wheelbarrow.

"I'll get another pitchfork and give you a hand. We'll have these stalls cleaned in half the time."

"Thanks, but Ben wondered if you could lend him a hand over at the stallion barn when you were finished with the hay. The stallion kicked out a couple boards in his stall. Ben thinks one or two others might be weak." She would gladly have traded places and let Dobie finish cleaning the stalls. Unfortunately carpentry wasn't one of her talents. Abbie knew she was more apt to smash a thumb than pound a nail.

"I'll get that fixed and come back to help you."

"Thanks." She smiled absently in his direction and scooped up a pile of manure from the stall's straw bed, then swung the pitchfork over to the wheelbarrow to dump it.

The rhythm took over: scoop, lift, pitch, scoop, lift, pitch. Abbie didn't even hear Dobie leave the stall. In the background, the radio played some twangy country tune. A radio was always going in the barns, tuned to a music station to soothe the horses and keep them company. But Abbie had stopped listening, thinking, feeling, and smelling a long time ago. Like a robot, she simply scooped, lifted, and pitched.

As she swung another forkful of manure and soiled straw into the wheelbarrow, out of the corner of her eye she saw a man leaning against the stall door. She stuck the pitchfork under another pile, then realized the man was MacCrea. She froze, her heart suddenly lurching against her ribs. She turned and looked again to make sure she wasn't seeing things.

"Hello, Abbie." His deep voice felt almost like a caress.

"MacCrea." She was flustered. Her heart was pounding as hard as a galloping horse. She felt all shaky inside, and she didn't like it. She didn't like wanting anyone this much. It left her too exposed. She shifted her grip on the pitchfork handle and bent again to her task, but this time she slowed her rhythm way down, making a project out of sifting the horse apples from the straw.

MacCrea watched her, the way he'd been watching her for the last several minutes, stimulated by the sight of her lissome body, remembering the way it looked without clothes, the way it had taken him and drained him. All week she'd haunted his trailer. Everywhere he'd looked, he'd seen her — on the sofa, by the door, in front of the sink, and most of all, in his bed. Each phone call, each rumble of a car, he'd expected to be her.

"It's been a week since I've seen you," he said.

There was the smallest break in her action as she swung the pitchfork over to the wheelbarrow. With a practiced twist of the handle, she dumped the manure onto the growing pile, then let the tines rest on the top and glanced in his direction, her look guarded. "You knew where to find me."

He wanted to walk over to her and pluck the wisps of straw from her dark hair, but MacCrea knew he wouldn't stop there. "I finally realized that you weren't going to get in touch with me."

"It was your move." The straw rustled as she once again turned and searched for more waste. "If you only wanted a one-night stand, I wasn't about to make any demands on you, MacCrea."

Too damned much pride, MacCrea suspected and wondered why her back wasn't bowed by the weight of it. But he knew he admired it. Abbie was different from other women he'd known. It *had* been his move, but none had ever let him make it. They'd always arranged to bump into him accidentally or made up an excuse to see him or call him. Abbie had a ready-made excuse to do that. She could have gotten in touch with him to give him more names. But she hadn't. And here he was.

"I never had any intention of seeing you again." That's what he'd told himself when Abbie left that night. He'd enjoyed her, but it was over, and that was the end of it. How many times had he said that this past week? Every time he remembered her, and that was too often.

"So why are you here?" She paused, her back still to him, both gloved hands gripping the pitchfork, then she laughed, a short, hollow sound. "That's right. I forgot. You wanted names from me."

"Yes, I wanted that." He didn't like talking to her back, and he didn't like not having her full attention. He pushed away from the frame of the stall door and crossed the space between them in two long strides. Startled, she didn't try to resist when he took the pitchfork from her hands and tossed it aside. He dug his fingers into her arms, feeling the heat of her body flow through them, and turned her to face him. Everything seemed to go still inside him as he stared down at her, taking in the glistening sheen of her complexion, the parted softness of her lips, and the boundless blue of her eyes. "But that's not why I'm here and you damned well know it."

"I do?" It sounded as if she breathed the words, as her expression became all soft and warm.

For a split second, he was furious with himself for not staying away. He had no business getting involved with her. He couldn't afford the distraction of an affair just now. Between running his drilling company, trying to get this lease locked up and the capital raised to drill a well on it, and getting this new computerized testing process of his off the ground, he didn't have the time to devote. Hell, in his line of work, he was never in one place that long. And he wasn't in a position yet to settle down and run his operation from behind a desk. He'd learned by experience that long distance invariably killed a relationship. But he just couldn't get Abbie out of his head. She'd meant more than a one-night stand, whether he wanted to admit it or not.

"Don't play dumb, Abbie. You knew I'd come."

"I knew . . . if you felt anything at all, you would."

He was taken aback by her candor. He had expected a denial, not a frank admission of tactics. But when hadn't she been full of surprises? He felt the touch of her hands on his stomach and his control snapped. Raising her the necessary few inches, he covered her lips with his mouth, tasting, drinking, and eating their softness, driven by a hunger that hadn't been fed for a week.

But a kiss didn't come anywhere close to satisfying his hunger. He broke it off, aware of how rough and labored his breathing had become, and how hard he'd grown. He started to rub his cheek against her hair, but a straw poked him. Impatiently, he plucked it from her tousled hair.

Her arms tightened around him as she pressed her head closer against his chest. "I'm a mess," she said, her voice partially muffled by his shirt.

"Funny, you don't feel like a mess." He ran his hands over her, remembering the feel of her body and the way she'd fit him as snugly as a glove. He molded her to him, pressing her against his hips, trying to ease the aching in his loins.

She moaned softly, "Oh, MacCrea, I want you, too." Shifting in his arms, she drew him down to her lips and arched her body even closer to him.

He'd heard all he needed to hear. Neither the time nor the place meant anything to him as he loosened the tail of her blouse to touch the heat of her flesh. She turned her lips away from his mouth, murmuring, "Not here," but he ignored her faint protest and nibbled at her throat. She pushed away from his chest in forceful resistance. "No." This time her voice was stronger.

A man's angry, drawling voice came out of nowhere. "Take your hands off of her!"

The warning had barely made an impression on MacCrea when someone grabbed his arm and jerked him around. He had a split second to focus on his assailant before a fist filled his vision. A long-ingrained fighting instinct took over as MacCrea jerked his head back to avoid the blow and it glanced off his jaw.

The sandy-haired man in the battered straw cowboy hat swung wildly at him and yelled, "Run, Abbie!"

MacCrea blocked the fist with an upraised arm and quickly jabbed the man in the stomach, but not before his head was snapped back by a third swing that found its target. But the jarring contact didn't stop him; it only made his heart pump faster and speed the flow of adrenaline through his system. His blurred vision saw only his opponent. He slammed his fist into the man's midsection again and followed it with a left to the jaw and another right to the head that threw the man backward against the wall, knocking his hat off. Bareheaded, he slumped against it, his legs buckling as he tried to shake off the blow.

MacCrea went after him. He'd been in too many brawls to quit when his opponent went down. This was the time to finish him off and make sure he didn't get up again. Suddenly Abbie was in his way.

"Stop it, MacCrea!" she shouted angrily. "Can't you see you've beaten him?" He paused, dragging in a breath to fill his laboring lungs, just starting to get his wind and to feel good. Abbie turned to the other man and crouched beside him. "Dobie, are you all right?"

"Yeah." But the man didn't sound at all certain of that. MacCrea started to smile in satisfaction, then winced instead, for the first time feeling the cut on the inside of his lip. That stinging sensation was followed instantly by the ache in his hands, his knuckles sore from their jarring contact with the man's face. MacCrea flexed them and tried to shake out the stiffness.

It irritated him the way Abbie was fussing over the other guy. "Just who the hell is this character?" He pressed his fingers against his split lip and explored the extent of the cut with his tongue, tasting a trace of blood.

The man looked at him as if realizing just that second that MacCrea was still there. He made a move toward him, but Abbie pushed him back. "It's all right, Dobie. He's . . . a friend." The man she called Dobie relaxed, but MacCrea noticed that his expression remained hostile. If anything, it became more so as he straightened to his feet, shrugging off Abbie's attempt to help him.

"I'd like you to meet MacCrea Wilder. MacCrea, this is Dobie Hix, our neighbor. He's been coming over to help Ben and me with the horses."

"Hix." MacCrea acknowledged the introduction with a nod of his head, and the man mumbled something in reply, but didn't offer to shake hands.

MacCrea noticed the look Hix darted at Abbie. It would have been obvious to a blind man that Hix was crazy about her. Or maybe it was just obvious because he recognized the symptoms. Just when he thought Hix was going to leave and he'd have Abbie to himself again, the old man appeared in the stall doorway. His sharp eyes seemed to take in the situation in a flash, although his stoic expression never changed.

"Your mother says we should clean up for supper now," he informed Abbie.

"Thanks, Ben." Then she turned expectantly to MacCrea. "You will join us, won't you?"

This was his chance to bow out, to leave before he became involved any deeper with her. Common sense told him to clear out, but MacCrea heard himself accepting the invitation. All during the long walk to the house with Abbie and her two cohorts, MacCrea cursed himself for being twenty kinds of fool.

The very minute Abbie set foot in the house, she left him to cool his heels in the living room. He spent a good fifteen minutes listening to Babs Lawson chatter away about nothing while avoiding the staring match Hix kept trying to instigate.

He was about ready to make his excuses and leave when Abbie sailed down the staircase into the room and the sight of her blocked all other thoughts from his mind. Her skin glowed with a scrubbed freshness and her wet hair was skimmed back from her face and plaited in a single braid, the severe style softened by wispy curls around her temples and neck. She had changed into a simple cotton frock in a vivid shade of green with a row of white buttons down the v-neck front. She breezed past him, leaving in her wake the clean smells of soap and some sexy perfume. MacCrea watched her, staring at the way her breasts strained against the material of the snug-fitting dress top.

He stayed. She sat next to him at the dining room table, their chairs crowded close together, her thigh brushing against his. It was unquestionably the longest meal MacCrea had ever had to sit through, trying to participate intelligently in the table talk.

"No, thanks." MacCrea refused the second cup of coffee Babs Lawson tried to pour him and pushed his chair away from the table. "The food was good — too good. As a matter of fact, I'm afraid I'm going to have to walk some of it off. Join me, Abbie?"

"Thanks." Abbie slipped her hand into his, squeezing it lightly. He started for the back door, but she paused next to Ben's chair. "We'll check on the foal."

Ben nodded, then glanced at Dobie's downcast expression as the door clicked shut behind them. He liked their neighbor. Dobie Hix was an honest, hardworking, God-fearing man, but Ben knew that he did not have the strength of will to handle a spirited, headstrong woman like Abbie. He had the gentleness but not the firmness. She would walk all over him.

As for this MacCrea Wilder, Ben wasn't sure about him. He'd seen him only a few times, yet he'd sensed a restlessness about the man. Other things pulled him. Abbie needed someone strong and dependable so she could remember how to be soft and trusting. This man was strong, but Ben questioned how long MacCrea Wilder would be around.

"I think I'll get some fresh air, too." Dobie Hix rose abruptly and headed for the door. He grabbed his hat off the hook, then paused. "That was a lovely meal, Mrs. Lawson. Thank you."

"You're more than welcome, Dobie."

Ben wasn't certain whether Dobie intended to add to his collection of barely visible bruises, so he pushed back his chair. "I will join you, Dobie."

He followed Dobie onto the veranda and stood beside him at the top of the steps. The sun was down and moonlight silvered the grounds — and the couple walking body against body across the clearing. Dobie stared at them and impatiently tapped his hat against the side of his leg.

"Maybe it isn't my place to be saying this, but I don't like him, Ben." He shoved his hat onto his head and pulled it low.

Ben wondered if Dobie noticed that the pair was headed for the office annex, not the broodmare barns where the sick foal was. "She is a woman grown."

"Yeah, I guess so." Dobie clumped off the porch. "I'd better be getting home. See you in the morning."

"Good night, Dobie." Ben remained on the porch.

As they entered the dark annex, MacCrea attempted to turn Abbie into his arms, but she eluded him and caught hold of his hand to pull him deeper into the shadows. He followed reluctantly.

"Where are we going?"

"Here." A doorknob turned, a latch clicked open, and he breathed in the smell of leather. "It's my father's private office." She led him inside, then released his hand. He could barely make out the myriad of shapes, distinguishable mainly by their differing shades of darkness. "Wait here."

He could hear her footsteps as she moved confidently into the room. There was a snapping sound and the soft glow of light from a small green-shaded desk lamp spread over the room. He glanced quickly around the room, noticing the desk and chair, the paneled walls covered with pictures and trophies, and the leather sofa, its cushions empty and inviting. He looked at Abbie, partially backlit by the desk lamp, then glanced at the ribbons and trophies on the near wall.

"That's some collection."

"Yes." Abbie looked at them briefly. "I won most of them, the ones in the English pleasure and park classes."

"You must be quite a horsewoman."

"I can ride with the best of them." Her smile gave her reply a totally different meaning.

"So I've discovered."

"The door has a lock," she said.

MacCrea shut the door behind him and turned the lock. This time they wouldn't be rudely interrupted by her neighbor or anyone else. She was still standing in front of the desk when he turned back into the room. He walked over to her, paused, then ran his hands over her bare collarbones and up her neck to cup her face. Bending, he kissed her, taking little bites of her lips and feeling the rapid beating of her heart. At last he came up for air, and a tremor shook him. She looked into his eyes, and he had the feeling she could see all the way into his soul.

"You have the bluest damned eyes." He kissed their corners, closing them, and slid his hands onto her shoulders, his thumbs caressing the hollows. Conscious of the slight rise and fall of her breasts, he let his gaze travel down to them and center on that hint of cleavage behind the first white button. Then his fingers were around it without his being aware of moving his hand.

"No." She stopped him before he could free the button, and stepped back from him. "I'll do it."

A protest formed, but MacCrea never got it out as he watched the swift deftness of her hands reveal that she wasn't wearing a bra under that dress. Christ, she wasn't wearing a damned thing! he realized as the dress slithered to the floor and she stood completely nude before him, bathed in the soft lamplight.

He swore and she laughed. Then he had her in his arms. After that, it all became a blur of raw passion: the shedding of his clothes, the entwining on the leather couch, the kissing and fondling of bodies, the rhythmic rocking in unison, their climax, which forever trapped in his memory images of her nipples so erect with arousal, the side-to-side turning of her head, the arching thrust of her hips, and the look of raw wonder on her face.

MacCrea and Abbie lay nestled together on their sides like two spoons, the narrow couch not giving them any room to sprawl in contentment. He felt a tingling in the arm that pillowed her head, the warning of the nerves that they were going to sleep, but he didn't move. Hell, he didn't want to move from her.

Frowning, he absently studied the top of her mussed hair, the dark strands pulled loose from the single braid. He tried to analyze his feelings and understand why, with her, everything seemed different. True, Abbie went out of her way to please him, but so had other women, and succeeded as well. So what did she give him that others didn't or hadn't? Maybe it was the way she loved him with more than her body. All her emotions, her passion, went into it. She gave him everything — every part of her. But there wasn't any room in his life right now for a wife and family.

Marriage. My God, was he really thinking about marrying her? He concealed his shock and felt Abbie rub her cheek against his arm like a purring cat.

"After Daddy's funeral, I came here to think. Until that day, I didn't know he had another daughter. All along I thought I was the only one. It was hard for me to accept. It still is," she mused. "She was his favorite."

"How do you know that?" He felt her shrug a little.

"I know," was all she said. "You've seen her, MacCrea . . . you've seen Rachel. You know how much I look like her." He was struck by her phrasing: "I look like her" and not "she looks like me." "Every time Daddy looked at me, he saw her. Do you?"

"No." Until she'd mentioned it, he'd completely forgotten she had a half-sister, let alone the resemblance between them.

As Abbie turned in a tight circle to face him, needle-sharp pains shot through his arm. Wincing, MacCrea shifted onto his back to ease the pinching in his arm and pulled Abbie partially onto his chest. Using her forearms to prop herself up, she searched his face, her own expression warm and loving. He didn't want to notice that, any more than he wanted to notice the rounded contours of her breasts hanging full before him.

"I'm glad we made love here, MacCrea." She leaned forward and kissed him, her lips soft, her breath fresh. He felt himself growing hard again and tried to will it to stop. "Now when I come here, I'll remember this. I'll remember how good it was." She laid her head on his shoulder, pressing her firm breasts against his chest.

"Abbie." He knew he wanted to go on seeing her. But if he ever had to choose between his business future and her, he knew Abbie would lose. He wouldn't sacrifice his ambitions, his dreams — his life — for her. She'd give and he'd take. Wrong or not, that's the way it was going to be. But it wasn't necessary to make that choice yet. Maybe it never would be.

She made a protesting sound and snuggled closer to him. "I know it's late and I have to get up early in the morning, but I wish we could stay here all night."

"What are you going to be doing this next week?"

"Lane is supposed to come. Hopefully, he'll have this mess straightened out with Daddy's estate." Her mood changed. MacCrea sensed her restlessness.

"That's your days. What about your nights? Are you free?"

"No, I'm very expensive." She sat up, her smile mocking him.

"Are you, now?" The lightning change of topic and tempo kept him alert. She stimulated him mentally as well as sexually.

"Yes. And don't you forget it." She picked up his pants and tossed them to him.

15

But Lane Canfield didn't come to River Bend until the end of the week. Now that he was there, sitting in the living room, Abbie felt uneasy, her nerves on edge. She didn't know what was going to come out of this meeting with him, but something had to. This waiting and all the attendant uncertainty was becoming a strain on everyone.

As she listened to her mother chattering away, playing hostess, she wanted to scream at her to stop, but she couldn't. Her mother had been in such good spirits all morning that Abbie dreaded the moment when they would vanish. Which they surely would. She had noticed that Lane hadn't touched either the coffee or the pecan tart he'd taken. Abbie had trouble convincing herself that he simply wasn't hungry or thirsty.

"Now, Lane, what was it you wanted to talk to us about?" Babs smiled and sipped at her coffee, blithely indifferent to the tension that was twisting Abbie's stomach into knots.

"Unfortunately, what I have to tell you isn't good," Lane began, setting his cup and saucer on the end table by the tasseled arm of the sofa.

"What are you trying to say?" Abbie demanded. "Is Daddy's estate going to be tied up in some litigation?" All along she'd suspected Rachel would contest the will and demand a share of the estate. Now it was happening. Abbie was sure of it.

"No. Nothing like that." He appeared to dismiss the possibility out of hand.

"Then what?" She frowned.

"It's taken some time to get a clear picture of exactly what the financial condition of the estate is. And I'm afraid it's worse than was first thought."

"What do you mean?" Mentally Abbie braced herself as she watched him closely.

"I'm sure you know that when Dean sold his father's company, he received a very large sum of money —"

"Twelve million dollars," Abbie remembered.

"Taxes, commissions, and various other costs had to be paid out of that, so actually he netted less than that," Lane stated. "Over the years, he has repeatedly dipped into that capital. Even though he borrowed money to build the improvements at River Bend — the new stables, et cetera — the actual breeding and showing of his horses was a constant cash drain. His law practice operated in the red as well. Add to that some unwise investments and an extremely high standard of living, and . . ." He paused, as if unwilling actually to voice the rest.

"You're saying there isn't any money left?" Abbie asked, hoping it wasn't true.

"I'm saying he was heavily in debt. His mortgage payments to the bank are past due. Property taxes are owed. There is virtually no source of income."

"You mean we're broke?" She doubted she understood him correctly.

"I'm sorry. But the assets will have to be sold to satisfy the claims against the estate."

"What has to be sold?" Abbie questioned, dreading the answer, yet needing to know precisely what he meant. "The horses? Some of the land? You just can't mean we'll have to sell River Bend."

"I'm afraid I do."

"No." Abbie couldn't believe it. She darted a stricken glance at her mother. Babs looked white. "Momma." She didn't know what to say to her.

"Is it that bad, Lane?" Babs watched him anxiously.

"Yes, Babs, it is." His expression was grim, regret evident in the way he avoided her gaze. "You know I'll help in any way I can."

"I know," Babs said dejectedly.

But Abbie still couldn't believe it was true. Things couldn't be that bad. She stared blindly at the papers Lane took from his brief-case, physical proof of his claim, evidence in black and white of monies owed, complete with names, dates, and figures. Her mind reeled with the words that sprinkled his conversation: mortgages, overdue loans, past-due bills, property taxes, delinquent payments.

All the talk of liabilities and indebtedness was followed by a dis-cussion of terms such as "appraisal of assets," "inventory of stock and equipment," and "estate auction." But once Abbie waded through the business and financial language, she saw that Lane was saying they had to sell the only home she'd ever known, the beautiful Ara-bian horses she loved, the little corner of the world she lived in. Everything that was familiar to her, everything she'd ever loved, had to go under the auctioneer's hammer. River Bend was to be sold, the home that had been in her family for generations. This was her life he was talking about so coolly and unemotionally. Didn't he see that? She listened to him in frozen shock, rooted in her chair, unable to think, with the constant whirl of questions spinning in her head.

What was going to happen to them? What about Ben? Where were they going to live? What would they do? Where could she find a job? Doing what? Where would they get the money to eat? How could they move all this furniture when they didn't know where they were going? Why had this happened? How could her father have done this to them? How could he have done it to her mother?

But Lane never offered answers to any of her questions as he kept talking, now using phrases like "possible proceeds left after satisfy-ing the creditors." He was so calm and matter-of-fact about it all that none of it seemed real. This wasn't happening to them. It couldn't be.

"Don't worry about anything, Babs," Lane insisted. "I'll handle all the details. Someone will be out in a couple of days to take a complete inventory and estimate the fair value of everything. I promise you we'll get the best prices we can."

"Promise. How can you promise anything?" Abbie angrily pro-tested the way he kept trying to assure them everything was going to be all right. It wasn't all right. "How can you sit there and tell us not to worry? It isn't your home that's being sold! It isn't your world that's being turned upside down!"

"Abbie." Her mother was stunned by her outburst.

"I don't care, Momma. We're about to lose everything, and he's telling us not to be upset about it! Well, I am!" She couldn't take any more of his bland pap and bolted from the house.

Hot tears burned her eyes as she ran blindly to the stables. All she knew was that she had to get away and think — off by herself, away from everyone and everything. She grabbed a hackamore from the tackroom wall and ran to the paddock, hounded by the pounding questions in her head, driven to panic by the desperation and uncertainty. Somewhere there was an answer, a solution, a way out of all this — and she had to find it. They just couldn't lose everything. It was all a mistake, a dreadful mistake.

Her fingers were deft and sure even in her present turmoil as she hurriedly buckled the hackamore on the silver head of her filly and led her out of the paddock. She looped the reins over the Arabian's arched neck, grabbed a handful of mane, and swung herself onto the filly's back. With a prod of the heel and a pull on the reins, she turned her silver-gray horse toward the gate to the large back pasture.

Vaguely she was aware of Ben running toward her and shouting, "Abbie, what are you doing? Where are you going with that filly? Come back! Too young, she is!" Nothing he said registered. It was just more words, none of them having any effect on her overwhelming need to run as fast and as far as she could.

Somehow she opened the gate without even being aware of doing so. One minute it blocked her path and the next, the long pasture was before her. She urged her mount into a gallop, unconsciously whipping the reins across the marbled flank. The surprised filly leaped forward and stretched into a run.

Everything was a blur to Abbie: the startled horses scattering out of their way, the trees standing motionless, and the water running in the creek that fed into the Brazos River. She saw nothing beyond the pricked ears in front of her, felt nothing other than the wind whipping her long hair, and heard nothing beyond the pounding hoofbeats. Faster and faster they ran.

The filly stumbled, breaking stride and throwing Abbie forward. As she clutched at the sleek neck in an effort to regain her balance, Abbie felt the wetness, the slime of lather, and realized what she was doing. Pulling back on the reins, she managed to slow the winded and excited filly to a stop, then hurriedly slipped off her back, dragging the reins with her.

"Easy, girl. Easy, Breeze. It's all right now." Abbie tried to quiet the filly as she danced nervously away from her, dark nostrils flaring wide to show the red inside, gray sides heaving, black skin glistening wetly through the silver neck hairs.

Another set of hooves pounded the ground behind her. Abbie turned as Ben rode up on the old gelding they kept as a stable pony. He dismounted, stiff with anger, and strode over to her. "What you think you do, Abigail Lawson?" But his eyes were already focusing on the young Arabian horse. "You want to ruin this filly? Too young she is to be ridden so hard."

"I'm sorry, Ben." She watched anxiously as he ran a practiced hand down the filly's slim legs, all the while crooning softly in Polish. When he straightened, Abbie searched his stern expression. "Is Breeze all right?"

"Now you worry," he snorted in disgust. "Why you not worry before?"

"I'm sorry. I wasn't thinking."

"No, you think. You think only of yourself. Always when you get angry and hurt inside you make someone else suffer. To you it does not matter. It is only that you want to feel better. You do not deserve such a filly as this one."

"Maybe I don't." Her throat tightened. "But she's mine. She belongs to me." She wrapped her arms around the filly's quivering neck, unable to hold back the tears anymore. They streamed down her cheeks. "Breeze is all right, isn't she, Ben?" She turned to look at him.

"Yes." He relented slightly from his hard stand. "I felt nothing. It is lucky you weigh so little. The bones of a two-year-old have not finished their growing. This you know. We ride them little bits. We do not racing around the pasture go."

"I know."

"You will walk her to the barns. You will not ride her. And you will rub down her good."

He was lecturing her as if she were still fourteen years old and didn't know any better — as if she didn't know how to take care of a horse. But the flare of resentment quickly died as Abbie was forced to admit that her actions hadn't shown she did.

Dejectedly she gathered up the reins and turned to lead the filly back to the barns. Yet when she looked over the pasture at the horses she'd known since they were foals, the creek where she had played as a child, and the trees she'd climbed, she was overwhelmed by a terrible sense of loss. Soon she'd have to leave all this, she realized — leave everything she'd always known and taken for granted. To go where? To do what? It still didn't seem real.

"Why all the tears, tell me?" Ben asked.

"We have to sell out. Daddy owed too many people when he died.

There isn't any money to pay the debts. It all has to be sold to pay the creditors. Everything has to go — including us."

"Is this true?" He frowned.

Abbie nodded. "Lane told us when he came. We're bankrupt. I knew there were problems, but I never thought . . . I never dreamed it was this bad." She looked at Ben, the old man who'd rode out all the previous storms with her and given her strength. "What's going to happen to us? What's going to happen to you? You've been the uncle I never had. What am I going to do without you?"

"Child." He gathered her into his arms. Abbie wanted to cry some more, but now she couldn't. This time he couldn't reassure her. It wasn't going to be all right. "Your poor momma," he said. "How frightening for her."

"Momma." She hadn't even considered what effect the news would have on her mother. Her own shock had been too great. In a vague way, she'd recognized that this meant she was her mother's only means of support now. She not only had to look after herself, but her mother, too. It wasn't fair, but whoever said life was fair? "River Bend, the horses, they're all to be sold. All except River Breeze. She belongs to me." She pulled away from Ben and turned to the filly.

"She will be a good mare on which to build a new broodmare herd."

"Don't, Ben." Abbie nearly choked on the lump in her throat. "This is no time for foolish dreams. Right now I've got to worry about finding a roof for our heads and food for our table. And Momma. I've got to worry about Momma, too."

Babs pressed her fingertips against the throbbing in her temple, then lowered her hand and pushed herself out of the chair. Instinctively she wanted to forget everything Lane had said, pretend the situation wasn't as bad as he had portrayed it. But she couldn't. Not this time. No one was going to make it all right for her — not Dean, not R.D. She had no one but Abbie.

As the front door opened, Babs turned toward the foyer, recognizing the familiar tread of Abbie's footsteps. But Abbie walked past the living room and started up the stairs.

"Abbie," Babs called after her and heard the hesitating footsteps and the sound of their return.

Then Abbie appeared in the archway, looking all windblown and tired, still wearing that troubled frown.

"I was worried about you. You were so upset when you left." She had seen her daughter angry before, but never so distraught. "I wanted to be sure you were all right."

"I guess I am." She shrugged vaguely. "I just had to get away by myself and sort things out." Her dark hair was all snarled and tangled, and Babs could see the tear streaks on her cheeks and the lost look in her eyes as Abbie wandered into the living room, looking around her as if she had to memorize every detail. She reminded Babs of a frightened little girl — her little girl. "I can't believe we have to sell River Bend. This is our home. If we sold the horses and all the land except for the little piece the house is on, why wouldn't that be enough?"

"Don't you remember, Lane explained about the large mortgage on the house?" Babs's heart went out to her daughter.

"There has to be a way we could assume it. This is our home." Behind all the anger, there was despair. Then Abbie sighed bitterly. "How could Daddy do this to us, Momma? I don't understand. Did he really hate us that much?"

Babs breathed in sharply. Never once in all these years had she suspected that Abbie felt she was unloved, too. How was it that she could have a daughter and know so little about her feelings? Babs wanted to reach out to her now and reassure her that it wasn't as bad as she thought, but she wasn't sure how.

"I believed Lane when he said that, had your father lived, he would have obtained the funds to pay all these debts. In his own way, he cared about us." She couldn't say "love." Any love Dean had felt for her died long ago. He had stayed out of duty, guilt, and probably pity. Babs had never wondered whether Dean actually loved Abbie. She'd simply assumed he did. If he hadn't, maybe she was to blame for that. He didn't love her, so maybe he couldn't love the child she had given him either. But it accomplished nothing to dwell on the past. Babs knew she must think of Abbie now.

"As for this house, you would have left it again someday, Abbie, when you found another man you loved and wanted to spend your life with. You would have married him and moved away . . . to a home of your own, just as you did with Christopher. It isn't as if you would have lived here all your life if this hadn't happened."

"But you would have. What about you, Momma? You love this house. The curtains, the wallpaper, the furnishings — you picked out everything. This is your home. How can you leave it?"

"I don't mind, really." She said it to reassure Abbie, but almost the instant the words were out of her mouth, Babs realized they were true. "After R.D. died, all I ever knew here was loneliness. I don't think I want to live with the memory of that around me all the time."

"Momma, you can't mean that."

"I do." She was equally surprised by the discovery. "It's a drafty old house, impossible to heat in the winter and impossible to cool in the summer. It's always damp and miserable. The plumbing is bad and the windows are always warping shut." There was so much wrong with the house it was a wonder she'd never noticed it before.

"But . . . where will we go? What will we do?"

"I don't know." She forced a smile and fell back on the phrase that had always been her talisman. "Everything will work out for the best. It always does."

"I hope so." But Abbie couldn't be as confident. She didn't have her mother's optimistic attitude. A snap of the fingers wasn't magically going to produce a job or a place to live. She'd have to go out and look for them . . . and, at the same time, keep the farm going, get the horses in sale condition, and prepare for the auction. Everything had to be in tiptop shape if they hoped to get good prices.

16

Silence assailed her when Rachel entered the steakhouse. Pausing, she glanced at the sea of white tablecloths and empty chairs in the dining area. A faint murmur of voices came from the adjacent lounge. Rachel glanced hesitantly at the doorway to the bar.

She knew she was early for her dinner date with Lane, but she hadn't been sure how long it would take her to find the restaurant. With Houston's lack of any zoning laws, she'd already discovered that restaurants, or any type of business, could be located in the middle of some small residential area.

Even though she hadn't noticed Lane's car parked outside, Rachel decided to check in the lounge to see if he was there. As she moved toward it, she nearly walked right into a man coming out. His hands came up to catch hold of her arms and stop her.

"Sorry, miss. I'm afraid I wasn't looking where I was going."

"No, it was my fault," she insisted, her pulse racing at the near collision.

Embarrassed, she stepped back, freeing herself from his hands and darting a quick look at the man dressed in black denim jeans and a loose-fitting white shirt open at the throat and gathered at the shoulder seams. A low-crowned cowboy hat sat on the back of his curly brown hair, hair the rusty color of cinnamon. Young and brashly good-looking, he stepped aside with a little flourish, his glance skimming the jade-green jersey wrap dress she wore. Self-consciously

Rachel walked by him into the nearly darkened lounge, avoiding contact with the interested gleam in his hazel eyes.

Two men stood at the bar and one sat at a back table. All three looked up when Rachel entered the room. None of them was Lane. Feeling their speculative stares, Rachel abandoned any thought of waiting in the lounge until Lane arrived. Never particularly adept at turning aside unwelcome advances, she hurriedly retreated to the foyer.

The man in the cowboy hat walked out of one of the swinging doors that led to the restaurant's kitchen. Again Rachel felt his interest centering on her when he noticed her standing at the entrance to the dining room. Guessing that he must work there, she gathered her courage as he approached.

"Excuse me, but . . . would it be all right if I sat down at one of the tables?"

All in one sweeping glance, he took in her, the empty restaurant, and the entrance to the lounge. "The restaurant part won't open for another ten minutes yet. I don't think the boss would mind if you sat down."

"Thank you." She smiled politely, not quite meeting his eyes as she started to walk past him.

"Could I bring you anything to drink? A cold beer? A glass of wine?" he asked.

Rachel hesitated, but since he'd offered, she decided it couldn't be an imposition. "A glass of white wine, please."

"Coming right up." He sauntered off toward the lounge.

She watched him a moment, the way he was dressed making her wonder if he was the bartender. She hadn't noticed one behind the bar — not that she was interested in what he did for a living. It meant nothing to her one way or the other. She entered the dining room and chose an empty table by the wall.

She had barely sat when the man in the cowboy hat reappeared. She glanced at the wineglass in his hand and unfastened the clasp on her shoulder purse to search out her wallet, using it as a distraction to avoid his gaze. "How much do I owe you?"

"It's on the house."

"I can't let you do that."

"It's the boss's way of apologizing for the fact that he couldn't seat you right away. He likes to keep his customers happy." He offered her the glass, holding it by the stem. There wasn't any way she could take it from him without touching his hand. She reached for the glass, her fingers barely brushing his, but even that brief contact made her feel awkward and ill at ease.

"Thank him for me, please. But this wasn't really necessary. I'm the one who came early, before the restaurant opened." She clasped the wineglass tightly in both hands and stared at the pale, nearly colorless liquid.

"I think he wanted to make sure you stayed." He continued to stand there, watching while she sipped nervously at the wine, anxious for him to leave. "My name's Ross Tibbs, by the way."

"How do you do, Mr. Tibbs."

"No, that isn't the way it's supposed to work. You see, I tell you my name, then you tell me yours. Let's try it again." He smiled, and two very attractive dimples appeared in his smooth cheeks. "My name's Ross Tibbs."

"Rachel. Rachel Farr," she responded, not knowing what else to do.

"I thought to myself, what big blue eyes you have."

"That's very flattering of you, Mr. Tibbs." But his compliment made her feel all the more uncomfortable.

"Ross," he insisted. "I'll bet your nickname is Blue Eyes."

"No. Just plain Rachel."

"You're not plain by a long shot. I could write a song about you. I'm a songwriter and singer. I play here on the weekends, give the place a little atmosphere and class. Of course, that'll only be 'til the end of July. After that, my agent's booking me into Gilley's. See, there's a good chance Mickey Gilley's going to record one of my songs on his next album." He said it all with a kind of pride and modesty that didn't make it sound like he was bragging.

Now that she knew he was a performer, she understood why he could talk to her with such ease, and say exactly what he was thinking. She envied that lack of reserve with strangers. At the same time, she wished Lane would come. She felt so much safer with him.

"That's wonderful." She was glad for him, even though she knew her voice lacked sincerity.

"I don't start singing until around eight o'clock, but I always come early to grab a bite to eat and give my food a chance to digest before I have to perform. Why don't you join me? I'd like the company, and there's no need for you to eat alone either. It makes for a long meal."

"Thanks, but I'm waiting for someone. He should be here anytime."

"That's just my luck." Ross Tibbs smiled ruefully. "The pretty ones are always spoken for."

"You're very kind." She wished he'd stop saying things like that.

"I'm not kind. Envious is more like it." His admiring look flustered her even more. "And, listen, if the guy is stupid enough not to show, the invitation stands. Okay?"

"He'll be here," Rachel asserted with more conviction than she felt.

There was always the possibility that Lane might not be able to make it. As busy as he was, a hundred other things might have come up that were more important than having dinner with her. He might be tied up at the farm, unable to get away. That had happened to her before with Dean — too many times to count. He had constantly made plans to see her, then broken them at the last minute. She wished she hadn't arranged to meet Lane here, at a public restaurant. It would be so embarrassing if he called and canceled.

Just as she was getting anxious that he wouldn't come, Rachel saw Lane enter the restaurant. "Here he is now," she said to Ross Tibbs, as Lane approached her table. "Hello." She watched his eyes light up with that special look that made her feel as if she was the most important person in the world to him, a look reserved for her alone. It gave her confidence and assurance. She could say or do anything and he'd still feel the same. "I was afraid you might not make it."

"Nothing would have kept me from you." He kissed her lightly on the cheek, the heady fragrance of his expensive cologne washing over her. "If necessary, I would have moved heaven and Texas to get here."

"And I'll bet you could." She laughed, proud that it meant so much to him to be with her. After all, he was Lane Canfield.

"I hope I didn't keep you waiting long." His attention strayed from her, and she saw his gaze narrow ever so slightly on Ross Tibbs.

"No. I was early," she said, and unwilling to have Lane think she might have something to hide, she added, "Lane, I'd like you to meet Ross Tibbs. He's the singer here. He was kind enough to keep me company while I was waiting for you to come. Mr. Tibbs, this is Lane Canfield."

"Mr. Tibbs, I'm in your debt." Lane held out his hand.

Ross took it and stared at him. "Lane Canfield. *The* Lane Canfield?"

"The same," Lane admitted with neither apology nor pride, just a mere statement of fact.

Ross released a low whistle under his breath and shook his head, obviously impressed. "It is an honor to meet you, sir. Everybody in Texas knows who you are."

"I doubt that everyone does." Lane smiled politely, then glanced at Rachel. "I see you already have a drink. I could certainly use one myself."

Rachel noticed the look of curious speculation on Ross Tibbs's face, as if he was trying to guess what her relationship to Lane was. For the first time she was aware of their age difference — a young woman with an older man. She hated the idea that people might think it was something sordid and cheap when it was nothing of the sort. Lane Canfield was a wonderful man and he meant a great deal to her. His age had no bearing on that. Why did people have to judge others and turn something special into something dirty? she wondered as Ross Tibbs moved away from the table, retreating toward the lounge. All her life they'd done that to her. It wasn't fair.

"He's a good-looking young man," Lane remarked. "You probably should be having dinner with him instead of me."

"Don't say that, please." It hurt, and she blinked at the tears that so quickly stung her eyes.

"Rachel." He sounded surprised and bewildered as he reached over and covered the hand she rested on the table. "I was only joking."

"You weren't, not really." She knew better. "You feel self-conscious about being seen with me in public. I'm sure you're concerned that people will think you're foolish."

"I don't give a damn what people think. I never have, Rachel, or I would never have built the companies I have," he insisted sternly. "Only one person's opinion is important to me and that's yours. I know you deserve someone young, with his whole life still ahead of him — not someone like me, who's used up most of his. My feeble attempt at a joke was my way of acknowledging how lucky I am that you are with me and . . . it was also my way of saying that I would understand if you ever decided to choose him, or someone like him, instead of me."

"I won't. I'm sure of that." She saw the way he smiled at her, almost patronizingly. "I suppose you think that's amusing."

"No. I was just remembering when I was your age, I was that sure about things, too. Now I'm older, and I know better. You can't be sure of anything, especially what the future holds."

She longed to deny that and swear that he would always be special to her, but she was afraid such a declaration would sound childish and silly. "I know it's true, but I wish you wouldn't say that."

"Now is enough, Rachel," he said gently. "When you think about it, all anyone has is now. The past and the future don't really matter. Let's enjoy tonight and worry about tomorrow when it comes."

"*If* it comes."

"If it comes," Lane conceded, then released her hand as a waitress approached their table. Rachel missed the warm pressure of his fingers. As he ordered a drink, she wondered if she would ever be able to explain to him the void he filled in her life. "So tell me, did anything new and exciting happen today?"

"Yes. Or, at least, I think it's exciting. As of this morning, Simoon and Ahmar are on their way here from California. I've made arrangements to board them temporarily at a private stable until I get a place of my own. It's going to be so good having them here. I've missed them," she stated simply.

"When will they arrive here?"

"In three or four days. The driver's going to take it in easy stages so the long haul won't be too much of a strain on them."

"You've talked so much about them, I'm looking forward to finally seeing them."

"I want you to meet them. But . . . I know how busy you are, and this isn't really very important in comparison." She hated the idea that he might have suggested it just to humor her.

"It's important to you. That makes it important to me." Lane leaned forward and laid his arm on the table, extending his hand to her. Rachel slid her hand into his palm and his fingers closed around it, the pressure warm and reassuring. The waitress returned with his drink, but this time Lane didn't let go of her hand. When the woman set the drink before him, he thanked her absently and dismissed her with an indifferent nod. "As I was saying before we were interrupted, I'm interested in everything about you, Rachel."

"I know you say that."

"It's true." He understood her hesitation. He'd had trouble coming to terms with it himself. In the beginning, he'd tried to convince himself that his interest was motivated by a sense of responsibility and compassion. But it was much more complicated than that. Other women had wanted him, but Rachel actually *needed* him: his knowledge, his guidance, and his affection. The butterfly was slowly emerging from her cocoon, and Lane knew he was responsible for her transformation. Watching it, he felt renewed himself — strong and vital again, losing his jaded outlook. Out of all the women he'd known, she was the first to arouse the man in him, both emotionally and sexually. "How many times do I have to tell you that before you believe me?"

Warmth flowed from his hand. It seemed to fill her up until she thought she would burst with happiness. Not a wild kind: the feeling was more contented, like sitting in front of a fire on a cold night, close enough to feel all toasty and warm inside, but not so close that the heat burned.

"Maybe a thousand," Rachel teased.

His eyebrows shot up, amusement deepening the corners of his mouth. "I believe you're flirting with me."

She laughed shyly. "I guess I was."

"Don't stop. I like it."

"Now you're flirting with me."

"I know. I like that, too." He picked up his glass. "Shall we drink to our mutual flirtation?" Lifting her wineglass, she touched it to his, then sipped at the dry Chablis, her eyes meeting his over the rim. There was something warm and intimate about the moment that gave her confidence.

"I wish we were alone." She wanted to be held and kissed — loved.

Lane took a deep breath, then seemed to have trouble releasing it as an answering darkness entered his eyes. "I think we'd better change the subject," he murmured as he reluctantly released her hand and leaned back in the chair, putting more table between them. "What else did you do today?"

She was tempted to test the full extent of her ability to disturb him, but she was afraid she might find out it wasn't that great. "I spent the biggest share of today riding around looking at various properties for sale with that realtor you recommended. She must have shown me ten different parcels outside of Houston. Unfortunately none of them was what I had in mind."

"What are you looking for?"

Another River Bend, but Rachel couldn't bring herself to admit that. Ever since she'd gone there that afternoon, the sight of it had lived with her. Nothing she'd seen since had come even close to being comparable.

"I'd like to find about a hundred acres with some buildings already on it, not farther than an hour out of Houston. It sounds easy, but something has been wrong with every piece of land I've looked at: either the price is more than I want to pay, or it's too far out, or it's too heavily wooded and the cost of clearing it and turning it into pasturage is too high. I don't know." She sighed, all her insecurities and feelings of inadequacy flooding back. "Maybe the whole idea is impractical. After all, who am I? A twenty-seven-year-old woman with two million dollars and no practical experience in breeding Arabians. I not only have to buy land and horses, but I need to hire a qualified manager, trainers, and grooms as well. I'm just dreaming if I think I can do it."

"Dreams are never practical, and they shouldn't be. But they do come true. Hold on to it, Rachel. You can make it happen if you try, but only if you try."

"Do you really believe I can do it?" No one, not even Dean, had ever encouraged her so totally. As her glance swept over his thick, silvered hair and strong face, Rachel finally identified the thing that attracted her so. The look of eagles — that was the quality a person sought in a stallion, a rare blend of nobility, pride, and strength. And Lane had it.

"Yes."

"Deep down, I think I can, too. I know it won't happen overnight. It takes time to establish a breeding program and prove that it works. A lot of it is trial and error. Dean taught me that. The knowledge I gained from him is going to be very useful. Look what he accomplished on a hundred acres, how successful he was. There's no reason I can't do the same." Rachel saw the frown that flickered across Lane's face, erasing the smile of interest and encouragement that had been there seconds ago. "What's the matter? Don't you agree with that?"

"I do." The smile came smoothly back, yet Lane seemed slightly distant.

But she wasn't reassured. She knew she must have said something wrong. Why else would he frown? But what could she have said? She tried to recall exactly what she'd been talking about when Lane reacted. It was something about Dean and River Bend. River Bend . . . Lane had been there today. Was that it? Had she unconsciously reminded him of something that had happened there? Had she reminded him of Abbie?

Resentment rose in her throat, but she forced it down. She'd had to accept that all her life. Why should she think it would be any different now?

Somehow she managed to get through the meal without letting on how hurt she felt — hiding it just as she'd done so many times in the past with Dean. As she left the steakhouse with Lane, she caught a glimpse of Ross Tibbs in the lounge, singing and accompanying himself on the guitar. She remembered how much she had been looking forward to spending the evening with Lane — and realized how anxious she was now for it to end.

Lane followed her back to her hotel in the Galleria. When he suggested having coffee in her hotel suite, Rachel wanted to plead tiredness, but realizing how kind he'd been to her, she felt too guilty to refuse.

Lane was standing at the window of the suite's luxurious living room, looking at the light-studded nightscape of Houston, when room service arrived with the coffee. Rachel poured each of them a cup and carried them over to the window. As usual, their conversation was centered on her plans for an Arabian horse farm. Rachel couldn't help wondering if that was the only subject Lane could think of to talk to her about.

"Have you ever considered taking on a partner?"

"What do you mean?" She frowned.

"I mean, why don't you and I become partners in this farm of yours?"

"What?" Rachel couldn't believe she'd heard him correctly. "Why would you want to become involved in it?" If it was only to help her, she knew she couldn't let him.

"Everyone knows that breeding operations are excellent tax shelters if managed properly. In my position, I can certainly use the write-offs. So you see, it's to my advantage to become involved. It would be a joint venture, with you overseeing the operation and me contributing part of the capital."

"You're serious."

"I am very serious."

"Are you sure this is what you want to do?" Rachel clutched at his hand, hardly daring to believe him.

"Only if you want me for a partner."

"There isn't anyone else I'd rather have than you, Lane." Inside, she was exploding with happiness. She couldn't imagine anything more wonderful than always having Lane there to turn to whenever she had a question or a problem. All her life she'd wanted to share this dream with someone. Doing things alone was no fun. She'd done them that way all her life and she knew. She wanted to plan with someone, work with someone, and share success with someone. "You can't know how happy you've made me, Lane."

"I'm glad. I want you to be happy."

"Earlier tonight, I had the feeling you had something on your mind." She'd been so certain it was Abbie, but now . . . "This was it, wasn't it?"

"I . . . have been giving the idea considerable thought lately."

But Rachel caught the slight hesitation. All her life she'd been sensitive to such things, quick to pick up the smallest nuance of phrasing — the careful wording that made a statement neither the truth nor a lie.

"I thought I might have said something wrong or maybe . . . there were problems at River Bend." Watching him closely as she voiced her suspicions, Rachel saw the faint break in his expression.

"Why should you think that?"

She wasn't fooled by his smooth smile. "It was River Bend. Something happened today that you don't want me to know." He was keeping things from her, shielding her the way Dean had, and she hated that. "What is it?"

"Yes, there are some problems there, but I'd rather not talk about them right now. After all, we have plans to make, critical things to decide . . . such as what are we going to name our farm?"

Rachel tried to go along with him. "South Wind." She'd picked out the name years ago. "According to legend, the Prophet Mohammed claimed that Allah summoned the south wind to him and the angel Gabriel grabbed a handful of it. From that, God created the Arabian horse." But she couldn't muster her usual enthusiasm for the subject.

"I like it."

"It's no good, Lane," she said. "If you don't tell me what happened, I'll just wonder about it. Did they say something about me?"

"No, Rachel, it isn't that at all. I didn't want to talk about it now because this is a big moment for you. I want you to enjoy it."

"So do I." But there had never been a single occasion in her life that hadn't been shadowed by Dean's other family. And it seemed that nothing had changed. "But I have to know."

"All right." He sounded grim. "It seems your father was heavily in debt when he died. He was behind in his payments. Everything is heavily mortgaged. It will all have to be sold to pay his creditors."

"But" — Rachel stared at him in disbelief — "how could that be? It's impossible. He couldn't have been broke . . . not with all the money he left me."

"That money was tied up in a trust for you. He couldn't touch it."

"Abbie, her mother — what about them?"

"I'm confident that after the assets are sold off and the accounts settled, there will be enough money left to enable them to find a new home and carry them for a while."

"River Bend is to be sold." She couldn't imagine such a thing happening. "Dean loved that place." Even more than he'd loved her mother, refusing to leave it for her. "It's been in his family for generations. It doesn't seem right that someone who isn't a Lawson should have it." The instant the words were out of her mouth, the thought flashed in her mind. "I'm a Lawson — by blood." She turned to him eagerly. "Lane, let's buy it."

"What?" An eyebrow shot up in surprise.

"Don't you see? It's perfect. Not only can we keep it from falling into a stranger's hands — someone who wouldn't love it and care for it the way Dean did — but we'd also have all the facilities standing there ready for use. There wouldn't be the expense of building. Plus River Bend already is a recognized name in the Arabian horse world. Time won't be lost establishing a reputation for ourselves. It's so obvious I'm surprised it didn't occur to you."

"Obvious, perhaps, but is it wise? That's something we need to think about."

"What is there to think about?" Rachel argued, not understanding why he didn't agree with her. "It's logical, practical, and sound. Even I can see that." Then she guessed his reason for hesitating and stiffened. "You're worried about how they'll react to me buying River Bend, aren't you?"

Lane set his coffee cup aside and took her gently by the shoulders. "All I'm saying is that we should think it through carefully. River Bend was Dean's home. It's natural that you would feel a special attachment to it. And I love you for wanting it to stay in the family. But I don't want you to make an impulsive decision that you may later regret. Right now, your reaction is mainly an emotional one. It isn't imperative that you make up your mind tonight. River Bend won't be sold for several more weeks yet. You have time and I want you to take it. Will you do that for me?"

"Yes," she agreed reluctantly, and turned away from him to stare out the window. "But I know I'm not going to change my mind. I don't care what they think. Maybe that sounds heartless, but . . .

River Bend is going to be sold anyway. They're going to lose it, so what possible difference could it make to them who buys it? At least if I do, it will still be in the family. They should be grateful for that."

"Maybe. But let's sleep on the idea for a few days and talk about it then."

"All right." She breathed in deeply and nodded.

"I meant what I said a few minutes ago."

"I know. And I will think about it."

"I wasn't referring to that." Lane smiled faintly, his gaze running over her profile in a caress.

"Then what?" With so many other thoughts crowding her mind, Rachel didn't try to guess.

"I meant it when I said I love you."

He said it so softly, so gently, that for a full minute, its meaning didn't register. When it did, Rachel was stunned. "Lane," she whispered and turned to touch his face in wonder that a man like him could love her.

As he kissed her long and deep, she wrapped her arms around him and slid her fingers into his thick hair. That he should love her was such an amazing thing that she was afraid to believe it.

"Lane, are you sure?" She ached inside that it might be so.

"You are the woman I love," he insisted and smoothed the hair away from her face, then kissed her brow, nose, and cheek with feather-light touches of his lips.

"But I'm illeg —" His lips silenced the rest.

"You're a love child," he murmured against them.

Her breath caught in her throat. She drew back to stare at him. "My mother always said that."

"She was right. You were born out of love and intended for love. And I'm going to show you that."

The proof was offered by his lips and hands, caressing and arousing a desire in her that Rachel hadn't known she could feel. When Lane's hand stroked her breast, it was as if in adoration of her shape, and Rachel reveled in the feeling.

"I love you, too, Lane." Delicious shivers danced over her skin as he nibbled at her neck and ear.

"Do you?" He drew back, bringing her face into focus. "I want to believe that, but I'm older than you — much older. Are you sure you don't see me as a father figure?"

"Why do you have to say things like that?" she protested, hurt and angry that he should doubt her. "I look up to you, yes. But is it wrong for a woman to look up to the man she loves?"

"No, it's not wrong, if that's what it is."

"Why are you trying to put doubts in my mind?" She hated the way he was making her question her feelings. For her, it was enough that she felt them. Emotions weren't meant to be analyzed.

"Have you ever been in love before?"

"No." Twice she'd been close, but love had always eluded her — always.

"Then how can you be sure you know how it feels?" he reasoned. "I'm going to be out of town for a couple days. When I get back, we'll see how you feel then. If it is love, examining it won't hurt it . . . or change it." Shifting his hold on her, he hooked an arm around her shoulders and turned her away from the window. "Walk me to the door before I decide to take advantage of your moment of weakness."

Rachel almost wished he would. When he kissed her good night, she couldn't recapture her earlier pleasure in his touch. He'd given her too much to think about: her feelings for him and River Bend.

At nine-thirty, MacCrea saw the flash of headlights through the trailer windows. On the phone earlier, Abbie had told him she'd be there by nine. He started for the door, then turned abruptly and walked into the kitchen instead, irritated by how much he wanted to see her and hold her. After she'd made him wait this long, he'd be damned if he was going to run out there to her like some lovesick swain. He pulled a bottle of beer out of the refrigerator and waited for the trailer door to open.

When she walked in, everything else went out of his mind. She was slim and petite, but filled out in all the right places, as the low neckline of her peasant blouse revealed. Her dark hair lay thickly about her shoulders, all loose and soft, the way he liked it.

"Hello." That was all she said.

"I was beginning to wonder where you were." As he moved toward her, MacCrea noticed the tiredness in her eyes and the faintly troubled look in her expression despite the smile she gave him.

"It took longer than I thought. We have another sick foal. Ben thinks it might be pneumonia."

She slid her arms around his middle and tipped back her head for his kiss. MacCrea was happy to oblige. She responded, but not with the fervor and greedy passion he'd come to expect. She seemed unnaturally subdued. Something was on her mind and it wasn't him. A little annoyed, he released her and walked over to the kitchen counter.

"How about a cold beer?" He popped the top off his bottle with an opener.

"No. The last thing my head needs right now is alcohol." She sounded discouraged or angry, MacCrea wasn't sure which — maybe both. She turned toward the table. "What's this? Flowers?" She touched the spray of wildflowers in the amber glass as if assuring herself that they were real.

"I decided the place needed a man's touch." He moved over to stand next to her, breathing in the shampoo scent of her hair.

"They're beautiful." But her smile was barely more than a movement of the mouth.

"Careful. You might get carried away by so much excitement," MacCrea taunted.

"I'm sorry." She sighed, her glance sliding off him. "I guess I'm tired tonight."

That wasn't tiredness he saw; it was tension. Abbie was wound up tighter than a spring. Talking wasn't what he'd had in mind when she arrived, but until she relaxed a little, something told him she'd just go through the motions of making love. MacCrea didn't want that and decided, if they had to talk, it might as well be about a subject that interested him.

"You said Canfield came today. Did everything go all right?" He started to raise the bottle to his mouth, but he stopped in midmotion as Abbie turned abruptly away from him, suddenly agitated and angry.

"He showed up all right." Her voice vibrated with the effort of holding her feelings in check. Then just as abruptly as she'd turned away, she turned back and headed for the refrigerator. "I think I will have that beer you offered."

Curious, MacCrea watched her. While she took a cold bottle of beer out of the refrigerator, he opened the overhead cabinet and took down a glass. He watched as she snapped the cap off with the opener. The sharp popping sound seemed to release some of the built-up pressure inside her as well.

"What happened?" MacCrea pushed the glass across the counter toward her.

Abbie hesitated, then poured the cold beer into the glass, the foam rising thickly. "It's hardly a secret, I guess. In a few days, the whole damned state of Texas is going to know about it. You see, Mac-Crea," — she paused, the bitterness in her voice thicker than the foam on her beer — "we're broke. That's what Lane had to tell us today."

"What do you mean by broke?" He frowned, aware that different people had different definitions of the word.

"Broke as in head-over-heels in debt. Broke as in everything has to be sold to pay off the debts. Broke as in penniless — homeless." She gripped the bottle of beer tightly, her hand trembling with the vehemence and anger that had come from her.

"I think I get the picture," MacCrea said quietly, feeling a little stunned by the news.

"I doubt it," she retorted caustically. "Everything has to be sold: the house, the farm, the land, the horses, everything. I had a feeling we were going to have problems with Daddy's estate, but I thought they were going to come from Rachel. I thought she'd contest the will or make some sort of trouble. But I never expected this. Not once."

"It's rough." He knew better than anyone that right now words were meaningless. Abbie wasn't listening.

"I'll bet she knew all along. Lane must have told her. No wonder she didn't try to get a share of the estate. She already knew there wasn't anything to get." She picked up the glass of beer and drank down a quick swallow, then stared at the glass. "You know why there isn't any money, don't you? It's because he spent so much on her and that mistress of his. He probably showered her with expensive presents — like that filly he gave her."

"She was his daughter."

"So am I!" Abbie exploded. "But she always got everything! Did you know he was killed while he was on his way back from seeing her?"

"No."

"Not me. It was never me." She looked close to breaking, her voice choking up. "I had nothing of him when he was alive. Maybe it's fitting that I have nothing of his now that he's dead." She lifted her shoulders in a vague shrug, showing her helplessness. "I just don't know what to do."

It wasn't like her. But MacCrea could appreciate her dilemma. She'd never faced anything like this before. Other people's problems rarely had any effect on him, but this time was different. He couldn't be impervious to her situation. He took the glass from her hand and gathered her into his arms, struggling inwardly with the protective instinct she'd aroused. She leaned against him and rested her head on his chest, absently rubbing her cheek against him.

"There's so much to do I don't know where to start," she said miserably. "Somewhere I've got to find a job and a place to live, but doing what and where?"

"The last part's easy. You can move in with me." The idea of having her here all the time appealed to him.

"What about Momma and Ben? I don't think this trailer could accommodate four people. And there's Jackson. He was going to retire as soon as he received the bequest Daddy left him."

"I wasn't thinking about them."

"But I have to. At his age, Ben isn't going to find another job. And Momma has never worked a day in her life." Her arms tightened around him as she pressed herself closer. "Hold me, MacCrea. Just hold me."

That was all she asked. He cradled her to his body and swayed gently, rocking her ever so slightly. MacCrea didn't say anything. There was nothing he could say.

17

*A*s Abbie skimmed the list of horses that had been compiled from the records by Lane Canfield's assistant, the name of her filly River Breeze stood out sharply among the Arabic names her father had given the rest. She stared at it first in surprise, then puzzlement. Obviously it was a mistake — one that needed to be corrected immediately.

With the list in hand, she left Ben's office in the stable annex to look for Lane or his assistant, Chet Forbes. Both were somewhere on the premises along with three other members of his staff, taking a complete inventory of everything on the place. The current plan called for two separate estate auctions to take place, the first to be a dispersal sale of all the horses, their tack, and related equipment, and the second, the sale of River Bend itself and its individual items.

Hearing voices coming from the tack room, Abbie crossed to its doorway and paused to glance inside. A portly man in shirt sleeves lifted four show halters off their wall hook, Ben identified them, and another man marked them down on his clipboard sheet — a tedious, time-consuming project.

"Four show halters," the man repeated as he wrote it down.

"One of those is silver," Ben corrected. "It is most expensive."

As the heavy-set man examined the halters again, Abbie explained, "It's tarnished. We'll have to polish it before the auction." She made a mental note of yet another thing that had to be done.

The list was getting long. "Have you see Lane or Chet Forbes?"

"Yeah, they're in the other office." A chubby hand motioned in the direction of her father's private office.

"Thanks," Abbie said, already walking away, striding quickly to the office door. She knocked sharply twice, then reached for the doorknob as a muffled voice invited her inside. Lane stood behind the desk going over some papers, with the man in wire-rimmed glasses, Chet Forbes, seated in the chair. Both looked up when she walked in. "Excuse me, but I was just going over the list of horses you gave me. You have River Breeze included. That's the filly *I* own. Daddy gave her to me last year."

"I wonder how that happened." The pale young man took the list from her and glanced at it briefly, then began going through the folders on the desktop. "I used the owner registration papers and the foaling records to compile the list."

"You probably saw my registration papers on Breeze in with the others, caught the name Lawson, and added it to the list without looking at it any closer."

"That's possible." Chet Forbes opened the folder and deftly leafed through the clipped papers, scanning the names as he went. "Here it is. River Breeze." After carefully examining both the front and back of the certificate, he looked up triumphantly. "I was right. The horse is registered to Dean Lawson and nothing has been filled out transferring the ownership to any other party."

"That can't be." Abbie took the folder from him and looked at the back of the certificate, but her name didn't appear on the line reserved for the buyer of the horse. "He gave River Breeze to me."

"Did he say he was signing the registration over to you?" Lane walked around the desk to look at it.

"That was last year. I don't remember exactly what he said. But you don't give somebody something and keep the title in your own name," Abbie insisted.

"Did you ever ask about the owner registration?"

"No. I assumed he sent it in. I never gave it another thought. I mean, it would have come here and . . . Daddy would have put it away for me. If I had wondered about it at all, that's what I would probably have thought happened." She looked at Lane, suddenly made wary by his questions. "She is mine."

"I don't know what to say, Abbie," Lane said, stalling. "You don't appear to have anything in writing to back up your claim to the horse — nothing with Dean's signature. The registration papers are still in his name. Legally, it would appear that the horse belongs to his estate."

"No." She choked on the angry denial.

"I'm sure Dean got busy and overlooked it. I'll see what I can do, if anything," Lane promised. "But you must understand this horse is a valuable animal — a valuable asset, if you will, not that much different from a building. You wouldn't expect a claim to a building to be regarded as valid if you had no title or documentation to back it up. I'm afraid the law will look at this in the same way."

"And Rachel: I suppose Daddy signed over the papers on the filly he gave her." Abbie couldn't keep the bitterness out of her voice.

"I couldn't say." Lane took the folder from her and handed it back to Chet.

"We matched up all the horses on the farm to the registration papers in the file. There were two baby horses —" Chet began.

"Foals." Abbie snapped out the correct term.

"Yes . . . two foals that needed some forms filled out for registration, but other than that, we found no discrepancies between the papers we had and the horses on the place," he finished.

"I believe you," she replied tightly, her voice shaking with the anger and resentment boiling inside her. "But she still belongs to me."

Lane met her challenging stare. "I'll do everything I can to make sure you keep your horse, Abbie."

"Please do." As she started toward the door, Lane accompanied her.

"Chet and I were just talking about hiring some extra help to get the horses ready for the sale."

"We'll need it," Abbie stated, walking out of the office and heading for the outer door to the breezeway. "Ben and I can't get all the horses trimmed and groomed by ourselves. As it is, we won't be able to get them in top show condition in a little over a month."

"I'll see that you have the help you need," Lane promised as they emerged from the annex.

"Thanks." But Abbie was distracted by the sight of MacCrea's black pickup parked next to Lane's car. She hadn't expected to see him until later that night, their late-evening rendezvous becoming almost routine. When she saw him coming from the house, she quickened her step, breaking into a welcoming smile. "MacCrea, what are you doing here? You didn't say anything about stopping by today."

"I thought I'd surprise you." Pausing in front of her, he regarded her in that lazy way he had that made Abbie feel warm all over. "You did."

"Good." Possessively, MacCrea curved an arm around her shoulders and pulled her against his side with an apparent disregard for Lane's presence. Then he bent his head, as if to nuzzle her hair, and whispered, "I missed you." He straightened to smile crookedly at her, knowing she couldn't say the same without being overheard. Abbie made a face at him, secretly smiling, and MacCrea chuckled.

As Lane joined them, Abbie turned. "Lane, I'd like you to meet MacCrea Wilder. MacCrea, Lane Canfield."

MacCrea removed his arm from around her shoulders to shake hands with Lane. "It's a pleasure to meet you, Mr. Canfield."

"Mr. Wilder."

"I don't know if I've told you anything about MacCrea or not, Lane, but I meant to." Many times, Abbie realized, but each time she'd seen Lane, too many other things had cropped up. "He's a drilling contractor as well as a wildcatter. And he's come up with a new invention — some sort of a testing process. MacCrea can explain it better than I can."

"I doubt that Mr. Canfield is interested in hearing about it, Abbie," MacCrea inserted as he calmly sized up the older man. "It isn't exactly in his line."

"Daddy was going to put him in touch with some people he knew who could help MacCrea develop and market it. You know a lot of people in the oil business, Lane," Abbie reminded him. "Maybe you could arrange some meetings for him."

"I might be able to," he conceded. "It certainly never hurts to look at something. Maybe we could get together sometime and you can explain it all to me."

"Why don't I give you a call at your office the first of next week and set up a meeting?"

Abbie didn't hear Lane's response as the battered pickup owned by Dobie Hix came rattling into the yard. She frowned, wondering what he was doing there at this time of day. It was too early to feed the horses. But she was even more bewildered when she saw her mother sitting in the cab of the truck with Dobie.

"Excuse me." She turned away from Lane and MacCrea with only an absent glance in MacCrea's direction and headed for the pickup.

"Abbie, the most wonderful thing just happened." Her mother clambered out of the cab, all astir with excitement. "I've found a place for us to live."

"You did?" Abbie glanced sharply at Dobie Hix as he walked around the hood of the rusted truck. Hurriedly, he pulled off his hat. As the sunlight flashed on his hair, bringing out the red in its strawberry-blond color, Abbie wondered what he had to do with all this.

"Yes, and it's perfect," Babs Lawson declared. "Dobie just showed it to me. It's small. We'll have to get rid of some of our furniture, but we really don't need anything bigger. There's even a room for Ben."

"Where is this house?" Abbie didn't mean to sound skeptical, but she wasn't sure her mother understood all the things that had to be considered in selecting a place to live.

"It's over at my place," Dobie answered. "Some of my hired hands live on the farm with their families. I furnish them living quarters as part of their salaries. But this particular house is vacant now, and I thought if you wanted, you could live there. It ain't much — not like what you been used to, but —"

"Dobie, I don't know what to say." Abbie shrugged helplessly.

"I'll have to charge you rent for it. But it'll be fair. I need something to cover the costs of the utilities."

"If you didn't let us pay, we wouldn't even consider staying there." She wasn't about to accept charity from anyone, even a close neighbor.

"I know that, Abbie. But I think you'll like the house." Dobie gazed at her earnestly, anxious to convince her of the fact. "And I don't keep much livestock anymore, so the barn's practically empty. You can keep your horse there at no charge. It's just standing empty anyway."

"Do you see what I mean, Abbie? It's perfect for us," her mother declared happily.

"It sounds like it," Abbie was forced to agree. But she didn't understand why she didn't feel more relieved that a solution may have been found for the problem of where they would live. After all, it meant one less thing she had to do. She should have been happy that her mother had taken it upon herself to look into it. Instead she found herself wanting to find fault with the choice.

"If you want, I can run you over so you can look at it," Dobie offered.

"Maybe later. I'm busy now."

"Sure." Dobie glanced in the direction of Lane and MacCrea and reluctantly nodded. "Anytime you want to see it, you just come over."

"Thanks, Dobie. I will."

"Well." He smiled and played with his hat. "Guess I'd better get going."

"Dobie, thank you for taking me over to see the house." Babs reached out to shake his hand. "Don't worry, I know Abbie is going to like it as much as I do."

"I hope so." He pushed his hat onto his head and headed around the truck to the driver's side, saying over his shoulder, "See y'all later."

The truck's engine sputtered uncertainly, backfired, then chugged to life. Still struggling with the mixed feelings she had about the house, Abbie watched while he reversed away from the fence and aimed the truck down the farm lane.

"Wait until you see it, Abbie." Babs was still excited about the house and obviously proud that she had found it. "I know it's smaller than we're used to, but we don't need all the room we have now."

"I know. Maybe tomorrow morning we'll have time to go look at the house together." She started to turn away and rejoin MacCrea and Lane.

"This is certainly our day for company, isn't it? Who do you suppose that is?" Babs wondered.

As Abbie glanced down the long driveway to the road, Dobie's pickup took the shoulder of the narrow lane to let the other car pass. Abbie stopped abruptly, all her muscles and nerves growing tense.

"Probably somebody to look at the horses." Like last time, Abbie thought as she worked to keep her voice calm and evenly pitched. "Why don't you go up to the house and fix us some iced tea, Momma? And ice that cake you baked this morning. Lane would like that."

"That's a good idea."

With her mother successfully sidetracked, Abbie walked quickly toward the car slowing to a stop in the yard. She felt almost rigid with tension when Rachel Farr stepped out, a picture of freshness untouched by the hot afternoon sun. Resentment simmered near the surface as Abbie looked into the face that was so like her own.

"What are you doing here, Miss Farr? I thought you understood that you weren't welcome here." She blocked Rachel's path, realizing MacCrea and Lane were standing a few feet away only after Rachel darted a quick glance in their direction.

"I know, but I had to talk to you."

"My God, you're . . ." The barely whispered words came from behind Abbie. As she swung around, she caught the stricken look

Babs turned on her — a look of shock at the resemblance between the two.

"Momma, I told you to go to the house." She hated seeing her own mother look at her that way. She had tried to spare her this. Why hadn't she listened?

"I'm Rachel Farr, Mrs. Lawson."

Abbie turned on her. "Why don't you just leave? We don't want you here."

"If you'd let me explain —" Rachel began again.

"We aren't interested in anything you have to say."

"Rachel." Lane came up to her.

"No, Lane. I told you that I've thought this through very carefully the way you asked," Rachel told him quietly, her tone firm despite a nervous tremor in her voice.

Abbie stared as Lane took Rachel's hand and clasped it warmly. "All right," he said.

There was an intimacy in the exchange, a sense of closeness, that left Abbie shaken and confused. She had guessed Lane and Rachel had talked before. But she had always assumed their meetings had dealt with her father's will, just as Lane's meetings with her and Babs had. Yet that look, the way he held her hand and stood beside her — he was obviously more than a family friend. What made Rachel so special? Why did Lane like her better, too?

"Lane has explained to me the financial situation you are in . . . with all the debts," Rachel began hesitantly. "And I know the prospect of River Bend being sold at public auction can't be pleasant. Rather than have it all go up on the sale block, I'd like to buy it."

"With what? My father's money?" Bitterly Abbie recalled that Lane had told her that Dean had made separate provisions for Rachel.

"Most of the money will come from a trust fund he established for me, yes," Rachel admitted.

"Most of the money," which meant Rachel had received a sizable fortune, Abbie realized. River Bend had been appraised at well over two million dollars. And Rachel wanted to buy it. Even at his death, her father had made sure Rachel had money, even though he'd left them with nothing. Did she need any more proof than that, that her father hadn't loved her?

Abbie felt something snap inside, unleashing a torrent of hatred and anger. "I'd burn River Bend to the ground before I'd let you have it! Now get out of here! Go before I have you thrown off! Do you hear? Get out! Get out!" She couldn't think straight. She couldn't see. She wasn't even aware of the rising note of hysteria in her voice as she screamed at Rachel, watching her shrink against Lane for protection.

Suddenly MacCrea was between them, his hands digging into her arms with punishing force. "You've made your point, Abbie."

She trembled with the violence that raged inside her and choked her voice. "Just get her out of here."

But it was Lane who walked Rachel to her car and helped her inside. A diamond-bright trail of tears streaked Rachel's cheeks, but Abbie knew her own pain went deeper than tears. Glancing at her mother, she saw the drained and broken look on her face.

As the car pulled away and Lane started back to them, Babs turned weakly away. "I think I'll go to the house," she said.

"Yes, Momma," Abbie said tightly, then sagged a little herself when MacCrea released her arms. As Lane rejoined them, she eyed him suspiciously, now fully aware of where his loyalties were.

"I'm sorry you feel the way you do, Abbie," he said. "I know that Rachel was anxious to have River Bend stay in the family."

"She was anxious over that, was she? How very noble of her to be concerned about the family home. What about Momma? How do you think she feels knowing that Daddy left Rachel enough money to buy River Bend, but Momma didn't get a thing? Hasn't she gone through enough hell knowing that Daddy didn't love her? Did she have to be reminded that he had provided for his mistress's child, but not for his own wife and daughter?" Abbie raged bitterly.

"I know how you must feel —"

"Do you? I doubt it. Because now I feel the way Momma does. I can't stand this place. I can hardly wait until it's sold and everything on it."

Abbie walked away from them, aware that MacCrea hadn't said a word. But she didn't care what he thought — not right now. She hadn't realized it was possible to hate so much.

18

And sign here." Lane flipped to the last page of the partnership agreement and indicated the x-marked line that required Rachel's signature. Rachel signed her name in the blank and straightened from the massive walnut desk in his office. "That's the last one." He stacked the copies of the agreement together as she laid the gold pen on his desk. "Here's your copy," he said, handing the top one to her. "Happy?"

"To have you for a partner, of course." Rachel smiled and turned to look out at the city, knowing that only one thing could make her happier: owning River Bend.

"We'll have to have dinner together tonight and celebrate."

His voice sounded closer, and she realized that Lane had left his desk and joined her. Rachel smiled at the thought that his plushly upholstered desk chair was too expensive to squeak. She looked around his office, admiring its clean, contemporary look. Like the building, the spacious executive office was done mostly in glass and chrome, its corner setting giving it a wide view of downtown Houston. She liked the symmetry and style of the room, everything in proportion, including the huge desk.

"I'd like that." She turned to him, then paused. "You haven't said whether you've talked to Abbie since . . ." She let the sentence trail off unfinished, knowing she didn't need to remind him of the disastrous encounter with her the previous week.

"I called yesterday to let her know we were sending her the proofs on the sales catalogue so she can check it for errors. The names of some of those horses would twist any man's tongue and send him scrambling for a dictionary . . . Arabic, of course." When she failed to smile at his attempt at humor, Lane sighed. "You haven't changed your mind, have you? Even though you know how they're going to feel?"

"No. I still want us to buy it." When she closed her eyes, she could still see Abbie's face, the contempt and rage that had been on it. If anything, it only made her more determined to have it. "I suppose you think that's wrong of me."

"No. No, I don't." Lane seemed to consider his next words before he spoke. "As a matter of fact, after you left that day, Abbie informed me that she and her mother hated the farm. She said she couldn't wait for it to be sold."

"She really said that? How could she?" Rachel was at once astounded and angry by the statement she regarded as blatant disloyalty. "River Bend is Dean's legacy. His family has owned it for a hundred and fifty years. How could she want to see it sold to some stranger?"

"I don't know. But that's what she said."

"Well, I'm not going to let it happen. I can't." She glanced down at the newly signed document in her hand. "I know you think I'm being silly and sentimental. Maybe we should just tear up these partnership papers, because I know you don't approve of buying River Bend —"

"You're wrong." He folded his hand around her fingers, tightening her grasp on the document. "I see no reason why we shouldn't buy it, especially when you want it so much."

"Do you mean that?" She searched his face anxiously.

"How could I look into those blue eyes and say no?" he chided.

"Lane." She breathed his name in an exultant laugh, then kissed him, pressing her lips ardently against his, loving him more at that moment than she ever had. Through the thin silk fabric of her dress, she felt his hands traveling along her back and arching her against the shape of his body. She wanted to hold on to this moment, with its heated closeness and consuming happiness. The world was hers now. If there was one dark spot in it, it was knowing that Abbie had been the one who had succeeded in convincing Lane to buy River Bend when she had failed.

Gently Lane tugged her arms from around his neck as he reluctantly withdrew his mouth from her moist, clinging lips. "I have yet to seduce a beautiful woman on my office couch," he said thickly, "but if we keep this up, you'll be the first."

Her own pulse racing, Rachel noticed the answering desire that darkened his eyes and weighted their lids. She felt like a temptress. One curl of her finger and she could get him to do anything she wanted. She reveled in the feeling even as he firmly set her away from him.

"I'm quite sure that I'm the happiest woman in the whole world right now, Lane. I not only have you, but soon, River Bend will be ours, too. Sometimes I wonder if this isn't all a dream . . . that maybe none of this is happening . . . that you didn't kiss me a minute ago."

"I found it very real. Everything else is, too, I promise you." He gazed at her for a long moment, then walked over to his desk, as if needing to put more distance between them. "I'll arrange for an agent to bid for us at the auction."

"Speaking of auctions, when I glanced through the list of brood-mares to be sold, I saw several that I think we'd be interested in acquiring. Of course, I'm basing that strictly on their bloodlines. I've never actually seen them. Naturally, I would want to before we bought them."

"You're saying you want to attend the horse auction," Lane guessed.

"Yes. But considering the way Abbie behaved the last time I was there — ordering me off the premises — you know she isn't going to want me there."

"She can't bar you from it. It's a public auction, open to anyone, and that includes you."

"Maybe you should remind her of that the next time you talk to her."

"I will. Now, I don't mean to chase you off, but I have another meeting in" — he paused and glanced at the gold Piaget watch on his wrist — "five minutes. I'll pick you up at seven for dinner."

"I'll be waiting." She walked over and gave him another kiss, sensing that he wished it was longer and more passionate than the chaste kiss she bestowed.

On her way out of his office, Rachel collected her alligator purse from a chair. Over and over she kept reminding herself that soon she would be the new mistress of River Bend and Abbie would be out. She would have Dean's home. She would carry on the family traditions. And she would run the River Bend Arabian Stud. She felt an exhilarating sense of power. For the first time in her life, she felt she could do anything, be anything. Nothing could stop her: not the shame of her past, not Abbie — nothing.

As she swept through the outer office, she barely glanced at Lane's secretary and the man standing at his desk. In the lobby, she pushed the "down" button for the elevator and waited for it to come. She was still waiting when she was joined by someone else. She glanced absently at the man and instantly recognized him as the one who had intervened the other day with Abbie. According to Lane, Abbie had been seeing him regularly.

"You're MacCrea Wilder, aren't you?" she said, recalling the name Lane had told her.

"That's right." He nodded briefly, something hooded in his glance — or maybe she got that impression from the hat brim that shaded his dark eyes.

Rachel found it impossible not to compare him physically to Lane. Wilder was taller, broader in the shoulders, and more narrow in the hips than Lane. His thick hair was dark and wavy; Lane's was silver and straight. Lane was smooth-shaven and Wilder wore a full mustache, but he lacked that distinguished air that Rachel found so appealing in Lane. It was obvious to her that Abbie preferred the rugged, virile type.

"Lane mentioned that you've been seeing Abbie."

"I have," he confirmed, looking straight into her eyes.

She had expected him to scan her face and take note of the features she shared in common with Abbie. But he didn't. It was as if he saw no resemblance at all. For some reason she was thrown by that and fought to rid herself of that resurfacing sense of inferiority.

"Our elevator's here."

With a small start, Rachel noticed he was holding the doors open for her. She quickly stepped into the empty elevator, followed closely by MacCrea. She watched him punch the ground-floor button. Belatedly, she recognized the combination of tan blazer and blue jeans as being the same as that worn by the man in Lane's outer office.

"Were you the one talking to Lane's secretary when I came out of his office?" she asked as the doors slid shut.

"Yes."

"He said he had a meeting. Was that with you?" If so, it had certainly been a short one.

"No. I was making an appointment to talk to him later in the week."

"About Abbie?" she guessed.

"No. It's a business matter."

"I remember: Lane said you wanted to talk to him about some invention of yours. It had to do with drilling oil wells, I think he said."

"That's right."

"I know he sounded very interested in it," Rachel recalled thoughtfully, remembering that Lane had indicated he might become personally involved in the development financing and marketing of it. "Would you object if I sat in on your meeting with Lane, Mr. Wilder? This might be something I'd like to get into — purely as an investor."

"I don't mind, as long as Lane doesn't."

"He won't mind," she stated confidently, fully aware that Abbie would. Rachel smiled, discovering that she liked the idea.

19

The cool of the central air-conditioning greeted Abbie as she entered the kitchen through the back door. A roast baking in the oven was redolent of the tang of cooked onions. She picked her way through the boxes stacked by the door, all of them bearing the meticulous scroll of her mother's handwriting, identifying the cartons as containing sale items. Abbie searched the counter by the wall telephone, but the day's mail wasn't in its usual place.

Impatiently, she pushed open the connecting door to the formal dining room and checked the table and bureau top for the mail, then continued into the living room, her boots clumping loudly, then softly, then loudly again as she went from hardwood floor to area rug to hardwood floor again.

"Abbie, is that you?" her mother called from the upstairs landing.

"Yes, Momma." She crossed to the foot of the staircase. "Where did you put today's mail? Ben said there was a packet from Lane's office in it."

"It's on the table in the foyer." Babs came down the steps, dressed in a pair of slacks that looked like relics of the forties, with a scarf tied around her head like some Aunt Jemima character.

Abbie didn't know where her mother was finding the clothes she'd been wearing lately, but she suspected they were coming from the old trunks her mother had dragged out of the attic. She walked over to the side table and started leafing through the mail.

"I'm so glad you're here, Abbie. Which bedroom do you want for yourself at the other house? You never did say when we went over to the Hix farm to look at it," she reminded her as Abbie ripped open the manila envelope bearing the return address of Lane Canfield's office and pulled out the printed sales catalogue. "I'm trying to decide which dresser sets to keep and which to sell. Yours will fit in one room but not in the other. Same for mine, but the guest bedroom set will work in either."

On the third page of the catalogue, Abbie found River Breeze's name listed in bold type. Even though she had suspected that the filly would be included despite her claim of ownership, something died inside her when she actually saw it in print. Two days ago, Lane had called to inform her that the probate court seemed to be taking the position that the filly was too valuable to be regarded as a family pet. Yet Abbie had hoped.

"Abbie, did you hear me? Which bedroom do you want?"

"I don't care." She let the pages of the catalogue flip shut, then dropped it on the table with the rest of the mail. "You choose the one you want and I'll take the other."

"Is something wrong, Abbie?" Frown lines creased her forehead as Babs glanced from her to the catalogue and torn envelope on the table.

"Wrong?" Abbie shook her head vaguely. "I'm not sure I know what's right or wrong anymore, Momma." She reached for the front doorknob. "I'll see you later."

Abbie walked out of the house onto the wide porch feeling beaten. Everything was going from bad to worse, it seemed, and she wondered when it was going to stop. When was something good going to happen to her?

As she reached the top of the steps, she heard the hinges creak on the picket gate and looked up. MacCrea was striding toward her, tall and vigorous, a smile splitting his strong face. Here was something good, she realized and suddenly became aware of the bright shining sun and the blue of the jay on the lawn.

She practically ran down the steps, but by the time she reached the last one, he was there. And that step eliminated his height advantage and put her on just the right level to throw her arms around his neck and kiss him long and strong, putting everything she had into it. After a startled instant, he responded in kind, returning the driving pressure of her lips and wrapping his arms tightly around her and molding her to his body.

When she finally dragged her lips from his mouth, she was trembling. "I've missed you, Mac," she murmured. "I haven't seen you for two days. Where have you been?"

"If this is the kind of welcome I get, I'm going to leave more often." His low-pitched voice was a little husky.

"You hadn't better." She needed him. Abbie hadn't realized how much until now.

"I've got some good news. As of this morning, a major drilling-fluid company in Houston has agreed to field-test my computerized system for checking the downhole performance of mud — and market it, if it proves successful. The financing and everything has all been arranged."

"Are you serious?" For a split second she hardly dared to believe him, but the glint of satisfaction in his eyes told her it was true. "That's wonderful! Mac, it's fantastic!"

"You're damned right it is. And you and I are going out on the town and celebrate, starting now," he declared.

"This minute?" But she realized that was exactly what he meant. "MacCrea, I can't. I've got a thousand and one things I have to do this afternoon. Later, after the horses are fed tonight —"

"We're going now." His half-smile was lazy and confident.

"You're crazy. I can't leave all this work for Ben." Abbie tried to push away from him, but his arms were locked together behind her back.

"He'll manage. And if some of the horses go hungry tonight, it's not going to hurt them. You're coming with me and that's final."

"I am not — and that's final!" She didn't like his high-handed attitude. It smacked of dictatorship, and no one told *her* what to do, not even MacCrea.

His smile faded. "If that's the way you feel," — he paused, and she felt his arms loosen their hold on her, his hands retreating to her waist as he took a step backward — "I guess I'll just have to take matters into my own hands."

Suddenly she was being lifted. Abbie tried to struggle, but it all happened too fast. One minute her feet were on the steps, and the next she was slung over his shoulder like a sack of grain.

"MacCrea Wilder, you put me down this minute," she ordered through gritted teeth and pushed at his back, trying to lever herself off his shoulder, but he had a viselike grip around her thighs. Abbie held herself stiffly, refusing to kick and beat at him like some hysterical female.

"Sorry."

"You're not the least bit sorry," she spat, bobbing against his shoulder as he climbed the porch steps. "And just where do you think you're taking me?"

"To get you cleaned up. You smell like a horse."

"And you smell like a . . . a . . ." She couldn't think of anything vile enough as he paused to pull the front door open wide, then carried her inside. "Dammit, MacCrea, will you please put me down now?" She wanted to hit him, but she knew how ineffectual any resistance would be.

"If I do, will you go upstairs and get ready?"

"No."

"That's what I thought." He shifted her to rest a little higher on his shoulder and headed for the staircase. "Hello, Babs," he said calmly.

Abbie twisted around to see in front of him. Her mother was halfway down the steps, staring at them in shocked bewilderment. "Momma, make him put me down," she demanded.

"I'm kidnapping Abbie and taking her out for a night on the town, but first I have to get her cleaned up." The lazy confidence in his voice made it easy for her to imagine the look on his face. "If you could just tell me which bedroom is hers, I'd appreciate it."

"The second door on the right at the top of the stairs."

"Momma!" Abbie was shocked at her betrayal.

"It will do you good to go out. You've been working too hard lately." Babs smiled at her as she walked by, continuing down the stairs.

"See? Even your mother agrees with me."

"My mother —"

"Careful," MacCrea cut in. "After all, she is your mother. It's not nice to call her names." At the top of the stairs, he turned right and headed for the open door to her bedroom.

"How dare you lecture me on manners?" Abbie protested angrily as he kicked the door the rest of the way open with his foot. "That makes about as much sense as some urban cowboy telling a real one how to crease his hat." Once inside the bedroom, MacCrea still didn't set her down or stop. "This is getting ridiculous," she muttered through her clenched teeth, the blood rushing to her head. "Will you just put me down?"

"In a minute."

Suddenly she had a glimpse of another doorway coming up — the one to her bathroom. "MacCrea, what are you doing?" she yelped in panic.

He swung her off his shoulders and set her down in the shower stall. "I told you, I'm going to get you cleaned up," he reminded her complacently.

Certain he was bluffing, Abbie faced him squarely. "You and whose army?" The taunt was barely out when he swung her around to face the shower head and reached for the faucets. "MacCrea, no! Don't!" She grabbed at his hand, trying to stop him from turning the faucet on. "My clothes, you can't!" She screamed in shock as a full blast of cold water sprayed down on top of her. Sputtering with anger and a mouthful of water, Abbie groped for the faucet handle and finally managed to turn it off *after* she was already drenched to the skin.

Her hair was plastered in a wet sheet covering her eyes. She pulled it apart in the middle to glare at MacCrea, standing safe and dry outside the stall, his arms folded across his chest and his expression disgustingly smug.

"Now you'll have to get cleaned up and change clothes."

"Ya wanna bet?" She threw him a killing glance as she shook the excess water from her hands, but it didn't help. More just ran down from her wet blouse.

MacCrea reached out a hand and rested it on the shower faucet, his towering bulk effectively blocking her exit from the shower. "Honey, I'll even give you odds," he drawled. "Believe me, I would enjoy scrubbing you from head to foot. Truthfully, that idea isn't half-bad."

Just for an instant Abbie let herself fantasize that MacCrea was in the shower with her, his hands massaging the soap into her skin, lathering her breasts, and rubbing over her pubic bone. "Is that a threat, or a promise?" she countered, challenging him to go through with it at the same second that Jackson appeared in the bathroom doorway.

The usually unflappable houseman stared at them, his lips parted in astonishment. "Jackson," Abbie whispered, suddenly realizing that her wet blouse was virtually transparent — and she wasn't wearing a bra.

MacCrea glanced over his shoulder. "Did you want something, Jackson?" Inching sideways, Abbie shifted to hide behind MacCrea, feeling oddly embarrassed — for both herself and Jackson.

"I . . . I thought . . . I heard a scream."

"It was just Abbie," MacCrea explained. "Nothing for you to worry about. I'll handle it."

"Of course, sir," Jackson replied, recovering his poise and withdrawing with just a hint of a bow.

"Poor Jackson," Abbie said sympathetically. "I've scandalized him totally." As MacCrea laughed under his breath, she glared at him. "It's your fault. You're a bastard, do you know that?"

"And you're an ill-tempered bitch." His mustache twitched with his halfhearted effort to contain the mocking smile that played upon his lips. "It looks like we were made for each other." Straightening, he took his hand away from the faucet. "Now get out of those wet clothes and get cleaned up."

As he walked out of the bathroom, he closed the door behind him, leaving her alone. She stood there, dripping in the shower, unable to think about anything except that one remark he'd made. She wondered if he meant it . . . if he really believed they were made for each other, or if he had merely said it in jest. She didn't want it to be an idle joke. On the heels of that realization came the recognition that she was definitely in love with him — more in love than she'd ever been in her life. She felt suddenly afraid and defensive. She wasn't sure she wanted to love anyone this completely. It left her exposed and vulnerable.

Hurriedly she peeled off her wet clothes and stepped under the shower again. As she ran the soapy sponge over her body, she couldn't rid herself of the thought that its pleasing roughness might have come from MacCrea's caressing hands if Jackson hadn't shown up. She tried to tell herself it was just as well, but it didn't ease the ache she felt.

She stepped out of the shower and toweled herself dry, then wrapped another towel around her head and one around her body, sarong-fashion. As she walked out of the bathroom, Abbie saw the lacy underwear lying on her bed: bra, panties, slip, even a pair of sheer silk stockings. Then she heard the scrape of wire hangers being pushed along a clothes rod, the sound coming from her walk-in closet. Frowning, she walked over to it and saw MacCrea inside, going through her clothes.

"What are you doing?"

"Trying to find something for you to wear tonight." He pulled a red strapless dress of silk chiffon, layered in ruffles, from the rack. "This isn't bad."

"I'll pick out my own clothes, thank you." Abbie took it from him and hung it back up, nagged by the thought that maybe he'd done this with other women he'd known in the past. She was surprised by the surge of jealousy and possessiveness she felt. She couldn't stand the idea of MacCrea being with anyone else.

"Not that feathered thing, though," he said, slipping his arms around her middle, crossing them in front of her waist and pulling her back against him. The towel came untucked, but his arms held it in place. "You smell like a woman now," he murmured. "All you need is a little touch of perfume here." As he nuzzled the ridge of her bare shoulder, Abbie instinctively arched into a caress. "And here." He nibbled at the pulsing vein in her neck, sending chills of pleasure dancing over her skin. "And maybe a dab . . . here." His hand slid up between her breasts and hooked a finger over the towel, dragging it farther down as he traced a line down the center of her cleavage.

When he lifted his head, breaking off the stimulating nuzzling of her neck, Abbie turned within the circle of his arms to face him, the towel slipping more. "Don't stop now. I was just getting warmed up."

"Aren't you ever satisfied?" He gazed down at her with easy confidence.

"Did I imply I wasn't satisfied? I am, you know . . . at least most of the time," she added deliberately to tease him.

"Only most of the time?" He arched an eyebrow in amusement. "That's not how I remember it."

"Maybe you need to refresh my memory." She started unbuttoning his shirt.

"If I don't walk out of this bedroom in five minutes, especially now that the shower's not running, what is your mother going to think? And Jackson?" His eyes darkened perceptibly as his gaze traveled rapidly over her face, her bare shoulders, and the ever-lower-drooping towel.

"Momma is a woman. She understands. As for Jackson, I've already scandalized him. Besides" — she paused and slid her hands inside his shirt, spreading it open to expose his muscular chest — "it doesn't usually take longer than five minutes, does it?"

"You little witch." His voice rumbled from deep inside his chest, richly laced with humor. "You are going to eat those words."

"I'd like to," Abbie said, looking up at him with half-closed eyes, their lids weighted with passion. She reached for the buckle on his belt and MacCrea swore softly, achingly.

*   *   *

Two hours later, they were seated at a table in the crowded steak-house, waiting for their drinks to arrive. Abbie opened her menu and glanced over the selections.

"Don't tell me you're still hungry," MacCrea mocked.

"For food," she retorted. "Dessert comes later."

"Now that's a proposition if I ever heard one." he chuckled as his glance strayed from her. "It looks like I'm about to have competition. Who is he? An old flame of yours?"

Abbie turned, expecting to see someone she knew, but she didn't recognize the man in the dark cowboy hat banded with silver conchos. Yet he was grinning at her like a long-lost friend.

"Hello, there. Remember me?"

"No, I don't think so." Abbie stared at him, searching for some resemblance to anyone she knew.

"Ross Tibbs. I sing here in the lounge. We met —" He stopped, uncertainty flickering across his face. "You're not her, are you? Across the room, I thought for sure — Man, you look enough like her to be her twin."

"Well, I'm not," she replied stiffly, fully aware that he must have mistaken her for Rachel.

"I'm sorry. I know I probably sounded like I was giving you the oldest line in the book, but you really do look like this lady I met named Rachel."

"Don't worry about it, Mr. Tibbs. It's happened before." She was thinking about her father when she said that, remembering how many times he'd stared at her with that strange look in his eyes . . . as if he was seeing someone else.

"I can sure understand that," the singer replied, smiling ruefully. "Again, I'm sorry I bothered you, Ra —" He caught himself and laughed self-consciously. "I guess I can't call you that, can I?"

"The name is Lawson. Abbie Lawson."

"Say, you wouldn't happen to be related to the Lawsons that have that Arabian horse farm outside of Houston?"

"Yes. River Bend is owned by my family." But only for a little while longer, she remembered, feeling again the emotional tear over losing it.

"I've been by the place a time or two. You've got some beautiful horses there. Didn't I see a notice somewhere that you're having an auction to sell them off?"

"Yes. Next week." She didn't even have to close her eyes to see River Breeze's name on the list.

"I might see you there," Ross Tibbs declared. "I always wanted to own an Arabian. Not that I could afford one, no matter how cheap they might sell. But a man can dream." As the waitress arrived with their drinks, he stepped to one side. "Listen, I . . . won't bother you any longer. If you get a chance after dinner, stop by the lounge and catch my act."

"We'll see," MacCrea inserted.

"Enjoy your dinner," he said, moving away from their table.

Aware of the way MacCrea was quietly studying her, Abbie tried to shake off her brooding thoughts. Forcing a smile, she lifted her glass to him. "Since this is supposed to be a celebration, don't you think we should drink to your success?"

"I do." He touched his glass to hers.

Abbie took a sip of her bourbon and water, then cupped the moist sides of the glass in both hands. "You know, you still haven't told me any details about how this all came about — or who all you're dealing with. I know you met with Lane last week. Did he set the whole thing up?"

For a fraction of a second MacCrea seemed on guard, his glance sharp, then the impression was gone. "Yes, he was involved in it from the start."

"Maybe I was wrong about him," she conceded absently.

"What do you mean?"

"He was trying to find some way I could keep my filly, but she's being sold with the rest. I questioned how hard he really tried to help, but, considering what he's done for you, maybe there wasn't any way he could arrange for me to keep River Breeze."

"So what happens now?"

"I don't know." Abbie shook her head, frustrated by the blank walls that seemed to surround her. "I'm not sure I can afford to buy her. A filly always brings more than a colt, unless you have an outstanding stallion or show prospect. And with her looks and bloodlines, she's bound to bring anywhere from ten to twenty thousand dollars — maybe more." She tried to smile. "We'd better talk about something else. This subject is too depressing."

"Did I tell you my regular toolpusher reported back to work the first of the week? He's on crutches, but he gets around pretty good. Which means I won't have to be on the site twenty-four hours a day."

"I like the sound of that already."

20

"What do you mean, she wants to come to the sale?" Abbie demanded, trembling with anger. "She —"

Lane held up his hand to stop the tirade. "Before you fly off the handle, remember that this auction is open to the public. She has every right to come if she chooses to do so and you can't stop her. I am only advising you of her plans because I hope to avoid any ugly scenes such as the one that occurred the last time she was here."

Recognizing that he had a valid point — it was a public auction — Abbie made an effort to control her temper, but she was almost choking on her own gall. "Why? What possible reason could she have to come to it?"

"She's interested in buying some horses," Lane replied.

Everything went still inside her. She was afraid even to draw a breath. "Which ones?"

"She didn't say."

What if one of them was River Breeze? Her anger turned ice-cold. For the first time since Lane had announced Rachel's plans to attend the sale, Abbie was thinking clearly, sharply, her mind racing swiftly to find some way to keep her filly from ending up in Rachel's hands.

"I'd like to know what you're going to do, Abbie," Lane said.

For a split second, she thought he was asking about the filly, then realized he was referring to Rachel. "Like you said, Lane, it's a public auction. Just tell her to stay away from my mother and me. Is there anything further we need to discuss?" she asked, an icy calm dominating her attitude.

"No, I think we've gone over everything."

"Good. I have work to do." Turning on her heel, Abbie pivoted away from him and walked briskly toward the stables. She had an idea, but she was going to need help to carry it out.

She found Ben in one of the foaling stalls, doctoring a minor cut on the foreleg of a young stud colt. "You are a clumsy boy," Ben said to the colt, the soothing tone of his voice belying the chiding words he spoke. "You must learn not to run into things or you will hurt yourself very badly sometime."

"I need to talk to you, Ben," she said when he released the colt. The horse charged across the large box stall to hide behind his mother, then peeked around her rump to eye Ben warily as he moved to the door.

"That one is what your father called an accident waiting to happen." Ben stepped unhurriedly out of the stall and slid the door shut. "Always he is cutting and scraping himself."

But Abbie wasn't interested in discussing the accident-prone colt. "We only have four days before the auction. Lane just told me that the grooms he hired will be arriving the day after tomorrow. Before they come, I want to get River Breeze out of here."

"Get her out of here?" His gaze narrowed sharply. "What are you saying?"

"I'm saying I don't want her anywhere on the farm when they arrive."

"What is going on in that head of yours?" Ben asked suspiciously.

"I've thought it all through," Abbie said. "When the Germans invaded Poland at the start of World War Two, what did you do? You evacuated all the horses from the stud and tried to find a safe place to hide them. That's what I want to do with River Breeze. If she isn't here, she can't be sold at the auction."

"It is not the same, Abbie. There is no war. If you would take the filly from here, you would be stealing her. That is wrong."

"Wrong. How could it be wrong to steal my own horse? And River Breeze is mine. You know that Daddy gave her to me, regardless of what the ownership papers say," Abbie reasoned, maintaining her calm. Anger never got her anywhere with Ben.

"This is true," he admitted reluctantly, still troubled by her proposal.

"Then how can I be accused of stealing my own horse?" She could tell he was wavering. "I need your help, Ben, but I'll do it alone if I have to."

"Where will you take her?" he asked gruffly.

"To Dobie's. He's already said I could keep her in his barn once we move. Momma has already taken some of our things over to the house. We can simply tell him that we want to bring River Breeze over there now so we don't have to deal with moving her later. He doesn't have to know anything different."

"You would lie to him?"

"No. I simply wouldn't tell him the whole truth."

"What do you think you will accomplish by doing this?" Ben tipped his head to the side and watched her closely.

So far he'd been satisfied by her answers, but Abbie knew this one was critical. On it, he would base his decision. If she didn't obtain at least his tacit approval, she doubted that her plan would succeed.

"I'll buy time," she said. "You know that I don't have much hope of outbidding anyone at the auction. If I can keep her hidden until after the sale, maybe I'll be able to buy her on terms. Or maybe we'll make enough money off the sale to pay off the creditors and she won't have to be sold. Don't you see, Ben, I have to take the chance that there will be a way?"

There was a long pause before he answered, as if he were mulling over all her arguments in his mind. "We should move her tonight . . . after it is dark."

Relief broke the iron control she'd exercised over her emotions. Abbie threw her arms around him and hugged him tightly. "I love you, Ben. I just knew I could count on you to help me."

A crescent moon hovered above the eastern horizon, a curved blade of silver against a midnight sky studded with stars. Beyond the pool of light cast by the tall yardlight next to the broodmare barn, a dark-colored pickup truck with a two-horse trailer in tow was parked.

Ben stood in the shadows of the vehicle, holding the lead rope attached to the filly's halter while Abbie smoothed the navy-blue horse blanket over the filly's back, concealing the silvery coat that stood out so sharply against the night's darkness. She fastened the belly strap and loosely buckled the chest strap, then drew the top of the blanket up to the arched crest of the filly's neck and fastened it securely under the throatlatch. The filly nosed Ben's shoulder as if seeking human reassurance about this unusual nighttime activity.

"That night we left Janow under the cover of darkness, the horses seemed to understand the need for silence, as this one does," Ben recalled, speaking in a hushed voice. "We left at night so the German Luftwaffe could not observe our flight. Mr. Rhoski, the manager of Janow, led the way in his carriage. Then my group, we followed with the stallions, riding one and leading another. After us came the mares, foals, and other young horses, most of them tied to carts carrying fodder for the march, pulled by the half-Arabians at the farm. It was a sight to see, Abbie. Two hundred fifty of Poland's best Arabians streaming out of Janow to be swallowed by the night.

"All along the road that night, we met hundreds — thousands — of our fellow countrymen from western Poland, fleeing from the Germans. They told us of the bombings by the Luftwaffe of the highways, the planes diving and shooting their machine guns at the people trying to escape. We did not go near the highways, but stayed on the country roads. When dawn was near, we hid the horses in the forests. We hid there all day. I was tired after traveling all night, but I could not sleep. I kept listening to the roar of the German planes, wondering if they would see us in the trees. When darkness came, we marched again, but that night the stallions were not so eager to travel. They did not prance and push at the bit as they did when we left Janow. I think they knew that the road to Kowel was a long and dangerous one — and that they would need all of their great stamina and courage to reach the safety on the other side of the Bug River."

"All set. We can load her in the trailer." Abbie patted the filly's withers and stepped back. Cloaked in the dark horse blanket, River Breeze blended in with the shadows, only her silver-gray head and tail visible against the darkness. But in the dark trailer, that little bit of white would barely be noticeable.

"Open it and I will lead her in." Ben shortened his hold on the lead rope.

As Abbie stepped out from behind the trailer and moved to the tailgate, a pair of headlight beams laid their long tracks on the winding lane. "Wait," she whispered to Ben, her nerves screaming with tension as he started to lead the filly out from the shadows. "Someone's coming. Stay there until I find out who it is."

"Maybe it is Dobie come to find out why we are so late." The filly pricked her ears at the sound of a running engine and Ben cupped a silencing hand over her muzzle.

"Maybe." But the vehicle didn't sound like Dobie's truck. Her mouth felt dry and her palms sweaty. Abbie tried to summon some saliva as she stepped away from the horse trailer and wiped her hands on the hips of her jeans, waiting for the vehicle to come under the tall yardlight next to the house. "It's MacCrea." She hadn't been aware of how scared she'd been until her knees almost buckled with relief when she recognized his truck.

"Do you realize you were supposed to meet me almost two hours ago?" MacCrea slammed out of the truck. "I couldn't figure out what happened to you, whether you'd had an accident, your car broke down, or what. Then I call the house and your mother says you're still here."

"Something important came up and I . . . forgot. I know I should have called you. I'm sorry." There wasn't anything else she could say.

"You forgot? Well, thanks a lot." He stopped inches in front of her, his hands on his hips in a gesture of anger and disgust. Then he shook his head, as if unable to believe any of this. "This happens to be a first, you know. I've never been stood up before. Naturally you would be the one to do it."

"I didn't do it on purpose. I honestly forgot."

"What came up that was so important?" he demanded.

Abbie was conscious of Ben standing only yards away in the shadow of the horse trailer, holding River Breeze. "One of our horses went down. We were afraid it was colic."

The filly picked that moment to snort. Abbie stiffened as MacCrea glanced toward the horse trailer. "Did you hear that?"

"What?" But she knew playing dumb wouldn't work. "It was probably one of the horses in the barn."

"This isn't where you usually park the horse trailer." MacCrea studied her suspiciously. "What's it doing hitched up to the truck?"

"We were using it today." A second later she heard the restless shifting of hooves as the filly grew tired of standing quietly. She knew MacCrea had heard it, too. She was almost relieved when Ben came walking out from behind the trailer, leading the blanketed horse. She was trapping herself in a snare of lies and she wanted it to end. "So we decided we might as well haul River Breeze over to Dobie's place before we unhooked the trailer." She walked over to the trailer and unlatched the endgate so Ben could load the filly.

"Wait a minute. I thought she was being sold at the auction." MacCrea frowned. "Was Lane finally able to arrange for you to keep her?"

"Something like that." She was reluctant to tell him of her plan. The fewer people who knew about it, the better chance she had to keep the horse hidden.

"All right, Abbie." He caught her by the wrist and forced her to turn around and look at him. "What's really going on here?"

"I told you. We're taking River Breeze over to the Hix farm," she replied, trying to appear tolerant of his supposedly stupid question.

"It's nearly midnight."

"A few minutes after eleven is not midnight."

"That clever little mind of yours is at work again, isn't it?"

"I don't know what you're talking about," Abbie declared.

"You know exactly what I'm talking about." But he turned to Ben when he emerged from the trailer after tying the filly inside. "Maybe you'd like to explain to me what's going on here?"

"It is for Abbie to say," Ben replied, but his look prodded Abbie to tell the truth.

"It's simple, MacCrea," she said, her voice becoming curt. "If the filly isn't here, she can't be sold."

"I should have guessed," he said grimly. "There are bound to be questions. Horses don't just simply disappear. How are you going to explain it?"

"Horses get loose all the time. A fence was down or a gate was left open and she got out. There are any number of ways she could get away." The strain of secrecy and the stress of lying followed by the forced admission all combined to make Abbie feel defensive.

"In the meantime, you're going to have her hidden away."

"That's right — until after the sale, when I can arrange to buy her."

"And what happens if someone finds out what you're doing?"

"They won't find out unless you tell them." The questions, the tension became too much. "Look, Rachel is coming to the auction to buy some horses. She isn't going to get River Breeze!" She twisted her wrist free of his hand and swung the endgate closed, then slid the locking bolt into place, shaking inside with emotion. Finally she turned back around to confront him. "Well, MacCrea?"

"I take it you're in this with her, Ben," he said.

"The filly belongs to her. Sometimes risks must be taken to do what is the right thing."

"Are you going to tell Lane?" Abbie needed to know where he stood.

"Why should I?" MacCrea countered.

"You think we're doing something wrong —" she began.

"I never said that. I think it's a damned-fool stunt, and you two are going about it like a pair of amateurs. I'm surprised you aren't dressed in black and have grease smeared on your faces. It would have been a helluva lot less suspicious if you'd simply ridden the horse over there and had your redheaded friend drive you back. Just how much does your friend know about this?"

"Nothing." She knew she had MacCrea's support even though he hadn't said it in so many words. She felt her confidence return. "I've let him assume that Breeze belongs to me, and any question about it has been resolved."

"Once you report the horse missing, what happens if someone asks him whether he's seen it?"

"That won't happen, because I'm not going to report that she's missing until the morning of the sale. With the pressure of getting all the horses ready for the auction, there won't be time to organize anything. Ben and I can pretend to look for her." So far he hadn't asked her a question that she couldn't answer. Confident that she had every contingency covered, Abbie grew impatient with the delay. "Everything's set. It's too late to change the plan now. Dobie is waiting for us, and if we waste any more time here, he's going to start asking questions. Come on, Ben. Let's go." As Ben headed for the driver's side, Abbie walked the length of the trailer to the passenger door, aware that MacCrea followed her. The interior light flashed on when Abbie opened the cab door. MacCrea held it as she climbed onto the seat, then turned to look at him. "I'll see you when I get back. You'll be here, won't you?"

"No. I'm coming with you, so move over." He climbed into the truck, barely giving Abbie time to scoot to the middle.

Leaving the headlights off, Ben drove slowly away from the stables with the horse trailer in tow. As soon as they were beyond the illumination of the yardlights, he slowed the truck to a crawl and sat hunched over the wheel, staring intently ahead to keep the truck and trailer aimed down the center of the narrow lane, with only the dim starlight to show him the path in the darkness.

"There usually isn't much traffic on the road at this hour of the night, but we don't want to take the risk of someone driving by and seeing us leaving here with the horse trailer," Abbie explained to MacCrea.

"They're liable to take more notice of you because you aren't running with lights." He grabbed the dashboard in front of him. "Watch the ditch on the right!"

Ben swerved the truck away from it and drove even slower. "It was like this in Poland. The night was so dark you could not see the ditches by the road. And so many people, too, fleeing with what possessions they could save. Wheels of the carts were always sliding off the road into the ditch."

"Ben took part in the evacuation of the Arabian horses from the Polish stud farm during World War Two when the Germans invaded Poland," Abbie explained in a quick aside to MacCrea.

"It took us three nights to reach a place where we could cross the Bug River, traveling only after dark and hiding the horses wherever we could during the day. German planes filled the sky over Poland like flocks of birds when autumn comes, but they did not fly beyond the Bug River. After we crossed it, we could travel during the day. We were maybe two days from Kowel, our destination, when we heard the artillery fire and learned that the Russians had invaded eastern Poland. So close we came, only to turn around and make the long trek back to Janow. We all agreed if the horses were to be captured, we would rather have them taken by the Nazis."

"In the First World War, the Soviet armies overran the stud farms and slaughtered nearly all the horses," Abbie added.

"When we returned to Janow Podlaski, the Germans were there." Ben turned onto the road and continued to drive without lights. "The commandant ordered us to move all the horses to the Vistula River, which was another hundred and fifty kilometers west of Janow. The horses needed rest. They had marched far and long, and the manager refused. It would have been better if we had gone, but we did not know the Germans and Soviets had made a treaty. Everything east of the Vistula was to be under Russian occupation. We tried to save the horses from them, but the Germans surrendered the studs to the Russians. It was only a few weeks later, the line was changed to the Bug River, but when the Soviet forces left Janow, they took with them the horses — spoils of war. That is how the great Ofir arrived in Tersk, a war prize stolen from Poland."

"Fortunately for the Arabian horse world, some seventy horses, too exhausted, lame, or too young to endure that first evacuation attempt, had been left in the care of farmers along the way. The Polish stud was able to recover most of them, including Balalajka, the dam of Bask, probably one of the greatest stallions since Skowronek," Abbie explained as the truck rumbled over the old bridge that spanned the creek.

"Yes, the owner of Balalajka was given sugar and alcohol in trade for her. We were able to obtain many horses in this way, so we could start breeding Arabian horses again."

"We're coming up on the intersection," MacCrea warned, then added dryly, "This is Texas, Ben, not Poland. I think it would be safe to turn on your lights anytime now."

"We are away from the farm now. It would be okay, I think." Reaching down, he pulled the knob that activated the lights. As the beam illuminated the road ahead of them, the truck picked up speed.

"This is more like the second time Janow was evacuated, isn't it, Ben?" Abbie smiled at him, his craggy face now bathed in the faint glow from the dashboard lights.

"That time we went by train. Thirty-one boxcars it took to carry all the horses. That was in 'forty-four. The Soviets had driven the Nazi armies out of Russia and were marching into Poland. It was a good thing we were able to escape with the horses. Much heavy fighting occurred around Janow Podlaski. The barns were destroyed by the artillery shelling, and some houses at Janow, also."

"What about Dresden and all the bombings there? You were in Dresden then. It was probably just as bad if not worse than Janow," Abbie said.

"I have the feeling you know the story better than Ben does," MacCrea mocked.

"I should," she retorted, smiling. "When I was a little girl, they were my bedtime stories. I was raised on his exploits during the war."

"We are here," Ben announced as he swung the truck and trailer onto the dirt driveway that went a quarter of a mile back to the headquarters of the Hix farm.

"Dobie waited up for us. There's a light on in the house," Abbie observed. "We might as well go straight to the barn, Ben."

A porch light flashed on as they drove past the main farmhouse to the old wood and stone barn, nearly dwarfed by the large machine shed next to it. Ben made a looping circle and parked near a side door. Abbie climbed out of the truck after MacCrea, then waited as Dobie loped across the farmyard to meet them.

"I figured you'd be here an hour ago. Did you have problems?" Dobie darted an accusing look at MacCrea as if convinced he was the cause for Abbie being late.

"We got tied up with a few things that took longer than we expected. I'm sorry you had to wait so long for us to get here, Dobie."

"I've got a place all fixed up for your filly in the barn," Dobie said.

The area was large and roomy, nearly twice the size of the box stalls at River Bend. A short partition in the middle divided one side into two open, double stalls complete with mangers and feed troughs. Abbie led River Breeze inside. The blanketed filly stepped daintily across the straw-covered floor, snorting loudly and breathing in all the new smells.

Abbie tied the lead rope to one of the manger rings, then removed the blanket and handed it over the manger to Ben. After she made sure the filly knew where the water bucket was located, she put some grain in the feed trough and turned her loose to investigate the new surroundings.

"I think she likes it," Dobie said as the filly nibbled at the grain, appearing to relax a little.

"She will." Abbie was concerned about that. "Thanks for letting me keep her over here."

"Now or later, it doesn't really make much difference." Dobie shrugged. "Do you want me to turn her out in the morning?"

"No, don't do that," Abbie said, conscious of MacCrea's taunting glance. "I think it would be better if she stayed inside . . . at least until she gets used to her new home."

"If that's what you want."

"It is." She gave the filly a final hug and crawled over the manger to join the others. "It's late, and all of us have to work in the morning. Thanks again for everything, Dobie."

"If there's anything else I can do for you, you just ask."

As they walked out of the barn, MacCrea muttered close to her ear, "That poor fool would jump off a cliff if you asked him to."

"And you wouldn't," she guessed.

"No."

"That's what I thought." But she really didn't mind.

21

On the surface, the scene at River Bend appeared to be one of confusion, but the pother was organized. In the center aisle of the broodmare barn, a horse stood tied and waiting while one of the grooms curried another. Farther down the aisle, a second groom combed out the tangled mane and tail of a third horse. The low hum of a pair of clippers came from the stud barn where a third groom worked, trimming the bridle path, fetlock feathers, whiskers, and any excess hairs under the jaw of another horse. Outside, the local farrier hooked the foreleg of an already groomed and trimmed mare between his legs and snipped away at an overgrown hoof while his young helper held the mare's head.

Abbie checked, but the mare's halter had no yellow tag tied to it, indicating she was to remain barefoot. In the assembly-line system they'd established, once the horseshoer was finished with a horse, it would be taken to the stud barn and bathed by the fourth groom, then confined to a stall.

The gusting wind riffled the sheets of paper attached to the clipboard Abbie carried. Impatiently she smoothed them down, then checked the list again for the name of the next horse. Somewhere a horn blared, breaking across the whinnies and snorts of the horses, the buzz of the clippers, and the rasp of the farrier's file. It sounded again and again, a sense of urgency accompanying the tooting blasts.

Frowning, Abbie looked up as Dobie's old pickup came roaring up the driveway.

It squealed into the yard, the nearly bald tires spitting back the loose gravel. Impelled forward by a sense of foreboding, Abbie started toward it, then broke into a run when it rattled to a stop and Dobie poked his head out the driver's window.

"There's been an accident!" he shouted. "Your horse is hurt. You better come quick!"

"My God," Abbie whispered. Fear, cold as an icy finger, shivered down her spine. She stopped and whirled toward the barn. "Ben!" she yelled for him just as he emerged from the stud barn to learn the cause of all the commotion. "It's River Breeze! She's hurt!" She spun back to Dobie. "Have you called the vet?"

He shook his head with a vagueness that indicated it hadn't occurred to him. "I came straight here."

She tried to check the panic welling up inside her. Grotesque images of the filly down, thrashing in agony, flashed before her mind's eye as she raced around to the other side of the truck, yelling over her shoulder at the horseshoer, who had stopped work. "Call the vet and tell him to get over to the Hix farm right away! It's an emergency!"

She scrambled into the cab with a winded Ben right behind her, hauling himself onto the high seat beside her. Before Ben could get the door closed, Dobie stepped on the accelerator and the pickup shot forward, its spinning tires spending up a fresh storm of gravel.

"What happened?" Ben asked the question Abbie hadn't been able to voice, afraid of the answer she might hear.

"I don't know. I'm not sure," Dobie said. "I had hooked up the windrower to the tractor and drove it out of the shed. Maybe it was the noise — all the clanging and rattling from the tractor and windrower. I was already past the barn when I heard this scream. I looked back and —" He cast an anxious glance at Abbie. She stared at him intently, waiting for the rest of the words that would finish the scenario running in her mind, feeling as if her heart was lodged somewhere in her throat. "I'm sorry, Abbie." He looked to the front and tightened his hold on the steering wheel with a flexing motion of his fingers. "She was laying on the ground, kicking and struggling. The bottom half of the Dutch door was sprung open and cracked at the top. I'd left the top of the door open so she could get some air and see out. I guess she spooked at the noise and tried to get out."

"No." She didn't want to believe the accident was as bad as Dobie had described. She was sure the filly wouldn't have tried to jump the half-door; the opening was too small. A bad sprain, some cuts and bruises, that's probably all River Breeze had suffered.

"I think she broke her leg," Dobie added hesitantly.

"You don't know that," Abbie retorted. "You didn't check."

"No. I left her with one of my hired hands and came for you."

"Can't we go any faster?" Outside the truck windows the fence posts were a blur, yet the nightmarish feeling persisted that no matter how fast they traveled, the farm was still far away — and getting farther instead of closer.

All the way, Abbie kept remembering how close the machine shed had been to the barn. Except for a tractor, the filly had never been around farm machinery before. Naturally she would have been frightened by the banging clatter of such strange contraptions. Abbie wished she had thought of that, but she had been too concerned about secreting her horse.

By the time they drove into the yard, Abbie was frantic. She strained for a glimpse of the filly, hoping against hope to see River Breeze on her feet. But her silver-gray Arabian was on the ground. Abbie didn't even hear the cry of anguish that came from her throat. She practically pushed Ben out of the truck in her haste to get to the filly. Her legs were shaking so badly she wasn't sure they would support her as she ran to the downed horse, taking no notice at all of the man standing next to River Breeze.

The filly nickered and lifted her head when Abbie reached her. Abbie took one look at the dark eyes glazed with pain, the neck dark with sweat, and the tremors that quivered through the filly, and knew her horse had gone into shock.

"Quick! Get a blanket," she said to the hired man, then saw the rifle in his hands. She stared at him with a mixture of outrage and shock. "What are you doing with that?"

"The horse needs t' be put out o' its mis'ry. Ain't nothin' you can do fer it. Her front leg's busted." He gestured with the rifle, directing Abbie's attention to the filly's bloodied chest and legs.

Abbie's stomach was heaving convulsively as she almost threw up at the sight of the grotesquely twisted leg, lying askew like some ragdoll's. She fought off the nausea that left her knees weak and her skin cold and clammy with sweat.

"You're not going to shoot her. You don't destroy horses anymore just because they break a leg, so take that rifle and hang it back on your rack. And get a blanket like I told you." She knelt on the ground beside the filly and cradled the horse's head on her lap. "The vet will be here soon, girl," she crooned, reassuring herself as much as the filly. She concentrated on soothing the horse while Ben examined the extent of the injuries. The man left, but it was Dobie who came back with the blanket to cover the filly. Ben draped it over River Breeze, then straightened. Abbie looked up to search his face.

"The cuts are minor," he said. "Already the bleeding has stopped. One, maybe two are deep enough to leave a scar."

But his failure to comment on the broken leg was a telling omission. "Breeze is young and strong. She'll make it," Abbie said, sounding calm and determined even though, inside, she was scared — terrified that she might lose the filly she'd fought so hard to keep. "She'll make it. You'll see. She is descended from the great war mare Wadudda. After a desert raid, she was ridden over a hundred miles without stopping once. Her right leg was injured during the raid, yet she covered that distance in eleven hours. River Breeze has that same courage and heart. I know she does." Abbie clung tenaciously to that thought. She could build her hopes on it. She wasn't going to give up until the filly did.

"We will see what the doctor says," Ben replied.

Abbie refused to hear the doubt in his voice as she sat cradling the filly's head in her lap and brushing away the buzzing flies, mindless of the growing numbness in her legs, her heart twisting at every grunt of pain from the filly. She maintained her vigil, suffering along with River Breeze, while an eternity passed before the veterinarian arrived.

After a cursory examination, he was no more encouraging than Ben had been. Straightening, he looked at Abbie and simply shook his head.

"Broken legs can be set on a horse. They do it all the time," she insisted, challenging the vet to deny it.

"The break in the leg is too high. Supposing that I could get the bone set, I don't see how I can immobilize that shoulder area. I'm sorry, Abbie, but it doesn't look good," he stated reluctantly.

"But there is hope." Abbie grabbed at the slim straw he'd let slip.

"If this was a gelding, I wouldn't hesitate a bit in recommending putting the horse away. If by some wild chance the break healed, the horse would be a cripple the rest of his life. But I hate the thought of destroying a young valuable filly like this one with all her foal-producing years still ahead of her. But I'll tell you like I've told your father, I don't believe in prolonging an animal's agony when I know nothing can be done for it."

"But you don't know that," she argued. "How can you when you haven't even tried? You can set her leg and we'll rig up a sling to keep her off it until it can heal."

"Don't you be trying to tell me my job, young lady."

"Somebody should," she raged in desperation. "Just because this is an animal, that doesn't make you God, holding power of life and death over it."

"In the first place, setting a broken leg and rigging up a sling doesn't solve anything. That's when the problems start. Horses aren't people. You can't strap them in a bed and rig them up in traction and expect them to sit still for it. They're animals — dumb animals. And an animal in pain usually goes berserk. They panic and start kicking and lashing out, and usually wind up doing more damage to themselves. Sure, you've heard stories about horses with broken legs that have recovered and lived useful lives. But you haven't heard the stories about all the ones that didn't make it, that went crazy and had to be destroyed — like that Thoroughbred filly, Ruffian, a few years back."

"But we don't know River Breeze will do that."

"We'll see what we can do, Abbie, but don't get your hopes up."

The rest of the morning and afternoon was a living nightmare for Abbie, helpless to do anything but watch and wait. Since the front leg was injured, transporting the filly to Doc Campbell's clinic in town was out of the question. There was too great a risk that more severe damage would occur on the journey. After a half-dozen phone calls, Doc was able to locate a portable X-ray unit. When it finally arrived at the farm, the resulting X rays showed both front legs were broken. The left foreleg had suffered only a hairline fracture, but both the ulna and the radius bones were broken just below the shoulder joint in the right leg.

Abbie sat with the filly while Doc Campbell got on the telephone again and consulted with several fellow practitioners whose opinions he trusted. He came back with a course of action, admittedly radical, and sent Ben back to River Bend to fetch the farrier and Dobie to the welder in the machine shed with a hastily sketched diagram of the splint he wanted made. A Thomas splint, he called it, explaining to Abbie that it was an appliance frequently used on dogs and cats with broken front legs. By then, she was too numb inside to object that River Breeze was a horse, not a dog or cat. Reaction had set in, and all she wanted was for him to do something for her filly — anything.

Propped against a corner of the stall, Abbie sat huddled in a wool blanket — the same blanket that had covered the filly earlier. Exhausted from the long ordeal, she let her head roll back against the rough boards and closed her eyes just for a minute. A faint sound, a rustle of straw, and she snapped them open, instantly ready to spring to her feet.

But the filly was motionless, her gray head hanging listlessly, still under the lingering influence of the anesthesia. Both front legs were encased in plaster, with a pair of long metal splints curving in a high hoop up the gray shoulder and extending down to the hoof, attached to the shoe. A belly sling, fastened to a crossbeam overhead, supported most of the filly's weight.

Even though River Breeze had always been gentle and well-mannered, Abbie realized that it would take a horse with the tolerance of Job to put up with all those contraptions. Maybe she was wrong to put the filly through all this stress and pain. Maybe she should have let Doc Campbell put her to sleep. She stubbornly rejected the thought, determined that her filly would live no matter what it took.

She heard a footstep and called out softly, "Dobie, is that you?"

"It's me," MacCrea answered, coming around the corner of the stall's partition, his tall shape backlit by the bare bulb overhead.

"How —" She was suddenly too choked for words.

"I called your house earlier to let you know I was a man short on the afternoon shift and would be tied up tonight." He moved quietly over to crouch down beside her, sitting on his heels. "Your mother told me what happened. I'm sorry I couldn't get here any sooner."

"There wasn't much you could have done anyway, except maybe given Dobie a hand welding the splints." She was just glad he was here with her now.

"How's she doing?" He nodded at the filly.

"She's going to make it," Abbie asserted, again feeling that swell of determination.

"What are you going to do now?"

"Stay with her." She stared at the young filly all trussed up in the sling and splints, a sorry-looking sight. "I have to. A lot of horses go crazy with the pain and trauma and try to destroy themselves. I have to make sure that doesn't happen."

"That's not what I meant," MacCrea said. "Everybody knows the horse is here."

She hadn't thought of that. "So help me, MacCrea Wilder, if you say 'I-told-you-so,' " she threatened angrily. Too many times today she'd wondered whether an accident like this would have occurred if she hadn't brought River Breeze over here. All day she'd lived with the terrible irony of knowing she had done it to keep the filly and might lose her as a result.

"I'm not. I'm only wondering how you're going to handle the situation now."

"I don't know. Who would buy a cripple? Doc Campbell warned me that even if she makes it, there's no telling how well the bones will knit. There's a chance her legs will never be strong enough to support the weight of pregnancy."

"Make a full disclosure of everything the vet said and put the filly in the auction," MacCrea said.

"What?" She stared at him, regarding his suggestion as tantamount to betrayal.

"You said it yourself: Who'd buy her now? You should be able to pick her up cheap."

"I could," Abbie mused, then sighed. "The auction is only a day away. There's so much to be done yet. I know Ben can handle it, but I should be there to help." She was tired and confused, torn by responsibility. Too much had happened today, and it left her feeling drained and numb inside.

"You look tired. Why don't you get some sleep?"

"I can't." She shook her head, weighted with weariness. "I have to stay here and keep an eye on Breeze."

"I wasn't suggesting you should leave. Move over." The straw on the stall floor rustled with their movements as MacCrea wedged himself into the corner and shifted Abbie inside the crook of his arm, nestling her against his shoulder. "Comfortable?"

"Mmmm." She snuggled more closely against his side, drawing the blanket over both of them. Absently she rubbed her cheek against his cotton shirt, soothed by the warmth of his body and the steady beat of his heart. "I suppose you think I'm crazy for sitting up with a horse."

"Would you sit up with me if I was hurt?"

"Probably not." She smiled.

"That's what I thought." His voice rumbled from his chest, warm with amusement. Then she felt the stroke of his hand on her hair, lightly pressing her head more fully to the pillow of his chest. "Try to rest, Abbie."

Obediently she closed her eyes and felt the tension, the need for watchfulness, slipping away. MacCrea was here and she could relax.

Slowly, gradually, he felt her grow heavier in his arms and the rhythm of her breathing deepen. He tried to ease the cramping in his muscles with a flexing shrug of his shoulders, but there was no relief from the hard boards pressing into his back. He didn't know why Abbie hadn't chosen to keep watch from the soft comfort of a haystack instead of this damnable corner of the stall.

A scrape of metal against the cement floor of the stall was followed by the sound of hooves shifting in the straw. MacCrea glanced at the silvery horse. Her head was up, her ears were pinned back, and the white of one eye showed in alarm. Twisting her neck around, the horse made a weak attempt to bite the splint's iron hoop that rubbed against her shoulder.

"Hey, girl. Easy," MacCrea crooned. Her ears pricked at the sound of his voice as she swung her head around to look at him, blowing softly. "She's sleeping. Don't wake her up."

After a few seconds, the horse let her head droop again, the list-lessness returning. MacCrea watched her closely for several more minutes, but the horse made no further attempts to fight the immo-bilizing makeshift harness. As Abbie stirred against him, he gently smoothed the top of her head and drew her closer still.

22

Although the auction wasn't scheduled to begin for another hour yet, an assortment of parked cars, pickup trucks, and horse trailers already filled the farmyard, a few overflowing onto the shoulder of the narrow lane, when Rachel arrived. She found a space between two vehicles parked near the house and maneuvered her car into it.

As she stepped out of the car, a hand touched her arm. Startled, Rachel turned sharply, half expecting to be confronted by Abbie. Instead she found herself gazing into Lane's smiling eyes, happy lines fanning out from the corners like so many rays from the sun.

"Lane." She breathed out his name in a mixture of delight and relief.

"Surprised?" He kissed her lightly.

"And glad," she admitted as he drew back to run an admiring glance over her, sweeping her from head to toe.

She met it confidently, aware that her choice of attire was both casual and elegant, as well as practical and feminine. Padded at the shoulders and graced with a high stand-up collar and turned-back cuffs, her ivory blouse was done in a softly draping silk charmeuse. A wide brown leather belt circled the shaped waistline of her camel skirt, which then fell gracefully full to midcalf. Instead of shoes, she wore a sophisticated version of flat-heeled riding boots. A silk scarf, the same ivory shade as her blouse, held her hair back at the nape of her neck. Her only jewelry was a pair of heavy gold earrings, sculpted in layers.

Since she'd moved to Houston, she'd thrown out or given away all her clothes and bought a whole new wardrobe. No more inexpensive California casual for her: now that she had some money, it was Texas chic, thanks to the helpful and instructive suggestions she'd received from clerks at several of Houston's more exclusive department stores — clerks vastly different from the disinterested, gum-chewing salespeople in the stores where she used to shop. Knowing what to wear, how to wear it, and when to wear it — and knowing that because of it she always looked her best — had done wonders to improve her self-image.

"You look stunning, as usual," Lane declared, then tucked a hand under her elbow and guided her toward the idly milling crowds near the stables.

"I didn't know you'd be here today. You never said anything about it when we talked on the phone last night." She looked at him curiously.

"Under the circumstances, I decided it would be wise for me to come and ensure that there wouldn't be any problems." He didn't say "with Abbie," but Rachel knew that's what he meant. "And, as Dean's executor, I felt I should be on hand to see how the auction went."

"Of course." A small crowd had gathered at the rail of the riding arena to watch a horse and rider working in English tack. Rachel paused with Lane to observe the pair, her attention first drawn to the flashy bay mare, then shifting to the rider. It was Abbie, dressed in jodhpurs, riding helmet, and white shirt, minus the customary jacket, her dark hair pulled back in a low bun. As she rode along the near rail, Rachel noticed that her face looked haggard and she had dark hollows beneath her eyes. "Did you see her, Lane? She looks awful." The words were out before she realized how tactless the remark was. She tried to cover them. "Is she ill?"

"No, I think she's just tired. She hasn't had much sleep lately, I understand." He hesitated, then added, "Her horse was injured in a freak accident a couple days ago. Both front legs were broken. She's been sitting up nights with her ever since."

"What happened?"

"The way it was explained to me, the horse got out of the pasture sometime in the night and strayed onto the adjoining farm. The neighbor caught her the next morning and put her in his barn, then called here to let them know the horse was safe. Before they could go get her, the horse was frightened by the noise from some farm machinery and tried to get out of the barn."

"How terrible." Rachel shuddered to think of such a thing happening to her mare.

"Yes. . . . I think Chet needs to talk to me about something," Lane said, indicating the man motioning for him. "Do you want to come along?"

"No. I think I'll wander through the barns and look over the horses." Rachel took the sales catalogue from her purse and folded it open to the page containing the names and sale numbers of the three mares she was interested in buying.

"I'll catch up with you later. You'll be all right?"

"Of course." She smiled, liking the way he was so protective of her. It made her feel secure and loved.

More than a dozen prospective buyers were scattered along the wide corridor, surveying the horses in the stalls, when Rachel entered. Inside, she checked the sale numbers of the horses on her list again, then started down the cement walkway, pausing in front of each stall long enough to read the number on the horse's hip. Along the way she caught snatches of conversation.

"This mare should nick well with our stallion. Her breeding —"

"— pretty head, but her legs are —"

"— always said, if you don't like the looks of a horse in the stall, don't buy it."

Rachel stopped in front of one of the last stalls in the row. The flaxen-maned chestnut mare stood at an angle that made it difficult for Rachel to tell if the last number on her hip was a five or a nine. As she moved to try to get a better view of the number, someone else came up to the stall to look at the horse. She paid no attention to him until he spoke.

"Hello, beautiful."

At first she thought the murmured words were addressed to the mare, although his voice sounded vaguely familiar. Idly curious, she glanced sideways at the man and encountered his gaze. As he pushed the dark cowboy hat with the concho-studded band to the back of his head, Rachel recognized the curly-haired singer, Ross Tibbs.

"Mr. Tibbs." She was surprised at how clearly she remembered him.

"I thought we agreed that it was Ross to you." He smiled, looking at her as if nothing and no one else existed, the sensation distinctly unnerving. "It's been so long since I've seen you, I was beginning to wonder if I hadn't dreamed you."

She was disturbed by the flattery inherent in his remarks. "I never expected to run into you at a horse auction. Why are you here?"

"Same reason you are, I expect. I came to look over the horses. I've always wanted to own an Arabian. I was kinda hoping I might be able to pick one up for a song." He winked at her, then smiled ruefully. "That was a joke. A poor one, I admit. Singer . . . song."

"Of course." She laughed uneasily.

"From the looks of all these folks that've shown up, there's not going to be much chance of me picking up a bargain. But, it never does any harm to window-shop now and then." Turning, he braced an arm against the stall, his head resting on a board near her head. She'd never noticed how dark and thick his eyelashes were — long like a woman's. "I'd like to take you out to dinner after the auction's over."

"I can't." She was surprised and briefly embarrassed by the invitation.

"Why?"

"I'm . . . with someone." She stared at the open collar of his shirt, her eyes on the smooth, taut skin of his throat and neck.

"Who? Lane Canfield again?"

"Yes."

"Just what is he to you? Your sugar daddy or what?" He sounded almost angry, and the muscles along his jaw tightened visibly.

"No." Rachel didn't like the connotation of that term. It implied she was his mistress, his plaything. But what was she to him? "We're . . . friends. That's all."

"Friends, eh? That can cover a lot of ground, you know." Ross swung partially around, trapping her against the wall of the stall. "He's too old for you, Rachel."

"He isn't old," she insisted, but she recognized the shakiness of that argument. "Besides, maybe I like older men."

"I'm pushing thirty. I fit that category." He leaned closer and she felt smothered by his nearness, unable to breathe. Reaching up, he lightly traced the curve of her cheekbone with the tip of his forefinger, following it all the way to the lobe of her ear. "You remind me of Sleeping Beauty still waiting to be awakened by a kiss from her prince. I never read any fairy tale that had a prince with white hair in it."

She felt hot all over as her heart beat rapidly. He was staring at her lips and Rachel could almost feel the pressure of his mouth on them. She was frightened by the things she was feeling. Was this how her mother had felt with Dean — so overwhelmed by emotion that she abandoned everything, including her pride and self-respect? That wasn't going to happen to her. She wouldn't let it.

"Don't say things like that." She pushed away from the stall and hurriedly brushed past him, not stopping until she'd put several feet between them. Against her will, Rachel looked back.

"I'm sorry." He lifted his hand in a helpless, apologetic gesture. "I didn't mean any harm."

"Please, just leave me alone." She walked out of the barn and nearly ran into Lane on his way in.

"I was just coming to look for you." His initial smile faded slightly as his interest in her sharpened. "Is something wrong?"

"Of course not. What could be wrong?" Rachel forced a smile, surprised that she could do it so convincingly, and linked her arm with his to steer him away from the open barn doors before he could catch sight of Ross Tibbs.

She didn't want Lane to know she'd been talking with Ross or he'd guess why she was upset. Knowing that a moment sooner and Lane would have found them together made it all the more imperative that he not find out. At the same time, Rachel didn't understand this feeling of guilt just because for a brief instant she'd been attracted to — and tempted by — Ross. After all, nothing had happened.

"I thought Abbie may —"

"I haven't seen her." She began to breathe easier as his smile came back.

"The auction is scheduled to start in another ten minutes. I think we'd better head over to the sales ring if you want a good vantage point."

"Yes, we probably should."

As they walked toward the sales ring, they were joined by others converging on the same destination. Rachel noticed the looks Lane received and heard the murmurs of recognition. The first few times she'd been out in public with him, the stares and whispers had bothered her, but she'd grown used to the attention he attracted — the respect, admiration, and envy with which he was regarded. In fact, she was actually beginning to enjoy it.

"Testing: one, two, three. Testing. Testing." The auctioneer's voice came over the loudspeakers. "Well, folks, it looks like we're ready to start. We've got some fine horses for you today. And we'll start with Lot Number One. Coming into the ring now is the incredible stallion, Nahr Ibn Kedar, the five-year-old son of the stallion imported from Egypt by the late Dean Lawson himself. This magnificent stallion is being shown under saddle by Dean's daughter, Abbie Lawson."

Recognizing that he was dealing with a knowledgeable group of buyers, the auctioneer wasted little time extolling the pedigrees and show records of the Arabian horses that entered the ring one after another. And rarely did he interrupt his rhythmic chant to exhort higher bids from the participants. The quickness of his hammer to declare a horse sold instilled a feverish pace to the bidding and allowed few lulls between bids.

As Abbie rode out of the sales ring on the final horse to be shown under saddle, Ben waited to take the reins. She flipped them to him and dismounted, feeling exhausted. The heavy humidity from the moisture-laden clouds overhead was taking its toll on her, as well as the tension of trying to get the best out of every horse she rode.

"It goes well." Ben patted the mare's neck, then turned to lead the horse to the barn. Abbie fell into step beside him. "The auctioneer does not give them time to think how much they are bidding. We get good prices."

"I noticed." She should have been pleased about it, but she wasn't, and she blamed the indifference she felt on her tiredness. "Is the next lot ready for the ring?"

"Yes."

She spied the bale of hay shoved up against the stable door. It offered an escape from all the hubbub and confusion going on inside the barn. "If you don't need me, I think I'll just sit and rest for a minute."

"We can manage," Ben assured her.

"Thanks." She smiled wanly and angled away from him, walking over to the lone bale.

As she sank onto the compressed hay, Abbie removed the hot riding helmet and laid it on the bale, then leaned back against the barn door. For a time, she stared at the crowd gathered around the sale ring and idly listened to the auctioneer's singsong voice calling for higher bids on the mare and foal in the ring.

Then her attention wandered to the barns, the white-fenced pastures, and the old Victorian house — the place, the land, the buildings that comprised her home, the only real home she'd ever known.

Suddenly it was all a blur as tears filled her eyes. Tomorrow it would be sold and a new owner would take possession of it.

Leaning forward, she scooped up a handful of dirt — dirt that turned into thick gumbo when it rained. She rubbed it between her thumb and fingers, feeling its texture and consistency, the way she'd seen her grandfather do a hundred times or more. When she'd ask him why he did it, he'd put some in her hands and say, "Now, feel that. It's more than just dirt, you know."

"It's Texas dirt," Abbie would reply.

"It's more than that. You see, that dirt you're holding, that's pieces of Lawson land." Then he would hold it up close to his face, smell it, and taste it with the tip of his tongue.

"Why did you do that, Grandpa?" she would ask.

"Because it's good for what ails you. Remember that."

Abbie remembered, closing her hand into a fist and squeezing the dirt into a thick clump in her palm.

"Mind if I join you?"

Startled to hear MacCrea's voice, Abbie sat up and brought her hands together, hiding the dirt clutched in her palm. "What are you doing here?"

"I had an errand to run in town, so I thought I'd stop by and see how the sale was going." He moved the riding helmet to one side and sat down next to her. "There's a lot of people here."

"Yes." Uncomfortable under his inspecting glance, she looked down at her hands.

"Are you all right?"

"I'm fine," she assured him with a quick nod. "Just tired, that's all." She said nothing to him about the dirt she held so tightly, doubting that he'd understand. From the little she'd learned about his childhood, she knew he'd never stayed in any one place long enough to form any deep attachment to it. He couldn't appreciate the strong bond she felt for River Bend, her home, her heritage.

Ben emerged from the stables and walked over to them. "I wanted to remind you that he will sell your filly after this mare leaves the ring."

"Thanks." Abbie pushed to her feet and headed directly for the sales ring. MacCrea walked with her, but she paid no attention to him. She worked her way through the crowd and reached the edge of the ring just as the auctioneer rang the hammer down, selling the mare and foal to the high bidder.

"The next filly to be sold — number twenty-five in your

catalogue — was unfortunately injured in a freak accident two days ago," the auctioneer explained. "The veterinarian's report, which I have in front of me, states that both front legs were broken. Both have been successfully splinted and cast, and the veterinarian expresses a guarded optimism over the filly's chances of recovery."

Practically rigid with tension herself, Abbie closely observed the crowd's reaction to his announcement. Most shook their heads skeptically and a few turned away from the ring. No one appeared to be even slightly interested in River Breeze, not even Rachel, whom Abbie spotted standing on the opposite side of the ring, talking to Lane.

The auctioneer then went into a lengthy description of the filly's breeding, concluding with, "Regardless of this filly's injuries, I think you will all agree she has the potential to make an outstanding broodmare. Now what do I hear for an opening bid?"

Abbie held her breath as he and his assistants scanned the throng, but silence greeted them. Anxiously she waited until his second call for a bid was met with silence, then she signaled a bid of a hundred dollars.

"I've got a bid of one hundred dollars right over here. Who'll gimme two? Who'll gimme two?" The chanted call rolled off his tongue. As soon as it became apparent there were no takers at two, he halved it. "I've got one. Who'll gimme one-fifty? One-fifty?"

As MacCrea had predicted, no one wanted the injured filly. Within a scant few minutes after the bidding started, it was over.

"Breeze is legally mine now." Abbie turned to him, a smile lifting her tired features.

"So are the vet bills," MacCrea reminded her.

"I don't care," she declared, blithely defiant of such practical considerations. "She's worth it — and more." She still held the dirt in her hand, sweat turning it into a ball of mud. But she wouldn't let it go.

23

All morning long, ominous gray clouds loomed over River Bend, casting an eerie half-darkness over the tree-shaded grounds. Distant rumbles of thunder, like deep-throated growls, threatened rain. The auctioneer's podium stood on the veranda of the great house, facing the striped tent that had been erected on the front lawn to shelter the bidders in case it rained.

All day long, Rachel had watched people traipsing through the house, faces peering out at her from turret windows, children racing around behind the second-floor parapet, and hands tapping at wood to check its solidness. But she had yet to venture inside herself. When she set foot inside that house for the first time, she was determined not to be surrounded by irreverent gawkers.

A hush settled over the crowd gathered under the tent as the auctioneer announced the next item to be sold: River Bend itself. Rachel felt her stomach lurch sickeningly. All this waiting, the tension, the uncertainty had worn her nerves raw. She glanced anxiously around for Lane and saw him talking with Dean's widow. Twice Rachel had seen her and that Polish stud manager who had worked for Dean, but she had yet to see Abbie on the grounds.

A boom of thunder reverberated through the air, chasing those on the outer fringes farther under the canvas roof. Behind her, Rachel heard a man say, "I wouldn't be surprised if that isn't R.D. up there, pounding his fist on a cloud. You know he's looking down on this — and not liking it one whit."

Just for an instant, Rachel took the remark as a personal slur against her, then reminded herself that the man couldn't know she intended to buy River Bend. As the auctioneer continued with his legal description of the property and its buildings, she tried to locate the man Lane had pointed out to her earlier — the one who would actually do the bidding for them. But she couldn't find him in the crowd. The last time she'd seen him, he'd been smoking a cigarette near the old carriage house that had been converted into a garage.

Panicking at the thought that maybe he didn't know the bidding was about to start, Rachel caught Lane's eye and signaled him to join her. She waited impatiently as he worked his way through the crowd to her side.

"Where's your man Phillips? I don't see him."

"He's on the far side of the tent. I saw him there just seconds ago. Stop worrying." He took her hand and gave it a reassuring squeeze.

"I can't help it." She held on to his hand, locking her fingers through his, today needing his strength and his confidence.

When the auctioneer called for the first bid, it started to rain — at first just making a soft patter on the tent roof, then turning into a steady drumming. The sky seemed to grow darker.

The woman in front of Rachel turned to her companion. "Let's go find Babs and tell her we're leaving," she said in a low, subdued voice. " I don't want to stay for this. It's like all of Texas is crying."

Rachel tried not to let the woman's comment demoralize her. Those were just rivulets of rainwater running down the windowpanes of the mansion, not tears. This was the moment she'd been waiting for all her life . . . even though she hadn't always known it. Nothing and no one was going to spoil it for her.

"I haven't seen Abbie," she remembered. "Is she here?"

"She didn't come today," Lane replied.

Finding out that Abbie had stayed away from this auction made Rachel feel that she'd won a minor victory. Her dream was well on its way to coming true, in a way she had never dared to imagine. Yesterday she had acquired three broodmares, all with foals at their side and checked in foal to Nahr El Kedar, increasing the number of Arabians she owned. And today, River Bend itself would belong to her. Now she would have that part of Dean's world that had always been denied her. She wanted to hug herself and hold on to that triumphant feeling, but she was too nervous, too anxious. Instead she gripped Lane's hand a little harder and listened to the bidding.

Higher and higher it went, finally narrowing the field to three bidders, their agent among them. When Rachel realized the price had climbed to over a hundred thousand dollars more than Lane had expected River Bend to sell for, she started to worry. Then the agent, Phillips, dropped out of the bidding. Pierced by a shaft of icy-cold fear, Rachel wondered if she had come this close, only to lose it after all.

"Lane, why isn't he bidding?" she whispered, afraid of the answer.

"He doesn't want to drive the price up more."

She realized it was some sort of strategy, but the suspense was almost more than she could stand. But when the gavel fell, knocking off the final bid, the auctioneer pointed to the bald-headed agent as the successful bidder. Weak with relief, Rachel sagged against Lane.

"Happy?" Lane smiled at her with his eyes.

"Not yet. I think I'm afraid to be," she admitted, aware that she must sound terribly unsophisticated to him, but it was the truth.

"Maybe it would seem more real to you if we went inside and looked around your new home."

"Not now. I'd rather do it later . . . after everyone leaves." She didn't want any strangers wandering through the rooms when she explored the house. She wouldn't feel that it really belonged to her if they were there.

"If that's the way you want it, we'll wait."

Late that afternoon, the last of the cars headed down the long driveway, carrying the auctioneer and his staff. The rain had stopped, but drops of water continued to plop down from the wet leaves of the giant trees in the yard. Overhead the clouds lingered, forming a charcoal-colored canopy over River Bend.

Nervous and excited, Rachel felt as giddy as a teenager as she waited for Lane to unlock the front door. When he held it open for her, she glanced hesitantly inside, in her mind seeing Abbie's apparition standing in the doorway, ordering her away.

But this was no longer Abbie's home. From now on she would do the ordering. Rachel walked inside to take possession of it. In the large foyer, she paused and gazed at the impressive staircase with its balustrades of ornately carved walnut. She tried to visualize Dean walking down those steps to welcome her, but the image wouldn't come.

Hiding the bitter disappointment she felt, Rachel followed Lane through the rest of the house, so huge compared to the apartments she'd always lived in. In every room, the wood of the parquet floors, the richly carved door and window moldings, the wainscoting, and the fireplace mantels gleamed with the patina that came from years of loving care. Yet the bare walls and windows seemed to stare back at her. With no furniture, curtains, or paintings in the house, their footsteps echoed with a stark, lonely sound.

"Once all the paperwork is finalized and you officially take possession, you can have an interior decorator come out," Lane said as they climbed the staircase to the second floor. "I'm sure there will be changes you want to make."

"Yes," Rachel said absently, but she doubted it would be anything drastic. She wanted to keep the house just the way it was. She planned to limit any decorating to choosing curtains, rugs, and furniture.

But when she entered one of the bedrooms on the second floor and felt prickles crawling up the back of her neck, she changed her mind entirely. She knew without being told the room had belonged to Abbie. Her Dior perfume still lingered in the air.

She crossed to the French doors that opened onto the narrow balcony within the parapet and pulled them open, letting the rain-freshened air sweep into the room. She paused there a minute, staring at the high limbs of the towering ancient oaks, some stretching out their arms so close to the house she had the feeling that she only had to reach out her hand to touch their shiny leaves. Drawn by the stillness, the peace of the view, Rachel wandered onto the railed balcony. Through the trees, she could see parts of the winding lane, the stable complex and paddocks, and the empty pastures.

As she leaned against the parapet, Lane walked up to stand beside her. "You haven't said very much."

She turned to face the house, half sitting and half bracing herself against the rail. "I guess I'm still finding it hard to believe this all belongs to me — to us," she corrected quickly.

"Yes, to us," he said thoughtfully. "I've been wondering . . . ," Lane began, then started over. "Have you ever given any thought to making our partnership a permanent one?"

"What do you mean?" Rachel frowned. "I thought it was. All the documents we signed, didn't they —"

Lane smiled ruefully. "I'm putting it badly, I'm afraid. I wasn't referring to our business partnership. I meant you and me. I think you know that I love you, Rachel. But do you love me?"

"Yes." She thought he knew that. Lane Canfield was everything a woman could ever wish for in a man. He was so good *to* her and *for* her — not just because he was fulfilling her dreams, but because he'd made her feel that she was someone very special.

"Do you love me enough to marry me and be my wife?"

"Do I!" She nearly went into his arms, but she checked the impulse, suddenly wary. "You mean it, don't you, Lane? This isn't some joke, is it?"

"I couldn't be more serious." The gravity in his expression convinced Rachel of that. "I've never proposed to another woman in my entire life. You would eliminate a lot of the misery I'm going through right now by simply telling me yes or no."

"Yes." Gazing at him, Rachel wondered if he knew how much he had given her: first a belief in herself and her dreams, then River Bend, and now the respect and legitimacy of his name. No man had done so much for her before — not even Dean.

In the next second, his arms were around her and his mouth was on her lips. She reveled in the adoring ardency of his kiss, overwhelmed by the knowledge that of all the women he could have chosen, Lane Canfield wanted to marry her. At last she drew back a few inches to look at his face, so strong and good and gentle. "I do love you, Lane."

"I suppose we should make this official." He reached into his jacket pocket and pulled out a ring. Rachel gasped as fire leaped from the circlet of diamonds that surrounded the large sapphire. Lane took her hand and slipped it onto her ring finger.

"It's beautiful." The words sounded so inadequate, but she couldn't think of anything else to say.

"I've been carrying that ring around with me for the last two weeks, trying to convince myself that it wouldn't be a mistake to marry you. You deserve to be happy, Rachel. If you'd be happier with someone else . . ."

"No one could make me as happy as you do," she insisted, refusing even to consider the possibility. "I am going to be so proud to be your wife. Mrs. Lane Canfield. I love the sound of it."

"So do I. Now about our wedding . . ."

"We can fly to Mexico tonight and elope if you want." Rachel almost preferred that. She didn't want to be reminded that she had no father to give her away, no family and few friends to invite.

"No. I want you to have a wedding with all the trimmings. Nothing elaborate, you understand. Just a simple ceremony and a small reception afterward with a few of our close friends in attendance. I want you to come to me in a bridal gown, all white satin and lace."

"Whatever you say, Lane."

"I'll do my best to make you happy, Rachel. I want you to know that. There will be times when my work will take me away from you, maybe for several days in a row, and for one reason or another you usually won't be able to come with me. You understand that, don't you?"

"Of course."

"I know how lonely your life has been. I don't like the idea that as my wife, you may be lonely again."

"I'll have a lot to keep me busy, between the horses and turning this into a home for us." As long as it was only his work that kept them apart, Rachel could accept the separations. What was really important was that she had his love.

"You're a remarkable woman," he murmured, drawing her into his embrace once again. She kissed him while secretly doubting she was all that remarkable, but it was important that he believed she was.

"Lane." She kissed him fervently, straining to give back part of the joy he'd given her. When she finally drew away from him, she knew she had aroused him. The evidence was there in the disturbed light in his eyes and the quickened rate of his breathing.

"It's moments like this that make me wish this was our wedding night," he whispered and set her slightly away from him.

Rachel was touched by the way he refused to anticipate their wedding night. She considered his attitude wonderfully old-fashioned and proof he was worthy of her trust. Yet in another way it bothered her. Sometimes she thought there was something wrong with her, that she wasn't desirable enough. Otherwise, if he loved her as much as he claimed, he'd be tempted to take her. But she didn't press the issue even now, fearing his rejection as well as his possible discovery of her own inadequacies at making love.

24

The headlight beams raced ahead of the car as Abbie sped down the highway, the overlapping tracks of light a blur in front of her eyes. Instinctively she was running — running like a child trying to escape from the unkind taunts of her playmates. But no matter how far or how fast she went, she could never get away from the hurtful words.

For the last ten days, she'd listened to the swirl of rumors going around, speculating on the identity of River Bend's new owner. It was common knowledge that the man Phillips, the successful bidder at the auction, had been acting on behalf of an unnamed client. Today, when she and Babs had gone to Lane's office to receive a final accounting on her father's estate after all costs and debts were paid, she had learned the truth.

As she had feared all along, Rachel now possessed River Bend. But what Abbie hadn't known was Lane's involvement. The two of them owned it jointly. More damning than that, he had blandly announced that he and Rachel were getting married in September. At that point Abbie had walked out of his office, unable to endure his presence a second longer.

Lane Canfield. A trusted family friend. He had turned against them and joined with Rachel. It seemed that no matter which way she turned, she was faced with betrayal. She should have known the day of the funeral when he'd told her about Dean's long love affair with Caroline Farr exactly where his sympathies lay. She should have seen when he leaped to Rachel's defense that day at River Bend that he wasn't looking out for their interests. Rachel came first with him — just as she had with her father.

Maybe she could have eventually learned to live with the fact that her father had another child. Maybe she could have even accepted the fact that he had loved Rachel more than he ever had her. But the fortune he had left Rachel, while she had received nothing from him, the ownership of River Bend going to Rachel, and Rachel's impending marriage to a man who was supposed to be a trusted family friend — combined, they were all more than Abbie could tolerate. Her initial resentment of Rachel had grown into a consuming hatred.

If Rachel thought Abbie was going to move away from the area and start a new life someplace else, she was wrong. And if she thought Abbie was going to forgo any further involvement in the breeding and showing of Arabian horses because Rachel was getting into it, she was wrong there, too. Whether Rachel realized it yet or not, she had a rival almost literally in her own backyard. There hadn't been anything Abbie could do to prevent the things that had happened. But now she intended to fight Rachel every step of the way, reminding Rachel by her presence alone that she was the intruder, the interloper, in Abbie's world.

A mile before she reached the drilling site, Abbie could see the glow from the platform's floodlights lighting up the night sky. It shone like a beacon guiding her to a safe haven, the way growing brighter the closer she got. Finally the clearing was directly in front of her car, the bright lights from the derrick spilling onto the dusty trailers and the pickups parked at the site.

After parking in front of MacCrea's office trailer, Abbie stepped out of her car and walked directly to it. She didn't bother to knock, knowing she wouldn't be heard above all the noise. Instead, she walked right in.

There was no one in the front half of the trailer. When she looked toward the rear, she saw MacCrea sprawled across one of the single beds, fully clothed and sound asleep. She walked back to where he lay and, for a moment, simply watched him. She had never seen him asleep before. His dark, wavy hair was all rumpled; his shirt, pulled loose from the waistband of his pants; and his muscles, lax. His chest rose and fell with the even rhythm of his breathing. Abbie smiled at the scowl on his face.

Things had gone badly for her lately. But watching him, she realized that she'd been so caught up in her own problems she'd forgotten that MacCrea had lost nearly everything after his father died. Yet he had battled the odds and built the company back up. She knew it hadn't been easy, especially at the beginning.

To be honest, her own situation wasn't as bad as it could have been. Besides River Breeze, she had her own reputation in the show ring. This last week, she and Ben had contacted several of the small Arabian horse breeders in the area and let them know their services were available to condition, train, and show outside horses. With the fall show season approaching, quite a number of the breeders expressed a definite interest in hiring them.

And they weren't totally broke. Babs would receive almost fifty thousand dollars from her share of the estate, money left over after all the creditors were paid from the auction receipts. If Abbie had stayed instead of walking out of Lane's office in such a huff, it might have been more. But her mother had insisted that Jackson receive the full amount of his bequest, and instructed Lane to take the amount necessary from her proceeds to make up the difference. It was a grand and noble gesture, one that Abbie had difficulty arguing with. Still, she didn't think it had been necessary for her mother to be *that* generous.

So, her mother had a small nest egg. Abbie had River Breeze, and after a bout with a fever, the filly was improving. Plus she had Ben for a partner. And, most of all, she had the man lying before her, frowning in his sleep, ready to fight some more.

Slowly and carefully she lowered herself onto him, letting her weight settle gradually. She gently smoothed the furrowed lines from his forehead with her fingers, not letting her touch be too light, to avoid tickling him. As she rubbed her lips over his mouth, letting them trace its outline, she felt him stir. His hand moved hesitantly to the small of her back, then glided along a familiar course up to her shoulders. Abbie knew he was awake even before he began to lip at her mouth and draw it to his. She kissed him, receiving a languorous response, like a flame slow to kindle and long to burn, heating her more thoroughly than any passionately demanding kiss could.

Finally MacCrea shifted onto his side, drawing her with him so her head rested on the same pillow facing him. "Hello," Abbie said softly.

"Now that's how a man likes to be woke up." His voice was still husky with sleep. He looked deep into her eyes, so deep that Abbie felt certain he could see all the love she felt for him. "I've missed you, Abbie." Emotion charged his words, and she felt her breath catch in her throat, hearing in the admission how much he cared for her even though he hadn't actually used the word *love*.

"I've missed you, Mac," she whispered.

His hand exerted pressure on her back a second before his mouth moved to claim hers. Abbie gave to him all the feelings she'd held inside, her heartbeat quickening and the blood running sweet and fast in her veins. There was nothing hurried about the long, full kiss; no sense of urgency pushed them. Abbie sensed that he, too, found something warm and satisfying in this closeness and sought only to enjoy it.

The loud racket from the drilling rig suddenly flooded the trailer. MacCrea pulled back, frowning.

"Hey, boss!" a rigger in a hard hat called as he stepped into the small kitchen, stopping short when he saw Abbie lying on the narrow bed with MacCrea. His head dipped as he looked hurriedly away. "Sorry. I didn't know ya had company." He retreated a step, uncertain whether to stay or go.

"What is it, Barnes?" Partially rising, MacCrea propped an elbow beneath him. Abbie lay beside him, not at all upset by the interruption, wrapped in the comforting feeling that she had the right to be there in his bed.

"We could use you out on the rig for a minute, that's all," he mumbled and turned to leave.

"I'll be right out," MacCrea told him. When the door closed, shutting out the noise from the rig, he looked down at her, a dark glow shining in his eyes, and added softly, "Much as I'd like to stay right here."

"And much as I'd like to keep you here, I won't." Levering herself up, she brushed a kiss across his cheek, then swung her feet onto the trailer floor.

MacCrea was only a step behind her when she entered the kitchen. She moved to the side to let him pass, her gaze following him as he grabbed his hard hat off the table and stepped to the door.

"I shouldn't be long." He smiled briefly in her direction, but Abbie could tell his thoughts had already shifted from her to the rig. "Put on some fresh coffee, would you?"

It was hardly a question since he was out the door by the time she said, "Okay."

Minutes later the electric percolator bubbled merrily, the wafts of steam rising from its spout sending the aroma of coffee throughout the trailer. Abbie tidied up the kitchen, then poured herself a cup of the freshly brewed coffee and carried it into the front office area of the trailer. Drawn by the photograph of MacCrea and his father, she wandered over to the filing cabinet and, for a time, studied the picture propped against the wall on top of it. The love, the deep bond, between father and son was so obvious that she couldn't help feeling a sharp pang of envy.

Fighting it, she turned away and walked over to MacCrea's desk, suddenly needing his closeness, the reassurance of his love. Impulsively Abbie sat down in the worn swivel chair behind his desk, its cushion and padded back long since fitted to the shape of his body. She rocked back in it, sipping at her coffee as she absently perused the papers and file folders scattered across the desktop.

One of the folders bore the label "CTS documents." CTS was the acronym for MacCrea's computerized testing system, Abbie remembered. Out of idle curiosity, she slipped the folder out of the stack and opened it to glance through the papers. She knew the project meant a lot to him, yet he'd never discussed the deal he'd made. As she leafed through some sort of partnership agreement, one of the signatures on the last page leaped out at her: Rachel Farr. Abbie stared at it in shock, certain there had to be some mistake. MacCrea couldn't . . . MacCrea wouldn't . . . She straightened slowly, the pages clutched tightly in her hands, her gaze riveted to the name Rachel Farr.

The trailer door opened and MacCrea walked in. Abbie turned her head, unable to speak, unable to think, unable to do anything except stare at him, frozen by the damning evidence in her hands. But he didn't seem to notice as he removed his helmet and gave it a little toss onto the sofa.

"I told you I wouldn't be long." A lazy smile lifted the corners of his mustache as he paused beside the desk, then glanced briefly at the papers in her hand. Without a break in his expression, he turned and walked into the kitchen area, saying, "The coffee smells good."

"What is this, MacCrea?" Abbie pushed out of the chair and followed him to the door, then stopped, still in the thrall of a shock that deadened her senses.

"That?" Half glancing at the papers in her hand, he lifted a cup of steaming hot coffee to his mouth, but didn't drink immediately from it. "It's a joint ownership agreement on the patent for the CTS."

"I know that." She shook her head and wondered if he had deliberately misunderstood. "I'm not talking about his signature. What is hers doing on it?"

"By 'hers' I assume you mean Rachel's." His voice was calm and even, the name coming from his lips with ease. "Since it's a list of owners, naturally Rachel's name is on it."

His casual announcement shattered the numbness that had kept all her emotions in check. Now they raged through her. "What do you mean, 'naturally'?" Half-blinded by anger, Abbie couldn't even make out the hated name on the list. "Are you saying she's one of your investors? That you — you —" She searched wildly for the words that would express the absolute betrayal she felt.

"That's exactly what I'm saying." MacCrea sipped at his coffee.

"You took money from her." She trembled violently as she made the accusation, hating him for standing there so calmly, as if he'd done nothing wrong. All along she thought he truly cared about her, but it was obvious he didn't. "How could you?" Abbie stormed.

"Simple. I wanted to get this project off the ground and out to the drilling sites. I never made a secret of that."

Abbie knew he hadn't, but admitting that just made everything worse. Infuriated by his phlegmatic attitude when he had to know what this was doing to her, Abbie slapped the coffee mug from his hand, mindless of the arcing spray of scalding liquid and the loud crash of the cup as it struck the opposite wall and broke.

"And you didn't care who you got the money from either, did you?"

"Not one damned bit!" MacCrea flared, her anger at last penetrating.

"Now I know why you didn't tell me anything about your *deal*." The contempt she felt matched the violent anger that quivered through her whole body. "You were very careful not to let me know who all was involved, weren't you? You did it *knowing* how I would feel about it. How could you?"

"Easy. This was business," MacCrea stated emphatically.

"Business. Is that what you call it?" She had another name for it: betrayal, the ultimate betrayal. "All that time you spent in Houston, you were meeting with her, weren't you?" She felt sick to her stomach just thinking about the two of them together. She could imagine how Rachel must have gloated over it, knowing she had stolen someone else who had supposedly belonged to her alone.

"There were others involved in those meetings," he snapped. "I wasn't alone with her, if that's what you're implying. I told you: it was business."

"Am I supposed to believe that?" Abbie taunted.

"I don't give a damn whether you do or not!"

"That's obvious." She could tell that he had no intention of altering the situation, a situation that meant he would have continued contact with Rachel. "And it's equally obvious that you don't give a damn about me either!"

"If that's the way you want to look at it." There was no yielding in his hard stand. There wasn't even a glimmer of regret in his expression, not even a hint of apology for his actions.

"This invention of yours was always more important to you than I was. I was a fool not to see that. Well, now you've got it!" She hurled the papers at his face and stalked quickly to the trailer door. Gripping the handle, she glanced over her shoulder, consumed by the pain, jealousy, and anger that were so firmly intermixed she couldn't tell them apart. "I hope they keep your bed warm at night from now on, because I won't!"

She charged out of the trailer into the floodlit night, fighting the tears and trembling that threatened to overwhelm her. She could still see him standing there, towering over the strewn papers and broken pottery shards from the mug, his expression thin-lipped and angry. But she had crossed that fine line, now hating him with all the passion with which she had once loved him.

In the trailer MacCrea stared at the door, his fingers curling with the urge to go after her and shake her until her teeth rattled out of her head. Instead he turned, the papers crackling underfoot. He glanced at them, then, in a burst of frustration, he rammed his fist into a cabinet door, the pressed wood cracking and buckling under the force of the blow.

25

*A*bbie looked on as the filly stood quietly while Ben cleaned and applied disinfectant to the large ulcerated sore under the foreleg caused by the rubbing splint. So far, River Breeze had adjusted well to the splints and lately had managed to hobble a few steps with them.

As Ben straightened to his feet, the messy task finished, the filly nuzzled Abbie's shoulder. The affectionate gesture seemed to be one of gratitude. Smiling, Abbie cradled the filly's silver head in the crook of her arm and lightly rubbed the arched neck with a small circular motion to imitate the nuzzling of a mare on her foal.

"You know we're doing all of this to help you, don't you, Breeze?" Abbie crooned, her chest tight with the pain of betrayal that just wouldn't go away. It was as fresh this morning as it had been two nights ago when she'd left MacCrea's trailer for the last time. If anything, the anger, hurt, and bitterness had grown stronger. When Ben left the stall to dispose of the soiled gauze pads, she pressed the side of her face against the filly's sleek neck. "You would never do that to me, would you, girl?" She drew comfort from that knowledge.

"Looks like she's healing real good."

Startled by the sound of Dobie's voice, Abbie stiffened. She hadn't heard him walk up to the stall and wondered how long he'd been standing there.

"Yes, she's coming along nicely." She gave the filly one last pat, then stepped away, feeling the strain of trying to behave normally so no one would guess that she had broken off with MacCrea. She couldn't talk about it — she didn't want to talk about it yet. "I planned to talk to you today about renting this barn and that section of pasture along the Brazos."

"But I already told you that you were welcome to use both. Neither one of them is of any use to me."

"But that was when we were talking about keeping only my filly here. Several local breeders have contacted us about training and showing their Arabians this fall. So far it looks like we're going to have about a dozen horses. Since Ben and I are going to have to rent facilities somewhere, I thought it would be much more convenient and more logical if I could work out some sort of arrangement with you to keep them here."

"If that's the case, I don't see why not," he replied with a falsely indifferent shrug. As tight as Dobie was with money, Abbie had been certain he wouldn't turn down the opportunity to make an extra dollar. She hadn't misjudged him. "Course" — he glanced around at the interior of the old barn — "this place isn't in very good shape."

"Ben and I can fix it up. We'll pay for the improvements." With what, she didn't know. But that was a worry she'd leave for another time. Maybe by then she'd have sold her Mercedes. "But we would expect a break on the rent because of it."

"I promise I'll be fair with you, Abbie. Anything is better than the nothing I'm getting for it now."

"I suppose that's true."

Knowing that now it was simply a matter of dickering over the price, she felt a little more relieved. It would be good to wake up in the mornings and once again hear the whinny of horses. She had missed that since leaving River Bend. And she could imagine how much harder it must have been on Ben. For nearly all his sixty-odd years, he'd been surrounded by horses — Arabian horses. The care and training of them were both his vocation and avocation. Without them, he felt useless and lost.

The side door of the barn banged shut. Abbie turned, expecting to see Ben. Instead it was MacCrea coming toward her, his long, lazy stride eating up the space between them. Stung, she felt all the hurts coming back, that terrible ache, and the rawness of wounds too fresh even to have begun to heal.

"What do you want?" She heard the brittleness in her voice — rigid and cold like a thin shell of ice. That's the way she felt. She looked him in the eye, taking care to ignore the probe of his dark gaze and not to let her glance slip to the heavy brush of his mustache to watch his mouth when he spoke.

"I want to talk to you."

Beside her, Dobie took a step toward the door. Abbie stopped him. "You don't have to leave, Dobie. I'm not interested in hearing anything he has to say." Pivoting sharply, she swung away from MacCrea.

"I had hoped you would have cooled off enough by now to let me explain a few things to you."

She swung back to face him, cold with rage. "There's no explanation you could give that would justify anything."

When she started to walk away from him, MacCrea grabbed her arm. "Dammit, Abbie —"

"Take your hand off me!" Burned by the contact, she exploded in anger. Releasing her arm, he drew back. "Don't touch me, MacCrea. Don't ever come near me again. Do you hear? I don't want to see — or hear from — you. Just get out! And stay out!"

MacCrea looked at her for a long, hard moment, then snapped, "With pleasure."

In the next second, Abbie was staring at his back as he walked out of the barn. She continued to tremble, but it was more in reaction than anger. MacCrea was gone. She kept reminding herself that she should be relieved to have him out of her life. But why wasn't she? With the exception of Ben, the men she'd known had never brought her anything but grief, from her father to her husband and all the way to MacCrea. She swore she wouldn't be any man's fool again.

Dobie came over to stand beside her. "Are you okay, Abbie?"

"Of course," she answered sharply.

"He wasn't right for you. I always knew that," Dobie said. "The man's a wildcatter. His kind are never in one place very long — always moving on to find the next big strike. A woman like you needs a home — a place you can sink your roots in and raise a family. You need a man to look after you and —"

"I'm perfectly capable of looking after myself. I don't need any man to do that." More specifically, she didn't need Dobie. And she could almost guarantee where he was leading this conversation. "If you'll excuse me, I have work to do — and I'm sure you do, too."

"Yeah, I . . . I do." He nodded, then glanced at her hesitantly before he turned to walk to the door. "I'll talk to you later about the rent for this."

"Fine."

After coming to terms on the rental, Abbie had insisted that a lease agreement be drawn up, covering both the barn area and pasturage, and the house they were living in. Although she doubted that Dobie would go back on his word, she preferred not to take anything on trust.

For the next two weeks, with the help of a laborer to do the heavy work, she and Ben had repaired the barn, fixed the fences, built small paddocks, and spray-painted everything in preparation for the arrival of their new charges. Even then, the facilities were barely adequate to fill their most basic needs — certainly nothing to compare with what they'd had at River Bend.

But the hard physical work left Abbie too exhausted to think about anything — not her former home or its new owners nor even MacCrea. With the approach of noon, Abbie trudged to the house while Ben went to the barn to check on the filly one more time. Every bone and muscle in her body felt bruised, but she had the satisfaction of knowing they had accomplished the impossible. When the first of the horses arrived tomorrow, the place would be ready and presentable.

Pushing open the back door, Abbie walked into the small kitchen, but no cooking odors met her. Babs always had lunch ready for them when they came in at noon. But this time her mother sat at the chrome table in the kitchen, holding the receiver from the wall-mounted telephone to her ear with a raised shoulder while jotting down something on the notepad in front of her.

"Yes, that sounds fine," she said into the phone. When she heard Abbie push the door shut, she started to turn around, then grabbed for the phone to keep it from slipping off her shoulder, the coiled cord pulled taut. "What? . . . All right. Let me call you back after I've had time to check on this." She told the party on the line good-bye as she walked over to hang up the phone. "I didn't realize what time it was, Abbie. This morning has just slipped through my fingers like butter." Hurriedly she began gathering up her papers and notebooks from the table. "I'll have lunch ready in just a few minutes. I'm afraid it'll have to be something cold."

"That's all right. I'll set the table for you."

"Just sit down and rest. You've worked all morning as it is."

Abbie was too tired to argue and gladly sat down in one of the chrome dinette chairs. "Who was that on the phone?" But Babs had her head buried in the refrigerator. She came out of it juggling bowls of potato and macaroni salad and a pitcher of iced tea.

As Abbie was about to repeat her question, Babs finally answered, "You've been so busy lately I haven't had a chance to tell you that Josie Phillips called me last week and asked if I'd help her plan a party for Homer's birthday next month. Her youngest daughter is in the hospital and Josie has a houseful of grandchildren. So I said of course I would."

"It should be fun for you." Abbie smiled wanly, vaguely resenting the fact that her mother's friends called only when they wanted something from her.

"She's . . . she's offered to pay me, the same amount it would have cost her for a professional party consultant for something this size: fifteen hundred dollars. And I'm in charge of arranging and coordinating everything."

"Fif — Momma, that's wonderful. But are you sure you want to do that? I mean, isn't it going to be awkward working for your friends?"

"Men do it all the time in business," Babs insisted logically. "Ever since Josie called me last week, I've been thinking: what is the one thing I am really good at? Giving parties. Your father and I used to give three or four really large parties every year, and who knows how many little dinner affairs? When I think of how much money we spent a year just on entertaining . . . why, your wedding alone came to almost five hundred thousand dollars. If your father had only said something to me — but how could he? I never wanted to discuss business or finances."

"You can't blame yourself, Momma. I don't think Daddy realized what kind of situation he was in financially." Or if he did, she doubted that he would have admitted it.

"I've never talked about it, but I think you know that my family didn't have very much when I married your father. It wasn't the money. I would have married him if he was as poor as a wetback. But suddenly I didn't have to worry about whether we could afford to buy a new dress or coat — or anything, for that matter. It was like playing with Monopoly money. There was always more if you ran out. Sometimes, I was even deliberately extravagant because I knew he was spending money on —" She stopped abruptly, catching herself before she referred to Rachel or her mother by name. "Any-way, that's all over. And I'm looking at this birthday party for Homer as sort of a trial run. If it works out the way I think it will, then I'm seriously considering going into business for myself."

"You mean that, don't you?" Abbie said as she realized it was true. As preposterous as the combination of Babs and business sounded to her, she couldn't laugh at it.

"I most certainly do. In the last thirty years, I've probably had more experience at it than any professional consultant in Houston. I know all the caterers and suppliers personally. And I can track down anything, no matter how unusual. That's no different than a scavenger hunt. And look at the people I know — people who have been to my parties in the past. They already know what I can do."

"Momma, you don't have to convince me," Abbie laughed. "I believe you can do it, too."

"For now, I can work right out of this house. I know you've been talking about finding a job in addition to your work with the horses, and I was wondering whether . . . you'd like to go into business with me — assuming, of course, that this works and I'm offered more parties."

"I'll help all I can. And I have the feeling you're going to need it. With the holidays and the debut season only a few months away, I'll bet you'll be flooded with jobs the minute the word is out."

"That's what I'm hoping, too." As the back door opened, she started guiltily. "Here's Ben already and I don't have lunch on the table yet." She hurried back to the refrigerator to bring out the sandwich makings.

"How was Breeze?"

"She was fine. Just a little lonely, I think." He walked over to the sink to wash his thick, stubby hands.

Babs opened the top cupboard door next to the sink and began taking down the glasses and plates from the shelves. "I meant to ask you, Ben, when you went to the lumberyard yesterday, did you happen to drive by River Bend?"

"Yes, I did," he admitted slowly, darting a look at Abbie out of the corner of his eye. She tried to pretend she wasn't listening. She even made an effort to concentrate on something else — anything just so she would be reminded that River Bend no longer belonged to them.

"When I was by there the other day, I swore they were taking down some of the trees by the lane."

"They have chopped down several." Ben nodded affirmatively.

"But why?" The protest was torn from Abbie. Those old, twisted pecan trees and ancient oaks had been there forever.

"I was told they are widening the lane. I was also told they are making many changes in the house. Painters and workmen, they are everywhere."

Feeling sick to her stomach, Abbie pushed out of her chair and mumbled some excuse about changing out of her dirty clothes before lunch. But the truth was, she didn't want to hear any more. It hurt too much.

During the next two weeks, it became impossible for Abbie not to learn about the activities of her neighbors. The morning edition of the *Houston Chronicle* carried a story about the wedding of Rachel Farr and Lane Canfield. The article described the wedding and the reception that followed as a small but elegant affair attended by a few intimate friends of the bride and groom. The article didn't identify any of the guests by name, but Abbie was willing to bet that MacCrea had received an invitation to it.

The newspaper briefly mentioned, as well, that after the couple returned from their European honeymoon, they would be dividing their time between their Houston residence and their new country home, presently being renovated.

The latter was just about the only thing anyone wanted to talk about — from Dobie and the owners of the Arabian horses she and Ben had under training, to Josie Phillips and the various service companies they were dealing with in connection with the party. The only time she escaped it was in the mornings when she worked with Ben, training and exercising the horses.

She didn't try to pretend she didn't know about the changes going on at the farm, but neither did she initiate the subject in conversation. Sometimes she suspected people brought it up in front of her just to watch her reaction. And sometimes it was difficult not to let the bitterness and resentment show. Especially when she learned the gazebo was being torn down to make room for a swimming pool, and carpet was being laid on those beautiful parquet floors. But what could she expect from someone who cut down centuries-old trees just to widen a road?

According to the latest word she'd heard in Houston that afternoon while running some errands for her mother, the Canfields had returned unexpectedly, cutting their honeymoon short due to some pressing business matter. Their early arrival had apparently thrown everything into an uproar at River Bend. The renovations that were supposed to have been finished by the time they returned were nowhere close to being complete.

As she drove back, surrounded by the night's blackness, the windows rolled down to let the fresh air rush in, she tried not to think about any of it. Yet there was an awful sinking sensation in her stomach. She'd been dreading the time when Rachel would actually take up residence in her former home. She was back now, and that moment was only days away from becoming a reality.

As the newly erected entrance pillars to River Bend came into view, a lump rose in Abbie's throat. She glanced through the break in the trees, a break that hadn't existed until they had chopped down some of the old giants. She could just barely make out the white rail of the balustrade and part of a two-story turret. Her home — once.

Then she noticed the unusual storm cloud that blackened the sky beyond the house. Summer storms rarely came out of the north. She slowed the car and peered through the windshield. A yellow-orange light flickered in one of the turret windows. At first, Abbie wondered if some of the workmen were putting in overtime to get the job done, then she caught the acrid smell of smoke.

"My God, no." Instinctively she slammed on the brakes to make the turn into the newly widened driveway.

As she sped up the freshly black-topped road, the smell of smoke became stronger. She could see it rolling out from under the porch roof. Stopping the car short of the picket fence, she stared at the yellow tongues of flame licking around the front windows.

She climbed numbly out of the car and hurried to the porch, but the heat from the flames and the choking black smoke forced her back. She stepped back, staring in horror at the fire consuming her home, completely helpless to stop it. She had to get help. She raced back to the car and drove as fast as she could to the Hix farm. Once inside, she ran straight to the phone and dialed the number for the rural fire department.

"Abbie, what's wrong?" Babs hurried to her side. "You look white as a ghost. Were you in an accident?"

"No —" Abbie started to explain when she heard a voice on the other end of the line. "Hello? This is Abbie Lawson. I want to report a fire . . . at River Bend." She clutched the receiver a little tighter, conscious of her mother's horrified look. "I just drove by there. The whole first floor of the house was on fire."

"No!" Babs gasped.

"We're on our way," the man said and hung up.

Slowly Abbie replaced the receiver, then looked at Ben, who had come to stand next to her mother. "They'll never make it in time to save it." She made the pronouncement with an odd feeling that she couldn't explain. It was a strange mixture of guilt, sorrow, and apathy. "It's funny, isn't it? I would have done anything to prevent her from moving into that house, but not this. I never wanted it to burn down, Ben. I really didn't."

"I know." He nodded.

"Do you think we should go over and see if there's anything we can do to help?" Babs asked uncertainly.

"No. Momma. There's nothing we can do." Abbie walked over to the window that looked out in the direction of their former home. She could see the smoke billowing up like a dark cloud to block out the stars. Beneath it, there was a faint red glow. She didn't know how long she stood there before she heard the distant wail of a siren, but it seemed like an eternity. By then, the glow was brighter and the cloud was thicker.

When morning came, the pall of the fire hung over the countryside, tainting the air with the smell of charred wood and smoke. The greenbroke bay filly snorted and sidestepped nervously as Abbie swung into the saddle, but the young horse quieted quickly when Ben rode up alongside on the plump chestnut mare. She shortened the length of rein. "Ben, I want to ride over to River Bend."

"I thought you would," he said. "We can ride across the fields."

Both horses were fresh and broke eagerly into a canter without any urging from Ben and Abbie. With only two gates to negotiate, the mile that separated the Hix farmyard from her former home was quickly covered. But the burned-out devastation was visible when they were less than a quarter of a mile away.

The stallion barn was the only building still standing, but it hadn't escaped damage. Its roof was blackened, and its sides, once painted a pristine white, were now scorched brown and smudged with dark smoke. All that remained of the stables, office annex, and the equipment shed were blackened timbers and charred rubble.

The brick chimney stood like a tombstone over the mound of ash that had once been her home. But the trees, the beautiful old ancient oaks that had graced the yard — Abbie wanted to cry when she saw their seared and withered leaves and charred trucks.

The fence between the two properties was down. Abbie waited until Ben had walked his mare across the downed wires, then let the filly pick her way over them. The water-soaked ground was a mire of trampled grass and ashen mud. The young filly shied nervously from the burned remains of the house and edged closer to her older companion, not liking anything about this place.

Abbie reined the filly in, halting the young Arabian well away from the rubble. Several vehicles were parked on the other side of the smoke-blackened picket fence. Some men were over by the barns, poking through the timbers, a few of which were still smoldering. Three more men were going through the ashes of the house, with its blackened porcelain sinks, bathtubs, and toilets. She stared at the large, gaping hole gouged out of the lawn in the backyard: the site of the new swimming pool. It reminded Abbie of an open grave waiting to receive the remains of the house.

"It's worse than I thought it would be," she remarked to Ben.

"Yes."

"Hey, Ben! I thought I recognized you." Sam Raines, one of the volunteer firemen, came trotting over to them. His glance skipped away from Abbie to look back at the chimney. "It didn't leave much. By the time we got here last night, the whole place was in flames."

"We could see it. It looked bad."

"Sparks were flying all over. When that hay caught fire, I thought we were going to lose everything. We probably could have saved the stable, but we ran low on water. We had to concentrate what we had left on the one you see. You know, it's ironic. If they'd gotten the pool in, we probably would have had enough for both."

"Do you know what started it?"

"That's what they're trying to figure out now." He gestured to the men picking through the charred rubble of the house. "As near as we can tell, it started in one of the back rooms where the painters kept their thinner and paint rags. Who knows?" He shrugged. "The wiring in that house was old. There could have been a short, or somebody could have dropped a cigarette near those thinner rags. These old houses are fire hazards. I say it's a darned good thing no one was living in it. I'll bet it went up fast."

There was almost nothing left of the place she'd known from childhood: the house was burned to the ground, the stables and sheds completely destroyed. She could deny many things, but not the ache she felt inside.

The hinges on the picket fence gate creaked noisily in the stillness. At first Abbie was struck by the ludicrous sight of the silver-haired man holding aside the gate for the stylish brunette in a white silk blouse and pleated tan trousers. They started up the walk together, looking like a couple coming to call, but the sidewalk led to ash and rubble. When the woman turned her head, Abbie saw her face, white with shock and dismay. It was Rachel, a strikingly different Rachel. The coiffed hair, the clothes that had "designer" written all over them, the scarf around the neck, the bracelets on her wrists — she looked like some willowy fashion model.

Rachel saw her and stopped abruptly, then started across the muddy lawn toward her. Lane attempted to stop her, but she pulled away from him and continued forward. Abbie could tell Rachel was angry to see her there. Yet she was surprised at how calm she felt.

As Rachel approached head-on, the nervous young filly started to swing away, but Rachel grabbed the reins close to the chin strap and checked its sideways movement. "You did this," Rachel accused, her voice vibrating. "You started the fire."

"No!" Startled, Abbie tried to explain that she had been the one who turned in the alarm, but Rachel wasn't interested in hearing anything she had to say.

"You threatened to do this. There were witnesses, so don't bother to deny it. You couldn't stand the thought of me living in this house, so you set fire to it." She was trembling, her hand clenched in a fist. "God, I hate you for this. I hate you. Do you hear?" Her voice rose, attracting the attention of the men going through the burned rubble. Rachel roughly pushed the filly's head to the side, starting the horse into a turn as she released the reins. "Get out! Get off my land and don't you ever come here again!"

Angry and indignant, Abbie opened her mouth to defend herself, but Ben touched her arm, checking her denial. "She will not listen," he said. "We go now."

But Abbie wasn't content to leave it at that as she collected the reins. "Believe what you like, but I didn't do it!"

She reined the Arabian filly in a half-circle. It moved out smartly, eager to leave this place, with its heavy smell of smoke and currents of angry tension. Abbie held the young horse to a prancing walk and kept her own shoulders stiffly squared and her head up as she followed Ben across the downed fence. Not until they were well out of sight did she give the filly her head and let her break into a gallop.

As they raced across the stubble of the mowed hay field, the wind whipped away the tears that smarted in her eyes. She knew the accusation would stick. No matter what the official cause of the fire was determined to be, people would still look at her as somehow being responsible. It wasn't fair.

26

MacCrea stepped down from his truck to the sound of pounding hammers and whining saws. In front of him, like the phoenix bird rising from the ashes, stood the partially framed skeleton of a Victorian-style house similar to the one that had once occupied this same site. The house now under construction was like it in every detail, from the wraparound porch and balustrade to the twin turrets and cupola — except it was half again as big.

Simultaneous with the construction of the house was the erection of a huge barn in the same architectural style a hundred yards away. The one building not destroyed by the fire had been razed to make room for this new, massive structure. Nothing remained that had been there before except for the few old trees that had managed to survive the ravages of the fire.

The place crawled with carpenters, other laborers, and tradesmen. MacCrea stopped an aproned carpenter who walked by, balancing a long wooden plank on his shoulder. "Where can I find Lane Canfield?"

The man jerked his bandaged thumb toward the house and walked on. MacCrea took a step, then paused as a slender woman with dark hair emerged from the structure. Just for an instant, he was thrown by her resemblance to Abbie, and felt the stirring of old feelings. Grimly, he clamped his mouth shut and forced his gaze to the man behind her, Lane Canfield. Silently he cursed the fact that this happened every damned time he saw Rachel, certain he would have forgotten Abbie months ago if it weren't for her.

Lane lifted a hand in greeting, then Rachel claimed his attention. She seemed upset about something, but MacCrea couldn't hear what she was saying until the couple came closer.

". . . shouldn't wait to hire a night watchman. I want one now," she was insisting forcefully. "You know as well as I do that she's just waiting until the construction is further along before she does something."

"Rachel, there is no proof that she started the fire." There was a tiredness in Lane's voice that indicated this discussion was an old one.

"I don't need proof. I know her. She hates me." She seemed frustrated by her failure to convince her husband and turned to MacCrea in desperation. "Ask MacCrea. He'll tell you."

"Don't drag me into this," he said, shaking his head. "I don't get involved in personal disputes. I'm out of it and I want to stay out of it." But for him, the expressions of loathing and distrust, of resentment and anger, were echoes of the past. The difference now was that they came from Rachel instead of Abbie.

"I don't care if either of you agrees with me or not. I want somebody on guard here at night to make sure nothing happens." But she was no longer demanding; she was pleading with Lane. "Surely that isn't asking too much. After all, this is going to be our home."

"All right." Lane gave in, seemingly incapable of refusing Rachel anything she wanted. "I'll have the superintendent hire one right away."

"I'll go tell him for you. Thank you, dear." She gave him a quick peck on the cheek, then hurried away, heading back to the house to find the superintendent.

More than once MacCrea had observed the lack of passion in their relationship. Admittedly there were displays of affection between them — touching and hand-holding — and they seemed happy enough together. But as far as MacCrea could tell, there was something missing. Maybe he just remembered the way it had been with Abbie: whenever he was with her, he didn't want her to leave, and whenever he wasn't with her, he wanted to be.

Obviously Lane and Rachel were satisfied with something less. He wondered whether their age difference had anything to do with that or if it was simply a reflection of their personalities. Lane was very businesslike in his approach to things, and Rachel was somewhat reserved and quiet, although more and more she seemed to be coming out of her shell.

Either way, it wasn't any concern of his, MacCrea decided, and glanced at Lane. The man looked vaguely troubled as he watched his wife disappear inside the partially framed structure.

Sighing, Lane turned back to MacCrea and said, almost reluctantly, "She's been like that ever since the fire. She's obsessed with the idea that Abbie's to blame for it. Of course, it isn't as if she hasn't had cause to think that way. Abbie has . . ." Lane paused and smiled ruefully. "But I didn't ask you to come by to talk about her."

"No." He reached inside his windbreaker and took the papers from his pocket. "Here's the proposal. I think you'll find it pretty much the way I outlined it to you over the phone yesterday."

He handed him the papers and watched Lane's face as he skimmed the first page. Not that he expected to see a reaction: Lane was too canny for that.

But he did raise an eyebrow at MacCrea. "Are you certain your testing system doesn't work? This offer could be just a way of squeezing you out."

"I thought of that. But when negative reports started coming in from the field tests, I went out on test sites and checked it myself. It doesn't work. But they still like the concept. Rather than risk a possible infringement suit sometime in the future, they want to buy the patent rights on it now." MacCrea didn't mention that the drilling fluids company had initially suggested that he stay and work with the project. But he wasn't a scientist. Besides, he knew the longer he stayed around here, the longer it would take him to get Abbie out of his system once and for all. "In my opinion, I think we should accept the offer."

"You're probably right," Lane conceded.

"I know I am."

"So what will you do now?"

"I've acquired the mineral rights to some property in Ascension Parish. I plan to put a deal together and drill a development well there."

"From what I've been able to gather, the land men with a lot of big oil companies have been trying to get their hands on the oil and gas rights to that property for years now. How did you manage to get it?" Lane asked curiously.

"The old lady that owns it took a liking to me." MacCrea didn't think it was necessary to inform Lane that the old woman had once taken care of him when he was a child, sick with a bad case of bronchial pneumonia.

"I wouldn't mind getting in on it," Lane said. "I'd consider backing you on this, assuming, of course, that we can agree on a split."

Covering his surprise over the unexpected offer, MacCrea shot back quickly, "It all depends on how greedy you are."

"Or how greedy you are." Lane smiled. "Think it over and give me a call. We'll sit down and talk numbers and percents."

"I don't have to think about it. You have the money and I have the lease, the drilling rig, and the crew. I'm ready to talk a deal now. Maybe you need to think it over."

"Tomorrow, be at my office at ten. We can talk privately — without all this confusion." Gesturing, Lane indicated the construction going on around them.

"I'll be there," MacCrea promised.

27

As Abbie turned River Breeze loose in the small pen, the half-dozen horses in the adjacent corral crowded against the fence and nickered for the gray filly to come over and talk to them. The filly hesitated and swung her head around to look at Abbie as if reluctant to leave her.

"Go ahead." Abbie petted the silvery neck. "I have to leave anyway."

She stepped away from the filly and ducked between the board rails to join Ben on the other side of the pen. The filly moved haltingly over to the fence, her gait stiff and awkward. The casts had been off for a month now. Each day, her legs had gotten stronger, her coordination was better, most of the sores had healed, the swelling was reduced. Abbie knew the filly would have a permanent limp and there would always be some disfiguring enlargement of the forelegs but that didn't matter. Watching her move about on all four legs was the most beautiful sight Abbie had ever seen.

"She's going to make it, isn't she, Ben?"

"Yes. She will improve every day." He nodded.

"Do you think by this spring she'll be strong enough that we can get her bred?"

"I think so."

"We'll need to start deciding on a stallion. I want her bred to the best. I don't care how much the stud fee is." Then she sighed. "There's always the possibility she won't be fertile. We've had to give her a lot of drugs."

"We will have to wait and see."

"Yes." But she wished, just once, that he would offer an opinion. "Nobody expected Breeze to get this far. I want to start making a list of stallions that will nick well with her, Ben. We're going to breed her in the spring." She said it with confidence and determination, yet she had the uneasy feeling she was daring fate to intervene.

But when she saw the smile of approval that broke across Ben's lined and craggy face, she knew he shared her optimism. "The list I have already begun. It is God's miracle that she walks. We must believe that in His time, she will also become in foal."

Abbie smiled faintly. "Sometimes I wish I had your faith, Ben." It was mostly grit that carried her. She couldn't trust blindly. She hadn't been able to do that for a long time, she realized with a sigh, and pushed away from the fence. "I'd better get ready. I promised Momma I'd give her a hand at the party tonight."

Every tree and shrub along the driveway leading to the private estate in River Oaks was etched with tiny fairy lights. The sprawling house with its Spanish architectural details was decked in its holiday finery, too. Garlands of greenery strung with lights draped the porte cochere that welcomed the arriving party guests. With Thanksgiving barely over, this was the first party of the holiday season.

A Christmas tree, nearly twenty-five feet tall, dominated the glass-ceilinged *gran sala*. There, Rachel gave her mink jacket to a waiting maid and lightly grasped Lane's arm as they joined the rest of the guests milling throughout the expensive and lavishly decorated house.

Briefly she touched the Van Cleef and Arpel's diamond-and-emerald brooch that anchored the plunging sweetheart neckline of her gown, assuring herself it was still firmly in place, at the same time conscious of the weight of the matching earrings pulling on her lobes. Ever since their marriage, Lane had showered her with presents: clothes, jewelry, furs, expensive perfumes, and other trinkets. At first she had felt uncomfortable with all the gifts, remembering too well the way Dean had tried to buy her love and ease his conscience with them. But Lane took such joy in bringing her big or little gifts that Rachel thought it unfair to question his motives. Yet the doubt remained.

A waiter offered them a glass of champagne from his silver tray.

Rachel took one, needing something to occupy her hands, but Lane declined. "I think I'll get a drink from the bar. Will you excuse me?"

"Of course." Invariably he left her alone at these social gatherings, though not always intentionally. Usually he ran into a business associate or someone he knew, and she was forgotten while he stopped to talk. To her regret, Rachel had quickly learned it was always business with him. That was his idea of a good time.

Meanwhile, she had to suffer through these evenings as best she could. She looked around, remembering that MacCrea was supposed to be here. At least he was someone to talk to. But she saw few familiar faces as she glanced around the room. She was still a stranger among them, not totally accepted yet.

When women had discussed her in various private powder rooms, they had accused her of being aloof and unapproachable. Little did they know that she didn't say much, unless the subject was art or Arabian horses, because she didn't know the people or the events they were talking about. Rather than show her ignorance, she said nothing. And there were some, she knew, who were covertly hostile to her — mainly those still loyal to Abbie and her mother. But they couldn't cut her, not Lane Canfield's wife. Rachel tilted her head a little higher. Whether they liked it or not, she belonged here as much as, if not more than, they did. She'd show them. In time, they'd have to accept her as one of them.

The soft strumming of a guitar came from one of the rooms that opened off the grand entry. Rachel gravitated toward the sound, taking advantage of the diversion it offered so that it wouldn't appear as obvious that she had no one to talk to.

In one corner of the spacious family game room, a small country band played for the couples dancing on a cleared area of the terrazzo floor. As Rachel wandered into the room, the singer stepped up to the microphone. She felt a little shock go through her when she recognized the slim man in the black tuxedo. Even at this distance, the black cowboy hat with its concho-studded band that had become Ross Tibbs's trademark was unmistakable. She should have guessed he'd be the entertainment tonight. Ever since the song he'd written had climbed to the top of the country charts, he'd become a mini-celebrity in Houston, despite the fact that the song had been recorded by another artist.

She knew she should leave, walk right out of the room, but his clear baritone voice, rich with feeling and warmth, reached out to caress her and draw her closer. She moved along the wall until she found a place she could stand and watch him safely, inconspicuously.

But when the song ended, he turned to acknowledge the applause and looked directly at her. For an instant he was completely motionless, staring at her as if he was seeing her in a dream. Rachel wanted to look away, break the eye contact, but she couldn't . . . any more than she could control the sudden fluttering of her pulse.

Again he stepped up to the microphone. "I'd like to do another song for you that I wrote. As a matter of fact, I'll be recording it myself next week when I go to Nashville. It's called 'My Texas Blue Eyes' and goes something like this." He nodded to the band to begin, then glanced directly at Rachel and said softly into the microphone, "This is for you, my own Texas blue eyes."

Her skin felt as if it had suddenly caught fire. She looked around to see if anyone else had noticed that he'd dedicated the song to her, but all eyes were on him. Then he started singing:

> *Tell me, boys, have you ever seen her,*
> *The lady with those eyes of Texas blue?*
> *She'll steal your heart if you ever meet her,*
> *And leave you all alone and lonely, too,*
> *My blue eyes, my Texas blue eyes.*

> *I want to listen to your sighs*
> *And feel your body next to mine,*
> *But you're too far away to touch.*
> *Why do I love you, oh, so much,*
> *My blue eyes, my Texas blue eyes?*

The sweet longing in his voice, full of the passion and pain of loving, pulled at Rachel. She didn't want to feel the sensations he was evoking. They were too strong — and too wrong. Abruptly she turned and blindly picked her way through the crowd that had gathered to listen. At last she emerged from the room and paused to draw a calming breath and stop the pounding of her heart.

But his voice followed her:

> *I know that she will always haunt my dreams,*
> *That lady with those eyes of Texas blue.*

Moving as swiftly as she dared, Rachel crossed the atriumlike *gran sala* and went in search of Lane. When she didn't find him near the bar, she checked the formal dining room, with its stunning cut-crystal chandelier presiding over a long buffet table. She stiffened in surprise when she saw Abbie on the far side of the room, speaking in a hushed voice to one of the waiters.

Dressed in a peplumed jacket of quilted gold silk, belted at the waist and heavily padded at the shoulders, and a black velvet skirt, Abbie looked like one of the guests. For a split second, Rachel questioned how Abbie had received an invitation to the party. Then she remembered that Abbie and her mother hired themselves out to oversee all the arrangements for parties such as this one. Rachel couldn't help smiling a little as she watched the waiter acknowledge an order given by Abbie with a discreet nod of his head before she moved away.

On her way to the bar to double-check the liquor supply, Abbie stopped one of the maids and directed her to some dirty plates on a coffee table. As her mother explained their role to prospective clients, their duties were to assume all the responsibilities of the hostess, leaving her completely free to mingle with her guests. They would see to it that there was an ample supply of food and drink at all times, and make certain that ashtrays were regularly emptied and soiled plates and empty glasses quickly cleared away. Every facet — from valet parking so the driveway wouldn't be clogged with cars to the checking of wraps at the door, from the policing of the men's and ladies' rooms to keep them tidy and clean to the handling of belligerent guests who had had too much to drink, and from the initial planning of the party to the cleaning up afterward — became their obligation.

But assuming the role of hostess didn't mean that they physically did anything themselves. Still, when Abbie noticed an empty champagne glass set on the pearl-inlaid top of an antique Moroccan chest, she picked it up and carried it to the bar with her. Babs was elsewhere in the house making her own inspection tour of the rooms. Abbie usually worked behind the scenes, handling the food and drink, and rarely ventured out of the kitchen. But she'd just learned from the liquor caterer that he'd inadvertently brought only two cases of bourbon. Knowing her fellow Texans' capacity for the whiskey made with fermented corn mash, she was concerned that they might run short and wanted to check on how the supply was holding up.

She set the empty champagne glass on the counter and waited for the head bartender to finish talking to the guest at the opposite end of the long bar. When he finally turned away from him, Abbie suddenly had a clear view of the man.

MacCrea. She felt as if she'd been stabbed, the pain — the longing — was so intense. She stared at his face in profile, so compellingly masculine with its blunt angles and powerful lines. Every detail, every feature was achingly familiar to her, from the dark brush of his mustache to that curled lift of his crooked little finger.

She tried to blame her reaction on the shock of seeing him after all this time. What had it been, around three and a half months? She didn't understand how she could still love him after what he'd done. "Out of sight, out of mind" . . . she thought she had succeeded so well at that. Now she realized he'd never been out of her heart. But was it really any different from the way she had been with her father — loving him even when she hated him?

The head bartender walked over to her. "Did you need something, Miss Lawson?"

"Yes." But she momentarily forgot what it was as she saw MacCrea watching her, his gaze half-lidded, but not concealing the intentness of his stare. Unwilling to let him know how much seeing him again had affected her, Abbie assumed a businesslike attitude and focused her attention on the bartender, but out of the corner of her eye, she saw MacCrea push away from the bar and walk toward her.

"Hello." His low voice caressed her. She didn't even have to close her eyes to remember the feel of his rough hands stroking her skin.

She made a determined effort to ignore him. "How is the bourbon holding out?"

"Just fine," the bartender replied.

"Good." She refused to look at MacCrea. It didn't matter. All the rest of her senses were focused on him. She was aware of every sound, every movement he made. Finally gathering her composure around her like protective armor, she turned to face him. "Was there something you wanted?"

"You," MacCrea said calmly, matter-of-factly.

A thousand times she had turned aside similar remarks from men without batting an eye, but this time she couldn't — not from MacCrea. And she wasn't going to let herself be hurt again. He'd already proved she couldn't trust him. She turned sharply and walked swiftly away from the bar, not slowing down for anything until she reached the dining room.

"Going somewhere?" MacCrea said. Abbie swung around in surprise. With all the noise and confusion of the party, she hadn't heard him following her. But there he was, towering in front of her, studying her with a glint of satisfaction.

"I'm busy," she insisted stiffly, angered that he was making an issue out of this when he knew she didn't want any more to do with him. She turned her back on him and began fussing with the garnish around the bowl of pâté.

"You're not as tough as I thought, Abbie," he drawled.

"I don't particularly care what you think — about me or anything else."

"You're afraid of me, aren't you?"

"Don't be ridiculous," she snapped.

"Then why did you run away just now?"

"It certainly wasn't because I was afraid of you."

"Prove it."

"I don't have to." She was trembling inside with anger as well as his nearness. "Go away and leave me alone."

"I can't. I'm a hungry man." He spread his hand over her back, then let it glide familiarly down to her waist.

She couldn't remain indifferent to his touch, so she picked up the bowl and turned around with it, breaking the contact to face him. "Have some pâté then."

Smiling faintly, he took the bowl from her and set it back in its garnish nest, then braced a hand on the table behind her and leaned toward her. "Is that any way to talk to a fellow guest?" His breath smelled strongly of whiskey.

"You've been drinking."

"Of course. This is supposed to be a party, isn't it?" His glance swept the other guests milling about the area before coming back to her. "People usually drink at parties, don't they?"

"Yes." She looked away, angry and hurt that he was here saying all these things and stirring up her emotions because he'd had too much to drink — not because he still cared or because he wanted to make amends, but just for the hell of it.

"It's too bad you don't feel like joining me. You'd have a lot to celebrate. You see, my downhole testing system failed to pass its field tests."

She experienced a mixed reaction to his news. Although she was glad Rachel had lost the money she'd invested in it, she felt sorry for MacCrea. She knew how much the system had meant to him, and how hard he'd worked on it.

"What, no cheers?" he mocked. "I thought you'd be happy to hear it."

"I am," she said because it was what he expected her to say.

"Happy enough to have a drink with me?" MacCrea challenged, arching an eyebrow.

She hadn't realized how hard it would be to resist him, knowing she couldn't trust him, but somehow she managed it. "I'm not paid to fraternize with the guests. If you'll excuse me . . ." But when she tried to brush past him, he caught her arm.

"What do you mean by 'paid'?" A deep crease pulled his brows together as his gaze narrowed on her in sharp question.

"I happen to be a working woman with the responsibility of this party on my hands." She could feel the heat of his hand through the quilted silk of her jacket. She felt burned by the contact, and the memory of his pleasantly rough caresses. "I believe I told you once before to leave me alone. I hope I don't have to repeat myself." She hated the betraying tremor in her voice.

"I remember," he said smoothly, slowly taking his hand away, his level gaze never leaving her face. "I remember a lot of things, Abbie. More than that, I think you do, too."

Not trusting herself to respond to that, Abbie turned and retreated to the seeming chaos of the kitchen. The meeting with MacCrea had left her shaken — more shaken than she cared to admit. She tried to busy herself with something, anything that would get her mind off him . . . the way he had looked, what he was doing there, and why he had spoken to her at all. She wondered if he was regretting having done so. It hurt to think he might.

She picked up a silver coffee pot from the counter and carried it over to the tall stainless-steel urn to fill it, ignoring the constant comings and goings of the uniformed maids and waiters. As she turned away from the urn, she saw Rachel standing in the doorway, watching her.

Abbie stared at the elegant woman before her, taking in her dark hair skimmed back to emphasize the perfect oval of her face, the sparkling earrings of teardrop emeralds surrounded by glittering diamonds, and the figure-hugging gown of forest-green panne velvet that bore the unmistakable mark of Givenchy.

Suddenly Abbie was painfully conscious of her surroundings —

and the coffee pot in her hand. She had known all along that sooner or later Rachel would be a guest at one of the parties. But why did it have to be tonight? And why did she have to come face to face with her in the kitchen, of all places?

Or had Rachel sought her out here deliberately? Abbie was almost certain she had. What better way for Rachel to remind her that they were no longer on equal footing? What better way to humiliate her? If that was her intent, she had succeeded, but Abbie was determined not to let her see that.

"Did you want something, Mrs. Canfield?" she inquired, icily polite.

"I was looking for the powder room, but I must have taken a wrong turn somewhere. Perhaps you could direct me."

Abbie longed to challenge that lie, but she smiled instead. "I would like to, but, as you can see, I'm busy," she said, indicating the coffee pot she was holding. "However, I'm sure one of the maids would be happy to show you where it's located." She called one of them over and instructed her to guide Mrs. Canfield to the powder room.

"How thoughtful of you," Rachel said coolly. "But then, you do seem to be very thorough in your work. The next time Lane and I decide to have a party, perhaps I'll give you a call."

Abbie felt the digging gibe and reacted instinctively. "Something tells me we'll be booked."

Rachel laughed softly, a low taunting sound, then turned with a graceful pivot and walked down the hall, a bewildered maid trailing behind her. Abbie's face felt hot, and she knew the flush wasn't caused by the heat of the warming ovens.

When Rachel rejoined the party, she drifted aimlessly from the fringes of one group to another, listening in on conversations without taking part except to smile or nod whenever her presence was noticed. Careful to stay well away from the family game room where Ross Tibbs was singing, she wandered over to the long bar and saw MacCrea at the far end, nursing a cup of coffee.

"Coffee, MacCrea? Haven't you heard this is a party?" But she felt no more festive than he obviously did.

"I never listen to rumors," he replied dryly, lifting the coffee cup to his mouth and taking a sip.

"Have you seen Abbie yet? But of course you have. You spoke to her earlier, didn't you?" Rachel said, watching closely for his reaction.

"Briefly." He nodded, his expression never losing its brooding look.

"Abbie and her mother are in charge of this party tonight. You'd think it would be awkward for them to work for people who were once their friends. I understand, though, that they've traded considerably on those friendships in order to get these parties. You'd think they would have more pride."

"Maybe pride doesn't pay the rent," MacCrea suggested.

"Maybe it only burns down houses that don't belong to you anymore," Rachel countered, the anger and bitterness over the destruction of the original Victorian mansion at River Bend resurfacing. "Excuse me. I'm going to look for Lane."

As she walked away, she saw Ross Tibbs coming toward her. She paused uncertainly, then realized there was no way to avoid meeting him.

"I was beginning to think you'd left. I'm glad you didn't," he said, looking at her in that warm way that always made her feel uncomfortable.

"I thought you were singing."

"Just taking a break between sets. This is quite a place, isn't it?" He glanced around the high-ceilinged room tastefully decorated with garlands and wreaths for the holiday season.

"Yes."

"You'd think with all these Christmas decorations there would be some mistletoe hanging somewhere, wouldn't you? But I've yet to see any. Have you?"

"No. No, I haven't. Excuse me, but I'm looking for my husband."

As she started to walk by him, he said, "I'm glad you liked the song I wrote for you, Rachel."

She stopped short. "What makes you think I did?"

"Because it made you so uncomfortable you had to leave the room."

She wanted to deny it. She wanted to tell him that it hadn't affected her at all. It was just another song — like so many other country songs. But the words wouldn't come. Instead she walked away, almost breaking into a run.

A little after midnight, Babs walked over to Abbie in the kitchen. "The party will be breaking up in another hour or so. If you want to go ahead and leave now, I'll finish up here. I know you've been up since six this morning, working with the horses."

"I am tired," Abbie admitted, conscious of the pounding in her head that just wouldn't go away. "If you're sure you can manage . . ."

"I'm sure. You run along home."

Ten minutes later Abbie left the house by the service entrance and walked along the path to the garage where she'd left her car parked. It seemed strangely quiet outside after all the clinking and clanking in the kitchen and all the laughter and noise from the party in the rest of the house. There was a faint chill in the early December air, but it felt good. She was almost to her car when she noticed the man leaning against the black pickup, one long leg negligently hooked over the other. Abbie stiffened in surprise as MacCrea casually straightened and came forward to meet her.

"I was beginning to wonder how much longer you'd be," he said.

But Abbie didn't respond. She didn't trust herself to talk to him. Instead she started for her car, walking briskly and clutching the key ring like a talisman.

"I've been waiting for you to come out." His breath made little vapor clouds in the air.

"If I had known you were here, I would have called a cab." She stopped beside the car and fumbled to locate the key to unlock the door, her fingers numb and cold.

"No, you wouldn't." He stood beside her, his hands in the pockets of his jacket. "You aren't the kind that runs, Abbie."

"You don't know me as well as you think you do." She tried a key but it wouldn't fit in the lock.

"Don't I? Right now, you're hating yourself because you still want me."

"You're wrong!" she insisted, stung into denying it.

"Am I?" He caught her by the arm and pulled her away from the car, toward him. She gripped the folds of his jacket, feeling the tautly muscled flesh of his upper arms, and tried to hold herself away from him. She could feel the mad thudding of her heart as she looked up at him, torn by conflicting emotions. "I don't think so, Abbie. I really don't think so."

She saw the purposeful gleam in his eye and knew she didn't have a hope of fighting him. He tunneled a hand under her hair and cupped the back of her head in his palm. As he covered her lips with his mouth, Abbie tried to remain passive and show him that she didn't care anymore. But it had been too long since she'd felt the warm pressure of his lips. She'd forgotten how good his kiss could make

her feel. She missed the sensation of having his arms around her
. . . of being loved.

Yielding to him at last, she returned his kiss and slid her hands
up to his shoulders, no longer trying to keep him at arm's length,
instead seeking the contact with his hard, lean body. As his arms
gathered her close, she rose on tiptoe, straining to lessen the difference in their heights. All the passion and emotion were back, but
with them, too, came the knowledge that they wouldn't last — they
couldn't last.

When he dragged his mouth from her lips, Abbie pressed her head
against his chest, trying to hold on to this poignant moment a second
longer. "Tell me now I was wrong, Abbie," he challenged huskily.
"Tell me you don't still care."

"The way I feel doesn't change anything. You still can't understand that, can you?" she said.

"Because of Rachel, I suppose."

She heard the grimness in his voice. It hurt. "Yes. Because of
Rachel." She kept her head down as she pushed away from him, but
he caught her by the shoulders.

"I thought by now you'd be over this stupid jealousy of yours,"
he muttered.

"It may be stupid to you, but it isn't to me," Abbie flared bitterly.
"As long as you have anything to do with her, I'll have nothing to
do with you. And don't try to tell me you didn't talk to her at the
party tonight or that you don't go to River Bend to see her, because
I've seen your truck there several times."

"And when you have, it's because I had business to discuss with
Rachel *and* Lane. But, yes, you're right in your way of thinking. I
was with her. Do you know what I think about when I'm around
her? What goes through my mind?" he demanded. "You. Always.
And you don't know how many times I wished to hell that it wasn't
so. What makes it even crazier, she's not like you at all."

He sounded so convincing . . . or maybe she simply wanted to
believe him. "I don't know what to think anymore." She was tired
and confused. Too much had happened all at once, and she knew
that right now she wasn't in control of her emotions. They were
controlling her.

"There's no reason for you to be jealous of her. There never was,
except in your head. Put it in the past where it belongs. All that's
over now." His hands tightened their grip as if he wanted to shake

her, then they relaxed, their touch gentling. "And if you have to think about something, Abbie, think about this. I love you."

For a split second, she resented him for telling her now. It tipped the balance of her emotions. Yet the rest of what he said was true, too. His business with Rachel was over. His testing system had failed. There was no more reason for him to have anything to do with her.

"I love you, too, Mac," Abbie murmured. "Don't you know that's why it hurts so much?"

"Abbie." As he lifted her off her feet, Abbie wound her arms around his neck and hung on to the man who had given her so much joy and pain — the man she loved. She kissed him fiercely, possessively, thrilling to the punishing crush of his arms and the driving pressure of his mouth as he claimed her as his own. She was sorry when he let her feet touch the ground again, but the look in his eyes made up for it. "You're coming with me."

But as he started to walk her to his truck, she suddenly remembered. "Wait. What about my car?"

"To hell with your car." MacCrea didn't break stride. "I'm not letting you out of my sight. I'm not going to take the chance that between here and my place, you'll change your mind."

Abbie wondered whether she would have second thoughts if she had time to think about it. It felt so right walking beside him, his arm around her, that she doubted she would. He loved her. With Rachel out of the picture, maybe they could start over. And this time they could make it work.

When they climbed into the truck, MacCrea insisted she sit next to him. Abbie happily snuggled against him, feeling like a teenager out with her boyfriend, stimulated by the close contact with him and the kneading caress of his hand, his arm around her, close enough to steal a kiss now and then as they made the drive to his trailer.

The drilling site was pitch-dark: not a single light shone in the clearing that once had been brightly lit at night. The truck's headlights briefly illuminated the dismantled rig loaded on a long flatbed behind a snub-nosed truck cab.

"You've finished drilling here?"

"Yep. We went to depth and came up dry."

But he wasn't interested in discussing the well as he stopped the truck, then proceeded to carry her into the trailer and all the way to the bed. There wasn't time for anything except making love — now — immediately. It was as if the months of separation lent a sense of haste and urgency to the consummation . . . that only through the coupling of their bodies could they bridge the angry pride and bitter jealousy that had driven them apart before.

Later they took the time to explore and enjoy each other all over again: a lovemaking filled with all the kisses, caresses, and fondlings that had been missing from the first. The climax was a long time coming, but when it arrived, Abbie knew it had never been so good between them before.

Afterward she lay in his arms, feeling wonderfully relaxed and content. From the sound of his deep, even breathing, she guessed MacCrea was asleep. Smiling faintly, she closed her own eyes and started to turn onto her side and join him.

His encircling arm tightened around her and pressed her back onto the mattress. "Don't leave," he said in a voice heavy with sleep. "Stay with me tonight."

"I can't leave, silly." Abbie's smile widened as she turned her head on the pillow to look at him, his face a collection of shadows in the darkness of the trailer. "You wouldn't let me drive my car here, remember?"

His response was a throaty sound that indicated he'd forgotten she was dependent on him for transportation. "I should have carried you off like this weeks ago."

"Is that right?" she teased.

"Mmmm." The affirmative sound was followed by a long silence. Abbie thought he was drifting back to sleep, but then he spoke again, his voice a low rumble coming from deep in his chest. "I'm leaving for Louisiana this next week. I want you to come with me, Abbie."

"I don't see how I can," she said, feeling a sharp pang of regret.

"Why not?" Slowly he let his hand wander over her rib cage, letting the persuasion of his caress work on her resistance. "I'm sure we can find some minister in the parish willing to marry us."

"Are you proposing?" She couldn't believe her ears.

"Only if you're accepting. If you're not, I take it all back." He sounded amused, and Abbie didn't know whether he meant the proposal or not.

Afraid of taking him seriously, Abbie chose the middle ground. "I want to go with you. You have to believe that, Mac. But I just can't pick up and leave the way you can. I have responsibilities and commitments here."

"Like your mother, I suppose."

"Yes. Plus Ben, and I have contracted with several owners to train and show their Arabians." It didn't bring in a lot of money by the time all the costs were deducted, but she'd managed to earn enough to pay the high veterinary bills on River Breeze. The rest she planned to save to pay for the filly's stud fee. But she didn't go into all that with him. It didn't seem necessary. No matter how much she loved him or wanted to go with him, she just couldn't right now. "Do you have to leave next week? Can't you postpone it? What's in Louisiana? Why are you going there?"

"Oil. What else?"

"You can find that right here in Texas," she argued. "You don't have to go to Louisiana, do you?"

"I've acquired the oil and gas rights to a hot piece of property there."

"But it's still going to take you time to raise money to sink the well."

"Not this time. I have a financial backer."

"Who?" She felt suddenly tense.

MacCrea hesitated just a little too long. "It's no secret. Lane Canfield's putting up the money."

Abbie sat up and flipped on the wall light at the head of the bed so she could see his face and make sure this wasn't some cruel joke. MacCrea threw up a hand to shield his eyes from the sudden glare, but she saw there was no smile, no teasing light in his eyes. "You're serious, aren't you?"

"Would I lie about something like that?" He frowned.

"No. You never lie," Abbie said as she realized it, the anger rising in her throat like a huge, bitter lump. "You just let me think things that aren't true. The way you let me think you were through with Rachel — that you weren't going to have anything more to do with her."

"Are we going through all that again?" he asked grimly.

"No. No, we're not." Stiff with anger, Abbie swung out of bed and began grabbing up her clothes.

MacCrea sat up. "What the hell are you doing?"

"Can't you guess?" she shot back. "I'm leaving. I'm not going to stay around here and listen to any more of your half-truths. I've trusted you for the last time, MacCrea Wilder. Do you hear me? For the last time!"

"You haven't got a car, remember? You can't leave."

"Just watch me." Hurriedly, she pulled on her skirt and silk jacket, not bothering with her nylons. Instead she wadded them up in her hand as she started for the door.

"If you walk out that door, Abbie, I won't come after you again," he warned.

"Good." She reached for the handle.

"That damned jealousy is destroying you, Abbie. Why can't you see that?"

She stepped into the night and slammed the door on his angrily shouted words, then hurried to his truck. The keys were still in the ignition. She climbed in and started the engine. She saw MacCrea in the sweep of the headlights as he came charging out of the trailer. She gunned the engine and whipped the truck in a tight circle, driving away before he could stop her.

28

That night, Abbie dreamed about MacCrea. They had gotten married, and after the ceremony he had led her under some moss-draped trees toward a small white cottage where he said they were going to live. The front door stood open. Then Abbie saw Rachel waiting inside, and MacCrea told her that she lived there, too — that all three of them were going to live together "happily ever after." Abbie had broken away from MacCrea and started running, but MacCrea had chased her. At first she'd been able to run fast enough to keep him from catching her, then he had started growing taller and taller — and his arms got longer. Soon they were going to be long enough to reach her. She could hear Rachel laughing with malicious glee.

A hand touched her shoulder and Abbie screamed. The next thing she knew she was sitting bolt upright in bed, completely drenched in sweat. "I don't know about you, Abbie, but you just scared the life out of me." Babs stood beside the bed, clutching a hand to her breast and laughing at the sudden shock to both of them.

"I . . . I was having a nightmare." A nightmare steeped in reality. Still a little dazed, she glanced at the sunlight that streamed through her bedroom window. "What time is it?"

"A few minutes before nine. I thought I'd check and see if you wanted to go to church with Ben and me this morning."

"I think I'll skip church this morning."

"I'm sorry I woke you." Her mother moved away from the bed. "Go back to sleep if you can. And don't worry about Sunday dinner. It's in the oven."

As the door shut behind her, Abbie slid back under the covers, but she knew she couldn't go back to sleep. She wished desperately that she could forget last night. She'd almost gotten over all the pain and bitterness from the last time. Now it was back, more potent than before.

At least she had the consolation of knowing MacCrea was leaving the state. She wouldn't run the risk any longer of accidentally running into him, or seeing him somewhere with someone else — or with Rachel. He'd be out of her life, this time for good.

Abbie stayed in bed until she heard Ben and her mother leave the house. Then she went into the small bathroom off the hall, where she washed her hands and splashed cold water on her face, trying to get rid of that dull, dead feeling. She opened the mirrored door to the medicine cabinet over the sink and started to reach for her toothbrush, but she stopped short at the sight of the flat plastic case on the bottom shelf — the case that contained her diaphragm.

Especially during the first years of her marriage to Christopher, she had wanted a baby very much but had failed to conceive. Christopher claimed that his doctor had found nothing wrong with him and said their childlessness must be her fault. It was shortly after she'd begun taking fertility pills that she'd found out he was cheating on her. Initially Abbie had blamed herself, thinking that her inability to get pregnant had driven him to seek other women. Christopher had sworn that he loved her and that the others had meant nothing to him, and promised to be faithful. She waited, continuing to use birth control, unwilling to risk starting a family while their marriage was on such shaky ground — only to catch him playing around again.

Nearly certain that she was sterile, she had taken precautions with MacCrea only during the most crucial times. Now, with a sudden sinking sensation, Abbie calculated where she was in her cycle. Lately she'd paid little attention to it; it hadn't seemed important, since she wasn't going with anyone. She never dreamed last night would happen.

Now she was forced to face the very real possibility that she was pregnant. She pressed a hand to her stomach, feeling frightened and half-sick. After all this time, she was about to find out whether the problem *had* been Christopher's, or hers . . . only it wouldn't be Christopher's child growing in her womb. It would be MacCrea's.

She didn't want to think about it. She didn't even want to consider the possibility that she had finally gotten pregnant. But she had to. If she was pregnant, what was she going to do? What did she want to do? What was right? What was best? She reeled from the endless questions that hammered through her mind, finding no easy answers to any of them.

Before long, the possibility became more than just a fear as Abbie started waking up in the mornings plagued by a queasy feeling in her stomach. Several times she wasn't sure she was going to make it through the morning workouts, but she always did. When Babs remarked on her pallor, she blamed it on tiredness and overwork. But she knew she couldn't hide the truth much longer. Sooner or later people were going to guess, if they hadn't already.

The flashy gunmetal-gray gelding she was riding snorted at the tractor chugging across the adjoining cotton field. Abbie slipped a hand under his cream-white mane and petted his arched neck, speaking softly to the young horse to quiet him as she glanced at the man bouncing along on the tractor seat. Dobie waved to her. She lifted a hand briefly in response, then turned the Arabian gelding toward the barn, less than a quarter-mile distant.

During times like these, when she wanted to be alone and think, she was glad Ben believed horses should be ridden as much as possible over open country and not endlessly worked in arenas, traveling in circles all the time. He claimed nothing soured a good horse quicker than arena work, insisting it became just as bored as the rider with the monotony of it. Abbie agreed with his philosophy, although today her reasons were slightly selfish.

As Abbie rode into the yard, she saw Ben in the small work pen they'd constructed next to the barn. He was working with a yearling filly being trained to show at halter. A marvel to watch, he relied on none of the more severe methods she'd seen some trainers use — no chains under the jaw, no head jerking, and no harsh whipping. Instead, he used a long buggy whip to get the horse's attention, cracking it behind the filly's back feet, and rarely ever actually striking her with it. Most horses quickly learned that as long as they paid attention to Ben, the whip was silent. Once Ben had the horse's attention, it was a relatively simple matter to teach her to face him and to direct her movements by altering his body position, creating a conditioned response.

Abbie dismounted near the barn and watched from the sidelines as she unsaddled the gelding. As usual, Ben kept the training session short, preferring not to tax the horse's attention span. He finished at the same time Abbie started to rub down the gelding.

After he turned the filly back in with the other horses, he joined her. "The ride was good? Akhar went well for you?"

"Yes." Abbie paused at her task and pushed up the sleeves on her heavy sweater, conscious of the tenderness in her breasts.

"Do you feel better now, after the ride?"

"I feel fine. I did before I left," she insisted defensively, aware of the intent way he was studying her. In the last couple of days, she'd caught Ben watching her closely several times. She thought he suspected something, but maybe she was just becoming paranoid.

"When a person has problems, it is good to go riding sometimes."

"Problems? What makes you think I have any? No more than usual anyway. I'm just tired, that's all." But more so than normal. She felt she could sleep for a week and not be rested.

"It is natural for you to be," he said, and Abbie darted a wary glance at him. His usually impassive features wore a troubled frown of concern. "You have the look of a female when —" He stopped abruptly as if suddenly hearing the words coming out of his mouth.

There was no point in keeping the truth from him, Abbie realized. He'd already guessed. With a sober wryness she faced him squarely. "I hoped since I wasn't a horse, you wouldn't be able to tell by looking that I was pregnant. I should have known I couldn't fool you."

"It is true then?"

"Yes. MacCrea Wilder's the father." She knew Ben would never ask. "He was at the party we hostessed in River Oaks early this month." It seemed a lifetime ago instead of a little less than three weeks. "I thought . . . It really doesn't matter what I thought. I was wrong."

"Does he know?"

"No," she answered quickly, forcefully. "And he's never to know, Ben. No one is. I want your word that you'll never tell anyone, not even my mother, who the father is."

"If this is what you want, I will do it," Ben agreed, but with obvious reluctance. "But what will you do?"

She'd thought it through thoroughly, considered all her options, and reached her decision. "I'm going to keep the baby, of course." No matter what else in her life had changed, she still wanted a baby. In the end, it had been as simple as that.

"But a young woman with no husband, you know what people will say," he reminded her sadly.

"Then I'll just have to get myself a husband, won't I?" Abbie declared, feigning an insouciance that couldn't have been farther from her true feelings. At the sound of the tractor chugging in from the field, she turned and glanced at the driver. "He's a likely candidate, wouldn't you say?"

"He has asked you?" Ben questioned.

"No, but that's a minor detail." She shrugged that aside, the same way she shrugged aside her feelings. If she sounded hard and uncaring, it was because she had to be. With a baby on the way, she had to be practical. She couldn't afford the luxury of personal feelings — neither her own nor Dobie's. "I can handle him."

"But do you want a husband you can handle?" Ben frowned.

"I don't want any husband at all," Abbie declared somewhat hotly. "But since I have to have one, I might as well marry someone I can manage."

"You would not respect such a man."

"I don't have to respect him. I just have to marry him." But she didn't mean to sound so scornful of Dobie. "Besides, Dobie would be a good father."

Late that afternoon, after the horses were fed, Abbie walked by the machine shed on her way to the house. When she saw Dobie inside, tinkering with some part on the tractor, she hesitated. More than anything, she wanted to go to the house and lie down for a while, but this project of hers wasn't something that she could afford to postpone. Altering her course, she entered the machine shed.

"Hello, Dobie."

He straightened quickly at the sound of her voice and hastily wiped his greasy hands on an oil rag. "Hello, Abbie." He smiled at her warmly. "I saw you out riding this afternoon."

"I saw you, too." She returned the smile, then came to the point. "I was wondering if you're busy tonight. I'd love to go somewhere to have a drink and maybe dance a little. But I don't want to go by myself. It wouldn't look right. I thought . . . maybe you'd like to come, too."

For a moment he was too surprised to speak. "I'd love to," he said finally as he pushed the battered Stetson to the back of his head, revealing more of his strawberry-blond hair. "Maybe we can leave early and have dinner somewhere first."

"That sounds good," she said, agreeing readily.

"I'll pick you up about seven. How would that be?"

"Fine. I'll be ready."

When Dobie picked her up that night, he was driving the brand-new pickup he usually kept parked in the garage under a protective dust cover. Dobie was all slicked up himself in a western-cut jacket, a sharply creased pair of new jeans, and shiny snakeskin cowboy boots. Even his red-gold hair had the sheen that said it had been freshly shampooed.

The evening didn't turn out to be the trial Abbie had expected. She couldn't have asked for a more attentive escort. Dobie was always opening doors for her, holding her chair, and fetching her drinks. Over dinner, they talked mostly about his farm and the current commodities market. At a local country bar, they two-stepped and slow-danced, but he was always careful not to hold her too close. Abbie decided that she had rejected his attentions a few too many times in the past, making him leery now.

On the way home, she actually felt guilty for the way she was using him. She almost wished Dobie wasn't such a gentleman. But this was something she had to do, for the sake of everyone concerned.

She waited as Dobie came around to help her out of the pickup. He opened the door and reached for her hand. "Well, here you are back again, safe and sound."

Abbie climbed out of the truck, then continued to hold his hand once on the ground. "I want to check on Breeze before I go to the house. Would you like to come along?"

"Sure," he agreed cautiously, as if uncertain about what she expected of him.

She released his hand and started walking toward the barn. "I really enjoyed myself tonight. I hope you did, too, Dobie."

"I did," he assured her, lagging about a half a step behind her. "It's been a while since I've been out, too."

Reaching ahead of her, he opened the Dutch door. Abbie stepped inside and flipped on the light switch. Several horses snorted and thrust their heads over the mangers to gaze inquiringly at them. Abbie passed all of them as she walked down the aisle to her filly's stall. River Breeze nickered a welcome and pushed her velvety-soft nose into Abbie's hand. "How are you, girl?" Abbie crooned and scratched the hollow above one of her big liquid brown eyes.

"She really likes you." Dobie watched from the side. "I've never had much to do with horses myself — not since I got bucked off of one as a kid and broke my leg. We took her to the sale barn and sold her that very next week."

"You should have gotten back on." She turned slightly, angling her body in his direction. "After your leg healed, of course. Just because you got hurt once doesn't mean you'd get hurt again."

He looked at her, then down at the floor, and shifted his weight from one foot to the other. "Some things just aren't worth the risk."

"Why haven't you ever gotten married, Dobie? You have so much to offer a woman, besides a home and this farm. There must be dozens of girls who are just waiting for you to ask them."

"Maybe," he conceded. "But I've never wanted any of them." Hesitating, he glanced at her. "There's only been one girl I ever wanted to marry. I think you know that."

"You could have also changed your mind."

"I haven't." His voice sounded thin.

"I'm glad." She had to make herself smile encouragingly. She kept telling herself that everything would be all right if she could just get this over with.

He moved hesitantly closer and leaned a hand against the stall partition near her head. He looked at her for a long moment, then swayed uncertainly closer, and carefully pressed his mouth against her lips for a very few seconds. As he started to move away, Abbie cupped the left side of his jaw in her hand.

"I'm very glad, Dobie," she whispered and brought her mouth against his lips, moving it over them, gently persuading.

For an instant, Dobie was too startled by the initiative she'd taken to respond. Then his arms went around her and she was gathered against him. He kissed her roughly, fiercely, almost frightening Abbie with his unbridled ardor, like a man too long without water and guzzling down the first glass given to him.

Abruptly he broke it off. "I'm sorry, Abbie. I —"

"Don't be." She pressed against him when he started to pull away from her.

"I've wanted to . . . kiss you and . . . hold you for so long. And now — Why now, Abbie?" he questioned.

"Sometimes, Dobie, you get so used to having someone around you that you . . . don't notice them." Abbie chose her words carefully. "You know they are good and kind and wonderful, but . . . you just take them for granted. You don't appreciate all the really good things about them. I guess that's the way I've been with you."

"Is it?"

"Yes." She nodded affirmatively. "Ever since my divorce, I think I've been afraid to trust a man again. But these last few months, living here and seeing you every day — I guess it's opened my eyes."

"I figured I never had a chance with you."

"You were wrong." She laid her head against his shoulder, unable to look at him anymore and lie. "You were very wrong, Dobie."

"All this time, I —"

"I know." With a lifting turn of her head, she sought his mouth and closed her eyes tightly when he kissed her.

She felt like a cheat. But she firmly reminded herself that she wasn't. Dobie was getting what he wanted, and that was her. Maybe she wasn't all that he bargained for, but that's just the way life was.

As one kiss led to another, his caresses grew bolder. Soon it was a simple matter for Abbie to draw him down onto the pile of straw next to the manger. She hadn't realized seduction could be so easy — or that she'd feel so empty and sick inside afterward.

As tears pricked her eyelids, Abbie turned her back on him as she sat up and pulled on her blouse. She could hear him dressing behind her, the rustle of straw, the thump of boots being pulled on, and the race of a zipper. She buttoned her blouse slowly in an attempt to delay the moment when she'd have to face him and pretend how much she'd enjoyed it.

"Abbie." He knelt on the straw beside her. "Are . . . are you sorry?"

That was the last question she expected. She wanted to scream at him for being so damned considerate. "No, of course not," she replied.

And it was the truth. She'd do it all over again if that's what it was going to take to get a wedding ring on her finger. She wasn't going to subject herself to the embarrassment and humiliation of having an illegitimate child. The county had talked enough about her family. They weren't going to talk about her. By the time she had this baby, she was going to have a husband.

With renewed resolve, she turned to Dobie. "Are you sorry?"

"No." His smile, his whole expression, was filled with adoration. "I could never be sorry. I love you, Abbie."

"You have no idea how much I wanted to hear you say that," she declared fervently.

*   *   *

Three more times in the next few days, Abbie arranged to be with Dobie. Finally, on the day before Christmas Eve, she convinced Dobie that marrying him would be the most wonderful present she could have. That afternoon they were married by a justice of the peace and spent their wedding night at a Galveston motel.

When they drove back to the farm that gray and drizzly Christmas morning, Abbie was legally Mrs. Dobie Hix. She had the ring on her finger to prove it. But if anyone bothered to look closely at it, they could see it was only gold-plated, like her marriage.

29

*L*ow clouds shrouded the windows of Lane and Rachel's Houston penthouse, obscuring the view of the city beyond. MacCrea stared at the thick clouds a few more minutes, then moved restlessly away and prowled about the living room. Over twenty minutes ago Lane had been called to the telephone by his houseman. MacCrea glanced at his watch, wondering how much longer Lane was going to be tied up. Irritable and impatient, he tried to blame his short temper on the damp and gloomy weather that had blanketed the Gulf Coast for more than a week and turned his drilling site into a swampy quagmire.

A key rattled in the door. MacCrea turned as the door swung open and Rachel walked in. The midnight-blue raincoat glistened from the droplets of moisture that beaded on the water-repellent material. As she started to unbuckle the wide belt that cinched the raincoat tightly around her waist, she noticed him standing there.

"MacCrea, this is a surprise. Lane didn't tell me you were coming."

"He probably forgot."

Unobtrusively the houseman appeared to take Rachel's raincoat and closed umbrella. "Did you receive the Christmas package we sent you?" She surrendered them automatically, with barely more than a nod at the quiet servant.

"Yes, and thanks for the sweater. I liked it." In truth, MacCrea couldn't even recall what color it was. Christmas had been just another rainy day to him, spent alone, without a tree or decorations like those that still adorned the Canfields' apartment.

"I'm glad." She glanced around the living room. "Where's Lane?"

"A long-distance call came in for him. He shouldn't be much longer." MacCrea hoped he wouldn't be. He was uncomfortable with Rachel and the memories of Abbie she evoked. "How's the house coming?"

"Luckily they got it all closed in before the rains started, so it's coming along fine." As she wandered over to him, there was something catlike in the way she studied him. "Have you heard the news yet?"

"News?" He arched an eyebrow, a little voice warning him that this news had something to do with Abbie.

"It seems my neighbor eloped over Christmas."

"Eloped. You mean she got married?" He reeled inwardly. Of all the things he'd braced himself to hear, that wasn't one of them. After the shock came anger. "Who to?"

"That redheaded Hix boy."

"That little —" MacCrea clamped his mouth shut on the rest, clenching his jaw so tightly his teeth hurt.

"You know why she married him, don't you?"

"No." Hell, she didn't love that little wimp. She couldn't.

"She did it to get back at me."

"How?" He frowned, not following her jealous logic.

"Practically all the land those Hix brothers own was once part of the original Lawson homestead. She only married him to get her hands on that land. You know how much she hates it that Lane and I have River Bend. Now she's going to see that we don't get our hands on any more of the family's former holdings."

"I see." It made sense to him. It was just the sort of twisted little plan Abbie would come up with. He knew just how eaten up with jealousy she was. Rachel was the reason Abbie had refused to marry him and destroyed everything good they had; now she was the reason Abbie had married Hix. "The stupid little fool," MacCrea muttered to himself.

"What did you say?"

"Nothing." Absently he shook his head, not wanting to believe the news. She was married now. He tried to tell himself that he was well rid of her, and all her stupid jealousies and hatred. He could almost convince himself of that. Almost.

30

*A*bbie waited until the second week in January to go to the doctor and obtain a medical confirmation of her pregnancy. When she told Dobie, he was ecstatic. He insisted they go over to her mother's house and tell her the good news. His absolute joy when he told Babs and Ben was almost more than Abbie could cope with. At the first opportunity, she escaped from the living room and slipped into the kitchen on the pretext of making coffee.

Ben came in. "Are you not feeling well?"

"I'm fine," she insisted impatiently, tired of all the questions about her health. She had answered too many of Dobie's already. From the living room came the sound of his laughter, rich with jubilance, but it just irritated Abbie more. "Listen to him. I never dreamed he would be so proud and happy."

"It is a wonderful thing to be having a baby."

"Yes, but the way he's acting you'd think he was the father."

"Is that not what you wanted him to think?"

For a fraction of a second she paused, then hurriedly pried the lid off the coffee cannister. "Yes." But she wondered how MacCrea would react if he knew about the baby — whether he'd be bursting at the seams the way Dobie was. But she'd never know, because he wouldn't find out about it. That's the way she wanted it — for herself and the baby.

* * *

Later that night, Abbie lay in the double bed with her back to Dobie. She knew he wasn't asleep. He was like a little boy on Christmas Eve, too excited about Santa's impending arrival to close his eyes. She felt the mattress shift under his weight as he turned toward her. His hand moved over the top of the covers to touch her arm.

"Please, Dobie, I'm tired." She couldn't bear the thought of him making demands on her tonight.

"I know, honey. I was just thinking that from now on you need to take it a little easier."

"Yes." She didn't feel like talking, certainly not about the baby anymore.

"I've already told your mother that she'll have to find somebody else to help her with the parties 'cause you won't be able to."

Stunned by his announcement, Abbie rolled over to face him in the darkness. "You did what?"

Ever since they'd gotten married, he'd been hinting that it wasn't necessary for her to work anymore. She was his wife now, and she should be content to stay at home and cook and keep house for him. He'd give her whatever spending money she needed. Considering the way he squeezed a dollar, Abbie knew that wouldn't be much. For the most part, she had simply ignored him, believing that in time, he'd get used to the idea of his wife working.

"I told her you couldn't work like that anymore and stay up 'til all hours of the night at those parties. You need your rest now. And tomorrow you'd better call the owners of those horses you've been keeping here and tell them to come get them."

"I will do no such thing! The Scottsdale Show is less than three weeks away, and I've promised two of the owners that I'll show their horses there. It's one of the biggest Arabian horse shows in the whole country. And I've worked long and hard to get these horses ready for it. The stalls have already been reserved, the entry fees have been paid, and a hauler has already been lined up to take them there. Even if I could find somebody else qualified to show them at this date, I wouldn't."

"You aren't really taking off to Arizona for two weeks and leaving me here alone? You're my wife now." Even in the shadowed darkness of the bedroom his disbelieving frown was visible.

"Yes, I am going. You knew all along I planned to," she reminded him. "You're welcome to come." But she doubted that he'd be willing to leave the farm for that length of time — or spend the money to go.

"But with a baby on the way, you shouldn't be bouncing around on those horses."

"In the first place, Dobie Hix, I don't bounce. And in the second, I'm not going to quit working with the horses — or my mother. So you might as well get that out of your head right now."

"I'm only thinking of you. You need to stay home and take care of yourself," he argued.

"No, I don't," she stated emphatically. "I am a normal, healthy woman who is pregnant. It isn't an illness, Dobie. As a matter of fact, the doctor said that as long as I exercise and eat sensibly, every-thing should be fine. Until he tells me differently, I'm going to keep working. Besides, I'd go stark, raving crazy if I had to sit around this farmhouse day in and day out." That was the truth, but she hadn't meant for it to come out so harshly. "And there's Ben to consider. Those horses are his source of income."

"He could always work for me on the farm."

Abbie knew Ben would hate that. "If he couldn't work with horses, I think he'd die. They're his life, just like this farm is to you."

Dobie rolled onto his back and stared at the textured ceiling, his frustration almost palpable. "I swear I just don't understand you sometimes, Abbie," he muttered. "What are people going to think? You're my wife, and here you are working — and gallivanting all over the country."

"I don't care what they think. I'm going to keep working, and that's final. I don't want to discuss it anymore." She turned on her side and punched the pillow into shape, then lay her head on it and determinedly closed her eyes. When he started to say something, she cut him off with a sharp "Good night, Dobie."

But the topic became a running argument between them. At one point Dobie reminded her that *he* owned the farm, and if he didn't want horses on it, that's the way it was going to be. Abbie had quickly pointed out that he had signed a legal agreement, leasing her the barn area and pasture. And if he chose not to renew the lease when it expired in seven more months, then she'd find somewhere else to keep the horses.

When he brought up the parties, she asked him exactly how he expected her to pay the stud fee to have River Breeze bred in the spring. Was he going to give her the ten or twenty thousand dollars it was going to cost — plus boarding and transportation expenses? In his opinion, it was a stupid waste of money.

The situation between them didn't improve when he saw all the cocktail and evening dresses she was packing to take to Scottsdale. She was supposed to be going to a horse show. Abbie tried to explain to him about the gala parties that were an integral part of the Scottsdale Show scene. But he didn't think his wife should be going to parties — not even with Ben as her escort. By the time she set out to drive to Arizona with Ben, she and Dobie were just barely on speaking terms.

In Arabian horse circles, the Scottsdale Show at Paradise Park was considered one of the most prestigious, and some claimed expensive, shows in the country and the premier sales arena in the nation. The giant parking lot next to the showgrounds was jammed with horse trailers and vans bearing license plates from all four points of the compass, from as far away as Canada. The trailers ranged in size from a simple single-horse trailer to luxury models capable of hauling six horses with room left over for living quarters.

Arriving a day before the show actually started, Abbie and Ben checked into an inexpensive motel a couple of miles from the park, her small single room a vast change from the plush condo she had usually stayed in when she had attended the show with her father. But many things had changed in her life.

The first two days of the show were hectic ones, getting the horses settled in, clipped, and groomed, with more exhibiters arriving all the time, florists delivering huge potted plants to various stables to aid in the transformation of common stalls into showcases, and carpenters and electricians swarming all over the place like so many flies in a barn. Outside the main show ring, the bazaar area was growing as more booths opened for business, selling everything from syndicate shares to fried ice cream, horse tack to mink coats, and oil paintings to tee shirts.

But those first days were fun days, too, for Abbie. At every turn, she ran into someone she knew. All of them had heard about her father's death, and the subsequent sale of River Bend and its Arabian stock, but it didn't seem to matter to them. They were glad to see her, glad to see she was still competing, even if it wasn't on horses her family owned.

After competing in a late afternoon class, her first in the show,

Abbie telephoned the horse's owners and informed them that their mare had made it through the first elimination round, then grabbed her dress bag and overnight case and hurried over to the ladies' shower trailers to get cleaned up. Desert Farm Arabians was holding an aisle party that evening to present their stallion, Radzyn. Abbie was anxious to attend and see the stallion that she regarded as a top choice for her young mare.

When she saw the striking blood bay stallion, he was all she had hoped he would be and more. Despite the crowd that had gathered around him, partially blocking her view, she was impressed by his regal arrogance as he stood with his head held high and his ebony tail flagged.

"What do you think of him, Ben?" She glanced at the elderly man beside her, still wearing his same serviceable tweed jacket. His one concession to the party had been the tie he added.

He studied the horse critically. "He does not have the classic *jibbah* I would like to see," he said, using the term that referred to the prominent forehead, a distinctive feature on an Arabian horse.

"Breeze does. And Radzyn has the level croup and well-sloped shoulders. Breeze has the classic features, the long hip and short back. Where Radzyn is weak, she's strong — and vice versa. They should make a good nick, I think."

Slow to make up his mind, Ben finally nodded. "I think so, too."

"Good. That much is decided anyway." She hooked an arm with his, her dress sleeve of scarlet silk jacquard at odds with his worn tweed sleeve with its suede elbow patch. The other guests were wearing everything from tee shirts and jeans to sables and Gucci. "Now all we have to figure out is how we're going to pay the stud fee. They want fifteen thousand for a live foal guarantee or ten thousand without it."

She steered him toward the buffet table, a familiar hollow feeling in her stomach. It didn't seem to matter how much she ate anymore; she just couldn't seem to satisfy the ravenous appetite she'd acquired with her pregnancy.

"We will find a way. Do not worry," Ben assured her. "You will see when April comes."

"I hope so," she sighed and began piling the daintily cut sandwiches on her plate, adding a dollop of caviar on the side.

On the opposite side of the buffet table, a woman nudged her companion. "Look. Isn't that the new owner of River Bend?" she said, using a toothpick-speared meatball to point to her.

Abbie turned around to look in the direction the woman had indicated. There stood Rachel, a snow-white ermine stole draped low on her arms, revealing a black lace dress studded with sequins over a strapless underdress of rose satin.

"What's she doing here?" Abbie felt first cold, then hot. "She doesn't have any horses competing here, does she?"

"No. But I have heard that she has come to buy."

"The sales. Of course, she'd be here for them," she said.

And Abbie was also painfully aware that her own name wouldn't be on any of the invitation lists. Even if she was able to wangle a ticket from someone to attend one of the major sales — extravaganzas that rivaled any Broadway production — it would be in the bleachers. She certainly wouldn't be able to sit in the "gold card" section, the way she used to. Gaining admission to that favored area required a financial statement worthy of a Rockefeller — or Lane Canfield. But Rachel would be there, diamonds, ermine, and all.

For the rest of the show, Abbie was haunted by Rachel. No matter where Abbie went, she was there: in the stands, on the showgrounds, or at the elaborately decorated stalls of the major horse breeders. And she was always in the company of some important breeder — several of whom Abbie had once regarded as her friends. Finally, Abbie stopped going to the parties just to avoid being upstaged by Rachel.

Still, she wasn't able to escape all the talk about her. She had gone on a buying spree, purchasing some twenty Arabians either at the auctions or through private treaty. In the process, she had spent, some claimed, two million dollars . . . and became the new "darling" at Scottsdale.

Even though Abbie managed to come away with placings in two of the classes, she was glad when the show was over. Her pride had suffered about all it could stand. She needed to go home and lick her wounds.

Home. Looking around the old farmhouse, Abbie found it hard to think of it as home. River Bend was home. In her heart it would always be. But she tried not to think about that as she unpacked, because that meant thinking about Rachel.

At least her return had brought one consolation. Dobie didn't seem inclined to renew their argument. Although she sensed that he still totally disapproved of her activities, Abbie hoped he had finally realized she wouldn't change her mind. She was never going to be the stay-at-home, dutiful little wife and mother he thought she should be. The sooner he accepted that, the better their lives would be.

"Abbie! Hello? Are you here?" her mother called from the front part of the house.

"I'm back here in the bedroom." She scooped the pile of dirty clothes off the bed and started to dump them in the hamper, but it was already filled to the top with the two weeks' worth of Dobie's dirty laundry. Abbie dropped them on the floor beside it, wistfully recalling the days when there were maids to cope with all this.

"Are you resting? I . . ." Babs paused in the doorway and stared at the luggage and garment bags strewn about the room.

"Not hardly. I'm just now getting around to unpacking." She snapped the lid closed on the empty suitcase and swung it off the bed. "It took me all morning to clean the kitchen. Did you see the dust all over? It must be an inch thick. When Dobie lived here by himself, he used to keep this house neat as a pin. But he marries me and he suddenly becomes completely helpless around the house."

"Men can be like that."

"Totally uncooperative, you mean," Abbie muttered, trying to hide her irritation. "I hope business picks up some more. I can hardly wait until I can afford to hire a housekeeper."

"Couldn't you talk to Dobie about it? Surely he —"

"— would pay someone else to do the work he thinks I should do as his wife? No, Momma. I'm not going to waste my breath trying."

"I know that . . . you and Dobie have been having some problems. Most couples do when they're first married. There's always an adjustment period when two individuals start living together under one roof. Lately I've realized that it can't be easy for Dobie having his mother-in-law living next door."

"He'll get used to it." Abbie removed her evening dresses from the garment bag and inspected them for stains before carrying them over to the closet to hang up.

"Perhaps. But while you were gone, I found a small, one-bedroom condominium in Houston. I talked with Fred Childers at the bank and showed him what I've managed to earn from the parties. Of course, I'll have to use some of the money I received from Dean's estate to make the down payment, but the bank is willing to loan me the balance."

"Momma, you aren't moving," Abbie protested.

"I think it's best."

"For whom? And why? Whose idea is this? Yours or Dobie's?

Momma, I'm going to continue to work with you. And if Dobie doesn't like it, that's his problem." She needed a source of income, more than what she could earn training and showing horses for others, if she was ever going to have the funds to pay the stud fee and buy more broodmares. She had every intention of building a breeding operation that would not only rival Rachel's but eventually surpass it. Rachel had it all now — the horses, the power, the money, the influence — but Abbie vowed that her turn was coming. Someday, all of Scottsdale was going to be talking about her.

"Dobie had nothing to do with my decision, although I honestly believe you two will get along better if I'm not popping in and out all the time. Besides, it will be much more convenient and practical for me to live in Houston. There won't be the time and expense of driving back and forth, not just for the parties themselves but to meet with the caterers and the suppliers, too. And I won't have all those long-distance charges on my telephone bill."

Abbie couldn't argue with any of that. Yet she smiled. "I wish you could hear yourself, Momma. Babs Lawson, the business-woman." She had always loved her mother, but now that love was coupled with a new respect and admiration. "I'm proud of you, Momma. I really am."

"Look at who I had for a partner." Babs smiled, then paused, her expression turning thoughtful. "The truth is, both of us have changed a lot these last several months — for the better, I might add."

Reaching out, Abbie warmly grasped her mother's hand, finding that they were on equal ground.

Within two weeks, Babs had moved to her condominium apartment in Houston. For Abbie, it was a strange feeling to have her mother out there in the world — on her own. She had more difficulty adjusting to this new independence of her mother's than Babs did.

31

The rusty old pickup truck with a single-horse trailer in tow labored up the long incline, shuddering in the strong draft of each car that whizzed by it. On both sides of the wide swath the highway made through the mountains, the landscape was an arid and unfriendly collection of rock and sand, dotted with the scrawny clumps of sagebrush, prickly pear, and scrub grass.

Driving with the windows down, a pair of sunglasses shielding her eyes from the glare of the sun, Abbie kept glancing at the temperature gauge, waiting for the truck to overheat again. A hot wind, laden with dust from the Arizona desert, blew in and whipped at her ponytail, tearing loose strands of dark hair and slapping them against her face. She ignored it, just as she ignored the throbbing ache in her lower back and the uncomfortable soreness of her full breasts, intent only on coaxing the truck to the top of the grade. She glanced in the rearview mirror, checking on the horse trailer in tow and the gray filly traveling inside it.

As they topped the rise, Abbie shifted out of low gear and sighed in relief. "It should be all downhill from here," she said to Ben, riding on the passenger side. Within minutes the desert community of metropolitan Phoenix came into view, sprawling over the mountain-ringed valley before them, a collection of towns all grown together. "I guess we don't have to wonder anymore whether Dobie's old pickup will make it this far. I just hope we don't have to make a return trip in the heat of summer. It's hot enough now in April." She doubted the pickup would be able to negotiate many of the mountain passes when summer temperatures sizzled over one hundred degrees.

"We will drive only at night then," Ben replied, unconcerned.

"I should have thought of that." Abbie smiled ruefully, recognizing that she was mentally as well as physically tired from the long trip.

Four days it had taken them to make the journey from Texas, stopping frequently along the way to avoid putting too much stress on the filly's legs and giving her a chance to rest and graze along the roadside. Except for some stiffness and minor swelling, River Breeze had weathered the trip well so far, better than Abbie had expected. Trailering long distances was hard on any horse and doubly so for a crippled filly like River Breeze.

In retrospect, Abbie was glad now that she hadn't been able to afford the cost of hiring a professional hauler to transport the filly to the stud farm in Scottsdale. He probably wouldn't have made the trip in stages the way she and Ben had, nor would he have taken the extra care they had.

The trip was definitely worth the time and trouble it had taken. No part of it had been easy. Right from the start, she'd had the problem of trying to find a horse trailer she could borrow. She didn't have a trailer hitch on her car, nor the extra money to buy one and pay to have it installed.

When she had tried to talk Dobie into letting her take his new truck, he had refused, then told her she was welcome to take his old one, fully expecting her to turn that down rather than take the risk of the beat-up old truck breaking down on the road somewhere. Out of spite, and sheer stubbornness, Abbie had accepted it. She knew he would worry about her, and it served him right. Maybe he'd learn someday that nothing was going to stop her.

After driving since before dawn, they had stopped at a truck stop late that morning so Abbie could shower and change into her last set of clean clothes. Now that she was entering her fifth month of pregnancy, she couldn't squeeze into her regular clothes anymore and only had three maternity outfits to her name. She'd saved the nicest of the three for today, an embroidered tunic top with a pair of matching blue maternity slacks.

As they entered the outskirts of Phoenix, the traffic became heavier. "This is almost as bad as Houston." Abbie felt for the map on the seat and handed it to Ben. "Here's the city map. I've marked the route we need to take to get to Charlie Carstairs's farm. With all this traffic, you're going to have to watch for the signs and tell me where to turn."

Circulating fans whirred, maintaining a constant air flow through the stallion barn. At the far end of the double-wide aisle, a stable hand hosed down the brick floor to further cool the barn.

But all eyes were on the black bay Arab that had been led out of its box stall for their inspection. Rachel watched intently as the stallion arched its swanlike neck and danced on its back legs. Keeping a snug hold on the lead shank, the groom led the stallion around in a circle, then brought the animal to a stop directly before her.

The sight of him was so magnificent it nearly took her breath away. A faint thrill coursed through her veins as she stared at the black fire that burned in the stallion's velvety eyes, then lifted her gaze higher to the small ears, shaped like half-moons, pricked in alertness. Rachel inhaled the strong scent of him, a scent headier than any expensive perfume Lane had ever bought for her.

The large nostrils flared as the dark stallion lifted his small, refined head and trumpeted a call that quivered with longing. When she heard the answering neighs coming from the mares in the nearby barn, Rachel understood, feeling an odd twinge of envy.

Turning to Lane, she smiled faintly. "I think I recognized Simoon whinnying just then. I wonder if she knows she was answering her future lover."

"Somehow I doubt it," he replied dryly, his look one of gentle tolerance and amusement for her fanciful thought.

Rachel knew it was probably a foolish notion, but she wished, just once, he would go along with her. Then she immediately regretted being even faintly critical of him. From the very beginning, Lane had indulged her every whim when it came to horses, regardless of the cost or inconvenience. Just like this trip. Even though he had assured her he had some business to take care of in Phoenix, Rachel knew he was coming along to please her. He gave her so much that often she felt guilty she had so little to give him in return.

"Well? What do you think of Basha 'al-Nazir, Rachel, now that you've seen him close up?" Charlie Carstairs stood with his arms folded across his barrel chest, the large gold nugget he wore on a chain around his neck winking in the light as he angled his shoulders in her direction.

"He's truly magnificent." But in her mind, she was imagining the foal that would come from this union.

"You can put him back in his stall." Charlie gave the order to the manager of his stud farm, Vince Romaine. With a wave of his hand, the short, thin man passed the order on to the groom holding the stallion, as spare with his words as Charlie was voluble. "Every time I see that stallion I wonder if I really want to sell him," Charlie declared with a shake of his head. "But with Radzyn winning the championship here at Scottsdale, I've talked myself into concentrating my breeding program more on Polish-bred Arabians. That seems to be what the market wants today. And Radzyn has a lot of Polish blood in his breeding. As a matter of fact, Patsy and I are planning to go to Poland this fall and attend the sale at Janow. I'd like to pick up some good broodmares there to breed to Radzyn. The horse business is crazy, Lane. Five years from now everyone will probably be wanting Egyptian, and I'll be kicking myself six ways to Sunday for selling Basha. Then again, it may be Spanish- or Russian-bred Arabians."

"Don't ask for my opinion," Lane said, curving an arm around Rachel's shoulders as they all started toward the door leading outside. "Rachel is the expert on horses in our family."

"I just know what I like," she replied.

"And I'm not about to fault your tastes. After all, you picked me for a husband," Lane teased.

"Careful," Charlie warned, "or she's liable to start thinking she's made a mistake."

Even though she knew he was only joking, Rachel felt honor-bound to deny his remark. "I'd never think that. I couldn't."

"That's what she says now, Lane, but wait until some handsome young stud walks by. You mark my words. She'll start wishing she was single. You should have seen my Patsy carry on the other night over that new singer, Ross Tibbs. He's playing at one of the clubs in Phoenix. That's where we met him. Then he came out to the farm to look at the horses. Why, the way Patsy acted, you'd have thought he was God's gift to women."

After an initial start of surprise, Rachel struggled not to react to the news that Ross Tibbs was in town. She cast a furtive glance at Lane out of the corner of her eye, but there was no indication that the singer's name meant anything to him. Why should it? For that matter, why should she let it mean anything to her? He was just someone she'd met — a man who'd made a pass at her. Others had and she'd forgotten them. She would have forgotten him, too, if he hadn't started making a name for himself in the music business, she told herself as they emerged from the shade of the barn into the hot glare of the desert sun.

"What d'ya say we go to the house and have a drink. Patsy makes a mean margarita," Charlie declared, rubbing his hands together in a gesture of anticipation.

"Maybe we should wait." With a nod of his head, Lane indicated the pickup truck with a horse trailer in tow coming up the driveway. "It looks like you have more visitors arriving."

The pickup was an old model that showed its age in the rusted-out fenders and rust-splotched door panels. A thick layer of dust hid its true color, making it impossible for Rachel to tell if it was dark green or dark blue. As it pulled to a stop in front of the adobe building that housed the farm's offices, the battered old truck looked pathetically out of place against the well-manicured backdrop of the horse farm, where even the sandy ground outside the stalls was raked in a herringbone pattern.

"More than likely it's some backyard breeder with a mare to be bred. We get them from all over the country. I've seen them arrive hauling the horse in the back end of a pickup. You should see some of the nags they bring. Ewe-necked, Roman-nosed, and apple-rumped . . . it's a crime to have such animals registered as purebred Arabians," Charlie complained bitterly. "The worst of it is, is that most of them think that by breeding that excuse of an Arabian to one of my stallions, they're going to get a top-quality foal. Once in a while, they'll end up with a mediocre foal, maybe even a good one. But those recessive genes are still there, and sooner or later, those bad traits are going to sprout up again. Usually in the next generation. But you can't tell them that. The old plug is probably the only horse they own — the only one they can afford. The backyard breeder may be the backbone of our industry, but, damn, I wish they'd be more selective in what they breed."

Fully aware that a year ago she would have been one of those backyard breeders Charlie was talking about, Rachel kept silent. She could have been the one climbing out of the pickup truck instead of that woman in the blue pants and matching top with her dark hair pulled back in a ponytail and wearing sunglasses.

"Go take care of them, Vince," Charlie ordered.

"Right." Separating himself from them, the stud manager walked swiftly toward the parked truck and trailer.

Rachel watched as the woman took a step toward them, then stopped and waited for Vince Romaine to come to her. The woman handed the manager some papers from her purse, but she was too far away for Rachel to hear what was being said. It was easy to imagine herself in the woman's place. There was even a slight resemblance between them, Rachel thought. Then the woman turned, presenting her with a side view that made her pregnant state obvious.

As the silvery mare was led out of the trailer, Charlie said in disgust, "Look at that mare. She's crippled in front. What did I tell you? We see everything here."

Rachel barely had a chance to look at the horse before Lane called her attention to the stocky, square-shouldered man holding the lead rope. "That old man . . . doesn't he remind you of Ben Jablonski?"

In that instant, everything clicked into place: the old man, the crippled filly, the dilapidated pickup, and the dark-haired woman. It was Abbie. As the realization shot through her, it was like a scab being torn off a newly healing wound and the sore stinging afresh. She glared at the woman who had always been the bane of her life.

"What is she doing here?" Rachel protested under her breath.

But Charlie heard her and turned sharply. "Do you know them?"

She was spared from answering as Vince Romaine came walking back. "They've brought a young mare they want bred to Radzyn, and they've got cash money to pay the stud fee. They didn't book in advance. So I thought I'd better check and see what you wanted me to do," he said.

"Did she give her name?" Lane asked.

"She said it was Hix," the manager replied. "She claims she knows you."

"I thought so." When Charlie glanced inquiringly at Lane, he explained, "She's Dean Lawson's daughter."

"You're kidding." He stared at the pregnant woman standing next to the battered truck. "I didn't realize she was having such a hard time."

"Maybe it's what she deserves." The retort was out before Rachel even realized she'd spoken. She could guess how heartless she must have sounded to her host, but she wasn't about to retract the statement. As far as she was concerned, it was the truth. "Excuse me, please. I'm going to the house."

As she walked away without waiting for a response, she heard Charlie say, "Find an empty stall for the mare."

*   *   *

Shock gave way to cold disbelief when Abbie noticed the silver-haired man standing next to the tall, heavy-set Charlie Carstairs. It didn't seem possible it could be Lane Canfield — not here. At this distance, she couldn't make out his facial features clearly, but there was a definite resemblance. And that mane of white hair was so distinctive she didn't see how it could be anyone else. That had to be Rachel with him. Instinctively Abbie knew she was right.

When Charlie Carstairs turned to confer with Lane and Rachel, Abbie braced herself for a fight. She knew if Rachel could find a way to deprive her of something she wanted — like having River Breeze bred to Charlie Carstairs's stallion Radzyn — she'd do it.

Abruptly Rachel split away from the others and started walking toward the large adobe ranch house. Abbie wasn't sure if it meant she had succeeded in her attempt or failed. Then Vince Romaine approached her again, and Abbie was forced to divide her attention between the stud manager and Rachel.

"Is there a problem, Mr. Romaine?" she demanded before he could say anything.

"No. Bring your mare and I'll show you where to put her. We keep all outside mares isolated from our home herd. Less chance of spreading disease that way."

Abbie didn't like the possibility that had just occurred to her. She started moving away from the short, thin man. "Excuse me. Ben, take Breeze and go with Mr. Romaine. I'll be right there," Abbie promised over her shoulder, then moved quickly to intercept Rachel.

But Rachel saw her coming and stopped. "What do you want?"

"Nothing," Abbie snapped, just as crisply. "I'm leaving my mare here to be bred. And if anything happens to her, I'll know you're responsible."

She'd invested more in the filly than just money. There was all the heartache and worry, all the hopes and dreams tied up in her, too. Abbie knew she couldn't stay and guard the young mare, protect her from Rachel. Rachel had taken or destroyed everything else that had ever belonged to her. River Breeze represented the future. She couldn't let anything happen to her.

"I have no intention of going anywhere near your mare. That's something you would do," Rachel stated coldly, then stared at her contemptuously. "The smartest thing MacCrea ever did was to walk out on you."

Abbie struck out blindly, slapping her hard across the face. For a split second she thought Rachel was going to react in kind. Abbie wished she would.

But Rachel didn't retaliate. Instead, she turned away and walked briskly toward the ranch house. Abbie watched her go, the anger draining.

Rachel had it all wrong about MacCrea. She had been the one to walk out on him. Yet it had hurt to hear Rachel speak his name. The very fact that Rachel had referred to him with such familiarity was proof of all her suspicions.

That evening, Rachel sat in front of the vanity mirror in Charlie's guest bedroom, raking the brush through her hair until her scalp tingled. She still smarted from Abbie's insinuation that she would harm her mare to get even for the fire.

She heard a shoe hit the floor and glanced at Lane's reflection in the mirror. He sat on the side of the bed, one leg crossed while he untied the laces of his other shoe. His expression was thoughtful as he looked up, meeting her glance in the mirror.

"You never did tell me what caused that scene with Abbie this afternoon."

After faltering for an instant, Rachel roughly pulled the brush through her hair again. "She was just being spiteful. I'd really rather not talk about it, if you don't mind."

"I wouldn't be too upset about it, if I were you. Women in her condition tend to be quicker to . . . take offense, shall we say?" He dropped the other shoe on the floor. "I must admit, though, I had no idea until I saw her today that she was expecting a baby. Did you?"

"No, I didn't. But as sudden as that wedding of hers was to Dobie Hix, I wouldn't be at all surprised if she had to get married." She knew that was a catty thing to say. She also knew Lane didn't like to hear her talk that way. When she sought his reflection in the mirror, she was surprised to see he was smiling. She turned sideways to look at him. "Did I say something amusing, Lane?"

"What?" For a moment, the sound of her voice seemed to startle him, then he recovered. "No, not really." He started unbuttoning his shirt.

But it had been something . . . something to do with Abbie. Rachel was positive of that. She had to find out why thinking about Abbie would make him smile like that. "Why were you smiling just then?"

"I was thinking about her husband — how proud and thrilled he must have been when he found out he was going to be a father."

His tone of voice was very calm and matter of fact, yet Rachel thought she had detected something wistful in it. Was it possible that he envied Abbie's husband? With a start, she realized that in all the months they'd been married, they'd never once talked about having children, not even when they were going over the new plans for the house. The extra bedrooms had always been referred to as guest rooms.

Somehow she'd had the impression that Lane didn't want children. It was nothing he'd said. She had simply assumed he didn't want any.

Truthfully, she'd never examined her own feelings on the subject. She supposed that, in the back of her mind, she'd always thought she'd have children someday just like any other person. But her dreams, her desires, had always centered on raising prize Arabian horses. Getting pregnant and having a baby was something she'd never tried to imagine. She shied away from the picture in her mind of Abbie, her figure all distorted by her pregnancy, her belly swollen almost to the size of a watermelon, and her breasts large and heavy.

But her feelings weren't important. It was Lane's she wondered about. "Would you like it if we had a baby?"

He paused in the act of pulling his shirttail free from his pants and stared at her with sudden alertness. "Are you trying to tell me something?"

"No." She laughed self-consciously and turned back to face the dressing table, certain she hadn't imagined that bright glint in his eye. "I was just wondering if it would bother you. You've always been so sensitive about the difference in our ages that I thought maybe it might."

Slowly he walked over to stand behind her chair. Rachel watched him in the mirror as he gently and caressingly placed his hands on her shoulders. When he lifted his glance to study her reflection in the mirror, his expression was impassive and unreadable.

"Would you like to have a baby, Rachel?"

"Only if you would." She couldn't honestly say she did. At this point, she was happy with things the way they were. But, if it would please Lane . . . if he wanted a child . . . after all he'd given her, she owed him that. "If you wouldn't be happy about it —"

"Not happy? I've always considered becoming a father to be the happiest moment in a man's life," he declared. Then his face crinkled with a smile that was warm and deeply affectionate. "You have no idea how much it means to me that you would want to have my child. But at my age . . . I'd be a doddering old man by the time a child of ours graduated from college. That wouldn't be fair — not to you or our child."

"Are you sure? When you talked about Abbie —"

"I probably sounded a little envious. I admit that when I first saw her, for a split second, I let myself imagine it was you. But I also know it wouldn't be right." He paused to study her image in the mirror. "Do you mind? I assumed that you regarded the horses as your children, that they could fill that part of your life."

"In a way, that's probably true." She'd never thought about it and didn't now. Turning, she grasped the hand that rested on her left shoulder and gazed up at him. "I just want to make you happy, Lane."

"Darling, I am. You're all I need for that." Bending, he kissed her warmly and firmly as if trying to convince her that he meant it. But Rachel didn't believe him. "It's late," he said as he straightened. She recognized that ardent look in his expression. "Don't you think you should be getting ready for bed?"

"Of course."

Avoiding his eyes, she gathered up her toiletry case and went into the adjoining bathroom. She set the case on the marble-topped counter next to the sink and turned on the faucets. Letting the water run, she opened the case and reached for the jar of cleansing cream inside. She hesitated when she saw her container of birth-control pills. Not once had Lane denied that he wanted a child. She remembered the look on his face when he'd referred to Abbie, admitting that he'd wished Abbie had been her.

Silently vowing that that would never happen again, Rachel pushed the pills out of their cardboard holder one by one and flushed them down the toilet.

Every morning, Rachel went to the stables to check on her mare, Simoon. Finally, the day before they were scheduled to leave, the charcoal-dark horse did not lay back her ears or squeal and kick when she was led alongside the padded trying bar that separated her from the "teaser," a stallion of slightly inferior breeding quality used for trying mares and determining which were in season. This time, Simoon responded to the teaser stallion's interested nickerings and leaned against the protective bar. Standing with her hind legs apart, the mare lifted her nearly black tail and urinated, showing a definite "winking" of the clitoris. The mare was ready to be bred.

When the dark-gray mare was led into the indoor breeding yard, Rachel was as nervous, excited, and apprehensive as she had been on her own wedding night. Initially she felt self-conscious about being present, but none of the handlers paid any attention to her as they prepared the mare, wrapping a bandage around her tail to keep the hairs out of the way, attaching the covering boots to her hind feet, and finally washing her vulva, hindquarters, and dock with antiseptic solution.

Suddenly the shrill trumpet of a stallion rang through the barn. With a quickening pulse, Rachel turned toward the doorway leading into the enclosed yard as Simoon nickered an answer. The black bay stallion seemed to explode into the yard, all fire and animation at the end of the groom's lead. With the water-dampened sand floor muffling the sound of his hooves, the stallion appeared to float above the ground, his legs lifting high, his neck arched, and his long tail streaming behind him like a black plume. The groom led the stallion in a tight circle and shook the whip at him as a reminder.

When the groom finally walked the snorting, plunging stallion toward the mare, Rachel experienced a faint shiver of anticipation. She remembered reading somewhere about an Arab sheikh who had invited guests to his tent to witness the mating of his prize war mare with a stallion of a valuable strain.

Standing on the sidelines, watching the courting stallion's sniffings and nuzzlings of the mare, she felt the same sense of moment. Amidst all the squeals and nickerings, she had the feeling she was about to observe the consummation of a royal union. All the ceremony was there: the ritualistic preparing of the bride, the grand entrance of the groom, and the presence of all the attendants.

Staring, Rachel waited for the moment when the stallion was fully drawn, not looking away or closing her eyes the way she did with Lane. This time she had to see everything. The instant the stud groom observed the tensing of the back muscles, the full erection, and the absolute readiness of the stallion, he allowed the eager stud to make his jump onto Simoon, the stallion instinctively swinging into position behind her as he did so.

Simultaneously, the handler on the other side grasped the mare's dark tail and held it out of the way, cautiously avoiding the stallion's hooves, while the man at Simoon's head checked her initial forward movement, preventing her from moving more than a step or two away from the mounting stallion. Rachel tensed in empathy and talked to the mare in her mind, mentally offering all the assurances she would have spoken to Simoon if she could.

Easy, my beauty. Don't be frightened, she thought, unconsciously straining against the imagined invasion, yet knowing it had to come. I know it hurts but it won't last long. He knows what he's doing. It'll be over soon. It always is. Just hold on a little bit longer. That's the way, my Simoon. As if hearing her thoughts, the dark-gray mare stood passively beneath the humping stallion. Rachel felt a quickening rush as the stallion's long tail flailed the air in an up-and-down motion, signaling his ejaculation. Yes. Yes, accept his seed, she told Simoon silently. Let it in now. You won't be sorry. I promise. Just let it come in. There, now, it's over. It wasn't really so bad, was it?

The bay stallion rested a moment atop the mare, then swung off. Rachel felt oddly flushed as the stud groom led the stallion away from Simoon and rinsed the stallion's sheath with a specially prepared wash. When she turned back to her mare, a handler unbuckled the boots on her hind feet and walked the horse out of them. As they started to remove the white bandage wrapped around her tail, Rachel noticed the man in a cowboy hat standing on the other side of the indoor yard.

In that stunned instant, when she recognized Ross Tibbs, she felt as if she had just touched an electric fence. Even though she had known he was in Phoenix, she had thought . . . she had *hoped* she wouldn't see him.

"Mr. Tibbs, what a surprise to see you here." She put on the brightly fixed smile she'd acquired since attending so many social functions with Lane.

"Mrs. Canfield." He mimicked her formality — deliberately, she suspected. "I read in yesterday's society column that you and your husband were here. It's been a long time since I've seen anyone from home. It gets lonely on the road after a while. You get to where you'd give anything just to see a familiar face."

Loneliness was something she'd known all her life, but she couldn't admit to it — not to him. A groom led her mare over to the exit. "Excuse me. They're taking my mare back to her stall. I want to see her settled in."

"Mind if I come along?"

She did, but she found it impossible to refuse. "Not at all."

Ross fell in step with her as she crossed the sandy yard, following behind the darkly dappled rump of the charcoal-gray horse. "I really like the look of your mare. I've been thinking about buying that stallion, Basha 'al-Nazir, off Charlie. But with the price he's asking, I'm not sure I can swing it yet, even though he's offered me some good terms."

"You were really serious when you talked about wanting to buy some Arabians last year." At the time, she thought he'd just been saying that to make an impression on her.

"Serious? Hey, it's been one of my dreams for . . . I don't know how long," he declared with an expansive wave of his hand. "Don't get me wrong. Music is my life, and always will be. But horses are my love. I can't explain it. That's just the way it is."

"I understand." Completely. The only difference for Rachel was that horses were her life as well as her love.

He asked her about Simoon's breeding, then about the other mares she owned. One question led to another. Rachel didn't remember leaving the stud barn or passing the broodmare barn or entering the separate facility where the outside mares were stalled. It was as if she had been magically transported from one place to the other. Although Lane had always willingly listened to her expound on her favorite subject — Arabian horses — she discovered it was different talking to someone who shared her obsession with the breed. Even when she and Ross disagreed on the attributes of a particular type or bloodline, it was enjoyable.

Once Simoon was back in her stall, together they looked over the other mares in the stable. As they approached the iron grate of one of the stalls, a mare the color of silver lifted her head and blew softly, her large, luminous dark eyes gazing at them curiously. Unconsciously, Rachel stopped short of the stall's partition.

"Now this one's a beauty," Ross declared, walking up to the stall to look over the barred top.

She stared at the mare that belonged to Abbie, watching the flare of the large nostrils as the young Arabian tried to catch their scent. Every time she'd come into the barn, the mare had nickered to her. Once Rachel had walked over to the stall, but the instant the mare had smelled her hand, she turned and hobbled to the far corner of the corral. Rachel hadn't gone near her since then.

Ross peered over the top of the stall, then turned back to Rachel, frowning in surprise. "Her front legs . . . she's crippled."

"Some freak accident, I heard." She didn't want to talk about the mare or her owner.

"That's too bad."

"Yes." Rachel walked on to the next stall, without waiting for him. A moment ago, she had been so relaxed with him. Now, she was all agitated and tense again.

"Remember the last time we were in a stable together?" The pitch of his voice changed, becoming more intimate.

"Please," she said in protest, remembering too clearly how she had felt when he'd touched her that day.

She felt the probing of his gaze, but she refused to meet it. "Charlie tells me that all Canfield knows about a horse is that it has four legs, a head, and a tail. What do you have in common with someone like him?"

"Please don't talk that way, Ross."

"You'll never convince me that you love him. You couldn't."

Out of the corner of her eye, she caught the movement he made toward her and turned sharply to face him.

"What do you know about it? You don't know me and you don't know Lane," Rachel protested in a voice choked with her warring emotions. She briskly walked away from him, breaking into a near-run before she reached the barn doors.

32

A booming clap of thunder from the May storm drenching Houston rumbled through the office building as MacCrea Wilder entered the reception area, his dark hair glistening from his dash through the rain, its wave more pronounced. "I know I'm late, Marge." He held up a hand to stave off any comment from Lane Canfield's secretary. "The traffic's backed up all the way to the airport this morning."

"You should have seen it when I came to work," the redhead sympathized and reached for the intercom to announce him as she waved him to the inner door. "Go right in. He's expecting you."

"Thanks." He crossed the space with long, loping strides and pushed open the door to Lane's office. Lane was just getting up from his desk when MacCrea walked in. "Sorry I'm late."

"With this storm, I wasn't even sure your plane would be able to land." Lane came around the large desk to shake hands with him. A sheeting rain hammered the windows behind him, obscuring the rolling, black clouds that darkened the sky over Houston.

"Neither did I." MacCrea shrugged out of the damp linen blazer and tossed it over one of the two armchairs in front of Lane's desk. Hitching up his trouser legs, he sat down in the other, uncomfortable in his rain-soaked silk shirt. "I have some good news to report. Just before I left this morning, I got word that the number three well came in. So far, we're batting a hundred and it looks like it's just beginning."

"Well, it appears congratulations are in order all the way around." Smiling widely, Lane reached back and picked up a wooden box containing hand-rolled cigars and held it out to MacCrea. "It may be a few months early for a proud father to be passing out cigars, but have one anyway."

Surprised by the announcement, MacCrea halted in the act of taking a cigar. "A father?"

"Yes." The smile on his face seemed to grow wider. "Rachel's expecting a baby." After MacCrea had taken a cigar, Lane snipped off the end for him, then struck a match and held the flame under the cigar to light it for him.

"I'll be damned," MacCrea said between puffs.

"That's what I said," Lane chuckled. "Rachel's been deathly sick for nearly two weeks now. She thought she had a bad case of the flu. Finally, three days ago, I convinced her to see the doctor. He suspected she was pregnant, and yesterday, the lab tests confirmed it."

"When's the happy event to take place?" Recovering from his initial surprise, MacCrea settled back in the thickly cushioned armchair and studied his financial partner, vaguely amused by Lane's obvious pride and delight. His reaction seemed totally out of character for the no-nonsense man MacCrea had become accustomed to dealing with. Maybe he'd act the same way if he found out he was going to be a father.

"The latter part of January. Imagine me . . . a father after all these years." Lane shook his head in amazement and walked back around his desk and sat down. "Most men my age are awaiting the birth of their first grandchild. And here I am, about to become a father for the first time in my life. I have to admit I've never been so excited about anything in my life."

"Congratulations — to both of you. Or maybe I should say all three of you," MacCrea suggested wryly.

"Thank you. Rachel is as happy about it as I am, I'm glad to say. Of course, this morning sickness has really gotten her down." When he glanced at the photograph of his wife on his desk, MacCrea's attention was drawn to it. As always he was unsettled by that initial resemblance to Abbie: the dark hair, the facial structure, and especially the deep-blue eyes. "She's anxious about her horses and the work going on at the farm."

"How's it coming?" He tapped the ash from his cigar into the crystal ashtray on Lane's desk, the question dictated by politeness rather than any desire to know.

"The contractor expects the house to be completely finished by November. Which means we'll be able to spend the Christmas holidays there. Rachel is really looking forward to that."

"Then you haven't had any more problems?"

"You mean with Abbie?" Lane guessed.

Dammit, MacCrea cursed silently, knowing that was exactly who he had meant. Before he'd left Louisiana this morning, he'd sworn to himself that he wasn't going to ask about her.

Taking his silence as an affirmative response, Lane said, "You know she's expecting a baby, too . . . sometime in early fall, I think."

Abbie pregnant — with that farmer's child. "No. No, I didn't know." He suddenly felt sick inside. He couldn't explain it, not even to himself. He just knew he wanted to get this damned meeting over with and get back on that plane and fly the hell out of here, fast. It was over. Any lingering doubts he may have had vanished in that instant.

It was one thing when she had another man's ring on her finger. But when she carried another man's child . . . MacCrea laid the cigar down in the ashtray and let it smolder. Sooner or later, it would burn itself out. "You said you had some papers we needed to go over," he said, reminding Lane of the purpose of his visit.

Part Two

33

The wind-driven dust swirled about the legs of the brightly festooned Arabian horses and whipped at the tassels and fringes that adorned their fancy bridles, breast collars, and long saddle blankets — elaborate trappings that were rivaled only by those of their riders, dressed in native costumes of flowing kuffieyahs and abas. The crowd outside the entrance to the main arena on the Scottsdale showgrounds parted to let the prancing horses pass.

"Look at all the beautiful horses that are coming, Mommy," Eden said excitedly.

Quickly, Abbie grabbed the hand of her five-year-old daughter and pulled her out of the path of the oncoming horses. "I swear I'm going to put a lead rope on you if you don't start listening and stay right beside me like you've been told."

Inadvertently Abbie glanced down at Eden's hand . . . and the crooked little fingers that curled ever so slightly higher than the others — from her father, from MacCrea. She had inherited the trait, along with her wavy hair, from him. Abbie wished she hadn't. She wished she could forget Eden had any father other than Dobie. She didn't want to be reminded that MacCrea Wilder even existed, but this had become impossible. His oil strike in Louisiana almost five years ago and his subsequent successes had placed his name on the lips of practically everyone in Houston.

"But I can't see," Eden pouted.

Abbie could appreciate that for a child, this crowd must seem like a forest towering around her. "You can see. The horses are going to pass right in front of you."

Single file, the horses and riders paraded by them, a glitter of gold, silver, and copper ornamenting costumes of brilliant red, blue, purple, and shiny black. With a swing of her dark ponytail, Eden turned to look up at Abbie and pulled at the sleeve of her blouse.

Obligingly, Abbie leaned down so Eden could whisper in her ear. "Windstorm is more beautiful than these horses, isn't he, Mom? If we dressed him up like that, he'd win for sure, wouldn't he?" she said, referring to the five-year-old stallion out of Abbie's mare River Breeze.

"I bet he would, too." Abbie smiled and winked in agreement.

"He's the best horse in the whole world," Eden asserted without a trace of doubt.

"Maybe not the best horse." Although deep down she believed that, too.

"He is, too." Eden stubbornly refused to listen to such disloyal talk.

"We'll see." Only Abbie knew how close that statement was to being the truth. All the top stallions in the country were here at Scottsdale to compete in the prestigious show. Windstorm had already won several regional championships, but a win here would give him the recognition he deserved.

It had been a long, expensive road just to get this far. But she was well on her way to having the high-quality Arabian breeding operation she'd dreamed of owning. She had leased more land from Dobie, built a new broodmare barn and a stud barn, purchased ten well-bred broodmares, and leased three more plus a stallion. And she'd done it all with money she'd earned herself, either from the thriving party business or from the high prices she had received from the sale of each year's crop of foals. She'd sold them all except Windstorm and a full sister to him foaled last year.

Abbie remembered all too clearly that trip to Scottsdale six years ago: sleeping in the back of that rusty old pickup truck in sleeping bags, eating cold sandwiches, hauling her crippled mare in a borrowed horse trailer, and watching every penny to be sure they'd have enough left to pay for the gas home. This time, she had a healthy bank account . . . and an Arabian stallion that just might win the championship. And she'd done it all the hard way, with no help from anyone except Ben — not even Dobie.

Sometimes she suspected Dobie resented that as much as he resented the success she'd had. She knew that secretly he had hoped she would fail. And his pride was hurt, too, by the amount of money she had made from the sale of the foals. He wouldn't let her spend a dime of it on Eden or the house, insisting it was horse money and that he alone would support his family. Abbie didn't argue.

It had stopped being a marriage a long time ago, if it ever had been one. She and Dobie lived in the same house, shared the same bed, and occasionally used each other to satisfy their physical needs. That's all it was. That's all it ever would be. Sometimes Abbie wished there were more to it, but, as long as she had the horses and Eden, she could manage to forget that something was missing from her life.

"Come on." She took Eden by the hand as the last of the horses and riders in the native-costume class went by. "Let's go find Ben."

"Where is Ben?" Eden hurried anxiously ahead, pulling at Abbie's hand. "Do you think he's lost?"

"I doubt it. He's probably waiting for us in front of the stallion barn."

Abbie guided Eden through the milling crowd on the showgrounds. The atmosphere was circuslike, with its array of sparkling costumes, brightly colored tents, and fast-food booths, all set against a backdrop of desert blue sky and waving palm trees. Exhibiters, owners, and trainers dressed in riding costumes, tee shirts and jeans, or the latest designer creations mingled with the sightseers: the tourists, curious townspeople, and horse fanciers, old and young, out for an afternoon's outing and a close-up look at the equine descendants from the Arabian desert right here in their own desert country. And a look they got, along with all the glamour and mystique that surrounded the Arabian breed.

As they approached the first stallion barn, Abbie spied Ben standing in the shade, waiting patiently. Bending down, she pointed him out to Eden. "There he is. See him?"

In answer, Eden tugged her hand free and ran ahead to meet him, her ponytail bouncing up and down and sideways. Smiling, Abbie watched her young daughter, clad like a miniature adult in riding boots, jodhpurs, and a string tie around the collar of her white blouse. She remembered the times when she had run to Ben with that same eager affection her daughter now showed. And Ben was as patient and gentle with Eden as he had been with her, if slightly more indulgent. There was no doubt about it in Abbie's mind, Eden had him wrapped around her little finger. Her crooked little finger, Abbie remembered, sobering with the thought.

"Mommy, Ben knew we would come here," Eden declared when Abbie joined them. "Ben knows everything, doesn't he?"

"Everything." Even the identity of your real father, Abbie thought, recognizing that over the years, he had been the trusted keeper of many secrets.

She lifted her glance to him and felt the tug of memories, old and new. Always he'd been her rock, square and stalwart, constant as the tides. While everything changed around him, he remained the same. There was hardly any evidence of the passing years in his craggy face. Abbie conceded that his gray hair had turned a little whiter, and she noticed that when he walked now, his feet shuffled a little, no longer striding out with their former firmness of step. His age was definitely catching up to him. She hated to see it. It was funny the way she could accept her mother's graying hair, but expected Ben to stay young forever.

"Will I ever know as much as you do, Ben?" Eden frowned.

"Someday, perhaps." He nodded sagely.

"Shall we go inside and have a look at Rachel's would-be contender for the championship?" Abbie suggested, knowing that if they waited until her daughter ran out of questions, they'd be here a month or more.

The long exhibition hall was lined with lavish showcase stalls the entire length of the building on both sides. Each farm represented had rented three, four, or more stalls, only one of which was used for the stallion on show. The rest were transformed into extravagant booths, each uniquely furnished and decorated, to promote the breeding farm and its stallions.

As they passed one that had been draped and roofed in black cloth to resemble the tent of a Bedouin sheikh, Eden tried to drag Abbie inside so she could investigate the plush cushions with the gold-tasseled corners. Another had been turned into a library, complete with rich walnut paneling and shelves of books lining the walls around a mock fireplace. Others were sleekly contemporary in their decor, making use of glitz and glamour to attract the eye of the passerby. The people strolling past the booths looked and marveled at the elaborate displays, but the real stars were still the stallions.

Halfway down the row, Abbie spotted the large booth that looked like a Victorian parlor, right down to the period antiques and silver tea service, and the dainty canapés offered as refreshments to visitors. Abbie scanned the dozen or so occupants of the River Bend booth, recognizing the farm's manager and several others, but Rachel wasn't among them. With all the big sales and exclusive private parties held in conjunction with Scottsdale, Abbie hadn't expected Rachel to spend much time in the farm's booth.

Nearly everyone in the River Bend booth sported the scarlet satin jacket emblazoned with the name Sirocco, the stallion Rachel had in the halter competition. Abbie had lost count of the number of people she'd seen on the showgrounds wearing those jackets. The farm was giving them away to anyone who would agree to wear it around the showgrounds. An expensive promotional tool, but a very effective one. The jackets were so plentiful, it was as if a scarlet tide were sweeping through the Scottsdale.

Rachel was sparing no expense to win the crown for her stallion. For months now, her advertisements of Sirocco had littered every major Arabian publication. The cost of this campaign had to run in the hundreds of thousands of dollars. Abbie couldn't hope to compete against Rachel financially, and she knew it. She wasn't poor by any means, but she didn't have the limitless wealth that Rachel had.

Abbie skirted the activity in the booth itself and went directly to the whitewashed stall emblazoned with the words RIVER BEND's NAHR SIROCCO. A scroll of iron grillwork topped the upper third of the stall. Beyond the curved bars, Abbie caught the gleam of a blood-red coat. Before she could get a closer look at the stallion everyone was predicting to be supreme champion of the show, Eden yanked at her hand.

"I want to see, Mommy."

"Come on, short stuff." Bending down, Abbie picked up her daughter and swung her onto her hip, groaning as she did so. "I hope you realize how heavy you're getting."

"I know. That's 'cause I'm getting big. Ben says someday I'm going to be taller than you are."

"I wouldn't doubt it," Abbie agreed, inadvertently recalling that MacCrea was a tall man. Determinedly she turned to study the blood bay stallion in the stall.

As if aware of his audience, the stallion turned, presenting them with a side view of his magnificence. His long black mane and tail rippled in shiny waves, and the black of his legs glistened like polished ebony. In contrast, the deep red of his satiny coat gleamed like a banked fire. His head was small and fine, held high as he looked on them with disdain.

Previously, Abbie had seen only photographs of the stallion — taken in the winner's circle. In all the competitions Windstorm had won, her stallion had never come up against her archrival's. Rachel had campaigned Sirocco almost exclusively on the West Coast under the skilled tutelage and handling of Tom Marsh, universally considered the best in the business, and who charged his clients accordingly.

Two other small but successful breeders like herself came up to the stall to view the stallion that was the talk of Scottsdale, even though he had yet to appear in his first class. Abbie eavesdropped intentionally.

"I have to admit Sirocco is impressive," one said reluctantly. "He has that air that says 'Look at me.' "

"Oh, he'll win. There isn't much doubt about that," the other replied. "Even if there were a better stallion in the class, he'd still walk away with it. Everyone tries to pretend that judges aren't influenced by somebody's money or reputation. Once they see Tom Marsh lead this stallion into the arena with all of Canfield's millions behind him, I say they'll mark the champion on their cards right then."

"You're probably right."

"I know I am. They're never going to let a stallion from some small farm win. And I don't care how great the horse is either."

As the pair moved away, Abbie tried to convince herself that all their talk was just so much sour grapes. Windstorm had as good a chance of winning as Sirocco. It took a lot of money to show a horse, but money still couldn't buy a victory. A loss didn't necessarily mean the better horse had won. Usually it was a matter of opinion. Some judges put emphasis on different things.

"I don't like him," Eden decided, the corners of her mouth turning down. "He looks snooty, don't he, Mommy?"

"Doesn't he," Abbie corrected her grammar automatically.

"Doesn't he?"

"A little, I suppose." But she found it difficult to fault the stallion's look of arrogance. In its own way, it was very compelling, although she much preferred Windstorm's look of noble pride — that rare "look of eagles" that evoked a sense of both power and gentleness.

"Windstorm will beat him, won't he, Mom?" As far as Eden was concerned, Windstorm was a wonder horse. It was understandable in a way. She'd been around the stallion all her young life, hiding behind his legs to play peek-a-boo as a toddler and riding on his back at the age of three whenever Abbie led the stallion to and from the pasture. Abbie even had a snapshot of Eden curled up asleep using Windstorm as a pillow.

"We'll see," Abbie said and turned to Ben, seeking a less prejudiced opinion. "What do you think of him?"

"Handsome, proud, the classic head, flat croup, well-set tail. He would be many people's ideal Arabian."

"Yours?" Abbie didn't want to hear praise for the stallion.

Ben gave a faint, negative shake of his head. "For me, his neck is too long. With it, he may look pretty, but it makes his balance not good. Too, he is a little sickle-hocked and the bone, it is weak. He could break down easy, I think. But, a man who knows what he is doing could disguise that in the show ring so the leg would not look so straight."

"How does he stack up against Windstorm?" She was beginning to feel the strain of her daughter's weight on her arm and hip. She swung her to the ground to relieve the pressure. "Just stand here for a while," she told Eden when she started to protest.

"Some will think his neck is too short." Ben shrugged. "Others will think sixteen hands is too tall for an Arabian. Some will not like Windstorm because he is a gray."

"I know." Abbie sighed. In the end, it all boiled down to opinion. And nobody knew whose was right.

"Mommy, can I go watch television over there?" Eden pointed to a booth across the way where a television was playing back a tape of that particular farm's stallion.

Abbie hesitated, then decided there wouldn't be any harm in it. Eden would be close enough that she could keep an eye on her. Besides, it might keep her active daughter entertained for a little while. "All right, you may go over there and watch it. But no farther, do you understand? And don't bother anybody, either."

"Yes, Mommy," she promised solemnly, then took off at a run.

Abbie watched to make sure Eden did exactly as she had promised. Once Eden had plunked herself down on the carpeted floor in front of the television set, Abbie felt sufficiently assured that she turned back to Ben, dividing her attention between him and the blood bay stallion in the stall.

"I've heard Sirocco's disposition isn't all that good." Abbie knew that anyone who'd seen how gently Windstorm behaved with Eden, a five-year-old child, couldn't question her stallion's temperament.

"I wonder what this one knows about being a horse. What has his world been? Horse trailers, stalls, lunging at the end of a rope, and being paraded around an arena with people all around him whistling and shouting. When do you suppose he ran free in a pasture the way Windstorm does when he is home? Or when has anyone ridden him across the country just for the fun of it, the way you do with Windstorm? Always for him, it is shows and training. Would you not get sour, too?" Again Ben shook his head. "I do not blame the horse for being ill-tempered. I have never yet seen a show horse that was not a little bit crazy in the head."

"That's true." Although she didn't have Ben's years of experience, Abbie had seen some horses, mostly fillies, that had come off of successful careers in the show arena. They'd been around people so much they couldn't relate at all to other horses. Some had even been terrified when they were turned loose in a pasture with other horses.

"Somewhere is that stallion they imported from Russia this winter. I want to see him, too." Ben turned to survey the other booths down the line.

"I think it's on the other side, about three down. I'll get Eden and meet you there."

But Eden wasn't ready to leave. Before Abbie could insist on it, a couple who had purchased one of River Breeze's foals saw her and stopped to show her the latest pictures of the filly, now a classy-looking two-year-old, entered in the Futurity Filly class at the show. It was a proud moment for Abbie, since it meant two of her mare's offspring would be competing at Scottsdale: Windstorm and this filly, Silver Lining.

"Where's Ben?" Eden wanted to know.

"I thought you were watching television." Abbie frowned, surprised to find Eden at her side.

"Ahh, it's a rerun," she complained.

"Do you remember my daughter, Eden? These are the Holquists, Eden. They bought that filly you used to call Pepper, remember?"

"Yeah. Hi. Where's Ben?"

"He's looking at another horse."

"Can I go find him?"

"No. You stay right here." Abbie ignored the face Eden made to protest the order and resumed her conversation with the Holquists, knowing their success with this filly made them likely candidates for the purchase of a future foal. "I'm planning to have her bred again this spring. We tentatively have her booked with a son of Bask, but Ben wants to look at that new Russian stallion they've imported before we commit ourselves."

"There's Ben. I'm gonna go see him." Eden dashed off before Abbie could grab her.

"I don't know if it was such a good idea to bring her along or not," Abbie sighed as she watched her daughter disappear in the crowd, not altogether certain that Eden had seen Ben, but trusting that she had. "She's been like this ever since we arrived."

"There's so much excitement and so many things to see, you can hardly blame her," Mrs. Holquist replied.

"I suppose not. There's one consolation in all this, though. She will go right to sleep tonight."

The woman laughed. "She probably will. I just wish I had half her energy."

"Me, too." Abbie thought she recognized Ben at the far end of the row, but with so many people wandering about, she couldn't get a long enough look at him to be sure. "I'd better go after my daughter. We'll catch you later, maybe when we come by to see your filly."

"Good luck."

"Thanks. Same to you." She hurried off to search for her elusive daughter and Ben.

MacCrea walked into the long barn and paused to look around. Idly he started down the wide corridor, joining the meandering flow of people that hesitated here and stopped there. Oddly, MacCrea felt in no hurry to reach the booth and find Lane Canfield. He wondered at the impulse that had brought him here. His meeting with Lane hadn't been dictated by necessity. He could have postponed it for a couple of weeks, even a month with no harm done, but that would have meant meeting Lane in Houston. Maybe that was what he had wanted to avoid. It had been nearly three years now since he'd been back. Sometimes it seemed a lot longer — and sometimes it didn't seem long enough.

Someone bumped against his shoulder. "Sorry."

"It's okay." MacCrea paused, but the man walked on. He felt something pull at the pant leg of his jeans. Glancing down, he saw a little girl looking up at him. Her eyes were big and blue . . . and held the faintest shimmer of tears.

"Mister, can you see my mommy?"

"Your mommy." MacCrea was surprised by the question.

"Yes. You see, I'm afraid she's lost," the little girl explained with a worried look.

"It's your mother who's lost. For a minute there, I thought it was you," MacCrea said, amused by her unusual view of the situation.

"No. I left her over there when I went to see Ben." The little girl pointed to her left. "Only I couldn't find Ben, and when I went back, Mommy wasn't there. Can you help me find her?" Again she tilted her head way back and turned those round blue eyes on him.

Of all the people walking around, MacCrea wondered why on earth this kid had picked him to help her. What he knew about kids wouldn't fill the container for a core sample. But he couldn't resist the appeal of those beguiling blue eyes. He crouched down to her level and tipped his hat to the back of his head.

"Sure, I'll help. I always was a sucker for blue eyes." Smiling, he tweaked the end of her button nose, then scooped her into the crook of his arm and straightened, lifting her up with him. "We'll see if we can't find someone to make an announcement over the loud-speaker. How does that sound, midget?" He looked at her, conscious of the small hand that rested on his shoulder. She gazed back at him solemnly.

"I'm not a midget. I'm a little girl."

"Is that right?" MacCrea replied with mock skepticism. "How old are you?"

"I'm five-and-a-half years old."

"What's your name?"

"Eden. What's yours?"

"MacCrea Wilder," he answered, amused by the rapid comeback.

"MacCrea is your first name?" She frowned at him as he walked toward the barn's main entrance to look for an official of the horse show.

"Yup."

"That's a funny name. So is Eden, though. My daddy says it's the name of a garden and it's a silly name to give a girl. Mommy says I shouldn't listen to him."

"Well, I agree with your mommy. I think Eden is a nice name for a girl."

"Do you really? Mommy says people say things sometimes just to be nice, but they don't really mean them."

"Your mother sounds like she's a very smart woman."

"She is. Smarter than my daddy, even."

"And I'll bet that's really saying something."

"Naw." Eden wrinkled her nose. "My daddy doesn't know anything about horses. He's nice though."

"That's good."

"Where do you suppose my mommy is?" Eden half turned in his arm to look behind them.

"I have the feeling she's probably frantically looking for you."

"Maybe we should go back and see if we can find her." She squared around to gaze at him earnestly.

"I think it will be quicker and easier if we just have her paged over the loudspeaker and let her find us." Feeling her intent stare, MacCrea glanced sideways at the child. "Something wrong?"

"How come you have a mustache?"

"I suppose because I didn't shave it off."

"Does it tickle?"

"I've had a few girls tell me that it does."

"Can I see?"

Surprised by the request, MacCrea stopped. He wasn't sure whether to laugh or not as he looked at the bold little mite in his arms. He could see she was totally serious. "Go ahead." He shrugged.

He watched her face as she tentatively reached out to touch the ends of his mustache. It was a study of concentration and intense curiosity. Then he felt the faintest sensation of her small fingers moving over his lips as she ran the tips over the bluntly cut hairs of his mustache. A smile of amazement broke across her face as she pulled her hand back.

"It did tickle a little, but it was kinda soft, too. How come?"

"I don't know." MacCrea frowned. "Tell me, are you always like this with total strangers? Hasn't your mommy ever told you that you shouldn't trust people you don't know?"

"Yeah," she admitted, unconcerned. "She says I talk too much, too. Do you think I do?"

"Far be it from me to contradict your mother," he said dryly.

"What does 'counterdick' mean?"

"It means telling someone the exact opposite of what someone else has told him. In other words, if your mother told you something was good and I said it was bad, I'd be contradicting her. That wouldn't be nice."

"Oh," she said with a long, slow nod of her head, but MacCrea doubted that she'd actually understood.

He shifted his hold on the child, boosting her to ride a little higher within his encircling arm. "Come on. Let's see if —"

"Eden!" The frantic call came from behind them.

"Wait," Eden ordered as she looked back. "There's my mommy!"

Turning, MacCrea spotted the slim, dark-haired woman just breaking free of the crowd. When she saw him, she stopped abruptly. A kick of recognition jolted through him. Abbie. For an instant he forgot everything, even the child in his arms, as he stared openly, drinking in the sight of her after all these years — two months over six, to be exact.

He was surprised to find she had changed so little in all that time. She wore her dark hair shorter now, the ends just brushing the tops of her shoulders. Even though the voluminous folds of her split riding skirt disguised the slimness of her hips, the wide belt that cinched her small waist revealed that she had retained her shapely figure. And her eyes still held that blue fire that he remembered so well. If anything, the years had added a ripeness and strength to her beauty that had been missing before.

The shock of seeing him had drained the color from her face. MacCrea watched it come back in a hot rush. "Where are you taking her? What are you doing with my daughter?" Before he knew what was happening, she was grabbing Eden out of his arms and clutching her tightly.

"I didn't know she was your daughter." He was still slightly dazed by the discovery. "I suppose I should have guessed when I saw those blue eyes."

"We were going to have the man call your name over the loud-speaker, Mommy," Eden said, momentarily claiming Abbie's attention. "I'm so glad we found you. I was starting to get worried."

"She thought *you* were lost," MacCrea inserted, feeling the impact of her glance as it swung again to him. God, but he wanted to hold her again. He didn't realize how much until this very minute, when the ache was so strong, he actually hurt inside. But her wary look made him hold himself back.

"Why didn't you stay with me the way you were told? Then none of this would have happened," Abbie scolded, her accusing glare indicating very clearly that it was this meeting with him that she wished had never happened.

"But when I couldn't find Ben, I came back and you were gone," Eden asserted, pouting slightly at Abbie's censure.

But Abbie wasn't interested in her explanation. "Why was she with you?"

MacCrea exhaled a short, laughing breath. "It wasn't my idea. She came to me. I don't know why. Maybe I looked like someone she could trust."

"Unfortunately she's too young to know any better." The bitterness in her voice dashed any hope MacCrea had that time might have altered her opinion of him.

"His name is MacCrea. Did you know that, Mommy? It's a funny name, but I like it. He thinks my name is nice, too. Don't you?"

"Yes." He found perverse satisfaction in knowing that Abbie's daughter liked him.

"Why are you here?" A second after she asked the question, Abbie glanced in the direction of the River Bend display, guessing the answer. The line of her mouth thinned even straighter. "Somehow I doubted that you had acquired an interest in Arabians."

"We have an Arabian stallion," Eden told him excitedly. "He's the most beautiful horse ever. Would you like to see him? His name is Windstorm."

"Yes, I would, Eden." Accepting the invitation, MacCrea smiled lazily in the face of Abbie's grim, angry look.

"I'm sure Mr. Wilder has better things to do than look at our horse, Eden. He's a very busy man."

"But he said he wanted to," Eden insisted, then smiled proudly. "It isn't nice to counterdick someone, Mommy."

"You mean contradict," Abbie corrected automatically.

"That's what I said. Counterdick."

"She's a clever girl . . . just like her mother," MacCrea observed. "Where is this horse of yours, Eden?"

"He's in a different barn. We'll take you there, won't we, Mommy?"

"Maybe another time, Eden." Her glaring look warned MacCrea not to insist. "Right now we have to go find Ben. Mr. Wilder understands. Don't you, Mr. Wilder?"

"No." He wasn't about to let her out of the invitation so easily.

"Look —" she began, barely controlling anger, only to be interrupted by the old man who came shuffling up behind her.

"Good. You have found her." He laid a gnarled and age-spotted hand on Eden's shoulder. "We were worried about you, child. How many times has your momma told you not to run off like that, eh?"

Abbie was irritated that Ben should pick this minute to arrive, but he was so relieved to find Eden with her that it was difficult for her to be angry with him. Yet she had to make him aware of the situation. "You remember Ben Jablonski, don't you, Mr. Wilder." As Ben stared at MacCrea, Abbie saw him appear flustered and unsure for the first time.

"Of course. Hello, Ben. It's good to see you again." MacCrea stepped forward to shake hands with him.

Ben glanced questioningly at her. Abbie gave a faint shake of her head to let him know that, as yet, MacCrea did not know her secret. "How do you do, Mr. Wilder." Stiffly Ben shook his hand.

"He wants to see Windstorm, Ben." Eden turned excitedly to Abbie. "Now that Ben's here, we can take him to our barn now, can't we, Mommy?"

Abbie longed to tape her daughter's mouth shut. Failing that, she appealed to MacCrea, hoping that he'd stop being stubborn and accept the fact that she didn't want him around at all. "We wouldn't want to take up your time uselessly, Mr. Wilder."

"I'll be the judge of that."

"Very well, we'll show you the horse." She was unwilling to create a scene with Eden looking on, and she realized that MacCrea knew that. The alternative was to get this over with as quickly as possible. She swung Eden to the ground. "You're too heavy to carry."

"She can ride on my shoulders," MacCrea offered.

"No." She refused too quickly and tried to temper it, knowing that she couldn't risk MacCrea being that close to Eden. "It'll do her good to walk and burn up some of that energy." She pushed Eden at Ben. "We'll follow you and Ben. Be sure and hold tight to his hand."

As Eden skipped alongside Ben to take the lead, Abbie fell in with MacCrea. But she couldn't look at him. She couldn't even breathe. She had never guessed seeing him again would be so painful. In so many ways, he looked the same as she remembered. Maybe his face looked harder, carved by a few more lines. But the lazy smile was the same, and that charm that both mocked and challenged.

She'd been terrified when she'd seen him holding Eden — terrified that he'd somehow found out she was his daughter and intended to take Eden away from her. Even now she was frightened by the thought. And that fear was stronger than any other feelings seeing him had aroused.

"We sorta skipped all the pleasantries," MacCrea said as they walked out of the stallion barn into the brilliant Arizona sunlight. "Maybe we should start over. How are you, Abbie?"

"Married."

"So I heard. Is your husband here with you?"

"No." The last thing she wanted to discuss with MacCrea was her farce of a marriage. "He's at home. It's a busy time at the farm. He couldn't get away." She felt as if she was sitting astride a horse with a hump in its back — all tense and waiting for it to explode in a bucking spree, not knowing when it was going to happen or which way it would jump first, but knowing it was coming and knowing she had to be ready for it or she'd end up being thrown.

Eden turned around and said, "That's our barn, isn't it, Mommy? That's where Windstorm is staying, isn't it?"

"Yes, honey."

"Wait until you see him, MacCrea. He's the most beautiful horse there ever was," she declared.

"His name is Mr. Wilder, Eden." Abbie couldn't bear to hear her daughter address him so familiarly.

"She can call me MacCrea. I don't mind."

"I do. And I'll thank you not to interfere when I'm correcting my daughter," Abbie retorted.

Quickening her steps, Abbie crossed the last few yards of sand and entered the dark shade of the barn's interior ahead of MacCrea. Ben released Eden's hand and she ran ahead to a stall a third of the way down on the left side. "Windstorm, we're back. And we've brought you a visitor."

In spite of herself, Abbie smiled when she saw the stallion lift his head and nicker at the child running toward his stall. In her opinion, Windstorm was as close to perfection as any horse she'd ever seen, but of all his attributes, she considered his gentle spirit to be the most precious.

While the stallion had all the fire and flash of an Arabian, it seemed to come from a joy of life and a love of freedom rather than from any sense of wildness. And every one of his first crop of foals out of grade mares had inherited not only a lot of his look but also his disposition, including one out of a dam that was notoriously ill-tempered. The real test of any sire was his ability to pass many of his good traits on to his get. Abbie had the feeling that she was the owner of just such a prepotent stallion.

Abbie walked over to the stall to admire her stallion, something she was unashamed to admit she never tired of doing. At five years, Windstorm had grayed out to an almost pure white, with only a few streaks of silver-gray still visible in his long mane and tail. The blackness of his skin was revealed in the darkness of his muzzle and around his eyes, making them seem even larger.

"How's my man?" Abbie crooned as the stallion lowered his head to let her scratch his favorite place, just below the ear.

"I knew you had to have one in your life," MacCrea murmured, his voice coming from directly behind her. She hadn't realized he was so close, but a quick backward glance confirmed he stood mere inches away.

Her heart started pounding so loudly she couldn't hear anything else. Somehow she knew that all she had to do was turn around and face him, and she would once more feel his arms around her and know again the excitement of his kiss. That was all it would take — just one move on her part, one silent invitation. And some traitorous part of her soul wanted her to make it.

But Abbie wouldn't let herself be fooled into loving him again. Instead she stepped sideways, moving well away from him. "You were so interested in seeing my stallion, Mr. Wilder, go ahead and take a good look." She was surprised at how calm her voice sounded, considering the way she was shaking inside.

As MacCrea stepped up to the stall, Eden clambered atop the bales of straw next to him so she could see over the wooden partition. "Isn't he beautiful?" she declared. "I saw him the night he was born. There was an awful storm, and the wind blew and blew. That's how he got his name, Windstorm."

MacCrea frowned. "You must have been awfully small yourself."

"I was a little baby," she admitted. "But Mommy says I laughed and laughed when I saw him 'cause I was so happy about it." When the stallion affectionately nuzzled the top of her head, Eden grabbed his nose and pulled his head down, then lovingly rubbed a chiseled cheek. "Stop it, you silly boy," she scolded, then said to MacCrea, "See how you can see all his veins. That means he's dry. That's a good thing."

"You certainly know a lot about horses."

"I do," she agreed. "I have a pony of my very own. His name is JoJo. You'd like him, too."

Watching the two of them, with their heads so close together, Abbie wondered how MacCrea could fail to see the resemblance. To her, it was much too obvious: the dark, wavy hair, the full, thick eyebrows, the same chin and mouth. And the hands — Abbie caught the faint curling of Eden's little fingers as she fondled the stallion's head. She couldn't let him find out. She just couldn't.

"Eden, come down from there." She had to separate them, get Eden far away from MacCrea.

"But —"

"Don't argue with me. Just do as you're told. You've bent Mr. Wilder's ear long enough." As Eden reluctantly scrambled off the bales, Abbie caught hold of her hand and led her over to Ben. "Take her to the car and I'll meet you there in a few minutes."

"Good-bye, Mac — Mr. Wilder." Eden half turned to wave to him.

" 'Bye, Eden. I'll see you again sometime."

Something snapped inside her, releasing all the emotions she'd been holding so tightly in check. They swamped her as she swung around to face MacCrea. "No, you won't! You leave my daughter alone. Leave me alone."

She knew her voice had quavered badly, but she wasn't aware of the sudden rush of tears into her eyes until MacCrea cupped the side of her face in his hand and wiped away a tear with his thumb. "You're crying, Abbie. Why?" The gentleness of his voice, the concern in it, almost proved to be her undoing. She longed to lose herself in the touch of his hand.

But she couldn't. Neither could she answer him. Instead she pulled away from him and pivoted toward the stall, turning her back on him. She hadn't dreamed that after all this time — after all he'd done to her — she could still be so physically attracted to him. Why was her psyche so twisted that she kept loving men she couldn't trust?

"You haven't forgotten either, have you?" MacCrea asked.

"I never tried," she lied.

"Will you have dinner with me tonight . . . for old time's sake? You can bring your daughter and Ben along if it will make you feel safer," he mocked gently, confidently.

"The only 'old times' I'm interested in are the ones where you were gone. Why don't you arrange for that to happen again?"

"Hold it. You were the one who walked out," he reminded her tersely.

His anger gave her the control she needed to face him once more. "I was, wasn't I? I guess I just didn't like the way you used people."

"You accuse me of using people. What about you? Or don't you want to admit the real reason you married that farmer? You don't love him. You only married him to get your hands on land that originally belonged to your family."

"I don't have to ask who told you that. So why don't you go find Rachel? She's the one you came here to see anyway."

"I'm here to meet Lane."

"Then go find him. But stay away from me." She walked off briskly, her throat tight and a dull ache in her heart. It hurt more than she cared to admit that she hadn't guessed wrong. MacCrea was here to see Lane and Rachel.

34

With a nod of his head, MacCrea absently acknowledged the hotel maid's greeting as he walked down the wide corridor to the double doors of the suite at the end. He knocked twice and waited, gnawed by the restlessness that had been eating at him since he'd left the showgrounds.

"Who is it?" The thick doors muffled the woman's voice, but he still recognized it as Rachel's.

"MacCrea Wilder." He still wasn't sure why he was there — why he hadn't headed straight for the airport and boarded the first plane out of Phoenix. Maybe he just didn't want Abbie to have the satisfaction of driving him out of town.

The security chain rattled a half-second before the left door swung open to admit him. Rachel moved away from it as he stepped inside. Her high heels made almost no sound on the thick carpet as she crossed to an oval mirror on the wall.

"The bar is fully stocked. Help yourself." She nodded in the direction of the paneled bar located in the corner of the suite's spacious sitting room.

"Thanks. I think I will." MacCrea tossed his hat on a rose-colored chair as he walked over to the bar and poured himself a glass of Chivas and water. "Where's Lane?"

"He's still in Houston." She removed an earring from the jewelry case on the side table in front of her and held it up to her ear.

MacCrea stopped with the glass halfway to his mouth. "He told me he was going to be here."

"I know. We were supposed to fly in together. But Alex has a bad case of the sniffles and Lane was afraid to leave him. You know how he dotes on his son."

Unconsciously MacCrea crooked an eyebrow at the hard, clipped edge of resentment in her voice, and the almost total lack of concern she expressed for her son. It was in such contrast to Abbie and her highly protective attitude toward her daughter.

"You don't sound worried about him." He sipped at his drink, studying her thoughtfully over the rim of the glass.

"Naturally I'm concerned when he's ill, but it isn't as if he's being left alone. Mrs. Weldon is a registered nurse. She is more than qualified to look after him. But Lane doesn't see it that way. Alex is his son."

"He's your son, too," MacCrea reminded her.

"Is he?" The words seemed to slip out. She attempted to cover them with a forced laugh. "Can you imagine a child of mine being terrified of horses? When he was two and three years old he used to scream his head off if one came within five feet of him. No, Alex is very much Daddy's boy."

"It won't always be that way."

"I wish I could believe that." She sighed heavily, suddenly no longer trying to mask her feelings. "You know that old saying, MacCrea, 'Two's company and three's a crowd'? I'm the one who makes it a crowd."

She looked so lonely and vulnerable that MacCrea couldn't help feeling a little sorry for her. "Lane does love you."

"Yes." Her mouth twisted in a smile that wasn't very pretty. "I'm the mother of his child. And that's a poor reason to love a woman, MacCrea." After trying on several earrings, she finally chose a pair of Harry Winston diamond-studded Burmese sapphires and clipped them onto her ears, then removed the matching diamond and sapphire necklace from the jewelry case.

"I suppose." But her comment made him wonder about other things — like the possibility that Abbie loved Dobie because he was the father of her child.

"When did you arrive?" She looped the necklace around her neck and fastened the clasp.

"About three or four hours ago. I figured I'd find you and Lane at the showgrounds, so I went there to look for you first. I ran into

Abbie." He wasn't sure why he had told Rachel that. He hadn't intended to mention his meeting with her.

"I heard she was here." The icy-sharp bite to her voice left little room for doubt about her feelings toward Abbie. Not that MacCrea had expected her animosity toward her to have mellowed in any way over the years.

"Have you seen her stallion?"

"Oh, yes." She laughed shortly, with more bitterness than humor. "She's made sure I have."

"What do you mean?" He frowned at the curious statement.

"She makes a point of riding that stallion in the field right next to River Bend. I know she does it deliberately. She could ride that horse anywhere, but she has to do it right in my own backyard." Rachel swung away from the mirror and faced him, holding her head unnaturally high. "Believe me, she's never going to win the championship."

"You sound very confident of that."

"I am. The horse business is no different from any other business. Your success depends on the people you know and the amount of money you have available to promote your stallion. . . . Do you have any plans for this evening?" Rachel asked as she walked over to a chair and picked up the beaded evening bag lying on the seat.

"Nothing particular." He shrugged.

"Good. Then you can be my escort tonight since Lane isn't here." She picked up her mink jacket and handed it to him. "The Danberrys are having an aisle party. Ross Tibbs, the country singer, is supposed to be there."

"The one from Houston?" MacCrea set his drink glass down to help her on with the fur jacket.

"The same. He has a good-sized farm in Tennessee now where he raises Arabian horses. I've run into him a few times at some of the bigger shows." Pausing, she glanced at MacCrea over her shoulder. Just for an instant, the shadowed blue of her eyes reminded him of Abbie. "You will take me, won't you, MacCrea? I hate to go to these affairs alone."

"Sure." For some reason he was reluctant to try to get a flight out tonight. And his other alternative — spending the night alone in a hotel room — appealed to him even less.

Rachel blinked as a flashbulb went off directly in front of her, momentarily blinding her. The stall area was jammed with people sipping champagne, munching on caviar, and wearing everything from Lauren to Levi, high fashion to no fashion. Everybody who was anybody in the Arabian horse business had come to the private party, making a curious gathering of celebrity entertainers, business giants, and the social elite hobnobbing with the top trainers, stud managers, and professionals in the business.

"I was told this champagne is for the lady with the bluest eyes. Where do you suppose I could find her?" The familiar voice came from behind her.

Rachel turned, her pulse hammering erratically. "Ross. How wonderful to see you again." She tried to inject the proper amount of pleasure into her voice as she accepted the wineglass from him. "Someone mentioned you might come to the party tonight. Did you just arrive?"

"No. I've probably been here about forty-five minutes."

"Really?" She pretended she hadn't known, even though she'd seen him arrive and made a special effort to ignore him. He didn't look or dress that much differently from when she'd first met him, but the trappings of success were visible. The bright blue shirt was silk, not polyester; the jacket was genuine suede, not an imitation; the jeans carried a designer label instead of J. C. Penney's; and the conchos on his hatband were solid silver, not silver-plated. More than that, everybody knew who Ross Tibbs was, and nearly all of them wanted to make sure Ross knew who they were.

"Where's your husband?" he inquired, his gaze never leaving her face, his intent study of her as unsettling as it had always been.

Rachel sipped at the bubbly wine, her palate sufficiently educated to recognize it was not one of the better champagnes, yet its effect on her was just as heady. "He's still in Houston. He plans to join me here in a few days."

She was tired of making excuses for Lane's absence from these affairs. If it wasn't business then it was little Alex that kept him away. Lane never seemed to have time for her anymore. His priorities were very clear to her: Alex was first; business, second; and she came in a poor third. Maybe it was wrong to feel jealous of her own son, but she had never anticipated that Lane would love him more than he loved her. Yet he did. There must be something wrong with her, some reason why people always loved someone else more than they did her. It wasn't fair.

"Tell me about this yearling filly of yours, Ross," she said, struggling to make conversation. "Everyone is talking about her."

"Have you seen her yet?"

"No."

Before she could react, the mink jacket that she had casually draped over her arm was in his hands. "Come on. We're going over to the barn so I can show her to you." He slung the fur loosely around her shoulders and kept his arm there to guide her toward the exit.

"Now? But . . ." Rachel protested half-heartedly, secretly wanting to be coerced into accompanying him and feeling vaguely guilty because she did.

"Wait until you see her." Ross propelled her through the crowd, talking over her faint objection. "She's a jewel. That's what I named her: Jewel of the Desert — in Arabic, of course, but I can't pronounce that."

Out of the corner of her eye, Rachel noticed MacCrea standing off to one side of the party crowd, talking to some man. She looked in his direction and saw that he was watching them. This was exactly the sort of situation with Ross she had wanted to avoid. That's why she had asked MacCrea to escort her to the party — to be her buffer, her shield. But now that it was happening, she didn't want it to stop. Yet she worried that MacCrea might tell Lane that she had gone off alone with Ross. She tried to convince herself that she had nothing to hide from Lane. After all, she was just going to see Ross's filly. It was perfectly innocent.

"Ross, please." She hung back, forcing him to pause as she glanced anxiously again in MacCrea's direction. "I really should let MacCrea know where I'm going. He brought me here. I just can't run off like this. What will he think?"

"Where is he?"

"Over there." Rachel pointed to him.

Changing course, he walked her over to MacCrea. "I'm taking Rachel to see my filly. Want to come along?" Rachel held her breath, partly afraid he'd accept and partly afraid he wouldn't.

MacCrea shook his head. "No, thanks. One horse looks the same as another to me."

"Tell you what, Wilder. There's no need for you hanging around here getting bored. I've got a car and driver right outside. I can make sure Rachel gets safely back to her hotel." Turning on a smile, Ross looked sideways at her. She was extremely conscious that his arm was still around her shoulders. "If that's okay with you, of course."

"I suppose it really doesn't matter how I get back," she began uncertainly, unable to tell by MacCrea's impassive expression what he actually thought. "I wouldn't want to inconvenience either of you."

"Whatever you want to do will be fine with me." MacCrea shrugged his indifference.

"Good. I'll take her back then." As they walked away, he tipped his head close to hers and murmured near her ear, "Didn't I tell you I'd handle it?"

"Yes." Maybe it was wrong to feel the way she did, but she was glad he had.

Any lingering misgivings fled the instant she saw the year-old Arabian. Totally enchanted by the bronze bay filly's exquisitely classic looks, she could talk of nothing else. She wanted to buy the horse on the spot. When Ross refused, insisting the filly wasn't for sale at any price, she begged him to breed the filly to her stallion, Sirocco, when she turned three, and Rachel made him promise that he'd sell her the foal.

Somehow she lost all track of time. She didn't even realize they never made it back to the party until she handed Ross the room key to her hotel suite. By then, it was too late to be concerned about any comments other guests might have made about the way she and Ross had disappeared without a word to their hosts.

"I think our arrangement calls for a drink, don't you?" Ross pushed open the door and followed her into the suite.

"I do, but you'd better make mine weak," Rachel declared, sighing blissfully as she tossed the mink jacket onto the sofa. "I already feel light-headed, and I'm not sure if I should blame the champagne or the prospect of a foal out of our two horses." She walked over to the small bar and leaned on the countertop to watch him prepare the drinks, barely able to contain the sense of excitement she felt. "Are you certain there's no way I can persuade you to sell that filly, Ross?"

"I can't think of anything I'd love more than to have you try. Lord knows, you're the only one who could tempt me into changing my mind." With the drinks in hand, he came out from behind the bar and walked around to her. Not more than a hand's width separated them when he stopped.

His nearness, the intimate look in his eyes, the feather-light brush of his fingers when she took the glass from him — all combined to stimulate the desire she'd tried to control from the outset. "You almost make me want to try," she admitted, catching the husky note of longing in her voice and knowing it shouldn't be there.

Reaching up, he lightly touched an earring with the tip of his finger. "Has anyone ever told you that your eyes are bluer than these sapphires?"

"Yes." Lane had, and Rachel wished Ross hadn't reminded her of that. All in one motion, she shoved the glass onto the counter and sidestepped Ross to walk over to the oval mirror.

As she stared at her reflection, she caught the diamond sparkle of the Harry Winston earrings and reached up to remove them slowly, one by one. Another gift, that's all they were. Gifts and empty words were the only things she received from Lane anymore, and all she had ever wanted was his love.

This was the way it had been with Dean, too, she realized, suddenly recognizing that she'd come full circle. Her reflected expression became grim as she considered the awful irony of the situation. She was as lonely now with Lane as she had been with Dean, forced to be satisfied with the scant remnants of his time and affection. All the expensive presents in the world couldn't make up for the love she'd been cheated out of again. What was wrong with her? Why couldn't anybody love her? She railed silently at the unfairness as she struggled to unfasten the safety clasp on her expensive necklace, a necklace she now hated.

"I'll do that for you." Ross's reflection joined hers in the mirror as he came up behind her.

When Rachel felt the warmth of his fingers on her neck, for an instant everything inside her became still. She stared at him in the mirror, absently studying his boyishly handsome features, remembering that reckless, happy-go-lucky smile that so often curved his mouth and that brashly flirtatious way he usually looked at her. She caught herself wanting to touch his curly brown hair, no longer hidden beneath his cowboy hat, and discover for herself if it was as soft and thick as it looked.

As she stood with her hand at her throat, holding the necklace in place, she considered the wedding ring Lane had placed on her finger. Once that ring had signified happiness and security to her. Now, when she looked at it, it meant nothing to her — just another pretty bauble Lane had given her to placate his conscience.

With its ends no longer fastened, the weight of the necklace sagged against her hand. She curled her fingers around the cold, hard stones and pulled them slowly away from her throat. A wonderful warmth replaced the inanimate feel of the necklace as Ross bent his head and pressed his lips against the side of her neck where a second ago the necklace had lain. Shuddering with the intense pleasure the kiss had evoked, she turned to face him, desperately needing to be loved by someone.

"Why did you do that?" She clutched the necklace tightly while his hands moved over the bare points of her shoulders, lightly rubbing and kneading her flesh with an odd reverence.

"Because I love you, Rachel. I've always loved you. You're the inspiration for every song about love, heartbreak, and loneliness I've ever written. I love you," he repeated, his voice so soft, yet so forceful. "And, right or wrong, I want to make love to you. If it's not what you want, tell me now. I don't know how much longer I can stand being this close to you without holding you and loving you."

"Ross, don't say you love me if you don't mean it. I couldn't endure that." She choked on a sob.

"I love you, my beautiful, beautiful blue eyes." He moved even closer, his mouth so near to hers that she could feel the warmth of his breath on her lips. "Let me show you how much I love you."

"Yes," she cried softly, and hungrily kissed him, going into his arms and clinging to him desperately, unable to get enough of the loving passion he showered on her. "I need you," she murmured against the smoothness of his shaven cheek. "You don't know how much I need you, Ross."

Lifting her off the floor, he cradled her body in his arms and carried her over to the bedroom door, kicking it open with his foot, kissing her all the while. It was like a romantic scene in a movie, only it was happening to her. She was the one being carried off by a man who loved her more than anything in the world.

Letting her down gently, he turned her to face him and took her in his arms, his lips caressing her brow and cheek with feather-soft kisses. She was trembling, frightened and excited by her own daring, as she felt his hand gliding up the back of her strapless gown, seeking and finding the zipper. The sound it made as he pulled it down reminded Rachel of a cat's soft purr. That's what she felt like — a purring cat rubbing herself against him and wanting to be stroked and petted.

As the loosened gown of velvet and satin began to slip, his hands helped it fall the rest of the way until the Blass original lay in a pile around her feet. A shiver rippled over her bared flesh in reaction to the sudden coolness. Needing his warmth, she pushed open his soft suede jacket and wound her arms tightly around his middle, pressing her body against him and feeling the heat of his body flowing through the thin silk of his shirt.

He cupped a hand under her chin and lifted it so he could once again kiss her lips. When his hat got in the way, he took it off and sent it sailing into a corner of the darkened bedroom, the silver conchos flashing in a whirling circle of reflected light, spinning off into the blackness.

As he shrugged out of his jacket, Rachel felt the play of the lean muscles in his back and closed her eyes, wanting to make sensations the reality. But his hands forced her to stand away from him, giving him room to pull apart the snaps holding the front of his shirt closed.

When she saw the curly dark hairs that covered his chest, she turned away and slowly began to remove her undergarments, her apprehension growing. She had gone too far to stop now, and truthfully she didn't want to stop, but she was afraid of standing naked before him — afraid he wouldn't want the plain Rachel he saw. Without the jewels and the designer gowns, that's all she was: the Rachel that nobody ever loved or wanted.

Yet she had to know. Slowly she turned to face him, grateful for the concealing shadows in the dimly lighted room. She heard him draw in his breath. Tentatively she looked up, but his arms were already going around her and his mouth coming down to cover her lips hotly, his tongue licking them open then plunging inside with a fervor and an urgency that caught her up in the force of his desire.

Then he lowered her onto the bed and joined her, his hands running all over her body as if they couldn't get enough of her — caressing the roundness of her breasts and rolling her hardened nipples between the calloused tips of his fingers, stroking her bottom and gliding between her legs, his fingers seeking the velvety moistness of her. Rachel shuddered uncontrollably at their entry, her hips arching instinctively to take them in.

He did not give her that pleasure for long, and she made a vague protest when he took his hand away. But already he was shifting to lie between her parted legs, his bone-hard shaft probing for the opening. Rachel tensed. She didn't mean to resist him, but she couldn't help herself. The reaction was automatic. As he entered her, Ross stretched out to lie on top of her. She tried to respond to the movement of his hips; she honestly tried, desperately wanting it to be different with him, desperately wanting to achieve climax with him inside her and enjoy more than the sensuous nibbling along her neck. For once in her life, she didn't want to fake it.

His hands slid down to cup her bottom, holding her cheeks to meet the grinding thrust of his hips and directing their movements. As the sweet pressure started to build, Rachel clutched at him, digging her fingers into his shoulders to hold him there, afraid he'd stop, afraid the wonderful rhythm would break. But it didn't. It didn't.

"Yes, yes, yes," she cried out without meaning to and felt the tempo of his thrusting hips change, driving deeper, lifting her higher, until the marvelous agony of it all exploded in a rush of pure rapture. Within seconds Ross shuddered against her, convulsed by his own throes of satisfaction.

As she lay in his arms, savoring that sensation of absolute fulfillment, she felt truly loved. Drenched in the scent of their lovemaking, she breathed it in, the musky odor headier than the most expensive Parisian perfume. She turned onto her side so she could see him, this man who had made her feel like a woman. She ran her hand over his chest, enjoying the sensation of his bare skin and silken hairs.

He caught hold if it and carried her fingertips to his lips. "I wish I were a poet, Rachel," he murmured. "I wish I knew the beautiful words to describe the satin smoothness of your body and the sweet perfection of your breasts. But the words that come to my mind sound so ridiculously corny —"

She covered his mouth with her hand. "Just love me, Ross," she whispered. "Love me." She said the last against his mouth as she took her hand away and replaced it with her lips.

✦ 35 ✦

People swarmed about the motel lobby, some arriving, some departing, and others entering or leaving the adjoining coffee shop. From her seat on a couch in the lobby, Abbie could see the elevators — when someone wasn't blocking her view, that is, which was nearly all the time. Impatiently she flipped through the morning edition of the Phoenix newspaper while she waited for Ben to come back. She couldn't understand what was keeping him. He'd only gone to get a jacket from his room. She had wanted to exercise Windstorm before the work arena became crowded with other horses and riders getting ready for their morning classes.

"Do you see Ben yet, Mommy?" Eden stood on the cushioned couch and leaned sideways against Abbie, trying to see around the people walking by.

"No, dear."

"Windstorm is gonna be wondering where we are, isn't he?"

"Yes. Now sit down. You know you're not supposed to stand on the furniture." Abbie absently turned another page of the newspaper and shook it flat.

"But I can't see, then," Eden reasoned, "and you told me to watch for Ben."

A grainy newspaper photograph practically leaped off the page at Abbie. She didn't hear Eden's reply or notice that she didn't sit down as she was told. She was too distracted by MacCrea's likeness staring back at her, exact in every detail, from the lazy gleam in his dark eyes to the complacent slant of his mustached mouth. He seemed to be mocking her, as if he knew she'd see this photograph of him . . . and the woman with him, none other than Rachel Canfield.

She told herself she didn't care, that he meant nothing to her anymore, that all she had to do was turn the page again. Instead she folded the paper open to the photograph and read the caption. "Rachel Canfield, wife of industrialist magnate Lane Canfield, escorted by millionaire wildcatter MacCrea Wilder to a party held last night at —"

"Look, Mommy!" Eden excitedly tapped her shoulder. "There's MacCrea!"

"I see him." She shifted her eyes back to the picture.

"MacCrea! Wait!" Eden bounced across the cushion in her scramble to get off the couch.

Startled, Abbie looked up as Eden darted toward a man crossing the lobby. MacCrea. "Eden, come back here!" She hurried after her, but it was too late. MacCrea had already seen Eden and stopped.

"Hello, short stuff." Smiling, he rumpled the top of her dark, wavy hair. "Don't tell me your mother's lost again." When he glanced up, he looked directly at her. Although his expression never changed, Abbie sensed shutters closing and a mask dropping into place.

"No." Eden laughed. "She's sitting right over there. We're waiting for Ben." As Abbie caught her daughter by the shoulders and pulled her back out of MacCrea's reach, she realized she still had the folded newspaper in her hand. "There you are, Mommy. See, she's not lost."

"Come on, Eden." She took her firmly by the hand. "You're bothering Mr. Wilder."

Resisting Abbie's attempt to lead her away, Eden looked at him and frowned. "Was I bothering you?"

"No, of course not."

"Don't encourage her," Abbie warned, keeping her voice low to conceal her anger.

"How come you got that?" Eden pointed to the garment bag slung over his shoulder. "Are you going somewhere?"

"Yes, I'm leaving. I have a plane to catch," he replied, addressing his answer to Abbie.

"But aren't you going to stay and see Windstorm win?" Eden protested.

"I can't. I've finished all my business here and I have to get back to work."

"Business?" Abbie scoffed bitterly. "That's not what the morning paper called it. Here. You can read it for yourself." She shoved the newspaper at him. "Maybe you'd like to tell me again how little contact you have with her!" She had no intention of waiting around to see what kind of trumped-up explanation he would make. As she scooped Eden into her arms, she saw Ben coming into the lobby and headed directly for the front door to their car parked outside.

"Mommy, how come you don't like MacCrea?" Eden asked as Abbie lifted her onto the seat.

At almost the same instant, MacCrea walked out of the motel and signaled for a cab. Abbie watched him, with more pain than anger. "You wouldn't understand, Eden," she said regretfully and climbed into the car with her daughter.

36

*M*ornings, afternoons, and evenings, Rachel grasped every opportunity to be with Ross. The lavish parties and equally glamorous sales that were an integral part of the Scottsdale Show scene enabled her to meet him discreetly. Always arriving and leaving separately, they attended the elegant gala held at the Loews', an elaborate fete given at the Wrigley mansion, the staid brunch at the Biltmore, an intimate dinner party in a luxury condo, and countless casual aisle parties and formal receptions.

They arranged to sit at the same tables in the exclusive "gold card" sections and view the Arabian horses offered for sale in spectacularly staged productions against backdrops of larger-than-life reproductions of art masterpieces, a recreation of the Palace of Versailles, and sleek contemporary settings of chrome and crystal. They sipped champagne together and ate chocolate-dipped strawberries while celebrity entertainers performed for them and Arabians came floating onto the runways through mists of white fog.

They sat together in the show stands and offered each other moral support when their respective horses competed in elimination classes to qualify for the finals. But then there were the nights — the madly passionate nights when Ross made love to her so thoroughly and so completely that she found it impossible to doubt the depth of his love. It seemed that nothing could mar this happiness she'd found.

She slipped the satin nightgown over her head and felt the sensuous material slide down to cover her naked body. Absently she adjusted the narrow straps over her shoulders as she turned back to the king-size bed where Ross lay, watching her.

"You are supposed to be getting dressed," she chided softly.

"I was trying to decide if you're more beautiful with clothes or without."

"And?"

"I can't make up my mind." He raised himself up on an elbow and reached for her hand to draw her close to the bed. "Why don't you take that gown off so I can decide."

"No, you don't." She leaned away from him, slightly pulling from his hand without making any real effort to get free. "It's late, almost midnight. And I have to get up in the morning. Tomorrow's the big day." Sirocco was scheduled to compete in the finals of the halter class.

"So?"

"So, I need my sleep. And so do you."

"Why don't I sleep here tonight with you? I want to wake up in the morning and find you lying beside me."

"Ross, we can't." She wished he wouldn't ask. "Suppose you're seen leaving my suite in the morning. What are people going to think?"

"The same thing they think when they see me sneaking out of your room in the middle of the night." He pulled her down onto the bed and began kissing her arm. "You don't really think we're fooling anybody, do you? By now, everyone's seen the way I look at you with all the love in my heart shining in my eyes."

"I suppose." But she didn't want to consider that.

"I do love you, Rachel. And I don't care if the whole world knows it."

"Ross, I — " As she reached up to stroke his face, the telephone on the nightstand rang shrilly. Rachel jumped, startled by the harsh sound. For an instant, she could only stare at it as it rang a second time. She glanced hesitantly at Ross, noting his suddenly sober look, then picked up the receiver, cutting off the bell in the middle of its third ring. "Hello?"

"Rachel, darling, did I wake you?" Lane's voice came clearly over the line.

"Yes," she lied, clutching the phone a little closer and turning more of her back to Ross. "Is something wrong? Alex — is he all right?"

"Yes, he's fine," Lane assured her. "As a matter of fact, he didn't even run a fever today."

"Then . . ." If it wasn't an emergency — and from the sound of his voice, it wasn't — why was he calling her at this hour of the night?

"I tried to reach you several times today."

"You did? I . . . I'm sorry. I've been on the run so much today that I never checked to see if I had any messages. I would have called but . . ." She hadn't wanted to talk to him. She didn't now, not with Ross lying here.

"I thought that was probably the case. And I'm sorry to call you so late and get you out of bed, but I wanted you to know that I'm flying out of Houston tomorrow. I'll have to stop and pick up MacCrea at our field in West Texas. I have some papers to go over with him. But we should be landing in Phoenix around noon."

"You will?" She didn't know what to think, what to say.

"I promised you I'd be there for the finals. Don't I always keep my word?" Lane chided affectionately.

"Yes, of course," she replied.

"You don't sound very happy about it."

"Oh, I am," she said in a rush. "It's just that . . . I'm only half-awake. Why don't I pick you up at the airport tomorrow?"

"I'd like that." He sounded satisfied with her explanation. "You go back to sleep, dear, and I'll see you tomorrow — correction, today."

"Yes. Good night."

"Good night, dear."

Rachel waited for the click on the other end of the line before she slowly replaced the receiver on its cradle. As she brought her hands back to her lap, she unconsciously touched the wedding ring on her finger.

"Your husband?" Ross guessed.

"Yes. He's flying in tomorrow."

The mattress dipped beneath her as Ross pushed himself into a sitting position behind her. He ran his hand up her arm in a caress that was no different from countless others she'd experienced, yet this time Rachel felt tense at his touch. That telephone call had complicated the situation. Not ten minutes ago it had all seemed so simple: Ross loved her; that Lane was her husband had seemed totally immaterial. But it wasn't.

"Are you going to tell him about us?" Ross asked, slipping aside the strap of her gown to nuzzle her shoulder.

The thought frightened her. What if she was wrong? What if Ross didn't really love her? This had all happened so quickly; how could she be sure? Agitated by his suggestion, Rachel pushed off the bed and took several steps away from it. "I don't see how I can, Ross. MacCrea will be with him," she reasoned with a forced calm.

"Rachel —"

"Please, Ross, I think it would be best if you'd get dressed and leave now." Nervously she twisted her hands together, unable to look at him.

"No." She heard the rustle of bedcovers being thrown aside and the squeak of the bedsprings, followed by the faint thud of his feet hitting the floor. "I'm not going anywhere until we get a few things straight." As she started to turn, he caught her arm and swung her the rest of the way around to face him. He wore a desperate look as he searched her face for some clue. "Just what are you telling me? 'It's been fun, but good-bye'? Because I'm not going to accept that. I can't just walk away and forget any of this happened. I love you. It isn't just a passing thing with me."

"Ross, I want to see you again, too. But, with Lane here, that will be impossible. And you have that television special to tape and all your other commitments to keep. It's not going to be as easy for us to meet after tonight."

"You could always leave Lane and come with me." He tried to draw her into his embrace, but Rachel flattened her hands against his chest to keep some distance between them.

"I want to be with you, Ross. I need you, more than you'll ever know. But, if you really love me, don't ask me to do that. I can't, not now anyway. It's too soon. There are too many other things to consider. I'm not even sure if I know this is right — for either of us."

"If I love you and you love me, it has to be right."

"You don't understand." She shook her head. "Once I thought I loved Lane, too. I want to be sure this time."

"Darling . . ." He started to argue, then paused and sighed heavily. "All right, I won't rush you, but it isn't going to be easy. Because I won't be happy until you're with me every day and every night. I know I'm not as rich as your husband is, but I'm not poor by any means, not anymore. I promise you you'll have everything you've ever wanted. Just name it and it's yours."

"I don't want anything." She didn't understand why every man thought he had to buy her love with expensive presents.

Another twenty minutes passed before Rachel was finally able to persuade Ross to get dressed and leave and she had time alone to think. As she lay awake, she almost wished she'd never gotten involved with him. True, she had been happy, but she'd been happy other times, too, and it had never lasted. Why hadn't she remembered that sooner?

37

*A*bbie's legs felt as if they were made out of Eden's Silly Putty. And if the flutterings in her stomach were caused by butterflies, then Abbie was certain they were the biggest butterflies in the whole world. She'd been nervous before, but never like this.

She shivered, but it was from nerves, not the cool desert air. For at least the tenth time, Abbie brushed an imaginary speck of dirt off Windstorm's white satin coat and checked his polished black hooves while she waited for the stallion class to be called.

"This is it, Ben," she said grimly, wishing she felt as calm as he looked standing there holding Eden in his arms. "Windstorm has to win. He just has to. I couldn't stand it if Rachel walked away with the championship."

"He'll win, Mommy." Eden leaned over and petted the stallion's neck. "I just know he will. He's the most beautiful horse ever."

"Beauty alone does not make a stallion great, child," Ben lectured sternly. "If Windstorm should win this title, what would it prove? That he has courage, stamina, heart? No. It is the racetrack and only the racetrack that would show his true worth. This class is no more than a beauty contest."

"I'm not going to argue." Abbie knew she had about as much chance of changing Ben's mind on that as she did of convincing a bulldog to let go once he'd clamped his jaws on something. "But if he wins here and we race him this summer, we can have both."

"I'll bet he can run faster than any horse in the world," Eden declared.

Abbie started to correct her daughter, then changed her mind. She didn't feel like explaining why a Thoroughbred could run faster than an Arabian. Over the years, Thoroughbreds had been selectively bred for speed, even though the lineage of every one of those horses traced directly back to three Arabian stallions. Arabians, too, were born to run, but their physical differences gave them an astounding ability to carry weight and amazing endurance. But trying to make a five-year-old understand that would take too long.

"Hadn't you two better go get your seats?" Abbie suggested, wanting a few minutes alone to settle her nerves, if she could, before the class was called. "You be good and stay with Ben. Promise?"

"I promise." Eden wrapped her arms around Abbie's neck and gave her a big hug and a kiss on the cheek.

As she watched them leave, she realized that for the first time she was going head-to-head with Rachel, her stallion against Rachel's. She had to win. She couldn't lose to her again.

All around her, grooms feverishly brushed, combed, and polished their respective stallions whether they needed it or not, while the trainers jiggled lead ropes, swished their whips, or quieted a stallion already too fired up by the electric tension in the air. Alone, without a cadre of stable hands to assist her, Abbie smoothed the stallion's long forelock, arranging it to fall down the center of his forehead.

It felt as if her heart leaped into her throat when the call for the stallion class finally came. An eternity of seconds seemed to tick by before it was her turn to lead Windstorm into the arena. "Okay, fella," she whispered as she swung him in a tight circle to head for the in gate. "Show them who's the best."

"Heads up!" someone shouted as Abbie ran toward the arena gate, giving the stallion plenty of slack.

Windstorm bounded past her, a white flame of motion, neck tautly arched, mane and tail flying. As he charged into the arena ahead of her, Abbie knew their entrance looked to all the world as if he had bolted on her. But the lead never went taut as the stallion swung back to her and reared briefly on his hind legs.

When she heard the roar of appreciation from the crowd in the stands, Abbie smiled. "They're yours, Windstorm. Make 'em notice you." He trotted after her, floating over the arena floor as she moved to the outer perimeter of the oval ring. She knew they made an eye-catching pair — a sixteen-hand white stallion and a petite dark-haired woman. And she knew Windstorm loved the noise and attention of the crowd. The more they cheered, the more animated he became, firing up as only an Arabian could.

"Go get 'em, Abbie!" a man yelled to her as they passed his seat.

Abbie stopped Windstorm a short distance from the next stallion to wait for the rest of the qualifiers to enter the arena. Officially, the judging didn't begin until the two-minute gate closed. She glanced at the section of seats where Ben and Eden were supposed to be sitting. About ten rows up, a small arm waved wildly. Smiling, Abbie started to bring her attention back to Windstorm, but something — a movement or a sound from the seats to her right — distracted her.

With a sense of shock, she discovered MacCrea staring back at her. All the faces around him were a blur. His alone was distinct. What was he doing there? Why had he come back? Half turning in his seat, he looked in the general direction of Ben and Eden's seats. Abbie felt her heart knocking against her ribs.

At that instant, the man sitting beside MacCrea leaned over and claimed his attention. Abbie recognized that distinctive mane of white hair. Lane and Rachel were seated with him.

"The gate is closed," the announcer stated, his voice booming over the public-address system. "The judging of the stallion halter class will begin now. The judges ask that you space your horses along the rail and walk them, please."

On either side of her there was movement. Fighting the sudden attack of nerves, Abbie led an eager, dancing Windstorm in a snug circle, then walked him along the rail, letting him show off his leggy, smooth stride. The stallion was ready to get down to business, but she wasn't.

How many times had Ben told her not to look at the crowd? Don't pay any attention to them, he'd said. It's just you and your horse. Block everything else out. Don't worry about what the other horses are doing or how they're showing or whether the judges are watching you. Make him look his best at all times. Concentrate on the horse.

It began: the walking, the trotting, the posing with all four feet in picture-perfect position, tail up, ears pricked, neck stretched, first en masse, then singly. As always, the class seemed to go on forever, straining nerves and heightening tension.

At last the announcement came. "The judges have made their decisions. You may relax your horses while their scores are compiled."

Immediately Abbie stepped to the stallion's side and absently rubbed a white wither. Her legs were shaking and her stomach was all tied up in knots. Windstorm swung his head around to look at her as if to say, "Are you okay?" She wanted to bury her face against his neck and cry — with hope or relief, she wasn't sure which. Instead she stood there, trying to hide all the anxiety that came from not knowing the judges' result.

Almost unwillingly, she glanced down the line at Rachel's blood bay stallion. The Arabian surveyed the crowded stands with absolute arrogance. She couldn't help noticing how confident the stallion's trainer looked. She felt better when she saw him nervously moisten his lips. Her own were dry as paper.

The minutes dragged by with agonizing slowness as Abbie and everyone else waited for the judges' scores to be tallied. When the announcer declared he had the results, the crowd noise fell to a murmur. Before he announced the Reserve Champion and Champion Stallion, he began naming the Top Ten Stallions, first explaining that the stallions placing in the top ten were all regarded as equal in status regardless of the order in which they were named.

Seven stallions were called, then eight, each followed by cheers and whistles from the crowd. And after each, Abbie held her breath, wanting the championship too desperately to settle for the honor of Top Ten Stallion.

"Next, number four fifty-seven, Windstorm!" Abbie froze as her number was called, everything inside her screaming *no,* her heart sinking to the pit of her stomach. "Shown by owner and trainer, Abbie Hix."

In a blur of tears, she led Windstorm out of the line, deaf to the applause and a few boos of disappointment. They had lost. Engulfed by a terrible sense of defeat, she didn't even remember the ribbon presentation and picture-taking ceremony. She didn't hear the Reserve Champion Stallion named. Nothing registered until the Champion Stallion was called.

"This year's Champion Stallion is number three fifty-eight, Sirocco!"

As the announcement was made, Windstorm bounded into the air, nearly jerking the lead out of Abbie's loose grasp. Instinctively she checked his forward motion, forcing the stallion to swing in an arc in front of her. With a raking toss of his head, Windstorm came to a stop, then trumpeted a challenge at the bay stallion trotting proudly in the spotlight, as if disputing the decision.

Her stallion's reaction was almost more than Abbie's nerves could take. As quickly as possible, Abbie exited the arena, unable to acknowledge the congratulations offered her. For some, Top Ten Stallion might be better than nothing, but not to her . . . never to her. All her life, she had lost to Rachel. She hated the taste it left in her mouth.

Blessedly, Abbie had a few minutes alone in the stall with Windstorm to regain her composure before Ben and Eden arrived. No matter how bitter the disappointment was to swallow, she couldn't let her young daughter see how upset she was over Windstorm's placing.

The hardest thing Abbie ever had to do was to look at the tears in Eden's blue eyes and smile. More than anything she wanted to cry with her daughter. "It's about time you two got here. We've been waiting for you."

"I don't care what anybody says. Windstorm is the best horse ever in the whole wide world." Eden's lower lip quivered.

"He's *one* of the best," Abbie stressed carefully. "And he has a ribbon to prove it. Come on. Help me pin it on his stall so everyone who walks by can see it." As she started to lift Eden out of Ben's arms, she met his glance. For a split second she faltered, knowing that he saw through her charade.

"Remember what I said."

She nodded. "I know. It proves nothing."

"There can be no question of the winner of a horse race. It is the horse what crosses the finish line first. In Poland, it is a stallion's record on the track and his foals that prove his worth as a sire. That is the way it should be here."

"I know." Just as she knew that more and more Arabian horse breeders, including some of the big ones, were turning away from the horse-show arenas and to the racetracks to test the worth of their stock, as their counterparts in Europe and the Middle East had been doing for hundreds of years. Gathering Eden into her arms, she gave her the ribbon and helped her to hang it on the front of the stall. "What do you say we all go get something to eat?" she suggested, wiping the last traces of tears off Eden's cheeks.

"I'm not hungry," Eden said, still pouting.

"Not even for a hot-fudge sundae with whipped cream and cherries on top?" Abbie looked at her askance, doubting her daughter's sweet tooth could resist such a temptation.

"A whole one . . . just for me?"

"I think this celebration might call for a whole one."

"Didja hear that, Ben?" Eden turned excitedly to him. "I get to have one all to myself and I don't have to share it."

"It will take a very big girl to eat a whole sundae by herself."

"But I'm getting bigger every day."

"You certainly are," Abbie agreed and set Eden down. "And a big girl like you doesn't need to be carried."

As they left the barn to head for the parking lot, Eden skipped along beside Abbie, swinging her hand as if she didn't have a care in the world, the prospect of a treat banishing all sorrow. Abbie envied that ability to forget and put it all behind her. She'd been like that at Eden's age. Unfortunately she'd outgrown that too many years ago. A special treat couldn't make the hurt go away anymore.

With their path blocked by the crowd milling in front of the stallion barn, Abbie was forced to slow her pace. She paid little attention to the shrieks of joy and late congratulations being exchanged by those around her, intent only on keeping her small party together and not getting separated in the crowd. Suddenly she found herself face-to-face with Rachel.

After an initial look of surprise, Rachel's expression became serenely composed, mannequin-smooth and smug. "Are you leaving already?"

Abbie stiffened at the insinuation she was running off to lick her wounds, angered most of all because it was true. "Yes."

"We're holding a little celebration in the stallion barn. Would you care to join us?"

Abbie was tempted to accept the invitation just to aggravate Rachel, but she resisted the impulse, knowing that Rachel would love the chance to rub her nose in the defeat. "What are you celebrating? Winning a beauty contest?"

"My, but that sounds remarkably like sour grapes," Rachel taunted. "I wonder why I have the feeling you wouldn't call it that if your stallion had won."

Vaguely Abbie was aware of MacCrea looking on, as well as Lane Canfield and Ross Tibbs, but she was too intent on this confrontation with Rachel to take much notice of them. "You're wrong. I've always regarded the halter class as a beauty contest. It judges a horse's looks, not his athletic ability. Win or lose, I had every intention of racing Windstorm this year. And that's precisely what I'm going to do. But I'm curious what your plans for Sirocco are now."

"I'm taking him home, to River Bend" — she stressed that deliberately — "so he can rest before the National Finals this fall. That's all he has left to win."

"Except a race. It doesn't matter though. I think you've made the right decision." Abbie smiled complacently at the look of surprise that flashed across Rachel's face. "You and I both know your stallion couldn't stand up under the rigors of racing. If I were you, I'd be afraid of him breaking down, too."

"You don't know what you're talking about," she retorted stiffly.

"Don't I? My father had a breeding program very similar to yours. He believed in breeding beautiful horses." Abbie paused, smiling. "I believe in breeding Arabians. Like you, he never did understand the difference."

"That's a lie!" Her voice lifted angrily.

"My mommy doesn't lie," Eden protested.

"Be quiet," Rachel snapped at her.

"You have no right to talk to my daughter that way."

"Then why don't you teach her some manners?" she shouted.

"Don't you yell at my mommy!" Eden tore loose from Abbie's hand and flung herself at Rachel, her arms swinging like a windmill.

Before Abbie could grab her and pull her away, MacCrea lifted Eden into his arms. "That's enough." Shifting Eden onto his hip, he took Abbie by the elbow and propelled her ahead of him through the crowd.

"Let go of me!" Abbie struggled to pull free, but his fingers dug deeper, numbing the nerves in her arm and making it tingle painfully.

"Not until I'm damned good and ready," he growled, leaving her in no doubt that he meant exactly what he said. As long as he held Eden, Abbie realized, she didn't have any choice but to go wherever he was taking her. He didn't stop until they were nearly to the parking lot and well clear of the crowd.

The instant MacCrea released her, Abbie whirled around. "I want my daughter. Give her to me."

Staring at her, his eyes cold and angry, he continued to hold Eden. "You're two of a kind," he muttered. "I oughta drag both of you over my knee and give you the paddling you deserve."

"I wouldn't try it," Abbie warned.

"Why are you so mad at my mommy?" Eden looked confused and a little frightened.

MacCrea paused and briefly eyed Abbie, then glanced over his shoulder as Ben hurried toward them, puffing slightly. "We'll meet you at the motel, Ben. These two are riding back with me."

"I'm not going anywhere with you, MacCrea, until you give me my daughter," Abbie asserted.

He just smiled. "I'm no fool, Abbie. She's my guarantee that you come with me. I've got a few things to say to you and you're going to listen."

"That's kidnapping."

"Kidnapping, blackmail, call it any damned thing you like. But that's the way it's going to be." He started walking toward the parking lot. Abbie hesitated, then hurried after him.

"All right, you win," she said as she drew level with him.

"I never doubted that for a minute. The tan car in the second row is mine."

When they reached the car, MacCrea set Eden in the backseat. "Can't I sit up front with you and Mommy?"

"Nope. Little girls ride in the backseat." He started the engine.

"Where are we going, Mommy?"

"Back to the motel." At least, she hoped MacCrea would take them straight back. She didn't really trust him.

"What about my sundae? You said I could have one with hot fudge and cherries and everything."

"If you'll sit down and be quiet, short stuff, I'll buy you a giant-sized sundae with nuts on it, too," MacCrea promised.

"You shouldn't bribe her like that," Abbie said angrily as Eden quickly sat back in the seat.

"It can't be any worse than what you're doing." He followed the arrows to the parking-lot exit and accelerated onto the street.

"What's that supposed to mean?"

"Knowing you, you're probably damned proud of yourself." Anger thickened his low voice. Abbie glanced briefly at him, noticing the ridged muscles in his jaw. "You weren't content until you dragged your daughter into your stupid, jealous feud with Rachel, were you? Teach them to hate while they are young. Isn't that the way it's done?"

"I didn't start it. Rachel was the one who wouldn't leave Eden out of it."

"None of it would have happened if you hadn't been looking for a fight. And don't deny that you goaded Rachel deliberately. I was there."

"That's right. Defend poor little Rachel," Abbie retorted sarcastically, fighting to suppress the sobs of frustration that caught in her throat.

"I'm not defending her."

"What do you call it then?" But she didn't care to hear his explanation. "I don't even know why I'm talking to you. How I raise my daughter is none of your business."

"Maybe it isn't, but every time I look at her, Abbie, I see you — the way you must have been before you were warped by this jealousy and your heart got all twisted with hate. Do you honestly want your daughter to grow up with the bitterness and hatred you feel?"

"No!" She was stunned that he would even think that.

"Then you'd better wake up and look at what you're doing to her," he warned. "Your jealousy is going to destroy her the same way it destroyed us."

Abbie started to remind MacCrea that he had been the one who betrayed her, but what was the point? It was over. He hadn't understood then, and he certainly wouldn't understand now. If anything, the years in between had proved she couldn't trust him.

At the same time, she couldn't argue with him about Eden. Someday she would have to tell her daughter who Rachel was. If she didn't, Eden would hear the whole sordid story from someone else. But MacCrea was right; she shouldn't let her bitterness and hurt color it.

Eden leaned over the middle of the seat back. "Are you talking about that lady that yelled at you? I didn't like her. She wasn't very nice."

Abbie caught the I-told-you-so look MacCrea threw at her. "You shouldn't say things like that, Eden," she insisted tautly.

"Why? You didn't like her either, did you, Mommy?" She frowned.

"Get out of that one if you can, Abbie," MacCrea challenged. She couldn't — and he knew it.

"Look! There's our motel." Eden pointed at the sign ahead of them.

Abbie nearly sighed with relief as MacCrea slowed the car and turned into the driveway. No longer did she have to wonder whether he truly intended to bring them straight here. The instant he stopped the car, parking it in an empty space near the lobby entrance, Abbie climbed out of the front seat and opened the rear door to claim Eden. She resisted the urge to gather Eden into her arms and run away from him into the motel. Instead, she walked Eden to the sidewalk that ran alongside the building, holding her firmly by the hand. There, she paused to wait for MacCrea.

"Tell Mr. Wilder good night and thank him for the ride." She tried to act normal even though every nerve in her body was screaming for her to get Eden out of his sight.

"But what about my sundae?" It was all Abbie could do to keep from shaking her.

"That's right. I promised I'd buy you the biggest sundae in town if you were good, didn't I?" MacCrea said.

"I wouldn't worry about it. The coffee shop is still open. I can buy her one there. After all, you do have a party to attend, and we don't want to keep you from it."

"What gave you that idea?"

"You were with her. You know she expects you." Her voice vibrated with the anger she tried to contain.

"Maybe so, but believe me, I won't be missed," he replied, then smiled at Eden. "Besides, I'd much rather buy a little girl some ice cream than drink champagne toasts to some horse."

"And I'd rather you didn't."

"Anyone would get the impression you're trying to get rid of me."

"I am." She tightened her hold on Eden's hand.

"Do you want me to leave, Eden?"

"Don't bring her into this," she protested angrily.

"Why not? She's the one I invited."

"I don't care!"

Eden pulled on her hand, demanding Abbie's attention. "Mommy, why don't you like him?"

"Yes, 'Mommy,' tell her why you don't like me. I'd be interested to hear how you'd answer that," he said dryly.

Frustrated by his stubborn persistence, Abbie couldn't even begin to try. The reasons were all too tangled. "Why are you doing this? Why can't you just leave us alone?"

MacCrea paused, as if her question had suddenly made him examine his motives. "I don't know." He shrugged faintly. "Maybe because you want it so badly."

Was she too anxious? Had she aroused his suspicion? Did he wonder if it was something more on her part than just a desire not to have anything more to do with a former lover? She couldn't risk learning the answers.

"Join us if you want. But don't expect me to make you feel welcome." She pivoted sharply and started toward the motel door, dragging Eden with her.

"Look, Mommy. Here comes Ben." Eden waved gaily at the driver of the car pulling into the lot.

38

Except for two men sitting at a counter drinking coffee and four more people at a table on the other side of the room, they had the restaurant to themselves. Abbie sipped at her coffee and glanced toward the kitchen, wondering how long it could possibly take the waitress to bring Ben's banana cream pie and Eden's hot-fudge sundae . . . and how long it would take her daughter to eat it. It couldn't be soon enough to suit her. Maybe she should have ordered something to eat just to have something to do to make the time pass more quickly, but the way her stomach was churning, she doubted she could keep it down.

It was difficult enough sitting next to MacCrea, aware that he had maneuvered her into accepting this situation. Why hadn't she been smart enough to see it coming? Why had she allowed it to happen? Why hadn't she recognized that he was up to his old tricks? He knew that where Eden was concerned, she was vulnerable. As yet, he just didn't know why. And she couldn't let him find out.

"Are you staying at this motel, too?" Eden asked MacCrea, the two of them carrying on the only conversation at the table.

"I sure am."

"So are we. When are you going? We're leaving tomorrow. We've been gone a long time. Daddy is really going to be happy to see us when we get back. Isn't he, Mommy?"

"He certainly will." Unconsciously she twisted the wedding band on her ring finger. The instant she noticed MacCrea's glance shift to her hand, she realized what she was doing and reached again for her coffee cup. "And we'll be glad to see him, too, won't we?" She smiled at Eden, forcing an enthusiasm into her voice that she was far from feeling.

"You bet!"

When the waitress came out of the kitchen, balanced on her tray was a large goblet filled with vanilla ice cream covered by a layer of chocolate fudge and crowned with a tall swirl of whipped cream, sprinkled with nuts and topped by a red cherry.

"Look at the size of that sundae. Are you sure you can eat it all?" Abbie asked skeptically as she scooted Eden's chair closer to the table.

"Uh huh, I'm a big girl."

"It looks bigger than you," MacCrea remarked when the waitress set the sundae down on the table in front of her, but Eden corrected that problem by kneeling on her chair.

"Can I eat the cherry first, Mommy?" She picked up the long spoon, its length ungainly in her small hand.

"Yes. Just pay attention and don't get that sundae all over your good clothes," Abbie cautioned, knowing she was probably wasting her breath.

"I think I'll save it for later." She plucked the cherry from the whipped cream by its stem and laid it on the table, then proceeded to wipe her sticky fingers on her dress.

"Use your napkin." Abbie pushed it closer to the goblet, conscious of MacCrea's low chortle.

When Eden plunged her spoon into the sundae to dig out her first biteful, an avalanche of melted ice cream, thick chocolate, and whipped topping spilled over the rim of the goblet on the opposite side. Eden caught it with her fingers and pushed most of it back inside the glass, then licked the mixture off her fingers.

"Mmm, it's good."

"It looks good," MacCrea agreed.

"Want a bite?" Eden offered him the huge glob of ice cream and fudge on her spoon, then somehow managed to get it to her own mouth without dropping it when he politely refused.

Within minutes, Eden had almost as much of the sundae all over her face and hands and the table as she did in her stomach. Abbie desperately wished that her daughter was still young enough to be spoon-fed. Watching her eat by herself was an exercise in patience, and Abbie's was already sorely tested. She looked over at Ben, seeking a diversion.

"How was the pie?"

"It was good but not as good as your momma's."

"How is your mother?" MacCrea asked.

"She's fine." Abbie held out her cup as the waitress brought the coffeepot to the table.

"Do you know my grandma?" Eden spooned another partially melted mouthful of ice cream from the goblet, half of it dripping across the table as she tried to aim it at her mouth.

"Yes."

"I don't get to see her very much." Eden released a very adultlike sigh and absently stirred the melting remains of her sundae. As she scooped out another dripping spoonful, she glanced over at MacCrea and paused, with the spoon in midair. "Look, Mommy." Wonder was in her voice as she used the dripping spoon to point at him. "MacCrea has a crooked finger just like me."

For a split second Abbie was paralyzed by Eden's pronouncement as she stared at the little finger curling away from the handle of the coffee cup MacCrea was holding. Then she noticed the puzzled blankness in his expression and realized the significance of the comparison hadn't registered yet. There was still a chance it wouldn't if she acted fast.

"Eden, you're dripping ice cream all over the table." Quickly she grabbed the small hand holding the long spoon, covering the little finger so MacCrea couldn't see the way it arched, too. "Pay attention to what you're doing. Just look at the mess you've made."

"But, Mommy, did you see his finger?"

Abbie talked right over Eden's question, praying that MacCrea wouldn't hear it. "I think that's enough ice cream for you, little lady. You're just playing in it now." Out of the corner of her eye, she saw MacCrea set his coffee cup down, a frown deepening the lines in his forehead.

"What's she talking about?"

She ignored his question as she took the spoon from Eden's sticky fingers and put it back in the sundae dish, then reached for a paper napkin. "I bet you have more ice cream *on* you than *in* you. You've got chocolate from ear to ear. I wouldn't be surprised if you have it in your hair. And look, you've spilled some on your good dress. What am I going to do with you?"

Abbie went through the motion of wetting the napkin in her water glass and attempting to wipe the worst of the sticky residue from her daughter's face and hands. But Eden knew she had MacCrea's attention and centered all of hers on him. When she opened her mouth to say something to him, Abbie immediately smothered the attempt with the wet napkin, pretending to wipe the chocolate ring around her lips.

When the napkin had rapidly shredded into nothing, Abbie stood up and scooped Eden off the chair into her arms. "I think we'd better go to our room and get you cleaned up. It's past your bedtime anyway." Ignoring the objections Eden attempted to raise, she turned to MacCrea and met his narrowed gaze. Her heart was thumping so loudly she was certain he could hear it. "I'm sorry," she said without knowing why she was apologizing to him, of all people. "Thank Mr. Wilder for the sundae, Eden, and tell him good-bye. We'll be leaving early in the morning, so we won't be seeing him again." She hoped.

"But —"

"Eden." Abbie shot her a warning look, but an instant later she had trouble swallowing as MacCrea straightened from his chair and towered in front of them.

"Thank you for the hot-fudge sundae, Mr. Wilder," Eden mumbled dejectedly.

"It was my pleasure. Maybe next time your mother won't spirit you away before you get a chance to finish it."

"Yeah." But Eden didn't sound too hopeful.

"Good-bye, Eden." As MacCrea extended his hand to her daughter, Abbie felt her heart leap into her throat.

"No, you'd better not," Abbie intervened quickly. "You'll get all sticky." She darted a frantic look at Ben. "Are you coming?"

But MacCrea paid no attention to Ben. Instead he stared at the small hand on Abbie's shoulder. Abbie didn't have to look to know that, at rest, the first joint of Eden's little finger always jutted upward at a very noticeable angle. When his glance swung to her, he appeared puzzled and faintly stunned. Abbie held her breath, her mind racing, trying to think what she could do when he finally figured out the truth. Ben stepped in to distract him.

"I wish to thank you for the pie and coffee. It was good."

"You're welcome," he replied absently.

"Yes, good night, Mr. Wilder, and thank you for the coffee." Abbie moved away from him before she finished talking.

"Wait a minute." He started to come after her, but the waitress detained him.

"Your check, sir."

Once outside the coffee shop, Abbie broke into a running walk, hurrying down the long corridor to her motel room with Eden jouncing on her hip. She looked back once to make certain Ben was the only one behind her. But she knew she wouldn't feel safe until she and Eden were inside the room and the door was shut and locked.

Her hand shook when she tried to insert the room key in the lock. Impatiently she set Eden down so she could use both hands. She glanced up briefly when Ben joined her. Beyond him she saw MacCrea striding purposefully toward them.

"He knows," Ben said.

She knew he was right, and knowing it just made her all the more angry — angry at herself, Ben, MacCrea, Eden . . . everyone. Why did he have to find out? Why couldn't he have just stayed away? Finally she got the key to turn in the lock and pushed the door open, but she made no attempt to shove Eden inside. It was too late. MacCrea was there. Still she refused to look at him, refused to acknowledge him.

"I think you'd better take Eden with you, Ben, so Abbie and I can talk privately," MacCrea stated, his voice clipped and hard.

"We have nothing to discuss," Abbie snapped.

"We damned well do, and you know it." His voice rumbled at an ominously low pitch as if he were controlling his anger with difficulty. "If you want to have it out right here and now, that's fine with me."

Left with no alternative, Abbie gave Eden a little push in Ben's direction. "Go with Ben, honey. He'll help you wash up. I'll come by to get you in a few minutes." She waited until Ben had Eden securely by the hand, then she pivoted and entered her motel room, MacCrea following a step behind her.

As the door slammed shut with reverberating force, the blood ran strong and fast through her veins, pumping adrenaline through her system. She had hoped this confrontation with MacCrea would never be necessary, but now that it was here, she was ready for it — in an odd way, almost eager for it.

"She's my daughter, isn't she?" MacCrea accused.

Abbie whirled around to face him. "She's *my* daughter!"

"You know damned well what I mean." He was angry, impatient, his lips thin and tight, the muscles working along his jaw. "I'm her father."

"You're nothing to her. You're just some stranger who bought her a sundae. Dobie's the only father she knows. It's *his* name that's on her birth certificate."

"That's why you married him, isn't it? The poor sucker probably doesn't even know the way you've tricked him and used him, does he?"

Fighting a twinge of guilt, Abbie looked away and asserted forcefully, "My baby needed a father and a name."

"Dammit, she already had one! She had *me!* She had the right to *my* name!" Grabbing her by the shoulders, MacCrea forced her to look at him. "You damned little fool, you know I wanted to marry you. I loved you."

"But I didn't want you — or any more of your deceit and half-truths." It was odd how fresh the pain of his betrayal felt to her at that moment. The ache was as real as if it all had happened yesterday.

"But you wanted my baby."

"I wanted *my* baby."

He dug his fingers into her shoulders. "Deny it all you want, but the fact remains, I am her father. You can't change that."

"What difference does it make?" she argued. "Twenty minutes ago you had no idea you even had a daughter. Why is Eden suddenly so important to you now? You don't even know her."

"Whose fault is that? Or are you going to try to blame me for that, too?"

"She doesn't need you. There's nothing you can give her that she doesn't already have. She's happy and loved, well fed and clothed. She has a home and a family, people who care about her. You'd just hurt and confuse her. You'd never bring her anything but pain."

"You're talking about yourself, Abbie," MacCrea accused. "And I don't mean just our relationship, but the way things were with your father. It's that damned jealousy again."

"Maybe it is. Maybe I don't think any child needs a father, least of all men like you and my daddy."

"Hasn't it ever occurred to you that your father might have loved both you and Rachel? That, just maybe, he behaved the way he did because he was torn with guilt?"

"You don't know anything about it! How can you defend him?"

She struggled briefly, trying to shake off the numbing grip of his hands, but he wouldn't let her go. He forced her to stand there and face him.

"I know how I felt walking down that corridor, for the first time realizing that I had a daughter and thinking that I should have been there when she was born; that I should have been there when she took her first step and said her first words; I should have been there when she cried. But I wasn't and I couldn't be. And I felt guilty even though it wasn't my fault. If I feel that way, imagine how your father must have felt over Rachel."

"That's not the way it was." She resented his attempt to defend a situation he knew nothing about, especially when she knew he was doing it to satisfy his own selfish desires. "He loved her, not me. All I ever got from him was a reflection of his love for her because I looked like her."

"He didn't love you both?"

"No," Abbie retorted sharply, too incensed by this entire conversation to think straight. "You can't love two people at the same time."

"You love Eden, don't you?"

"Yes."

"And your mother?"

"Of course." The instant the words were out of her mouth, Abbie saw the trap he was setting for her.

"And Ben?" he challenged. She glared at him, refusing to answer and damn herself with her own words. "Admit it, Abbie. You love him, too."

She couldn't deny it, and her continued silence seemed to be an act of betrayal against the one person who had always been there when she needed someone. She looked down at the gold buckle on MacCrea's belt and grudgingly replied, "In a way."

"In a way," MacCrea repeated her phrase with satisfaction. "That makes three people you love. How do you explain that?"

"It's not the same," she said defensively.

"No, it isn't. You love all three of them equally but differently, don't you?"

"Yes," Abbie said, quickly seizing on his explanation.

"Then isn't it possible your father loved you and Rachel equally but differently?"

"You always twist everything around." She felt strangled by the bitter anger that gripped her throat as she lifted her gaze to the ruthless lines in his face. "She was his favorite. He was always giving her things."

"Maybe he was trying to make up for the fact he wasn't there all the time. Maybe he was trying to cram all his affection into a few short hours."

"Look at the money he left her, while Momma and I ended up with practically nothing!" Tears burned her eyes until she could hardly see — hot tears caused by the pain of wounds that had never truly healed.

"For your information, he set up that trust fund for Rachel when she was born. That money was in place long before he got into financial trouble."

"How would you know?" Abbie jeered.

"I asked," MacCrea shot back.

"Then why didn't he do the same for me?"

"Probably because you were his legitimate heir and he figured you would end up with everything he had. Which, at the time, was probably considerably more than the money he placed in trust for Rachel. And maybe, just maybe, he did it because he knew what a spiteful little bitch you were going to turn out to be, and he knew that if he didn't make provisions for Rachel, you'd see to it she never got a cent — the same way you tried to keep me from finding out about my child."

"You're lying!" She struck out blindly with her fists, briefly landing blows on his arms and chest. Cursing under his breath, MacCrea hauled her roughly against him, using her own body to pin her arms against his chest. "Let me go!" Abbie continued to struggle, however ineffectually.

"I ought to . . ." But he didn't bother to finish the threat, instead using action to silence her.

Abbie made a vain attempt to elude the downward swoop of his head, but he grabbed a handful of hair and yanked it, arching her neck back as far as it would go. As he kissed her, his teeth ground against hers and his mustache scratched her skin. The brutal assault was a deliberate attempt to inflict pain. Abbie refused even to think of it as a kiss. She'd known too many of MacCrea's kisses to confuse this with one. The pain was in such contrast to the exquisite pleasure she had once known in his arms that Abbie couldn't help recalling the latter. He wanted to hurt her, but Abbie knew it was her heart that ached the most. She tried desperately to remember how much she hated him and forget the sensation of his heart thudding beneath her hands.

Breaking off the assault, he dragged his mouth across her cheek and down to her throat. "Damn you, Abbie," he muttered thickly against her skin. "Damn you to hell for doing this to me."

At first she didn't know what he was talking about as her bruised lips throbbed painfully. Then she felt the rubbing stroke of his hand on her spine — the beginnings of a caress. No! Abbie thought wildly. She couldn't, she wouldn't let herself be fooled by him again.

With a violent, wrenching twist of her body, she broke free of his arms, catching him by surprise. When he took a step toward her, she backed up two. "Stay away from me. I hate you. I can't stand the sight of you! Get out of here! Just get out!"

"You're good at that, aren't you? You've had plenty of practice at ordering people out of your life."

"Get out." She wanted to throw something at him, but instinctively she knew that would only provoke him.

"I'll leave." But he made no move toward the door. Unconsciously Abbie held her breath, not wanting to say anything that might change his mind. "But this isn't over."

"It was over more than six years ago."

"You're forgetting: there's still the matter of my daughter that needs to be resolved."

"Stay away from her." Abbie tried not to give in to the sense of panic she felt.

"You can shut me out of your life, Abbie, but I'm not going to let you shut me out of Eden's. You'd better get used to the idea."

"No." She knew how weak her protest sounded as he turned and walked the few steps to the door.

He opened it, then paused to look back at her. "You'll be seeing me again," he promised grimly.

No! Inside, the denial was an angry scream, but not a sound came out of her mouth as Abbie watched MacCrea walk out of the door. The door swung closed on its own. In a panic, Abbie ran after him, jerking the door open and rushing into the wide corridor. When she saw him striding away from her, she stopped.

"MacCrea, don't!" she called after him. "If you have any feelings for her at all, stay away. Don't hurt her just because you want to get back at me." She noticed the faint hesitation in his stride and knew he had heard her. But he kept walking. She didn't know whether she'd gotten through to him.

Turning, she glanced at the door to Ben's room, fear knotting her throat. She couldn't face Ben yet — or Eden either, for that matter. She needed some time alone to think this whole thing out.

The next morning, before first light, they checked out of the motel and drove to the showgrounds. By the time a red sun peeked over the eastern mountains to cast its eye on the city of Phoenix below, Windstorm was loaded in the horse trailer and they were on their way out of town.

For the first hour, Abbie kept one eye on the road and one on the side mirror, half-expecting to see the reflection of MacCrea's rented car coming after them. She didn't draw an easy breath until they crossed the state line. As she relaxed slightly, the tension easing from her neck muscles, a small foot pushed itself against her thigh. Smiling, Abbie glanced down at her sleeping daughter, curled up in the middle of the seat with her head pillowed on Ben's leg.

"She's so tired," Abbie said absently. "I knew she would be, getting up that early this morning. At least we won't have to hear her ask every five minutes, 'How much farther do we have to go?' "

"We did not leave so early because you wanted her to sleep," Ben stated. "You thought MacCrea would come back this morning."

"I wasn't sure. I couldn't take the chance." She paused. "He says he wants her."

"What did you expect?"

"I don't know," she admitted. "I never thought he'd find out."

"What will you do now?"

Abbie shrugged. "Maybe he'll change his mind. Why should he care anyway? He doesn't even know her. He can't possibly love her. Most men would be glad to let someone else take care of their child. They don't want the responsibility — financial or otherwise. Maybe after he has time to think about it, he'll feel that way, too, and forget all that stupid guilt."

"Guilt?" Ben frowned at her. "Over what?"

"He claimed he felt guilty because he wasn't there when she was born and a lot of other nonsense like that. I'd really rather not discuss it, Ben," she insisted impatiently, but the denial was no sooner out of her mouth than she remembered the other things MacCrea had said, specifically that whole argument they'd had over her father and Rachel. It had gnawed at her off and on all night long. "Ben . . . do you think Daddy loved both me and . . . Rachel?"

"Yes."

"But . . ." Abbie was thrown by his matter-of-fact response. "He gave her so much more than I ever got. How can you say that?"

"If you have a horse that is strong and one that is weak, to which one would you give more grain?"

"The weak horse, naturally."

"Correct."

Was he saying that Rachel was weak? Abbie wondered. She had started out with less and therefore received more? She realized that MacCrea had said almost the same thing, but in a different way. Was it possible she had been wrong to resent Rachel all this time?

39

As an airliner rumbled down the runway for takeoff, the thundering of its jet turbines shaking the air, a black limousine drove onto the concrete apron and stopped next to the private jet emblazoned with the logo of Canfield Industries. The driver stepped out and quickly opened the doors for his passengers.

Ross Tibbs climbed out first, then turned to help Rachel. When she placed her hand in his, his fingers closed warmly around it. He made no attempt to conceal the adoration in his look, and she felt a little tingle of excitement that he would show his feelings so openly with Lane standing only a few feet away. It was so reckless and daring of him that, even while it made her afraid, it also made her glad.

"What did I tell you, darling? Perfect flying weather," Lane declared, coming around from the other side of the long car to join her, followed by MacCrea. "Just look at that blue sky. And the pilot promised it's going to be like this all the way to Houston."

"I'm glad." But she almost wished it would cloud up and rain so she would have an excuse to stay behind — and steal a few more moments with Ross.

"Rachel is a white-knuckle flyer, I'm afraid," Lane said, smiling at her with an amused tolerance that she recognized too well. From the very beginning of their relationship, his attitude toward her had always been vaguely patronizing. Over the last few years, she'd grown tired of it.

"That's hardly true anymore, Lane." But she knew she was wasting her breath. He simply refused to recognize that she had matured into a sophisticated, worldly woman. He continued to play a fatherly role — that is, when he condescended to spend any of his precious time with her at all.

"I'm not the best of passengers either," Ross said, "so you're not alone in that, Rachel."

"I am not afraid of flying." If *he* started treating her like a child who needed her fears dispelled, Rachel swore she'd scream.

"In that case, if we ever fly anywhere together, you can hold my hand." As Ross gave her fingers a little squeeze, Rachel suddenly realized that he still held her hand. She darted a quick look at Lane to see if he had noticed, but it was MacCrea, standing slightly behind him, who appeared to be watching them with speculative interest. Rachel wondered how much he knew — or guessed.

Before Rachel could respond to Ross's comment, the pilot joined them. "All your luggage is aboard, Mr. Canfield. We can leave whenever you're ready."

"Thanks, Jim. We'll be right there," Lane said as the limousine driver closed the trunk and quietly took up his post by the door.

"I guess we have to leave. Ross, thank you for everything." Rachel pressed her other hand on the one still holding hers, then impulsively kissed him on the cheek. In a way, she didn't care whether Lane thought she was being too familiar or not. There was a little part of her that even hoped he'd be jealous.

"It was all my pleasure. You know that, Rachel." Reluctantly, Ross released her hand.

"You will stay in touch." Hearing the earnest plea in her voice, Rachel tried to cover it. "You know how interested I am in your filly."

"I'll keep you posted on her progress. I promise."

"Ross, let me add my thanks to Rachel's." Lane held out his hand to him. Ross hesitated a fraction of a second, then shook it. "We really appreciate the lift to the airport. I just hope it wasn't too much of an inconvenience for you."

"Not at all."

"If you're ever in the Houston area, give us a call. You know you're welcome at River Bend anytime."

"I just might take you up on that invitation," Ross declared, his glance skipping briefly to her. "It's been a long time since I visited my old stomping grounds."

After MacCrea had added his good-bye to the others, there was no more reason to linger. As she walked with Lane to the steps of the plane, Rachel felt torn. She waved to Ross one last time from the doorway of the private jet, then entered the plush cabin and took her usual seat. Once she had her belt fastened, she leaned back in the velour-covered seat and sighed wistfully.

"Something wrong, dear?" Lane inquired.

"No, nothing," she denied quickly, then saw he wasn't even looking at her. Already his briefcase was open on the tabletop in front of him and a sheaf of documents was in his hands. "I'm just tired, that's all. The party broke up so late last night . . ." She paused, suddenly noticing the way MacCrea was watching her. "I don't know whether I should even talk to you, MacCrea. You never did come back last night."

"I was detained."

"I don't suppose I need to ask by whom?" The mere recollection of that whole scene with Abbie last night made Rachel prickle with anger. God, how she hated, loathed, and despised that woman.

"No, you don't."

"What did you two talk about?"

"That, Rachel — to put it as politely as I know how — is none of your damned business." He wasn't in any mood to parry her questions about Abbie with nonanswers.

"MacCrea, you wouldn't be so foolish as to have gotten involved with her again? After the way she and that little brat of hers behaved last night, I don't —"

"Leave Eden out of it, Rachel," he warned.

She drew back slightly, her eyes widening at his threatening tone. "I never realized you were so sensitive about such things." Her curiosity was piqued.

Irritated with himself for arousing it, MacCrea pushed out of his seat. "Maybe I just don't like the way you and Abbie drag an innocent child into your petty feud. Excuse me. I think I'll sit in the back. I'm not exactly good company this morning." He moved to one of the rear seats in the cabin and strapped himself in.

Within minutes the private jet was airborne and streaking eastward. For a time, MacCrea stared out the window, watching the gray track of a highway below. Somewhere down there on one of those roads was Abbie . . . with his daughter. *His* daughter. He had a child. She was a part of him, his own flesh and blood.

He recalled the first time he saw her, a midget-sized blue-eyed beauty seeking help to find her lost mommy. At the time he'd wondered why she had picked him out of that whole crowd of people. But it was only right since he was her father. Instinctively she must have been drawn to him. Abbie could deny it all she wanted, but there was a bond between them.

But what was he going to do about it? What should he do? All night long he'd wrestled with the problem, but he was no closer to solving it than he had been twelve hours ago when he'd left Abbie's motel room.

"If you have any feelings for her at all, you'll stay away." That was the last thing Abbie had said to him. MacCrea wondered if she was right. If he tried to assert his paternal rights, what would that do to Eden? How much would that hurt her? She was a smart little kid, but there was only so much a five-year-old could understand.

But how could he walk away? He couldn't turn back the clock and forget last night had happened. He couldn't pretend Eden didn't exist. He lifted his gaze to the stretch of blue Texas sky above the horizon — a sky almost as blue as her eyes. He pictured her in his mind: the mischievous glint in her blue eyes, the rosy-cheeked innocence of her smile, and the bobbing swing of her dark ponytail. Damn, but she was a cute little mite, MacCrea thought. Almost immediately he could see Abbie's face next to Eden's, the same blue eyes, the same dark hair, but with a look of fearful wariness — the look of a mother willing to fight to keep her child from harm. He couldn't blame Abbie for wanting to protect Eden, but, dammit, what was he supposed to do? She was his daughter, too.

40

In the distance, a Caterpillar continued to growl over the former hayfield, its blade scraping away the thick stubble and taking the top layer of soil with it as the machine carved out the dimensions of the oval training track being built on the site. A quarter-mile away stood the Victorian mansion of River Bend, within easy sight of the track and vice versa.

When she had chosen the site, Abbie knew that Rachel would think she was building it there to antagonize her, but she had chosen that particular parcel of land because it was relatively level, well-drained, and far enough from the creek that it wouldn't flood in heavy rain. The track's proximity to River Bend was purely accidental, whether Rachel wanted to believe that or not.

As the compact car pulled out of the yard with the reporter for one of the major Arabian horse publications behind the wheel, Abbie sighed wearily. "I don't know about you, Ben, but I feel like I've put in a full day. Lord knows she has enough material to write several articles."

"Eden is home. There goes the school bus," Ben said.

"I think I'll go meet her." She started down the lane at a fast walk.

Ever since MacCrea had discovered that Eden was his daughter, Abbie had become overly protective and possessive of Eden, wanting to know where she was and whom she was with every minute. It had been almost ten days since MacCrea had found out about Eden.

As yet, she hadn't seen or heard from him. She wanted desperately to believe it meant he was going to stay away.

Ahead of her, Abbie saw the reporter's car swing to the right-hand side of the lane to make room for an oncoming pickup truck. She didn't recognize the truck, but the pigtailed little girl waving gaily at her from its cab was definitely Eden. As Abbie waved back, she glanced at the driver. She suddenly felt icy-cold all over, as if a blue norther had swept in and chilled the air thirty degrees. She stared at MacCrea as he slowed the truck to a stop. The very thing she had feared the most had happened; MacCrea was here and he had Eden with him.

"Mommy!" Eden poked her head out the cab window. Abbie forced her legs to carry her over to the passenger side of the truck. "Look who came to visit us."

Her throat paralyzed by fear, she couldn't say a thing as she stared past Eden at MacCrea. "Hop in," he said.

With numb fingers, she opened the door and climbed into the cab. Eden scooted into the middle to make room for her and started chattering away like a magpie, but Abbie didn't hear a word she said. She thought she had prepared herself for this eventuality, but now that it was here, she wasn't sure what to do.

"Mommy, aren't you going to open the door?" Eden demanded impatiently. In a daze, Abbie realized the truck had stopped moving. They were parked in front of the house. As she stepped down from the cab, Eden was right on her heels. "Come on, Mommy. I promised MacCrea I'd show him my pony."

Abbie reacted instinctively. "First you have to change out of your school clothes, young lady." She pushed Eden in the direction of the house.

"Aw, Mom." She hung back, digging in her heels in protest.

"You know the rule, Eden." The crunch of gravel warned Abbie of MacCrea's approach as he came around the front of the truck.

"I know," Eden mumbled, then abruptly spun around to gaze earnestly at MacCrea. "It won't take long. I promise. You'll be here when I come back, won't you? You won't leave, will you?"

"No. I'll be here." His low-pitched voice came from a point only a few feet to her left. But Abbie wouldn't turn her head to look at him as Eden broke into a smile and ran for the house.

Abbie stood rigid, the banging of the back door reverberating through her heightened senses like a shock wave. She was afraid to move, afraid she might say or do something rash as she felt Mac-

Crea's attention shift to her. She tried to ignore him, but just knowing he was looking at her made her aware of the wisps of hair that had worked loose from the sleek bun at the nape of her neck during the gallops on Windstorm for the photo session. The high collar of her blouse suddenly felt tight around her throat, the black jacket and gray riding pants too constraining.

The instant he turned away from her, she knew it, the sensation of his scrutiny lifting immediately. "You've made a lot of changes around here. I see the old stone barn is gone."

Turning, Abbie tried to look at the place through his eyes. "We tore it down to make room for the new broodmare barn."

All three of the new structures — the broodmare barn, the stables, and the stud barn — were painted the color of desert sand and trimmed in a dark umber brown. A coat of creosote darkened the wooden fencing around the paddocks, the arena, and the lunging pen. The whole place had a practical, efficient look to it. Abbie knew she had accomplished a great deal. She was proud of it — until she realized that MacCrea was bound to judge it by River Bend's ultra-modern facilities, and there was no way hers could compare to Rachel's.

"You're not interested in all this, MacCrea, so why don't you just tell me why you're here?" she demanded tightly, looking squarely at him for the first time. She was stunned by his haggard appearance, the gauntness in his cheeks and the hollows under his eyes.

"I tried to do it your way, Abbie," he said. "I've stayed away. But it's not going to work. I can't forget she's my daughter, too."

"No." It was no more than a whispered protest — a faint attempt to deny all that he was implying.

"I'm going to be part of her life."

"You can't!"

"Can't I?" His challenging gaze bored into her, then made a lightning skip to a point beyond her as a faint smile touched his mouth. "You just watch me."

Almost simultaneously, Abbie heard the slamming of the back door and the rapid clatter of booted feet on the sidewalk. She swung around, catching sight of Eden running toward them, her pigtails flying. One pantleg of her patched jeans was caught inside her boot top and the other was out.

"That was fast, wasn't it?" Eden declared as she reached MacCrea. Barely slowing down at all, she grabbed his hand and pulled him in the direction of the stable. "Come on. I want you to see Jojo. He's the nicest pony in the whole world. I'd let you ride him, but you're too big for him.

"That's all right. I'd rather watch you." MacCrea smiled.

Belatedly, Eden glanced over her shoulder. "You're coming, too, aren't you, Mommy?"

"Yes." She wasn't about to leave MacCrea alone with Eden.

But she deliberately held herself aloof from them, taking no part in their conversation. She was along strictly to chaperone them and help Eden saddle her thirteen-hands-high, Welsh-Arabian pony. Not by word or deed did she want to imply that this had her approval. And she certainly didn't want to make it a threesome.

Watching and listening to Eden, Abbie found it difficult to ignore how obviously taken her daughter was with MacCrea. She tried to convince herself that it didn't mean anything. Eden liked everybody; she always had. That's all there was to it. There was no special bond between them. Abbie repeatedly told herself to stop looking for something that wasn't there.

"She's quite the little horsewoman, isn't she?" MacCrea remarked, smiling as he watched Eden canter her pony around the arena.

Hearing the note of pride in his voice, Abbie wanted to cry in frustration. He was talking just like a father. "She is a very good rider for her age." To say less would be to deny the same pride she took in Eden's accomplishment.

As Eden circled the arena again, MacCrea shifted to stand closer to her and leaned his arms on the rail. "Just look at her, Abbie," he murmured. "That's a part of us out there — our flesh and blood."

Abbie stared at Eden and saw the dark hair that came from her and the waves in it that came from MacCrea, the blue eyes that were like hers and the crooked little fingers, like MacCrea's. She had refused to look at Eden in that way before. Now she saw that the evidence was irrefutable. Slowly she drew her gaze from Eden and turned to look at MacCrea. She found it difficult to meet the dark intensity of his eyes. At the same time, she couldn't make herself look away.

"We made her, you and I, Abbie." Something in the quality of his voice turned the words into a caress.

Suddenly it became frighteningly easy to imagine herself in his arms again. "Don't . . . say that." She took a step sideways, putting more distance between them. "Don't even think that way."

"You know it's true." He continued to lean against the rail, appearing oblivious to the tension that screamed through her.

She moved to the arena gate. "Eden! That's enough for today. Come say good-bye to Mr. Wilder. He has to leave now."

Kicking her pony into a gallop, Eden rode over to the gate. "Can't he stay just a little bit longer? I wanted you to set up some jumps so I could show him how high JoJo can jump."

"No. It's late." Abbie caught hold of the pony's bridle and led him out of the arena.

"But can't he stay for supper?"

"No." The last thing she needed was to have Dobie find out MacCrea was here. Out of the corner of her eye, she saw MacCrea push away from the fence and wander leisurely toward the gate. "I've already asked him. He can't." She glanced sharply at him, warning him not to dispute her claim.

"Maybe another time, Eden," he said.

"Then you will come see us again?" she asked eagerly.

"You can count on it."

"Mac —" Abbie didn't have a chance to say more.

"As I was about to explain to your mother, I'm moving back here to live." He said it so calmly that, for a split second, the full impact didn't register.

"You can't." Abbie stared at him, horror-struck by the thought.

MacCrea smiled lazily, but the look in his eyes was dead serious. "That's one of the advantages a wildcatter has. He can headquarter his company anywhere he wants. I've decided to move it here. It's time I settled down and found a place to live."

A thousand angry protests came to mind, but Abbie couldn't make a single one of them — not with Eden there. "Do you think that's wise?" she asked tersely.

"Wise for who?" he countered softly, then smiled with infuriating confidence. "I'll be in town for a couple of days looking around. Maybe we'll run into each other."

Abbie was so angry she couldn't even talk. He knew damned well she couldn't let his decision go unchallenged. She'd have to see him and try to talk him out of moving back. Somehow she had to convince him it would be a mistake.

MacCrea said something to Eden and moved away, heading across the yard to his pickup. Abbie watched him climb into the cab of his truck, relieved to see him go, but, at the same time, recognizing that she'd have to see him again.

"How come you didn't tell him good-bye, Mommy?"

"Mac, wait!" She suddenly realized she didn't know where he was staying. But it was too late. The roar of the truck's engine drowned out her call. He didn't hear her, and Abbie wasn't about to run after him.

"How come you called him Mac?" Eden looked at her curiously.

"I . . . don't know." Abbie hadn't realized she had. "I guess because that's his nickname." Yet she had rarely ever shortened his name — except when they were making love.

"I think that's what I'll call him, too," Eden stated decisively.

Abbie wanted to object, but how could she? Every time she turned around she seemed to have dug herself deeper into a hole. Somehow she had to find a way to get out of it.

"Unsaddle JoJo and put him back in his stall, honey. We still have the horses to feed and supper to fix before your daddy comes in from the fields."

The Truesdale building was a two-story brick structure built around the turn of the century. Once it had housed a bank, then later it had been remodeled into a retail shop with rental offices in the rear. When the retail shops had closed, the entire building had been converted into cheap office space. The last renter had moved out this past summer, but no one had bothered to scrape the name of the termite-and-pest-control company off the large plate-glass window in the front of the building.

But from the time Abbie was a child, she had been fascinated by the stately cornices that adorned the old building. Her eye was drawn to them again as she parked her car in the empty space in front of it. Stepping out of her car, she glanced around, looking for Mac-Crea's truck, but it was nowhere in sight, even though it was seven minutes after one. When she had finally reached him through his office that morning, he had agreed to meet her here at one. She walked up the steps to the main entrance and hesitantly tried the door. It swung open at the push of her hand.

She went inside and closed the door, then paused to listen. She could feel the damp chill in the stale air and doubted that anyone bothered to heat the empty old building. A loud clunk came from somewhere near the far end of the long, dark corridor before her.

"Hello? Is anybody here?" The echo of her own voice came bouncing back at her. It was like shouting into an empty oil drum. The bare rooms magnified the sound of the footsteps she heard, giving them a hollow thud. "MacCrea? Is that you?"

"Yeah. I'll be right there." The walls partially muffled his answer, but she was still able to recognize his voice. An instant later, he emerged from a shadowy alcove at the far end of the corridor and walked toward her, brushing at the sleeves of his jacket. "Sorry. I was checking out the plumbing. I didn't hear you come in. The realtor left me the key, so I thought I might as well look around a bit. What do you think of it?"

"I . . . I really don't know." She hadn't come here to discuss that.

"It's a stout old building. It wouldn't take much to whip the place into shape." MacCrea looked around, as if assessing the amount of work that needed to be done. "There's more space here than I need, but it will mean I'll have room to expand later on." Pausing, he turned back to her. "I've signed the papers to buy this building."

"No. You can't move here. I told you this morning that we had to talk. How could you do this?" All her well-thought-out arguments vanished with his announcement. "Why couldn't you have waited until we had a chance to discuss this?"

"There was nothing to discuss as far as I was concerned."

"Why can't you be reasonable? Don't you realize how impossible you're making things? Not just for me, but for Eden and everyone else involved. You can't just come waltzing back here and demand to see her," she raged helplessly.

"Why not? She's my daughter." He shrugged indifferently.

"I should have known that would be your reaction." Abbie swung away from him, outraged by his callous attitude. "You never did care about anybody's feelings except your own. You go around creating all these problems, then let others suffer for them."

Blindly she charged into a vacant room and threw her purse down on one of the wooden crates stacked against the wall. Hearing his footsteps behind her, Abbie stopped and turned to face him.

"I didn't create this problem, Abbie," he stated. "You did when you married Hix and passed our child off as his. I had no part in that decision. Now it's blowing up in your face. That's why you're so upset. You never should have married him."

He was right, and she hated him for it. "I suppose you think I should have married you," she retorted.

"If you had, you wouldn't be in this mess right now."

"No. I'd be in a worse one." She hugged her arms tightly around her middle, trying to hold in check all the violent churning tearing her up inside.

For a long moment, MacCrea said nothing. Then he wandered over to the wooden crates and stared at the lettering stenciled on the

sides. "That last time we were together, after that Christmas party
. . . that's when it happened, wasn't it? That's when you got pregnant."

"Yes." She was abrupt with him, impatient that he should even
bother to talk about such a minor detail.

"I've thought a lot about that night lately." Turning, he half sat
and half leaned against the stacked crates.

"Have you?"

"You're bound to remember it, too."

"I remember how it ended," she snapped defensively. Then a hor-
rible thought occurred to her. "Who have you told about Eden? Does
Rachel know?"

"I haven't told anyone." Reaching out, he caught hold of her hand
and pulled her over to stand closer to him. "That's one thing I never
have understood, Abbie. What the hell did Rachel ever have to do
with us? What did she have to do with the way I felt about you —
or the way you felt about me?"

"If you don't know by now, you'll never understand." She strained
to twist her wrist free of his grip, but he merely increased the pressure.

"I want to know," he insisted. "Explain to me what she had to do
with *us*."

"I can't!" All that didn't seem important to her anymore.

"Let me ask you a question. If she had a horse you wanted, would
you buy it from her?"

"What difference does it make? She'd never sell it to me." Abbie
didn't know why she was even letting herself get involved in this
senseless discussion.

"For the sake of argument, assume she would. Would you buy the
horse?"

"If I wanted it, yes."

"Even though you hate her and don't want anything to do with
her?" MacCrea challenged.

"I don't hate her." The instant the words came out of her mouth,
Abbie was surprised by them — surprised because she realized they
were true. She didn't know when or how it happened, but she didn't
hate Rachel anymore. "Besides, buying a horse from her, that's business. It has nothing to do with personal feelings."

"My dealings with her were — and still are — strictly business.
How many times did I try to explain that to you? But you wouldn't
listen to me. Why, Abbie? Why?"

"I don't know." She tried to give him an answer that made sense. "Maybe I couldn't then. Maybe I was too young — and too ready to believe the worst. So many things happened that year, I —" Realizing there was no way to pick up all the scattered pieces of the past, she pulled away from him. "What difference does it make now, MacCrea?" she said. "It's over."

He was on his feet and his hands were on her waist, turning her to face him before she was even aware he had moved. "It doesn't have to be, Abbie."

When she looked into his eyes, she could almost believe him. As she watched his mustached mouth descend, she made no attempt to avoid it. She let it settle onto her lips, its gentle pressure at once warm and evocative, stirring up feelings she thought she'd buried years ago. It had been too long since she'd known such tender passion, or felt the gentle strength of his caressing hands moving over her body, reminding her of the pleasures she'd once known in his arms. She pressed against him, aching with the need to love this man that had gone too long unfulfilled, and once she had loved him so very, very much.

"I want you, Abbie." He held her tightly, rubbing his mouth near her earlobe, his mustache catching loose strands of her hair. "I've never stopped wanting you, nor loving you, not once in all these years. And you still feel the same way about me. You can't deny it. Nothing's changed, Abbie. Not one damned thing."

But that wasn't true. "You're wrong." Abbie pushed back from him. "Things have changed, MacCrea. I'm not the same woman I was then, and you're not the same man. We've changed. I've grown up. I think differently and feel differently about things now. You don't know me. You don't know what I'm like now — what I want or what I need."

"No? I'll bet I could make some damned good guesses," he mocked. "Take your hair, for instance. Every time I've seen you lately, you've got it pulled back in this prim little bun. I'll bet you never wear it loose anymore, all soft against your neck." He trailed his fingers down the taut cord in her neck, stopping when he reached the high collar of her blouse. "And you wear a lot of turtlenecks and button your blouses all the way up to your throat. Your jackets are tailored like a man's. I bet if I looked in your closet I wouldn't find a single pretty dress that shows off your figure."

"You're wrong. I have several."

"New ones?"

"That's beside the point."

"Is it? You're a passionate woman, Abbie. But you've locked it all inside, beneath those high collars and that prim bun. You don't love that farmer husband of yours. You never have."

"What are you suggesting?" Abbie demanded. "That I leave him?" But she could tell by his expression that that was precisely what he meant. "And after that, what am I supposed to do? Come back to you?"

"Yes, dammit." He scowled impatiently, then tried to wipe it away. "Can't you see it would solve everything? The three of us would be together, you, me, and Eden, the way it should have been."

Abbie stared at him for several seconds, then pulled away from him and walked to the center of the empty room, unable to hold back the bitter laugh that rolled from her throat. "Why? Because you want your daughter?"

"Is it so damned impossible to believe that I might want you both?"

"No, it isn't impossible. Look, maybe you have the right to see your daughter and get to know her —"

"You're damned right I do."

"You also hold the power to force this whole situation out into the open. If I agree to let you see Eden, will you give me your word that you won't let on that she's your daughter — at least not for a while?"

"And if I gave you my word, would you believe me?" he asked, arching an eyebrow skeptically.

"I'd have to."

"That sounds remarkably like trust."

"You'd also have to let me choose the time and place to meet her." Unconsciously she held her breath as MacCrea studied her thoughtfully.

His answer was a long time coming. "Yes."

"Good." Abbie breathed easier, for the first time believing there was hope. "I'll be in touch. I promise."

"Abbie." He caught up with her in the corridor. "Before you go, there's one other thing. When I saw you in Phoenix that first time, long before I found out Eden was my daughter, it was you I wanted. Think about that. And think about this." He kissed her long and deep, not letting her go until she was kissing him back.

❖ 41 ❖

As Rachel passed the study, she noticed the door was ajar. She stepped back and pushed it the rest of the way open, but there was no one in the walnut-paneled room. Hearing the rustle of a starched uniform, she turned from the door just as one of the maids came around the corner of the back hallway.

"Maria, have you seen Mr. Tibbs?"

"Yes, ma'am. He's in the front parlor."

"Thank you." Quickening her steps, Rachel walked swiftly toward the high-ceilinged foyer. Intent on the double doors that led to the parlor, she almost walked right by the small boy standing by the front door, struggling with the zipper of his winter jacket. She stopped short of the double doors and swung back to face her son. "Where are you going, Alex?"

He darted an anxious glance at her, then lowered his chin, burying it in the collar of his jacket. "Outside," he mumbled, the mop of brown hair shielding his pale blue eyes from her sight.

"Did Mrs. Weldon say you could?" Rachel frowned, wishing he'd stop acting as if she were going to hit him. She'd never struck him in her life.

He bobbed his head up and down in an affirmative reply. "She said I could take the truck Uncle MacCrea gave me and play with it outside."

She glanced at the large toy pickup truck with oversized,

"monster" wheels sitting on the floor near his feet. "You be careful and don't break it."

"Yes, ma'am."

"Can't you call me Mommy or Mother — something other than ma'am all the time?" Rachel insisted impatiently. "I know Mrs. Weldon is trying to teach you to be polite, but sometimes, Alex, you carry it too far."

"Yes, ma'am," he mumbled again.

Seeing it, Rachel felt absolutely helpless. She tried to be a good mother to her son, but she just couldn't seem to reach him. There were times when she wondered whether this timid, sensitive child belonged to her. It was so irritating to know that Lane could do no wrong in Alex's eyes, and she could do nothing right. Sometimes she even wondered why she tried. Neither of them cared about her — not really.

As Alex continued to fumble with the zipper, Rachel walked over to him. "Let me help you with that."

At first he pulled away, but Rachel persisted. She arranged his collar so it would lay smooth, then paused, with her hands on his shoulders.

"There you go." She smiled at him. When he smiled hesitantly back at her, she had the urge to give him a quick hug. As she started to pull him toward her, he hung back. Suddenly it all felt awkward and forced. Rachel straightened abruptly, unable to endure his rejection of her. "You can go outside and play with your truck now."

Still smarting from his rebuff, Rachel turned and walked stiffly to the double doors. As she entered the parlor, she forgot all about Ross being there. She gasped in surprise when her wrist was seized and she was spun halfway around.

"There's no escape, blue eyes," Ross declared, smiling as he locked his arms behind her back. "This time I've got you."

"Ross, you're —" But he silenced her protest in the most effective and demanding way, kissing her with an ardor that melted all her previous stiffness. Sighing contentedly, she relaxed against him and nestled her head on his shoulder. "I've missed you," she whispered.

At almost the same instant, she heard a faint noise near the doorway. Too late she remembered the door was still open. Maria, Mrs. Weldon — anybody could have seen her kissing Ross. Guiltily she pushed away from him and turned, half expecting to see one of the maids retreating from the doorway. Instead she saw her son, poised uncertainly on the threshold.

"Alex, I thought you were going outside. What are you doing here? What do you want?" she demanded sharply.

He backed up a step, his gaze falling under her glare. "I thought . . . maybe you'd want to come outside and watch me play with my new truck."

"No!" She knew she answered too angrily, but she couldn't help it. "Not now. I'm busy." Alex continued to stare at both of them as he backed up farther still.

"Maybe another time, sport," Ross inserted.

Rachel couldn't stand the way the child looked at her. Those pale blue eyes, the color of washed-out denim, seemed filled with hurt and condemnation. "Alex, please. Just go outside and play."

He took another step backward, then turned and ran for the front door. Rachel stood motionless, waiting until she heard the door shut and the clump of his boots on the porch outside; then, only then, did she hurry over and close the double doors to the parlor. She leaned weakly against them and half turned to look at Ross, a wild fluttering in her throat.

"You shouldn't have been so hard on the kid," Ross said gently.

"You don't understand. He doesn't like me. What if he tells Lane?" Agitated, she moved away from the doors, clasping her hands tightly together.

"What can he tell him?" Ross stopped her and loosened her clenched hands, holding them in his own.

"I can't help it." She sighed, feeling frustrated and confused. "You don't know how glad I am that you're here, but at the same time, I'm worried that Lane might find out about us."

He lifted her right hand to his mouth and pressed his lips into the center of her palm. "Would it be so terrible if he found out about us, Rachel? After all, I love you and you love me."

"I want to be with you, darling. You have to believe that. But it isn't as simple as you make it sound. If I walked out that door with you, I'd lose everything: my home, River Bend, Sirocco, and —" She had been about to say, "and all the rest of the horses."

But Ross broke in, "I know . . . your son."

"Yes, Alex, too." She felt guilty that she hadn't even considered him. But she'd always regarded him as Lane's son. River Bend, the horses — they were hers. But Lane would never let her have them; she was certain of that. "Darling, you know all you have to do is call and I'll meet you whenever and wherever I can. We love each other. Isn't that what counts?"

"I'm just greedy, I guess. I want you all the time."

"Silly, you have me all the time. I'm always thinking about you — except when I'm with Sirocco and my other horses," she teased.

Ross chuckled. "I never dreamed I'd have a stallion for a rival."

"Now you know." She laughed softly, relieved that Ross was slowly beginning to accept the idea that she could never divorce Lane. Naturally he didn't like it. She didn't either. But it was the only way things could be.

Looking back, she understood so well what Dean had gone through. This land, this home had been in his family for generations. How could he risk losing it in a divorce settlement? He had been deeply in love with her mother. Two people didn't have to be married to be happy. In time, Rachel was certain she could convince Ross that this arrangement was best. If he truly loved her, he'd accept it and not expect her to give up everything she'd ever dreamed of having.

"Do you have any idea how frustrating it is to sleep under the same roof with you and not in the same bed?" Ross drew her back into the circle of his arms and began nuzzling the little hollow behind her ear. "Let's go up to my room, lock the door, and make love the rest of the afternoon."

"You know we can't do that." Deftly she eluded his attempt to draw her into another embrace and stepped free of him. "Lane and MacCrea might come back anytime now."

"I've been here three days and all we've managed to do is steal a few kisses. Rachel —"

"I think we'd better talk about something else." She walked over to the front window and lifted the sheer curtain aside to gaze outside. There was no sign of Alex anywhere in the front lawn. A movement in her side vision drew her glance to the adjoining field west of the house. The dark ring of the oval track stood out sharply against the tan stubble of the former hayfield.

"Any suggestions?"

She ignored the faint edge to his voice. "Last night, when you were talking to MacCrea after dinner, did he give any reason why he suddenly decided to move back here?"

"No. Do you know?"

"I have the feeling he's gotten himself involved with Abbie again," Rachel said tightly, aware that he'd announced his decision shortly after he'd disappeared with Abbie that night Sirocco had won the championship. "He's a fool to get mixed up with her again."

"Speaking of Abbie, did you see the article on her in the March issue of the Arabian horse magazine?" With a wave of his hand, Ross indicated the magazine on the coffee table, the one with the color photo of Sirocco on its cover.

"This one?" Rachel picked it up, frowning in surprise. "I read the piece they wrote about Sirocco, but I haven't had time to look through the rest of it."

"I read it last night — while I was trying to fall asleep." His pointed remark indicated she was the cause of his insomnia as he took the magazine from her and flipped through the pages. After locating the article, he handed it back to her. "She's going to get a lot of mileage out of her decision to race her stallion. There are some great pictures of her training track under construction. 'Abbie's folly': isn't that what you call it?"

"Yes," she muttered absently as she quickly began skimming the article. Between the photos and the text, it was five pages long, a full page more than the cover story on Sirocco.

"You have to admit it's a good piece," Ross said when she'd finished it.

Rachel flipped back to the beginning and read it through again, her ire growing with each infuriating word. "They make that old Polack sound like some sort of a guru. And did you see this quote of hers?" Rachel read it aloud: " ' "Racing will have to play a major role in the Arabian horse scene in America the same as it does in Russia, Poland, and Egypt. It's part of Nature's selection process, the survival of the fittest. Races are won by the strong and the swift. Here, in the United States, we put too much emphasis on the beauty of the Arabian horse," claims Ms. Hix. "Too many of our recent national champions have had serious conformation faults — serious enough that they would automatically be eliminated as racing prospects by any knowledgeable horse trainer. Yet our judging system has proclaimed these stallions to be the best we have. If they are the best, then I'm afraid we're in serious trouble." ' End of quote."

"She's only saying publicly what a lot of people in the business have been saying privately for years."

"Is that so?" Rachel angrily tossed the magazine onto the coffee table. "You are aware that she's referring to Sirocco in this article. She just doesn't have enough nerve to use his name. She can't stand it that her stallion lost to mine. Now she's doing everything she can to make Sirocco look inferior. I'd love to make her eat those words."

"Unfortunately, that's not likely to happen."

"Why isn't it?" she demanded, resenting his implication that Sirocco couldn't beat Abbie's stallion.

"Well, because . . . you're not going to be racing Sirocco. You've got the Nationals to get ready for. Besides, you don't risk injuring a valuable stallion like that on the racetrack."

"I suppose you think he'll break down, too."

"I didn't say anything of the kind." Ross raised his hands in a gesture of surrender. "Why are we arguing about this? You aren't going to race him, so —"

"Who says I'm not?" she retorted.

Totally bewildered, Ross sat down on the velvet cushions of the antique sofa. "I thought you did."

"Maybe I've changed my mind. If I put Sirocco in training, I'd get twice the publicity she would. Finding a trainer is no problem. I can hire the best in the country."

"You're not serious." He frowned.

"Why not? Sirocco's grandsires raced in Egypt . . . and won." The more she thought about it, the more determined she became. "She said something in the article about entering her stallion in the Liberty Classic at Delaware Park the Fourth of July, didn't she?" She reached for the magazine again.

"I think so."

"Sirocco's going to be in that race, too." She scanned the article again, then underlined the name, date, and place of the race.

"He's your horse, Rachel, but . . . are you sure you know what you're doing?"

"I know exactly what I'm doing. It's going to work out perfectly — in so many ways. Don't you see, Ross? Not only will I get tons of publicity out of this for Sirocco, but it will also give us a chance to meet somewhere away from here — away from all the people who know us. I'll have to send Sirocco somewhere to be trained. And he'll have to run in a couple races before the Liberty Classic. Lane won't think a thing about it if I fly there every other week or so. We can be together — alone — the way we were in Scottsdale."

"You don't have to say any more. I'm sold."

Rachel stared at the color photograph of Abbie. "I'd give anything to see the look on her face when she finds out." She laughed deep in her throat, relishing the thought.

*   *   *

A warm breeze, heavy with moisture from the Gulf, lifted Windstorm's silvery mane and sent it rippling back across Abbie's hands as she rode the stallion across the field, holding him to a trot. With the afternoon sun beating down out of a pastel sky, the heavy fisherman's sweater provided all the warmth she needed. It was one of those rare, fine days East Texas natives bragged about to their friends and relatives in the North, still shivering in March from the bitter chill of winter.

Slowing the stallion to a walk, Abbie started him around the training track, moving in a clockwise direction. Eden quickly joined her, the pony traveling at a jog-trot to keep pace with Windstorm's long strides. "If they had races for ponies, JoJo would win for sure, wouldn't he?"

Accustomed to her daughter's nonstop chatter and endless questions, Abbie let them wash over her, answering when it was necessary and nodding absently when it wasn't. The afternoon was too beautiful to let anything irritate her, least of all Eden's company.

As they rounded the first turn and started down the backstretch, Eden grew impatient with the slow pace Abbie set and cantered her pony ahead. Watching her, Abbie smiled. Eden always wanted to come with her when she exercised Windstorm, but invariably she grew tired of riding around the track and looked for something more challenging to do — like exploring the wooded creek bottom or stacking the leftover boards from the track rail in a pile for her pony to jump.

Somewhere a horse whinnied shrilly. Abbie glanced at the group of yearlings that crowded close to the white fence of the adjoining pasture at River Bend. The twin turrets of the Victorian-style mansion drew her attention, the peaks of their cone-shaped roofs poking into the pale blue sky.

"Hey!" Eden's sudden, sharp call snapped her attention back to the track. "What are you doing? Who said you could play here?"

Twenty yards ahead, Eden had stopped her pony and turned it crosswise on the track, blocking the trespasser from Abbie's view. Abbie dug a heel into Windstorm's side and the stallion bounded forward, quickly covering the short distance.

Before she reached her daughter, Abbie spied the young boy, Eden's age, with a toy truck clutched in his arms. The boy backed up quickly as if afraid she was going to run him down as she reined Windstorm to a halt beside Eden's pony. His eyes were saucer-round as he apprehensively glanced from Abbie to Eden and back, then darted a quick look over his shoulder as if gauging the distance to the track's outer rail and his chances of making it.

"What's he doing here, Mommy?" Eden demanded with proprietorial outrage.

"I . . ." The boy's mouth worked convulsively as he tried to get an answer out. "I was . . . just playing in the dirt with . . . my new truck. I didn't hurt anything."

Feeling sorry for him, Abbie smiled gently. "Of course you didn't. You just scared us. We didn't know you were here." But the boy didn't look altogether sure that they could possibly be as scared as he was. "What's your name?"

"Alex," he said reluctantly, backing up another step.

Abbie unconsciously lifted her head and glanced toward River Bend. Rachel's son was named Alex. Turning back, she studied him thoughtfully. Except for his light blue eyes, she could find little resemblance to Rachel. Yet he had to be her son.

"You live at River Bend, don't you?"

He bobbed his head in hesitant affirmation, then qualified his answer. "Sometimes."

Abbie vaguely recalled hearing that, even though Rachel spent a great deal of her time here, she sent her son to a private school in Houston during the week. "Does your mother know you came over here to play?"

"No." He stared at the ground. "She doesn't care. She doesn't care about anything I do." The mumbled answer carried with it a jumble of self-pity and resentment that caught Abbie by surprise.

"Oh, I'm sure she cares a lot," Abbie insisted, but Alex just shook his head in silent denial, forcing Abbie to consider how much more time Rachel spent at River Bend with her horses than she did in Houston with her son. "I'm glad to meet you, Alex. My name's Abbie and this is my daughter, Eden."

"How come that truck has such big wheels? It looks funny," Eden declared, frowning curiously at the truck he held.

"It's supposed to. That way it can go anywhere and run over anything. And it's fast, too. Faster than any horse," he retorted, eyeing her pony.

"That can't be faster than JoJo," Eden scoffed. "It's just a toy."

"Well, if it was real, it would be."

"Where'd you get it?"

"It was a present."

"Can I see it?" Kicking free of the stirrups, Eden jumped off her pony and walked over to look at his toy.

Abbie started to call her back, recognizing that Rachel would be upset if she knew Alex was here. Then she asked herself what harm it would do if Alex stayed a little while. Eden would certainly enjoy playing with someone her own age, and Alex probably would, too. Just because she and Rachel had had their differences in the past, there was no reason to drag the children into it.

When Abbie suggested that the two of them play in the track's infield, Eden blithely agreed and bossily shepherded Alex into it, leading the pony in tow. It never occurred to Eden that Alex might not want to play with her. Once again Abbie started the stallion around the track, this time at a rocking canter.

As Abbie cantered Windstorm past the first furlong pole, she noticed the white Mercedes driving slowly along the country road that ran past the field. She knew of only one car like it in the area, and it belonged to the Canfields.

Instinctively she checked Windstorm's stride and turned in the saddle to glance at the boy and girl playing in the infield, making mountains out of the clods of dirt for the toy truck to climb. She suddenly realized that she had no idea how long Alex had been playing here before she and Eden arrived. Someone might have discovered he was gone and come out to look for him. Why hadn't she obeyed that first impulse and sent him home? Rachel would be furious when she found him here.

As the Mercedes rolled to a stop, the trailing plume of dust ran over it, enveloping the vehicle in a hazy cloud. Abbie reined the stallion in and swung him back toward the infield. She started to yell to Alex to run for home, then she saw how flat and open the stretch of ground between the track and the white-fenced boundary or River Bend was. He'd never be able to cross it without being seen.

The settling cloud of dust partially obscured the man who climbed out of the passenger side of the car. Then, strangely, the Mercedes pulled away, leaving him behind. Abbie recognized that long, easy stride that had all the grace of a mountain lion. She felt a new tension race through her.

Unconsciously she tightened her grip on the reins and Windstorm sidestepped nervously beneath her, his ears flicking back and forth as his attention shifted from her to the man vaulting the fence and starting across the field toward them. As MacCrea approached the track, Abbie observed how rested he looked, compared to the last time she'd seen him. His handsome features now emanated strength instead of tiredness.

"Hello." He stopped on the opposite side of the track rail, his hands pushed negligently into the pockets of his leather jacket.

As she looked down at him from astride the stallion, she found the height advantage unsettling. She was too used to looking up at him. She swung out of the saddle and stepped onto the dirt track, gathering together the loose reins to avoid looking at him. "You were with Lane?"

"Yes, we had some business to finalize. You obviously meant it when you told Rachel you intended to race your horse." His glance made a cursory survey of the completed track.

"Yes."

MacCrea ducked under the rail and absently stroked the stallion's warm neck. "Looks like he's coming along all right."

"He is." She was conscious that his attention never really left her, not even when he seemed to direct it elsewhere.

"I got the picture of Eden you sent me."

Abbie was relieved that he'd finally mentioned Eden. She was tired of talking around the reason he was here. At the same time, she didn't want to be the one to introduce Eden into the conversation. "It's a school picture. I thought you might like to have one." She had hoped it might placate him a little and keep him from demanding to see Eden too often.

"Where is she?"

"Over there, playing." Abbie nodded her head in the direction of the infield.

A frown flickered across his face. "Who's the boy with her? That can't be Alex."

"I know I should have sent him home, but I didn't think it would hurt anything if they played together a little while." She turned as Alex hesitantly petted the pony's nose.

"I'll be damned," MacCrea swore softly. "Now I've seen everything."

Stung by the amused disbelief in his voice, Abbie reacted angrily, regarding it as another dig against her. "And just what does that mean?"

"Alex. He's always been afraid of horses. Now look at him."

"Alex is probably like a lot of boys," Abbie guessed. "He doesn't want to admit to a girl that he's scared. It would be too embarrassing."

"You're probably right."

Just then Eden saw MacCrea and let out a squeal of delight. "Mac!" She ran across the infield, pulling the pony along by its reins. Alex lagged behind, steering wide of the animal's hindquarters. Intent on the children, Abbie wasn't aware MacCrea had moved away from her until she saw him walking across the track to greet Eden. She led Windstorm over to them, reaching them as MacCrea swung Eden into the air and stood her on the top rail. "How did you get here?" Eden looked around for his company pickup.

"Magic." He winked.

Eden eyed him skeptically, then turned to Abbie. "Mommy, how'd he get here?"

"He walked."

"I knew it wasn't magic." She directed a sternly reproving look at MacCrea, then giggled. "You're silly."

"So are you." He tweaked her nose.

"No, I'm not." She jumped down from the rail and grabbed his hand. "I want you to meet my friend. He's got a truck and the wheels are bigger than it is. Wait until you see it." Turning, Eden waved at Alex, motioning for him to join them. "Come show him your truck."

But Alex hung back. "Alex knows I've already seen his truck," MacCrea said.

"When?" Eden demanded in surprise, then frowned. "Do you know Alex?"

"I sure do." He smiled.

"Do I have to go home now?" Alex raised his head, reluctance in every line of his face.

MacCrea glanced briefly at Abbie. She had the impression that he, too, was unwilling to break this up. "Your father's home. He will be wondering where you are. And your mother's probably missed you, too."

"No, she hasn't," Alex said, again with a bitter resentment that Abbie recognized too well. He added something else that sounded a lot like "She never misses me," but Abbie couldn't be sure.

"Just the same, we probably should leave," MacCrea said quietly, then cast a sidelong glance at Abbie. "You understand?"

"Of course." If they did start looking for Alex, she knew it was better that they didn't find him here.

"Does he have to go now? Can't he stay a little longer?" Eden pleaded in protest. "I wanted to take him to the slough by the creek. He doesn't think there's any alligators in it and I wanted to show him. Please."

"Maybe another time, Eden." He laid a hand on top of her head and gave it a little push down.

Eden grimaced at the refusal, then pursued the carrot MacCrea had offered. "Maybe you can come over tomorrow, Alex, and we can go then. We'll be here, won't we, Mommy?"

"Yes," Abbie admitted uneasily, realizing she was going to have to have a talk with her daughter. She dreaded trying to explain to Eden why Alex's parents might not want him playing with her. How could she make Eden understand, when she no longer understood it herself? Yet once she had hated Rachel with all the venom of a Texas rattler. Her hatred for Rachel was gone, but she feared their long-standing feud was about to start poisoning their children, and she didn't know how to stop it.

"Will you come, Alex?" Eden persisted.

"I don't know if I can." The boy shuffled his feet uncomfortably and stole a look at MacCrea.

"Please try," Eden wheedled. "We'll have lots of fun."

But Alex was obviously unwilling to commit himself as he chewed on his lower lip. MacCrea stepped into the void. "Come on, sport. We'd better go."

Stymied by Alex, Eden turned her persuasive efforts on MacCrea. "You'll come see us again, won't you?"

"Of course. Real soon," he promised, then glanced at Abbie, knowing it was up to her to set the time and place. "You know how to reach me."

She assumed it was through his Richmond office, but she simply nodded in affirmation rather than ask.

As they crossed the field, Alex walked with his head down and the truck tucked under his arm. The closer they got to the fence, the slower he walked, practically dragging his feet and forcing MacCrea to shorten his stride even more.

"You're very quiet," MacCrea remarked. It was something of an understatement. Alex hadn't said one word.

Beyond the dark trunks of the shade trees in the lawn, the large Victorian manor house glistened whitely in the sunlight. Alex eyed their destination with a look that was filled with misgivings. As his glance dropped away from the wide veranda with all its fancy gingerbread trim, he sighed heavily.

"Mother is gonna be mad at me 'cause I was over there." The corners of his mouth were turned down as far as they could go.

"What makes you say that?" MacCrea frowned sharply.

" 'Cause I don't think she likes that lady."

"How do you know?"

"Sometimes when she sees her riding her white horse over there, her mouth gets all tight and her eyes look mean. And she . . . she says things about her."

MacCrea wondered how many more people besides himself were going to pay the price for Abbie and Rachel's bitter rivalry before it was over. For the time being at least, Abbie appeared to be unwilling to involve the children in it. But he knew her too well. All it would take was one push from Rachel and she'd shove back. Abbie wasn't the kind to turn the other cheek. She always struck back, and, dammit, he didn't want Eden getting caught in the crossfire.

"Are you going to tell her where I was?"

It was a full second before Alex's anxious voice registered. MacCrea paused a second longer, then smiled thinly. "Not if you don't want me to."

A smile of gratitude and relief broke across the sensitive planes of the boy's face. MacCrea wondered briefly whether he was right to encourage him, then decided it couldn't be any more wrong than what Rachel and Abbie were doing.

As they reached the fence, MacCrea heard Rachel calling for Alex. Then Lane's voice joined in. "Sounds like they're looking for you, sport." He picked up Alex under the arms and hoisted him over the fence. The search seemed to be concentrated in the backyard and over by the barns. "Better hurry. I think your father is in the back."

Alex broke into a run, darting between the young trees planted several years ago to replace the ones destroyed in the fire. As the boy angled for the rear of the house, MacCrea followed, taking a straighter route.

"Alex!" Lane called, his back turned to them.

"Here I am, Daddy!" Alex raced past the gazebo with its lacy white latticework, heading straight for his silver-haired father.

Turning, Lane saw him and called over his shoulder. "Rachel! I've found him. He's over here!" As he crouched down on one knee to greet Alex, Rachel hurried from the direction of the barns with Ross behind her. "We've been looking all over for you, Alex. Didn't you hear us calling?"

"I . . . I came as fast as I could." Breathless from running and uncertain of his reception, Alex moved hesitantly within reach of Lane's hands, then let himself be drawn closer when Rachel approached them.

"Alex! Lane, is he hurt? What happened?"

"He's fine," Lane assured her.

"How could you run off like that, Alex?" Rachel demanded, her anxiety turning to anger now that he was found. "Where have you been?"

Alex avoided her accusing look. "Playing . . . with my truck," he answered.

"Yes, but where? We've been looking everywhere for you," she stated impatiently. Alex darted a fearful glance at MacCrea, then clamped his mouth tightly shut. "You had us all so worried, Alex. I thought you were outside playing in the yard, but when your father came home and we couldn't find you . . . I was afraid you were hurt or something — especially when you didn't come when we called."

"I'm sorry." He edged closer to Lane. MacCrea noticed the way Rachel's lips thinned. The door shut on the concern that had been in her expression. A coolness replaced it.

"Now that your father's home I'm sure you won't be running off to your secret place to play." She straightened and turned to Ross. "I think I'll go to the barn and talk to Mr. Woodall about my plans for Sirocco. Would you like to come along?"

"Sure."

As the pair set off together, Lane watched them, expressionless except for the pained look in his eyes. With difficulty he pushed to his feet, fighting the stiffness in his aging joints. "Come on, son." He took Alex by the hand. "Let's go in the house and get you cleaned up. It looks like you've been grubbing in the dirt."

MacCrea swung alongside as they headed for the house.

❖ ⬧ 42 ⬧ ❖

A roar came from the crowd in the racing stands, cheering on the horses running for the wire, as a groom led the gleaming white stallion past the stalls to the paddock area. Abbie walked alongside, the blue-on-blue jacquard silk of her dress and the silk scarf tied around the band of her wide-brimmed hat matching Windstorm's racing colors.

Her nerves were as tautly drawn as piano wire, and the palms of her hands were damp with perspiration. She was certain that she was more nervous than Alex had been last week when Eden had persuaded him to ride double with her on JoJo. Afterward Alex had said to her, "Maybe if I learned to ride, my mother would like me better." His comment had seemed an ironic echo of the past. Long ago, Abbie had turned to horses as well, in hopes of gaining her father's approval.

Alex had become a regular visitor, sneaking over to play with Eden whenever he could. Sometimes Abbie wondered whether she was right to let him come, but Eden needed a playmate her own age as much as Alex did, and his timidness balanced her boldness, each of them learning something from the other. But . . . there was Rachel to consider.

There was always Rachel, Abbie reminded herself, suddenly restless and agitated. Why was she letting thoughts about Rachel spoil a dazzling, beautiful June day? Windstorm was running in the next race. Why wasn't she enjoying the excitement instead of getting herself all worked up over Rachel?

But Abbie knew the answer to that one. This morning she'd learned from a fellow Arabian horse owner that Rachel's stallion, Sirocco, had won his race yesterday — by three lengths. In two and a half weeks, her stallion would be racing against Windstorm in the Liberty Classic, providing Windstorm finished well in this prep race today. He has to, Abbie thought, determined that he would not only win this race, but the Liberty Classic as well — the race that everyone was calling the Champion of Champions race. Windstorm was going to be that Champion. Abbie couldn't stand the thought of losing to Rachel again.

Eden tugged at her hand. "Mommy, do you think Mac's here?" A perplexed frown creased her child-smooth features as she scanned the small crowd that had gathered outside the paddock.

"I don't know." But Abbie knew he was supposed to be.

For the last three and a half months, she had arranged these "accidental" meetings so MacCrea could spend time with his daughter as she had promised, a task that had become increasingly difficult since Dobie had learned a month ago that MacCrea was back in the area. Twice Dobie had questioned her about him, wanting to know if she had seen or talked to him. Abbie admitted that she had, but she had tried to make it sound like that's all there was to it. She doubted that Dobie believed her. His unspoken suspicions and her own sense of guilt had added more strain to an already unstable marriage.

Abbie couldn't decide what to do about it. In the beginning, she had secretly hoped that MacCrea would get tired of playing father and go away, and things could be the way they were. But watching the bond between MacCrea and Eden grow, she knew now that wasn't going to happen. Sometimes she wondered who she was deceiving by maintaining this farce: Eden, Dobie, or herself.

"But Mac always comes to watch Windstorm race. Why isn't he here today?" Eden persisted, plainly troubled by his absence. More evidence of how much she looked forward to being with him.

"I don't know," Abbie repeated. "Maybe he was too busy."

When she had talked to him earlier in the week, MacCrea had told her that he planned to fly in from a drilling site in Wyoming and anticipated arriving around noon. Bad weather may have delayed him, since he was making the trip in the company plane instead of a commercial airliner. But if he'd run into a storm, why hadn't he called and left a message for her? Unless . . . Abbie remembered the photograph she'd seen in the morning paper of a private plane that had crashed during a storm. She suddenly felt cold — and a little frightened.

A large hand pressed itself against the back of her waist. Startled by the contact, Abbie turned into the curve of its arm and stared at MacCrea, alive and well, smiling that lazy smile that was so achingly familiar.

"MacCrea. You made it safely after all," she murmured, relief sweeping through her.

"Did you think I wouldn't?" His dark gaze centered on her with an intensity that gave Abbie the feeling that he could see right into her heart.

For a split second, everything was blocked out. She didn't even hear Eden clamoring to be noticed. "I . . . We . . . Eden wondered whether you were going to come today or not."

"Only Eden?" As the pressure of his hand on her back increased slightly, Abbie had the fleeting impression he was going to kiss her. Instead, he reached down and scooped up Eden.

"You really didn't think I wasn't going to be here today to cheer for Windstorm, did you?" MacCrea chided Eden. "You were the one who made me an official member of his rooting section."

"I know. But I looked and looked and didn't see you anywhere. And Mommy said maybe you were too busy to come."

"She said that, did she?" He hoisted Eden a little higher in his arms and partially turned to include Abbie in the range of his vision. "She was wrong. No matter what, I'll never be too busy to come. I can't stand up my favorite girl, now, can I?"

"You were awfully late," Eden reminded him. "It's almost time for the race. They've already taken Windstorm into the paddock so they can put the saddle on him."

"I know, and I'm sorry about that. I got caught in traffic on my way here from the airport. There was an accident and the road was blocked."

"Is that what kept you? I thought —" Abbie broke it off abruptly, not wanting to reveal the fear she'd had.

"Yes?" MacCrea prompted, casting a curious look in her direction.

"Never mind. Let's go into the paddock. I want to speak to the trainer before they give the call to saddle up." As she started toward the enclosure, she was forced to wait while a groom led another Arabian entrant through the opening.

"You're slipping, Abbie." MacCrea stood beside her, still carrying Eden in his arms. "You're going to have to watch yourself more closely."

"Why? What do you mean?" She frowned.

"The way you looked at me when I arrived, a person could get the idea you were glad to see me." His voice mocked her, but his gaze didn't.

Abbie didn't try to deny it. She couldn't. It was true. Just for an instant, she'd foolishly let her emotions rule. That was a mistake — a mistake she could easily make again with MacCrea. There were times when she wished she could just take Eden and run away — run from MacCrea and Dobie and this whole convoluted mess. But there were her mother, Ben, and the horses to consider. She wished MacCrea had never come back. Everything had been so simple before. She was trying desperately to hold on to that, but he was complicating her life in ways she didn't want.

In the paddock, Abbie conferred briefly with Windstorm's trainer, Joe Gibbs. She wasn't sure what she accomplished except to gain his reassurance that he considered the stallion fit and ready for the race — and to escape MacCrea's company. After weighing in, the jockey joined them, wearing blue-on-blue racing silks and carrying the light racing saddle and number cloth.

As the trainer personally saddled Windstorm, Abbie watched from the side, feeling totally superfluous. Still, she was reluctant to leave just yet. She glanced around the paddock at the half-dozen other Arabian horses entered in the race, all but two of them seasoned veterans of the track with respectable records. The favorite, a handsome chestnut with a slightly plain head, had lost only two races so far this season.

"You seem nervous," MacCrea remarked.

She glanced at him from under the brim of her hat, noticing that Eden was no longer with him. Ben was now the one being besieged by her endless questions. "Nervous, anxious, excited, worried," Abbie admitted, but she knew MacCrea was responsible for part of her tension. "Windstorm has some stiff competition today."

"You don't sound very confident. Have you forgotten that he's won all three of his previous races?"

"No. But he's never raced a mile before either — or against horses of this caliber. I have cause to be concerned. I don't think you realize how important this race is. How well he does here will decide whether we run him in the Liberty Classic on the Fourth."

"I thought he was already entered."

"He is. But if he can't handle distance, we'll pull him. The Liberty is a mile and a quarter." She shifted her attention to the silver-white stallion, eagerly alert yet at the same time indifferent to the fussing of the trainer and groom. "He has to win. He just has to."

"You've heard then."

Abbie stiffened. She wanted to pretend that she didn't know what he meant, but she knew she could never fool MacCrea. "About Sirocco's victory? Yes."

Ben came over, firmly leading Eden by the hand. "We should go find our seats now. Soon it will be time for the race."

After wishing the jockey luck, they left the paddock area and made their way to their seats in the owners' boxes to await the parade to the post. Eden was too excited to sit down, leaving the seat between Abbie and MacCrea empty.

It was always a struggle for Abbie to pretend to ignore him, but today it seemed even more difficult for her. She tried to blame it on the rising tension she felt over the upcoming race, but she had the uncomfortable feeling that she had unwittingly admitted something during those few moments of fear earlier when she thought his plane might have crashed. For once she welcomed the distraction of Eden's nonstop chatter.

"Mommy, did you remember to bet the money Grandma gave you for the race?"

"Ben did earlier. He has the ticket."

"How much will she win?"

"Nothing if Windstorm doesn't, honey." Fully aware that that answer would never satisfy her daughter, Abbie glanced at the odds board. At the moment the number-four horse, Windstorm, was listed at seven to one. It was hardly reassuring to discover that the odds-makers obviously didn't regard her stallion as much of a threat. "She'll win somewhere around seventy dollars."

"Wow! Are you going to bet some money on Windstorm, too?"

"No."

"But you could win a lot of money," Eden protested.

"And I could lose it, too." But that wasn't the reason. Betting on her own horse just seemed to be inviting bad luck.

"Why? You know he's the fastest horse ever," Eden insisted. "He's going to win. I know it."

"A thousand things can go wrong in a race, Eden," Abbie tried to explain. "He could break badly from the gate or get caught in a pocket surrounded by other horses. A horse could run into him or one might fall in front of him. You just don't know."

"I do," she replied, unconcerned by such dire possibilities, and turned to MacCrea. "You're gonna bet on Windstorm, aren't you, Mac?"

"I already have." He pulled several tickets out of his shirt pocket and showed them to her.

"All of these! Can I hold them?"

"Sure." He gave them to her.

"How much money will you win?"

"A lot." MacCrea smiled.

"Boy, I wish I could have bet on Windstorm." Eden sighed longingly as she stared at all his tickets. "I wanted to take the money out of my piggy bank, but Mommy wouldn't let me bring it."

"I told you that you're too young," Abbie reminded her. "Children aren't allowed to bet money on horse races."

"Well, when I get big, I'm going to bet on Windstorm and win lots of money," Eden declared.

"Something tells me that there's a strong gambling streak in her," MacCrea said in an aside to Abbie.

"Obviously she inherited it from her father," she retorted, and instantly regretted the quick rejoinder and its reference to him.

"I agree," he replied, his gaze running intimately over her face.

As a warmth stole over her skin, Abbie looked away, concentrating her attention on the track. Just then, the first trumpeting notes of the Call to Post sounded, stirring the crowd to life once again. An Arabian horse carrying a rider festooned in a scarlet-and-gold native costume cantered onto the track to lead the procession of Arabian racehorses on their parade to the post. Their appearance drew a smattering of applause from the stands.

"Look, Mommy. There's Windstorm!" Eden cried excitedly, the first to spot the silvery-white stallion, officially listed as gray.

Snubbed close to his lead pony, Windstorm entered the track at a mincing trot, his neck arched in a tight curve, his long tail raised and flowing behind him like a white banner. One of the other horses shied at the noise from the crowd as the seven entries paraded past the stands on their way to the starting gate. But not Windstorm. He played to the crowd as if in a show ring instead of on a racetrack.

"Sometimes I wonder if we were wrong not to race him first," she said to Ben.

"Do not worry. He knows why he is here," Ben replied, studying all the horses through his binoculars.

Abbie thought she was nervous before, but she was twice as anxious now. When the horses reached the area behind the starting gate, cantering to loosen up, she shifted onto the edge of her seat. With only one other gray horse among the entrants and that one a dark gray, it was easy to distinguish Windstorm from the rest. But at this distance, Abbie could tell very little about him.

"How is he, Ben?"

"He is sweating a little. It is good."

"Let me see." She reached for the binoculars and trained them on Windstorm when Ben handed them to her. There was a telltale shadow on his neck, the sweat wetting his coat and letting the blackness of his skin show through. A little show of nervousness was good; it indicated alertness and an awareness of what was expected of him. But too much drained a horse's energy. Studying the white stallion, Abbie was forced to agree that Windstorm was by no means lathered. He looked ready. She hoped and prayed he was.

"Can I see, Mommy?" Eden tugged at her arm, jarring the focus.

"Not right now." Abbie briefly lowered the glasses to locate Windstorm again and noticed that the first horse was being loaded in the number-one post position. Quickly she raised the binoculars to observe Windstorm being led into the number-four slot without incident.

As the last horse went in, the track announcer's voice boomed through the stands. "They're at the gate, ready for the start of the fifth race." Her nerve ends picked up the expectancy in his voice, vibrating like a tuning fork.

An eternity seemed to pass as she kept the binoculars trained on the number-four position, watching the jockey's efforts to keep Windstorm alert and squared in the gate. The stallion's ears appeared to be on a swivel, constantly flicking back and forth, impatiently waiting for a signal from his rider. Finally he tossed his head, irritated with the delay.

Bells rang as the clanging gates sprang open and the horses burst out. "They're off!" A dull roar came from the surrounding crowd.

Abbie came to her feet, lowering the classes. "How'd he break? I didn't see." By the third stride out of the gate, three horses had surged forward to vie for the lead. Windstorm wasn't one of them.

"He broke well." Ben stood up, adding softly, "Do not hurry him. Let him find his stride."

Abbie heard him as she concentrated on the loosely bunched horses thundering toward the stands, but a full second passed before she realized he was talking to the jockey riding Windstorm.

". . . Windstorm is fifth; Kaslan is sixth . . . ," the track announcer droned.

The white stallion was along the outside, five-and-a-half lengths back of the leader, but running easily, neither gaining nor losing ground as the horses approached the first turn. Abbie raised the glasses once more to follow him.

"I can't see, Mommy."

"Stand on the seat beside Ben." Abbie shifted to her right to make room for Eden. The horses entered the backstretch stringing out in a longer line. "He's in fourth now." Unconsciously she clutched at the sleeve of MacCrea's shirt, trying to contain her excitement as Windstorm began to close on the leaders. "I think he's making his move. I hope it's not too soon." But the stallion was still running with his ears pricked forward, a sure indication that he wasn't yet extending himself.

She lost sight of him as the horses went into the final turn. He was just a blur of white on the outside, obscured by the horses on the rail. She felt an unbearable tension in her throat.

The two leaders came out of the turn, neck and neck heading down the homestretch. But there, flying on the outside, was Windstorm, stretched out flat, each thrust of those powerful hindquarters driving him closer to the leaders, his large nostrils flared, drinking in the wind.

The cheers of the crowd were a distant roar in her ears, no match for the drumming hooves pounding over the dirt track. As Windstorm closed on the leaders, Abbie lowered the glasses, unconsciously using them to pump the air and urge him faster.

At the seven-eighth's pole, the white stallion caught the leaders and started pulling away. The other jockeys went to the whip, but Windstorm's jockey continued to hand-ride him, driving for the finish line. He was a half-length ahead . . . one length . . . two.

Abbie screamed as Windstorm crossed the line, still pulling away. "He did it! He won! He won!" She turned to MacCrea, her excited cry becoming a jubilant laugh.

"Didn't I tell you he'd win?"

Thrilled by his decisive victory, Abbie couldn't contain her elation. She had to express it, let some of it out. Impulsively she flung herself at MacCrea. He hooked his arm around her waist, lifting her off her feet.

The instant her lips touched his mouth, she realized what she was doing and started to pull back. His hand cupped the back of her head, checking the movement. There was a moment of stillness, broken only by the thudding of her heart, as the rugged planes of his face filled her vision.

"Oh, no, you don't, Abbie," he whispered.

He kissed her, his lips moving warmly, possessively, over hers, taking what she had been about to give him. Abbie couldn't deny that she enjoyed it. She returned the pressure, savoring the pleasure that flickered through her.

The whole embrace lasted no more than a few seconds, yet it seemed a lifetime had passed when MacCrea finally set her down and shifted to include a laughing, squealing Eden. Together they hugged and laughed and rejoiced in Windstorm's victory, drawing Ben into their celebration. But the sensation of MacCrea's kiss lingered on her lips. Abbie couldn't look at him without recalling it. But what was more unsettling, she saw the same reaction mirrored in his eyes, too, each time he looked at her.

Together they all trooped down to the winner's circle for the presentation ceremony. When it came time for pictures to be taken, Eden insisted that MacCrea be included, but he excused himself, convincing her that he had to cash his winning tickets in.

Abbie watched him disappear into the throng, knowing as well as he did that there was no way she could have explained to Dobie why MacCrea was in the photograph. MacCrea was right, for all their sakes, to stay out of it. Yet as the photographer positioned them next to the silver stallion, Abbie found herself wishing he was there.

After the ceremony was over, the groom led Windstorm away to have the mandatory check for drugs. The stallion moved off at a dancing walk, still looking fresh and eager to run.

As she left the winner's circle with Eden firmly in tow, Abbie thought about the coming mile-and-a-quarter race, now less than three weeks away. "There can be no doubt about Windstorm running in the Liberty now," she said to Ben, shortening her stride to keep pace with his slower steps. "It's going to be a treat to watch Windstorm kick dirt in Sirocco's face when they cross the finish line. Windstorm beat his time for the mile by a full second today."

"Not only that, he set a track record at the mile for Arabians," the trainer, Joe Gibbs, chimed in, bringing up the rear.

"He did?" Abbie turned to stare at the trainer, stunned by the news. "I knew his time was fast, but . . ." She started to laugh. She couldn't help it. "Can you believe it, Ben?" She wondered what Rachel would think when she found out.

A track record. She could hardly wait to tell MacCrea the news. She sobered slightly, remembering the kiss, and absently ran her fingertips over her lips as if expecting to find a physical impression to match the one he'd left on her mind . . . and, if she was honest, on her heart.

Automatically, Abbie glanced in the direction he would come. The stable row was quiet, an island of comfortable sounds, removed from the din of the grandstands. Horses stood with their heads hanging over the stalls, swishing their tails or stomping their feet at buzzing flies, munching on hay or banging their water buckets. Occasionally there was the clop of hooves as a groom walked by, cooling out a horse, or the soft voices of passersby as they paused at a stall to stroke a velvety muzzle. The yelling and cheering belonged in the stands.

As MacCrea came strolling leisurely past the row of stalls toward them, Abbie felt the quick knocking of her heart against her ribs. She stared at him, a fine tension running through her. But the feeling wasn't unpleasant; it was more like a sharpening of her senses than anything else.

"Eden," she called to her daughter chattering away at the groom, relating Windstorm's life story, from the sounds of it. "There's MacCrea."

" 'Scuse me. I've got to go." She was off like a shot, running to meet him. "Did you collect your winnings?" she called before she even reached him.

"I sure did." He fanned the bills for her to see.

"Wow! Look at how much money Mac won, Mommy!"

"It's a lot, isn't it?" Abbie said as Eden skipped ahead of MacCrea to rejoin her. "Did you tell him our news?"

"What news?" Eden stared at her with a blank frown.

Bending down, she whispered in her ear. "Windstorm set a track record for Arabians."

"Oh, yes!" She turned to MacCrea, her eyes bright with excitement. "Windstorm set a record."

"He had the fastest time for an Arabian at the mile here at this track," Abbie explained, feeling again that little surge of pride over her stallion's accomplishment.

"That's great. Now we have three things to celebrate: Windstorm's time and my winnings."

"What's the third thing?" Eden frowned.

"I bought the Jeffords' property — house, acreage, and all." He looked at Abbie when he answered her. "Just about ten miles from the farm."

"I know the place," she said, even though she'd only seen it from the road.

"Maybe you can come by sometime and see it," MacCrea suggested, but Abbie wasn't about to commit herself to that. She didn't want to see where he ate or . . . where he slept. At her silence, MacCrea shifted his attention back to Eden. "How do you think we should go about this celebrating we have to do?"

"Well . . ." She pressed her lips together, considering the problem seriously. "We could all go get a bi-i-ig hot-fudge sundae and . . . maybe look at some toys. And we could go to a movie," she concluded proudly.

"Sounds good to me." MacCrea smiled faintly.

"Count me out. You two go ahead. Ben and I have to stay here and see to Windstorm." She always begged off so MacCrea could spend time alone with Eden.

"But I want you to come with us," Eden declared insistently. "It won't be the same if you don't."

"I'm sorry, but we can't go. Ben and I have to stay here." Abbie saw the tantrum coming on and braced herself for it.

"Then I'm not going to go either," Eden retorted, her expression defiant.

"Eden, you know you always have fun with Mac." She tried to reason with her.

"But I want all of us to have fun together like we did that time at the horse show."

"Don't be difficult, Eden." Abbie sighed, running out of patience with her recalcitrant daughter.

"If you won't come with us, we'll just stay here with you." She folded her arms in front of her, the gesture determined, and accompanied by a stubborn jutting of her chin.

"You're not spoiling anybody's fun but your own." But it was like talking to a mule. Abbie glanced helplessly at MacCrea, who seemed amused by their battle of wills. Just for an instant, she wondered if he had put Eden up to this.

"If you can't beat 'em, join 'em. Isn't that the way the old saying goes?" MacCrea said, his mouth crooking slightly beneath his mustache. "Come along with us. Windstorm gets along fine when you're not here. Why should this afternoon be any different?"

"I should have known you'd take her side in this," Abbie accused, but she couldn't summon any anger. She had the uneasy feeling that subconsciously she wanted to be talked into going. But to admit that, she'd also have to admit that she wanted to be with MacCrea.

"Please come with us, Mommy. They'll take good care of Windstorm. I know they will," Eden said, indicating the grooms with the stallion.

"Ben . . . ?" Abbie appealed to him for help.

"What is there to argue with?" He shrugged his square shoulders. "What she says is true."

"See. Even Ben agrees," Eden declared happily and took hold of Abbie's hand, then reached for Ben's. "You'll come with us won't you? We'll have lots of fun."

Eden was so obviously delighted at the prospect that Abbie felt it would be deliberately churlish to refuse. "You've talked me into it."

Together the four of them set off for the parking lot and the car MacCrea had rented, their destination a movie theater not too many miles from the track, one that MacCrea and Eden had discovered on a previous excursion in the area.

When they left the theater two hours later, dusk was spreading its mauve blanket over the sky, pushing aside the streaks of cerise. To Eden's dismay, Abbie insisted it was time they went back to their motel. She tried to convince Abbie she wasn't tired, but she fell asleep in the backseat within ten minutes.

MacCrea turned into the motel parking lot and drove past the lobby. "What room are you in?"

"One twenty-six. It's near that first side entrance." Abbie opened her purse to retrieve the room key. "Ben, would you wake up Eden?"

"Let her sleep," MacCrea said. "I'll carry her in."

Knowing how cranky and uncooperative Eden could be when she first woke up, Abbie didn't argue. "All right."

MacCrea parked the car near the side entrance and lifted Eden out of the backseat, then followed Abbie and Ben into the building.

Unlocking the door to room 126, Abbie walked in and stepped to the side to hold the door open for MacCrea, as Ben continued on to his own room. "You can put her down on the first bed," she said, indicating the double bed closest to the door.

When MacCrea started to lay her down, Eden made a protesting sound and clung to him. Gently he laid her down on the bed and untangled her arms from around his neck. Smiling absently, Abbie took off her hat and walked over to the suitcase lying open on the low dresser. Eden's nightgown, a long mock tee shirt, lay on top. As Abbie picked it up and started back to the bed with it, she noticed MacCrea sitting on the edge of the bed, pulling off Eden's socks and shoes.

"You don't have to bother with that. I'll get her ready for bed."

"I want to do it." The bedsprings creaked faintly as MacCrea shifted to glance at her, his angular features gentled by the underlying tenderness in his expression. "Is that her nightgown?"

"Yes." Abbie stared uncertainly at his outstretched hand.

"Putting Eden to bed is probably old hat to you," he pointed out, "but I've never had the opportunity to do this for my daughter before."

Abbie hesitated a second more, then handed him the nightgown and stood back to watch. Unwillingly, she was moved by the touching scene as MacCrea removed Eden's dress and slip, careful to disturb her as little as possible. He smiled at the frowning faces she made, his strong hands gentle in their handling of the sleeping child. Holding her, he pulled the nightgown over her head, slipped her arms through the sleeves, then laid her back down, sliding her legs between the sheets. Eden immediately snuggled into the pillow under her head. Bending, MacCrea lightly kissed her forehead, then straightened and pulled the bedcovers over her, tucking her in. He paused for an instant to watch Eden in sleep, then switched off the bedside lamp, leaving only the soft glow from the floorlamp between the two vinyl chairs to light the room. Moving with cat-soft silence, he came back to stand next to Abbie.

"Look at her," he murmured. "So small and innocent. A sleeping angel."

Admittedly that was the way she looked, the white pillowcase a halo around her dark head, her cheeks still baby-soft, her long-lashed eyes closed, all sweetness and innocence. But Abbie was well aware that Eden was no angel. Surely MacCrea didn't really think she was, but he had never seen her at her irritating worst. He'd only been exposed to her in small doses.

Surely he didn't think that today was an example of what it was like to be a parent. Certainly it had been fun and idyllic, but today was the exception rather than the rule. All he'd ever done was play at being a father. Living with Eden was something entirely different.

"Don't be fooled by her. She isn't always like this," Abbie warned. "You've never seen her when she's sick with the flu or a cold. She's whiny and demanding, always wanting this or that. Believe me, she's no fun at all then." Judging by his amused study of her, MacCrea wasn't at all convinced. Abbie hurried on, "Being a parent isn't all fun and games. That little temper tantrum you saw today — it was mild compared to some she's thrown when she didn't get her way. Just wait until she starts sassing and talking back. You won't think she's so cute and innocent then."

"Is that right?" The hint of a smile around the edges of his mouth seemed to mock her.

"Yes, it is," Abbie retorted, irritated that he might think she was making all this up. "And then there's the way she talks all the time. Look at the way she talked through the entire movie, asking why somebody did this or said that, wanting everything explained to her. Do you know that she even talks in her sleep? You've only had to put up with her endless chatter for a few hours at a time. Wait until you have to listen to her day in and day out."

"Talk, talk, talk," he said.

"Exactly. She just goes on and on . . ." Abbie forgot what she was going to say as he took her by the shoulders and squared her around to face him, all in one motion.

She stared at his mouth, surprised to find it so close, and watched his lips form the words, "Just like her mother."

Before she could react, he was kissing her, warmly, deeply. For an instant she forgot to resist, then she drew back, breaking the contact. "Mac, I think —"

"That's always been your trouble, Abbie." He didn't let her get away. Instead, he started nuzzling her neck and ear. "You think too much and you talk too much. For once, just shut up."

As he claimed her lips again, his advice suddenly seemed very wise. Why should she refuse herself something she wanted as much as he did, just because she didn't want to admit she wanted it? Denying it wouldn't change the longing she felt at this moment. As she allowed herself to enjoy his embrace, it was a little like coming home after a long absence. The joy, the warmth, the sense of reunion —

they were all there . . . and something more that she was reluctant to identify.

He tunneled his fingers into her hair and began pulling out the pins that bound the chignon. As her hair tumbled loose about her shoulders, he drew back to look at her, his eyes heavy-lidded and dark. "I've wanted to do that for a long time."

Still holding her gaze, he scooped her off her feet and carried her to the nearest armchair and sat down, cradling her in his lap. No longer did she have to strain to reach him and span the difference in their heights. She was free to touch him, to run her fingers through his thick, wavy hair and feel the rope-lean muscles along his shoulders and back. His roaming hands stroked, caressed, and kneaded her body as he and she kissed and nibbled as if hungry for the taste of each other. Then his fingers went to work on the bow at her throat and the buttons of her shirtwaist dress, undoing them one by one. When his hand glided onto her bare skin, a rush of sensations raced through her body.

Caught up in the building passion between them, Abbie had no idea how long they had been in the chair, necking like a pair of teenagers just discovering all the preliminary delights that made making love the wonder it was. But when she heard Eden stir and mumble in her sleep, her maternal instincts reclaimed her. She couldn't tune out the sounds her daughter made, or ignore her presence in the room.

When she tried to inject a degree of restraint into their embrace, MacCrea protested. "Let me love you, Abbie. It's what we both want."

"Not here." She drew back, earnestly trying to make him understand. "We can't. Eden might wake up." A mixture of irritation, disappointment, and frustration darkened his expression when he glanced toward the bed. "We'd better stop before . . . one of us loses control," Abbie suggested, no more willing than he was to end this.

"Me, you mean." His mocking reply had a husky edge to it.

"I didn't say that."

He sighed heavily, giving her his answer as he sat her upright. She swung off his lap to stand on her own, feeling shaky and weak. She wanted nothing more than to turn and have MacCrea gather her back into his arms. Instead, she walked him to the door, holding the gaping front of her dress together. As he paused with his hand on the knob, she had the feeling that he didn't trust himself to kiss her again.

"This isn't over, you know," he said.

"Yes." She nodded, recognizing that she didn't want it to be over.

A slow smile spread across his face. "It took you long enough to admit it." Then he was gone — out the door before Abbie could say any more.

Automatically, she locked the door and slipped the safety chain in place, all the while thinking about his last statement. For the last four months, ever since she'd seen him that first time in Scottsdale, she had been telling herself it was over between them. Now she knew better. She wanted him so much it had become a physical ache.

She walked over to the open suitcase on the dresser. As she started to pick up her lace nightgown, she noticed her reflection in the mirror. Her long hair was all disheveled; her lips looked unusually full; her eyelids appeared to be faintly swollen; and the front of her dress gaped open all the way to her navel. She had the definite look of a woman who had just been thoroughly made love to . . . perhaps not thoroughly, she corrected, conscious of the lingering need.

As she gazed at her reflection in the mirror, Abbie found herself coming face to face with reality. A part of her had never stopped loving MacCrea — and the rest of her had learned to love him all over again.

She went through the motions of getting ready for bed — washing her face, brushing her teeth, and changing into her nightgown —but she didn't go near it. Instead she laid out clean clothes for herself and Eden and packed everything else into the suitcase except the toiletries they would need in the morning, postponing the moment when she'd have to climb into that bed alone.

At first, Abbie didn't pay any attention to the light rapping sound she heard, thinking that someone was knocking on a door somewhere along the corridor. Then it came again, slightly louder and more insistent, accompanied by the soft calling of her name. Frowning, Abbie started for the door. Halfway there, she realized that the rapping was coming from the door to the adjoining motel room. She stopped in front of it and waited until the sound came again.

"Yes?" she said hesitantly.

"It's me, MacCrea. Open the door."

She fumbled briefly with the lock, then pulled the door open.

There he stood, leaning in the doorway to the next room and dangling a room key from his hand.

"I gave the desk clerk a hundred dollars and told him one twenty-eight was my lucky number. Is it?"

She stared at him, momentarily at a loss for even the simplest answer. Then she found it. "Yes." She was in his room — and in his arms — before she had time to consider the decision. But it didn't matter. It was where she belonged. Where she had always belonged.

43

MacCrea drifted somewhere between wakefulness and sleep, a heady contentment claiming him. He was reluctant to waken and break the spell of whatever dream he'd had that made him feel this good. Yet something — or someone — stirred against him and coolness touched his bare leg where heat had been. Instinctively he reached out to draw that warm body close to him again. The instant he touched her, he knew. He opened his eyes to look and make sure he wasn't dreaming. It was Abbie he held, nestled in the curve of his body.

In sleep, she reminded him of a more sensual version of Eden: the same dark hair billowing about her face like a black cloud, the same long-lashed eyes and full lower lip. Now fully awake and aroused by the recollection of last night's passion, MacCrea couldn't resist the urge to lean over and kiss the ripe curve of her lips.

She stirred beneath him, drowsily kissing him back. He lifted his head to study her, watching as she arched her back, stretching her arms overhead like a cat waking from a nap, the action brushing her breasts against his chest. Then she snuggled back down, her eyes more than half-closed.

"Is it morning?" she asked, her voice thick and husky with sleep.

"Does it matter?" Supporting himself on one arm, he ran his hand over her body, pausing long enough to arouse a sleeping nipple, then traveling back down.

"Yes." But her body language was giving him an entirely different answer.

"This is the way it should be every morning, Abbie: you and me in the same bed and Eden sleeping in the next room."

"I'd better get up. I don't want her waking up alone in a strange room." Shifting position, she reached for his wristwatch on the nightstand and glanced at the dial. "It's eight o'clock already. I need to get Eden up, finish packing, and get out to the airport in time to catch our flight."

MacCrea checked the move she made to get out of bed. "Take a later plane. Stay here with me awhile longer."

For an instant she gazed at him longingly, then she shook her head. "I can't." She rolled away from him to the other side of the bed. "Dobie's meeting us at the airport."

Disturbed by something in her tone, he stared at her slim back, watching as she picked the short nightgown off the floor and slipped it on. He wanted to pull her back onto the bed and make her stay. With some women that might work, but he knew Abbie wasn't one of them. Stifling his frustration, he reached for the pair of slacks lying on the floor and stepped into them.

As he pulled them up around his hips, coins and keys jingling in the pockets, he turned to study her. "You are going to tell him about us, aren't you?" She hesitated ever so slightly, but didn't answer. As she moved toward the connecting door between the two rooms, MacCrea didn't like the implication of her silence one damned bit. "Don't leave yet, Abbie — not unless you want this conversation to take place in front of Eden."

She paused short of the door and turned back as he came around the bed. "Why? What is there to talk about?"

But he didn't buy her attempt to feign ignorance. "About us, of course. Or didn't last night mean anything to you?" He was certain it had. He'd stake everything he owned on it.

"Of course, it did." She avoided his gaze, the action telling him more than she realized.

Confident now of her answer, he could ask, "Abbie, do you love me?"

She sighed and nodded. "Yes."

"You know this changes everything, Abbie." He watched the play of warring emotions upon her face. "You can't stay married to him now. You have to tell him the truth. You know that."

"I don't know any such thing," she retorted tightly.

MacCrea gritted his teeth, wanting to shake her until her own rattled. "What are you, Abbie? Too stubborn or too proud to admit you made a mistake? Or are you planning to be just like your father and stay married to someone you don't love and make everyone's life as miserable as your own?"

"That's not true," she flashed, startled into anger by his accusation.

"Isn't it? Then tell me just how long you expect me to go on living with this lie of yours?"

"I don't know. I haven't had time to think. I —"

"You'd better find the time, and quickly," MacCrea warned. "I've played it your way long enough. I'm not going to live the rest of my life this way, sneaking off to meet you whenever you can get away."

"Don't threaten me, MacCrea Wilder." Tears glittered in her blue eyes, adding a hot brilliance to them.

"It isn't a threat." Sighing, he took her by the shoulders, feeling her stiffness. "We love each other, Abbie. And I'm not going to let you do this to us."

"It just isn't as easy as you think it is," she said, continuing to protest faintly.

"But it's got to be easier than living a lie the rest of our lives."

She leaned against him and hugged him around his middle, like a child seeking comfort and reassurance. "I do love you, Mac. It's just so hard anymore to figure out what's right or wrong. I always thought I knew."

He kissed her. He didn't know what else to say or do.

The farmhouse bedroom stared back at her, its silence somehow heavy. The old hardwood furniture of mixed styles was nicked and scarred from years of use, but still more than serviceable. Dobie didn't believe in replacing something just because it was old. He waited until it was practically falling apart. The pretty chintz bedspread and pale blue linen curtains at the windows were her choices. At the time, getting them had seemed a minor triumph, but now, Abbie didn't care at all about them.

With enough clothes packed to last several days, she closed the lid of the suitcase and swung it off the bed. As she set it on the floor behind the bedroom door, her glance fell on the gold wedding band she wore. She twisted it off her finger, hesitated, then slipped it into the pocket of her white cotton shirtdress.

Downstairs a door slammed. Frowning slightly, Abbie paused to listen. When she heard footsteps in the kitchen, she went to investigate. She found Dobie standing at the sink, filling a glass with tap water, his battered hat pushed to the back of his head and hay chafe clinging to his sweaty skin.

"What are you doing here?" She glanced at the wall clock. "It isn't even lunchtime yet. Did something break down?"

He shook his head briefly, then drank down the water in the glass and turned back to the sink to refill it. "I saw the car leave. I thought maybe you'd gone off somewhere again." Suspicion was heavy in his tone.

"Ben took Eden to her swimming lesson. Afterward, he's taking her out for a hamburger and french fries, so they won't be back for lunch." It had been her suggestion. She hadn't wanted Eden anywhere around this noon.

"You could have fixed some here just as easy. And it'd been a lot cheaper, too."

Irritated by his niggardly remark, Abbie nearly told him that Ben was paying for the treat, but she checked the impulse. She didn't want to get sidetracked into a meaningless argument with him over money.

"We need to talk, Dobie."

"About what?"

"Us. Our marriage. It isn't working out." It was ironic. She'd been through this before. She wondered why this moment wasn't any easier the second time.

"You seemed satisfied until Wilder showed up."

She didn't try to deny that. "Maybe I thought things would change — that we just needed more time. But it hasn't worked, not from the beginning. You have to admit, Dobie, that I haven't been the kind of wife you wanted . . . someone who stays home, who's waiting here when you come in from the fields every night."

"Have I complained? I let you have your horses, and go traipsing all over the country —"

"Dobie, stop." She wasn't going to let this turn into one of their typical arguments. "Please, all I want is a divorce. Believe me, it will be better for both of us."

"It's Wilder, isn't it?" Dobie accused, his jaw clenched tightly. "You've been sneaking around and meeting him behind my back, haven't you? You want a divorce so you can marry him. That's it, isn't it?"

In a way, everything he said was true. Only none of it was the way he thought. "I love him," she admitted simply, quietly.

For an instant, he just stared at her, his eyes wide, his expression raw with pain. Then he swung around abruptly, facing the sink and gripping the edge of it, his head bowed and his shoulders hunched forward. Seeing him like that, Abbie wanted to cry, but she determinedly blinked back the tears.

"Dammit, Abbie," he said, his voice low and half-strangled by his attempt to control it, "I love you too. Doesn't that count for something?"

"Of course, it does. Why do you think this is so hard for me? I never meant to hurt you, Dobie. You don't know how many times I wished there was some other way."

"Then why are you doing this?"

"Because . . . it's the right thing to do, the fair thing."

"Fair for who?" He turned back to look at her, his eyes reddened with tears. "For you? For Wilder? What about me and Edie?"

Abbie glanced away, unable to meet his gaze. "We need to talk about Eden. I know how much you love her —"

"What do you expect? She's my daughter."

Mutely she shook her head, finding it almost impossible to say the words. But no matter how much it hurt him, she couldn't hide the truth any longer. "No, Dobie, she isn't."

"What?"

With difficulty, Abbie forced herself to look at him. "Eden isn't your daughter. I was already pregnant with her when we made love that first time."

"You're lying."

"Not this time. I wanted my baby to have a father and I knew you would be a good one. And you have been. It was wrong of me to deceive you like that, I know, but —"

"If I'm not her father, then who is?" Dobie demanded, still doubting. "Not Wilder —"

"Yes."

"But you can't prove it. And you can't expect me just to take your word for it."

"Look at the way her little fingers curl — MacCrea has one like it. I've never seen such a thing before. It's a Wilder family trait."

"My God." He whitened. "All these years . . ."

"I'm sorry," Abbie said. "More than you'll ever know."

*　　*　　*

When Abbie tried to reach MacCrea at his office, she was told he was at River Bend, meeting with Lane Canfield. There was a moment when she almost decided not to call him at all, but she needed to talk to him. Tense and anxious, she dialed the number.

Rachel answered the phone. Abbie recognized her voice instantly and had to fight the urge to hang up. "I'd like to speak to MacCrea Wilder, please. I was told he was there."

"Who's calling?"

Abbie clutched the receiver a little tighter. "It's Abbie. I need to speak to him. It's important."

"I'm sorry. He's in a meeting."

"I know that," she inserted quickly, fearing that Rachel would hang up on her. "Just tell him I'm on the phone."

There was no response for several long seconds. Then there was a dull clunk, but the line didn't go dead. Abbie could hear faint noises in the background, then distantly MacCrea's voice saying, "Abbie? Of course, I'll take it." A second later, there was a click and he was on the line.

"I'm sorry I called you there, but . . . I had to talk to you."

"Don't worry about that. Just tell me what's wrong. I can tell something is."

"I told Dobie this morning that I wanted a divorce. He knew right away that you were involved."

"What about Eden?"

"I told him you were her father, not him."

"And?"

She took a deep breath, trying to steady her nerves. "And he walked out of the house. He hasn't come back. I don't know where he went."

"Where are you now?"

"At Ben's house. We're going to stay here."

"Eden's with you?"

"Yes. She's in the living room, playing checkers with Ben." She glanced at the two heads, one gray and one dark, huddled over the checkerboard on the coffee table.

"I'll be right there."

"Mac, no. You can't. It will only make things worse if Dobie finds you here when he comes back."

"Dammit, Abbie, you can't stay there."

"We have to . . . at least until we can find somewhere to take the mares and colts. I probably should have waited and talked to Dobie after we had found other facilities for the horses." When she thought of all the time and money she'd spent building her breeding farm there, she wished she had postponed her discussion with Dobie.

"I've got that handled. You can keep them at my place. I want you to throw some things in a suitcase, get Eden and Ben, and meet me over there in a half hour."

"But —"

"Abbie, don't argue with me. I don't want to take the chance that anything might happen to you . . . or Eden. If I can't come there, then you're going to come stay with me. Agreed?"

Abbie hesitated, then realized that if Dobie did cause a scene when he returned, it would be better if Eden didn't see it. She and Ben could always come back to take care of the horses. "Yes."

"Good. I'll see you there in half an hour. And, Abbie —"

"Yes?"

"I love you."

She felt the tears come. "I love you, too, Mac." And she loved him even more because he wasn't going to let her go through this alone. She continued to hold the phone to her ear after MacCrea had hung up, unwilling to let go of the closeness she had felt between them. She heard a second click, breaking the connection. Someone had been listening in. Abbie stared at the phone. That person had to have been Rachel.

After carefully replacing the telephone receiver in its cradle, Rachel turned to face the pocket doors to the library, and listened to the muffled voices of Lane and MacCrea coming from within. As the doors were slid apart, MacCrea stepped out and Rachel moved away from the telephone in the foyer.

"Leaving already, MacCrea?" she taunted, irritated at the way he was rushing to Abbie's side. Then she smiled sweetly at Lane, coming behind him. "I'll see him to the door, darling."

"Thank you. I do have some calls to make." Lane paused to shake hands with MacCrea. "I'll be getting back to you in the next week or so — after I've had a chance to review everything."

"I'll be waiting to hear from you. If you have any questions, just call." Then MacCrea turned, his glance briefly pausing on Rachel.

Smoothly, she slipped her arm into the crook of his and started walking him across the tiled foyer to the front door, waiting until she heard the retreat of Lane's footsteps before saying anything. "So. You've gotten yourself involved with Abbie again."

"That's my business, Rachel."

"You're a fool, MacCrea," she declared, releasing a sigh of disgust. "She only wants your money. Surely you can see that. You know as well as I do that she's determined to establish a stud farm that will rival River Bend. But that husband of hers won't give her the money to do it, so she's picked you."

"I'd be careful about pointing fingers if I were you, Rachel." MacCrea unhooked his arm from hers and reached for the solid brass doorknob. "Because every time you do, the other three fingers point back at yourself."

Stung by that complacent, knowing look in his dark eyes, Rachel drew back to glare at him. "I hope you remember that I tried to warn you." But he was already out the door, closing it in her face.

Abbie was waiting in the shade of the deck when MacCrea pulled into the driveway and parked his car next to hers. As she watched him come striding up the walk, indifferent to the broiling heat and stifling humidity of the East Texas summer afternoon, she felt some of her anxieties slipping away. He looked so strong and vital, so capable of handling any situation, that she finally really believed that everything was going to be all right. It was crazy when she thought about it. She had always prided herself on being independent, not needing anyone. Now she found herself wanting to lean on someone. Not just someone; she qualified that quickly in her mind. She wanted to lean on MacCrea.

As he reached her, he glanced around and frowned. "Where are Eden and Ben?"

"We saw the stables in back when we drove in. You know Ben. He had to check them out. Eden went along with him."

"How's she taking all this?"

"She doesn't know what's going on." Abbie shook her head, staring at the white buttons on his shirtfront and wishing he would take her in his arms and hold her. "I haven't told her yet."

"We'll do it later . . . together," MacCrea said, exactly as she had hoped he would.

"She's so young, I don't know how much of this she'll understand, especially about you."

"We'll take it slow . . . a step at a time." He gazed at her. "To tell you the truth, Abbie, I wasn't sure you'd break with him, at least not right away."

"If I'd thought it through, I probably would have waited. With the horses and a mare due to foal, and the race two weeks away, my timing isn't exactly the best." But the truth was, she didn't want to have to sleep in the same bed with Dobie anymore — not now, not after being with MacCrea. "But I had to."

"If you hadn't, Abbie, in another two days, I would have," he stated firmly, leaving her in no doubt that he would have done just that. "God, I've missed you," he said in the next breath and gathered her into this arms, kissing her hungrily, deeply. Just for an instant, Abbie let herself forget everything except the love that blazed between them — a fire that heated every inch of her body and lit every corner of her heart. When he pulled away, his breathing had grown ragged — as hers had. "It seems a helluva lot longer than three days since I held you like this."

"For me, too."

"How long do you think it will take Ben to look over the stable?"

"Not that long." She smiled.

MacCrea sighed as he released her, removing temptation to arm's length. "It's a damned shame there aren't more than six stalls down there."

"I didn't even know the property had a stable on it."

"That was one of my criteria when I had the realtor looking for a place. Horses were bound to be involved somewhere in the bargain, whether it was just Eden or it included you. I know it isn't River Bend —"

"There's only one River Bend." She wished he hadn't mentioned it . . . and she wished she hadn't said that. "I'm sorry." She couldn't look at him.

"I thought you'd gotten over losing it."

"It was my home. You never get over something like that. You just go on." She looked down at her hands, remembering the feel of River Bend dirt between her fingers. "You go on and hope that someday you'll find a place that will mean as much." Forcing a smile, she turned her face up to him. "You haven't shown me your house, yet, MacCrea."

He studied her thoughtfully, then turned. "Eden and Ben are coming. We might as well wait for them."

Eden came running up to show them one of the long seed pods from the catalpa trees that shaded the lawn. When Ben joined them, MacCrea led them into the sprawling adobe ranch house, built around a center courtyard.

White stucco and dark heavy beams dominated the interior design, with French doors in nearly every room opening onto the courtyard. Large skylights had been cut into the red-tiled roof, letting in the sun by day and the moon and stars by night, again incorporating the outdoors into the house. Throughout, floors of Tercate clay tiles gave way to sections of hardwood and Indian rugs.

As soon as Eden saw the huge stone fireplace in the living room, she immediately wanted MacCrea to start a fire in it, but Abbie managed to convince her that despite the air-conditioning, it was too warm for one. The room was done with antique English and American pieces and deep suede sofas.

When MacCrea showed her the child's suite, all done in light pink and mauve, Eden was enchanted by the canopied bed.

"We shouldn't have any trouble persuading her to go to sleep tonight," Abbie remarked as they left the room.

"I counted on that," MacCrea replied, his glance warmly suggestive of the plans he had for their time alone.

"Where's Mommy going to sleep?" Eden wanted to know.

"In here." He opened the door to the master suite.

A rounded fireplace of white adobe brick was nestled in one corner of the room, with a couple of easy chairs in front of it. Fur rugs flanked the king-sized bed that dominated the other side of the room. Two large closets were linked by a separate dressing room leading to an exquisite marble bath.

"Isn't it grand, Mommy?" Eden declared, sighing expressively. "Mac has the nicest home I've ever seen."

"I'm glad you like it, short stuff." MacCrea scooped her up to ride on his hip.

"I do, but, what about Ben?" She frowned at him. "You haven't shown us his room."

"I will not be staying here tonight, Eden," Ben inserted. "We have a sneaky mare who would pick such a time to have her baby."

MacCrea turned to him. "Can you handle everything all right, Ben?"

Abbie looked on as Ben let the question hang unanswered for several seconds while he quietly studied MacCrea with a critical eye. "I think there will be no trouble. One of the grooms will take part of the foal watch for me. You look after these two, and I will look after the horses."

Later that night, after they had tucked Eden into bed, Abbie lay curled on MacCrea's lap, her head nestled against his shoulder and her lips still warm from the kisses he'd given her when he'd pulled her into the chair with him. A heavy sigh broke from her, betraying her inner restlessness.

"What's wrong?" MacCrea asked, tipping his head to peer at her face.

"I feel a little guilty about Ben being at the farm, dealing with Dobie by himself and sitting up half the night with the mare. All this is my doing. I should be there taking the brunt of it, not Ben."

"Ben isn't going to have any problems with him."

"I hope you're right." She sighed again.

"I know I am."

She tilted her head back to study the quiet strength that was an innate part of his features — the sculpted cheekbone and slanted jawline. "Ben respects you. I was never sure how he felt about you until I saw the way he looked at you today."

"It's mutual."

"I saw that, too." She smiled.

He cupped her cheek in his hand and let his thumb trace the curved line of her mouth. His hands were no longer calloused, but Abbie found their smoothness equally stimulating. He bent down and rubbed his mouth across her lips, deliberately withholding the promised kiss to tease her. Reaching up, Abbie slid her fingers into his hair and forced his head down until she felt the satisfying pressure of his lips devouring hers, their tongues melding as they tasted each other.

Reluctantly MacCrea pulled back. "How much longer do you think it will be before that daughter of ours is sound asleep?" His hand slid under the long white skirt of her dress and caressed the back of her thigh.

"Not long." Abbie wanted to block everything else out of her mind except loving him, but she couldn't. She snuggled against him again and absently rubbed her cheek against his shoulder.

"What are you thinking?"

Abbie hesitated. "I was just wondering what . . . Dobie is going to do. I'd feel easier if I knew."

"Abbie." MacCrea lifted her chin, forcing her to look at him. "You're with me, and that's the way it's going to be from now on. There's nothing he can do that will change that. Not Dobie. Not Rachel. Not anyone."

"I know." She turned her face into his hand and kissed his palm, then rubbed her jaw and chin against it. "When I called you today, I think she listened in."

"I wouldn't be surprised." MacCrea paused, wanting more than anything to kiss her and kindle the passion he knew he could arouse. But he knew it wasn't what she wanted from him just now. "I was going to wait to tell you after the deal was finalized, but Lane agreed, in principle today, to sell me his interest in Wilder Oil. There's still a lot of details to work out, but in three or four weeks, it should be all signed and official."

"What?" She stared at him, her blue eyes wide with disbelief.

"I offered to buy him out shortly after I moved back. It's taken me this long to raise the necessary capital to make the deal. With the nosedive oil prices have taken lately, banks aren't exactly eager to loan money on something like this."

"Can you afford to buy him out?"

"To tell you the truth, I'm in hock up to my neck." MacCrea smiled. "I hope the Arabian horse business is good."

"But . . . why are you doing this?"

"Can't you guess?" he teased. "I lost you twice because of my business dealings with Lane and Rachel. I'm not about to let that be the reason I lose you a third time."

"You don't have to do this."

"That's a risk I'm not willing to take."

"You're crazy, MacCrea." But there was love in her eyes.

"You're damned right I am. All because of you." Seeing that look on her face, he couldn't keep a rein on his desire any longer.

Kissing and caressing her, he dispensed with the barrier of her clothes, turning her faint protests about Eden into low moans of need. When she was writhing against him, he carried her to the bed, stripped off his own clothes, and joined her there, immediately reaching out to gather her close and feel the heat of her flesh against his. He nibbled at her throat and breasts while his hands stroked the smooth skin of her thighs and hips, letting the tension build until the ache was mutual.

As he buried himself inside her, she arched her hips to take him all in. They rocked together, the tempo building, straining. For one brief instant, before the paroxysm of intense pleasure claimed him, MacCrea somehow knew that it would always be this way with them — thrust matching thrust, passion equaling passion, and love rivaling love. And he didn't want it any other way.

Three days later, Dobie's attorney contacted Abbie and informed her of Dobie's terms for an uncontested divorce. She was to agree to the immediate termination of her lease on his property, relinquish all financial claims to any permanent improvements she had made on his land, forfeit any rights to property acquired since their marriage, remove his name from Eden's birth certificate, and waive any claim for child support. In return, she was to keep all of her Arabian horses, the related tack and stable equipment, and the monies earned from them, plus any personal items that belonged to Abbie or her daughter, and allow him reasonable visitation privileges with Eden. Abbie agreed.

44

*L*ike a monarch surveying his admiring subjects, the blood bay stallion gazed at the crowd gathered at the paddock rail. Magnificent and regal, he seemed totally indifferent to the saddle being placed on his back and the ministrations of the attendants — a king accustomed to being dressed by others.

"Isn't he just stunning, Lane?" she declared, unable to turn her gaze away from Sirocco to glance at her husband. "Have you ever seen him look so sleek and fit? He's going to win today. I know he is."

Hearing her voice, the stallion thrust his dark muzzle toward her, stretching out his long neck. Rachel moved to his head, rubbing him just behind the ear and studying up close the huge dark eyes and the network of veins on his face, so intent on her stallion that she didn't hear Lane's reply.

"We'll all be cheering for him."

"Who said beauty can't run?" she crooned softly. "We'll show her today, won't we?" She gave him a hug and a kiss. "Just for luck," she said and stepped back to stand next to Lane.

Out of the corner of her eye, Rachel caught a silver-white flash of movement and turned her head slightly to look at the white stallion, his head flung high, his nostrils widely distended as if trying to catch her scent. A little to the left stood Abbie with that old Polack guru of hers, Ben Jablonski. MacCrea was there, too, and the child. Rachel stared at the smiling and confident foursome, conscious of a faint bristling along her spine.

"May I give Sirocco a good luck pat, Mother? Will he let me?"

Distracted by the sight of her longtime rival, Rachel snapped an irritated, "Of course."

Then the unusualness of her son's request struck her and she turned to stare at Alex, dressed in short pants and a button-down white shirt, his brown hair neatly slicked in place. Warily, he approached the bay stallion and reached up to cautiously pet a muscled shoulder. "Good luck, Sirocco," he offered softly, then backed up quickly when the stallion dipped his head toward him. Alex stopped when he was safely between his father and Mrs. Weldon again.

"You have certainly gotten braver, Alex. I always thought you were afraid of horses," Rachel commented, wondering at the change in him.

He looked down, avoiding her gaze. "They're big, but they won't hurt you — not on purpose."

"I'm glad you finally realized that. Horses can be your dearest friends." She gazed at the stallion, this son of Simoon that meant so much to her, then glanced back at Alex in time to catch his small nod of agreement. "Has a horse become your friend, Alex?" Once she'd seen him duck under the fence to the broodmare pasture and disappear among the pecan trees. She knew how curious horses could be and wondered if one of them had come to investigate this small human who had entered their domain.

But her only response from Alex was a noncommittal shrug as he tucked his chin even closer to the collar of his white shirt. Frustrated, Rachel wondered why she even bothered to try to communicate with her son. He didn't want anything to do with her. He never did. Lane and his nanny, Mrs. Weldon, were the only two people Alex cared about.

Leaving the paddock area, they started making their way to their box seats in the grandstand. She knew that Ross would be waiting for them . . . as planned. Of course, she'd act surprised to see him and pretend that she didn't know he was in town — both of them ignoring the fact they'd been together last night.

It had been an absolutely wonderful evening, marred only by one small argument when Ross had attempted to give her the business card of a supposedly brilliant divorce lawyer. No matter how many times she tried to explain to him, Ross simply refused to accept the fact that she didn't want to get a divorce from Lane, not now and not later. Why should she? She had everything she could ever possibly want: her horses, her home, Lane, and Ross.

Rachel led the way as they approached the box. She spied Ross immediately, the cowboy hat on his head distinctly setting him apart from the crowd. He had on a pair of dark glasses, partly to shade his eyes from the bright July sunlight and partly to avoid being recognized by the large holiday crowd at the racetrack.

"Lane, look who's here." But she didn't wait for his reply, quickening her steps to hurry to Ross. "This is a surprise," she declared, briefly going into his arms and kissing the air near his cheek. "I thought you weren't going to be able to make it. You told me last week that you had a performance scheduled on the Fourth."

"I do," Ross said, speaking up for Lane's benefit. "I promised Willie I'd be on hand to sing at his annual picnic. If I leave right after the race, I can just make it. I told my pilot to have the plane fueled and the engines running so we could take off as soon as I got to the airport." As Lane joined them in the box, Rachel moved to the side to allow Ross to shake hands with him. "Hello, Lane. It's good to see you again. With your busy schedule, I wasn't sure you'd be here today either."

"There was no chance of that, Ross. I've always made it a point to be with Rachel at events that are important to her."

Startled by his statement, Rachel looked at him — startled because it was true. Even though Lane hadn't been at every single horse show or race, he had been present for the major ones despite his busy schedule. Until this very moment, she hadn't realized that.

Minutes later, the horses paraded onto the track, its condition officially listed as fast. Immediately she gave them her undivided attention, excluding every other thought from her mind.

As the horses were led into the starting gate, Rachel lifted the binoculars to watch the proceedings, using them as well to hide the mounting tension that stretched her nerves thin. Sirocco had to win this race. Right now, it was more important to her than winning the Nationals this fall.

When the gates sprang open to the loud clanging of bells, it felt as if her heart leaped into her throat and stayed there, a strangling ball of apprehension. The eleven horses appeared to explode as one out of the gates and ran stride for stride for several yards. Then she saw Sirocco surge forward to take the lead, a black-tipped flame racing in front of the field.

A chestnut came up to challenge on the outside. Rachel scanned the rest of the field, finally locating Abbie's horse, running in fifth or sixth position. Someone had told her that he usually came off the pace.

The other nine horses in the field didn't really mean anything to her. In her mind, this race was between Sirocco and Windstorm. As the horses rounded the first turn and headed down the backstretch with Sirocco still running in front, Rachel briefly lowered her glasses and stole a glance at Abbie, standing in a nearby owner's box. Even at a distance, she looked animated and excited, tense with emotion. Rachel felt like a statue by comparison, unable to let her feelings show. She wanted to yell and cheer, too, but she couldn't.

Instead she trained the binoculars on the blood bay stallion leading the field by three lengths. But that distance was quickly shortened as other horses made their move on him coming out of the turn for home. The silver-white horse along the rail charged closer with every stride. But Sirocco's jockey didn't see him. He was concentrating on the black bay charging up on the outside to challenge Sirocco.

Rachel wanted to yell a warning to the jockey, but she couldn't seem to open her mouth. The white stallion got a nose in front, but Sirocco came right back to race neck and neck with him, muscles bulging and straining, hooves pounding and digging the hard dirt.

An eighth of a mile from the finish line, Sirocco's jockey went to the whip. The bay stallion seemed to respond with a fresh burst of speed, but he couldn't shake off his challenger. The white stallion stayed right with him. Suddenly Sirocco appeared to stumble. The jockey tried to pull him up, but in the next stride, he fell, tumbling headfirst onto the track, directly in the path of the onrushing field.

"No!" Rachel screamed, trying to deny what her eyes were seeing as she struggled free from the pair of hands that gripped her. "Not Sirocco! *No!*"

Abbie never saw Windstorm cross the finish line in front. She felt numb with shock, her gaze riveted in horror on the fallen horse and rider, both lying motionless in the wake of the field. A hush had fallen over the crowd as several track personnel rushed to the downed victims.

"What happened, Mommy? Why isn't that horse getting up? Is he hurt?"

Hearing the fearful uncertainty in her voice, Abbie held Eden closer. "I'm afraid so, honey."

"Will he be all right?"

"I don't know." The jockey was attempting to get up despite the efforts of two men to make him lie still and wait for the ambulance speeding onto the track. But there was no discernible movement from the stallion. Abbie looked over at Rachel's box. Sirocco wasn't even her horse, but she could feel the pain, remembering her own terrible ordeal when River Breeze lay hurt.

Lane was at Rachel's side, an arm around her for support, as he cleared a path for them through the gawking crowd. Distantly Abbie could hear Rachel's hysterical, sobbing cries, "I've got to go to him. Please. I've got to go to him."

"Oh, God." Abbie turned away from the sight. She felt Mac-Crea's hand touch her shoulder.

"They'll want you down in the winner's circle for the cup presentation."

"I can't." She shook her head from side to side, protesting the need for her to be there. She'd won. At last she'd beaten Rachel. But she just felt sick inside.

"You have to. Windstorm won. The accident doesn't change that." Taking her by the elbow, MacCrea steered her out of the box toward the winner's circle below. Abbie knew he was right, but that didn't make it any easier.

Outside the winner's circle, she stopped, ignoring the attempts of a track steward to hustle her inside. The enclosure gave her a full view of the activity on the track. She could see the bay stallion lying in the dirt, the sunlight firing his red coat. The track veterinarian crouched beside the horse and several others stood around him. As two paramedics helped the jockey into the ambulance, Lane and Rachel walked onto the track.

"MacCrea, please. I have to know how serious it is. Will you go see?"

He regarded her solemnly for an instant. "Of course."

As MacCrea walked away, Abbie reluctantly allowed herself to be ushered into the winner's circle along with Ben and Eden. When Windstorm came prancing in, tugging at the groom's lead, lathered but still eager, she felt a rush of pride. She had bred and raised this stallion, a winner on the racetrack and in the show ring. Tearfully she hugged the Arabian stallion.

"We won, fair and square." The jockey was all smiles as he glanced down at her. "We were going past him before he went down."

"What happened? Do you know?" she asked.

He shook his head. "I heard a pop . . . like a bone snapping. He was a game horse, but we woulda won anyway. I asked Storm for more and he had it to give. The bay only had heart left."

"Like a bone snapping": the phrase echoed and reechoed in her mind. She tried to remind herself that a broken bone didn't necessarily mean the end of Sirocco. Look at River Breeze. "What about the jockey?"

"Joe, one of the stewards, said it looked like he broke his shoulder and maybe got a concussion out of it. Angel's tough. He'll be all right. I've seen worse spills."

A track official came over. "We're ready to make the presentation now, Mrs. Hix, if you'll just step over here."

As Abbie turned to follow him, the jockey repeated his earlier statement. "We woulda won anyway."

Numbly she accepted the congratulations from the race's sponsor, along with the silver trophy cup and the winner's share of the purse, and posed for the obligatory photograph, but she couldn't smile for the camera — not when, beyond it, she could see Rachel on the track, kneeling beside her stallion, mindless of the white linen suit she wore.

At last it was over. Abbie paused outside the winner's circle, watching as the jockey dismounted and pulled off the saddle to weigh in officially. A groom spread a blue blanket over Windstorm's lathered back and led him away.

"Aren't we going with Windstorm back to the barn, Mommy?" Eden frowned up at her, puzzled by this change in their routine and the strange undercurrents in the air.

"Not now. I want to wait for MacCrea." He was walking back across the track toward them now. She had to know what he'd found out.

"How come you look so sad, Mommy? Aren't you happy that Windstorm won?"

Sighing, Abbie tried to come up with an answer. "I am happy that he won, but I'm also sorry the other horse got hurt." But it wasn't just any horse. Sirocco was Rachel's stallion. Abbie didn't know how to explain to Eden why that was so significant. "Wait here with Ben while I go talk to MacCrea."

Ignoring Eden's protest that she wanted to come, too, Abbie walked forward to meet MacCrea. She searched his face for some clue as to the seriousness of Sirocco's injuries, but his expression showed her nothing. Unconsciously she tightened her hold on the silver trophy cradled in her arm as a truck pulled to a stop near the fallen horse, its bulk blocking the stallion from her sight.

"How bad is it?" she asked.

But MacCrea didn't answer until he was directly in front of her. When he gently gripped her shoulders, Abbie tried to brace herself mentally. "He's dead, Abbie. He broke his neck in the fall."

"No." It came out in one long, painful breath. "Oh, God, no." She sagged against him, moving her head from side to side, trying to deny it. "It can't be true. It can't."

"It is. I'm sorry."

"Why?" she cried, doubling her hand into a fist. "Why did it have to happen?"

But there were no answers to the questions she asked. Again, her gaze was drawn to the track as she pushed away from MacCrea. This time she understood the reason for the truck. It was there to haul away the dead stallion. Soon the horses in the next race would parade onto the track and everyone would be hurrying to place their bets, the tragedy of this race temporarily forgotten. But Abbie knew she would never forget that moment when Sirocco went down, or the tangle of legs as the onrushing horses struggled to jump the obstacle suddenly in their path, the stumbling, the near collisions, the wild swervings, and then, in the settling dust, Sirocco lying there, motionless.

Through a misting of tears, she saw Rachel, slowly walking her way, supported by Lane, her usually composed features wracked by grief. As she moved to intercept Rachel, MacCrea stopped her.

"Where are you going?"

"Rachel . . . I have to talk to her. I never wanted this to happen."

"Abbie, no. It's better if you don't."

But she wouldn't listen to him, pulling away to walk to them. Lane saw her first and paused, but Rachel stared at her without appearing to see her at all.

"Rachel, I . . . just wanted you to know that . . . I'm sorry." The words sounded so inadequate when she said them. "I'm truly sorry." But repeating them didn't seem to give them more weight.

Yet they must have penetrated, as Rachel looked at her with bitter loathing. "Why should you be sorry? Your horse won the race. That's what you wanted, isn't it?"

"I wanted him to win, yes, but . . . not this way." But the cup was there in her arms, evidence of Windstorm's victory.

"Why not?" Rachel challenged, her voice threatening to break. "Didn't you set out to prove that your stallion was better than mine? You've done it, so just go away and leave me alone. Sirocco's dead.

Do you hear? He's dead. He's dead." She sobbed wildly and collapsed against Lane, hysterical now with grief.

This time when Abbie felt MacCrea's hand on her arm, she let him lead her away without a protest. "It's my fault," she said miserably.

"It was an accident, Abbie, an accident. It could have happened to any horse in the field, including Windstorm. I'm not going to let you blame yourself for it."

"But it was my fault. She would never have raced Sirocco if I hadn't goaded her into it. Remember that night right after Sirocco won at Scottsdale, when I told her that he'd won a beauty contest, that he didn't have the conformation to race? My God . . . I even told her he'd break down if she did race him. I forced her into this."

"She made her own decision. She knew the risk she was taking and raced him anyway. You can't hold yourself responsible for that."

But Abbie knew better.

⬧ 45 ⬧

The morning breeze skipped across the swimming pool, then paused to riffle the pages of the purchase agreement on Lane's lap and scurried on. Automatically, Lane smoothed the pages flat as he continued to stare at the slight figure in the distance, huddled beside the freshly turned earth.

His half-lensed reading glasses sat on the umbrellaed poolside table next to him. He had yet to read the first page of the document on his lap. Not that he really needed to. He'd already gone over the agreement thoroughly the day before. He'd merely intended to look it over once more before MacCrea arrived this afternoon for the signing. But his concern for Rachel made it next to impossible to concentrate on business matters for any length of time.

"Watch me, Daddy!" Alex shouted.

With difficulty, he forced his attention away from Rachel and turned in time to see his son cannonball into the pool with a mighty splash that sprayed water far onto the deck. He waited until he saw Alex surface and dog-paddle vigorously toward the ladder.

"That's enough diving for today, Alex," he called to him. "You aren't that good a swimmer yet." If dog-paddling could be called swimming. "Get your inner tube and go play in the shallow end of the pool."

When Lane saw his young son trotting to the opposite side, he let his attention revert back to Rachel. She hadn't moved from her silent vigil by the grave.

"Excuse me, Mr. Canfield." Maria, the housemaid, approached his chair, the thick rubber soles of her white work shoes making almost no sound as she crossed the deck. "Mr. Tibbs is here." She partially turned to indicate the man following her dressed in new jeans and a pearl-snap western shirt.

"Thank you, Maria." Lane absently moved the papers off his lap and rose to greet his guest. "Hello, Ross. I wasn't aware you were expected." Briefly he shook hands with him, then motioned to the deck chair next to his. "Have a seat."

"Sorry, I can't stay." Ross removed his cowboy hat and briefly ran his fingers through his curly hair, then used both hands to turn the dark hat in a circle in front of him, inching it around by degrees. "I just stopped by to see how Rachel is. I know how upset she was over Sirocco. I only wish I could have stayed —"

"I understand." Lane found it strangely ironic to be standing here talking to Ross about Rachel. Although why not? They were two men who loved her. "She has taken the stallion's death very hard."

"Where is she?"

"Over there. By his grave," he said, pointing out the general location with a nod of his head. "She insisted on having him brought back for burial here at River Bend. At the time, I didn't see any harm in it. Now I'm not so sure it was a good idea."

"Do you mind if I go talk to her? I've brought something with me that might . . . well, make her feel a little better."

"Go ahead." At this point, Lane didn't care who brought Rachel out of her deep depression as long as someone did. He couldn't stand to see her this way.

With a self-conscious nod, Ross acknowledged the comment, then pushed the hat onto his head and walked away, cutting across the lawn toward the unmarked grave set off by itself near the fence line to the back pasture, halfway between the house and the barns. Lane watched him go, wondering if he would succeed, wondering if Rachel would wind up in his arms — this time for good. Yet she had turned to him, not Ross, when the accident occurred. Surely that action had to have been an instinctive one. At least, that's what he kept telling himself.

"Daddy. Daddy, did you see the big splash I made?" Alex came running around the pool to him, his wet, bare feet making slapping sounds on the concrete.

"I certainly did." Lane made a concerted effort to give Alex his whole attention. Too frequently in the last few days Alex had been shunted aside, Lane's concern for Rachel taking precedence over him. "You nearly got me wet."

"I know." Alex grinned with a trace of impish glee. "Would you like to swim with me for a while?"

"I'd like to, but I can't. I have some papers to go over, but I'll watch you."

Alex thought about that. "I think I'll just sit here with you for a while and rest. Swimming is pretty tiring."

"Yes, it is," Lane agreed, smiling faintly as Alex climbed onto the deck chair by the table.

Resuming his seat, Lane picked up the purchase agreement, but left his glasses on the table. Alex tapped his hand idly on the tube-like arm of the deck chair and gazed off in the direction of the grave. "What did Mr. Tibbs want?"

"He came to see your mother. He brought her something that he hopes will cheer her up a little."

"She's awfully sad, isn't she?"

"Yes. She loved Sirocco very much. She was there when he was born. You were just a tiny baby then. So she'd had him almost as long as she's had you. It hurts when you lose someone or something you care about a lot."

"I wish there was something I could do to make her feel better."

Lane caught the wistful note in Alex's voice and understood the need he felt to contribute something, however small. "Maybe there is."

"What?" Alex looked at him hopefully.

"A lot of times when you're very sad, little things mean more than anything else . . . thoughtful little things that say you care. For instance, you could pick your mother some wildflowers and give them to her so she can place them on Sirocco's grave. Or you could make her a card —"

"I could draw her a picture of Sirocco and color it for her. That way she'd always have a picture of him to remember what he looked like," Alex suggested excitedly. "She'd like that, wouldn't she? I can draw really, really good, Mrs. Weldon says. And I'd draw this extra good."

"I know you would. And I think your mother would like that very much." Lane smiled.

"I'm going to do it right now." Before the sentence was finished,

Alex had scrambled out of the chair. He took off at a run for the house.

Watching him, Lane couldn't help thinking that it must be wonderful to be young and innocent enough to believe that you could find the answers for life's sorrows.

Rachel sat on the grass next to the long rectangular patch of freshly turned earth, something childlike in her pose: her legs curled up to one side, her head and shoulders bowed, one hand resting on the clods of dirt. A soft breeze ran over her dark hair, lifting tendrils and laying them back down like a mother lightly playing with a child's hair in an attempt to soothe and comfort.

As Ross walked up to her, she gave no sign that she was even aware of his presence. He paused, struck for a few seconds by the stark grief in her expression. There were no tears. He almost wished there were. He had the feeling they would have been easier to cope with than this intense sorrow that went so much deeper.

"Hello, Rachel."

At first he wasn't sure she'd heard him. Then she looked up. Her eyes were dull and blank, with almost no life in them at all. Even though she looked straight at him, Ross wasn't sure she saw him standing there. Then she seemed to rouse herself to some level of awareness.

"This is where Sirocco is buried. I'm having a marker made — a marble one, engraved with his name and the dates of his life, and a verse from a poem I once read. I've changed it a little to make it just for him." Almost dreamlike, she quoted the line, " 'If you have seen nothing but the beauty of his markings and limbs, his true beauty was hidden from you.' "

"It's beautiful."

"Feel the earth." She dug her fingers into the dirt. "It's warm . . . like his body was."

"It's the sun that makes it feel that way."

He started to worry about her, then she sighed dispiritedly and gazed up at him. This time the pain was visible in her expression. "I know," she said. "But sometimes I like to pretend it's from him."

"You can't do things like that, Rachel. It isn't good for you."

"I don't care. I want him to be here . . . with me," she declared insistently.

"Don't do this, Rachel. He's gone. You can't change that. I'm here with you. Please, come walk with me." Taking her by the shoulders, he gently forced her to stand up.

She offered no resistance, yet she continued to stare at the grave, reluctant to leave it as he turned her away. "He should be here, nickering to those mares in the pasture."

"I wish there was some way I could make you feel better — something I could say . . . or do. But I just don't know the right words." He felt helpless and frustrated, just like at the track. "You don't know how many times I wished that I hadn't left you that day, but I had to. There didn't seem to be anything I could do there. Lane was with you. I knew he'd look after you and see to everything."

"Lane's always there, every time," she murmured.

"I know." It bothered him that she had turned to Lane in those first shocked seconds after the accident occurred. She was supposed to be in love with him. "Look, I'm due back in Nashville tonight. My record company wants me to cut a new album and I have a meeting scheduled tomorrow with the producer. But if you want me to stay here with you, I'll cancel it."

"There's no need. It doesn't matter whether you're here or not. Nothing matters anymore."

She was so indifferent, so distant with him, as if he were a stranger, not the man who had held her in his arms and made love to her countless times in the past. They were walking side by side, his arm was around her, yet there was no sense of closeness. Somehow he had to change that.

"Come on. I have something to show you." He picked up their pace as they neared the palatial barn, but his statement sparked no interest from her. "Aren't you going to ask what it is?"

"What?" It was obvious she asked only because he prompted her.

"It's a surprise, but I can guarantee you're going to like it. Just wait and see if you don't."

But when Rachel spotted the truck and horse trailer parked outside the barn's imposing main entrance, she pulled back. "Somebody's here. I don't want to see them."

"It's okay. Honest. That's my rig."

"Yours? I don't understand." She frowned at him. For the first time, Ross had the feeling that he'd finally gotten through that wall of grief that insulated her.

"Remember I said I had a surprise for you." He motioned to the handler standing at the back of the trailer, gesturing for him to bring the filly out. "Well, here it is." Stopping, he turned to watch her face as the man walked the filly into her view. A puzzled look flickered across her face as she stared at the young Arabian, the morning sunlight flashing on her bronze coat. "It's Jewel," he said.

"Yes, but why did you bring her here?" She turned to him, her frown deepening.

"I want you to have her." As she drew back from him, still frowning, Ross went on. "I know how much you've always wanted her, and I meant it when I said she wasn't for sale. We're never going to have that foal out of her by Sirocco, so I'm giving her to you — as a present."

"No." She backed another step away from him, vaguely indignant and angry.

Puzzled by her reaction, Ross took the lead rope from the handler and offered it to her. "Please take her." But she shook her head and hid her hands behind her back. "I want you to have her, Rachel. I know she's not Sirocco, and . . . maybe I can't make it up to you for not staying with you after the accident, but let me try."

Something inside her seemed to snap. "Why does everybody always give me presents? Do you think you can buy me?" she cried in outrage. "Presents don't make up for all the hours I've been alone. I'm not a child that you can give a bauble to and think that will make the hurt go away. It won't work anymore!"

"I don't know what you're talking about," Ross said, confused and taken aback by her sudden outburst. "I'm not trying to buy you. I —"

"Then what do you call it? You feel guilty, so you want to give me your horse so you can ease your conscience. Well, I don't want your horse! And I don't want you! Just take your horse and get out of here. Don't ever come back! Do you hear? Not ever again!" Her hands were clenched into fists at her sides as she stood before him, trembling with anger, tears rolling down her cheeks.

"Rachel, you don't mean that. You're just upset." Stunned, Ross struggled to find an excuse for the abrupt change in her. "You don't know what you're saying."

"I know precisely what I'm saying," she retorted, her voice quivering with anger. "And if you don't have that horse loaded up and out of here within five minutes, I'm calling the sheriff and ordering him to escort you off this farm." She turned on her heel and headed for the barn, breaking into a run when she was halfway to the door.

"Rachel . . ." Ross took an uncertain step after her, unable to believe any of this was really happening.

"I think she means it," the handler said behind him.

Ross was forced to agree.

Sobbing in despair, Rachel ran straight to the section of the barn that housed the broodmares, not stopping until she reached the third one from the end. Hurrying frantically, she unhooked the webbed gate and went inside, pausing long enough to fasten it behind her, then throwing her arms around the neck of the dappled gray mare inside and burying her face in the charcoal-streaked mane.

"Simoon, Simoon," she cried brokenly. "Why do they always do this? Why? They keep trying to give me presents, when all I want is their love. Nobody really cares about me. Nobody." As she sobbed out her anguish and hurt, she felt the mare nudging her anxiously, accompanied by a soft whicker of concern. "No, that's not true, is it? You care, don't you, my beauty?" Rachel murmured, moving to face the mare and taking her head in both her hands, smiling faintly as the mare nuzzled at the tears on her cheeks, then, with a slurp of her big tongue, licked curiously at the salty wetness. "I love you, too, my Simoon. You've never let me down, have you?"

Straw rustled in the adjoining stall as the aging red gelding moved closer to the dividing partition and nickered for attention. Turning, Rachel scratched the underside of his grayed lip through the bars while she continued to rub the hollow behind the mare's ear.

"I know you care, too, Ahmar. I haven't forgotten you," she crooned, still intensely sad.

Overhead, circulating fans whirred, constantly moving the air and stirring up the strong smell of horse, hay, manure, and grain. Rachel turned back to the mare and rubbed her head against the mare's cheek, cuddling close to the Arabian, enjoying the slickness of her coat and the heat from her body, and breathing in her stimulating odor, finding a reassurance in the equine contact that she needed.

"Are you all right, Miz Canfield?"

Startled by the human intrusion, Rachel caught a quick glimpse of the groom standing at the stall entrance, then ducked back behind the mare, keeping her face hidden so he couldn't see her tears. She didn't want him or anybody else feeling sorry for her. She didn't need or want their pity.

"Yes, I am," she asserted. "I'd like to be alone. Please . . . go."

"Yes, ma'am."

Ahmar snorted as the groom passed his stall. When the gelding's attention swung back to her, Rachel knew they were alone.

"It always was the three of us, wasn't it?" she remembered, then reconsidered her statement. "Not always. For a while there were four. Now . . . Sirocco's gone. I miss him so much." She could feel the sobs coming again and hugged Simoon's neck. "Why did he have to die like that? It isn't fair. Your son's gone, Simoon. Do you understand that? Your son . . . and mine, too."

She began to cry softly, her tears wetting the dark gray hairs on the mare's neck. Here, she felt free to pour out her sorrows and her pain, free to grieve over the death of her beloved stallion and the betrayal by yet another man who hadn't truly loved her.

Simoon snorted and swung her head toward the stall opening, warning Rachel of someone's approach. Sniffling back her tears, she wiped frantically at her wet cheeks and eyes and struggled to summon a modicum of composure.

"Mommy?" Alex appeared, moving slowly down the wide aisle between the box stalls, cautiously looking to the right and left. "Are you here?"

She wanted to pretend she couldn't hear him, to slink into the far corner of the stall and hide from him — from everyone. But she knew she couldn't do that.

"Yes, Alex. What is it?" she demanded, her voice tight and choked from her recent cry.

At first he didn't know which stall her voice had come from, then he saw her. "There you are." He trotted eagerly to the webbed gate, trying to hide the sheet of paper in his hand behind his back. "I've been looking everywhere for you."

"If it's time for lunch, tell Maria I'm not hungry," she retorted sharply, impatient to be rid of him and be alone again. It was too difficult trying to hide all the hurt and pain she felt. She remembered the terrible agony of all his questions during the flight home: Why did Sirocco die? Why did he break his neck? Why did Mommy race him? Why was Mommy crying? Why did she love Sirocco? Why, why, why. She couldn't bear the thought of going through that ordeal all over again. Lane should be here to answer his questions the way he had on the plane.

"It isn't lunchtime yet. At least, I don't think it is. I brought you something." Stretching, he reached over the webbing, all smiles and eagerness, as he held out the paper he'd been hiding behind his back.

"It's for you. I wanted to wrap it in pretty paper with a bow and everything, but Mrs. Weldon said we didn't have any."

Another present, Rachel thought bitterly. Why were they all trying to buy her? "I don't want it."

His smile faded abruptly. "But . . . Daddy thought —"

"Daddy was wrong! I don't want any presents! Not from you. Not from anyone. Do you understand?" She was too blinded by the angry tears that scalded her eyes to see the stricken look on his face. "Go. Go back to your daddy. I don't want you here!"

Whirling around, she sought the comfort of Simoon's warm body. Distantly, she heard the sound of his racing footsteps as Alex ran from the stall, the paper fluttering into the stall to land on the bedding of wood shavings.

She was alone with her horses again, and that was the way she wanted it. She didn't need anybody. And she spent the next hour trying to convince herself and them of that.

When she heard footsteps in the brick aisle approaching the stall again, she railed silently at the world for not leaving her alone. She saw Lane come into view, his leonine mane of silver hair distinctly identifying him as he glanced anxiously around.

"Alex?" he called.

Rachel nearly laughed out loud. She should have known he wasn't worried about her. He only cared about his son. She shrank back against the wall, trying to make herself small, hoping he wouldn't see her. But the movement seemed to draw his attention. He turned and looked directly at her.

"Rachel, have you seen Alex? Lunch is ready. But when Maria called him, he didn't answer."

"I don't know where he is," she replied flatly, her voice sounding as dull and dead as she felt inside.

Lane frowned and stepped closer to the stall. "But he must be around here somewhere. One of the grooms said he was positive he saw him come — What's that?" He stared at something on the stall floor. Reluctantly Rachel moved around to the other side of the mare to see what he meant. A paper, crumpled in the center by a hoof, lay among the shavings. Rachel saw it, but she made no attempt to retrieve it as Lane unhooked the gate and entered the stall. "Isn't that the picture of Sirocco that Alex drew for you?"

"I guess." She shrugged as he picked up the paper to look at it.

"Then he was here? He brought this to you?" He glanced at her questioningly, seeking confirmation.

"Yes." She stared at the paper Lane held, resenting all that it represented. "I told him I didn't want it. I thought he took it with him."

"You what?" Lane glared at her in cold, disbelieving anger. "How could you do that? He made this for you!"

"I don't care!" she hurled angrily. "Why should I? All my life people have given me presents, thinking that would make up for everything. Well, it doesn't! It never has."

"My God, Rachel, he's just a child. He wanted to do something that might make you feel better. Are you so wrapped up in your own self-pity that you can't see that we hurt because you hurt? This was more than a child's drawing. It was his way of letting you know he cared!"

Never in her life had Rachel ever seen Lane so angry. All his angry words hammered at her like blows to the head. For a second, she thought he was actually going to strike her. She shrank from him, cowering a little.

"I didn't know," she said faintly. "I thought —"

"You thought," he repeated harshly. "You thought only about yourself. I wonder if you ever think about anybody else." He left her standing there, still reeling from his angry condemnation.

As MacCrea drove past the massive white pillars that marked the entrance to River Bend, he glanced at the clock on the car's dashboard. He was five minutes late for his one-thirty meeting with Lane. As he sped up the wide driveway, he noticed two, no, three men, spread out in a line, walking through the pasture on his left. Initially it struck him as strange, then he dismissed it, deciding they were probably trying to catch one of the horses.

When he pulled into the yard, he saw Rachel come riding in astride the dappled gray mare she frequently rode. The horse's neck was dark with sweat. MacCrea frowned, wondering what Rachel was doing out riding in the heat of the day like this . . . and those men in the pasture . . . something was wrong. Quickly, he turned away from the house and headed for the barn, arriving just as Rachel dismounted and handed the reins to one of the grooms.

As he climbed out of his car, MacCrea caught the last part of the question she asked the groom: ". . . seen anything?" The groom responded with a negative shake of his head and led the horse away.

"What's going on?"

Rachel turned with a small start, a frantic look on her face. "MacCrea. I didn't know that was you."

"Where's Lane?"

"He's out with the others, looking for Alex. He's disappeared. Nobody's seen him since before lunch. We've called and called but" — she paused, drawing in a deep, shaky breath — "I'm worried that . . . something's happened to him. I'll never forgive myself if it has."

MacCrea started to tell her that he thought he might know where Alex was. After all, the boy didn't know Eden wasn't living at the neighboring farm anymore. But there was the chance he could be wrong. If he was, telling Rachel his suspicion would just stir up more trouble. It would be better to check it out himself.

"He'll turn up."

"I hope so," she replied fervently.

"If you see Lane, tell him I'll be back later."

"I will." She nodded.

But MacCrea doubted that she would remember, as he walked back to his car and climbed in.

Abbie carried the last box of their belongings out of the farmhouse and stowed it in the backseat of her car. Pausing, she wiped the beads of perspiration from her forehead and glanced at the rental van parked in front of the broodmare barn. Two of the grooms were systematically going through the barns and loading up all tools, tack, implements, and equipment they found. From the looks of it, they were almost done.

Dobie was out working the fields. With luck, she'd be packed and gone before he finished. She hadn't seen him and didn't want to. Telling him she was sorry again wouldn't undo the damage she'd done to all their lives.

Hearing the sound of a car's engine growing steadily louder, Abbie turned to glance down the driveway. When she recognized MacCrea's car, she frowned in surprise. What if Dobie saw him?

She tried to hide her concern as she walked over to him. "What are you doing here?"

"I was hoping to find Alex. You haven't seen him, have you?"

"Alex? No. Why?"

"I just came from River Bend. They're turning the place upside down looking for him. Nobody's seen him since late this morning. I thought . . . he might have come over here to play with Eden."

"We've been here nearly all day. Besides, after the heavy rains the other night, the creek between here and River Bend has been running bank full." The instant the words were out, Abbie felt a cold chill of fear. "Mac, you don't think he would have tried to cross it. I know he's only a little boy, but surely he would see that it's too dangerous."

Looking grim, MacCrea opened the car door. "I'd better go look."

"I'm coming with you." Abbie hurried around to the other side.

MacCrea drove out of the yard onto the rutted track that led to the lower pasture and the creek. When they reached the gate, Abbie hopped out to open it, then scrambled back inside after closing it behind them.

"There's a natural ford right along there where we usually cross." She pointed to a section of the tree-lined creek just ahead of them.

Short of the area she'd indicated, MacCrea stopped the car. "Let's get out and walk."

The blue sky, the bright, shining sun, and the rain-washed green of the trees gave a deceptive look of peace and quiet to the scene. But the stream was no longer a narrow rivulet of water trickling slowly over its bed of sand and gravel. The run-off from the recent heavy rain had turned it into an angry torrent. Its roar almost drowned out the sound of the two slamming car doors.

Linking up in front of the car, they paused to scan the shaded bank and the swollen creek, its dark waters tumbling violently down the narrow channel, hurling along branches, dead limbs — anything that got in their path.

"Where do you think he is?" Abbie was more worried than before. "He has to know they're looking for him by now."

"'Let's hope he just doesn't want to be found."

"He wouldn't have tried to cross that," she insisted. "He's too timid." She couldn't find any consolation in that thought as she stared at a section of the bank on the opposite side that had caved in, undermined by the tremendous onslaught of water.

"We'd better split up and cover both sides." MacCrea headed for the creek's natural ford.

"Be careful," she urged.

Pausing, he smiled reassuringly at her, then waded into the rushing stream, picking his way carefully. At its deepest point, the water came up to his hips . . . well over a little boy's head. As she watched him fight to keep his balance in the strong current, she realized that Alex wouldn't have had a chance if he'd fallen in.

Safely on the other side, MacCrea waved to her, then looked around. Cupping his hands to his mouth, he shouted, "I found some tracks!

He's been here!" He gestured downstream, indicating they should start their search in that direction.

Abbie was more worried than before, aware that MacCrea had chosen this direction thinking that if Alex had fallen in, the raging torrent would have carried his body downstream. His body. No, she refused to think like that. Anxiously she scanned the bank ahead of her, keeping well away from the edge as she moved slowly along, paralleling MacCrea's progress on the other side.

Thirty feet downstream, she spied something yellow caught in a tangle of debris by the opposite bank. "MacCrea, look!" She pointed to what looked like a piece of clothing and unwillingly recalled that Alex had a jacket that color. She held her breath, wanting to be wrong, as MacCrea worked his way to the spot and snared the yellow item from the trapped debris with a broken stick. It was a little boy's yellow jacket.

"Alex!" Abbie called frantically. "Alex, where are you?" She hurried along the bank, mindless of the thickening undergrowth that tried to slow her, now doubly anxious to find Alex. The roaring creek seemed to laugh at her as it rolled ahead of her, a churning, seething mass of water, silt, and debris.

She thought she heard a shout. She stopped to listen, then noticed that MacCrea wasn't anywhere in sight. Had she gotten ahead of him in her search? Hastily she backtracked.

"Abbie!" MacCrea waved to her from the opposite bank, holding a muddy boy astraddle his hip. "I found him!"

She started to cry with relief and pressed a hand to her mouth to cover the sob. Alex was all right. He was safe. Finding a place to ford the stream, MacCrea carried the boy across. Abbie waited tensely on the opposite side, not drawing an easy breath until they were beside her. "Where did you find him?" she asked as MacCrea set him down.

"He was hiding in some brush."

Abbie stooped down to look for herself and make sure he was all right. Up close, she could see the streaks on his grimy cheeks left by tears. "We've been looking for you, Alex. We thought . . ." But she didn't want to voice the fear that was still too fresh. Smiling, she lifted the brown hair off his forehead, damp with perspiration, and smoothed it back off his face. "We'd better take you home."

Abruptly he pulled back. "No. I don't want to go there."

"Why?" Abbie was taken aback by his vehemence. "Your mother and father will be worried about you. You don't want that."

"She won't care," he retorted, tears rolling down his cheeks again. "She doesn't want me. She told me to go away. I did and I'm never going back!"

"Alex, I'm sure she didn't mean it."

"Yes, she did," he asserted, then, as if it was all too much for him to bear alone, he threw himself at Abbie and wrapped his arms tightly around her neck to bury his face against her and cry. "I don't want to go back. I want to stay with you and Eden."

Moved by his wrenching plea, Abbie glanced helplessly at Mac-Crea. MacCrea crouched down beside them and laid a comforting hand on Alex's shoulders as they lifted spasmodically with his sniffling sobs.

"That's not really what you want, Alex," he said. "Think how much you'd miss your father."

"He works all the time."

"Not all the time."

"He could come see me when he doesn't," Alex declared tearfully, obviously having thought it all out.

"Oh, Alex," Abbie murmured and hugged him a little tighter, feeling his pain. "I'm sorry, but it just wouldn't work."

"But why?"

"Because . . . you belong with your mommy and daddy."

"Come on, son. I'll take you home." But as MacCrea tried to pull him away from Abbie, Alex wrapped his arms in a stranglehold around her neck.

"No!"

"I'll carry him," she told MacCrea. Alex clung to her, winding his legs tightly around her middle as she walked back to the car with MacCrea. She continued to hold him once they were inside, cuddling him in her arms like a baby.

"I'll drop you off at your car," MacCrea said.

"No. I'm coming with you." She'd made up her mind about that at the creek. "There are a few things I want to say to Rachel."

"Abbie." His tone was disapproving.

She didn't need to hear any more than that. "I'm going." Nothing and no one was going to stop her, not even MacCrea.

A half-dozen sweaty men, exhausted by their search for the missing boy in the full heat of the day, hunkered together in the shade of a surviving ancient oak, guzzling water from the jugs brought by the house staff and silently shaking their heads in answer to the questions put to them by both Lane and Rachel. Few even looked up when MacCrea drove in with Abbie and Alex.

Abbie struggled out of the passenger side, with Alex still in her arms. At first no one noticed her, their attention all on MacCrea, who was nearest them. As she came around the front of the car, Rachel saw the boy in her arms.

"Alex! You've found him!" Relief flooded her expression as she broke into a run. "Oh, Alex, where have you been? We've been so worried about you."

"He was over at the farm," Abbie answered as Alex tightened his arms around her.

At the sound of her voice, Rachel finally noticed Abbie. Immediately she stopped, wary and suspicious. "Why are you carrying him? Give me my son."

As she tried to take him from her, Alex cried out and hung on to Abbie more fiercely. "No! I want to stay with you."

"What have you done to him?" Rachel glared.

"It's not what I've done, but what you've done to him," Abbie answered as Lane joined them, his sunburned face still showing the mental and physical stress of the search, his shirt drenched with perspiration.

"Is he all right?" he asked worriedly.

"He isn't hurt, if that's what you mean," Abbie replied. Alex didn't resist when Lane reached to take him from her. Abbie willingly handed him over to Lane, but Alex continued to hide his face from Rachel. "You should know that he's been sneaking over to play with my daughter for several months. I probably should have tried to put a stop to it, but I didn't want our children to become involved in our personal conflict."

"You. You're the one who's turned my son against me," Rachel accused. "I should have known you'd do something like this. All my life, everyone's always loved you. Dean — everyone. You've always had everything. Now you're trying to steal my son. I never knew how much I hated you until right now. Get out of here before I have you thrown out!"

"I don't blame you for hating me. I probably deserve it. But I'm not leaving until I've said what I came here to say."

"I'm not interested in listening to anything you have to tell me." She started to turn away, but Abbie caught her arm, checking the movement.

"You have to listen . . . for Alex's sake," she insisted. "He thinks that you don't want him — that you don't love him. You can't let him go on believing that. I grew up thinking my father didn't really love me. So did you. Can't you remember how much that hurt? That's what Alex is feeling now."

"He's never cared about me," she replied stiffly. "It's always been Lane."

"And you resented that, didn't you? Don't you know that Alex picked up on that? Children are very sensitive. But they're still just children. You can't expect them to understand your hurt feelings, when they haven't even learned how to cope with their own. He wants you to love him, and he thinks there's something wrong with him because you don't."

Rachel tried to shut out the things Abbie was saying. Each was a barb, pricking and tearing at her. But none of them was true. They couldn't be. "You don't know what you're talking about," she protested.

"Don't I?" Abbie replied sadly. "Look at us, Rachel. Look at how bitterness and envy have twisted our lives. When I think of all the things I've said, the things I've done, the way I felt. And I blamed you for everything. We're sisters. What turned us into enemies? Why are we always competing against each other? It can't be for Daddy's love. He's gone. But if he could see us now . . . Rachel, you have to know that this isn't the way he wanted us to be."

"Stop it!" Rachel pressed her hands over her ears, but she succeeded in only partially muffling Abbie's voice.

"Maybe he did love us both. It's taken me a long time to realize that. You need to believe that, too. Maybe you and I will never be sisters in the true sense of the word, but can't we at least stop this fighting?"

"You'd like that, wouldn't you?"

Abbie looked at her silently for a long moment. "Just love your son, Rachel," she said finally, emotionally drained. "And let him know it, the way Daddy should have."

Rachel turned and ran, her vision blurred by tears. It was a lie — a trick. It had to be.

As Rachel disappeared from sight near the barn, Abbie felt MacCrea's hand on her shoulder. "You tried."

She glanced at Lane, and the boy in his arms. She hesitated. "I'm sorry for creating a scene."

"Don't be," Lane said gently. "A lot of it needed to be said."

Just then, a clatter of hooves came from the barn. A second later

Rachel burst into view, riding her dark gray mare. For an instant, Abbie stared in shock. "She only has a halter and lead rope on that mare."

"Somebody, quick! Go after her!" Lane ordered.

Sobbing, blinded by tears, Rachel twined her fingers through Simoon's dark mane, holding on to it as well as the cotton lead rope. Digging her heels into the mare's sides, she urged her faster, needing to outrun the thoughts pounding in her head.

"It isn't true. She can't be right," she kept sobbing over and over.

But the drumming in her temples didn't stop as they raced headlong across the pasture, swerving around the towering pecans that loomed in their path and scattering the mares and colts that grazed among them. All the while she kept trying to convince herself that Abbie had said all those things just to confuse her. Dean couldn't have loved them both.

"Daddy." She buried her face in the whipping mane.

She didn't see the white board fence coming up, but she vaguely felt the bunching of the mare's hindquarters and the stiffening brace of the front legs as Simoon tried to get her hindlegs under her and slow down.

At the last second, the mare came to a jerking, sliding stop just short of the fence, unseating Rachel and pitching her forward onto the mare's neck. Simoon reared, twisting to turn away from the fence. Rachel felt herself falling and grasped at the one thing still in her hand: the lead rope. But the pull of her whole weight on it twisted the mare's head around, throwing her off balance. As Rachel hit the ground, the gray mare fell on top of her. Rachel felt first the jarring impact with the hard earth, then the crushing weight of the gray body pressing down on her, then pain . . . pain everywhere, intense and excrutiating. She whimpered her father's name once, then let the blessed blackness consume her.

Severe internal injuries and bleeding was the diagnosis. They operated to stop the bleeding and make what repairs they could, but her prognosis was uncertain. Lane refused to leave the private suite in the hospital's intensive-care unit. Special accommodations were arranged to let him sleep in the same room. But Lane slept little during the three days Rachel lay unconscious. Most of the time he spent by her bed, staring at her deathly pale face, the tubes sticking out from her nose, arms, and body, and the wires running to the monitors, their beeps and blips constantly assuring him that she was still alive when his own eyes doubted it. He'd never been a praying man in the past, but he'd become one as he watched over her, willing her to come back to him.

Her eyelids fluttered. Lane wondered if he had imagined it. When it happened again, he held his breath and gazed at her intently. A moment later, she tried to open her eyes. After the second try, she succeeded. Lane immediately summoned the nurse on duty and leaned closer to the bed.

"Rachel. Can you hear me?"

She appeared to focus on him with difficulty. Her lips moved, but no sound came out. He clutched her hand in both of his and called to her again.

"Lane?" Her voice was softer than a whisper.

"Yes, darling. I'm here." He leaned closer, tears springing into his eyes.

"I . . . knew you . . . would be." The breathy words seemed to require great effort.

The nurse came in and he was forced to move aside. Several times that day, she'd drifted in and out of consciousness. Lane regarded it as a hopeful sign. The specialists he'd hired admitted that the next forty-eight hours were critical.

Abbie shortened her stride to match Ben's slower pace as they crossed the parking lot to the hospital entrance.

"She's got to be all right, Ben." She'd said that over and over the last three days, every time she came to the hospital to see Rachel. But she'd received no encouragement until Lane had phoned the house tonight. "If only I'd let MacCrea take Alex back alone," Abbie said ruefully.

"Do not play this 'if only' game in your head." Ben's lined and craggy face was grim with disapproval. "There is nowhere for it to stop. 'If only' you had not gone there must be followed by 'if only' Alex had not run away, then 'if only' you had not allowed him to play with Eden. Eventually it must become 'if only' Eden had not been born, 'if only' your father had not died. No one can say where the blame truly belongs."

"I know." She sighed heavily. "But I still feel responsible for what happened."

"I remember well the day you learned that River Bend would have to be sold. You also went galloping through the pasture like a mad-woman. If you had fallen, if you had been injured, would you have blamed Mr. Canfield? He was the one who told you. Would you have blamed your father? Rachel?" He stopped to pull the glass entrance door open, then held it for her.

"That was different." Abbie halted to protest the comparison.

"The outcome was different, Abbie. You were not hurt on your wild ride." For all the sternness in his voice, his expression was filled with gentleness and understanding. "Abbie, you are not responsible."

"Ben." Her throat was tight with her welling emotions. " 'If only' Rachel had known someone like you when she was growing up."

"No more of that." He shook a finger at her, smiling warmly.

"Come on." Abbie hooked an arm around his waist. Walking together, they entered the hospital. The sterile atmosphere, the medicinal and antiseptic smells, and the muted bells, all combined to sober her. "I left word for MacCrea to meet us at the intensive-care nurse's station. I hope he got the message."

But he was waiting for them when they arrived. His dark glance swept over her in a quick inspection, a hint of relief in his expression. "I had visions of you racing through this traffic. If I had known Ben was with you, I wouldn't have worried so much."

"Have you seen Lane yet?"

"No. I just got here. Where's Eden and Alex?"

"Momma was at the house when Lane called. She's watching them." After learning the seriousness of Rachel's injuries, Abbie had persuaded Lane to let Alex stay with them rather than be looked after by servants, no matter how caring they were.

A nurse came to escort them to the private hospital suite. Lane emerged from the room as they walked up. Again, Abbie was struck by the change in him. Over the last three days, he seemed to have aged ten years, his face haggard and worn from the strain and lack of sleep. Even his hair looked whiter. The confidence, the strength that had been so much a part of him were no longer evident. Instead he looked vulnerable and frightened — and a little lost, like Alex had been.

"Abbie. Thank God, you're here," he said, grasping at her hand and clutching it tightly. "Rachel's been asking for you."

"How is she?"

But Lane just shook his head. Abbie didn't know how to interpret his answer, unsure whether he meant he didn't know or that Rachel's condition had changed. Hurriedly he ushered her into the suite, signaling to the guard outside that MacCrea and Ben were to be admitted as well.

He guided Abbie to the hospital bed, then reached down and took hold of Rachel's hand. "Rachel. It's Lane. Can you hear me?" There was a faint movement of her eyelids in response. "'Abbie's here. Do you understand? Abbie."

As Rachel struggled to open her eyes, Lane shifted to let Abbie take his place at her side. Abbie stared at the pale image of herself in the hospital bed.

"Abbie . . . my almost-twin sister." Rachel's voice was so faint Abbie had to lean closer to catch the words.

"Yes. We are almost twins, aren't we?" She tried to smile at that, even as her eyes filled with tears. "You're going to make it, Rachel. I know you are."

"Abbie." There was a long pause as if Rachel was trying to gather her strength. "You . . . were right . . . the things you . . . said."

"I don't think you should try to talk any more." It hurt to see her like this and remember all the confrontations they'd had in the past, when they'd hissed and arched their backs like a cat startled by its reflection in a mirror.

Rachel smiled weakly. "Lane and Alex are . . . going to need you. And . . . let our children . . . grow up together . . . the way we should . . . have."

"I will." Tears spilled from her eyes. "But you shouldn't be talking this way, Rachel. You're going to be fine."

She closed her eyes briefly, almost displaying impatience with Abbie's protestation. "I love . . . my son. Make sure he . . . knows that."

"I will."

She glanced dully around. "Lane? Where is he?"

Blinking rapidly to control her tears, Abbie half turned to look at Lane. "She wants you." She stepped back to MacCrea, letting Lane take her place. She leaned against him, grateful for the comfort of the arm he wrapped around her . . . and for the fact that they loved each other.

"Darling." Lane stroked her cheek, his hand trembling. "I'm here. You rest now."

"I do love you," she whispered.

"I love you too." He started to cry, silently. "We're going to have a lot of time together. I promise you."

A faint smile curved her mouth — a smile of regret, then, strangely, peace. "I have to go now, darling," Rachel whispered, then added so faintly that Lane wasn't even sure he heard it. "Daddy's . . . waiting."

You may purchase a
handsome and sturdy
book rack for your prized
books at $9.95 each.

Write to:
Book Rack Offer
P.O. Box 9039
Buffalo, N.Y. 14240-9039
Attn: Order Department